Reading
BOROUGH COUNCIL

Reading Borough Libraries

Email: info@readinglibraries.org.uk
Website: www.readinglibraries.org.uk

To avoid overdue charges please return this book to a
Reading library on or before the last date stamped above.
If not required by another reader, it may be renewed by
personal visit, telephone, post, email, or via our website.

A NAKED SINGULARITY

Sergio De La Pava

A NAKED SINGULARITY

MACLEHOSE PRESS
QUERCUS · LONDON

First published by the author in a limited edition in 2008,
and by University of Chicago Press in 2012
First published in Great Britain in 2013 by

MacLehose Press
an imprint of Quercus
55 Baker Street
7th Floor, South Block
London W1U 8EW

A CIP catalogue record for this book is available
from the British Library

ISBN (HB) 978 0 85705 280 3
ISBN (TPB) 978 0 85705 281 0
ISBN (Ebook) 978 1 78206 656 9

10 9 8 7 6 5 4 3 2 1

Designed and typeset in Minion by Libanus Press, Marlborough
Printed and bound in Great Britain by Clays Ltd, St Ives plc

Part One

The Lord looks down from heaven upon the children of men, to see if there are any that act wisely, that seek after God.

They have all gone astray, they are all alike corrupt; there is none that does good, no, not one.

– Psalm 14: 2, 3

Chapter 1

—noise background,

My getting out or what?!

Eleven hours and Thirty-Three minutes since meridian said the
clock perched high atop a ledge on the wall and positioned to look
down on us all meaning we were well into hour seven of this
particular battle between Good and Evil and, oh yeah, that was Good
taking a terrific beating with the poultry-shaped ref looking intently
at its eyes and asking if it wanted to continue. We were what passed
for Good there: the three of us and anyone we stood beside when we
rose to speak for the mute in that decaying room (100 Centre Street's
A.R.-3); and in that place, at that moment, Evil had us surrounded.

The puppetmaster pulling strings from behind the bench was a
bloated pink one on loan from the Bronx. The nameplate directly
before him announced J. MANOS in calligraphic gold. Its owner and
referent had decided no-one would taste freedom that arctic night
and had been slowly apprising us of that decision for the aforementioned seven-plus hours. And all that while he fostered this ugly habit
of echoing the end of his sentences, but only after the kind of delay
that fooled you into thinking you were in the clear, as in *bail is set in
the amount of ten thousand dollars . . . ten thousand dollars* and often
all emphatic(!) too.

7

The D.A. was essentially bony but with a slightly bulbous face beneath a mushroom hairdo that rose and expanded from dark root stem to bottle-blond cap. She displayed no discernible personality or affect as she uttered (through an inconsistent lip-distorting-yet-thankfully-dry-lisp) the customary declarations of mock moral outrage like *this defendant hath warranted on every one of his twenty three cathes, this defendant itha four-time predicate felon* and *this defendant hath used twelve different aliathes.* Unsurprisingly, these words – when spoken in those or similar combinations and to that audience – were more than sufficiently persuasive and as such invariably caused high numbers with commas to emerge from behind the nameplate. The numbers then attached to a *body,* one that by then had traversed the entirety of a creaking assembly line, and as a result the body stayed in.

[**bod-y** (bŏd´ē) *n., pl.* – **ies. 9.** *C.J.S.* Inarguably odious term used by N.Y.C. Department of Correction and other court personnel to denote incarcerated criminal defendants: *There are three hundred bodies in the system so we should be busy. He's bringing the next batch of bodies down now, I'll let you know if your guy's one of them.*]

And this was before anything even remotely insane had happened when I still occasionally thought about things like how it was that people were reduced to bodies, meaning the process. How you needed cops to do it and how their master, The System, needed to be constantly fed former people in order to properly function so that in a year typical to the city where the following took place about half a million bodies were forcibly conscripted. And if you learn only one thing from the ensuing maybe let it be this: the police were not merely interested observers who occasionally witnessed criminality and were then basically compelled to make an arrest, rather the

8

police had the special ability to in effect create Crime by making an arrest almost whenever they wished, so widespread was wrongdoing. Consequently, the decision on who would become a body was often affected by overlooked factors like the candidate's degree of humility, the neighborhood it lived in, and most often the relevant officers' need for overtime.

None of which tells you the exact process by which someone, let's say You, becomes a body, which account I sort of impliedly semi-promised, so imagine you are on the street, then in an *incident*, then a stranger's hand is on your melon making sure it doesn't bang the half-blue/half-white American-only car with the colorful bar across the top. Imagine that, easy if you try. Now the police have twenty-four hours to get you in front of a judge for your criminal court arraignment but if you're the perceptive sort you will monitor Time's ceaseless consumption of this period yet rightly detect no corresponding increase in ambient urgency.

Your first stop is the appropriate precinct where the arresting officer or A.O. stands you before another cop known as the Desk Sergeant. He tells him the tale of your alleged sin and the two, speaker and audience, join their heads to decide what section(s) of the New York Penal Law to charge you with. Now you've been informally charged and with that out of the way you may be asked to remove all your clothes (the propriety of this being debated at the time) and kindly spread open your ass. This strip search is one of several ways that additional charges can still arise so while you may have been arrested for a triviality like displaying an open bottle of Heineken to the public – a prosecution normally conducted in a decidedly minor key and resolved right at arraignments – your glove-clad searcher may now discover what you most sought to conceal, that you are currently *holding* one of the area's surfeit of readily-available-yet-technically-illicit anesthetics in amounts ranging anywhere from the ghostly residue of celebrations past to multiple powder bricks and in locations as presumably inviolable as within your underwear or even up your ass or maybe you possess one of the other less popular forms of the all-inclusive law enforcement term *contraband*. In that way can minor breaches be converted into major faults and this happens often, not occasionally. The police know this and are therefore unlikely to ignore even nonsense like the above Consumption of Alcohol in a Public Place (A.C. §10.125). People like you know this as well yet permit it to alter their conduct not in the slightest, ensuring in the process that the number of bodies will always remain fairly constant.

Another way you have to be careful not to pick up more charges is by resisting capture, even if only verbally, because such conduct can incite some of your lesser blue pacifists into a bit of retributory violence, with said violence then necessitating that you be charged with Resisting Arrest (P.L. §205.30) if only by way of explaining your injuries; which injuries better be minor lest they result in the added felony charge of Assault in the Second Degree (P.L. §120.05[3]), a more extensive explanation whereby a misdemeanor assault becomes a felony one by virtue of involving a police officer.

Still at the precinct, you are *printed*, each of your fingers rolled in black ink then onto vestal white paper. The resulting bar code is sent to Albany for the purpose of producing a *rap sheet*, an accordiony collection of onion paper that means everything where you are. It means everything because sentencing like Physics and other sciences builds on what came before so that the worse your past was, the worse your present will be, and no sane person doubts the rap sheet's depiction of the past since it's based on unalterable fingerprints and not relative ephemera like names or social security numbers. I say no *sane* person because when once confronted by an individual who steadfastly claimed not to recall in the slightest what I deemed to be a highly memorable conviction on his sheet and one that substantially increased his exposure, I asked him if he planned to launch a Lockean defense whereby he could not be held responsible for something he didn't remember as such act was not properly attributable to his personal identity at which point he gave me the blankest of stares in response then started saying increasingly odd things in rapid succession until I realized that he not only sort of knew what I was talking about, which was weird enough, but that he was undeniably insane and my ill-advised Locke reference was like the thing coming after the final straw to tip him over the Axis-II-Cluster-A edge, as it were, so that I thenceforth stopped doing things like that.

Now there's all this paperwork the A.O. has to fill out and he'll stick you in the precinct's cell while he fills. But first, if the case has any seriousness whatsoever, he and his friends want to accumulate evidence against you and since the best evidence is quite often the very words you emit, they mostly want you to make a statement, and trust me when I tell you that by the time they're through with you you'll probably want you to make a statement as well. Because while the police operated under something called the forty-eight hour rule which stated that an officer charged with any kind of official misconduct *cannot* be questioned about it for forty-eight hours – giving him time to, among other things, retain a criminal defense attorney – you are currently operating under a different forty-eight hour rule. This one says the police can harass, intimidate, lie, cheat, steal, cajole, make false promises, and delay your arraignment (where you would be assigned an attorney who would most assuredly *not* allow you to speak to the police) for forty-eight hours if that's what it takes to extract your statement. And it is following all that, not at the very instant you're arrested as mass entertainment would have you believe, that they will advise you of your Miranda rights so your ensuing statement will be admissible.

And this is as good a time as any for you, gentle reader, to learn that I can wander a bit while storytelling so that the very imminent digressive passage on the judicial creation of Miranda warnings can be entirely skipped by the uncurious without the slightest loss of narrative steam.

Digression begins. So Ernesto Miranda is the Miranda of the warnings and the same year a famous shooter(s) would later scatter John Fitzgerald all over Jackie he was twenty-three and creating smaller-scale mayhem. A high school dropout with the mental development of an eighth-grader, Miranda had already served one year on an attempted rape conviction. In a perpendicular universe, an eighteen-year-old Phoenix girl who I'm going to say strove to dress like the glossy girls she saw in magazines and to listen to the same records as her more desirable classmates indisputably acted as attendant to some movie theater's candy counter, the true home of such an operation's profits incidentally. She sold synthetic butter and liquid Real Things and when done tried to go home. Enter Miranda who interrupted her trip home. He grabbed her, dragged her into his car, and drove her out into the Red, Brown, and Purple of the Painted Desert where he raped her.

Fast forward one week when the girl briefly saw what she thought was the car driven by her assailant, a 1953 Packard. She reported this belief to the police, telling them the license plate of the car was DFL312. That plate turned out to be registered to an Oldsmobile but the police discovered that DFL317 *was* registered to a Packard – a Packard owned by Twila N. Hoffman, Ernesto Miranda's girlfriend. Off to 2525 West Mariposa (*Oeste* Butterfly) Street where Miranda was found to fit the description given by the girl. He was arrested and placed in a line-up. The girl said he most resembled the rapist but failed to make an unequivocally positive identification.

Detectives took Miranda into Interrogation Room Two where he was told he had been identified as the rapist and *asked* if he wanted to make a statement. He did, a signed written confession that took two hours to elicit following his initial denial of guilt and that

12

included a section saying he understood his rights. Miranda was charged and assigned an attorney. The attorney, Alvin Moore, had plenty on his neck, however, and for a well-spent $100 he objected that the confession had been illegally obtained because no-one told Ernesto, prior to his statement, that he had the right to an attorney. The trial judge said *no way* to that and after the jury consequently heard the confession, and was surely impressed by it, he got to prescribe twenty to thirty years in special housing as a remedy. Ernesto wondered if he could appeal and he could.

The A.C.L.U. grabbed the case and 976 days later they were in front of the court that never gets overruled with John Flynn saying, and this is a direct quote (no it isn't): "look dudes, and I refer to you thusly because this is way pre-O'Connor/Ginsberg, your Fifth Amendment deal is only protecting the rich and powerful: those who are brainy enough to know what their rights are or who have the dough to rent a lawyer." The Warren Supremes actually agreed and, in the kind of decision that makes maybe five people happy, held that before future police could torment some illiterate sap who nobody cares about into confessing his sins, real or imagined, they would have to inform him of certain rights not covered in your average eighth-grade Social Studies class. As is customary in these all-too-rare instances, Miranda's conviction was reversed and his case set down for retrial – a trial to be conducted without his now tainted confession, without any physical evidence of a struggle, and with a dubious identification. In a stroke of all-too-common prosecutorial serendipity, however, Miranda's common-law wife, the previously mentioned Twila, emerged to testify that Miranda had admitted the rape to her. The fact that she and Miranda were then involved in a *bitter* custody dispute – are these ever otherwise described? – was conveniently ignored and the new jury said something to the effect of where are your Supremes now because we agree with the first jury. Miranda was eventually paroled then, the same year his country celebrated its two-hundredth birthday party, stabbed and killed in a Phoenix bar fight. As the police arrested one of his assailants they took care to read him his Miranda rights in English and Spanish. *Digression ends.*

Of course so famous have these warnings become that it seems they're no longer really heard in any meaningful way so that although someone with a gun is pointedly telling you you have the right to remain silent, that is, you have the right to make their job harder, to make it more difficult for them to accumulate evidence and later proof against you, the right to decrease the chances that you will end in jail, you will still almost invariably decline to exercise that right. Instead when someone like me later asks you if you spoke you'll affirm then say things like: *he said I would get out if I made a statement* or *they knew I wasn't the shooter so he said I would get a misdemeanor if I told them about the robbery* or maybe *I had to tell my side of the story* or *my mother said to tell them what happened* or else *I told them what happened but I didn't write it so it's not a statement right?* or even *they said once I got a lawyer there was nothing they could do for me* and other similar, painful nonsense. You tell me these things and my chin drops because I'm not interested in what's good for your soul only what's good or bad for my case and your statement is bad for it.

And in what is possibly another mini-digression, here is, more specifically, why your statement is always bad or at least your classic no-win deal, regardless of its content: Realize that if what you said was good for you, you can reliably expect that it will never be repeated because the prosecution needn't present it at trial or even tell anyone about it. On the other far more likely hand where what you said damages your prospects, then you likely just reduced me to arguing that the cop misinterpreted or improperly influenced the content or, worse, just made it up out of whole cloth. Only I'm arguing this in Manhattan not the Bronx or Brooklyn meaning a substantial portion of the listening jury has graduate degrees and nannies and they don't think Police Officers do things like that and aren't about to be disabused of that notion by a criminal like you. So thanks. All by way of saying that statements are good evidence for the prosecution so the cops know to get them and thus do, with occasional help from an assistant district attorney sitting in front of a bargain videocam if the case is serious enough.

Back to that paperwork the A.O.'s filling out with you in a nearby cell. He's scribbling and hunting and pecking while asking you the occasional question (these are mostly *pedigree* questions like name, address, etc., which everyone in a robe agrees don't require preceding Miranda warnings) and you may not know it but your future's in them pages, those police reports. Because those reports are *Rosario material* and as such must be turned over to your attorney at some point, usually seconds, before trial. And even at that late stage believe me that these reports are usually his only true friends within the cruel, lonely world he operates in. Friends because in all their babblative beauty they make claims early and often that the cop now has to mirror perfectly or else gift him the inconsistency so that if it suits you he will stand there at trial and wave them at the cop like holier verity was never written boy. And the Rosario List that comes with the material will look substantially like this (well, without the explanatory parentheticals):

1. Online Booking Sheet: (mostly pedigree info but also details your capture including specific time and place).
2. UF61 or Complaint Report: (principally useful for the narrative of events it includes as relayed by the cop and/or those pesky civilian eyewitnesses).
3. Sprint Report: (transcription, in scarcely legible form, of all communications made via 911 operators and police radios including the infamous *one-under* that signals your descent into The System).

4. Memo Book Entries: (every uniformed cop has to record in a little pad everything of note that happens during his shift).

5. Aided Card: (only if someone was hurt requiring medical attention).

6. Vouchers, Property Clerk Invoices, Invoice Worksheets: (about any property recovered and most importantly by whom and from where).

Only longer.

Now the paperwork's complete and you're on the move because the A.O. is taking you to Central Booking. Central Booking is located at One Police Plaza and is the first of three post-precinct levels you must inhabit before meeting an attorney who will guide you through the final formal steps by which those who stay *in* are separated from those who get *out*. (Speaking only figuratively, these levels are concentrically circular and either expand while ascending or constrict while descending, depending on your vantage point). On this first level, you are handed off to cops previously, and likely disciplinarily, extracted from the street to work desks. They take charge of you while the A.O. leaves to meet with one of the assistant district attorneys working in the Early Case Assessment Bureau, or E.C.A.B., or Complaint Room, of the District Attorney's Office. Here, the newly assigned D.A., after interviewing the A.O., writes the criminal court complaint that formally charges you with a specific crime(s) and which includes a short narrative of the incident written in law-enforcementese and signed by the swearing cop. Note that this is why I earlier called precinct charges something like informal even though nobody else calls them that, my justification being that these arrest charges don't really amount to much in the final analysis since this D.A. is actually the one who decides what crime to charge you with or whether to even charge you at all. Consequently, it's the most common thing in the world to see charges that were inflated and overly optimistic, from the officers' standpoint, reduced to something far more realistic by the party actually being asked to prove the damn thing, making these arrest charges something more along the lines of a recommendation really. Anyway, the D.A. additionally fills out a *D.A. Data Sheet* that also becomes *Rosario* and that includes more facts about the case and what his colleague's bail request should be at the upcoming arraignment.

Back at Central Booking, your rap sheet returns from Albany and the cops check it to see if there are any outstanding bench warrants, arrest orders judges issue whenever a defendant stands them up at a court date. Now you can graduate to the next level located across the street in the building where this entire mess will come to fruition. This intermediate level is buried beneath your ultimate pre-arraignment destination and is colored to make you feel you're inside a lime. Here, you sit in a cell and wait to meet a representative of the Criminal Justice Agency who wants to interview you to produce a *C.J.A. Sheet*. This sheet informs the judge of the extent of your community ties and thus presumably the likelihood of your return to court, a critical factor allegedly used by the judge in determining whether or not to set bail on your case and if so how much. What you're rooting for here is a C.J.A. verdict of **RECOMMENDED VERIFIED TIES** although that doesn't exactly guarantee you anything either.

When this and other delays have been exhausted you're ready for the pens directly behind the arraignment courtroom. To get there you're walked down a perfectly symmetric hall that overhead, every eight or so paces, has metronomically intermittent, dimpled-plastic rectangles containing two tubes each of flickering light that end well before the dark base of the stairs. At the top of those stairs is a short hallway that leads to those two identical but transposed cells where you are told to wait until a lawyer like me calls you ad nominem into one of the six interview booths.

And on bad nights like that night with Manos you will scarcely have room to move as a great many other bodies wait there with you, the cell walls straining against the immured humanity; the number of bodies held therein so great you would not think so many could simultaneously do wrong. A teeming multitude with its components angling desperately for their just portion of the surrounding air and now you're ready to declare Hobbes victorious over Rousseau with scant need for further deliberation. Because people sleep face-down on the sticky floor, the ones who aren't too pained from active withdrawal, and you're handed a small carton of milk with an unsealed plastic bag of white bread squeezing baloney and cheese to bleed solar-yellow mustard while you smell those alien body parts you least wanted to smell, watch dirty hands tremble to hold bloody scabs, feel beset by voices indistinctly grouped in throng and in the corner, as if on display, is an uncovered toilet next to a payphone available to any member of that preterite crowd capable of inserting a quarter and willing to make a phone call while watching someone take, or more accurately *give*, a shit. But worst is that every time a body goes out to see the judge it comes right back in shaking its head and it doesn't take much to deduce that you will soon be doing the same. That's where you are, where You ended up.

Where I was, by contrast, was fifteen yards away staring at an empty basket and praying it wouldn't fill with more yellow (felonies) and blue (misdemeanors) papers describing additional bodies I would meet under duress so they could lie to me. But it did fill and the filling compelled me to action. And I'm going to *start* start here because I met Dane for the first time that night; that meeting and consequently the many subsequent ones a pure product of arraignment-schedule chance. We stared at the basket then each other and I realized that to that point he had said maybe five extra-judicial words. Consistent with that he absently grabbed an unfairly large share of the cases and went off to interview them without a sound.

Linda was a battle-scarred veteran of double digit years who had mastered the expected art form of appearing to be quite busy while doing little of value and was therefore nowhere near the basket. I took what remained, mostly yellow some blue, and went to the back to do the interviews. I planned to do them with extreme velocity too because I had done about a quillion already and wanted desperately to get the hell out of there. The first case I looked at was Darril Thorton, a yellow-back charged with Sex Abuse in the First Degree (P.L. §130.65). I called his name softly, hoping he wouldn't answer, but he immediately moved in, a let's-get-this-over-with look on his face. He spoke first, obviously yelling but still creating only a barely audible signal:

—noise background,

My getting out or what?!

My money's on what, followed by a pause long enough to be uncomfortable.

Oh c'mon I didn't do nothing man! This is bullshit you got to get me up out of here on the double yo, she's lying on me!

Easy, hold on, let's start at the top. Here's my card. My name's Casi, I'm going to be your attorney. Let's see, well, you're charged with Sex Abuse in the First Degree, that's a Class D violent felony.

Wait let me see this, holding the ivory rectangle up to the bar-streaked light and nodding negatively, uh-uh.

What uh-uh?

I don't want you man, starting to walk out but not really.

Why? What's the problem?

Because man, sitting back down, I wanted an 18B, only thing you guys ever did for me is send me upstate man. No offense but that's just keeping it real on your ass, pointing but not at it.

Well, whatever, you're sort of stuck with me so let's just see how it goes for a bit O.K.?

No.

Who's Valerie Grissom?

19

Man you alright. O.K., she's a crackhead. That's what I'm trying to tell you officer, I mean lawyer. She's making up some crazy stuff, everybody knows she's a fabricator and a confabulator. Everybody knows it!

You know that for a fact?

What, that she confabulates?

No, that she's a crackhead.

Everybody knows!

How do *you* know? You smoke with her?

I don't smoke man but I seen her smoke.

So she has a record?

Man she been popped tons of times, laughing but still managing to sound angrier somehow.

You know her date of birth?

Na man, I ain't know her like that.

She married, kids?

Kids somewhere I think but they ain't around.

What's your relationship to her?

Man we ain't related. Shit, what the fuck you think?

I mean how do you know her?

Just from the neighborhood man, everybody knows her she's always up in everybody's business.

How long you known her?

A few years man!

Just relax a bit. She's saying that two weeks ago at 322 West 119th Street . . . that where she lives?

She's sort of homeless but I think she stays there a lot with a friend of hers.

She's saying that you forced her down on the bed—

What?!

Let me finish. She says you threw her down on the bed, put your forearm across her neck and forced your fingers into her vagina.

How many fingers?

Just says fingers.

Can they do that?

Not specify how many fingers?

Yeah.

Yes.

Well that's crazy man. That's a complete and totally utter lie, I've never even been in a bed with her! What bed are they saying? I can't believe this! It's a total set up. Total. Set. Up. You have to get me out of here.

You *ever* had a sexual relationship with her?

Never.

The truth, Darril.

Never, I swear!

Well did the two of you have some kind of argument over something?

I haven't even seen her in like . . . let me see . . . two months?

So what's going on?

You tell me.

Well you're saying this woman with whom you've never had more than a casual relationship and haven't even seen in two months suddenly decided to falsely accuse you of essentially raping her. Does that make any sense? If the two of you have no beef and you've never been more than just acquaintances why would she possibly make this up?

I have a theory but I can tell by looking at you, which he then did exaggeratedly, that you will not accept it. I can see that in your eyes.

What's the reason?

Your eyes.

What's the reason she's lying?

Fine, The Hater.

What?

The Accuser.

The what-user?

The fallen and rebellious angel himself.

The hell you talking about?

The Prince of Darkness man. You heard of him right?

O.K. I have heard of him but what does that have to do with this?

Look I found the Lord O.K.? I'm about to become a minister as a matter of fact. And one thing I've learned, in my studies and etceteras, is that the Dark Prince gets into people man. Now I'm trying to get my life together. I been out of prison twenty-three months. You see I been reporting to parole and working as a mechanic right there on 118th Street. Why would I do this? Tell me that. I would have to be crazy to do that insertion and whatnot. I'm trying to stay clean but The Evil One sees that man. He sees that and he says *I'm taking this man down, this righteous man who hath turned to the good book must now falleth.* And that's why this is happening. But all I know is I never touched that woman. It's a lie, she's a false witness being brought to bear.

Well, whatever the reason, she's saying you did this and—

I done told you the reason, the very archenemy of God has—

O.K. whatever stop. The bottom line is that as a result of her statement to the police you've been charged with this and we're about to go in front of a judge who's going to decide what your bail is.

Bail?! But I'm innocent, they have to release me.

I doubt they'll see it that way.

So what exactly my looking at here man?

Numbers?

Yeah man, what else?

You been upstate?

I'm a mandatory persistent man. That's what you're going to see when you look at my raps so I'll just up and save you the time.

O.K. then you know the deal.

What kind of charge is that? Abuse?

D violent. Yeah, I see two prior violent felonies. Two to four on a rob two and you're currently on parole after doing five to fifteen on a manslaughter right?

First of all, that was an accident man. It was just a fight and I was defending myself. Second of all, both of those cases were before I found the Lord.

They still count. That's two violent felonies and this is another one so you are a mandatory as you said—

I know.

Which means you're looking at a minimum here of twelve to life and a max of twenty-five to life—

Fuck.

Right, so this is no joke and you're going to figure out Darril that the only way I'm going to possibly be able to help you is for you to start leveling with me a lot more than you have so far.

I'm telling you the truth. I didn't do this.

Listen, I don't have all night. There's got to be more to it than this. You're not giving me any possible credible reason why she would make this up.

I told you, the Archfiend.

By credible I mean a reason that doesn't involve him . . . so that it? Anything else?

I've told you everything I know. I didn't do this.

How can I get in touch with her to interview her? She have a phone?

I don't know. But she still stays in that building last I heard.

O.K., any questions?

What are my chances? Am I going home?

No.

No, just like that?

Be realistic, please, everything I just told you.

So what's my 180.80 date then?

Well you were arrested yesterday, Wednesday, so next Tuesday.

She needs to come to court that day or else they'll release me right?

Pretty much true. They need an indictment that day or else they have to release you, yeah. There's one exception but—

Let them know I'm going in the grand jury too.

Look my feeling is it would not be a great idea for you to testify in the grand jury.

Why do you say that? I'm innocent.

Well foremost the grand jurors are going to hear about your record in a way your trial jury never would and for that reason alone there's no way they'll dismiss the case. As a result the only thing you're going to accomplish is to give the D.A. an early version of your story.

I don't care what version they get because it's the truth. So there.

Maybe so but that'll be small consolation when you get indicted. Unbelievable.

Listen we don't have to decide anything right now. I'll serve cross and we'll discuss it next court date when we have more time and when I'll know more about the case. Deal?

O.K. but I'm testifying.

Alright. I'll talk to the D.A. before your next court date to see what they're offering.

I'm not taking anything!

Well then just to satisfy my curiosity O.K.? Any other questions before we go in front of the judge?

Just that I'm innocent.

O.K.

I know you seen my record and I *have* committed felonies. The robbery was a way to get money and I know it was stupid. The manslaughter? Fine, that was a fight and I cut him. All that was before I found the Lord by the way. Before. But this? This would be like pure evil to have done something like this to someone like that and I'm not

24

evil. I am not a person who traffics in evil, dig? So you have to believe I'm innocent.

O.K.

I mean it. You have to!

I believe you.

No for real don't just say it. You have to believe I'm innocent.

See you in front of the judge.

Wait a minute. I mean it man! I need a lawyer who believes in my innocence. You have to believe that to do this case.

You're wrong I don't, I just don't. It's not going to make me work harder on your case like in some stupid movie and it's certainly not going to make it more likely that you walk. In fact, if you really are innocent then it's probably going to hurt you and your case more than anything because, for one thing, I would probably be so distracted by the novelty of the situation I'd be rendered ineffective and, for another, your innocence might mean your devilish theory is true in which case we'd really be screwed because from where I'm sitting the devil appears be pretty effective, certainly more so than the average D.A. So stop, I beg.

I want another lawyer.

One's enough and if you mean a different one then that request is denied as well so just chill as much as possible for someone facing the rest of their life in jail and let me handle it. I know what I'm doing, although admittedly only in this severely limited area. Agreed?

Alright.

Anything else?

No.

Good Darril, now kindly step out so I can interview the next.

Ah Chut. AH CHUT!

Bless you motherfucker! Ha ha!

Mr Chut?

Yeh.

Is that you? Are you Ah Chut?

Yeh.

Here's my card I'm going to be your attorney. Do you speak English?

Nuh.

Cantonese? Mandarin?

Cantonese yeh Cantonese!

Well . . . O.K. . . . were you selling batteries on the subway?

Yeh. Wuh?

You sell battery subway?

Cantonese.

No, I know but there's no interpreter and I want to get you out of jail.

Yuh.

You sell battery on subway yes?

Yih.

And you don't have a license right?

Cantonese.

No license right?

No license no.

O.K. you go home soon O.K.?

Home?

Yeah you go home. O.K.?

Yah. Cantonese?

No. You're going to have to go home in English because there's no interpreter and it would take hours to get one.

Yeh.

O.K. step out.

Out? pointing.

Yes.

Glenn. BEN GLENN!

That's me,
You don't have to say it three.

How you doing Mr Glenn? Here's my card. My name's Casi and I'll be your attorney. You've been charged with Criminal Mischief in the Fourth Degree, that's a class A misdemeanor. This guy Hal Posano is saying you stood in the entrance to his pizzeria and wouldn't move. He's saying that when he and his workers tried to get you to move you kicked the door and shattered the glass. Is all that true?

The truth lies somewhere in between
I wanted some pizza but didn't have any green.

Is that what led to the argument? You couldn't pay for some pizza you had eaten? What happened? How do you end up kicking this guy's door in?

Frankly, I refuse to divulge any further the nature of my defense.
To trust a stranger like you simply makes little sense.

I can't help but notice, Mr Glenn, that you are speaking entirely in a kind of rudimentary spoken verse, is there a reason for that?

What you've just said is fully true.
I speak solely in rhyme how about you?

I tend not to. I also see, looking down now, that your last case was dismissed after a 730 examination. What that means is that a psychiatrist examined you and determined that you were too sick to face a criminal case and the case was dismissed. Right? Remember that? So I think what I may do is have a psychiatrist examine you again to see how you're doing, O.K.? The problem is that because of your record and because of the judge we're going to be in front of, it's unlikely you will be offered something that's going to get you out and if there's no disposition this judge is going to set bail so—

The judge can set all the bail he wants and I won't complain
When Batman wasn't fighting crime his name was Bruce Wayne.

True, I guess. If the judge sets bail, however, and you're homeless like you told C.J.A., then you're going to be in jail while the case is going on. So I think the best way to proceed from your standpoint is to have a psychiatric evaluation done. This way if you're too sick to know what's going on, the case will be dismissed and you'll be civilly committed to psychiatric care. On the other hand if you're fine, then we can try to get a plea that will get you out. O.K.? Mr Glenn?

Do your best but remember you are only epidermally covered bone
And perhaps the disease in me is one you too own.

O.K. Well it's not a very serious case so we'll see what I can do.
Listen Casi sorry to interrupt, a court officer stuck just his head in then kept it perfectly trained on me as if Glenn were a mere product of my imagination, but do you have Glenda Deeble, Robert Coomer, and Terrens Lake?
Yeah, what about them?
They're all specials so they're on the bench and we need to get them done before we can bring more bodies out.
Alright, Glenn had vanished while I spoke. The bench referred to here was not the judge's bench but rather the two L-positioned pews to the far left of it where all defendants were placed immediately prior to having their case called. Some, like the following, went directly there for various reasons rather than stopping in the holding cell and

28

were interviewed in a wooden kiosk-like structure located nearby. I went there.

Oh Casi I'm so sorry, Linda with hand on cheek cavity caused by open mouth, you took everything. Want to give me some of those?

It's alright I just have these three on the bench then another blue and I'm done.

Probably shouldn't do anymore anyway with tomorrow my last day.

What?

Yeah you didn't know?

No, didn't even know you were leaving.

Really? Yeah, tomorrow's my last day.

Wow, where you going?

I'm going to be a real estate agent.

Real estate? Get out, let me do these then tell me all about it.

Glenda Deeble?

Yes.

In there Glenda . . . here's my card I'm going to represent you.

How do you say that name?

Casi kind of like Lassie but not really, who's Ray Doherty?

That's my husband.

Cops are saying you helped him sell methadone to a person who turned out to be an undercover police officer. That true?

No it's not. He might have sold but I had nothing to do with it.

So what happened?

O.K., we had just come out of the methadone clinic which is like a block from where we was arrested. The clinic was going to be closed the next day so after we drank one inside they gave us each an extra one to take home and drink the next day, I guess today. Anyways as soon as we walk out this guy comes up and starts begging Ray for his methadone. He was like really insisting, offering to pay for it, and he looked like he was in really bad shape. I kind of walked away at this point because I been busted once before for selling my methadone and besides I couldn't sell mines anyway because, as you can see, I'm five months pregnant and if I go through any kind of withdrawal it could hurt the baby. So I think Ray might have sold to him but I'm not sure.

Where did you get arrested?

He talked to the guy then we tried to get to the train on Hudson but we were arrested right there, near the entrance. Something like five cops jump out of a van and throw us against a gate. They took my bottle of methadone, the one I need for today. Can I get that back?

No they're saying it's evidence. But you can get methadone inside if you're held in.

Wait, I'm going to jail?

I don't know yet.

I don't understand why I was even arrested. I didn't sell anything.

They're saying your husband did the actual selling but that you helped him by looking back and forth, in other words being a lookout. They're charging you with acting in concert.

Is that a felony?

Yeah a C felony, same as if you actually made the exchange.

So some cop was nearby and saw this happen, nodding yes.

No, the guy your husband sold to was an undercover pretending to be a drug addict.

Oh Christ, she looked up. Can they do that? Can they? I mean this guy was practically begging Ray to sell to him. I know for a fact he never intended to sell his stuff but the guy just kept asking him and finally I guess he convinced him to do it. Isn't that like *trapment* or something? She tilted her head and raised both eyebrows, can they do that to us?

Well the problem is you have a prior conviction for the same thing, selling methadone, and unfortunately that kind of effectively negates the defense of entrapment. It also means you're a predicate felon which means you're facing a minimum of three to six in this case.

Can't they bring it down?

They can, and I'll talk to the D.A. and try to get you a misdemeanor but for now the only thing we're really concerned with is your bail status.

I don't have any money for bail, I'm on S.S.I.

Yeah I'm going to try to get the judge to release you with a court date to return.

On my own R'n'R?

Right.

You think he'll do it?

I don't know, maybe, we'll find out shortly. Where do you live?

We live in one of those hotels. I have full-blown A.I.D.S. so D.A.S. pays for it and they give me my medication.

I see. And how's your health now because you look kind of yellow.

That's because I have Hepatitis. I just got out of St Claire's after a transfusion about a week ago.

Oh. Well the last thing we have to discuss is the grand jury. If I can't convince the D.A. to give you a misdemeanor then that means she's going to go into the grand jury and try to indict you on a felony drug sale. You have the right to testify in the grand jury and tell your side of the story in the hopes that they will dismiss or at least reduce the charges.

Doesn't it get worser for you if you do that?

It could, every case is different though. Here, I think—

I don't want to testify in no grand jury Casi.

Well you don't have to decide—

No way.

Why not? Listen if what you told me is true then—

It is true, it is, but I'm not stupid. Look at me. Things aren't exactly going good for me here. I know that if I go in there I'll just end up making things worse because that's what I do.

Let's just—

Because that's the way things happen in my life since I was maybe six. No not maybe, I was exactly six, that birthday forward.

I understand and that may be so but my experience is—

Things probably go well for you, I can tell just by looking at you, but for me if my luck wasn't bad I wouldn't be lucky at all. Everything I touch turns to shit. I know this.

I don't accept that.

You're right not everything, not these five months. I been good since I found out I was *with child*. You don't know how many times these months I says to myself, like, what could they say if I did everything right from here on out? For real, if I did everything right up to and beyond that day would I really be that different than those moms in their soccer vans? I'd be like them and my baby, at least, would have to look at me the right way, he wouldn't know. To him I'm just mom. He doesn't know. The things I've done. I seen that look. I want to be at the end of that look. And if I am and I return it the right way then that's something isn't it? That's one thing I would've done good and no-one could say different right?

I don't—

Right?

Definitely. But look, about the grand jury.

So I don't want to try anything tricky because, like I said, I know I'll just mess it all up when I'm this close to doing it right for once. I mean the only reason I was even there was to make sure I don't have any withdrawal that could hurt the baby. I'm close, I'm close. If you could just get me a misdemeanor and city time I would be really grateful and definitely take it, as long as I'm out in time you know? And I wouldn't be one of these people who complains about their lawyer neither. I would know it was a good deal and I would take it, even though I had nothing to do with this particular sale and even though I think it's wrong what that cop did, with the entrapping.

O.K.

Turns to shit.

I understand. And believe me, I'm not normally a big fan of putting people in the grand jury either but your instincts about a possible defense were generally right so I feel that perhaps maybe possibly you might if—

I don't want to, please.

Then you won't. That's all. You certainly don't have to. It's your decision to make. Do you have any questions before we go in front of the judge?

You think I'll get out?

Maybe.

If I have the baby inside, they take it.

I know. Anything else?

No, just thank you.

O.K., you can step out.

Robert Coomer?

Yes!

Close the door behind you Robert.

You have before you a completely innocent man and my question to you sir, if I may call you that, is this: *what . . . am . . . I . . . charged . . . with?*

Robbery.

I'm innocent.

David Sanders is saying you pulled a knife on him about two months ago and forced him to give you two hundred dollars.

An outlandish accusation.

Who is he?

Who is you?

My name is Casi, here's my card, I've been assigned your case. Now who's David Sanders?

It's a long story young man so what I'll do is give you the condensated version.

You're charged with Robbery in the First Degree, a B violent felony with a minimum jail sentence of five years in prison, so I think you should tell me at least the medium-length version.

As you like it young man. Now I met Mr Sanders, a.k.a. The Colonel, about eight months ago at the park.

What park?

Morningside Park. Now at this park many of us congregate to play chess. Everyone knows that any day of the week you can find Robert Delano Coomer there playing chess.

Who's that?

That's me.

Oh. Sorry, go ahead.

I mean geez.

Alright continue, where did you live at this time?

I lived in the park that's why I was always playing chess there. Anyway I noticed that this man, Mr David Sanders, would come and observe on quite a few occasions and so we got to conversating.

You became friends.

Now don't go jumping the gun that's the problem with you youngsters nowadays. We didn't become friends at all in fact we were in constant disputation.

About what?

Well the fact is I done come up with a new chess opening. And the truth is that this chess opening has confounded the grandmasters and dumbfounded the neophytes.

Great, so where's the problem?

Well the further fact is we had irreconcilable philosophical differences respecting just how good my opening was.

What's the opening?

You really want to know?

Sure.

And you won't tell anyone?

No.

You sure?

Yes. Even if I wanted to, the attorney-client privilege would prevent me. I would lose my license to thrill.

It's a queen's rook pawn opening.

Certainly unique but it seems like you would have a big problem with development.

You see that's exactly what he said! Whose side are you on anyway?

I'm on yours don't worry. I'm sure it's a good opening I just can't visualize it, keep going.

Damn straight it was a good opening, the best! Sixteen hundred years they been playing this game and it took a homeless brother in the park to come up with the perfect opening. Well I become very protective of my creation and whatnot and that done led to some argumentation between us. Anyway, after awhiles we reconciled our differences behind us, and he started letting me stay with him once in a while. Then I moved into his place for good.

Were you two involved?

Meaning?

Were you his boyfriend?

No, nothing like that, we was just friends. I ain't gay nor nothing. He was letting me live there while I tried to get back on my feet you know?

Were you working?

No he was working and would pay the rent. What happened was I came into some money by way of my brother. He's some kinda rapper though all I knows is growing up the boy couldn't rhyme *cat* with *hat*. So anyway David seen me dropping bills left and right and he felt I should have been directing some of that his way since I ain't never been paying no rent. Anyway, one day I come home and he's all in my shit taking out my money. We got into it and I hit him in self-defense but I never pulled a knife on him and I did take back the money but it was mines anyway. The truth is we both hit each other and the only thing that ended the fight is that we both started bleeding and he kinda panicked because I'm positive and he hasn't had the balls to get himself tested; *ignorance be bliss* that's what he say. So I moved out like that night and I moved in with another friend of mine who liked my rook opening a lot more than David.

When was that?

That was like two months ago.

Who did you move in with?

Warren Holliday but that didn't work out neither cause he's like a known felon and shit.

What does that mean?

Well he's a felon and it was knowed.

Why was that a problem? Everyone's a felon.

He just done crazy things that's all.

You seen David since you moved out?

Two days ago he came to visit me in the hospital.

Yeah why were you in the hospital?

I was on a roof with *the professor* smoking crack when the cops rushed up. I got a running start and tried to jump onto the roof of the building next door like in them action movies only I didn't make it. I fell three stories and shattered both my legs see?

How did David know?

Somebody must've told him. When he showed up I was shocked man. Cause this was like my nemesis you know what I mean? But he was saying he still loved me and that he didn't want me arrested and that when I got out of the hospital I could come and stay with him again since the apartment I was staying in is now a crackhouse and's been condemned to death. Anyway when they were going to release me from the hospital the police were there and they arrested me saying that David had filed a complaint against me like two months ago but they wouldn't tell me what for. I don't think he's going to impress the charges is what I'm saying.

Well if you're right and he doesn't testify in the grand jury within six days you'll be released.

I think that's what will happen because two days ago he was telling me how much he loved me and all.

I thought you two weren't involved like that? Well?

O.K. I lied, we were, but I wouldn't want that to be common knowledge throughout the community and whatnot.

Don't worry, both your opening and this other secret are safe with me.

Any questions before we go in front of the judge?

No, I understand.

Good then, but actually, I have a question.

What?

Professor?

He's a guy from the neighborhood who's always getting good rock . . . he once took a class in college.

I see, we're done.

Terrens Lake?

yeah.

Go in there . . . here's my card Terrens, don't lose it. My name's Casi, I'm going to be your lawyer. You're sixteen?

yeah.

Cops are saying you sold drugs to an undercover.

na, i don't sell drugs. T.N.T. just came up and swept a bunch of us up i wasn't doing nothing.

Who was selling there?

tons a guys be selling out there, it's a big spot.

What were you doing out there?

just hanging out with a friend.

Who?

we call him Boop.

What's his real name?

i d'know, just Boop.

Where does he live?

d'know, think downtown.

Anybody else there that you know who saw what happened?

na, yo i got a question though.

Yeah.

in the van they were saying to each other that i was a J.D. lost and shit. what up with that? if i'm a what do you call lost subject, what am i doing in the van right?

Lean back a second . . . is that what you were wearing when you were arrested?

yeah.

Including that shirt that says LAND OF THE LOST?

yeah.

There's your answer.

what?

The cop who buys radios a description to his arrest team of the guy he wants picked up for selling to him. The description is always J.D., as in John Doe, followed by the distinguishing feature of the seller, like your clothing in this case.

word?

Indeed.

damn. i'm going to kill my cousin for getting me this shit at Niketown.

Let me look at something . . . you have another drug sale pending?

uh-huh.

What's going on with that case?

i'm supposed to get probation on that.

You pled guilty?

yeah.

When's your next court date?

d'know, sat home on the fridge.

Who's your attorney on that case?

d'know his name but he's got red hair and a mustache.

You have his card?

na i lost it.

Who's the judge?

d'know.

What part?

damn, ninety-three maybe?

No such part, thirty-nine?

na, not thirty-nine.

Well you've got a big problem now right? When you took the plea on the other case the judge told you that one of the conditions you had to meet before you would get probation was to avoid getting rearrested right?

yeah! how'd you know?

And now you've picked up another sale. So basically the judge doesn't have to give you probation anymore, she can sentence you to state prison instead. Not to mention this case where you're facing a minimum of one to three.

but i wasn't selling this time. i didn't have stash or marked money on me nor nothing so how can they charge me with a sale?

They can and for someone who doesn't sell drugs you sure got the terminology down. Who do you live with?

my grandmother.

Why did you tell C.J.A. you live with your girlfriend?

cause i stay in both places while my moms is trying to get me back.

Get you back from where?

cause she gave up custody when i was a kid and now she's trying to get me back, we in family court next week. she's suppose to be in court right now with her common-law fiancé and whatnot.

Well is she? You see her?

na, i don't think so, but i can't see the whole space.

What's her name?

Tara.

Lake?

Simms

I'll look for her. We're going in front of the judge soon and he's going to decide how much your bail is. Any questions?

nah but could you tell the judge that i ain't trying to do no jail time cause i just had a son, he's three weeks old and he needs me and shit. i think my baby mama's coming too.

I will kid, step out.

Listen can I talk to you about a case, docket ending 654, Ah Chut?

Uh-huh.

This is a sixty-one-year-old first arrest. Unlicensed General Vendor. Can I get an A.C.D.?

Dithorderly conduct and time served.

I know but give me an A.C.D. This guy's sixty-one. He's been in the system twenty-nine hours.

I don't give A.C.D.s on U.G.V. I'll give him a 240.20 and time served.

Even for this guy? He's been in twenty-nine hours on a first arrest for selling batteries on the subway.

Sorry.

Well here's the problem. The guy doesn't speak a syllable of English which means if you're not going to dismiss it I have to get an interpreter which means twenty-nine is going to turn into thirtysomething.

Sorry, but that's the standard offer.

Brilliant. Keep up the work.

Rory Ludd. Ludd!

Yeah.

What's up? You in the park after it closed?

Yeah but right they can't arrest you for that?

Well they can, although my feeling is it may be indicative of some kind of frontal lobe damage on the part of the arresting officer.

That's right man, what you said about the lobe! I like this guy, looking back at his colleagues. This is ridiculous you can't even hang out in the park no more? I had no drugs on me, no beer, nothing! Can they do that? The cop just rolls up on me, tosses me, finds nothing then arrests me on some fucking park regulation. How long I been in here man?

Twenty-three hours.

That's not right man I'm going to sue, can you take the case?

Look, in about fifteen or twenty minutes we're going to be in front of the judge, they're going to offer you time served and you're going home.

Right but right this wasn't right?

Right but it will soon be over.

So with time served the case is over right and it doesn't go on my record?

No it does go on your record but your sentence is the time you've already been in.

But I didn't do anything man I was just walking in the park that's a crime now?

Look I know it's bullshit but why compound it Rory? Just take your time served and go home. You already have a record and God knows a damn park regulation violation isn't going to make it any worse.

You're right man I'll take it. Let me ask you this though: if I was some white guy in a suit and tie think they would have arrested me? But I hear what you're saying B and I'll take the time served.

Good, we'll be in front of the judge in a bit.

Ahhight.

Finish up, we'll go get some food.

Hey Dane.

How long you going to be?

What are you talking about?

Food.

We had dinner during the break you know, should have come if you were hungry.

What three hours ago? You call that dinner?

We did. Where's Linda?

She split, she had no more cases to do.

What envy I felt just now when you said that.

Envy?

Yes, envy.

Never feel envy.

No?

No, instead simply alter the environment giving rise to that emotion in a manner that removes its factual basis.

Nice sentiment but I can't leave.

You don't mean you *can't* leave right? Literally?

No I guess not, but I won't.

In that case you should be feeling an entirely different emotion and one a great deal more painful I'm afraid. Anyway what about that food? I'll explain to you what I mean there.

Sorry but I think I'll have to pass on the second dinner at one in the morning, thanks anyway.

Bizarre decision.

Docket ending 638 – Ray Thomas!

That's me Casi but I'll remember the spurned invitation.

You'll recover.

Tara Simms?

Yes.

Terrens Lake's mother right?

That's right.

I'm going to be his attorney. We're going to go in front of the judge in the next half-hour or so and he's going to decide whether to set bail or release your son. Does Terrens live with his grandmother?

Yeah with my mother. He told you I abandoned him I suppose, he tells everyone.

He didn't tell me anything, I'm just trying to verify his address so I can try to get him out.

What are they charging him with?

Drug sale to an undercover.

Did he have marked money?

I don't know yet. We'll find out when we get in front of the judge. Do you have any money for bail?

No.

Nothing?

No.

Does he go to school?

No.

Does he work, what does he do?

Hm-hmm that's what I say. I tell him he needs to get a job and stop hanging out with his friends but that's all he do.

Do you know who his attorney is on his other case?

No, all I know is he has . . . damn, what am I thinking?

Red hair?

No, red mustache. You know Terrens has a new baby boy?

Casi can you help this person?

Excuse me a minute Ms Simms, we'll talk again afterwards.

What's the matter?

I need to speak to judge.

What about?

I want to be arrested.

Arrested? For what?

I'm GUILTY!

Hold on, don't scream, let's go out in the hall to talk about this . . . what's the problem?

I want the judge to arrest me.

Why?

Because I want to be in jail.

Why do you want to be in jail?

My wife and her brother they're going to kill me.

Why do you say that?

I know.

Why would they want to kill you?

Because I'm guilty.

Guilty of what?

Just guilty.

You're not making any sense sir. Why do you think they want to kill you?

Have they said anything?

No. They don't say things they look at me a certain way. They say things that aren't the same thing but I know what they're really saying and I know what they're really thinking. They blaming me, they think I'm guilty but I'm not. But they thinking so much that I'm guilty that I have almost become guilty. I don't mean that I only *feel* guilty I mean that I have really become guilty because of them.

What are you guilty *of*?

You not listening.

I am but I don't . . . let me ask you this: do you have a doctor you see?

Yeah I have a doctor but that's not important.

Is he a psychiatrist who helps you?

Yes but he doesn't . . . no! I don't have doctor, no doctor.

44

Do you have his card with you?

I don't have a doctor I just told you! I want speak to judge, he can arrest me and put me in jail, that's where I . . . need to be!

Listen the judge doesn't arrest people and besides even if he did no-one gets arrested just because they think they'd be safer in jail. What you need to do if you're concerned about your safety is go the police precinct and file a report. But I will say that it doesn't sound as if these people have said or done anything to cause you to fear for your safety. Maybe what you should do is call this doctor who doesn't exist and tell him what you're feeling or talk to your wife about it. The precinct is like two blocks from here why don't you go there now because if you keep disrupting the court you might actually get your wish which believe me you would almost immediately regret. Goodbye.

Can you put me in jail?

No, I spring people, the very opposite of your request, but I think if you are legitimately scared you should go the police and tell them what you just told me or else talk to your wife or another family member about your concern, O.K.?

You a good man you are.

Your cases are up Casi.

I have to go back in there and do some cases. Here's my card, call me tomorrow if you still need help.

Good man!

Docket ending 645 – *People versus Darril Thorton*! Defendant is charged with Sex Abuse in the First Degree on the sworn complaint of Officer McAfee. Quiet in the courtroom! Counsel waive the reading of the rights and charges but not the rights thereunder?

Yes.

People any notices?

People are serving 190.50 felony grand jury notice. People are also serving statement notice: the defendant stated in sum and substance to Officer McAfee at the time of his arrest: *I never touched that bitch, she's a crazy crackhead. I'm on parole why would I do this?* The people are also serving identification notice. There was a confirmatory point-out identification by the complaining witness in this cathe. The point-out was at the corner of 118th Street at the time and place of arrest. Your honor, the people are requesting that bail be set in the amount of one hundred thousand dollars. The defendant is a two-time predicate felon and in fact is a mandatory persistent in this case. In addition he's had ten other misdemeanor convictions and has an extensive warrant history having warranted on virtually all of those cathes. He's currently on parole your honor for a manslaughter conviction. He's used different names, different dates of birth, and different social security numbers. In this case your honor, the complainant and the defendant are known to each other. The attack occurred in the complainant's home and she's concerned for her safety, we're asking that you issue a full order of protection.

Counsel?

I'm serving cross grand jury notice on the people and I'm asking that you release my client on his own recognizance. I understand my client has a serious record judge but you'll note that he's been on parole almost two years and he's been doing well; there haven't been any violations. As C.J.A. confirmed, he's also been working during this time as an auto mechanic on 118th Street . . . in fact, he now informs me that he was arrested while at work at the garage. As far as the accusations in this case, he vehemently denies them judge. You'll notice from looking at the complaint that there's approximately a two-week lag between the date of this alleged incident and the arrest of my client so that certainly casts some doubt on the truth of these accusations.

People?

I don't have any information on the reason for the delay your honor.

46

Well judge I would also like to know if there was any medical attention given to the complainant?

There was no medical attention your honor.

So this woman is making this accusation judge but there doesn't appear to have been any immediate outcry or any medical attention. Additionally, it appears that the complainant may not be the most reliable witness here in that I understand upon information and belief that she has a drug problem and criminal history. My client's address and employment have been verified by C.J.A. judge so I'm requesting that you release him.

Bail is set in the amount of fifty thousand dollars . . . fifty thousand U.S. dollars! Full order of protection issued. The defendant is to have no contact whatsoever with the complainant in this case. The case is adjourned to the 180.80 date in Part F . . . Part F.

P.D. take charge, one going in! Step in you can communicate free of charge with the Department of Corrections. Next case is docket ending 646 – *People versus Robert Coomer.* Defendant is charged with Robbery in the First Degree on the sworn complaint of Officer Molloy. Counsel waive the reading of the rights and charges but not the rights thereunder?

Yes. People notices? People are therving 190.50 felony grand jury notice. We are also serving statement notice: the defendant stated in sum and substance to the arresting officer at St Luke's Hospital at the time of arrest: *I took my money but there was no knife. He's mad because he don't like my rook opening.*

What was that?

Repeat that for the court reporter please Madame D.A.

R-O-O-K opening. I don't know what that means.

It's chess.

Fine.

The people are requesting that bail be set in the amount of fifteen thousand dollars your honor.

What?

Quiet Robert, let me handle it.

Although the defendant is not a predicate this is a very serious case. The defendant and the complainant are former roommates. Apparently, the defendant pulled a knife on the complainant and stole two hundred dollars from him. The defendant has several misdemeanor convictions and a warrant history your honor.

Counsel?

Judge I'm serving cross grand jury notice on the people and requesting that you release my client on his own recognizance. In this case we have a two-month delay between the date of this alleged incident and the arrest of my client. The people have offered no explanation for that delay. It's true there was a dispute in this case over money but it was money that belonged to my client and which the complainant wanted him to use to pay rent. The dispute became slightly physical but there was never any knife involved. If you look at his raps you'll see that my client really doesn't have much of a record: a few minor misdemeanors and certainly nothing that would suggest he is the kind of person who would pull a knife on a friend and commit a robbery. As you can see my client is on crutches and is not well physically. He was bought here directly from the hospital where he was being treated for two broken legs he sustained after falling off the roof of a building. Significantly, while he was in the hospital he was visited by the complainant in this case who offered to let my client move back in with him once he got out of the hospital. So, given that, I think it's certainly unlikely that the complainant will be pursuing these charges any further from this point. For those reasons your honor I'm requesting that you release my client.

People do you have any information about whether the complainant visited the defendant in the hospital and tried to resume their friendship?

No your honor.

Bail is set in the amount of fifteen thousand dollars . . . fifteen thousand, United States currency only, and the case is adjourned to the 180.80 date in Part F.

P.D. take charge, one going in! Step in you can communicate free of charge with the Department of Corrections. Next case is docket ending 651 – *People versus Terrens Lake*. Defendant is charged with Criminal Sale of a Controlled Substance in the Third Degree on the sworn complaint of Officer O'Dell. Counsel waive the reading of the rights and charges but not the rights thereunder?

Yes.

People any notices?

People are serving 190.50 felony grand jury notice. People are also therving identification notice. There was a confirmatory identification done by undercover officer 6475 at 23:12 hours at the corner of 147th and Amsterdam. The people are requesting bail in the amount of five thousand dollars. This is an undercover buy and bust and the defendant has another open sale on which he pled guilty and has yet to be sentenced. That case is on for sentencing in two weeks in Part 29.

Counsel?

Any buy money or stash recovered?

People?

Your honor there was no prerecorded buy money or drugs recovered from this defendant.

So it's a weak case against my client who denies that he made a sale. I'm serving cross grand jury notice on the people and I'm asking that you release him to the custody of his mother who is in the courtroom. He hasn't been sentenced on his other case so he's not a predicate. He's sixteen years old and therefore still eligible for Y.O. and probation notwithstanding this new case. You'll note judge that on his other case he made all his court dates so he's shown that he will return to court if released. As I mentioned his mother is in the courtroom and she's verified that he lives with his grandmother at

49

2218 Amsterdam Avenue. She doesn't have any money for bail but given the weakness of the people's case, his verified ties, and his age, I'm asking that you release him on his own recognizance.

Why did he tell C.J.A. he lives with his girlfriend; which C.J.A. was unable to verify?

He stays in both places but his primary residence is with his grandmother.

Bail is set in the amount of twenty-five hundred dollars, cash only . . . cash. Case is adjourned to 180.80 date in Part N.

P.D. take charge, one going in! Step in you can communicate free of charge with the Department of Corrections. Next case is docket ending 649 – *People versus Glenda Deeble.* Codefendant's case will be done at a later time. Defendant is charged with Criminal Sale of a Controlled Substance in the Fourth Degree on the sworn complaint of Officer Gooly. Counsel waive the reading of the rights and charges but not the rights thereunder?

Yes.

People any notices?

People are serving 190.50 felony grand jury notice. People are also serving statement notice. The defendant stated in sum and substance to the arresting officer at the 23rd precinct at 23:20 hours: *I've been arrested for this before, nobody saw what we were doing.* People are serving identification notice at this time. There was a confirmatory identification done by undercover officer 2516 at 22:55 hours at the corner of Canal and Hudson. People are requesting that bail be set in the amount of ten thousand dollars. The defendant is a predicate felon with an extensive criminal history for prostitution cathes including one just two weeks ago. She also has a warrant history and has used several different names in the past. This is a strong case where prerecorded buy money was recovered from the codefendant and stash was recovered from this defendant. For those reasons we are requesting that bail be set in the amount of ten thousand dollars.

Counsel?

I'm serving cross grand jury notice on the people and I'm requesting that you release my client. Frankly, the amount of the people's bail request is absurd in its excess. First, this is an extremely weak case against my client. Even if the allegations contained in the complaint are taken to be true, it is the codefendant who exchanges methadone with the undercover and it is the codefendant who takes money from the undercover and, in fact, that's where the prerecorded money is recovered at the time of the arrests. The people's allegation that my client had stash on her at the time of the arrest is borderline disingenuous or at least not fully ingenuous let's say. We know that the way these buy and busts work is that an undercover posing as an addict will approach people as they leave their methadone clinic on a day when they will be receiving an extra bottle. Therefore the fact that when my client is arrested she is in possession of methadone is not evidence of guilt but rather of innocence. If she had intended to sell her methadone then one would expect that she would have done so since she was obviously in the immediate vicinity of a willing buyer. So the characterization of the methadone that she possessed as *stash* is plainly incorrect. In the absence of any concrete evidence, what the people are left to allege is that my client looked up and down the street while the codefendant made the sale. That is clearly insufficient to constitute acting in concert judge. So I believe that this will ultimately prove to be a legally insufficient case and I would be shocked if the D.A. actually presented this case to the grand jury with respect to my client. As far as her personal circumstances are concerned you can see that she's obviously pregnant with her first child. She's in very poor health having only recently been released from the hospital following transfusions necessitated by hepatitis. Additionally, she also has a terminal illness that she's on medication for. As far as her community ties, although C.J.A. failed to confirm them, she has shown me identification from the hotel she lives in with her husband and which is provided by D.A.S. Given these factors, she's obviously not going to be able to make any bail so I ask you to release her judge.

Are you requesting medical attention?

I'm requesting that you release her which is the obvious—

I'm not doing that. Bail is set in the amount of five thousand dollars. Case is adjourned to the 180.80 date in Part N, that's N as in narcotics . . . narcotics.

Your honor why are you setting bail on such a weak case; where's she going to go?

Counsel, bail is set and I'm not going to listen to any further argument.

Well why not make five thousand the bond amount and set a far lower cash alternative?

I would characterize what you just said as further argument.

More like incredulity at your ruling.

Well keep expressing it and you're going to see the bail double.

In that case, being that my pregnant, terminally ill client is going to be incarcerated on this airtight, earth-shatteringly serious case I *am* requesting medical attention.

Medical attention ordered.

P.D. take charge, one going in! Step in you can communicate free of charge with the Department of Corrections. Next case is docket ending 653 – *People versus Ben Glenn*. Defendant is charged with Criminal Mischief in the Fourth Degree on the sworn complaint of Officer Jackson. Counsel do you waive the reading of the rights and charges but not the rights thereunder?

Yes.

People notices?

People are serving statement notice. The defendant stated, in sum and substance to the arresting officer at the time and place of arrest:

I kicked in the window for sure.
But look in me and see that my motives were pure.

Your honor the people are requesting that the defendant be 730'd. Apparently, the officers in this case indicate that the defendant was speaking very strangely and I see that his previous case was dismissed following a 730 examination.

Counsel?

Well I don't think it's the people's role to come in and request that a defendant be 730'd. The relevant question, it seems to me, is whether I can communicate with him and whether I feel that he understands the nature of the proceedings against him.

So what do you want to do with the case?

I want you to give him time served on a plea.

People?

We're recommending six months on a plea your honor. The defendant has a previous record and the window will cost four hundred dollars to replace.

Six months then.

No disposition. I'm requesting that you release my client on his own recognizance.

Bail will be set; do you have a further application?

I'm requesting a 730 examination.

The defendant is remanded and a 730 examination is ordered. Case is adjourned for two weeks to Part C for results of 730 exam.

P.D. take charge, one going in! Step in you can communicate free of charge with the Department of Corrections. Counsel do you need an interpreter on the Chinese case?

Can you get one?

Not anytime soon, we'll put it over to the lobster.

No, I can do without.

O.K. Next case is docket ending 654 – *People versus Ah Chut.*

Defendant is charged with Unlicensed General Vending on the sworn complaint of Officer Faddis. Counsel waive the reading of the rights and charges but not the rights thereunder?

Yes.

People?

People offer a 240.20 and one day of community service.

Where did this community service come from? You said 240.20 and time served.

If I said that, it was a mistake. The standard offer is a discon and one day community service.

The guy's been in jail twenty-nine hours.

What are we doing here counselors?

I'm trying to get the people to offer time served on a sixty-one-year-old first arrest who's been in twenty-nine hours.

As you know counselor it's their offer and there's nothing I can do about it. I'll give him time served on a plea to the charge.

No because then he gets a record.

The offer is a discon with one day of community service.

You can go home now but you'll have to do one day of community service.

Yeh.

My client is authorizing me to enter a plea of guilty to penal law 240.20, disorderly conduct, which is a violation not a crime, in exchange for the promised sentence of a conditional discharge with the condition that he perform one day of community service. He waives prosecution by information, waives formal allocution, and is ready for sentence.

Mr Chut do you understand what your attorney just said?

He waives allocution judge.

No he doesn't. I'm going to electrocute, I mean allocute him. Mr Chut do you understand that your legal representative has offered to enter a plea of guilty on your behalf in exchange for the prosecution's offer to reduce the charges in your case to the violation of disorderly conduct with the understanding that you will be sentenced to a conditional discharge the primary but not sole condition of which will be that you perform one day of community service?

Uh?

Do you speak and understand English Mr Chut?

Can we approach?

Come up.

. . .

Judge he speaks very little English that's why I waived allocution.

Well let's get an interpreter.

In my experience that will take at least several hours at one in the morning and he's already been in over twenty-four hours.

Well he clearly didn't understand what I just said so I'm going to second call the case for an interpreter and let the next judge deal with it.

Can't we just do the right thing here. Let him take the plea without allocuting, the case is over and all is well.

I'm not interested in doing *the right thing* as you call it; I'm going to do things correctly and that means not doing a case where the defendant doesn't understand what's happening.

Well then you don't have to second call it, just release him with a date to return.

I'm not doing anything further on the case without an interpreter. How do I know he'll even understand to return?

Then he's entitled to be released if you're not going to arraign him since he's been in more than twenty-four hours.

You know the correct procedure for such an application is a writ.

Yeah and I know it takes longer than getting an interpreter.

A couple more hours in jail isn't going to kill him . . . it's not going to kill him.

Of course none of this would matter if she would just give him an

A.C.D. which is what the case is worth anyway; even he will understand *dismissed.*

I gave him the standard offer and I'm not changing it.

You seem to have an unhealthy fascination with all things standard.

O.K. That's enough. Step back. Second call for Chinese interpreter . . . Chinese!

Second call, case is put over to A.R.-5! Step in. Final case is docket ending 652 – *People versus Rory Ludd*. Defendant is charged with a violation of Parks and Recreation Regulation T-108 on the sworn complaint of Officer Milton. Counsel waive the reading of the rights and charges but not the rights thereunder?

Yes.

People?

On a plea to the charge people recommend time served.

I've discussed it with him and my client is authorizing me to enter a plea of guilty to a violation of this park regulation.

Mr Ludd did you hear what your attorney has just said?

Yeah!

Yes?

Yes.

And is it true that you wish him to plead you guilty to violating this parks regulation?

I don't have any choice.

You most certainly do have a choice, you can tell him you wish to fight this case. Is that what you want to do? Fight the case?

No.

So you wish to plead guilty?

Yes!

And is it true that you were in the park after it had closed?

I didn't even know they closed the park! I wasn't doing anything; I don't understand what's going on!

Well they do close the park and you're no stranger to the system having been arrested . . . fourteen other times . . . so do you want to take this plea or not?

Yes. I was in the park after it closed and I'm pleading guilty but why did I have to be put through the system for something so stupid why couldn't they have given me a summons or a D.A.T. – a disappearance ticket?

I'm not concerned with that Mr Ludd. The fact is that whether it's usual or not the police did nothing improper here and whether they put someone through the system or give them a summons is left to their discretion. That said, do you still wish to take this plea?

Yeah.

Yes?

Yes.

Very well. The sentence is time already served and there is no surcharge on these cases . . . time served.

Step out of the well your case is over. That being the final case of the evening, A.R.-3 is adjourned until 5:00 p.m. A.R.-5 will commence in approximately fifteen—

TOTAL BULLSHIT!

Hold it! Hold it! Get him back in here! Counselor I'm going to hold your client in contempt of court and sentence him to fifteen days. Do you wish to be heard?

Judge, I don't think he meant to direct that to the court. I think he was just frustrated by the fact that—

Speak with your client because unless I get some kind of explanation the summary conviction and sentence will be imposed.

What are you doing? You were out the door.

I was just expressing myself man, I have a Fifth Amendment right to do that right? I spent a day in jail for no reason just because the cop didn't like my face or something.

Whatever man. This is a battle you can't win. What he wants is an apology, give it to him and I'll get him to take back the contempt otherwise you're going to stay in jail. Rory?

Fine.

Judge my client wishes to address you.

Mr Ludd?

I want to apologize to your honors for cursing in the courtroom. Like my attorney said I was just frustrated by the situation.

Well the situation was one of your own making young man. If you don't break the law you don't get arrested it's as simple as that. I do not stand for that kind of language either. This is a goddamn courtroom not some corner hangout! I don't care what you think those cops did or didn't do to you out on the street; when you come into my courtroom you show me respect because I am a man of respect. I think your attorney will tell you that I am an exceedingly fair-minded individual. How do you think you become a judge other than by demonstrating an extreme, almost-criminal, degree of impartiality but I will not have my courtroom turned into a circus by the likes of you. When I am confronted with such a situation I will wield my considerable power swiftly and decisively . . . decisive swiftness. You are going to have to learn to respect authority. The officer who arrested you and myself we are authority, ask your attorney. Now, are you sorry?

Yeah I'm sorry.

Yes?

Yes.

Fair enough, he's not a bad guy at that. Next time he'll obey the signs.

Fucking—

That's it! I find the defendant guilty of contempt of court and sentence him to fifteen days. Fifteen days to be served under the vilest conditions permitted by New York law. Get him out of here!

Step in! P.D. take charge one going in.

What were you thinking Rory?

I didn't think he could hear me. Can I take it back?

Judge you have to permit him to make a statement in his defense before you can summarily find him guilty of contempt.

He had his chance, I said get him out of here! We're done! Step up counsel I want to talk to you . . . son I really think that you are a great attorney in the making, if not great then certainly tremendous. But you have to learn when to leave well enough alone. None of these people is worth your career and another less patient judge won't stand for your little comments after every ruling you don't agree with. And something like trying to do a case without an interpreter is just plain wrong and borders on the unethical. Now if you ask around you'll hear I'm a fair judge. One of the best really. The best in fact and I say that despite being humble. I'm famous for that as well. I'm very proud of my humility and if I had to pick one quality of mine that has continually stood me in good stead and which has allowed me to achieve the status I have, I think I would point to that, my humility that is; either that or my intelligence. Now it's not every judge who would take the time to talk to you like this and I hope you realize that. That's another good quality that I have and which I try to fertilize as often as possible. So remember what I've just said here tonight . . . said here tonight. Good night.

Morning.

So how much is his bail?

Twenty-five hundred.

So ten percent of that and Terrens get out?

No. Here, twenty-five hundred means you have to pay the full amount in cash. Can anybody pay that?

No that's a lot of money.

I know but we'll be back in court on Tuesday and maybe we'll get lucky.

If they don't have an indictment on that day they have to release him.

Where's that?

Part N, second floor of this building.

I'll be there.

She turned and split making me the last night-court person in a courtroom duly filling with lobster-shift personnel. Now this shift ran from the a.m.'s one to its nine so many of the people milling about me then looked like warmed-over cadavers reanimated by some evil genius that they may haunt the living and they cast their vacant eyes on me amidst air still charged with the dim electricity of Transgression, the invisible contagion that permeated the room; all of which made me let's-say-eager to leave but when I did and stepped outside the immoral cold so set upon my flesh, forcing my shoulders to drop and squinch together, that I nearly beat an immediate retreat but didn't because it was getting pretty late if I hoped to snag one of the cabs that lined up outside 100 Centre for the end of night court, especially after a voice from across the street stopped me in my tracks with: "You good man you! Good man, I call you tomorrow!" It was the guy who was convinced his wife wanted an irreversible divorce and whom I had sent to the precinct. Whatever they told him he sure seemed happy as he waved frantically while walking away and I realized I never even learned his name; some good man I made.

I saw there was only one cab left but rather than run or even trot I just followed my geodesic towards it like a soulless galactic body. Floating forward in this manner the vast sidewalk below of lightning-shaped cracks and flat, adhered pebbles, receded, section by section, into my past; in the dim light the many black islands of spent gum, various in size and shape but consistent in frequency, seemed like so many portals to null space. And at the Ptolemaic center lay a steaming lump of rags that only suggested humanity. For out of that amorphous shape emerged two leg-like structures ending in dull orange Chuck Taylors, one of which had been purposely ripped open near the ankle to expose a gapingly open sore that wetly reflected streetlamp light. But wait, maybe his entire body was an open sore and the circle I was staring at the only healthy patch. I looked away. Just before the cab was a round, waist-high kid dressed from chubby head to toe in aggressive pink and testing the limits of acceptable distance from the only nearby woman emitting any maternal air. He stared back at me as if I owed him money and sang distractedly in a troubling falsetto. He sang: ♫ *You've got to accen–tuate the positive, eli–minate the negative . . .* ♫ and wasn't it like one in the morning on a Thursday night? I dropped into the cab and made my request. Suddenly behind me came an aural explosion directly into my bad ear: *Hi! This is Judd Hirsch! I know a thing or two about taxis, ha ha . . . ha, and I know that you should buckle up for safety.* I immediately thought of Latka Gravas altering his lifestyle to fit the fast lane with predictably grim results. Ah Latka! Ah humanity!

The driver was the very picture of energy, darkening at various times significant portions of the dividing screen with his seemingly limitless body while his bellow filled the rest of the cab in almost visible sound waves.

"You work in the courts huh chief?"

"Yup."

"You one of them there D.A.s working night court son?"

"No."

"Well you sure look like a lawyer. You know wearing that suit at one-thirty in the a.m. and all, tell you that."

Oh man. This was New York, you weren't supposed to have to talk to anyone when all you wanted was to stand mute but this pause was going into labor and my interrogator had locked his eyes on the rear-view in predatory wait, so:

"Yeah I'm a lawyer but I'm with the bad guys."

"What do you mean mac?"

"I'm a defender of the public."

"Uh?"

"I defend the public from—"

"What?"

"I'm a public defender."

"Really? Wow that must be something." He mulled it over noisily. "A public defender in New York City. I mean this has got to be like the crime capital of the world right bub?"

"Well—"

"I read somewhere that someone is killed every hour in New York City."

"That seems a bit—"

"This is one violent city."

"– actually absurdly—"

"Not for the weak."

"– high."

"That's great for you though right champ? I mean you get that experience."

"I guess."

"Cause you guys get paid shit right boss? I hear the trick is get that experience a few years then go into private practice, which is where the money is. Next thing you know, you're charging five, six hundred dollars an hour, that's real money," this guy wasn't even pausing for air, "take my brother-in-law for example, he's a lawyer. Not a public defender, a real lawyer. Anyways, that's a guy's really got his act together. Married to my sister, the fuck. They got two kids. He's like a what do you call *senior partner?* at one of those big Fifth Avenue firms. I think he does like trademark work you've probably heard of him his name's Jack. Anyway this guy really knows how to live. Big house over in Jersey he's got this seventy-inch Television with a perfectly flat screen that automatically turns on when your favorite shows are on so you don't miss them, you know, by accident. Seventy inches!"

"Yeah those guys make money," I said near tears. "Make your first left up there."

"Oh you don't know. We'll go to a titty bar and this guy will drop two, three thousand dollars easy. They love him there. Love! Best of all, his wife can't say shit. Not at the rate he's bringing the cash in! You know what though kid?" Now he turned and looked me directly in the eye while I cursed myself for not having listened to goddamn Alex Reeger. "You look like you're real young. If you work hard and make the right connections I bet you could end up just like him in a couple of years."

"This is it," I said trying to contain my exultation.

"Six bucks chief. Just remember what I said. You can be like my brother-in-law. You can be Jack."

"Thanks."

"I do have one question for you though before you go," all gravity now.

"What's that?"

"How can you represent someone you *know* is guilty?"

I took my four bucks change and returned half. I watched this guy take his dough but all I kept imagining was Jack's suburban construction raptly coming to responsorial attention for the suddenly resurgent Monolith as it chanted the rhythmic, synchronized intro to Sajak's *Rota . . . For . . . tunae!!* He asked again. I summoned the tattered vestiges of my concentration, looked him in the eye, and answered his question:

"Practice," I said.

The Yellow-Bellied Sapsucker (environs Brooklyn) is distinguishable
mainly by the fact it's got a yella belly and is sucking sap!
– The Sanitation Worker's Guide to Ornithological Species, Vol. XII

Chapter 2

It was marrow-petrifying, prayer-inducingly cold and I couldn't find
my goddamn keys. I was frantically patting myself all over and doing
so in historic Brooklyn Heights, an *idyllically tree-lined* neighborhood
immediately off and to the right of the Brooklyn Bridge. The archi-
tectural charisma of that ancient bridge, the clear view of Manhattan
across the East River and, most importantly, the residential neighborhood's proximity and transportational ease to nearby Wall $treet
all conspired to spawn seven-figure brownstones and the people
who could own them so that wherever you turned you saw what
looked like gray-haired grandmothers but were in fact the actual
mothers carrying their little blubber packages in chest-high kangaroo
pouches on the Trinidadian nanny's day off. Many longed to live in
this land of the silver-haired kangaroo and as a result the exalted
spectre of this neighborhood so hung over the surrounding areas
that when looking at ads for apartments located in neighborhoods
that were most decidedly not Brooklyn Heights you were nonetheless
assured *Brooklyn Heights Vicinity*. Consequently, for an apartment
roughly the size of a manila envelope I paid the kind of rent that
could pull some countries out of a recession and at that moment, it
occurred to me, I was paying it solely to provide shelter for Casper
the Friendly Ghost who bound my keys and likely lay on the wobbly

semicircle table near my front door.

I thought about Casper and wondered how someone with such soft edges could do this to me after so many years of one-sided friendship, thought about: *a two-year-old in my aunt's apartment; yellow flowered bed sheets delineating rooms and trapping icy air-conditioning: ¿is it three yet? No. Casper comes when the little hand is on the three and the big hand on the twelve. O.K. ¿which one is the three? : Do you love me? Yes. One to ten? ∞*

I remembered all that, watched the figurative mercury plummet while my powers of reasoning suffered greatly, and somewhere in there I semi-concluded that maybe it was all meet and just that I should sleep on the street that night like the open-sored guy outside arraignments. So I curled into a ball there by the door to start slumbering only I started shivering so bad I couldn't stop and the sound of my teeth like machine gun fire then a low guttural moan that I eventually realized was coming from me and those two competing sounds so disturbed me, so exacerbated the pain in my ear, that I decided I would make a more significant effort to sleep indoors that night.

Which was about the time I had an auditory hallucination informed by recent memory whereby a recondite voice said *hey being that we're friends now we should perhaps have a copy of each other's keys so we don't get negligently locked out and so forth* which in turn spurred the instant storyteller into acting like a cinematic Lotharian suitor by throwing icy acorns at the second-story window of one Alyona Karn in place of ringing a doorbell that never worked. Alyona's uncle was the proud owner of the general recipient of my acorn pelts and of my apartment contained within. In addition to being the sixty-year-old father of a preschooler he allowed Alyona to live there footloose and rent-free provided he would superintend. Alyona in turn, and unbeknownst to uncle, allowed two others, Angus Glass and Louis Sands, to live in the apartment without paying rent in exchange for their promise to pay all necessary bills and expenses; necessary meaning digital cable, satellite programming, broadband internet, phone, food, toothpaste, electricity, water et cetera. This pleased him to no end and more than once he bragged that *I have in essence extricated myself from our system of pay to play. Currency has no meaning to me. I am a twenty-eight-year-old who does not have a bank account yet my refrigerator is always full. Bills arrive in my name and get paid without me so much as opening the envelope. This – extreme nonconsumerism – is something that has come to be associated with illegality has it not?*

Now several acorns had successfully flown their sorties, cutting through the frigid air to form interrupted parabolas, when I began to conceive the inconceivable. Could they all be asleep? Not home? Was there a difference if either meant sleeping on the street? The three of them were good customers of Columbia University. Alyona was purchasing a doctorate in Philosophy with an emphasis on either the eighteenth century British empiricists or else the work of Sextus Empiricus I could never recall. Angus was a twenty-six-year-old under-grad gravitating without the slightest volition towards a Bachelor's in Psychology and Louie a graduate student trying to master business with both eyes towards his first and true love: Advertising. Alyona and Angus never left the house and, to my knowledge, the three of them never slept, certainly not while it was dark out, yet there I stood with diminishing acorns in raw gloveless hands and, to all appearances, vastly alone. And I was just beginning to reflect on how I came to be so alone when I heard the sweet, redemptive sound of a door opening followed by cognizable human words.

"What are you trying to do, break our windows at a time when their continued integrity is of the utmost importance?" The speaker allowed maybe a third of his face to appear from behind the door and I saw that it was Alyona. "Come on, you're letting the red out and the blue in."

I moved inside the door to hear it close behind me. "My hero," I said and emitted that little shudder you get with the initial blast of heat. He was shaking his head no as if I'd been all prodigal or something.

"You know what the key to getting inside a locked building is?" he said.

"Funny."

"So?"

"It's relaxing in my apartment," I said moving up the stairs to the promise of greater heat but careful not to outpace my rescuer as that would have been weird.

"Good thing you listened to me then huh? I'm starting to think I'm . . . um."

"Prescient?"

"Negative."

"Clairvoyant?"

"Maybe."

"Were you sleeping?" puzzled look. "No because you have that hat on, I didn't know those were worn anymore outside of comic strips."

"They're not. And no because we have a guest, courtesy of Louis."

"Let me guess."

"Gorgeous."

I spent the time on the stairs wondering if I could wait in the hall while Alyona got my key's identical twin then just run up to my third-floor apartment. Would that be rude and if so did that necessarily mean I had to go in since I had no legal or contractual obligation to avoid being rude nor had I promised anyone I wouldn't be rude and in fact rudeness must be a rather natural state of human being since time immemorial to have necessitated invention of the word *rude* right? And even if this one time I acted in this eminently common manner would that be sufficient, standing alone, to make me a rude person? Moreover, if I did go in how quickly could I split given that I had just worked about seventeen straight hours? I mean without being rude.

"Suit and tie at this hour," Alyona said opening the door. "That's got to be brutal."

"Not fun."

"Hope I can find them Casi, think they're in my room somewhere."

I went in with Alyona, almost instinctively, having never resolved my little internal debate. "Casi my good man," said Louie. "Come in dude, join the party."

"I am in," I said.

"I mean *in* in," he said. "This is Traci."

"Hey Traci how are you?" (The Traci part of this was a new trick I had recently picked up from a dental waiting room Glamour published the requisite decade earlier, which trick called for people like me to *repeat the name immediately for better memory retention* and shortly after reading that the dentist told me his name but I immediately forgot it because I couldn't repeat it with that little vacuum thing resting on my lower row of choppers.)

"Hello," Traci said.

"Casi?"

"Angus."

"Who's cooler, the Loch Ness Monster or Bigfoot?"

"I don't know."

"C'mon which?"

"I have no preference."

"If you had to choose, gun to your head."

"I guess I would then say Loch Ness but I stress that a gun would have to be involved."

"See?" said Angus pointing at Louis.

"Defend that choice because four out of five say Bigfoot," said Louis.

"Just cooler I don't know. I'm tired."

"C'mon make something up. But like the kind of things we say."

"The kind of things you say? Fine, how's this? The thought of a guy who looks at vaginas for a living dropping some toy in a body of water and spurring decades of debate in a certain underdeveloped segment of society reassures and comforts me with the power of designer truth. Happy?"

"Wait, it was a hoax?" said Louis.

"I will say this on Bigfoot's behalf however. There *was* a movie," said Angus a look of careful reconsideration on his face.

"Movie?" groaned Traci.

"Yeah, movie theater and everything. So we're all settled in ready for this movie to start when suddenly from a door near the screen comes this like huge eight-foot-tall guy bearing a striking resemblance to Bigfoot – the very same Bigfoot about to star in the feature we plunked down five bucks to see. Well for once this sort of thing works and of course there follows a rush of about fifty eight-to-ten-year-olds flooding into the aisle and running up the incline to the exit. Anyway goddamn Bigfoot gets the brilliant idea that he's going to like pursue the kids for a while, you know ham it up. Well long story short he steps on a box of melted Raisinets, becomes involuntarily airborne and lands on like some seven-year-old girl who proceeds to have what theater management termed *a brief respite in cardiactivity*. I think they banned those kind of promotional stunts at that theater for like the next thirty-five years. You can't do cool shit like that with Loch Nesses the way you can with Bigfeet. So basically I change my vote."

"Me too," said a resigned Louis. "I love hoaxes."

"You love hoaxes?" said Alyona. "What do you think fucking Bigfoot was? Some clown named Ray Wallace photographing his wife in a Sasquatch suit!"

"The hell's a Sasquatch suit?" said Traci.

"Like a leisure suit."

"No, more like a zoot suit."

"Or a monkey suit."

"Or your birthday suit."

"Or a chicken-skin suit."

Where we were was the living room, which had three different non-complementary throw rugs. In the center of the room, both literally and figuratively, was Television. Angus sat exactly 8.3 feet from its screen and precisely twelve degrees to the right of its imaginary extended midpoint. On the rare occasion he rose from that spot, the sofa maintained a little scoop where his ass belonged. According to Angus, this particular positioning of the viewer was said to create optimal video-aural receptory performance according to several well-respected studies performed by several similarly respected institutes. The rest of the room paid homage to its star as well. The furniture had been strategically positioned to encourage crystalline reception. The sofa seemed to lean towards Television like a needy plant towards the sun. Speakers of varying sizes appeared in odd places and assumed unlikely, almost pornographic, positions. The result was that Television's sound had you sensurrounded with resistance being futile Earthling. And on top of Television that night sat a new silver box; the red and green lightbars it contained vying for attention.

"What's that thing?"

"New H.D.V.D.C.R. man," said Angus. "The Casio Carousel, that's its name. This puppy can handle up to fifteen Entertainmentities at one time. I can press this button and go to any of the fifteen in an instant. I can also operate the device in such a fashion as to create a never-ending loop of entertainment. Again all at near instantaneity. The booklet even says that if I ever have to wait more than three seconds for one of the entities to play I get my choice of my money back or a part in their next commercial. Do you own a stopwatch?"

"It doesn't come with one?"

"Hmm."

"Have you heard of a Television that turns on automatically when your favorite shows are on?"

"I don't understand, why would you turn it off?"

Television: ♫ *Magilla Gorilla for sale . . .* ♫

"See. *That* I have a problem with," said an exasperated Louie as the channel changed three times during the course of his statement. "How can Magilla Gorilla be for sale just like that? What, you walk into a basic pet store and buy a gorilla?"

"Seriously, I agree," said Angus. "And if that were the case how much does a gorilla like that go for and where does this little girl get that kind of green?"

"She doesn't. It's bullshit. A gorilla like that. One that can talk? That simian's got to be worth a fortune!"

"Except Magilla couldn't talk," said Angus.

"Yeah I don't think he could talk either," contributed Traci.

"I bet he could talk if he had to. He probably just never had much to say," countered Louis.

"He *was* purple. That's got to jack the price up," said Angus.

"He wasn't purple dude you're thinking of goddamn Grape Ape," said Louis.

"I think they were both purple," said Traci.

"Here, let me try to find it again," said Angus.

"Casi?" from a tiring Louis.

"I don't know, black and white set." I drifted to the back of the apartment where Alyona searched his bedroom with increasing desperation. Our best-laid plan would crumble if Alyona didn't find the key I'd given him.

"I've looked everywhere," he said. "I have no idea where I put it and locating something in this mess is no small task."

"I have faith in you."

"You shouldn't."

"Got it, maybe Louis can hypnotize you to remember where you put them." (In addition to his lifelong love of advertising Louis had a new interest in anything hypnotic, alleging that the distinction between the two fields grew blurrier by the day. One day about two months past he had gone to a three-day seminar in Anchorage, Alaska given by someone named Gary Dullen, a self-proclaimed *hypno-guru*. Before he left he showed me the brochure which said *inter alia* that YOU TOO CAN LEARN HOW TO HYPNOTIZE OTHERS IN JUST 12 EASY LESSONS! AMAZE YOUR FRIENDS AND IMPROVE YOUR PERSONALITY! The premise, and the allure for Louis, was that you needn't wish to become a professional hypnotist to benefit from the seminar. Materials would be given, workbooks used, with the end result that your $239.99 – all major credit cards accepted – would be exchanged for a winning *hypnotic* personality, one that would win you the admiration of others, although they may not be entirely sure why they admire you.)

"No way," Alyona said. "I would sooner break your door down and deal with my uncle than let that guy mess with my head, he's that scary. Though not as scary as that other nut. Sometime I'll tell you."

"Well I'll give you your privacy as long as you promise a continued good-faith effort."

"Be not afraid for it has become almost personal at this point."

I walked back towards the living room while picturing, really almost feeling, my lumpy but loyal bed.

"Want an espresso?" said Louis from the open kitchen.

"It's two in the morning. I have to be at work in about seven hours."

"Is that a yes?"

"That's a no-but-thank-you. You guys plan to sleep at any point?"

"Tell him your plan, go ahead," said Louis motioning to Angus with his chin while measuring coffee grounds.

"Well the truth is I bought The Casio Carousel for a reason. Tonight starting in less than one half-hour, Channel Eleven, as they do every year though a bit late this year, is presenting a Honeymooners marathon, all thirty-nine episodes back to back and in order."

"And your plan?"

"On the surface what I'm going to do is record all of the episodes. Then, thanks to the Carousel's highly attuned C.E.S. or Commercial Extraction Sensor, I will replay the episodes without commercial interruption on a continuous self-propelling and repetitive loop." At mention of the sensor Louis had visibly shuddered then fired ocular evil in Angus' direction. "That's what I'm going to do on the surface," Angus continued unfazed.

"O.K. And below the surface?"

"I'm going to turn Ralph Kramden and possibly the three others into actual human beings."

"What do you think of that Casi?" asked Louis.

"Nothing."

"You must think something of it," said Angus.

"Nope."

"C'mon be honest."

"It's honestly late."

"Honestly? You think nothing?"

"Fine, I think it seems you really like the show but I also think you're being frivolous."

"It does sound frivolous, I admit that, but that's only because I haven't taken the time to properly explain," Angus said with the air of someone about to repeat something they had said earlier with far greater emotion. "What happens when two people become friends Casi? I say that at least part of what happens is that the two people become more *real* to each other. In a sense each feels that the other has become more of a human being. Anyone would agree with that but how does this happen? How does someone go from being a collection of flesh and bone who generally occupies the same space as us to being a real person who has an inner life that we, on some level, care about? Well I think the principal way this happens is through speech and language. After all, we can see the same person every day for years but if we've never heard them speak I maintain that if properly confronted we'd be hard-pressed to even think of them as human and we certainly wouldn't consider them friends. That sounds odd I know, but have you ever been in a room full of complete strangers who weren't talking? Did you ever then have a fleeting thought or feeling that maybe they didn't really exist at all the way you exist? On the other hand, people actualize through speaking. Actors know this. *How many lines?* they ask when considering a part, not how much face time. Hostages talk to their tormenters in the hopes of becoming more human and therefore harder to kill. These people seem to realize that the more we hear someone talk in a variety of situations the closer we become to them, the more *real* they become to us. Their speaking makes it harder to ignore their status as actual people with inner lives like ours. So why is that? The answer is probably obvious but I don't know what it is. Nevertheless, and more importantly, I'm going to make this process happen in the context of The Honeymooners. Sure I've seen all these episodes before but half-hour at a time and diffused among all this other stimuli. This time, however, I'm going to be running these episodes in a constant loop. I won't move a muscle while they play. There will be no commercials. The result is that over time Ralph Kramden and to a lesser extent the others will begin to seem, no, *will in fact become*, more and more real. And why not? I'll see them in a variety of situations. They'll be coming into my home! What could be more intimate than that?"

"You can't touch them for one."

"So what? How many times have I touched you? Are we not friends? Are you not real? These people will be constantly speaking to each other."

"Right, to each other not to you."

"That's irrelevant. There are people in this room right now as we speak solely to each other yet their perception of us as actual beings suffers not in the slightest."

"They can join in if they wish. If you try to join these Honeymooners conversations you'll only establish that you're insane."

"They *can* join in that's true, but if they choose not to does that make us any less real to them? I will not be joining in these conversations but I will observe them and listen to them for so long and in the absence of any other stimuli that the characters will eventually become *real* in an important sense of the word."

"O.K. how long?"

"As long as it takes. My guess is at least a hundred hours, or enough to see every episode seven times."

"You'll lose interest, become bored. You'll be highlighting the absent third dimension in these people and the illusion will be shattered."

"Two-dimensional, three-dimensional, what's the difference? People are people dude. Why discriminate against Ralph just because he happens to cause a different kind of image on my retina? Don't you think it's time people of different races, creeds, colors, and realities came together? Besides, the thrill of creation will keep me interested. Man is never more alive than when he is creating. I'll be a modern-day Prometheus but whereas he worked with clay I'll work with televisual analog waves and digital pulses. What could be more exciting than that? Besides if I start to falter, Lou and Traci have agreed to help."

"Help how?"

"If they see I'm getting tired, disinterested or whatever they're going to say things like *c'mon Angus you can do it, don't quit.* You get the idea."

"Big help."

"Turns out it will be. Listen to this psych study. First they get a bunch of volunteers together. These people agree that they'll put their bare feet in buckets of ice water and keep them there for as long as possible. Now I tried this the other day and can faithfully report that it hurts when you do that. Real pain. Anyway, they split these people into two groups. One of the groups is all alone so to speak. They stick their feet in the bucket, hold out as long as they can and someone times them. The other group does essentially the same thing only they have these people around them shouting encouragement. Well you can see where this is going as the cheerleader group substantially outperforms the other group."

"Substantially how? What are the actual numbers?"

"What do I know? *Statistically significant* as we say. The principle is the important thing. People need people after all."

"3-D people. When do you learn about these studies anyway? I never see you go to class."

"I haven't missed a lecture all year. Tell him Lou."

"He hasn't missed a lecture all year," deadpanned Lou.

"I've never seen you leave the house."

"That's the beauty. I don't have to leave the house to go to class. I take two classes both taught by the same teacher and he broadcasts all his lectures on the school's e-campus. I sit in front of the computer's twenty-nine inch flatscreen monitor at the allotted times and soak in all the knowledge with minimal interruption to my day."

"Wouldn't it be good to leave the house, interact with other students, discuss the lectures, ask the professor questions in person?"

"He has his own website you can ask him questions at any time during the week. That other stuff you're saying is vastly overrated. Information is everything. Give me the information. Supply it like any other product. The method of delivery is irrelevant. I'll *learn*, if you want to use that term, the information myself and who knows I may even use it someday. What do people have to do with it?"

"You're a psych major right?"

"Yeah so? I watch people every day on Television and don't say they're not in their natural state. Being on Television is fast becoming *the* natural state. In the future all life will be televised. Our mayor was on Television tonight saying that a camera can be more effective than a gun in the war against crime. He wants to put cameras everywhere then arm you and me with even more cameras to help the state fight crime. How will people act then? Well I have a better idea than most."

"They said it couldn't be done!" Alyona walking towards me with the key in his hand and never had my eyes feasted on sweeter sight. I wanted out and up real bad. In my weakened state, Angus had half-convinced me that Kramden and Norton would soon be in the room and I knew enough people. My left ear hurt too, I cupped my hand to it. "You've got to get that ear checked out man. Here you go." Alyona dropped the key in my other palm. I thanked him, offered brief goodbyes, and headed for the door with visions of bed in head when:

"By the way who's the worst guy you represented tonight?" asked Louis.

"Everybody was fine tonight."

"Who was charged with the worst crime though?"

"I had a guy charged with using the subway without paying."

"Bastard, what else?"

"Let's see, I had another guy selling batteries in the subway without a license."

"That's illegal?" joined Alyona.

"Yeah, twenty-nine hours in jail and counting."

"Dude I can't believe you're in favor of crime."

"He's not in favor of crime he just likes it."

"He doesn't just like it he adores it."

"You're both wrong, he doesn't admire it in any way. He abhors it like the rest of us. It's just that he recognizes it as a legitimate, albeit alternate, lifestyle."

"I have to go," I said.

"The other day someone stole my club, you believe that?" said Traci. "I don't mean that someone stole my car while The Club was on it. No, someone broke into my car for the express purpose of stealing my Club which I had neglected to place on the steering wheel and which was sitting on the back seat."

"Delicious irony actually," said Louie. "Undone by your own protective measures."

"Yes that from which you sought protection has instead inspired malfeasance," said Alyona.

"What are you a fucking biblical narrator?"

Television: *With Art Carney, Audrey Meadows* . . .

"O.K. guys I need monastery-type quiet," said Angus. "The marathon's about to begin."

"I'm gone, thanks for the shelter." I was out the door and up the stairs in record time. Put key in door and it opens was my new favorite technology. Casper was on the table alright that ghostly prick. The answering machine blinked plaintively. Scattered on the floor was mail. The mailbox was broken again and Alyona must have slid it under my door. In the middle was a familiar yellow envelope with its tiresome but nonetheless fear-inducing slogan: IF YOU THINK EDUCATION IS EXPENSIVE, TRY IGNORANCE. Inside, I knew a posteriori, would be threats: *your credit rating . . . collection agency* and other ominous warnings. I read this as if about another, without alarm or true belief. More mail alleging it was sensitive to time; I sympathized. From my machine came exhortations: *Don't forget about tomorrow . . . I can see you're not going to return my phone calls . . . please call immediately regarding your account.*

I figured I needed to wash my brain clean if I hoped to sleep. Needed to forget that there were Glenda Deebles the world over or at least get them temporarily out of my skull and for that I would need an attractive distraction. Music was always my first choice but I liked it loud and the ear was in no mood. I had not nearly enough concentration left for reading so on went Television and its replay of the nightly news.

Angus was right. Before an array of microphones in front of City Hall stood a lanky Toad. Toad was the mayor. New York City's electoral populace had not elected a fly-eating amphibian to run the city but they had selected someone named Toad, pronounced toe-add, to stand behind microphones in situations such as this and he now did so gladly, a slight smirk maybe building across his face. Video Vigilantes was a good idea he was saying and a grinning fat guy in a green beret was shaking his hand. Citizens needed to help the police fight crime. Citizens had greater leeway and could, in some instances, be more effective since their conduct was not governed by that obstructive Bill of Rights. Videotaping life was a step in the right direction. Those who weren't doing anything wrong had nothing to fear and those who were, well they would be exposed by the white light of the camera – a camera that incidentally never lied. The reporter then hit the streets to see what average Joe thought. There followed near-universal praise for the vigilantes and the Toad's stamp of approval. Crime was on the run.

But not completely because up next was *the horrifying story of the Dutch woman whose New York vacation has turned into a nightmare that just won't end,* the face said this with a solemnity that veered towards glee. Then they sped to Cindylou or whatever who was at the scene with the full story: *Thanks Chuck. A nightmare is exactly what Dutch tourist Lana Huber is experiencing. Behind me is the T.G.I.N. MONDAY'S in midtown where the twenty-three-year-old single mother stopped in for what police believe was a decaffeinated beverage. Police say Ms Huber left her ten-month-old daughter outside on the sidewalk in a stroller while she had her coffee. When she returned (dramatic pause) the baby was gone.*

Yes it appears that the female in question was in this establishment consuming a decaffeinated beverage while the child in question was left outside for a period of time. When the female returned to the scene the child in question was gone.

Any leads?

We're not going to discuss a pending investigation.

Reaction in the community was mixed.

Serves her right! You can't leave no baby out in the street like that. This is New York this ain't Iowa!

My heart goes out to her as a fellow mother. She may have made a mistake but nobody deserves to have her baby abducted in that manner. I certainly hope they can find the person who did this and I hope the baby's safe.

It just goes to show you that nobody's safe not even a baby.

Chuck, police are asking anyone who might have information on this missing baby to call 1-800-BAD BABY. The BAD is not meant as any kind of value judgment Chuck, its alliterative allure is simply designed to increase consumer awareness. From outside MONDAY'S in midtown this is Cindylou or whatever reporting.

Thank you. In Harlem a brutal slaying has shocked . . .

There followed grim descriptions of further mayhem and an almost heartfelt plea to stay tuned for a report on the record lows from their vaunted Weather-tis-Better-Center. I ignored this plea and flipped the channel to this hyper, ultra-white guy saying you could visit all sorts of calamities on your car but the Buffbuster would still clean it good as showroom new and I disliked this guy intensely but when I went to re-flip the bastard battery giving me remote control picked then to die and I was too spent to get up and exercise immediate control. But then the guy started engaging in these like spontaneousy demonstrations of the product in response to studio questioning and just like that I found I could tolerate him. Then he kept it up and now I felt bad for having judged him rashly because it seems all he wanted was for the autos of the world to be clean, which seemed admirable, and the studio audience must have agreed because their oohs and aahs increased until I almost reached for the phone and bought the damn device in what would have been, for me, three very difficult installments.

I was fading fast . . . Television still spoke but now without sound . . . the clock ticked insistently . . . a three and a twenty-eight . . . four minutes past my original grand introduction.

I was 24.

It is better for us both, therefore, to merge.

Chapter 3

I dreamt often those days and almost exclusively to ill effect.

O.K. class listen and observe closely First we trip the locus coerulus alarm to ensure unfettered exploration As you can see the top of the subject's head has been sliced open in a perfect ellipsoid Note that by purposely failing to cut entirely through the dorsal portion we can use the flesh to a hinge effect, allowing us to peel back the top of his cranium and peer inside What you see is, of course, mechanistic, intricately so but so nonetheless, nothing else and nothing more, hard wiring all of it But it's hard wiring we have to know cold if we are to succeed because success will most likely not arrive suddenly but rather gradually, and incidentally it had better arrive whatever the means for your pathetic sake Now some are easier than others but this one looks easiest of all Here's the cerebral cortex which we purposely dim so that only day to day affairs are of concern and it is within this very banality that we thrive See his amygdala? What he most fears threaten him with, dangle it, not as mere possibility but as overwhelming probability, a proven technique with this sort of specimen Look at the hippocampus sloshing in acetylcholine courtesy of his basal forebrain This will almost be too easy Always remember that we are here not to cure but to sicken So while normally at this point we begin to suggest the toxic, break down the healthy, and foster disorder, here an entropic chaos is already spreading virtually unchecked seeking its own heat death and this despite the fact that our own procedures are completely adiabatic and therefore blameless So why tamper?

To tamper would be to excuse in a sense Closing I've seen enough After all, there are rules We're not savages.

When I awoke I put my hands to my head. The pain there and in my ear was obscene but I at least felt relief to be alone on my bed and not on an icy slab of steel surrounded by questionable medical personnel. The woman in charge wore a ptosic eyelid that almost completely shut her left eye, she lifted her chin to compensate, and when my eyes began to shut again I feared I would return to her. I sat up quickly, inviting reality and looking for a toehold. I was concentrating, concretely thinking myself into the real as if exiting a theater into midday's bright city.

I felt disbelief at the clock's assertion of **9:45**. Impossible, I thought, because I hadn't really slept. I had merely lowered my lids, been pried open at the skull, then raised them again. The whole thing took maybe ten minutes but those numbers claimed hours. The digital clock I stared at had an invisible seconds-hand that circled ceaselessly, accelerating. Next to it Goya's postcard-sized Saturn had devoured the speaking part of his son, a bloody stump where the head once lay.

I was in a bad way from the night before so I tried to convince myself I had options. I could call in a comp day and stay home. But a quick look at my book revealed I had two out cases on – another Terrens-Lake-type kid and an emaciated credit card misholder serving an ersatz death sentence – neither of which could really be dumped on even a willing colleague. There was also the matter of a meeting that afternoon to discuss the death penalty appeal I had volunteered to help write; my brilliant ideas never ceased. I had to go in.

The radio came on and said the missing baby had a name. Everyone should keep an eye out for Baby Tula and all were beseeched to call the toll free number with any potential information on the bad baby.

I was almost tragically late so I took my time showering and getting dressed. Turning twenty-four was no minor disappointment. At twenty-one, Edward Van Halen erupted and placed all other similarly engaged guitarists into a group called *the rest*. At nineteen, Mary Wollstonecraft's daughter won her gothic bet decisively, giving birth in the process to a sentient seventy-thousand word monster that, more than two centuries later, still haunts readers. Then there was this kid named Wilfred. At seventeen, Wilfred Benitez embarrassed the great Colombian fighter Antonio "Pambele" Cervantes to become the scientifically gifted Junior Welterweight Champion of the World at a time when twelve different guys couldn't simultaneously make the same claim. They and so many others mocked me.

My response was to leave. I made sure to grab friendly Casper this time before moving down the two flights and out the door. It was angry cold again. Then from the second-floor window I heard Angus screaming down at me:

"Call in sick dude! Ralph's taking Alice roller skating, this is a great one."

"Thanks but I better not."

"It's your funeral."

"Come on Angus you can do it!" I heard Louie and Traci simultaneously exhort. "Don't quit," Louie added.

Angus was nuts, true, but maybe it was my funeral. After all there I was walking all slow and solemn then in a box being gradually interred and when the box hit bottom there had gathered there that day a slew of people, who if not grieving sure didn't look thrilled, to hear atonal dirges and accusatory liturgical phrases fill the air creating a quasi-commerce that I walked through to stand on yellow bumps meant to warn of danger where man-made wind screeched into and past my face until I was in another box this one moving horizontally within which I breathed on many and was breathed on in return before the box spit us all out still under Earth's crust but this time flowing from inside a mass towards stairs that led back to life. ✓

84

Each stair brighter yet colder than the one below it like the sun was daring you to see how little effect it was having.

Two men above me at forty-five degrees and brooking no passage while speaking so that every nearby ear was forced to listen:

"It's too damn cold for this time of year, too early in the year for this shit. I'm telling you man when I get dressed in the morning before I leave the house I put a goddamn lambskin condom on my dick to keep it warm. Y'ever seen a lamb complain about the cold? Still, it don't even work, I'm a start putting two of them on before I leave the house."

"Heard that."

"Now about this other thing, I'll say this. The man has to be large and in charge. It's like I tell my bitch. You my queen but I'm the King and that's the way it has to be man. The man has *gots* to be the boss you ask anyone. It's what you call the natural order of things and the woman have best understand that, dig?"

The listening guy claimed that he indeed dug and more discussion ensued until the woman rising alongside me, sick of exhaling loudly and circling her eyeballs, started asking them questions. The various voices got louder and the woman did this great thing where after she made what she felt was a particularly pointed remark, but which in reality was shot through with meekness, she would move the hair away from her face with a lovely hand, which maneuver was quite yummy. At the end of the stairs, on top of the city, she went left to my right and I watched her shrink wishing I would one day see her again. But where I was you could never arrange that kind of sequel. You just never saw the person again was what happened.

I walked through City Hall Park, past the iced fountain and through the gloved hands pushing flyers, to the lobby of the only building in the area that looked like it shouldn't even contemplate generating revenue. There was a new sign between the newsstand and the elevators. It said the entity that signed my criminally feeble

85

paychecks had floors four through nine and that its Complex One was on nine. It said the Attorney-in-Charge could also be found on that floor and that his name was Thomas Swathmore. I wondered if this last part hadn't been better written in pencil.

I grabbed the two tabs and started skimming them back to back in front of the elevators. Holding them that way you could almost feel the competition heating up between them. The Post was all over Tula with a picture of a rattle below a giant **OH BABY!** Inside was a description of the grim horror with quoted reaction all the way from Holland. There was a poll too. Thirty-three percent said the kid would turn up the very picture of health. Fifty-two percent said no way look into adoption and fifteen percent wanted the pollster to repeat the question; of those fifteen percent, seventy percent later admitted to having understood the question the first time. Meanwhile, sixty percent said it was wrong to do a poll on such a subject but participated anyway while forty percent thought it perfectly legitimate to do such a poll but wanted no part of it. The *Daily News* countered. Seems our mayor was the newly christened **CAPTAIN VIDEO** given his newfound interest in *video-enhanced law enforcement.* There was a map. The red areas were new smile-for-the-camera zones. The green areas would remain as before, i.e. patrolled solely by the naked eye. Lastly, the blue areas were in dire need of a video presence but the vigilantes were too afraid to be stationed there.

I stepped off on nine to see Denise's eyebrows rise and her mouth open slightly meaning I was precisely the person she was looking for but couldn't yet address because of the phone at her ear. Afterwards she smiled hello and "Malkum Jenkins called, he's in court waiting for you."

"Nice to know, that it?"

"Tom's looking for you."

"Great. Since?"

"Maybe quarter to nine?"

"Time is it now?"

"Forty-two after ten."

"I see, not good. Listen Denise if you'll be so kind as to keep this little conversation confidential, I will now rotate my body in the appropriate manner and return home."

"Sure."

"Already one of those days let me tell you."

"Sorry honey, he's in his office."

"Thanks."

I walked until the brief hall ended then popped my head forward to spy Tom's green door, three-quarters closed and adrift in a sea of varying browns. I listened and heard no speech that sounded as if it were being issued from behind clenched teeth then took exaggerated cat burglar steps to my office in the opposite corner. I was alone in there for a change although I saw it would be temporary. The furry jacket on the back of Leon's chair, the kind with the leather ovals that tell old-timers like its owner where the elbows go, meant he would soon return and the white sneakers with pink touches on Julia's desk meant she was nearby as well. I sat at my desk between theirs.

I stared at the jacket and just like that wanted to be Leon Greene, Esq. I wanted those life moments of highest suspense and relevance to be in my immutable past. Wanted to have been at that desk for thirty-five years and not find the slightest thing wrong with that. And in those years I would not once have worn casual clothes to work even if I wasn't going to court or meeting one of my clients, all of whom incidentally I would give the benefit of the doubt despite decades of empirical opposition, and in all that time I would never have raised my voice or used salty language at the office either. And I would bring that quiet dignity to the office every day without fail by the sharpest eight-thirty and would remove it no later than four-thirty, with the same forty-five minutes excluded for the lunch Helen would pack, and allow myself only one glass of wine a night with my light dinner

87

at five-thirty and maybe trade some words about our kids and their kids and draw steadily increasing paychecks and save for retirement and talk about pensions and never produce any evidence of having noticed that every square inch of the third inhabitant of that square, one Julia Ellis, was skin-raisingly gorgeous and at precisely that moment I realized I no longer wanted to be Leon.

Although Leon wouldn't be essentially hiding in that office avoiding Tom either. No, if Tom were looking for him, Leon would report front and center. Even if he was Casi and so never got to the office before ten and that day was pushing eleven and had a separate lengthy list of transgressions each singly capable of producing supervisory ire. So I pretended to be Leon. I stood up and took purposeful strides to the door where I almost ran into Dane.

"Where you off to in such a rush, to snatch up a square?"

"Yeah."

"Figured."

"What? Square? What square?"

"Right."

"What are you talking about?"

"Don't tell me you haven't heard about the pool, you do work here right?"

"What pool?"

"The macabre office pool your colleagues are running on Baby Tula's fate? Dead or alive being the major demarcation with all sorts of ensuing possibilities. Five bucks a square."

"That's what you came in here for? To see if I would attempt to exploit the disappearance of an infant for monetary gain?"

"Not in the slightest. I'm here because you remember the case I told you about last night, the one you should work with me on? Well I just got the video, let's eyeball it."

"Video?"

"Whole thing's on video, I told you."

"Oh."

"Come on, to the video room Robin."

"Have to see Tom first, I'll meet you in there."

I took a deep preparatory breath outside Tom's then a woman who seemed to recognize me but for whom I could not reciprocate handed me some papers and said *sign this* before spotting someone else and rushing off in that direction.

I walked through the door and immediately into a knee-high cardboard box. Now I was face-first in more boxes and crawling on them to the chair in the corner from where I looked at their owner and said:

"What the?"

"You O.K.?"

"Yeah, I meant to do that. What is all this?"

"Moving offices man, eighteen years in those boxes."

His walls were bare with light rectangles and squares where frames had hung.

"You been in here that whole time?"

"Been in here since I was you. Funny, people think it was some kind of symbolic gesture not moving to a better office when I kept getting bounced up but look at this shit, would you want to move it? Not that neatness—"

No. Tom's hair, it was as if he had managed to sleep on all sides of his head simultaneously. And the loop of his tie was always partially visible under his unbuttoned collar.

"Guess it could be worse," he said. "I could be packing involuntarily to leave for good, you know?" He grinned and put his feet on his desk.

I looked at the papers in my hand. Their title was PETITION TO DEPOSE T. SWATHMORE and below a little statement of facts was a lot of signatures.

"What do you got there?" he said.

"You looking for me?"

"Yeah, you know, if I ever come in here again, check the computer and see that you arraigned seventeen felonies in an arraignment shift—"

"Oh c'mon."

"You already have the highest caseload in the office."

"The cases kept coming in, what am I supposed to do? Brilliant Debi puts Linda in arraignments on her penultimate day."

Tom was talking and gesticulating and the rectangle at my feet with the center star of broken glass wanted it known that the trustees of Harvard College on recommendation of the faculty had conferred upon Thomas Swathmore the degree of Bachelor of Arts along with all the rights and privileges that thereunto appertained and I knew the law school felt similarly whereas the petition in my lap weighed down by signatures alleged *a pattern of abuse and intimidation* except with respect to *favorites*. I sensed silence and Tom looking at me.

"Right," I said.

"What do you mean right? Right is not responsive."

"No I mean, what are you talking about?"

"This mandatory you picked up."

"Right, what about him?"

"I have to take it from you."

"What are you talking about? I'm all over it."

"It's too much too soon."

"That's crazy. I'm going out to the scene today it's probably not even going to be indicted."

"What is it?"

"Sex assault, they're known to each other and there's a delay in reporting. No medical attention either. Like I said, I'm all over it. Don't worry so much."

"O.K. but keep Debi and Conley posted on what's happening. Alright?"

I turned the petition over, face down onto my lap.

"If you *were* packing involuntarily, big deal, you know Kevin Miller?"

"Sure."

"He says you're the best trial attorney in the city. For now anyway."

"Oh for now huh? Who the fuck talks to me like this kid?" He was laughing and looking around for invisible support.

"So it's true?"

"No, I doubt it's true."

"Let me quote, something like *the closest you can get to perfection in a complicated endeavor*, about Rollins I think."

"Probably, but I don't think so."

"Why not? You see Fallon on the news last night, all fake-outraged about his client's innocence, what a clown."

"Clown? No he's damn good, we came in here together."

"Get out, I didn't know that."

"Sure, in this very office."

"You were tight?"

"Still are, I'll tell him your feelings. No, we used to go on each other's investigations. Ten, eleven at night we're in neighborhoods you wouldn't believe. Now this Alabama death penalty project, did I hear you were involved in that too?"

"This picture, it looks like you're throwing something, what is this, who's this?"

I showed him the picture of the smiling girl whom he identified as his daughter.

"You yell at her?" I said.

"Ah, that was dumb, but I told myself when I became head that I would not run an untrained office you know? People here six, nine months already looking at their watches, I don't know what it is. So I lost it a bit there I guess. Speaking of, how exactly do you have time for a death penalty case?"

"Please, that's a group situation, three attorneys. We have a meeting this afternoon where we get the transcripts and all the discovery then each group does an appeal-type deal."

"That it?"

"Pretty much, there's this Murder Two."

"What?"

"Not mine, just considering working on it with another attorney."

"Who?"

"He's not on our floor, new guy, lateral from Florida."

"Florida? Don't know him, we get five new guys a day though."

"He's good."

"What's so good about him?"

"He's fearless, I hear, I think, what do I know?"

"Or reckless."

"Well I don't know," I started to walk out. "If I'm in it I'll make sure everything gets done and my guess is he can try a case."

"Look don't get the impression that I don't appreciate it because I do. I got about twenty attorneys going to their union reps and looking to file a grievance because their caseloads are too high. Then I got a handful like you who want to take on anything they can get their hands on and who are doing some truly great work. What I'm saying is you've been doing this two years not twenty and I know this will surprise you but you don't know it all, acquittals notwithstanding. So slow down and be very thorough. That's more important than being good in the way that you're good. And who you align yourself with is important too. My feeling on some attorneys is that they can be naturals and great fun in a courtroom but that kind of thing is overrated. How many cases go to trial? Two, three percent at most? What kind of work do you do on those hundreds of cases that don't go to trial? Isn't that a better indication of the kind of attorney you are?"

"What's with the bike still?" I engaged and disengaged the brake. "It's like two degrees out there."

92

"I love it. The air wakes you up and gets you going, ready to come in here and fight some more."

"All the way from the upper west?"

"Every morning."

"It's pretty beat up too, maybe a new one."

"Oh no, have to love my bike until it can't reciprocate."

I said I had court but was glad I could help, that his concern was appreciated and his advice would be heeded although we knew it wouldn't be because as long as they kept track of things like caseloads mine would always be the highest. Tom nodded and reiterated some things while I picked at the bike's rear tire. Then I walked out and down the hall shaping the petition into a ball and calmly sinking an uncontested eight-footer into the trash can just outside the video room.

NOW SHOWING:

On the screen is surprising quality – like decent public access; the angle is upper right-hand corner looking down. Looking down on the innards of a tiny bodega with two consumer aisles and one of those fridge/counters in front of the cash register located on the bottom right of the screen. There's no life in there. Behind the counter sits, according to his T-shirt, Superdad, or a fiftyish Hispanic man with a close-cropped gray afro. The once-black shirt has faded to a dark grey that emerges intermittently from behind the yellow and red pentagon logo. The short sleeves barely contain the wearer's carved arms and shoulders as he rocks back and forth on his wooden stool. He is alone and staring emptily.

Now the chimed door announces work and he slowly uncoils to attention, leaning forward against the counter. To the back they go, one in each aisle followed by purposeful loitering and Superdad's eyes on them all the while. More loitering. Marvyn Rane and Disangel Cruz are the two and they can't decide and Superdad is losing patience maybe starting to worry. Now Rane signals to Cruz with his chin and they rhyme towards the counter, the cash register, and the near-future decedent. Cruz has a bag of chips that he drops on the counter. Rane looks out the door then points to the cash register. Repeatedly. Point. Point. From behind the counter, a dismissal in response, signaling to the door with annoyed lips. Except Rane has a gun.

The gun does not come out and jut forward. The gun comes out and drives Rane backward, straightening his bony right arm with its electric current. It points at a stone face and Rane seems bigger now as Superdad shrinks. Cruz hops up and down like a fighter between rounds and Superdad moves to the cash register without looking away from Rane. It doesn't open. Rane is a statue – hardening and unforgiving. More hopping. Won't open. Gun moves closer to the counter with Rane following. Cruz wants out. He pulls at Rane's left shoulder but the right one stays frozen. Still tapping, now pounding, the register. Refuses to open. Rane waves Cruz off. Open. (The tape should end here or shortly thereafter when the money enters Rane's hand right?) Now Superdad has the bills so he's armed too and he extends them to Rane, his mouth silently moving. But the money no longer exists to Rane. Cruz's mouth moves. Rane's doesn't. His fist is full of the trite ending. He squeezes it. A white flash as if from a camera then the beginnings of a flame that's quickly snuffed.

Superdad's neck is black from all the red.

Hands wrapped tight around his neck to keep the red in. The universal sign for choking. Gargling and Thrashing. On the floor behind the counter, chin down and soaked shirt. Rane looking down, leaning over the counter and pointing again. Cruz part of the audience. Another squeeze and flash. Superdad's middle looks like his neck. Now he's on his side and crawling with Rane pointing again. But suddenly out the door they go – Cruz first.

On the ground Supe crawls to the white then red cordless phone.

His wet hand can't properly grasp it. It falls and he looks at it. The mouth moves but slower. Hands on and chin down but it can't work. Can't keep liquid life in when it wants out and the thrashing is a dull imitation of earlier vigor. The rejected money has scattered around him. His breathing is insanely heavy now. A paroxysm of desire. Then less and less. Pianissimo. Wrists down . . . palms up . . . eyes open. No more forevermore. Inexpensive Surreality Television. THE END.

Dane stared at me as if colorful chips were between us. "Something huh?" he said.

"Everything's some thing."

"Meaning it's not often you're confronted with your client's irredeemable actions in such unassailable detail is it?" He looked back at the barren screen. "You're an eyewitnesses in effect. It's not just represent a guy who did this, which you'd probably say is never a problem, it's squint your eyes and witness his interior darkness in all its glory. What are your options then? Do you embrace it, reject it, grudgingly accept it, and does it ultimately matter? Regardless, you're in right?"

"I'm pretty busy right now like I said last night."

"Perhaps there's a slight failure of comprehension here," he said. "You saw, did you not, the cash register finally open?"

"I did."

"Saw the money offered to Rane?"

"Yes."

"What you didn't see, of course, was either genius take that money and leave."

"No."

"So naturally when I get a case like this what I want, and what I have thus far been denied by those annoying pro forma protestations of innocence, is a look inside the shell of this person. Understand? Unlike most, I don't deny the attraction. What do you want?"

"In general?"

"From Rane."

"Nothing from Rane. Besides, he says it's not him and that could be true. I mean it *could* be," almost laughing.

"This is his mug shot."

"O.K., so much for that. So he'll take a plea."

"I suppose, but as I say that's hardly the most relevant considera-tion here. Think of what I'm offering you."

"Whatever, I guess."

"Good, very good. Lunch later?"

"Why not? If I'm not back by one meet me in front of one-eleven."

"Oh yeah, in the interest of full disclosure, Edwin Vega was the name of the bodega guy. I talked to the neighborhood. He was loved. He would give neighborhood kids jobs and he would coach in the peewee basketball league or whatever. He had kids too, ten-year-old girl and eight-year-old boy."

"Yeah the shirt."

"So you understand?"

"That he had kids? Yeah I understand. That makes him a father, I'm familiar with the concept."

"Then you can come with me when I return to the neighborhood," he chuckled. "What killed me last time was when this lady says to me *I can't believe this happened to him, he went to church every Sunday.* Believe that? In this day and age? Lot of good it did him huh? I mean can't you just picture it? Every Sunday this poor schlub packs his plump wife and two kids into their early-eighties Buick and off they go to the building with the pretty windows and the empty promises. Inside a guy in a colorful robe tells them everything is going to be alright because what happens here is essentially meaningless. Just bide your time you know? Then in walks this twerp who doesn't shave yet and what good is all that shit? A little bullet to the neck and what good is it all? These funny distractions you people create for your-selves are powerless in the face of clinical truth. The Ranes of this

96

world are that truth. There will always be Rane Casi."

"O.K."

"I mean have you thought about this guy, every day in his little bodega just trying—"

"Really don't want to think about him."

"So what do you say to what I'm saying?"

"I say I have to go to court."

"And?"

"And I don't care about Vega right now."

"Have it your way then."

"I will. Later."

"One o'clock at one-eleven."

And just like that, poof, he was gone.

In the elevator were two attorneys. I recognized one of them from the night before as one of the attorneys who'd come in for the lobster shift. He was a tall, square-jawed, game-show-host-looking guy. There was a Clarke and a Karl; he was one of them but I didn't know which and he was talking to another attorney, Lee Graham, whose name I knew only because he had recently achieved mild notoriety by fainting in front of a judge.

"How was the lobster yesterday?" asked Graham.

"Not bad, we didn't do many cases at all."

"It was slow?"

"Well it was actually funny. They beat the shit out of some guy in the back real bad so we just sat around while they had all these E.M.S. guys come in and take this poor sap away. Supposedly they shattered this guy's jaw and everything."

"The cops?!"

"No the other prisoners."

"Really?"

"Yeah don't faint on me now. It wasn't that big a deal."

"They charge anyone?"

"Nah, no-one would spill who done it."

"When did this happen?"

"Round three."

"Did you see the guy when they took him out?"

"Oh yeah. A real mess, both eyes closed, broken teeth, dried blood, the whole deal. Somebody wasn't happy with this dude."

"Wow. Who was it?"

"Some Oriental."

"What?!" I said.

"What what?" he said.

"What did you say about Oriental?" I said.

"Oh I'm sorry *Asian*. Fucking political correctne—"

"No, who was Asian?"

"The guy who got fucked up haven't you been listening?"

"Well what the hell was his name?"

"How do I know? He didn't show me any I.D. man. Who is this guy?" to Graham.

"Nobody said his name?"

"Choo choo or something. What the hell do I know?" he was full of laughter too.

"Chut? Ah Chut was that his fucking name?"

"Sounds right. Why does he owe you money or something?"

"Listen you worthless piece of shit, was his name Ah Chut or not?"

"Hey screw you man. No reason to get insulting here."

"Fuck," I said under my breath as I walked through the lobby towards the door.

"Who is that guy anyway Grammy?"

Worst part was I couldn't even remember what Chut looked like. Those arraignment faces always bled together like in an amateurish, speedy camera pan. *You go home* I remembered assuring him in that retarded way people talk to those who fall short of full comprehension of the language being used. I thought about it some and concluded I had messed up. I was supposed to get him home. No-one else cared or was supposed to. I was responsible for getting him home without excuses but didn't so now he was a mess to look at.

Just then, at that very moment, I became sick of my job and wanted a different one. More specifically I was sick of that kind of shit always happening. Until I quit, I thought, I could make a pledge like the kind comic book superheroes are always making, you know where they like pledge that *never again* will injustice flourish in their presence and then this pledge brings a clarity and meaning to the superhero's life that he or she could not have envisioned prior to the pledge. A Pledge. I decided to make one, a pledge, to myself really. And not an insignificant factor in this decision was the fact that the word *pledge* was really rather funny if you kept saying it repeatedly or in my case thinking it, so I felt a responsibility to somehow animate this word that had given me pleasure at a down time by actually making one. So anyway the pledge was that, in the mystical future, but the one that began like that instant, nothing detrimental or untoward would ever happen to a client of mine. I could make this pledge, I thought, because I would be physically present whenever such a deleterious event would threaten to occur. I would be there when somebody – judge, prosecutor, court officer, janitor – tried to make something bad happen and I would be there to stop it. I would simply stop it is what I would do. How I would do that would obviously depend on the situation. So no more errata I thought. No almosts or maybes. In the future I would always succeed; all regret and guilt would wither and die in the face of a crushing, compulsive efficiency.

I thought about how, when I was a squirt, minor bad things like misplacing a pair of gloves that still spanked, the price of which I'd been explicitly and repeatedly informed, would happen with alarming frequency and how I was often, as a result, placed on the defensive. *For the defense: they lost themselves, you still love me? ¡Of course papi! how much? This much. but there are mommies who are bigger than you and can stretch their arms wider, do they love their kids more than you?*

First up following The Pledge was Malkum Jenkins and 111 Centre Street, one of two buildings in New York County where state criminal cases were heard and home of Part 28 where Jenkins was presumably waiting. Part 28 belonged to Judge Sizygy and Friday meant it was his calendar day which in turn meant there would be a slew of teens and their families behaving like heated molecules inside his ridiculously tiny courtroom. (The thinking went something like this: let's take the J.O. [juvenile offender] part, the part that figures to attract the highest number of interested observers – familial and otherwise – due to the age of the defendants, and stick it in a courtroom appreciably smaller than any other so that inevitably the audience on calendar days [remember, *Friday*] will spill out into the halls creating barely restrained chaos, won't that be fun?) And Sizygy was probably the best judge around. He took an interest in the defendants and tried to help. He kept their families informed and even fielded questions from them. He took his time on every case, careful to do the right thing. He was, in short, a good man whose basic decency made contact with him a desirable pleasure. Everyone hated going there.

Malkum had to go because four months earlier he'd sold to an undercover during a buy and bust. He was arrested and charged with Sale 3° and some 18B got the case but no matter since Jenkins was nothing if not routine and thus entitled to the standard outcome for sixteen-year-olds who look disproportionately at the floor and sell the product that sells itself. Standard outcome was adjudication as a youthful offender, meaning no criminal record, and five years probation. Y.O. and probation meant Malkum stayed pure and out of jail but with someone to watch over him: a probation officer or P.O., where we were all the kids had them. Twenty-one days, that's how long Malkum reformed before we met. Once again he'd sold to the only customers who complain and his sweet deal had turned acrid. This time there was no R.O.R. at arraignments. Instead he received $5,000 bail and a head start on his expected jail sentence. Y.O. eligibility had been exhausted too, meaning the minimum was one to three years in state prison plus whatever he got on the forthcoming V.O.P. or violation of probation.

Malkum's predicament required that I employ the signature move of public defenders everywhere, unseemly begging. So I begged the D.A. – a decent, mousy woman with a visible heart – and she agreed to offer the kid an open C, meaning no mandatory minimum jail sentence, with the judge to determine his sentence. Then I begged the judge to send the case to Sizygy who had put Malkum on probation in the first and now represented our best chance at mercy. Several weeks later Sizygy was looking down at me shaking his head like the guy lending you money again even though you've never before repaid. But I had checked shame at the door and said judge this is Rene Collis from YOUTH FIRST and I think this is exactly what Jenkins needs because he's not a bad kid and they have drug testing, job training, and counseling and what say you? Sizygy agreed and Malkum was released to the program but not before confessing and with his sentence pending. Complete the program he was told. Show me something and you'll get another chance at probation, albeit as a felon this time. Of course, screw up and . . .

Now we were there for the first update from the program and the mere sight of Malkum sitting in the audience, wearing a green-polo-shirt-with-white-tie ensemble, represented an initial victory:

"Well good to see you," I said.

"yeah, hi."

"How's the program?"

"it's ahhight."

"You been going?"

"yeah i be going like every day."

"Really?"

"swear."

"And? Do you like it, is it good, what?"

"i don't know."

"Well can we at least agree it's better than jail."

"no doubt."

"Progress, who you living with?"

"my moms."

"Who else?"

"my grandmother and my little brother."

"How you getting along with your mother?"

"she all mad i ain't working and shit."

"When were you working?"

"like before i got locked up i was making mad money selling."

"Yeah and look where you ended up."

"i know. i ain't trying to go back to that. i'm looking to stay clean but my moms is hassling me about money twenty-four/seven yo."

"Tell her to call me. Never mind, I'll call her. For now just do whatever this program says or you're going to end up going back in, alright?"

"yeah."

"Is Collis here?"

"?"

"The guy from the program?"

"oh yeah. he said to tell you he would be right back."

"Did he say the update would be good?"

"yeah everything's good."

"O.K. have a seat I'll sign your case up. My guess is we'll be here awhile."

A good guess it turned out, with the judge taking his sour time and an endless procession of kids who could be doing better with some of them disappearing through the doors at the rear of the courtroom to the accompaniment of blubbering mothers. It was alternately excruciating and boring until I saw Garo Conley seated in the jury box and lecturing. Those around him occasionally opened their mouths and nodded in the negative, a common reaction in his vicinity. I wanted to hear so I sat behind him and his main audience.

"Macaroni and Cheese," Conley said.

"Come again."

"Macaroni and Cheese. It's an actual color. I did my research and those are the exact words used by Crayola to describe a color and moreover that's the color I'm proposing."

"Macaroni and cheese?"

"Yes a nice vaguely copper type orange," he said. "Like those chicks that spend too much time absorbing fake sun at salons. Maybe a little more reddish come to think of it."

"Why that color?"

"Why not? It's an attractive enough color. The color isn't the important thing anyway. The uniformity is what matters."

"Good God."

"I'm serious, imagine looking out into this courtroom's audience and everyone's the same color."

"Imagine it? I don't have to. They already are the same color. Black, like me."

"That's silly. First of all, strictly speaking, nobody's black, not actual black. But fine, imagine not just the audience but every single person you encounter being Macaroni and Cheese Orange."

"You're insane."

"Insane? It's called progress. All thanks to our friend deoxyribonucleic acid. Extract 44 discovered in '44 and you don't actually think that was a numerical coincidence do you? I'm talking about a second, this time lab-propelled, genesis. You'll be able to choose the genetic qualities your child will have. Think about that for a minute.

103

Everyone will be attractive, intelligent, athletic."

"Macaroni and cheese?"

"Macaroni and Cheese, right. Everyone."

"And?"

"And? And no more accidents of birth, that's and. What do you think makes life so unfair? The world we live in will finally be just. We'll make it that way genetically."

"But what does all that have to do with what I'm talking about?"

"Well that should be obvious. Since in the near future, there'll be no significant physical differences between people, the statement you just made would be meaningless. Remember it won't be a case of just the people in the audience of this courtroom looking alike, everyone the world entire will look alike. Gazing at another will be like gazing in a mirror, you might as well discriminate against yourself. Racism will be stamped out. I'm talking about it no longer existing!"

"Must we all look like you though?" a third party joined in.

"No, like a good-looking orangey person. You're laughing Henry but it's the only way. You have to remove the factual basis for racism and if four hundred years from now everyone looks the same that'll do it. Otherwise forget it. You can't regulate how people feel. The best you can hope for, in the absence of genetic manipulation, is what we have now."

"Which is?" asked Henry.

"Who's we?" the third added.

"*We* is this country. I'm not concerned with anywhere else. And what we have here is a situation where racism still exists but it doesn't really interfere with anyone's life. Oh Casi I didn't see you back there. This is Henry, Henry this—"

"Whatever," they said in unison and I never did get that third guy's name.

"What are you saying exactly?" said Henry.

"What I'm saying – and don't go crazy on me – is that racism as an

104

active, noxious force endorsed by society and government, subtly or otherwise, no longer exists the way it did for example in the nineteen-twenties. We've addressed these things. There's no longer segregation, for example, no-one's being told to give up his or her seat on the bus. Today, a group calling itself the freedom riders would look ridiculous, they'd have no cause."

"I can think of a dozen new ones they could take up," said Henry. "And you talk as if these situations are so remote they have no relevance to today. First, from the perspective of a nation's history these things happened yesterday. The desegregation you're so proud of was like pulling fucking teeth. Not until 1954 did the Court hold that six-year-old black kids were not being equally protected when they were forced to go to different and inferior schools than white kids, 1954! Although the decision was unanimous, the law clerk for one of the Justices advised him that the schools should remain separate rather than impose government-mandated desegregation. That law clerk is now the Chief Justice of the current court! Of course the schools reacted to this ruling with *deliberate speed* and it only took about twenty years for these southern schools to be dragged before a court one by one until they were all in compliance. This included a charming incident I'm sure you'll recall where the Governor of Arkansas placed the armed Arkansas National Guard in front of a high school to keep black children from entering an all-white school. Note, Conley, that I'm talking about governmental action here not private attitudes. In '63 George Wallace – the goddamn governor of Alabama and a constant presidential candidate – used his inaugural platform to proclaim his love for segregation now, tomorrow, and forever and his constituency cheered."

"I'll tell you Henry I think you're making my point for me," Conley was quieter now, less excited. "The very reason the things you just mentioned seem so outrageous is that they would be unthinkable in today's society. That's the very definition of progress. Remember, I'm the one who thinks that racism will always exist until eliminated genetically, so of course I concede that racism continues to exist in private individuals. I do maintain, however, that with respect to our social structure it's gone. The government does not endorse it and the laws are in place to oppose it. A lot of credit goes to the people who were instrumental in changing those laws."

"And who were in several instances smoked for their troubles," said the third guy all happy with his contribution.

"Yes. But the laws and society were changed and I no longer think it's accurate to term our government or society racist in the same sense the term might've been accurate fifty years ago. Do the laws always work? Does everyone follow them? Of course not, but that doesn't seem to be the most important issue as I see it. All we can do is set up a system that's as fair as possible. Listen no system can guarantee that there won't be some fat, toothless, inbred piece of shit from West Virginia who wants to kill all black people. All it can do is give everyone a fair opportunity. We have that."

"We don't have that," said Henry.

"We do Henry! Look at you. You've been an attorney for twenty years and have done very well for yourself, you could buy and sell me were it not for the fact that I'm not currently for sale. Racism hasn't prevented you from achieving quite a bit within the framework of our system and it doesn't prevent anyone else from achieving the same things. The reason is all the impediments have been removed. Listen I don't dispute that there were some serious problems in the past. The battle, which undoubtedly was righteous and constituted an absolute moral imperative, is over however, and we've gone as far as we can until science takes over. Now sit back and let The Human Genome Project do the rest."

"Hold on. Just stop right there because everything you're saying is wrong and wrong in important ways. The fact that there are successful people who look like the people in this audience means next to nothing. One of the things the Board of Ed argued against Oliver Brown was that the separate schools didn't harm children like his third-grader Linda. After all, they said, didn't George Washington Carver among others achieve greatness in spite of facing even greater obstacles than the kids then attending the lesser, segregated schools. Well many years have passed and the stakes are different but you're rehashing the same argument and it's weak. The relevant question is not whether back then a few extraordinary individuals could overcome a system strongly weighted against them or whether today an admittedly far greater number requiring far less talent can succeed. The real question is whether it's harder for the people in this audience to succeed be they extraordinary, average, or below average. If it is, and I think it obvious that it is, then that's untenable in a country that purports to provide equal opportunity for all. Now of course you'll dispute my claim that it is more difficult to succeed for them. You say the battle's over. I say not only is it not over but you yourself are stationed on the frontline of the battle and have been all these years. This room and the criminal justice system as a whole is the frontline. This is where modern-day segregation lives on."

"Well that's quite a bit hyperbolic don't you think?" said Conley.

"Is it?" He began to read from a pamphlet in his lap that had undoubtedly started the whole thing. "Let's take the example of Washington," he said, "our nation's capital named after our first president. Well the National Center on Institutions and Alternatives looked at them. What they found is that fifty percent of black men ages eighteen to thirty-five in D.C. were either incarcerated or under probation or parole supervision. Our government controls one out of every two such young men in that area."

"That seems way too high. Besides even if you're correct you're referring to a small sample that may not accurately reflect—"

"Fine, nationwide the number is one out of three. Additionally, Justice Department statistics show that nationally about eight out of ten such men will spend some time incarcerated during their life-times. What this does is—"

"That number seems a bit high. That can't possibly—"

"Please Conley," the third party rejoined the fray. "Why are you making him spout all these stats? Even if they would seem extreme to the average person you can't tell me that you, with this job, are surprised by these numbers, or that you truly doubt their accuracy. Like he says, look in the audience of this courtroom for Chrissakes. Go in the back and look at the pens. I worked arraignments last week. I did about thirty-five cases and all but maybe three of them involved minority defendants."

"Has your experience been any different Conley?" said Henry. "Think of your caseload."

"I don't think of my clients in terms of their color," he smiled, "they're all just people whom I have the highest obligation to defend."

"Well humor me for a moment and estimate what percentage of your cases involve black defendants."

"O.K. I accept your numbers. It does appear that roughly eighty to eighty-five percent of our clients are black but what does that mean? More importantly, why is that the case? I don't think, for example, that the police, who are often themselves black, at least around here, are ignoring crimes committed by whites or purposely looking to arrest more blacks than whites. The only logical conclusion if you agree with those figures is that blacks must be committing more crimes than whites. If that's the case then *it is* more difficult to be black in this country but it's not really the result of racism but rather the result of being part of a ravaged community. A community ravaged from within by its own members."

"The problem is those numbers don't accurately reflect the discrep-ancy you're referring to so something else seems to be at work," Henry said. "And moreover the discrepancy itself may be further evidence of what I'm alleging. More importantly, what I'm saying is these aren't just statistics, they have profound human effects." He looked to the third guy for some more support. "Because what happens as a result of—"

"Isn't that your kid?" Conley was looking at the defense table then me.

"Curses," I said. My kid was Jenkins who was standing at the table looking helplessly at the judge and wondering where I was. I slithered out of the jury box and stood behind the defense table at Malkum's side just as Sizygy was asking which attorney belonged to the case. Greetings were exchanged and Collis began his update speech. Things were not going as swimmingly as Malkum had painted but overall he was doing fairly well and Collis, who wore an absurd, stop-sign-red scarf, had a rare contented air that filled the courtroom. Malkum looked down at the table intently, eyes averted and knuckles cracking. But well enough is never lonely for long in this racket so Sizygy decided he'd chat Malkum up:

"Glad to see you're doing well," he said. "I see from this report that you only completed up to the ninth grade in school. Well, if you keep doing well with this program, they're going to help you get your G.E.D. Is that something you want to do?"

"yeah, yes."

"You bet it is, you know it's not too late for you son. You can still make something out of your life. I firmly believe that in this country everyone can make what they want of themselves provided they're willing to work hard enough." He was warming to his task now, convincing himself and maybe others, looking around while people nodded and Malkum looked downward. "What do you want to be?"

". . ."

"What are your interests?"

". . ."

"Answer me young man!"

"i don't . . . um," Malkum was looking for me to maybe feed him a line. I put my hand on his shoulder because that always looked good then whispered in his ear. I explained that everything was going relatively well, fine, but in that courtroom he had a speaking part. He had to talk a little about the error of his ways and the value of appropriate intervention. Malkum looked at me like I'd just grown a second head. Silence filled the room for the first time that day.

"Judge he wants to go to college," who said that?

I don't know why I said it but the mere sound of something like that gives it at least some truth value, and a foundering-if-free Malkum was somehow worse than an incarcerated one. At any rate, Sizygy was pleased now and the courtroom exhaled. So what if almost always the dumb just got dumber and dumber until they altogether ceased to form images if we were now confronted with the exception?

So that was settled more or less with the case adjourned two months for another update from the program. In the middle of all that a court officer had announced that we were the last case before lunch precipitating a palpably resentful exodus that left Malkum and me in a near-empty courtroom. And I didn't want to walk out with him so I pretended I had urgent business at the prosecutor's table which, in one of The System's obvious tells, was always millimeters from the jury box. I played with the pitcher of water and its satellitic cups then at an officer's urging took dilatory steps out into the hall where surely Malkum would no longer be.

"why'd you tell the judge i was going to college?" he asked.

"I said you wanted to, don't you?"

"shit no, i'll be lucky if i can get my G.E.D., that shit's hard."

"But if I asked you right now if you want to go where rich, eighteen-year-old women congregate to drink heavily what would you say?"

"course."

"Then I'm sticking by my statement that you *want* to go to college."

"yeah but why the judge all up in my grill and shit?"

"He does that, don't stress. You have my card, call if you need anything or if there's a problem with the program."

"oh yeah, my moms wanted me to ask if i have a criminal record."

"Yes, you do, quite a one."

"why?"

"*Why*? Man, how many times did we go over that before we took the plea? I told you, you have a record now and it stars a felony."

"oh, but what does that mean?"

"It means you're a fucking felon. All your future actions are felonious because taken by you. You can't do certain things. You can't vote, you can't hold certain government jobs, can't say you're not a felon. Get it now?"

"but that gets sealed after a while right? if i stay out of trouble?"

"No it doesn't, the only thing sealed is your fate. You're a sixteen-year-old felon, for good. Well your age will I hope change."

"oh."

"What's the face? You're the same person you were before I told you that."

"*can't vote?*"

"Vote? What's so fun about voting? You should never vote, everyone knows that. If you vote and your guy wins you can't later complain because you helped put him there. That's why I never vote, so I can later complain. Besides who were you going to vote for? The guy who ignores you or the one promising to build more jails for you as we speak."

" . . . "

"And don't even try using your record as an excuse either."

"i'm not i just didn't know all that."

"Well you have to listen when I talk, it's not all bullshit. We discussed all this to the point of nausea, mine, before you took the plea."

"nah i remember."

"Anything else?"

"nah, you know you got my boy T-Dog."

"What does that mean?"

"you're his attorney, he was picked up wednesday."

"Let me guess, Terrens Lake."

"yeah that's him, i toll him you was real good, he's all happy now."

"Good, we'll see how long that lasts."

"that's a cool suit too."

"O.K."

"good looking out b."

"Alright Malkum. Like I said, call if there are any problems. You know you can call even if there aren't any, if you want to let me know how you're doing or about anything else. You're doing well." That said I kind of tapped his shoulder and walked away making my way through the lobby.

Truth was I had to get away from that moment and in a hurry. It was that kind of bullshit social worker aspect of the job that had me ready to end it. I guessed that for the first time Malkum could feel the noose tightening around his neck and I was more than just a witness; I felt like the goddamned hangman.

Which reminded me of often being called on in school to be *the* Hangman. Which, as I viewed it, was a position completely bereft of prestige. But Sister Whatever must have been keen on the way I drew the ill-fated stick-figure hangee. Or maybe the words I chose to have the other squirts guess at, every wrong answer bringing the poor stick soul closer to its demise. Until I figured out that the squirts would always call the same letters out first. And so if my word had those letters in sufficient number even they could correctly identify it before I could finish drawing the victim's final limb. Making everyone happy.

Just outside the courthouse was a group of food vendors. Hot dogs, Italian sausage, and an actual line. I was on this line when a noisy group of fellow defense attorneys came by. Now I don't know anybody who is actually happy but I'm forever coming across clustered people roaring at some knee-slapping hilarity I must have just missed. Just to the left of the group was Dane, the only person I knew who appeared capable of laughing from under a seriously furrowed brow and who somehow seemed to be simultaneously with and apart from the group. What I had to do then was kind of slink off the line to avoid letting on that I had forgotten about lunch. He broke off from his fellow revelers and came right at me.

"I just had the second best idea I've had since I made the mistake of becoming an attorney," he said.

"On Rane?"

"No on lunch. Let's go to Katz's – easily the best deli in the free world."

"Agreed but that's all the way on Houston."

"So what? We'll jump in a cab."

"No way, I have to go back to court after this."

"So what do you propose?"

"Let's do Little Italy," I said and we did. Once we decided on the particular restaurant not a word was exchanged on the way there. For one thing it was so apocalyptically cold I wasn't sure words could survive if released. For another my ear was acting up again putting me in no mood for idle chat.

What I did instead was make a mental list of the myriad diseases that could be responsible for that damn ear. It had to be Thrombocytopenia, that ticking time bomb I'd been waiting to feel detonate ever since I stole an adolescent glance at that fucking medical chart. My only inheritance. Oh yes, a brilliant piece of diagnostic reasoning I then thought. A blood disease with no possible connection to my ear. No, I would have to go to the place where they hand out official verdicts on things like ears. Tests would be ordered, the kind you can't study for or cheat on. Then the grim, white-haired doctor would come in with a false air of professionalism and distracted eyes. Further tests. The passive voice would be used. My options discussed. Doctors stripped to their true function, estimates of time and pain.

As for any possible non-fatal causes I rejected them out of hand as I steeled myself for what would surely be an anticlimactic denouement. Then what? Then we arrived at the restaurant, a tiny, family-owned deal on Mulberry Street. Mobby cars parked bumper-to-bumper on both sides of Mulberry with disregard for the Italian-flag-colored hydrants. Eager waiters stood outside and tried to talk you into their restaurants with broken English while German tourists walked around with noses in their Fodor's looking for the place that sells the best cannolis, filled right before their expectant eyeballs.

Dane insisted we sit at a big table, something about nothing being worse than eating all cramped. Once seated we would need conversation.

"So what then is the best idea you've had since you became an attorney?" I asked.

"I'll tell you what it was," laughing. "Never mind, I hate that war story, am-I-not-great bullshit."

"But I asked."

"True, so I'm trying some dead case down in Florida, a one witness i.d. case but dead. Cabdriver robbed by his passenger. The robber gets out and, get this, slowly *walks* away. Course the cabdriver follows him in his cab while calling the police on his cell, fucking technology. Well, he loses sight of him for all of twenty seconds before the police nab my guy. He i.d.'s him and eight months later this hump won't take a plea and I'm stuck trying this piece of shit. Anyway the guy's got a horrible sheet and's a real pain in the ass. He's being railroaded et cetera, the usual deal. You know, I'm working with the D.A., you're familiar."

"Move on."

"Fine. Now to this day I don't know what ethnicity my client was

114

but one of the things that made the case so bad was that he was a unique kind of maybe Hispanic, maybe Eastern-European looking guy. Well I'm picking this guy's jury when I look at one of the prospective jurors and I swear this chump looks exactly like my client. I'm talking to the point where when I first saw him I thought what the hell is my client doing in the jury box? So I'm questioning this guy and he's like horrible for us. You know *they're all guilty, I love cops*, really horrible answers. But I'm sitting there and I'm thinking that the fact that this guy looks like my client's fucking doppelganger has got to be useful in some way. I don't know, I was thinking maybe during summations I'd point out the resemblance to show the jurors how a mistake could have been made, whatever. The gist of it is I put this nut on the jury. Now the D.A. is like this three-hundred pound woman who is literally salivating as if she just saw a well-marinated pork chop at the prospect of this guy deliberating on my guy's fate. Also my supervisor's watching the trial and he's like apoplectic when I put this guy on the jury. You're a loose cannon Dane, I'll have your attorney card! You know like the black police chief in those action movies. Anyway, the trial gets started. The D.A. puts some cops on and I'm getting buried as expected. Now she puts the complainant on and he's laying it on thick. The guy's driving a cab hundred hours a week to support thirteen kids who live in some grass hut overseas and subsist on twigs and my scumbag client's got to rob him of his night's take. Pretty emotional stuff. So she gets to the worst part for us. You know she asks him if the guy who did this horrible thing to him is in the courtroom and if so would he mind terribly pointing him out. Of course, I'm barely paying attention at this point because I'm all focused on my upcoming cross. But even I'm noticing that this guy's not saying anything. So I look up and this guy's standing up and looking all over the courtroom! Now I'm starting to get hope when he indicates that yes he sees the guy that robbed him. Well the D.A. takes her first breath in about thirty seconds and asks the guy to go ahead and point out the robber. Sure enough this sonuvabitch stands up, steps down from the witness stand, points to this poor sap, the look-alike juror, and says *that's him, that's the guy who robbed me!*"

"Get out."

"Serious, course mayhem ensues with the D.A. asking for a brief recess and me objecting saying that the witness' testimony speaks for itself and she shouldn't be allowed to talk to him. Finally the judge tells the jury to leave the courtroom while we discuss legal issues. Would you believe this juror stays put. He thinks he's about to be arrested for the robbery of this goddamn cabdriver! I mean he's disconsolate and staring at the court officers waiting for them to come and cuff him."

"Did they?"

"*Did they*?"

"Kidding."

"Well they didn't, but let me tell you the complainant was intractable. Even after being told that the guy he'd identified was a juror, he remained convinced it was some kind of trick and kept insisting that the juror was the robber."

"Good grief. So?"

"So they make my guy some great offer that gets him out of jail and he takes it. I'm convinced that to this day the cabdriver believes our system of justice is corrupt because we allow the defendant to serve as one of the jurors."

"That's great," I said and started wondering if I was supposed to come up with a comparable story because just then I couldn't and I was reasonably certain this deficiency wouldn't disappear as more time elapsed. "Sounds nutty down there."

"Not down there man just the job, how long you been doing this?"

"A little over two years."

"Oh man, you're just a kid."

"Older today."

"Really? Congratulations, I suppose, then."

"O.K."

"What's the number?"

"Twenty-four."

"Wow. Now how is that possible given that—"

"My mother lied," I said and we stopped talking because our food arrived. Dane took two bites, declared the food an unqualified success, then never returned to it. Instead he leaned back as if considering all that had come before and weighing several options.

"A birthday is an odd thing despite being inherently senseless," he finally said. "I'm referring to the way it looks you in the eye and demands retrospection whether you're willing or not."

"Well I have a strong will."

"It won't matter. I recently began my thirtieth ellipse around our sun, an anniversary that as you can imagine barks louder than the usual ones. Anyway it was a Sunday and one of those political news shows was on where they pretend to speak on important topics. They were talking about the President and his difficulties during his first year in office and one of the commentators said something like *this really hurts him because those close to him say he is a man obsessed with his legacy.* I thought about that statement a lot. What do you think about that statement?"

"I think I have no way of knowing if it's true or not."

"Course not but what do you think of this concept of a legacy? Because it totally intrigued me."

"What about it?"

"Simply everything. The first thing that struck me is that it is perfectly legitimate, and not at all presumptuous, for a President to worry about such a thing. After all, this man has a job whereby, one hundred, two hundred years from now people will still be assessing his performance. Think about that. It seems to me that whatever the assessment is becomes secondary to the fact there is one at all."

"Meaning?"

"Meaning take someone at random as an example. I elect myself. As you might have guessed it wasn't long before I started wondering what my legacy would be. How will history remember me? I'll tell you. It won't remember me at all. At all! As far as history is concerned I may as well not have existed. Now I know that to you that seems just about right."

"Well."

"But to me this fact is simply astounding. I mean as far as I'm concerned I'm downright enthralling. Now understand what I'm saying here. I'm not saying that when I objectively assess myself I conclude that I'm an enthralling person, although I do. What I am saying is that everything about me is incredibly enthralling *to me*. For example, I can stand in front of a mirror for forty minutes trying to figure out the best way for me to wear my hair. On the other hand, if you tried to engage me in even a thirty-second discussion regarding your hair, I'd instantly tell you to shut up. So there's this horrible dilemma whereby I think I'm the most important thing in the world and everyone else thinks I'm practically meaningless. But it's even worse than that. At least now I exist and am in some sense meaningless. Someday, I hope not too soon, I won't even exist and then I'll give new meaning to the term meaningless."

"Meaning to meaningless?"

"Go ahead, make fun, but this applies to you as well you know. We're all in the same boat."

"Maybe so but you think everybody worries about what you just said?"

"No, at least not in those terms. I understand that the overwhelming majority of people do not articulate this conflict or view it in quite this manner. This despite the fact that what I've said is particularly true of them. But while these people don't put their finger on this feeling they do experience it and it does impact their lives."

"Huh?"

"Look, people need to conform the external reality they face daily with this subjective feeling they likewise experience constantly. To do this they have two options. First, they can achieve what passes for great things. Now the external reality matches their feeling; they really are better than the rest and maybe they'll even be remembered as such. These are the ambitious people, the overachievers. These are also, however, the people who go on these abominable talk shows where they can trade their psychoses for exposure on that box, modernity's ultimate achievement. Note that this tack, being ambitious, is not the preferred course of action. The reason is it's the equivalent of sticking your neck out which we all know is dangerous. Instead many act like they have no ambition whatsoever. Their necks come back in and they're safe. Only problem is now they're at everyone else's level, which we've seen is untenable. The remedy of course is that everyone else needs to be sunk. This helps explain racism's enduring popularity. If I myself don't appear to be markedly superior to everyone else at least I'm part of the better race, country, religion et cetera. This in turn reflects well on my individual worth. There are other options of course. For example, you can constantly bemoan others' lack of moral worth by extension elevating yourself. Think of the average person's reaction to our clients. Do these people strike you as so truly righteous that they are viscerally pained by our clients' misdeeds or are they similarly flawed people looking for anything to hang their hat on? The latter obviously, they're vermin."

"A little strong no?"

"I for one choose the first option, I need to elevate myself above all others. As for you, you're one of the people who does view the dilemma in explicit terms and does worry about his legacy so the distinction is irrelevant as far as you're concerned."

"This you know how? We essentially met yesterday."

"Please. I don't see things? Hear things? You're trying to outrace the same demons I am and every day running out of more time. Only the unimaginative fear death when it's oblivion that cuts deepest. Next time you burrow into the subway picture the aerial view. Ants."

"Fine. For the sake of argument, let's say your analysis was achingly accurate. Then what?"

"Simple. You have to get yourself one of those legacies the guy was talking about. I'm not telling you something you don't already know. I've heard. Tons of trials, never lost a single one. I was the same way. But then you realize it's not working. Outside of our little insular community, the impact's simply not there."

"You take what you can get, most have far less."

"Yes, at first. But that's the thing about *more*, you can always have it and you always want it. More in this case is more recognition for more time."

Dane stopped now. He was pleased with himself and staring at me.

"You can't be boiling this down to fame," I said. "Do the famous strike you as happier than the rest because I don't see it."

"Happiness? Who's talking about happiness? For people like us I'm talking about trying to avoid abject misery."

"Speak for you Dane."

"I'm talking about the misery of suffering by comparison. For us, the whole thing takes place at a higher level. We're not concerned with the average person so put that to the side. But don't I have to explain, at least to myself, this disparity between the President who has a legacy and I who don't? Don't you?"

"He's accomplished more than I have."

"Why?"

"I've never tried politics. I have no interest in it. He must have a special talent in this limited area. Remember Dane, this isn't Alexander the Great conquering most of the known world or Napoleon cutting a swath through Europe for Chrissakes. This is a guy kissing untold quantities of ass to put himself in a position where

120

a woefully underinformed electorate can deem him slightly less offensive than the other guy trying out for the job. Besides all that, he's also been around quite a bit longer than me."

"No, no good. As for that last consolation, cling to it as long as you can because it will soon be gone. Moreover, it seems to me you have to admit that he and his kind are simply better than you are. Not better at one specific thing but just plain better. Are you prepared to do that?"

"..."

"Your silence speaks volumes. This is a man who is arguably the most powerful man in the world and you're not willing to admit he's more talented than you. I won't even mention lesser lights. What if I say it for you? These people are better than you! How does it make you feel when you hear those words? You want to say you're in a different field? Well I can name twenty attorneys who are considered better than you, whether accurately or not. Just think about that. How does that make you feel? If those people were looking at you right now, they'd be thinking how much better than you they are. You have other interests you say? You're not *really* a lawyer? Want to try something different? What are your interests? You like science? Are you Kepler, Newton, Galileo? Are you the one who realized that massive objects warp space-time? Philosophy? There's a lot left to do, that's true, but honestly the best you can hope for is to balance on the shoulders of René, David, Immanuel, and the like. And with both these fields you can only really even hope for *that* if you devote your whole life to its pursuit and it's already too late for you to do that. Music? Are you Ludwig van? Johannes Sebastian? Are you Wolfgang composing operas in his preteens? Are you at least Bruce Lee giving a demonstration of his newly minted Jeet Kune Doo at a 1964 martial arts tournament in Long Beach? If you were any of those people or their equivalent don't you think you would know it by now? Are you Fyodor—"

"I get the point."

"So you admit it then?"

"No, fuck them."

"Good because this torments me and the time has come to do something about it."

"Let me know how that works out for you."

"What are you doing tonight? Maybe we could—"

"I'm crossing the river to family."

"Family? Really? Your liar mother?"

"Among others."

"Family," he repeated as if I'd told him I had a werewolf butler. "I do have a fat cousin six or seven times removed in Austin with a disinterested wife and kids who are always barking at him. By the way, the fact that people continue to have kids in overwhelming numbers, despite the clear disadvantages, fits in nicely with my legacy theory vis-à-vis attempts to avoid death and/or oblivion."

"Are you incapable of light conversation? It's fucking Friday."

"You're right, what's the deal with your officemate?"

There was no way Dane was talking about Leon.

"He's a good guy," I said. "His rather lengthy story is as follows—"

"Not *him*, the other one, Julia Ellis. She's one of the most beautiful women in the world."

"You feel you've seen enough women to make that determination?"

"Sure. Look I watch the MusicTeleVision et cetera. Those are the world's most beautiful women, digitally and surgically engineered to make me want to buy something. Now I look at Julia Ellis and I see that she's as beautiful if not more beautiful than any of those women and I know she's not putting as much effort into it as they are so I conclude she must be one of the most beautiful women in the world. Follow?"

"I'm not prepared to say you're right but you may not be as wrong as you usually are."

"Does she have anything else going for her?"

"Besides her astonishing appearance?"

"Yes."

"She appears to have several other positive attributes."

"Really? That's odd."

"How?"

"Well I find extreme beauty fascinating."

"Is that so? How unique."

"No I mean beyond simply being attracted to it like everyone else. One of the things that seem true to me is that God doesn't often give the extremely beautiful much else. Nor does he, for that matter, give the hyper-intelligent or super-athletic much else either. Think about that. You never hear that the gorgeous supermodel is also diligently searching Theoretical Physics for its Grand Unified Theory. And when they cut to that guy from M.I.T. to explain the inexplicable doesn't he always look like something a hairless cat coughed up?"

"I don't know."

"Leave the knowing to me."

Now I guess I can be incredibly unobservant at times. So it wasn't until then, when there was a lull in the conversation and we were waiting for the check that I first realized what a bizarre portrait Dane's was. He seemed almost inhuman, not really subhuman or superhuman though; more like metahuman. His build was paradigmatically average like the cardboard cutout in your doctor's office. On it lay a skeletal face that seemed to disappear the longer you looked at it. From his skull straight ink-black hair and overseeing a sharp nose insane green-light eyes.

When we were done we started to walk back. I was going back to court, this time 100 Centre Street. Dane was going home with another aborted invitation rebuffed. We separated. On the way I ran into Sam Gold, Tom's cherubic underboss.

About Sam Gold I had recently learned exactly two interesting facts that I was still trying to properly contextualize and reconcile, videlicet: 1.) in over a quarter of a century at the office he had taken zero days off and 2.) his father had been *the* Manhattan District Attorney. Gold never handled an actual case or anything like that but his conciliatory skills were legendary and much in demand where I worked. He was glad he ran into me and could I do him a favor when I went back to court. Inside I said no with extreme prejudice but externally I agreed.

After Gold left I saw Dane again. He didn't explain or anything but instead just resumed as if there had been no interruption:

"Saw this movie late last night when I got home," he said. "It was atrocious of course and for a million different reasons I won't go into but one thing even the movies can't ruin is a good caper."

"Yes."

"A precise heist."

"Right."

"An impossible rescue."

"Correct."

"A desperate prison break."

"Definitely."

"Are we of like mind Casi?"

"On this yes."

"On everything, you'll see."

"Except they invariably screw it up because even when they depict a successful one it always involves at least one unexpected complication that must be overcome. The reason this is misguided is that the beauty of the caper and the other things you mention, what gives them their allure, is the notion that they can and will be pulled off seamlessly, with algebraic precision and exactly as planned."

"Interesting, constituting a triumph of what?" asked Dane.

"Intelligence, what else?"

"No, of will. Intelligence how?"

"If the right person plans it properly it will work, you can plan it into success."

"But then you need the will Casi. The will to execute it the one chance you get. This is where the adrenaline comes from and this is the universal attraction. This is why people love crime, the singularity of will involved. And don't tell me people don't love crime to the point of near obsession. Just look at the newspapers, the visual news, and all other forms of popular entertainment, crime is their favorite process. The only question left is whether crime is inherently a perversion, meaning error is necessarily built into it, or whether some degree of perfection can be achieved in that area."

"Meaning?"

"Meaning the commission of a truly perfect crime."

"Oh."

"Possible?"

"Guess anything's possible Dane."

"And everything."

"So get cracking on it, could be your legacy."

My, people come and go so quickly here!
– Dorothy in Oz

Chapter 4

So now imagine you are Raul Soldera meaning that although you are
dying, as promised, you are not doing it fast enough so that wherever
you turn people are upset by this and even you yourself end up not
really knowing what to root for since every upturn in physical health
leads to greater legal peril and so you spend time internally debating
things like whether 'tis better to be strong and caged or infirm but
free.

And one of the literally handful of things you own is a weathered
trumpet you use to play Salsa, your native Puerto Rico's creation, at
various nightclubs with various others but never without the assistance of one or more attractively controlled substances. And though
you are a legitimate musician you are not an immensely talented
one meaning your constant use of these substances achieves neither
mystique nor cliché but rather is a lot like that proverby thing
whereby *first you take drugs then the drugs take drugs then the
drugs take you* but all this happening in like three days really not the
years probably envisioned. So now stare at your owner, a seemingly
innocuous amount of white powder that you convert to injectable
fluid. A demanding owner that wants inside you at all times, that you
serve meekly in everything you do whether it's blowing into that
trumpet or selling Him to other chattel just so you can be near Him.
Until you sell to the wrong kind and one of the things the judge says
when you take the inevitable plea is that if you commit another felony

within the next ten years then you *must* be sentenced to State Prison and you say you understand and there will not be a next time. Which semi-vow you mean because you genuinely fear State Prison so imagine further that you in fact draw this demarcation into your life whereby in the ensuing eight years you continue to run afoul, as they say, of the law but only of misdemeanor incarnations of such. Meaning you will still sit behind a restaurant's dumpster near used condoms and inject your foot with your owner then shake your companion's chin to determine whether he continues among the living and in the absence of a final determination slowly peel his fingers from his needle to see if you might not be able to squeeze a few more drops for yourself but you will never again give to strangers for money, it being famously better to receive than to give in this context.

Now you are forty and essentially homeless and one night you spot a forgotten purse outside the nightclub you just played. Only the thing about the purse is not much in it save for the credit card with the woman's name in raised letters that you stick in your wallet to maybe feel a little important then forget about until its discovery months later by the latest A.O. on your latest failed buy who raises it to your face and makes a what-have-we-here type declaration while smiling, the fuck. The next day your improbably smooth-faced lawyer tells you you're charged with Criminal Possession of Stolen Property in the Fourth Degree and that this is an E felony with a minimum sentence of one and a half to three years in state prison but that he will likely get you out in five days, which he does. Then later he tells you the D.A. must be an idiot because you're indicted but he will delay things as much as possible, which he also does. Until the day when further delay becomes impossible as the case is scheduled for trial and they want to start it like that instant. And you don't want to take 1½ to 3 but you also don't want to go to trial and get more.

And you're sick. You're sick and your T-cell count is in like the teens and your mouth bleeds at inappropriate times and you didn't know you were positive, although it wasn't exactly a shock either, until those six days when your lawyer said something about medical attention then a doctor saw you and took blood and checked a lot of boxes for high-risk behavior then later told you it was bad, the blood. Now you are perceptibly wasting away with what look like white Rorschach inkblots on your face and have no stomach for a risky trial or prison sentence and instead just want the case to somehow disappear. Which it sort of does because after talking to the judge your lawyer tells you that because you are so sick you are being offered a special deal by the judge whereby you plead guilty and are promised the minimum sentence but your sentencing is deferred indefinitely while you provide intermittent updates on your medical condition until such time as . . . and then his voice kind of trails off as the two of you silently contemplate the obvious eventual ending of the litigation.

But these still become something like good times. For one, without the Damoclean sword of a potential trial and consequent state bid hanging over your head you actually start to feel better. You feel better and you play better and you stop with the junk and your sister lets you live with her as long as you continue to stop with the junk. You even start to semi-consistently play Jimmy's of all places and even though drinks are free for the band you drink club sodas with lime all night. You tell your lawyer he should come and watch one night. Then things really get better when you get switched doctors and you get Dr Weintraub who puts you on a cocktail, which you think is a funny name considering everything, and your T-cells go up like a lot and his letters to the court don't seem so dire and Judge Hilton, like the hotel, still smiles when she sees you every couple months and everything just seems so much quieter now.

But imagine that one day Judge Hilton is not there and she won't be back and instead it is Judge Cymbeline who will now *preside* as they say. The medical reports don't look so dire she says with slit-wrist serenity and adds that she disagrees with Judge Hilton. That she wouldn't have given you such a big break. This Dr Weintraub sounds almost optimistic she says. Why can't you go to prison now that you're feeling better? After all hasn't it been eight months since you took the plea and yet there's your heart still pumping, your compromised blood still flowing. That was not the deal. Your improving health requires that you be incarcerated and she's ready to do so. Imagine all that.

I did and remembered that after we dodged that bullet on the previous court date I had informed Soldera and his counselor, with uncertain terms decidedly not present, that he should get sicker if he wished to avoid going to prison. Preferably, I strongly suggested, he would be in the hospital, his home away from home and the only place that offered true amnesty, the next time he was supposed to be in court. So I fully expected to be greeted by a duly appointed representative who would give me the good news of Raul's hospitalization along with a little supporting documentation. But instead there was Raul himself, in the audience and smiling.

He stood and came to me. Raul was all eyes; they dominated his face as if his body had been reduced to its barest essential, seeing obstacles and getting out of their way.

"Good to see you but I was hoping you'd be in the—"

"I'm doing good. The new doctor is more better. He's got me on the cocktail and—"

"That's great but I'm worried that—"

"He give me this letter to give to the judge."

I looked at the numbers quickly. "The problem is this judge," I said. "When your condition improves she gets impatient and—"

"What's she going to do? Is she?"

"I don't know. Remember I told you last time that she can put you in jail to serve the 1½ to 3 if she—"

"But the other judge said—"

"That judge is gone Raul. Cymbeline's in charge of the case now and she can decide—"

"But you said—"

"I said that precisely this could happen. Damn it Raul, why didn't you do what I said? I was very—"

"Am I going to jail today?"

I thought of Ah Chut and The Pledge. "No I'll keep you out of jail. But next time either do what I say or tell your doctor to write more pessimistic letters!"

"O.K."

"I'm glad you're doing well and I'm sorry about this but—"

"Can I make a call while we're waiting to go in front of the judge?"

"Yeah but don't take too long. It doesn't look very busy in there."

I went inside the courtroom and signed in Soldera's case. I sat and watched Cymbeline and her Cheshire-grinned marionettes torture the lost like powerful boxers toying with overmatched opponents. After some time I realized Soldera hadn't come back so I went out to the hall to look for him.

I didn't see him.

I went back in and crossed his name off the list.

Then I went back out and looked for him some more. Nothing. He had disappeared.

The golden favor was a big one, *catching* a misdemeanor all-purpose part for an alleged afternoon hour prior to my death penalty meeting. In Manhattan there were five such parts with *all-purpose* code for nothing meaningful gets done but the nothing takes all day. Misdemeanors that had been arraigned but not disposed of were sent to these parts to take care of all pretrial matters. The parts typically handled about a hundred and twenty cases a day and did so with maximum confusion and disarray. In theory, the attorney on each of those cases would appear in the part to handle the case. Like most such theories, this one had little to do with reality. Reality was *catch, the catcher,* and *catch notes.* Each day an attorney was assigned to catch one of the parts, that person being the catcher. If the assigned attorney was unable to cover his case in one of these parts he would write a catch note that would tell the catcher what needed to be done on the case. The catcher would then cover the case to the satisfaction of no-one. The client was usually unhappy because where the hell was his attorney and when was client's case going to be called? The judge wasn't thrilled because the catcher knew nothing about the case aside from vague jottings on a piece of paper. The catcher was least happy because he was fucking catching and more demeaning and horrifying task had yet to be invented.

So there I was sifting through a pile of hieroglyphic notes and doing my best to ignore an increasingly agitated audience. Linda was there too.

"You know why you're catching?"

"Gold asked me."

"Know why?"

"No."

"Diane Zale refused to catch."

"Doesn't the schedule say Larry Halloran is supposed to be here?"

"Where've you been? He quit weeks ago. Diane was the reserve but she refused to come in and catch."

"What does that mean?"

"Well Conley informed her that she was the reserve and she informed him that she refused to catch. Then Swathmore went and talked to her and she said the same thing."

"To Tom?"

"Yup."

"And he said what?"

"You're fired."

"Is that even allowed in this place?"

"No there's already talk of a rescission," she laughed. "The union's negotiating and they're hinting about a sick-out on Tuesday."

"Aren't you broken up you're leaving? You'll miss all the fun."

"No I think I'm leaving just in time."

"Soon you'll be pressuring earnest bright-eyed couples to buy homes they can't afford. You know the ones near railroad tracks that you couldn't resell with a gun."

"No," she laughed. "You're bad."

I would've thought we were done then but she just kind of hung around the table there until I felt compelled to create more noise.

"So why are you splitting?"

"I've been here a decade and that seems like enough. It's draining to me. Every day dealing with people who are in so much trouble," she gestured to the audience for empirical support. "I know that sounds silly but it's true. I think it does something to a person to constantly deal with people who have made a mess out of their lives don't you?"

"I guess."

"See, you *guess*, but I *know*. That's the difference. I'm not like you, I don't have the stomach for this job. No I'm serious, I've seen you. You get sent out to trial you get excited, you like it. When I get sent out I get sick, literally. I just don't want this to be a part of my life anymore, I want to go back to the real world."

"Everyone gets nervous when they get sent out, that doesn't mean anything."

"I'm not talking about normal nerves here, I'm talking about terror. The first time I did a trial I'm about four months out of law school, twenty-six years old. I remember looking at my client and thinking am I really the attorney for this guy? It was petrifying to me to realize that it was really *me* who was in charge of this guy's defense. The first time I spoke during that trial I heard the words as if they came from another person, a very nervous person. After the trial I told my supervisor about this feeling I'd had and how it lasted throughout the entire trial. She said it was normal and would go away through experience. Well it's all these years later and I still get that feeling every time I pick up a serious case that doesn't look like it's going to plead out."

"Wow, that's not good."

"Uh, no. That's why I'm going to be worrying about mortgages and annual percentage rates from now on. I'm telling you this job's not healthy. You know I watched Lee Graham faint in court from the pressure. He's like me he's—"

"Wait, you were there?"

"Yeah, I was his second-seat."

"Pray tell."

"Really?"

"You're surprised?"

"I guess it's O.K. right? Anyway, it was an attempted murder where our guy was made an offer just prior to starting trial. So we spent the whole morning trying to talk the guy into a plea but he was adamant about going forward. Now when you have a disease you know the symptoms, and when someone with the same affliction comes along you're quick with the diagnosis. I'm looking at Lee and I'm totally seeing the signs. For one thing he's begging this guy to take the plea. I mean actual begging. It was very uncomfortable. He's doing this even though the guy didn't really have a bad case and the offer wasn't very good at all. Well the guy doesn't take the plea and we're supposed to start picking. Lee was literally green at this point. He was like shaking and stammering. He started telling the judge he couldn't start. The judge is like *you're starting* and calls for a jury. That's when Lee fainted. I had never seen an actual person faint before, have you? It's not like in the movies where the person gracefully falls perfectly backwards. The way Lee fainted it was as if all his bones had been suddenly suctioned out of his body."

"Then what?"

"The case was adjourned and on the next date the guy took a plea. I suppose the fainting unnerved him."

"Nobody's fool he."

"No, we told everyone Lee had been feeling ill but if you were there the real reason he fainted was obvious. Don't tell anyone. I saw the writing on the wall though. That would be me someday so I think I should get out before someone gets hurt. So I'm leaving."

Just then a burly court officer asked me to talk to a guy in the back who was making a commotion. The guy was in on a fugitive warrant from North Carolina. He'd been popped for having an open container of beer in the park. The police ran his information and found a warrant from North Carolina for a rape case. He was *remanded* (held without bail) in anticipation of North Carolina authorities picking him up and extraditing him back to their jurisdiction to face their version of justice. He had been in two weeks he said. But it wasn't him; he had never been to North Carolina. He was a different Edward Hill. He was a good one. Why was it taking so long? His lawyer said it would be straightened out when they compared his prints to those of the N.C. Hill. His lawyer was Solomon Grinn and his note to me was consummately useless.

When I came out from the back Linda was gone. Realizing it was for good kind of made me sad and sad in a way that was completely out of proportion to our relationship since we'd never really spoken much until arraignments the night before. This was one of my many problems. I could barely know someone – even border on disliking them – but if I then knew I was never going to see them again, those last few moments could make me pretty sad. For two years I barely exchanged words with Linda. Then two minutes before her final exit she opened her skull in front of me, as if I cared, to reveal that what I thought was gutless was gut-wrenching instead. I did Hill's case and a few others then my replacement arrived. Was I aware why we'd been pressed into duty he was asking but I was busy staring out the window:

> The window is a vertical rectangle showing an alley's airspace. Beyond it stir a great many white circles but out there the world's been inverted so that snow falls up. The circles appear from behind the bottom glass then rise, circuitously but inexorably, until out of all view, ascending from the littered street like loosed souls seeking heaven.

I was late for that death penalty meeting and when I walked into the conference room the speaker looked at me and stopped speaking, a formidable opponent to any stealthy entrance. I caught up. There were five groups of three attorneys each. Each group would work on the appeal of an Alabama death sentence. A member of the group would go to Alabama to meet with the client. The group would write and file a brief on the appellant's behalf and a member of the group would argue its merits before the appropriate Alabama appellate court.

My teammates were Melvyn Toomberg and Joe Ledo with our work product incredibly due in what felt like hours. The other catch was that after signing up to be part of our group, Ledo had subsequently quit about a week back. He had gone to Hollywood where he would write scripts with fame and fortune to follow meaning our three was two. Although Toomberg was more like one and a half there being no room in his cranium for anything other than The Law and his office therefore constantly housing a line of people hoping to hear his take on a legal issue which take he always preceded with a *don't quote me* although you could do just that as he was always right.

We got the files that day including a complete transcript of the trial. I rifled through it: **Twenty-two-year-old Jalen Kingg** it said. **Sentenced to death** it added quickly. Melvyn and I were of like mind. We would read over the weekend and talk on Monday.

As I walked out I saw Solomon Grinn who had been with the office seemingly before there was a right to counsel. The only thing skinny on this clown was his beard.

"You have a guy Edward Hill?"

"Yeah what's going on? He get picked up?"

"Picked up? He says it's not him."

"Oh that's right. He's probably full of shit but I did put that on the record at arraignments. He wouldn't waive extradition so now they have to get a Governor's warrant to get him back to South—"

"North."

"– Carolina, right."

"Well has the D.A. compared his prints to the Carolina prints?"

"I don't know what they've done but I put it on the record that he says it isn't him."

"Yeah but I think you should call the D.A. and make sure they compare those prints. All they have now is a name match. They have ninety days to get a Governor's warrant and that's how long they'll probably take. Meanwhile this guy might be in for no reason, think about that. I said all this to the assistant in the part and the judge but you know how that is. You'll probably want to stay on top of it with the assigned assistant."

"Yeah maybe you're right." He was looking away now, smiling at some other meathead and not really paying attention.

"So you'll do that or should I?"

"What?"

"You want me to do it?"

"What does that mean?"

"Means I'm not currently overcome with confidence you're going to take care of this."

"Listen I've been doing this since before your father—"

"Fuck off," I said leaving.

*

Would I work with him on the case? I was back in Swathmore's office. Death in the case he was mouthing about and death all around me too. Brown plants that had never been watered and ancient files closed tight and stamped **ARCHIVE** for good measure. I was opening and closing a binder on the floor with my foot and full of answers then questions. Yes I knew the case. Her own goddamn son. Wearing a yellow fisherman's cap like Paddington Bear while it happened. Seven years old. But wasn't Susan Hyves working on the case with him? Really? When did she leave? Hadn't he fretted this morning that I was too busy? Oh this was why? No, just asking. Yes. I would forget the murder two and work on this case instead. I would read it over the weekend and we would talk next week. Thanks, I guess, and all that.

From opposing ends, purple angelfish swim towards each other against a loud blue backdrop. Their mouths pucker then close again and again (breathing?) as they rush to meet in the middle. Just before making aquatic contact they veer off wildly in opposite directions swimming off the screen to be immediately replaced by others. The replacements look the same but aren't.

In front of this screensaver sat Conley and Debi Podurk and to their immediate left was Troie Liszt a new attorney who always wore white sneakers in court. They sat in the pink office that served as our Athenian Academy. (The walls of Conley's office were white like all others but immediately outside his sole window was a tremendous U.S. flag flapping in the constant wind and often completely obscuring the world outside; Conley kept the lights off but the room was rarely dark because angry-white solar rays would pierce through the red fabric of the flag and emerge to color the room rose.) Conley and Debi were supervisors entrusted with the responsibility of assuring the smooth functioning of the office so, as such, they had no actual work to do and what they did in lieu was sit in that office and debate everything from the ponderous to the absurd. Liszt was one of the constant visitors and contributors but everybody was welcome and seemingly everyone joined in at some point or another. There were unspoken rules. Debi and Conley could never agree on anything no matter how minor. If entering mid-debate you were not to interfere in any way with the gaining momentum by asking people to repeat arguments or by raising work-related issues. Lastly, you were expected to yell often and occasionally take an indefensible position you didn't wholeheartedly believe for the sole purpose of spurring passion and entertainment.

"The great unknown," said Debi.

"Oh please," said Conley. "You say that in hushed tones as if you're saying something truly awesome or meaningful."

"And you say what?" asked Liszt.

"I say that this great mystery that everyone tries to attach to it is totally overrated," Conley said this as if he were reminding all present that a triangle has three sides. "Speaking generally, death can be one of four things, three of which are highly palatable. First, it could turn out that death is really not much different than what we call life."

"Isn't it by definition very different, as in the opposite?" Liszt said.

"No. Not at all. Put aside for the moment spurious linguistic arguments. It could turn out that when you die you actually continue to function in essentially the same way albeit in some other form of reality. So while everybody's looking at your old body and bemoaning your absence you're actually doing quite well but doing it somewhere else. Note that this is not a bad situation. It's like moving from New York to Los Angeles. It takes some getting used to, at first you may be miserable, but eventually you adjust and the weather's better to boot."

"Of course your loved ones stay in this reality," said Debi.

"*What*-ones?"

"Loved ones."

"Loved ones? Big deal, you make new friends. The second possibility

138

is the one these religious kooks like Cleary try to sell you on. You know what I mean. Everybody's had harp lessons and white is everyone's favorite color. Peace, love et cetera abound. Although consummately boring, this possibility clearly beats the hell out of our current situation so again no complaints there right?"

"Not for most," said Debi.

"The third possibility is more like a tremendously strong probability and is the one all sane, sentient beings should subscribe to. In this one death is a real end. No more consciousness, no more anything. This one scares the shit out of people but it shouldn't. Someone explain to me what's so bad about not existing? I know it's bad to be sick or in pain. I know it's bad to be sad or in other psychic pain but I can't for the life of me get too worked up about the possibility of not feeling anything. As human beings we don't sit around in dread recalling the days before we existed."

"To recall something you have to experience it. To experience something you have to exist," said Debi.

"Precisely. If death is an end to all experience then that's not bad at all."

"Some of us enjoy life and its experiences and don't want them to end," said Liszt.

"That's absurd. Do you wake up after a long dreamless night and complain that you haven't experienced anything in the past ten hours? Of course not. A good deep sleep is as good as it gets. If death is just the longest, deepest sleep then sign me up right now, it's got to be better than this."

"I think we can all agree that you in a long, deep sleep is an attractive option," said Debi.

"Finally, comes the only possibility we should actually fear, the fourth and final one," said Conley, content for the moment to ignore. "In this possibility, death *is* a state of being and it *is* worse than life. Take your pick. Constant pain, psychological torture, whatever. There you have it. There goes the mystery. One of those four possibilities will be the truth just wait and see which one it is."

"Even if we gave you that these are the only four possibilities," said Debi.

"You have no choice," said Conley. "They're the only ones."

"Even so. Why would that signal the end of mystery? It's no minor thing to wonder whether you're going to be in a state of constant agony, bliss, or somewhere in between for a long time. Given those stakes, I think our preoccupation with the subject seems just about right."

"Oh relax. Three out of four possibilities is great! You can't ask for better odds than that. Given those odds, the way we cling to life borders on the embarrassing. I have an ancient uncle lying in a hospital bed severely decomposing but pulling out all the medical stops in an effort to last a few more weeks. He's got a hole in his throat for breathing, a bag coming out of his gut for shitting and he wants to know when he can go home. Why? He prefers certain and constant agony to a seventy-five percent probability of pleasant death! Where's the placid calm that's supposed to attach to the near-dead? To me it makes little sense. Some degree of curiosity is normal but the obsession my God. The books, the, the religious nonsense, the—"

"The D.V.D.s" Liszt jumped in. "The other day I rented a D.V.D. called UNFIT FOR TELEVISION: DANCES WITH DEATH. It was bizarre. It was all this video footage of people basically dying."

"Nothing's more basic," said Conley.

"For example?" said Debi.

"One dude was attacked by a shark, you saw copious blood in the ocean."

I was looking at what had no doubt caused this conversation. Television was in Conley's office holding rerun images of Rane's handiwork. Edwin Vega as Superdad behind the counter with both hands on his neck. He looked like so many people I knew. The action had been paused but I knew the ending. On Conley's desk, the paper

140

was open to a picture of Baby Tula and the offsprung story.

I knew the D.V.D. Liszt was talking about too. Angus had rented it and I was there the night he watched it. I caught the end of it.

Some years before, I'd been in Mexico on some mindless college bullshit. Posted everywhere, mostly on shredded telephone poles flooded with rusty staples, were signs selling someone who answered to **COLOSIO. COLOSIO** this. **COLOSIO** that. I finally asked one of my cabdrivers who this Colosio was and why it was necessary that his name be everywhere. He'd been running for President but not anymore. He was dead.

On the D.V.D. I saw why. From a very public, very crowded rally, the narrator tells you which one is Colosio and commands you to watch closely. As you watch, Colosio tries to make his way through this great amalgam of people. Another man approaches him from the right of the screen to within three or four feet. He shoots Colosio in the head. Red skull fragments land everywhere, scattering the crowd and ending the campaign. Everyone reacts. No-one grabs the shooter.

The next and last clip was from an outdoor railroad station. There are three separate tracks people are crossing without incident. A train approaches slowly on the first set of tracks nearest the camera then stops well short of the station. Seeing that this train has stopped for good, impatient people on their way to work continue to cross the tracks. Now you can sense another train approaching. You're not sure if it comes on the second or third tracks.

Then you see it. You see the train coming quickly towards the camera on the second set of tracks and from the same direction as the train that has stopped. You see this about the same time you notice a man and a woman crossing in front of the stopped train and walking towards the second set of tracks. Given the title of the disc you now focus on this man and woman who do not appear to be together. The man crosses the first set of tracks, notices the approaching train and stops suddenly.

"No," I said.

The woman breaks into a trot towards the second set of tracks with the suddenly loud train approaching. She's looking down at her bag. A distracted inventory of her possessions. It all happens so fast.

The train doesn't run her over, like the expression, it hits her. Her neck barely hangs on to her head. Her left leg flails across her body as she sails through the air: a lifeless skinbag of bones. Angus replayed it three or four times. Each time I moved towards the door then stopped and watched. It was the eyes. Angus could have played that evil clip of her derogation twenty times and I would have watched each one. I didn't want to. I had to.

The man next to her also watches as she flies through the air, his mouth is great wide open. She flies in the direction of the camera outracing the nose of the train.

She seems to gain speed just before going out of view.

By the time I finally got to my office Julia and Leon were gone. I listened to my messages. The first was a familiar voice from the night before. *You good man you* it said with further variations on that theme. He had gone to the precinct like I said and he felt much better. The police had been made aware of the situation with his potentially murderous wife and they were going to be *vigilante* he said. He still didn't tell me his name but he promised to call next week.

The other message was from Dane:

You didn't let me tell you why it doesn't work. Why it doesn't work when people have kids in order to escape oblivion. Superficially, it seems like it would work. The person who creates a child really does become more important in that someone is initially dependent on them for their survival. For a while someone exists who actually shares their view of themselves. Of course this little person will soon reassess that feeling and conclude that they and not the parent are the most important person in the world. The parent can now add someone else to the list of people who disagree with their self-assessment. Additionally, they're now saddled with the added burden of reconciling their view of their child with that of the rest of the world. These are the insane people who want you to faint when confronted with the superior intellect or beauty of their decidedly average offspring. Well of course there's more, but not now.

I erased these messages and gave some thought to where I was, where I was at that specific moment and where I would have to go. I had done nothing on Darril Thorton, my most serious case. Same for Kingg's appeal which we were being asked to turn around in what had to be record time, not to mention Tom's case on which I would surely be doing the brunt of the thankless-but-time-consuming work pursuant to customary practice. And now Soldera had evaporated.

Everybody was leaving or had just left. Their cases would be transferred and I would undoubtedly get some of them if I stayed. More people looking at me as if I had answers for the race against undefeated Time that we would undoubtedly lose. The office was morbidly quiet and I started to feel an anxious loneliness. I left.

On the elevator it was just Debi and me:

"Here's one," I said. "A doctor, an accountant, and a lawyer are in a roller coaster accident and meet their untimely end. They're in front of the pearly gates when St Peter approaches them with a proposition. Answer one question correctly and enter heaven where of course all is bliss. He turns to the doctor and says *name the twentieth-century luxury liner that sank after hitting an iceberg. The Titanic* the doctor says all happy and St Pete immediately lets him in. Then he turns to the accountant and asks *roughly what year was that? 1911* says the accountant hesitantly. *Close enough* says Pete and he lets him in to meet up with the doctor. Finally, he turns to the lawyer who's getting ready to join his friends and says: *name everyone who died*."

No reaction at all and at that very moment I decided to retract The Pledge as impossible to fulfill.

The snow had stopped and it wasn't quite as cold anymore so I decided I would avoid the subway and walk the mile or so over the Brooklyn Bridge. While walking towards the bridge I watched a man regaled in full Superman costume run past a woman and snatch her purse. The Man of Steal then ran faster than a speeding bullet into the subway station's yawning entrance, his billowing red cape squiggily trailing behind him as he disappeared. Everyone was kind of looking at each other not really sure of what had occurred and not wanting to besmirch the good name of a beloved superhero. I waited around for the requisite time when something bizarre happens, made the similarly expected eye contacts and shrugs, then kept walking.

Just off the bridge, on the Brooklyn side, was a park. I was cutting through this park when an errant wiffleball whizzed near my head. "It's all in good fun until someone loses an eye," I said as I threw the ball back to the smallest of the four kid players. They sized me up optically then asked if I would be the official pitcher. I was running late on time so I agreed. The kids couldn't have been older than ten or eleven but they sure took their wiffleball seriously.

At first my crafty southpaw delivery confounded these rapscallions. All except for one whose name I gleaned was Jimmy. Jimmy wore an orange baseball cap backwards and he strode to the plate with the confident swagger of all great athletes. Whenever he hit he made verbal and pantomimic reference to Ken Griffey Jr with the idea being that he was him. He crowded the plate too creating a temptation, which I somehow resisted, to deliver some serious chin music. Then he'd take my diluted offering and slap it somewhere for a base hit or worse.

Despite getting repeatedly tattooed by this kid I managed to keep the game close for both teams. Eventually the last inning arrived with the non-Jimmy team leading by a run. I promptly retired the first two batters then lost the plate. Now I was starting to really try, but you can't turn it on just like that and I couldn't get these damn kids out. The two kids on my team were actually exhorting me with things like *c'mon dude!* and *you can do it!* which was more than a little embarrassing. The other two kids led by Jimmy were talking serious trash at me and I have to admit it was somewhat unnerving. Mostly I just wanted to get the hell out of there before someone saw me locked in a life and death struggle with two pudgy ten-year-olds on behalf of two others.

The count was three-and-two with the bases loaded and Ken Jimmy Jr at the plate, his team still down a run with the payoff pitch upcoming. I was late. I had things to do. Had to get going across that river.

I went into my windup, looked up at the darkening sky like Fernando Valenzuela, and uncorked a filthy backdoor slider. It was ticketed for the low outside corner until it rudely dropped off the table. A suddenly overmatched Jimmy waved at it feebly and struck out to end the game.

Chapter 5

"Why, you're cooking?"

– ¡Of course *que sí*! But you're late.

"I know, got held up at work."

– ¿*Pero* don't you get out at five?

"It's not like that mom, I don't punch out at five on the dot. I have to get my work done before leaving."

– ¿You mean overtie?

"No, I don't. Be there in about an hour."

– ¿Didn't you get my message yesterday?

"Yes."

– ¿And you don't call me back?

"What's this? Telepathy?"

– I know *pero* the next day. I was worry. I hate that city. *El otro día* on the news.

"Be there in an hour."

– Don't forget Marcela and los kids.

"Forget. How could I forget?" I had.

– *Bueno*. Drive carefully *y que mi Dios lo bendiga*.

"How dramatic, I'm twenty-three miles away. If you're going to pray, pray there's no traffic."

– ¡Shhhhh! Don't be *malo*. I love you.

"Love you too."

*

Last time I saw Marcela I told her she needed to hurry up and pop out that third kid so that each of the three sibs would be precisely thirty-three months apart, the kind of symmetry I inexplicably craved. Instead she opened the door, still shaped like an inverted question mark, hugged me tight, then responded that Bill was at one of his jobs but she didn't know which because he left his cell at home which he never did except when he did. I sat at her wobbly piano and raised the white heart picture frame to my confused face.

"Who's *this* guy?"

"Very funny."

"Yeah but the copious hair, the missing weight."

"Speaking of, do you feel older little brother?"

"Every minute, this is the oldest I've ever been."

"Aw, you're so cute," she said and pinched my cheek. "Be ready in a minute."

She left the room and was replaced by Timmy. Timmy was severely precocious, a feature I generally disliked but in him detested. He stood in the open part of his tiny living room wearing a faded red jumpsuit with yellow balloons and stared at me as I moved to the couch. I knew he was about to say something because his mouth slowly yawned open and also I had a pretty good idea what the subject would be: his singular obsession.

"Is it true that everyone dies eventually?"

"Good grief."

"Is it?"

"So far so bad. Why?"

"What do you mean?"

"I mean that until now no-one's really made it past 115 years or so."

"So that means everyone dies."

"Not necessarily but it counts as damn strong evidence."

"Casi!" from Marcela.

"I mean darn strong kid."

"Why?"

"Why is it strong evidence?"

"No, why does everyone die?"

"No-one knows Timothy but what do you want life in perpetuity? If people didn't die where would we put the new ones? We're quite overcrowded as it is."

"So people die to make room for the newly born?"

"I'm not prepared to say that's the sole reason but it might be a factor."

"So the day my little brother is born someone will die?"

"No. Well. I mean someone *will* die that day but you won't know that person and the two events won't be related."

"But you just said it might be a factor."

"Don't be a wisenheimer, I got you a present."

"Mary too?"

"Yes, do you want yours or should I give it to Mary also?"

"No I want it."

"Here you go."

"Thanks! Wait what is it?"

"What is it? They're X-ray specs."

"What are X-ray specs?"

"They're great."

"What do they do?"

"Kids today. You put them on you get that there X-ray vision all the kids are talking about."

"What kids?"

"What kids he says. The kids at school, what other kids are there?"

"Nobody's talking about X-ray vision at school."

"Well they will be once they get a load of you wearing these and seeing through solid objects and the like."

"What will I see?"

"Put them on and find out. What are you waiting for? You're going to be able to see what's inside people."

"Bones?"

"Well yes but think big. If you squint hard enough you can see what's inside bone!"

"You mean mar—"

"Don't say it."

"Can I put them on later?"

"Course."

"Thank you for the present."

"You're welcome."

During this conversation, Timmy had been reluctant to even take possession of the magic specs. In mid-colloquy Mary had appeared and immediately cuddled up next to me on the couch with her head on my shoulder and her thumb in her mouth. Now Timmy took his X-ray capability with him and went to his room.

"Hi beauty."

The ensuing silence probably shouldn't have surprised or unsettled me the way it did, not given the mute weeks it was preceded by, but had this been a movie the screen would then have gotten all squiggly before revealing first an eight-month-old Mary delivering words to mass delight then ten months later asking compound questions without easy answers and recounting incidents in painstakingly verbose detail but always with lucid clarity, (back then you heard what she was saying but you couldn't really listen because to listen you had to pay attention and to do that you had to at least figuratively take your eyes off her which you couldn't, no-one could; you couldn't because she was a perfectly beautiful and angelic cherub with smiling eyes and rosy plump cheeks that sagged to just below her chin, *anyway* was her favorite word), until after a similar leap arriving at the recent past when she simply and suddenly forsook all language. She hadn't withdrawn, Alana once pointed out to less-than-zero reaction, and if anything she was more affectionate than before.

149

She appeared to still understand everything quite well and quacks were adamant that there was nothing physically wrong with her. Nonetheless her decision had an air of finality about it so that all her responses were nonverbal and should she need something she either mimed or did without.

"I got you something, want it?"

She nodded yes, eyes all wide.

What I gave her was a toyish necklace I had bought from an unlicensed general vendor on the street. He recognized me from one of his previous arrests and hence the alleged great deal. Were they hearts? If they were they looked anatomically correct and what was I thinking? Ridiculous really but now Mary raised her chin, pulled her anomalously long hair back with her chubby hands and waited for me to act.

I spun her around and fastened the clip around her neck. She turned, pulled my head down, planted a smooch on my cheek, then ran off to show her mom.

"That's very pretty, what do you say Mary?"

"She thanked me already."

"O.K.," Marcela said, aware I was lying. She came into the living room and opened her mouth but nothing came out and it slowly closed. Then three little empty bubbles appeared above her head leading to a giant bubble within which Marcela resolved to change the subject.

"Casi, did you ever call that doctor?"

"Doctor?"

"Yeah, did you call her?"

"Her? Who?"

"The doctor whose number I gave you. She's *single*," she sang this last word with the suggestion of manufactured intrigue. "She's Bill's cousin's best friend, you're supposed to call her for a date."

"That word's still used?"

"Of course, when are you going to call her?"

"How hideous."

"Why?"

"Exactly."

"What?"

"Why?"

"Because I'm a great matchmaker and I want to make this match."

"You know her?"

"No."

"So how are your matchmaking skills implicated?"

"I saw her picture."

"She has a picture?"

"She's beautiful."

"You have the picture?"

"No but I saw it and you can take my word for it."

"You were impressed."

"And she's a doctor what more do you want?"

"You ask her out then."

"She's very pretty."

"You mentioned, what does that mean?"

"It means what everybody thinks it means."

"Well I don't care for everybody or their beliefs."

"Casi, I went through the trouble of getting her number. Besides she knows I got the number and the reason I got it."

"How does she know that?"

"She'll be expecting your call, her feelings."

"I'll call."

"Yay! You never know maybe it'll work out."

"Work out?"

"The two of you might become a couple."

"Please, I'm calling, don't make it worse."

"Don't you want what everyone else wants? People are meant to be paired off you know, maybe that's your problem."

"We better go before your mother has a heart attack."

"Oh *my* mother now?"

So out the door and into the car to our grand mother's house we went. In the car no-one said anything. No-one said that everything in every direction looked uniform, that the ubiquitous minivans were all a species of gray with the sliding door on the same side, that the harried twenty-year-olds in playgrounds with kid rope-gangs dutifully trailing behind all wore the same plastic expression. No-one marveled that the birthday party for little Wendy Pennylipper was always at The Discovery Zone and always ended promptly at 4:00 and no-one wondered about the absence of felonious Supermen or wiffleball games contested in subfreezing Citibank temperatures. Instead we just existed quietly until I looked in the rearview and saw that the two squirts were already moving toward R.E.M. before Marcela looked at me with question-mark eyes:

"It's going to be O.K., I really believe that," she said.

"Yes."

"The not talking."

"I know."

"You think so too."

"Well I meant that I knew what you were talking about."

"So you're worried."

"No."

"I'm terrified."

"Don't be."

"It's not normal."

"What's normal?"

"Talking."

"Listen no kids her age talk."

"They *all* talk."

"No, not all of them. I bet some clam up."

"Sure, the few who can't talk. She can and doesn't. Who does that?"

"Certain monks for one and there are others."

"So I shouldn't?"

"Worry?"

"Yes."

"No. It's just Mary. Little Silent Mary."

"You're probably right," she shut her eyes and breathed out audibly. "I hope Alana comes, think she will?"

"Haven't heard from her."

"Me either. But she'll come, I bet, because of you. As for Mary I have faith in God."

In my head only I said *I like you Marcela, I mean I love you but I also like you, I like you because you say things like faith in God and when I hear something like that it's almost like I'm looking for subtitles, I like you because you wear an apron while you ask your kid if he finished his homework and I'm not built for that but I admire the hell out of it, best of all your eyes smile when your mouth does and have you ever noticed you passed that ultra-charming trait on to Mary?* When I was a little twerp I got lost at one of those antiseptic malls that place specialized in. The truth is I didn't get lost as much as I just decided to walk away from everyone I knew. The people I walked into kept getting bigger. They wore hairnets and nametags and kept crouching down to look me in the eye. All the lines you're only peripherally aware of came into focus and sharpened dangerously. I was afraid they would cut me because that's what sharp lines do. I wasn't crying but I was upset and I was walking faster and faster, circling, trying desperately to return to my point of origin. Resigned misery I felt. I was staring at the floor and decided I was going to dive in and try to quantum tunnel right through to the under side. But when I bent my stubby legs in anticipation I found I could fly. I rose above everyone, the earthbound, and started spinning. Then Marcela put me down and smothered me with love. The nametagged interlopers

153

receded and the globe again curved and softened. So I thought that whether her eyes smiled or not I would like her a lot. I reminded her of that incident.

"You were always doing that, in fact, oh my God," her hand went to her mouth. "I think we're coming up on that overpass from Television. Did you hear about it? You didn't? A kid fell off an overpass and was killed by an Intel truck. His friend was on the news and said that the kid was hanging from the side trying to remove some graffiti he had spray painted on there a couple years ago. Dom loves Sue or something was what he had written. They showed the overpass and I instantly recognized it from all the times I've driven by here. I even felt guilty because you know that momentary excitement you feel when a place you see all the time makes it on T.V.? Anyway I guess this girl Sue had broken up with him. The kid's mother was on and said he hadn't left his room in twelve days. Can you imagine? What do you do?"

"Count apparently."

"It's so sad. Timmy hasn't stopped talking about it. He keeps asking me if Sue is responsible and if so is she going to be punished. Look there it is!"

███████ Sue 4ever !!

"They're going to sue the city because they never removed the graffiti," Marcela added and all was again quiet as we neared our destination.

To turn onto Gluonn Street required significant vehicular precision for on each side of the impossibly skinny street were identical corrugated open caverns, the result of a misguided and subsequently abandoned construction project that the town evidenced no inclination to remedy. The car remained silent as I steered it with surgical care between the twin depths and though I eyeballed them and judged that each contained only an expectant six feet, I still felt that even the slightest slip of the wheel would send us hurtling endlessly downward, past the earthen crust to splash into a pool of boiling magma. "Careful," Marcela said lowly.

Half a block later I began to make out cars clustered like metal shavings near the magnet that was my mother's house. The house was the smallest on the block, probably in town, but it came armed with the loudest bark causing nearby houses and their inhabitants to recoil when it pulsated like it did now, illuminating the surrounding sky with the sounds of fortune. What sounded then was a family gathering loosely centered on my temporal crisis. The cars told this story: A blue Ford Escort that seemed to sputter even when off, registered owner Tio Chino also owner/co-creator of three of my cousins their names being Joann, Cybill, and Andres and their aforementioned father being married to Tia Margarita and he being the youngest child of the two old-timers ultimately responsible for this mess and whom in a long-ago uninspired fit of invention someone, a small someone doubtless, had monikered Buela and Buelo; and Buelo's green '51 Chevy in the driveway since he lives in the house with my mother who came to this country essentially on a dare from his wife's lips to the effect that you marry that man at the age of sixteen and well you can image the rest and her doing Buela one better and marrying that man – of whom nothing more will be said throughout but only out of deepest love and similar emotions even though the clarity of the image faded daily, like a photograph left under the sun – in a country where they were currently dropping like flies off highway overpasses and all this to the chagrin of the real head of the family and oldest sister Tia Miranda who decided to try and undo the geographically done and so boarded the next plane here to talk some sense to the newly wed, but little sister had decent powers of persuasion herself and before long Miranda was having apple pie and rooting for the home team at the ole ball game and subsequently birthing two more cousins with since-discarded male in the cigar-dispensing role and naming them Lorena and Vanessa and all this from an apartment located not more than ten feet from her sister's. Well there followed a genuine exodus of Colombian *tourists* who overstayed their I.N.S. welcome, the first being older-but-not-oldest sister Nia who married only long enough to expel sole daughter and cousin Melinda who later joins forces with redheaded Patrick, his black Lexus now parked facing the wrong way, to create not-yet-one-year-old Jaren whose grandmother was followed by youngest daughter and final aunt Ariana who at least waited until she was eighteen years and one minute old to take to the skies and now drove a red sports car with **SEXY** license plates and was unencumbered by reproductions. So all five gone from a now empty house and Buela spends the next twenty-odd years convincing Buelo to join them until finally they do, so that on weekends they, and others like newly arrived cousin Armando and his 70's Volkswagen van costumed like a giant hot dog, make my mother's house jump with *salsa* and *merengue* for your ears, *chicharrón* and *arepas* for your belly, and *aguardiente* for your soul.

Such was the case that night as the house's music crossed the street to where I pulled up behind the oversized frank, my front bumper coming to rest directly beneath the part where the little extra beef peeks out from inside the bun. Timmy woke up and immediately started singing:

> One two three . . . three two one
> Join with me and we'll have fun
> Join with me
> We'll have fun
> As th'Earth flies
> 'Round the sun
> Now I know my Alpha Beta C's
> Next time I want some money

Mary watched and listened but said nothing. Then she stuck her tongue out of the corner of her mouth like Charlie Brown, ran towards me and jumped into my arms. We walked into the house to find my mother frying. My mother didn't cook, she fried. If you weren't vigilant she'd fry your goddamn Lucky Charms in the morning.

What she fried on this night were *empanadas* and these are an unqualified good. If you disbelieve me then get your hands on this:

To serve as filling:

2 tablespoons olive oil (cheap kind)
1 cup peeled potatoes diced into ¼-inch dice
(Must get tiny yellow Colombian ones unless you can't in
  which case abandon the entire project)
2 cups sirloin steak similarly diced
½ cup finely chopped white onions
2 teaspoons ground cumin
1 cup ripe tomatoes seeded and diced

To create the dough that will surround the above:

½ teaspoon salt (Diamond Crystal or the lass with the inexplicable
  umbrella)
½ teaspoon freshly ground black pepper
1 teaspoon roasted garlic
2 cups cornmeal (finely ground)
½ tablespoon chopped parsley
2¼ cups hot chicken stock

To prepare:
1 large egg you'll beat lightly
More vegetable oil than you've ever eyed at once for frying.

And do this:

Boil the potatoes in a small saucepan with cold salted water until just tender, maybe 5 minutes, then drain. Concurrently, heat 1 tablespoon of the olive oil over medium-high heat in a large nonreactive skillet. Add the sirloin and cook until browned. Add the scallions and cook for 1 minute. Add the tomatoes and cook for 1 minute. Add the potatoes and cumin and cook for 3 minutes. Transfer to a bowl and let cool.

As to the dough, grab a large bowl and throw the dough ingredients in it. Mix them all until the dough is sticky but malleable. Refrigerate for 10 minutes to let the dough set. Cover your work surface with plastic wrap and slap the dough onto it. Cover with another sheet of plastic wrap and roll the dough flat with a rolling pin, using short strokes, until about ⅛ inch thick. Without removing the plastic wrap, and using a cup about 4 inches in diameter, cut out rounds of the dough.

Peel off the top layer of plastic wrap then remove excess dough between the circles and reserve. Using a pastry brush, brush the edges of each round with the beaten egg. Place a teaspoon of the filling on the lower half of each disk. Working on one *empanada* at a time, use the plastic wrap to fold the dough over to create a half-moon shape. Pressing through the plastic wrap, use the edge of the cup to seal the *empanada.* Remove from the plastic wrap and place on a baking sheet. Repeat with the remaining *empanadas,* rerolling the scraps of dough until none remains.

Heat many inches of oil in a heavy medium-size pot or in a deep fryer to about 365 degrees (to test use a bit of leftover dough, which should quickly puff and turn gold on contact). Fry four *empanadas* at a time until golden. Remove and drain on a wire rack. Repeat again and again then serve hot.

Do that and you'll have what we were having. Now please, make sure not to make the dough too thick or you'll ruin the whole enterprise. Also resist the temptation to substitute healthier alternatives to either the ingredients or the frying process. Do it right. And eat them right too meaning get yourself some lime (never lemon) or maybe a little bottle of Tabasco sauce. Now bite off the corner and add your condiment into the newly formed opening. Repeat this process until you can't.

On my mother's orange kitchen counter lay several dozen of the above. Bottles too and other assorted distractions. Now my mother was hugging both of Marcela's kids simultaneously, calling Mary *Maria* and Timothy some concatenation of phonemes I can't possibly hope to replicate.

Then she was coming at me. Tiny and round and looking no older than Marcela she squeezed my head and – ¡*Ay mi amor*, twenty-four jeers ago! You're still my little boy. Here eat. I made it especial for you.

Half an empanada sticking out of my face, I walked out of the kitchen and into near-hysterical humanity. The room was so loud that at first I looked for the fight that had erupted, but no, just the usual mayhem from everyone I mentioned before and more. The heavily made-up women all wore indecent-exposure-short skirts and heels in the smack of winter and looked like they should be elegantly twirling their hands in the vicinity of A New Car. These were mostly my aunts. There was music. Loud enough to interfere with conversation but really discouraging no-one and by simply changing the position of your head you could go from one multilogue to the next. A bottle of *aguardiente* the size of an equine thigh lay on the center table with a small bowl of limes.

Everyone was grabbing at me all hugs and smiles – an independent observer would think I had just been released from a P.O.W. camp –

confirming my age and handing me colorful boxes. Always with a card containing a handwritten message of devotional love. Alana was not there.

There were new people and they were introduced in painfully informal manner. Included was the latest boyfriend for Lorena whose name she repeated incessantly, surely motivated by fear that someone would mistakenly call this sap by a previous, now-defunct name. His name was undoubtedly Barry and he looked about as comfortable as a fourteen-year-old awaiting the result of a home pregnancy test. To my family he was a new toy with freckles that could be dragged from corner to corner and told bizarre stories in irreparably broken English and if things got too hairy and the words escaped, then in *español* and etiquette and viable communication be damned. When he wasn't being spoken to directly he still served as backdrop.

So there was constant yapping. Lots directed at me but precious little coming from my mouth:

"Mommy, right some people don't have a place to live?"

— I almost died during the delivery *Dios mío*. The next day they asked me if I had the name yet. I said *casi* because we were getting close to deciding. I kept waiting for them to ask me again but that's the name they put down.

— ¡No drink it fast like this! Forget the salt. All you need is *la lima* (never lemon) for right after.

Television was showing a computer simulation of aggrieved Dom's final flight. In it he holds on to the can of spray paint all the way down and when he lands he shatters like a hollow porcelain doll. Sponsored by Dell.

– ¡Nia says forget those antibiotics! *Eso es un* escam from the pharmacy companies. Just mix some shark cartilage with ginseng and drink it in three increasingly larger swallows.

"Where's Alana?"

"Right that some people live on the street mommy?"

Candles in front of a grainy portrait of the Virgin Mary. The blue and white liquefying into each other. And what's with the Davincian smile in this version?

– Pray to St Anthony and you'll find it right away.

– I don't know. They said it was a census or somesing. I lied.

"Don't you fear that we – the cousins – have been screwed up by all this confounded Catholic education with its sisters and fathers, even brothers . . . ghosts and hosts . . . virgins . . . trinities . . . chalices . . . wounds? I mean – they basically paid money they didn't have so our brains could be washed in lies. Didn't they?"

– *Fulana de tal* says that the police wait outside in the nightclub's parking lot. When you get in your car they immediately arrest you and take your car. ¿Can they do that?

"Screwed up how? Wouldn't one of us first have to evince the slightest hint that they received that schooling?"

– Americans love *el hot dog*. I sell them right out of the van.

– *¿Y Alana?*

"Who the hell's Vince?"

"Right that some people live underground in the subway?"

– Have another *aguardiente*. It's good for you.

Universal accord that these were the greatest *empanadas* ever ingested.

"Why not put some mustard on the van? I have yellow paint in my garage and I think it would help business."

"Right that those people don't have families?"

– *¿Otro aguardiente?*

"Listen to this. Air Security divides dangerous countries into four risk categories: crime, kidnapping, political violence, and wars or insurgencies. Colombia is the only country to appear in all four categories. Doesn't it border on the significant that our parents come from this place?"

 – *¿Americanos* love the mustard?

– ¿Lawyers in this country make a lot of money right?

– *Si. Mostaza.*

"Mommy what happens to those people when they die? What happens to their bodies? Do they have funerals?"

"I manage them. *Testy Wee Willie Wheeler and the Dissonant Tritones*. They're going to be big."

"Jeez Barry how am I supposed to know why she called you Fred?"

– No this is *merengue*. Just swing your hips from side to side to the music.

Fine the kid's a bit weird but what does happen to these bodies?

"I said she called me Vince. Who's Fred?"

– Down there the traffic cops give you change when you bribe them. ¡I'm not exaggerating, they'll go to the store and break a large bill!

– ¡Bill's here! *Pobrecito*, he works so hard.

– ¿*Por qué* do you represent those people?

"Boxing is the only real sport because you know men engaged in it from the very beginning. Somehow I don't see cavemen taking time off from battling with dinosaurs to swing a stick at a ball."

– I had to lie to get him in school early because I heard they were only making the Hispanic kids wait until they were five so they would fall behind the Americans. So I lied. I got him shoes with big heels and said he was five, small but five. Those *monjas* didn't care they just wanted the money.

"For every person I get to join I get $500 dollars! Everybody makes out."

– After he was sentenced to life in prison the Colombian government allowed him to build his own prison. ¡He put a bowling alley and a movie theater in it!

"I think if you come to this country you should have to speak American."

– *Miren este huevon.* (Now this new guy's the opposite of a hit.)

"Why so quiet cutie? . . . Mary?"

"I heard about that. One day there was a siege during a screening of a digitally restored *Wizard of Oz* and he just walked out."

"Whattya mean arithmathematically impossible?"

"Is Alana coming?"

– ¿Can I borrow the hot dog to pick up my girlfriend tomorrow? She loves tube-shaped beef.

Wilfred Benitez was born on September 12, 1958 in the Bronx, New York.

"The problem with this country is that we coddle our criminals. Everyone is all concerned with their rights and nobody's worried about the rights of the victims."

"That's a beautiful necklace Mary but what are they supposed to be? . . . Mary?"

– He refused to do the pledge of allegiance. I think second grade. ¡I had to go and talk to the nun principal or they were going to kick him out!

A blue and brown soccer ball with a two hour half-life and a Bic pen's chewed cap struggling to keep the air in.

– *¿Otro?*

"How come you're allowed to lie in court?"

– They killed him because he scored *un autogol* in the World Cup.

"Where do I find this *everyone?*"

Can a family be hyper-functional?

"Time's Alana getting here?"

– Recently Miguel Lora and Rafael Pineda but before that there was of course *Pambele.* ¡Our *país* has produced many great fighters!

– I know, down there a red traffic light is more like a suggestion.

Baby Jaren seems either unable or unwilling to hold his head in one place. The lumpy hair-speckled mass has no defined position just a wave of probabilities. Finally his eyes lock on an artifactual thirteen-inch Sony Trinitron, complete with requisite logo of supine red, green, and blue ovals and aluminum foil for an antenna, located about five feet away.

"This Wee Willer, why's he so testy?"

– *¡Ay* he's so esmart look at the way he stares at the T.V.!

– Drink this one, it's nice and cold. You won't even feel it.

– It's not just sports either. Don't forget *Gabo*.

"Any funny stories about representing the scum of the Earth?"

"Oh my God look. He's reaching for the remote control. How *cue!*"

And so it went. On and on without even hint of cessation until it somehow abruptly ended. First one or two left because *look at the time* then many followed suit and soon there was just the guest of honor in an empty living room. I had nodded affirmatively to too many liquid offerings and now the room had come off its moorings. It shook and tried to buck me off as I gingerly made my way to the sofa. I dropped onto it face down, remembering a trick I had learned and so keeping constant if tenuous limbic contact with the floor – like a silver screen couple in the code-of-conduct era – to combat the itinerant enclosure. I did this to find I wasn't really sleepy, just tired and altered. And very both. Then the room was incandescent.

The coupled beams of light were like the previous snow. They appeared from the bottom of the front windows then rose until they were fully *in* the room. When a car door opens there's that slight suction of air you hear which is soon followed by it's opposite expulsion just before metal and rubber click and fasten as the same door closes. I fell asleep in the seconds following this noise and dreamt that someone was tapping on the window by the sofa and calling my name.

So I looked at this window and saw an apparition. The raindrop-stained window created a second hologramic image of Alana. They stared at me as if all patience. I opened the window and dropped back into the sofa. Then I heard a familiar but now disembodied voice.

"So what of this twenty-fourth B-day? Happy or unhappy?"

"Huh?"

"You miss me?"

"Who are you?"

"You didn't think I'd fail to show my mug on a day like this did you? More fraternal faith than that one hopes."

"Whose lights?"

"Derek's."

"What's a Derek?"

"I strongly suspect it will soon prove irrelevant so I won't bother. But at least he was good enough to drop me here."

"You staying?"

"No, he's waiting. This is yours but don't open it until tomorrow."

"Is that ticking I hear?"

"So how was it?"

"Fine."

"Fine? Don't give me fine. C'mon do *as if I were there*."

"No way kid I'm barely conscious, too much *aguardiente*."

"Water that's ardent?"

"Right and still coating my esophagus too. Who's the fucker invented that shit?"

"Nonetheless, *as if I were there* please," she cupped her hand to her ear, the picture of foregone conclusion, but I motioned that an invisible key was locking my lips. "Please," she said, this time jutting her lower lip out when she was done.

As if I were there was a practice nearly as old as we were. Essentially it involved one of us recounting to the other a slice of space-time that person had missed and doing so to the extent that, in the end, the listener would in effect have missed nothing. A simulacrum of corporeal presence. Questions were generally held until the end. Now don't underestimate the level of detail involved here. The raconteur must season the word-for-word account with plainly irrelevant bits of data like people's position in the room, facial expressions, and

167

vocal inflections in a way that far eclipses even what you've heard to this point. So, because of the jutting lip and despite my compromised state, I did this for Alana with decreasing B.A.C. and increasing lucidity and when I was done she said this:

"Wow. But what kind of hot dog did Armando come in? You didn't say."

"Kind?"

"Sure there are different kinds. You've got everything from the watery, brown Sabretts of Midtown to the grilled, sheepskin-encased, red Nathan's of Coney Island."

"I don't think the van had that kind of detail Alana."

"You barely mentioned little Mary either. What does she have to say for herself?"

"The usual, nothing."

"Still not yapping?"

"Correct."

"I can picture the hysteria as we speak. So what? That's what I say. Maybe she just doesn't have anything to say at this point. You know when you first walk into a gathering? You don't let loose with an immediate verbal hemorrhage do you? Of course not, everybody hates those maniacs. First you kind of soak things in. I say Mary's still in her soaking phase and when she's done soaking and dries off we're in for some serious insights. Besides I was a little weird when I was a kid and I—"

"Was?"

"– turned out what passes for alright. On another topic I must admit I'm having trouble wrapping my cerebellum around this 24 thing. By that I mean you turning into this number. I mean if *you're* that old then it won't be that long—"

"Twenty-eight months."

"– before I'm that old. What do you make of this? Five years ago if you pointed to someone and told me that person was twenty-four I would have kind of felt sorry for them. Soon I'll be the person I once pitied!" While she was saying this, Alana was sort of climbing through the window and onto the sofa. Except now she looked stuck betwixt in and out with her body undulating like a seesaw and her belly and the windowsill serving as fulcrum. "No I'm actually liking this," she said when I tried to pull her in and so stayed there teetering noisily with her black Gene Simmons platform shoes flailing all kinetic behind her.

"Less *volumen* babe," I said maybe louder than any noise she was making. "You'll wake the entire house including me."

"Don't tempt me, I'll get this party started up again."

"That's what I'm afraid of," because she could have.

"But fine I'll whisper if you insist."

"I didn't."

"I'll whisper this," and she did whisper the ensuing but it was a strange whisper with her lips staying ventriloquist still and her eyes transfixed on what? "It's not a vanity thing you know?" she said.

"What isn't?"

"Do you?"

"What?"

"Know?"

"No."

"You do?"

"Know?"

"Yes."

"No."

"It's not some lame corporate-feast-on-your-insecurities-fucking-Pepsi-generation-youth-is-better garbage," Alana said, "that causes me to think about numbers. No, as I see it it's about intensity. I have to laugh when I hear somebody refer to *carefree youth* or some such nonsense. Youth is everything but. Six, seven years ago I would stay up all night wondering if some guy liked me or not. More than that really, I could have deliberated that entire time on what a look or phrase had *really* meant. Now some guy could propose to me and I'd probably tell him to shoot me a follow-up e-mail so I won't forget to get back to him. I get tired now. When I meet someone they always remind me of a previous someone in a way that makes any further investigation feel unnecessary," I could tell from Alana's intake of air that a lot more ramble was coming so I opened my ears a bit more and said nothing, the best course of action in those instances. "I read somewhere that the music I like now is the music I'll like for the rest of my life. My fucking brain or something like that won't find new kinds of music pleasurable from about this point on. What the hell is that? Good thing I like this music. C'mon youth wasn't carefree it was intense and intense is good. It's like this house. I never want to come here but when I do I end up liking it. Just to see everything through that prism again you know? A happy youth I must have had over-all. Or was I miserable but with a poor memory? Oh whatever. Remember that old record player in the lime green case, the one with the detachable knobs? I saw it in the garage the other day. In the garage Casi! I put it on and it worked. I mean I didn't have any records to really test it but it was spinning and that was amazing enough for me. I remember the oldsters would start in with the endless clave patterns and you and I would reach for that thing in protest. Then up to your room for a little Reader's Digest Edition of the L.V.B. piano sonatas, remember thinking R.D. was like good? And remember we would limit ourselves to the pre-Heiligenstadt Testament ones to exclude our runaway favorite, the cataclysmic Appasionata, with you being definitely partial to the Opus 28 Pastorale because it was supposedly after this one that he told Krumholz he would be taking a new path and me arguing that those kinds of ancillary matters were not fairly considerable and that some-times, just occasionally, overwhelming popularity is warranted and that the second 27, The Moonlight, with its initial melancholia was the greater work? Remember that? Well if you listen to them now I bet you'll be sent up to that room whether you're willing or not. And if you listen the right way then you're forced to actually *be* that person. Isn't that just the height of weirdness? That's what this house is, a giant green record player with detachable knobs, which is usually fine but can sometimes be the opposite. Sometimes it can be the realization that images seem blurrier now, sounds more muffled, and yet somehow we're inappositely picking up speed. We're picking up speed and you and I have been thrown out of the kitchen where we used to make ice cream floats, armed solely with A.T.M. cards that have our pictures on them and a little bar graph in the corner that's somehow linked to our fingerprints but only until they get the D.N.A. coding capability fully functional and maybe your green record player does still technically work but not really and don't pay it any mind regardless because I have a fifty disc C.D. player that positively compels neighbors to call the police and L.V.B. sounds twenty times better but not as *good* so I kill the lights and blast it anyway so that when the opening movement of the C minor Symphony nears its close at allegro con brio tempo I swear Casi that the sky is going to literally open up and forget all of Ludwig's later Ode to Joy crap because now it's God – for want of a better word – surveying the broken to regretfully diagnose a violent remedy then reaching down and *doing something* about this mess, no longer content to just watch, and you were right about Lincoln Center that time because yes it was great and how could it fail to be but it does have to be louder, or more accurately we needed more money to get closer and make it louder, loud enough that the notes come straight from heaven, replace your bone marrow and you start to question yourself as a physical being and I think the more time passes the louder and louder it will have to get in order to be heard above the din . . . hear that? That's the din."

"Who uses their car horn at this hour?"

"I didn't say he was overly bright."

"Stay over, tell him you're staying over."

"Nah, better go, but tell mom I'll call her tomorrow." She looked up with just her eyes. "I adore the phone, don't you?"

"I abhor it."

More din.

"Love you," she said through a hurried kiss. "Don't forget your present," she added as she swung backward off the window ledge then out of the window's raindropped mise-en-scène. I debated which interpretation to apply to that statement but now even quasi-sobriety proved fleeting and without Alana as distraction, and my foot incredibly on the sofa arm, a resurgent visual tremolo threatened to overrun me and the room I was in. I realized then that while Alana and I had done our little remembrance of lost time I had overlooked relevant things happening then and there and so forgot to ask if her work was selected for that gallery opening she had bated her breath for. More importantly, I forgot to ask her if she knew what happens to the homeless when they die. Do they have funerals? What happens to their bodies?

I sank further into the sofa, still eschewing contact with the floor. Your ear hurts I thought. The twin lights became one then quickly none, leaving the room in a permeating, haunting black. Then that car door sucking sound again.

Just think how you'll feel when even your basest desires are
quenched before they've even had the chance to fully form.
– Gary Dullen ®

Chapter 3 × 2 × 1

Someone once told me that whatsoever you fear most ardently young man (he was old) you will just as assuredly, in the long run, be forced to confront and in the ensuing years I had found those inchoately prophetic words to be, like most of that antediluvian nut's declarations, almost wholly without merit. Therefore, walking on the block of my apartment, thirty-six hours after Alana split, I felt confident I would not have to engage in more social interaction and for that I could thank the cold, which had spread so unchecked it was almost visible now. It drove the Sunday afternoon people indoors, this cold did, and made me feel like a sole post-apocalyptic survivor wandering the ruins of a once-proud civilization while bathing in the unmistakable lure of unobserved conduct. It was so alluring, this quiet solitude, that I found myself slowing to a complete stop that I might fully absorb the sensation until I realized that, incredibly, my body was no different than the ones that had obeyed the Fahrenheit and fled indoors.

But before I went inside, as I climbed the steps to my place, I saw that I hadn't really been alone after all because it was then that this old-timer suddenly materialized from in front of the doorway and walked towards me. I say materialized because even though I know I was looking straight ahead the entire time I climbed the steps, I didn't see this grim-reaper-looking fuck until he was practically on top of me, close enough that I could see intestinal steam escaping from the top of his bony head while he put me into increasingly sharper focus. Flat, disconcerting eyes this prick had, which I tried my best to avert but couldn't as he came closer and closer before finally resting inches from my face. I stopped trying to look away and spoke haltingly in what sounded and felt like an extraneous voice.

His response was a crookedly pointy forefinger coming up glacially then out towards my shoulder. He was trying to grab me this old-timer and only then did I realize that he wore a bare chest drained of all blood and protected by only sporadic patches of salty hair. Then he was opening and closing his mouth desperately like a grounded aquatic. His mouth quickened and quickened but all he could manage to emit was this horrible wheezing and all I could do was stand pillar-of-salt still until his hand landed on my shoulder. He squeezed my shoulder the way you might a roller-coaster harness and I found myself looking around, somehow fearful that I could be accused of wrongdoing. But he wasn't holding himself up, he was pulling me toward him. His other hand now rising, he was trying to hug me it seemed and I saw to my surprise that I was willing to be hugged. But then I thought better of it and kind of pulled away. It was then that the I'd-decided-centenarian showed an alacrity I had not previously thought possible. For after studying my eyes intently one last time, he wheeled away from me, jumped the four steps down to the sidewalk and ran away kicking his heels up. All this not slowly either. What the?

Inside I made my way up the stairs with minimal noise to see from the slanted rectangle of light on the hall floor that Alyona's door was open. The trick here was to get past that open door without being seen but to do so in a manner where if I *was* seen I could seamlessly enter the apartment as if I'd intended to do so all along. Also my face would have to portray that imaginary intent until and unless I was sure I had not been spied. So I probably looked a bit like a crab moving sideways into the doorway, where I saw Traci and walked right in to hear Alyona avoid availing himself of all available segues and say:

"Casi this is perfect. You had all that dubious Catholic schooling, don't you think the Second Coming of Christ has already occurred but nobody noticed it?"

"Just so you know where we are," Traci said. "I've had some of this *useless* schooling myself and I think that by definition the Second Coming is not something that people will be able to fail to notice."

"Why not?" said Angus who took care to keep his head perfectly still and focused on the screen. "I mean the whole thing's a joke don't get me wrong. It's like, no offense, some elaborate fairy tale. But the question is whether within this illusory framework the Second Coming could be missed? After all many missed it the first time."

"You're saying *could be* but Alyona's saying it already happened and we missed it," said Traci.

"Nonsense," Angus said. "We don't miss anything anymore."

"I think we miss a lot," said Alyona. "There's too much noise out there and we can only take in like one thing at a time. I'm telling you, I think it happened and we were like watching the Academy Awards or maybe the preceding Barbara Walters special. It slipped through the cracks."

"No way," said Angus almost anticipatorily. "Such an event would have to be announced. I've been listening and I haven't heard any announcement."

"On the contrary," said Alyona. "More than a few people have announced they were messiahs making a return visit. For example, a recent wacko claimed to represent the Second Coming, at least before he set himself and all his compound's inhabitants ablaze. Might not he have been telling the truth?"

175

"No," said Angus his head still immobile. "You can tell from his announcement."

"What more of an announcement do you want?" said Alyona.

"Television," Angus said with unmistakable respect.

"I don't think Jesus would go on Television," said Traci.

"Wrong," Angus said. "He absolutely would and the fact that none of these pretenders effectively exploited Television is incontrovertible proof that they were not the real deal. Remember, Jesus worked at a time that predated Gutenberg's printing press. He found himself in the midst of an oral culture. So what did he do? Did he go around passing out written pamphlets detailing what he believed to a bunch of illiterates? Of course not, he told stories. He told stories because that was the way people acquired knowledge back then. He told really interesting stories too. Parables that were compelling despite the fact they did not often engage with the truth. Parables that were likely to be remembered by people who did not, by and large, write things down. Now if Jesus is God, as many believe, then you can assume he knew what he was doing and did things in such a way as to ensure that his methods would have their greatest possible effect. What would such a person do were he to return to our modern world? Surely such a person would instantly align himself with Television, easily the greatest communication tool of all time. He couldn't write his message then and he couldn't write it now – not to a world of illiterates. What's he going to do? Tell some more of those nifty stories? Don't make me laugh. Images comprise the only effective language left and God would want to be effective. Television and its various offshoots, that's where you'd look for him if you thought he'd come back. Believe me, Jesus will speak Television."

"So he'd be a televangelist?" said Alyona.

"No, too limiting. Think more along the lines of a huge sitcom star. Bill Cosby at his peak et cetera."

"I think you both better hope you're right about this *illusory fairy tale* as you call it because otherwise it's straight to hell for both of you," said a head-shaking, laughing Traci. "As for a Second Coming, I haven't known what to believe for a long time but I still say that it's not the sort of thing that needs to be announced as I recall. It's more like the kind of thing that will make you either very happy or very sorry that you equated Jesus with a sitcom star."

"Interesting," said Alyona. "What Traci raises reminds me of . . . I think *Pascal's Theorem*? Anyway, the argument is this: God either exists or she doesn't. I either believe in her, and alter my life accordingly, or I don't. If I buy into God and it turns out she doesn't exist I'm at most inconvenienced and maybe disappointed. On the other hand, if I reject God and it turns out she does exist I could potentially be screwed. As a result I decide to hedge my bets and believe in God. What do you think? Shouldn't we subscribe to this? Angus? Casi?"

"Presumably," Angus said slowly, apparently thinking through the properly attributed but misnamed argument while responding, "an all-knowing God would know our selfish motivation and as a result fail to credit us. Therefore, unless we truly and viscerally *believe* we should live it up as if God is dead since we're not going to get credit for true faith anyway."

"I truly have no belief," said Alyona. "But now I can't help thinking that maybe my desire to believe that the Second Coming has come and gone without fanfare stems from a fear that I might ultimately end up having been on the wrong team. Casi, assuming all this nonsense were true, couldn't we still have missed it?"

I had counted and this was the third time I'd been directly addressed making further silence a probably prime example of luck-pushing, so:

"If true – an admittedly huge if," I said. "Then I think that Traci is on to something when she says it's not the sort of thing that could be missed. It won't be a repeat of Jesus walking around in sandals giving people fish. What they want you to believe is that it's essentially a clean-up operation. He comes in and basically separates the healthy from the sick then eternity takes it from there."

"There it is," Alyona said. "Typical Casi, says one thing and nails it." Each word was louder than the one before but still contemplative and a smile grew on his face as he spoke.

"What are you talking about?" Angus said.

"Don't you see? A separation of the healthy from the sick, the sinners from the sinned against and the virtuous from the vicious. Of course. That's precisely what it is! I'm sold. No further inquiry is required."

"So you retreat from your earlier position that this event has already occurred?" said Angus.

"Are you mental? I'm more convinced of it than ever. Listen, from what I hear God long ago stopped working in broad strokes. Even the most devout admit he no longer parts the skies and sets innocent bushes on fire. Rightfully so I might add. Only ambiguity can generate true faith. Any moron can accede to the painfully obvious. At any rate, why would this judgment day Casi refers to be any different? If God's recent track record is any indication we can expect more ambiguity. The simplicity of it all is both beautiful and obvious. I think it's clear that the healthy have already been separated from the sick. The problem is that all of us are the sick! Everyone here, everyone you see or hear, is the result of that separation. We've all been quarantined in this isolated world. It's fundamental. You can't let the diseased freely mingle with the robust and healthy. Somebody as bright as God definitely knows that and this world is the result of carrying that principle to its ultimate fruition. Life is hell after all."

"Stop exaggerating Alyona," said Traci. "The world's not that bad."

"Oh it isn't? Infants kidnapped outside of T.G.I.N.M., infants! Where do you think that baby is? You think it's going to end up being good news Traci? Want to hear what the possibilities are? I won't invent any of them either. I'll draw only from previous occurrences right here on our charming quarantined isle. And that's just this one limited area, I can go on. People baking in ovens—"

"So where are the healthy and robust living?" Angus asked.

"I don't know," Alyona said. "But you can't get there from here."

You couldn't get there from here. We all quit yapping and mulled that over awhile.

"What I love about the angels," Angus finally said gesturing to the screen with his chin, "and I refer of course to those owned by Charlie, is that they were never simply hired by a cuckolded husband to follow his wandering wife. No, their assignment was always the kind that required they go undercover as bikini models or high-priced call girls."

"Oh please," groaned Traci.

"A damn near perfect show I think," said Angus.

'Too obvious for my taste," said Alyona.

"Obvious? Seems positively subtle by today's standards."

"True, but that's just because sex was better back then."

"You mean sex as depicted by Television?"

"No I mean actual sex, making love, intercourse. It was better, higher quality."

"Hard to imagine fucking being any better than it is now," said Traci smiling slightly but not looking at anyone in particular or at all.

Traci's statement ground all conversation to a temporary halt, as any similar statement from a similar source to a similar audience invariably must. We all stopped and looked at her and I remember thinking I was seeing her for the first time. She wore tight, black, cotton, aerobicy pants with stretchy hooks around the heels of her feet. She sat on the sofa hugging the midpoint of her shins with her knees directly in front of her shoulders. Her legs tapered perfectly. Her rest was perfectly imperfect.

"What I'm saying," said a recovering Alyona, "is that the overwhelming noise we live with has made a fundamental pleasure like sex somehow less exciting, less satisfying, than it was for our libidinous forefathers and mothers. It seems to me that for sex and other pleasures to be enjoyed to the fullest, a certain contemplative quality to life must be present. If you doubt this imagine yourself for a moment having sex. Now imagine you wished to increase the pleasure you were feeling, feel it more intensely. What might you do? Well one of the things you'd probably do is close your eyes. What this does of course is shut out other stimuli. The visual quiet increases your sensual enjoyment and you concentrate more fully on the pleasure. The same is true for the removal of auditory noise as well. Well my feeling is that the average person has a much harder time doing this today than they would have decades ago. Today you close your eyes and shut off Television but the noise persists. It's part of our fabric now, our biology, and all other pleasures including sex are diminished as a result. We don't notice this derogation by the way and sex still feels great, don't get me wrong, but I think the difference is there nonetheless. Like the difference between seeing breasts when you're thirty as opposed to when you were thirteen."

"But aren't you really just identifying a saturation?" asked Angus. "Clearly the average person today is exposed to more sexual content than the average person fifty years ago. You may be right that the ease and constancy of this exposure may diminish our enjoyment of the real thing but overall we're still doing a better job of exploiting sex for our enjoyment. We just may not reach the peaks once possible. After all, the thirty-year-old is less impressed than the thirteen-year-old only because he's been there and done that. Nonetheless, the thirty-year-old has quantitatively experienced a greater deal of sexual enjoyment than his pubescent counterpart and that's what matters. Maybe visually and painstakingly inhaling the European supermodel does make it harder to get excited about Peggy Sue but isn't it better than never having seen a woman that beautiful?"

"That's all part of it, I agree, but I also think not the full story. I think that the prevalence of sexual content you refer to is more symptom than cause of the dulling of actual sex. We're obsessed with what we've ruined. In a village that was starving to death you might be able to interest people in a magazine with a pot roast centerfold. Similarly, as the ever-increasing ambient noise we endure continues to reduce the intensity of actual sex, we become more obsessed than ever with its simulations. Our obsession is a result of and an attempt to remedy the fact that we can't consumer our way into true sex the way we can everything else. I know what you're all going to say but put aside for the moment prostitution and similar conduct because I'm talking about real sex where both parties share a common motivation. That kind of sex cannot be purchased and this consumer impotence outstrips all others and leads to our current obsession. The problem is that unlike real sex, which has withstood the passage of time as our foremost attraction, this simulated and packaged version can have its attraction exhausted. When that happens, the stakes have to be raised. So whereas yesterday you were perfectly happy watching women in bikinis running on the beach on Channel 5, today you need to see completely naked women throwing chocolate pudding at each other on pay-per-view."

Television: *Come and knock on our door . . .*

"Yes!" said a gleeful Angus.

Television: *. . . take a step that is new*

"How much you want to bet," said Angus, "that during the course of this episode a misunderstanding will arise between the roommates, possibly involving Mr Furley and/or one or all of the satellite characters, and it will be a misunderstanding which could be instantly cleared up if one of the characters would simply say *wait, are we talking about the same thing here?* yet this will not be done until only two minutes are left in the episode? Also here's a critical question. The question is – and Traci you don't have to answer this – but Alyona, Casi," he paused as if giving a eulogy and mustering his last great recollection, "would you do Janet?"

"Sure," said Alyona.

"Really? Chrissy's so much hotter."

"Don't get me wrong Angus. I'd pork Chrissy *first* but that wasn't your question. What are you saying? You wouldn't ball Janet?"

"I guess I would, if I had to."

"What do you mean *had to*?"

"Well if she wanted me to bone her then it seems I'd have a moral obligation to do so."

"Moral?"

"Well maybe professional."

"O.K. that's my cue to leave," said Traci as she uncoiled off the sofa and towards the door. "Goodbye gentlemen, to use the term loosely, it's been a pleasure and tell Louis he needs to work on his timing. Bye Casi," she added then did this thing where she clasped and unclasped her hand towards me and just like that she was out the door and gone taking the newly birthed concupiscence with her.

"Well that was the only thing keeping me here, so I'll see you guys later," I said as I headed for the door.

"Nice going man. You frigging insulted her," Alyona said to Angus.

"What are you talking about dude?"

"What was all that would-you-do-Janet shit?"

"She wasn't insulted by that man. She's the same person who was singing the praises of fucking five minutes prior!"

"You crossed the line, simple as that," Alyona said. "Besides it was a stupid question. What man wouldn't give Janet the high hard one?"

"Ralph," Angus said.

"Who?" I said.

"Ralph. Ralph wouldn't do the horizontal horror with Janet. He's a happily married man."

182

"Ralph? Who's Ralph?"

"Ralph Kramden man."

"What the hell are you talking about?"

"Did you forget about Angus's grand experiment?" said Alyona. "Oh yeah, how'd that go?"

"You mean *how's it going?*" said Angus. "You happened to come in during a short break. I'm still watching them and have been continuously since Thursday night."

"And?"

"And it's working. It's just going to take a little longer than I thought."

"What do you mean it's working?"

"Well I can't say that Ralph has become fully human just yet but he's definitely getting close. Actually right now I'm a little worried about him. His friend Norton's big mouth has gotten him into a pickle and now he's scheduled to participate in a boxing match with this huge guy named Harvey."

"What the?"

"That's the most recent one," explained Alyona wearily and was that maybe a little fear I detected in his voice?

"He'll think of something," reassured Angus.

Television: *At participating stores only.*

"Wow they can't even make the food look good in the commercials anymore," Alyona said as the camera zoomed in on the golden potato skyline in the red container. "I *will* give McDonald's credit, however, for making no bones about the fact that for us food is first and foremost entertainment. I recently went to one of these restaurants and I was reminded how a lot of them have these playgrounds in the back. So I went into this McDonaldland as it's called and at first I was dumbfounded, like *what does this purple Grimace guy riding a seesaw have to do with cheeseburgers?* But really the marriage is perfect and beautiful in its honesty. I now think that McDonaldland may be the purest province in our land."

"Relax," said Angus. "McDonaldland is not some modern Utopia. It has its share of problems as well."

"Like what?"

"Well crime for one."

"Crime?"

"The Hamburglar," I sheepishly interjected.

"That's absolutely correct. The man's a menace."

"I forgot about him," said Alyona.

"Please," I said. "The guy's an idiot. How effective does he expect to be walking around in that prison garb?"

"He does positively announce himself Angus," said Alyona.

"Maybe so, but the fact remains he's been plying his sinister trade for like forty years and they still haven't been able to stop him."

"Well then maybe Mayor McCheese has to start running a tighter ship over there," countered Alyona.

"He can't. His hands are tied, all these concerns over the rights of the criminal."

"Tied hands? Are you nuts? Mayor McCheese is essentially a dictator. He's been in power like thirty years and I have yet to hear of any election. Also, the guy's surname prominently features the word *cheese*. Shouldn't he be dead of a heart attack by now?"

"First of all it's not a dictatorship. You have to account for Ronald McDonald. The government of McDonaldland is more like a . . . what do you call it?"

"Kakistocracy," I offered.

"Oligarchy," Alyona said.

"Thank you, yes. In fact, there are those who believe that Mayor McCheese is nothing more than a puppet of Ronald McDonald's. I believe those people are correct, incidentally. Goddamn Ronald McDonald runs that fucking city. It's his eponymous ballgame."

Television: *I'm living on the air in Cincinnati . . .*

"This is a great show," said Angus.

"I have to go," I said opening the door.

"Wait Casi. Before you go, what do you think happens to these people?"

"Who?"

"Like Herb Tarlek where is that guy now?"

"You mean the actor?"

After a long pause and I mean the kind of pause that makes you wonder whether you made yourself heard, Angus finally responded. "Not sure," he said almost silently.

In the hall I was immediately set upon by Louie. He looked relieved to see me – maybe just glad to be indoors – but also apprehensive about approaching his apartment door. After an exchange of minor pleasantries:

"Angus in there?"

"He is."

"He's watching The Honeymooners right? I'm telling you, the whole thing's getting a little weird I don't know if—"

"He's not watching it."

"He's not?"

"No, I think he said he was taking a short break."

"Well thank our good friend God for that at least. I mean it man. First he tapes them all sans commercials, of all things, and now he just plays them in a constant loop. I can't believe I was encouraging him at first. It's that damned carousel man. There's no stopping for air, it's truly constant."

"Casio makes some device huh?"

"You mean Sony."

"I could've sworn he said Casio Carousel. I'm always alert to all alliteration."

"Right."

"The Casio Carousel?"

"Yeah made by Sony."

"But it says Casio?"

"Right, it's the latest new and improved thing. It's actually quite beautiful in its subterfuge. It's called cross-pollination. Sony made the product alright, but for an outlandish fee they allowed Casio to put their name on it. Casio's happy because they have their name associated with a great new product. Sony's happy because they get to add this monstrous fee to their already massive profits."

"But people don't know it's made by Sony?"

"Oh it's in there but writ tiny and you have to know where to look. After all, Casio has to get bang for its buck."

"But doesn't Sony want the credit?"

"What for? They're already the unquestioned leaders in the field. There's really nothing more they can do to gain prestige and remember that the fee is outlandish."

"But aren't they helping a competitor?"

"Arguably, but not really enough to affect their own position in the marketplace. If anything, Casio may now hurt other healthier competitors in turn dropping the worth of those companies and maybe positioning them to be engulfed by Sony. I guess I exaggerated before. The more I think of it, the constant loop isn't that bad. Come in, I'll show you what I mean."

"No I have to go," I said.

"By the way, cold enough for you? That's my new thing. I take the weather, no matter what it is, and ask if it's enough for you."

"Good luck with that but did you happen to see a really old shirtless man out there?"

"What does he look like?"

"What does he look like? It's an old-timer wearing no shirt in five-degree weather, how many of them are there?"

"Never saw him. Don't worry, he'll be out there for a limited time only, that's for sure."

"What do you know about it?"

"Well I'm no doctor but it seems to me that a dude that old, in that cold, without a shirt, will likely be dead before the sun comes up."

"Dead? What then?"

"Huh?"

"I mean he's obviously homeless, no family or anything. What do they do with the body?"

"Speaking of, I never got the chance to ask you what you think of Traci."

"I think she just left for one."

"What do you mean?"

"I mean she left about ten minutes ago."

"No."

"Yes."

"Fuck. I fucked up. I'm fucked!"

"Sorry."

"Wait a fucking minute. Are you fucking with me?"

"No."

"Because if you're fucking with me, fucking tell me."

"I'm not fucking with you."

"Look if you *are* fucking with me, I'm going to ask you to fucking tell me that you're fucking fucking with me because there's nothing worse than being fucked with and not fucking knowing it, or even the fucking opposite which is not being fucked with but having fucking residual doubt as to whether or not you're being fucked with."

"Listen to me closely. I'm not fucking fucking with you you fuck."

"And you're fucking sure?"

"Fuck yeah."

"Fuck!"

A world where dog will set upon dog.
                                    — Eponymous

Chapter 7

Witnessed years back in a courtroom:

"You want the newspaper?"

"*El* newspaper, you wanneh?"

"You want the *periodico* or no?"

"What do you want me to do?"

"I'll visit you tomorrow, *sí.*"

"But what do I do with the newspaper?"

Overheard that day in a different but oddly similar courtroom:

"So I'm sent out to Part 49. Who's that?"

"McGarrity."

"How's he?"

"Not bad, tried a case in front of him. He lets you try your case but he's pretty dumb on the law."

"Let's you voir dire?"

"Only because he's not really paying attention. That said, if any legal issues arise, he'll reflexively rule against you unless you tape the controlling case to his forehead or something similar."

"Wait, did I hear *not bad*? I beg to differ."

"You've had him too?"

"Once was enough."

"What happened?"

"Well I'm expecting it to come back down on appeal any day now."

"Why? What's the issue?"

"I'd rather not say."

"What's *rather not say*? I've known you twenty years!"

"What's twenty years? I'd rather not say. I never even told my wife about this."

"You hate your wife."

"Exactly, she barely qualifies as a person in my eyes and I still couldn't bring myself to tell her about this. That's how painfully embarrassing it was."

"That settles it, now you absolutely have to tell me what happened in that case."

"You would force me to regurgitate a painful, traumatic memory? For Chrissakes, you've known me twenty years!"

"Listen, this entire situation is now clearly outside the bounds of morality. First of all, everyone who knows you, whether for twenty years or otherwise, knows you to be a superb raconteur, a master storyteller. Joe, what kind of storyteller is Ronny here?"

"Master."

"Precisely. Now in addition to this skill you possess, you dangle the carrot of an incident so deliciously embarrassing that years later you still can't bring yourself to relate it? Well what kind of friend are you to offer then rescind such entertainment? Haven't the last twenty years meant anything to you?"

"Aren't you supposed to be starting a trial?"

"What do you think I'm doing? Researching the judge that's what."

"Well I get paid to help with legal research."

"Oh is that so? Well of course then Ronald my good man. Here's a hundred. Now that's more than you made last month so make it good."

"Well I tried the case."

"What kind of case?"

"Rob One."

"Codefendant?

"No."

"Gun?"

"Knife."

"I.D. or what-happened?"

"What-happened, prostitution-gone-bad but really none of that matters."

"Continue Ronald."

"Well the evidence is over and now McGarrity's smiling at the jury – he always smiles when addressing the jury – and he's like, *We now come to the point in the trial where we hear the attorneys' summations* and he's looking at me. So I go up there but I don't feel very well at all."

"What's wrong?"

"Well I had dropped my daughter off at school the night before and—"

"How is Theresa?"

"Katie."

"Right, how is she?"

"Not good but it's either blow all my money on her school or put her in a rehab clinic, institutions which incidentally take the ripping off of money to unprecedented almost-artistic heights. You know they won't even guarantee results?"

"Why didn't you come to me Ron? I've got the best place. Serenity Mountain or some shit. These people are great, you'll never use anyone else. We put Julie in there and we swear by it."

"Julie?"

"Oh yeah, Percoset, Codeine, Cocaine – powdered only – Ibuprofen."

"Who's Julie?"

"My daughter."

"Tina has a sister?"

"There's no Tina, it's only Julie."

"Oh."

"Continue."

"Well by the time I get to Katie's room I'm positively ravenous."

"For?"

"Food. Now you would think a dorm at an all-girls school would have something better to eat but all they had were these Señor Smoke burritos."

"Hold it."

"You've heard of these. They're—"

"Forget the burritos. Did you say Katie goes to an all-girls school?"

"Yes, I did."

"Now your wife . . . um."

"Anne."

"Yes, good old Anne. Does she go with you to drop off Katie?"

"No."

"No?"

"No."

"Roommates?"

"What?"

"Does your daughter—"

"Katie."

"– have roommates?"

"Yes."

"Are they there?"

"Yes."

"What are they wearing?"

"All different things."

"Like?"

"I don't know."

"You're getting paid to know."

"Fine. Some are wearing those faded football shirts."

"Over what?"

"Seemingly nothing."

"No panties?"

"Well I'm sure panties."

"What else?"

"Others are wearing nighties."

"What kind?"

"What do I look like Calvin Klein? Nighties!"

"Is that all?"

"I guess others are wearing men's pajamas."

"The tops only or the full ensemble?"

"Full."

"What kind of footwear we talking about?"

"Some of those cute fuzzy slippers, but mostly bare feet."

"Painted toenails?"

"Predominantly."

"High arches?"

"Some."

"Now do you talk to them?"

"Of course, why do you think I'm driving Katie two hours to school and why do you think I insist on carrying her bags up?"

"How do you do it?"

"How else? I do that thing where you use your daughter as a crowbar to feign some sort of understanding of their experientially constricted lives. You know *ah yes, Katie too is thinking of doing a year abroad in Guatemala, how was it?* and declarations of this nature."

"A tried and true method. I've employed it countless times myself. The beauty of it is that, if done correctly, the overall impression left is *oh your dad's cool and funny and he really knows a lot about Guatemala* as opposed to, there's a fat, follicly challenged fifty-year-old who has the ability to talk to a dimwitted twenty-year-old about her career aspirations while not betraying that he is simultaneously imagining that same aspirant engaged in all forms of depraved debauchery."

"Correct, but again this is all digression. The point, to advance the plot, is that I find myself ingesting two of these Señor Smoke burritos."

"What kind?"

"Three Bean followed shortly by Jack Cheese. Now I don't mind telling you that, surprisingly, Mr Smoke makes a fine-tasting burrito, this despite the vagaries and flavor-robbing properties of cooking with microwaves. At any rate, the burritos pleased me greatly. More than that really; the consumption of these two burritos created an almost spiritual pleasure in my alimentary canal and created such affection in me for its creator that had Monsieur Smoke suddenly appeared in the room and asked me to drink some suspect Kool-Aid I would have at least swished it around in my mouth awhile."

"Then what?"

"Well once I'd exhausted all possibly legitimate reasons for still being there and am threatening to turn into the aforementioned fat fifty-year-old, I take leave of the scantily clad coeds and get in my car."

"Model?"

"Toyota."

"Make?"

"Land Cruiser."

"Luxury model?"

"Yes."

"Ronald."

"Thank you. Now I'm about halfway home."

"Time?"

"Oh Two Hundred hours."

"Two a.m."

"Thank you, now let the man continue. Continue Ronald."

"I come across a 7-Eleven."

"Open?"

"Twenty-four hours."

"In a row?"

"Yes."

"You stop."

"Yes. I stop because I'm hungry again and I'm thinking maybe bag of chips. As I enter the establishment, however, I come face to face with a cardboard Señor Smoke advertising his south of the border wares. As I face Herr Smoke shootout style and contemplate my next move, the two employees behind the counter are arguing over whose country first tested nuclear weapons only I can't figure out if they want to be first or not. Before long, I'm punching the oversized buttons on their microwave and contained within are two more Señor Smoke delicacies."

"What flavor?"

"This time Baja Beef and Huevos Rancheros. After paying the jingoistic combatants, I resume my journey while inhaling the two burritos. I arrive home and go to sleep without incident, mindful that the next morning I must sum up on my case."

"Of course."

"Now it's the next morning and my opinion of Señor Smoke has suffered a near-precipitous fall."

"You may have overmedicated."

"Yes, the thought does occur to me at the time that I might not be entirely without blame."

"Señor Smoke's not completely off the hook but you *were* complicit."

"Yes. Nonetheless, however the blame was to be later allocated, I got the distinct impression that my body would soon engage in open, gastrointestinal revolt. Naturally, none of this was helped by the normal butterflies one feels prior to giving a summation. So being the responsible attorney that I am, and cognizant of my upcoming performance, I took every opportunity to sit on the toilet in an attempt to proactively deal with the anticipated problem. Of course, none of these attempts work and we can now resume the story inside of McGarrity's courtroom as he signals for me to begin my summation, because it was then, as I began my carefully prepared closing remarks, that the previously mentioned revolt began in earnest."

"What exactly do you feel?"

"Well, for one thing, my rather large stomach is palpably convulsing to the point where the end of my tie is bouncing up and down. Luckily, the initial grimace on my face coincided with me saying that the People's case sucked or words to that effect. In addition, I now feel an overwhelming need to release the gaseous buildup of the last nine hours and the preferred route appears to be my anus. So now in addition to this childbirth-type pain, I'm also required to use my sphincter to slowly negotiate the gas out of my ass without making any noise. But of course, while I can control the noise, I cannot control the smell which is like something akin to digging up a dead skunk and performing an autopsy on it inside an Indian restaurant's dumpster. Now as luck would have it, the air-conditioning wasn't working and a fan had been set up and pointed directly at the jury box. The fan kept wafting the odor smack into the horrified faces of the jury. Of course, once I open the floodgates I can't stop and I'm ripping them machine gun style – but with a silencer. Eventually, the jury figures out that I'm to blame and they're looking at me like finding my client guilty won't be enough; they want *me* incarcerated. It also becomes apparent that while the release of gas provides some relief, I will soon need to divest myself of the actual burritos if I'm to ever see another sunrise. So now, as the jury's eyes begin to tear, I take a dramatic break and go over to where my client is seated as if conferring with him. Well he's all happy and says that the jurors seem to be really upset and responding to what I'm saying and some even look like they're crying. I now feel like I have at most two minutes before an emotionally scarring accident occurs so I ask to approach. Now when I get there I can't tell the judge I have to go to the bathroom because I will then have effectively removed all doubt in the courtroom that I am responsible for the almost ignitable smell currently enveloping the area. What I do instead is concoct a legal slash factual issue which has just come to my attention by virtue of discussion with my client and which necessitates a five-minute recess so I can rework my summation. With a little pleading I get my way and soon I'm in a full Olympic-Trials-type sprint for the bathroom all the while emitting loud and troubling noises. Well I barely make it on to the toilet before the Three-Bean-Jack-Cheese-Baja-Beef-Huevos-Rancheros explosion but I do and my troubles seem over."

"I still don't see where the reversible error comes in."

"Patience. When I'm done evacuating the burritos I feel about fifteen pounds lighter with a markedly sunnier disposition. I also realize, however, that the necessary clean-up will not be minor. Of course all that's available to me at the moment is standard court building one-ply toilet paper. One frigging ply! My God, one would think that by now at least two-ply would be the legally permissible minimum. What I needed then was something like eighty-two-ply. Anyway, mindful of this, and determined at all costs to avoid any fecal epidermal contact, I begin to unroll an obscene amount of toilet paper, in effect creating a toilet-paper catcher's mitt around my hand."

"This may be more detail than I can handle."

"Quiet, I paid good money for this. Continue, Ronald."

"So I take this catcher's mitt and I begin my task. Unfortunately, unbeknownst to me, the mitt has unraveled as I lowered it and about twenty percent of the mitt is currently in the fecal brown water. Now as I raise the mitt in order to fold it, the previously submerged portion comes up and drips its sordid contents onto my lap. Well I panic and immediately take off the mitt, which falls into the pocket

196

of underwear between my feet effectively drenching my underwear in putrid brown aqua-shit. Of course, fate picks this moment to send a bunch of rowdy teens into the previously empty bathroom. These kids are horsing around and wrestling and my new worst fear is that they'll come tumbling through the door to see me covered in shit and toilet paper with tears streaming down my face."

"Ha, ha, ha! What do you do? I love it! Ha, ha, ha!"

"What could I do? There was no way I was putting those underwear back on so I threw them to the floor. As for the rest I cleaned up as best I could. It took forever but eventually I made my way back in to the courtroom. When I got there I realized McGarrity had been a prick. He was pissed I'd taken so long so he brought the jury back into the courtroom to show them I was responsible for the delay. Well I saunter in, my pants soaked but relatively shit-free and my shoes so wet they're squishing as I approach the well, and I decide I'm going to ignore this monumental slap in the face and simply go right up to the jury box and continue my summation. Anyway by now the smell is gone but I notice that one juror in particular still has this look on his face like I kicked his dog. He's doing that thing where he's looking at me then looking at the judge as if to say *isn't someone going to do or say something*? I try to ignore it but it's becoming harder and harder to ignore. Then I notice that he's not really looking at my face but rather at my waist area. When I look down, God damn it to hell if I don't see my contaminated underwear hanging from the back of my pants."

"Noooo!"

"They had somehow become caught in my back pocket button during my panicked ministrations."

"What the hell did you do?"

"I did the same thing you would do if shit-soaked underwear was on your eight hundred dollar suit, I threw them off. Unfortunately, the fan got a hold of them and sailed them right onto the head of the guy making the face. Well the guy was so horrified that he in effect became catatonic. At this point the underwear, which is really the equivalent of waterlogged cotton shit, is on this guy's head in a way reminiscent of the way Fat Albert's friend wore his hat with each of the guy's eyes perfectly lined up with a corresponding leg hole. Understandably, the guy flips out and the rest of the jurors aren't exactly ready to vote me Lawyer of the Year."

"What the hell do you do?"

"I move for a mistrial but idiot McGarrity won't give me one. He replaces Fat Albert's friend with an alternate then smiles while he gives the jury a curative instruction."

"What kind of curative? *Please disregard the shit-soaked underwear incident during your deliberations?*"

"Words to that effect then he had them deliberate."

"And?"

"And what? They came back in like fifteen minutes and convict my guy."

"Holy shit."

"You said it."

"That thing's coming back down you can bet on that. Ha, ha, ha!"

"It better after the appellate lawyer made me relive the entire indignity for the sake of his brief. To add insult to injury the Fat Albert guy sued me for Negligent Infliction of Emotional Distress!"

"Ha, ha, ha! What happened with that? Did you settle?"

"Fuck that! I impleaded the deep pockets of fucking Señor Smoke as a third party defendant and the case goes to trial in a few months."

"Maybe you can get McGarrity to preside. Ha, ha, ha!"

Near the end of this I had surreptitiously put on headphones, and now, confident that the misadventures of the fat fifty-year-old fecund defecator were over, I headed Far Beyond The Sun with Yngwie Malmsteen. Listening to music in the courtroom is a major top-of-the-charts-no-no so when the court officer began to approach me I lied *911 tape* so I could be left alone.

Yngwie and I were waiting for Richard Hurd. Mr Hurd was a thirty-three-year-old drug addict with one tooth and three ears. The lonely tooth was an upper tooth and it was located in what seemed like the exact midpoint of his gums. The Third Ear requires further explanation. Although Hurd's two conventional ears were just that, if admittedly a bit small, his Third Ear never failed to elicit real horror from me and only some of that horror stemmed from the fact that it was, after all, a fucking *Third Ear*. The Third Ear was not small. It was large, located below the right ear it dwarfed, and oddly resplendent in its full tympanic glory. It was not functional, Mr Hurd had informed me, having none of the interior hardware – cochlea, ossicles et cetera – required to create bona fide auditory experience yet said ear did interfere with the functioning of its two healthier counterparts and generally compelled Mr Hurd to yell, presumably in an effort to hear himself. (Still Far Beyond The Sun but now Jens Johansson was on the keyboards). Impotence notwithstanding, The Ear cast a large shadow and was impossible to ignore. The Ear had large flaps of skin and cartilage that threatened to commandeer its owner's lower neck.

I was not waiting for The Ear to come in through the front door of the courtroom. The Ear was incarcerated in the pens behind the courtroom and I was waiting for corrections and court officers to bring its owner out so I could do the case. This was my only case for the day and it was going to be a plea. After protracted, soul-draining attempts to get Mr Hurd and his extra ear into the District Attorney's Office's Drug Treatment Alternative Program ("D.T.A.P.") had failed, he had agreed, to my immeasurable pleasure, to take 3 to 6. This decision pleased me because I did not want to try a case where the defense was that the police got the wrong guy and the wrong guy happens to have an extra fucking ear. That would have to be the defense too, because Hurd was adamant he had never made a sale, though that would soon have to change if he wished to take, and he claimed he did, the 3 to 6 currently being offered.

Now, still waiting to be horrified, I raised the volume to a dangerous level and crouched forward to blot out the outside world, only occasionally raising an eye to watch for Hurd. The keyboard interlude was done, the guitar taking over its final lick, and now the comparatively slower playing was beyond tasty. Of course this was all building to Yngwie's volcanic, inspired, notes-fretted-at-186,000-miles-per-second denouement. But no such luck because just as the music began a rapturous ascension to cataclysmic conclusion I spied Hurd as he actualized in the doorway leading to the pens. The court officer leading Hurd into the courtroom looked as if he'd just been force-fed twelve lemons, doubtlessly a result of ocular contact with aforesaid ear. Hurd sat at the defense table, mercifully to my right, as the case was called into the record:

THE CLERK: Number twenty-six on the calendar, Richard Hurd, also from the pens. Hurd, Richard Hurd.

DEFENSE COUNSEL: Casi (unintelligible) for the defendant.

MR ZORN: David Zorn for the People.

THE COURT: Come up.

(Conference at side bar.)

DEFENSE COUNSEL: I have an application.

THE COURT: Yes.

DEFENSE COUNSEL: My client has authorized me to withdraw his previously entered plea of not guilty and enter a plea of guilty to the crime of Criminal Sale of a Controlled Substance in the Fourth Degree in full satisfaction of the indictment before this court.

THE COURT: Mr Hurd, you've heard what your attorney just said. He's indicated that you wish to plead guilty to the lesser charge of Criminal Sale of a Controlled Substance in the Fourth Degree. Is that what you wish to do?

(The defendant conferred with his attorney.)

THE COURT: Mr Hurd listen to me. First of all, I'm going to have to ask you to keep your voice down in the courtroom because you're screaming. Of course you have the absolute right to consult with your attorney before making this decision. My understanding from my discussions at the bench with your attorney is that you've decided to plead guilty. You do not have to plead guilty, however, you can decide that you want the case to proceed to trial in which case we will set a trial date today. I assure you that I have no interest either way. If you accept the People's offer you will receive a sentence of 3 to 6 years in state prison. If you go to trial and lose you can be sentenced to up to 12½ to 25 years in state prison. However you decide it's all the same to me, but we do have a rather full calendar and I am going to ask you to decide now. Do you wish to plead guilty, yes or no?

(The defendant conferred with his attorney.)

THE DEFENDANT: Yes.

THE COURT: Very well. People can I have a copy of the indictment? Now before I can take this plea I have to ask you some questions. Again, at any time you can discuss with your attorney the answers to these questions. Now you understand, I hope, that by pleading guilty you are giving up certain crucial rights. You are giving up, for example, your right to possibly have evidence suppressed. Do you understand that?

THE DEFENDANT: Huh? I don't understand.

THE COURT: Your attorney has made motions in this case seeking to suppress certain evidence that the police have obtained. Specifically, I believe the motion in this case dealt with United States currency recovered from you and a statement attributed to you. Your attorney has moved to suppress this evidence on the basis that it was obtained in violation of your constitutional rights. Pretrial hearings have been

201

granted as a result of these motions. At the hearing, your attorney and the D.A. would litigate whether the evidence should be admissible. It is possible that at the end of that hearing the judge would rule that all or some of the evidence which is the subject of the hearing must be suppressed and cannot be introduced at your trial. When you take a plea, however, you waive your right to challenge the police conduct and no hearing is conducted. Do you understand that you waive that right?

THE DEFENDANT: They did violated my rights. They . . .

THE COURT: Talk to your attorney.

(The defendant conferred with his attorney)

DEFENSE COUNSEL: He understands.

THE COURT: Do you understand, Mr Hurd, that you give up that right?

THE DEFENDANT: Yes.

THE COURT: Fine. When you plead guilty, you also waive your right to a trial by jury. At a jury trial you would be presumed innocent until proven guilty. The People would have the burden of proving your guilt beyond a reasonable doubt and they would have to do so to the unanimous satisfaction of twelve jurors. At trial you would have a Sixth Amendment right to confront the witnesses against you. That means your attorney would be able to cross-examine the witnesses the People present in an effort to prove your guilt. Do you understand?

THE DEFENDANT: Yes.

THE COURT: Were a trial to be conducted in this case, you would also have the right to call witnesses on your behalf as well as to testify on your own behalf. Do you understand that you have that right and do you understand that you give up that right by pleading guilty?

THE DEFENDANT: Yes.

THE COURT: Do you further understand that at a trial you would also have the opposite right, meaning that if you did not wish to testify, you could not be compelled to testify. You have a Fifth Amendment right to remain silent. Do you understand that by virtue of this plea you now renounce that right?

THE DEFENDANT: How to pronounce it?

THE COURT: Renounce! Do you understand that you give up that right and no longer have it?

THE DEFENDANT: Yes.

THE COURT: Now are you currently under the influence of any medications, drugs or alcohol?

THE DEFENDANT: No thank you.

THE COURT: And are you entering this plea of your own free will? In other words, is somebody coercing you into pleading guilty or are you pleading guilty because that is what you want to do?

THE DEFENDANT: No, it's my will. My will is free. That is to say, I free will it.

THE COURT: Are you pleading guilty in this case because in fact you did commit the crime of Criminal Sale of a Controlled Substance in the Fourth Degree?

THE DEFENDANT: No.

THE COURT: Counsel I'm not taking this plea.

(The defendant conferred with his attorney.)

THE DEFENDANT: Yes, fine. Yes.

THE COURT: Are you sure? You don't seem sure.

THE DEFENDANT: Yes.

THE COURT: Well what happened?

THE DEFENDANT: I sold drugs just like they said.

THE COURT: How? What happened?

(The defendant conferred with his attorney.)

THE DEFENDANT: The guy came up to me. I didn't never say nothing to him but he said he wanted to cop and did I know where he could cop. And he said he wanted one so I took him to the guy in the store who I know sells because I bought from him many times previous. And that was it.

THE COURT: And did this person indeed buy drugs?

THE DEFENDANT: Yeah, he bought one for five dollars. But I never touched the drugs or took the money from the guy or anything so I still say I'm innocent.

THE COURT: Well you did this for remuneration isn't that correct?

THE DEFENDANT: I did it for the guy because he asked me. I don't even know what nation he was from.

THE COURT: Did you receive money for your role in the transaction you just described?

THE DEFENDANT: Ain't nobody rolled the guy! That crackhead got his drugs.

THE COURT: No, after the crackhead, um, the undercover officer, purchased the drugs did you receive any money for your efforts?

THE DEFENDANT: One dollar! Now answer to me this. How could I be guilty of a drug sale if *A* they wasn't my drugs to begin with and *number two* I only got one dollar!

THE COURT: Who gave you the dollar?

THE DEFENDANT: The dude who sells drugs! He gives me a dollar for every customer I bring him. He gave me the dollar after the covered officer bought the stuff and just before we was both arrested. I also want to put on the record, is this on the record your honors?

THE COURT: Yes. Everything is being taken down by the court reporter.

THE DEFENDANT: Then I want to stipulate that the person who gave me the dollar, my codefendant, is in here and he has made it be known to me, through the proper channels and whatnot, that he wants his dollar back because I bought him a cop as a customer. And I also want it stipulated that the street interpretation of that is that he will cause physical pain unto me if he gets the opportunity.

THE COURT: O.K., well that's totally incorrect usage of the word stipulate but your point is well taken and you can request protective custody through your attorney if you wish later. In the meantime, we'll continue with the allocution. The conduct you've described does constitute a drug sale under New York law so there's no legal impediment to the plea. Now you've been promised that on the day of sentencing you will be sentenced to an indeterminate prison term of three years to six years. Has any other promise been made to you to get you to plead guilty that we are not aware of?

THE DEFENDANT: Yes.

THE COURT: Yes? What other promise has been made to you?

THE DEFENDANT: No. No other promise but your honors why can't I get a drug program?

THE COURT: The reason you can't get a drug program is that you're a predicate felon.

THE DEFENDANT: I'm not! What does that mean?

THE COURT: It means that you have been convicted of a prior felony within the past ten years.

THE DEFENDANT: It's been eleven years!

THE COURT: Any time you've spent in jail the past eleven years doesn't count towards the ten.

THE DEFENDANT: Oh yeah, right. He did say that.

THE COURT: As a predicate you are subject to a mandatory state prison sentence in this case.

THE DEFENDANT: But what about the D-Trap my attorney said I could get.

THE COURT: You're referring to the D.A.'s office's D.T.A.P. program. Counsel were any attempts made to get a D.T.A.P. disposition?

DEFENSE COUNSEL: Yes. He was evaluated and rejected.

THE COURT: There you have it Mr Hurd. You were considered for D.T.A.P., which would have allowed you to enter an inpatient drug treatment program and if you had successfully graduated from the program, your case would have been dismissed in the interests of justice, but you were rejected.

THE DEFENDANT: But why was I rejected?

THE COURT: People what was the reason for the rejection?

MR ZORN: No community ties Your Honor.

THE DEFENDANT: But I am tied up to the community your honors. They called my mother and she told them I was tied.

THE COURT: Apparently they weren't satisfied Mr Hurd and unfortunately for you it is solely within their discretion whether or not to admit you into the program. That said, do you still wish to plead guilty?

THE DEFENDANT: I am pleading guilty your honors but I'm doing it because I think it would be a waste of money to have a trial over five dollars worth of crack. What I really need is a drug program because I want to turn my life around and the only reason I was doing what I was doing on the street was to support my habit. The habit has to be fed your honors as you know and I believe in working for my money. I could be out there robbing people but I'm not and I've always worked even though I am disabled. And not always at this your honors, I used to be a mail carrier back in the day but then I started using drugs and that was all I wanted to do. So I'm taking this plea to save the city of New York and the taxpayers money because I can't believe that the D.A., who I can see is a very tall man, would take to trial a case involving five dollars worth of crack, especially knowing how much a trial of that nature would cost. But I still think that I should get a chance to do a drug program because I've never been given that chance in any of my cases and the money that will be spent keeping me in jail could be spent addressing my real problem which is that I like, no need, to smoke crack every day and every chance I get, and if I have to point people to somebody who's selling the stuff so I can get one dollar and eventually save up enough to buy a vial then smoke it immediately and start saving up for my next one then I'll gladly do that, and I'll do it even though I know it could land me in jail for years because the only thing that matters at that moment is getting my next vial and I am not a Homo-sapiens-sexual your honors but if I need money to buy crack I will suck . . . .

THE COURT: That's quite enough Mr Hurd. I am not without sympathy for you and your plight, and believe it or not I agree with a lot of what you've said here. In fact I recently wrote an article for the New York Law Journal in which I addressed many of the same issues you've raised. One of the things I argue in this article, which will be on the front page of Thursday's issue by the way, is that the Rockefeller drug laws, which in the early 70's drastically increased the penalties for the conduct you engaged in, have flooded our prisons to the extent that there are eight times as many people incarcerated today than there were in 1970. Moreover, I argue that these laws, and the War on Drugs in general, have eviscerated our inner cities which, because of congestion, poverty, and other factors, are ideally suited for the sort of low-level drug-dealing targeted. Consequently, by focusing on these cities this war has had a disproportionate impact on the indigent and the African-American community of which you are a member. I also argue that the overwhelming majority of people incarcerated from these poor neighborhoods are either addicts looking to support their habit or young minorities who are especially susceptible to the perceived attractions of the low-level drug trade and that those who truly profit from the sale of drugs exploit these individuals for their personal gain and yet are rarely held accountable. So yes I do personally feel that the money spent to incarcerate individuals such as yourself for several years would be better spent on treatment for individuals who are addicted to drugs. That said I am not empowered, in this case and under these circumstances, to make a unilateral decision to sentence you to mandatory drug treatment in lieu of a state prison sentence. As I've explained to you that decision rests solely with the District Attorney and they have not seen fit to consent to such a sentence. Consequently, your choice is between pleading guilty and receiving a sentence of three to six or proceeding to trial with all that entails. Knowing that, do you still wish to plead guilty?

THE DEFENDANT: Yes, but I still say that Mr Zorro should have given me a drug program your honors.

THE COURT: First of all, Mr Zorn is the assistant who is standing up on all the cases in this courtroom today. He is not the assistant assigned to your case and likely had nothing to do with the decision to reject you for D.T.A.P. Second, I think we've more than adequately explained the reasons why that's not going to happen and there's no need to get started along those lines again. The plea is satisfactory to the court. Is it satisfactory to the People?

MR ZORN: Yes.

THE COURT: Enter the plea.

THE CLERK: Mr Hurd, in the presence of your attorney do you now withdraw your previously entered plea of not guilty and enter a plea of guilty to Criminal Sale of a Controlled Substance in the Fourth Degree in satisfaction of the indictment. Is that your plea?

(The defendant conferred with his attorney)

THE DEFENDANT: Yes.

THE COURT: Four weeks for sentencing. How's the 23rd?

THE DEFENDANT: That's fine your honors.

THE COURT: I was actually speaking to your attorney Mr Hurd. Any date is presumptively good for you. The 23rd counsel?

DEFENSE COUNSEL: That's fine.

THE COURT: Defendant is remanded. The 23rd for sentencing.

THE CLERK: That being the final case of the morning session, Part 46 is adjourned until 2:15.

(Audible groan from the audience.)

*

"Fucking Casi," from Dane who shook his head no while smiling from his seat in the first row. "You've got to control these guys better. A simple allocution shouldn't take longer than it takes to read this rag (gesturing with dog-eared Daily News) from front to back then back to front again."

"Guy said maybe five words to me the last six months," I said. "Must be the impending state bid that's got him all talkative."

"Yeah, well, he should get an extra year for taking so much time that I have to come back here in the afternoon."

"Let the guy have his fun. He rarely gets such a captive audience."

"True enough," conceded Dane. "What would you say if you were about to get three to six?"

"Nobody move or I'll shoot."

"Good old Preskill had no objection, she got to plug her article like some guest on Leno."

"Made my guy's day."

"What did he say?"

"I think he had no idea what she was talking about except that it was in some vague sense supportive. He was heartened, let's put it that way. I think he expects a last-minute reprieve on the day of sentencing. You know a disgusted Judge Preskill sticks her neck out, lobbies the state legislature, coerces the D.A., whatever, but somehow gets the guy with three ears into a drug program. His appointed savior."

"Is that what that was? That fucking thing on his neck. A god-damned third ear?"

"What's the big deal? You never seen a third ear?"

"Does it?"

"No."

There followed a not-too-brief discussion during which it was established that we'd have lunch together. This was followed by exten-sive analysis of the relative merits of our options and all this took far too long considering we were outside and the cold wind made my face feel like it was about to spontaneously bleed until finally an ultimatum from me to decide led to a decision to attempt a reprise – to the extent that sort of thing is even possible – of our lunch from the Friday past and so off to Little Italy we went.

On our way there we saw a strange thing.

"What in the holy hell?" said Dane.

What it was was one of those blue plywood walls construction sites are always putting up in the interests of gawker-prevention. Only this one was blood red with a small black-velvet curtain in the vertical and horizontal center. The curtain covered a port/peephole and above it in gold letters:

UNDER NO CIRCUMSTANCES SHOULD YOU LOOK INSIDE
TO SEE MAN'S GREATEST INVENTION SINCE
THE WHEEL. AGAIN, WE URGE YOU
NOT TO LOOK INSIDE
FOR ANY
REASON
!!!!

As we walked by some guy stood directly in front of the curtain. He stared intently at the immense golden words. His head lolled slightly to one side then the next as he read. Then he paused, threw the curtain over his head and looked in the hole.

We kept walking.

"Let's sit here again Casi."

"Fine."

"So what do the Preskills of the world want?"

"Huh?"

"Judge Preskill, she agrees with your client in many respects she says. What does she propose as an answer? Legalization?"

"I don't know. I guess you'll have to read her upcoming article, only promise not to fill me in."

"Given the source, I assume the article will be dim. But I've been ruminating on what she said and it's not incomprehensibly stupid."

"High praise indeed."

"Let's think about this for a moment, because I find that in our jobs it's important to constantly think things through and analyze them; instead of just getting by with the bare minimum required of each day, without scrutinizing the landscape we're operating in."

"Thanks for the tip."

"I'm going to show you something, really just as an intellectual exercise. Let's take it from the top and feel free to chime in if you disagree at any point."

"If you must."

"Preskill identified two things she disagreed with and which she presumably feels create injustice. Let's put aside any Socratic concerns over what it means for something to be unjust et cetera."

"Yeah definitely let's."

"The two things were the sentences given on drug cases and more generally the whole War on Drugs bullshit. Right? Right?"

"I'll chime in if I disagree remember?"

"Good. So regarding these matters where are people and how did they get to this point? I'll take these questions in inverse order."

"My favorite kind."

"This is how I bet they got in their present situation. At some point someone told a politician that it would be to his advantage to make drug policy one of his core issues. What this always means of course is a get-tough policy since *tough* is the only thing to get if you want to have a job. The idea caught on with those of his ilk and soon everyone had to have their own get-tough policy. These things always rocket to the top because anyone who opposes is accused of being a drug-lover or something similar, highly intelligent things like that. In this case the ascension of these harsh, anti-drug policies was abetted by the fact that most feel drugs really are a legitimate problem that leads to all sorts of social ills, so on the surface the steps seem necessary." He stared and I facially reminded him of the thing whereby I would only interject in the event of disagreement.

"At any rate," he continued. "War was declared on drugs, soldiers were drafted, money spent, and new laws passed. Sentences for drug-related offenses were increased and more resources were devoted to enforcing the existing illegality of drug use and sales. So what resulted? Let's only discuss and analyze that which we know intimately so as to avoid being the typical underinformed idiot. That means I'm going to limit myself to what this drug policy means and creates in New York of which I have first-hand knowledge. Note, however, that this doesn't decrease the legitimacy of my observations vis-à-vis the greater population. The reason for this is simple. You know how some motions must be decided while viewing the evidence in the light most favorable to the defendant?"

"Yes?"

"Well, as I'm sure you're aware, New York is widely considered one of the best places to be arrested in this country. This state's appellate courts, for example, often provide greater protection to defendants than is required by the federal constitution right? Therefore by looking at the situation as it exists at one of the polar extremes we can draw far more legitimate conclusions than if we looked at a random locale not easily susceptible to extrapolation. This is true, by the way, of all aspects of the criminal justice system not just drug cases; we can safely assume that any injustices suffered by our clients here in New York City would only be exceeded elsewhere and, at least with respect to the other places I've practiced, I have found this to be invariably true. So I think it a valid proposition, agreed?"

"You're really determined to flout your own procedure aren't you?"

"Very well. Here's what you've got. I handle only felony cases, and

I currently have about sixty or seventy of them in various stages. Of these cases, fifty to sixty percent are drug-related. Now when I say drug-related I'm not referring to criminal acts that arise out of drug addiction, I mean cases where the top count is either the possession or sale of drugs. My understanding is that these numbers generally reflect what other similarly situated attorneys experience. If that's the case, then we can assume that about one out of every two people charged with a serious crime in this city is a prisoner of this War on Drugs. Of course one of the first things to note about this high volume of drug arrests is their ultimate impotence. I don't know of anyone claiming that the drug trade in this city has been curtailed in any meaningful way. There are hundreds of drug spots in the city each of them moving thousands of dollars worth of drugs a day. The aforementioned fifty percent seem to be highly fungible and all these four-to-eight sentences mean is that someone else steps in and starts preparing for their state bid."

"True."

"So who are these people the police round up when they go on rooftops with binoculars, or pose as strung-out addicts to buy five-dollar vials, or beg some poor sap to sell them their extra bottle of methadone? Well one thing we know about them is they don't have any money. We know this first of all because we're their attorneys. It's hard to imagine any group of people being held in less esteem than we are by our clients. The overwhelming majority of them feel that we are either bumbling incompetents – after all if we're otherwise why aren't we in private practice making real money? – or, even worse, actively conspiring with the D.A. against them as evidenced by the fact that we know and appear to act friendly towards a lot of these people who are prosecuting them. Throw in that we are employed, at least in their eyes, by the same government. We also know that people tend to greatly overestimate the efficacy of private attorneys. Now despite these time-honored perceptions, I find that

I have no shortage of drug clients and that other attorneys, who I'm sure inspire far less confidence than I do, also have an abundance of drug cases. What this means is that these people, who were arrested for participating in the drug trade and who presumably profit from what is unquestionably a highly lucrative industry, are unable to scrounge up enough money to hire an attorney in a city that has more attorneys than mosquitoes, and this is the case even though they firmly believe their failure to do so will result in them going to prison for long stretches. Throw in the added fact that a substantial majority of this same population is being held in jail on bail the equivalent of which I spend in assorted bars in a typical week. Really though I only say all this in the interests of being thorough since we don't really need this recitation of facts to tell us that the majority of these defendants are indigent right? Seeing is believing and we can see that these people are primarily toothless drug addicts or twerpy teens who think they're being hard and ultimately these are the people that are getting sent upstate and who the police are cracking down on. So what do you say about this situation Casi? Someone like your thrice-eared friend peripherally participates in a drug sale in exchange for the grand sum of one dollar and now he's doing three to six."

"I think a D.A. might say *don't sell drugs that way you don't have to worry about being treated fairly by our judicial system since you won't be arrested* I think that's what they might say."

"And that kind of statement is always fairly persuasive I must admit."

"And it has the added benefit of making the speaker sound cynical and tough thus shielding him from accusations of naïveté, which is like the worst quality you can have, and all the while the speaker still feels morally superior because he doesn't sell drugs so chalk that up as another reason why he's a good person."

"Of course the problem, and I use the term loosely because I don't give the slightest what happens to these people, is this Casi. We've

214

already said that a lot of these people out there selling drugs, and seemingly a higher percentage of those arrested, are themselves addicted to drugs. And naturally the two things, the fact that the person is addicted to drugs and the fact that they have been arrested for participating in a drug sale or the possession of drugs, do not exist independent of each other but instead the person is possessing or selling drugs *because* they are addicted to them. Given that fact, how much free will, of the kind people like your speaker love to take shelter in, is actually involved here? We know, for example that a mother will leave her newborn alone in her apartment for days to go buy and smoke crack. Addicts will go days without eating to save their money for crack."

"I had a guy who had had a pacemaker installed on Saturday and came through on a 220.03 the following Wednesday. He showed me the freshly bandaged incision lest I disbelieve."

"I had a woman who traded her artificial leg for crack."

"The addict's options are limitless."

"Sell your mom's stereo."

"Pimp your thirteen-year-old daughter."

"Before he was interrupted your guy was going to say, after taking pains to assure everyone he was heterosexual, that he performs oral sex on men in order to finance his drug-taking activities."

"Thanks for reminding me."

"Now haven't you ever wondered what smoking crack feels like? Ever reasoned that it must be one of the greatest feelings in the world to cause such extreme behavior in the name of its pursuit?"

"I guess, have you?"

"I don't have to wonder, I've smoked crack."

"*What?* Now you've got my attention, tell me about that."

"Later. The relevant question for now is whether non-violent behavior such as directing willing buyers to willing sellers in order to feed what appears to be an extreme compulsion should give rise to these sentences and the collateral effects these sentences have on the affected communities."

"*Don't use drugs, just say no to them,* that same D.A. might say, *that way you avoid becoming addicted and all the other horrors you've described that end with you going to state prison.* As for the teen twerp, he'd tell him to go to school, get ahead et cetera and he won't feel compelled to get involved in a dirty business that can destroy his life. Those seem to be the kind of things these pointless fucks say."

"Now that one's laughable. Again I don't actually care about the so-called human toll but it does pain me to see the rules of logic violated. I assume your speaker is referring to not using drugs initially since we've already discussed how apparently difficult it is to stop using a drug like crack cocaine once you've started – a feat the likes of which is almost invariably beyond the willpower capabilities of the speaker of such a statement by the way and which they would readily admit if they were being honest with themselves. One advantage the speaker will have, however, is that he will most likely never have used, unlike me, a drug like crack. So what that person will essentially be saying is don't do something I've never done and have no interest in doing and which abstinence therefore, to me, seems easy. Of course, that apparent ease is built on a fallacy and one that is created by money and this takes me to my proposed solution." He checked his watch to make sure he had time to deliver his full proposal and I saw that what he was checking was an undeniable Rolex.

"You see, what the overwhelming majority of these people can't say is that they don't use drugs or that they've never used drugs. So I say the answer, certainly the most entertaining one at any rate, isn't legalization but rather criminalization. I'll show you what I mean. First, let's outlaw all drugs and see what happens, what do you say? Of course, the first thing we'll have to do is define what we mean by the term *drug* in this context. How's this? For the purposes of our new law, an illegal drug will be any substance ingested by a person that has the effect of, and which is taken for the purpose of, altering that person's physiology in a manner that person deems beneficial and which is taken in the absence of physical pain or malfunction. There you have it. Unless you had a legitimate medical purpose, and I'm talking exclusively about maintaining your corporeal health since all sorts of non-nutritive, highly altering substances are susceptible to justification in the name of that ever-elusive mental health, you would not be allowed to use any of the substances you've grown to first know, soon love, and finally worship. Now I would happily wager that, operating under this new definition, every adult you know is on drugs so what would happen in the days following the implementation of this new law? How about utter chaos?"

"But—"

"That's right, try utter chaos! I believe we'd see open revolt in the streets. You might as well outlaw eating. The only thing that would compare would be if you took Television and computers away from them. Think of the substances people would have to give up. Talk about kicking the crutches out from under a nation of invalids. Take your average dipshit to see what I'm talking about. The rooster crows and now this clown has some rising and shining to do, must report to his cubicle to ride that carpal tunnel. Only he was up the entire previous night worrying about how he's going to get that big promotion his wife wants so his energy level is currently nil. Well no matter really because he heads into his marbletop kitchen, the one with the center island, to brew your parental homeland's second most popular export—"

"How do you—"

"He guzzles his coffee and the caffeine kickstarts his limited brain so he's ready to face the day. This drug gives him energy that he wouldn't have otherwise. Let's examine this closely because I can tell from your look that although you know where I'm going with this, you're having trouble getting past the admittedly benign appearance of this situation. Remember he doesn't ingest this drug because he's sick and the drug serves a medicinal purpose. He's taking this drug because it will make him feel a certain way i.e. it will make him feel, at least in some sense, energetic as if he had gotten a good night's sleep the night before. Any run-of-the-mill coffee drinker will admit this. Put another way, this person's body has a highly normal reaction to its circumstances, only its owner doesn't like this reaction, is not willing to be discomfited in any way, so he takes a substance that allows him to avoid the unpleasantness for the moment. Of course, as is always the case, there's a cost and any hardcore caffeine user will tell you that if they discontinue use they are rewarded with consistent migraine-level headaches. So perhaps the apparent benignancy of the situation was misleading. After all what kind of substance, when spurned by a former lover, takes its revenge by attacking the spurner's head? Unconvinced?"

"Consummately so, move on counselor."

"Well you can see where this is going as our now-energetic protagonist is in his office waiting for the meeting that will decide his fate. Of course he's incredibly nervous, what with the wife and all, and his anxiety, abetted by his earlier drug use, is climbing steadily. Luckily he's the sort who's always prepared and he has just the thing for this situation. What he whips out are these little sticks. The sticks are specially formulated so that when sucked on in the manner of a nursing infant they deliver among other things the required drug which is nicotine. Now nicotine is just what the doctor ordered so to speak because although it is, like caffeine, a cerebral stimulant it has the useful property of being the only known drug that reduces anxiety without diminishing affect and this is good. Remember that with someone like dipshit, anxiety, whether justified or not, is a constant companion and as a result the sticks become a constant presence as well, creating both a physical and psychological need in the user that ensures their lofty status as beloved chemical appendage.

218

The drug works, not surprising given its popularity, that is to say the user's brain is altered in the way he wished, a way he finds pleasurable and a way that can eventually be summed up as going from needing nicotine to not needing it. This is critical. Ultimately, as is the case with all of the drugs I'll discuss, the physiological effects of the drug become unimportant and the only relevant physical and psychological states become need and the absence of need. Moreover, the latter state will ultimately only truly be achieved when the patient has just recently ingested the drug. Thus satiated, our friend can survive his meeting and any other obstacles that may come his way. Made of stern stuff this guy no? Of course the end of the meeting requires either celebration or consolation. In this city there are over ten thousand locations where you can buy, then imbibe, a liquid form of these nouns. Now when it comes to drugs favored by the multitudes, alcohol is the unquestioned leader with all other competitors rightly genuflecting before it. On T.V., white-skinned, yellow-haired females of dubious repute and their predatory admirers blissfully jump into skimpy swimwear in its presence as the stuff flows like a beechwood-aged, cold-filtered waterfall. For once Madison Avenue might not be exaggerating either because truth is they love the stuff. Here we don't have to speculate what would happen with criminalization because we saw what happened, as people decided *en masse* that this was one prohibition they could skip. So our friend goes to one of the countless places dedicated to providing this drug. I'm there almost every day. People sit around and pour the stuff down their gullets as quick as old Joe can keep it coming and if it would get their bloodstreams to kick the shit to their brains faster they'd pay extra. They'd pay extra because alcohol is a depressant and they need depressing. But more than that they need to disappear. They need to disrupt, if only for a limited time, their constant, tyrannical self-surveillance. The drunk person is not happy in the classic sense. Inebriation is instead prized for its liberating qualities. What they're

liberated from is insecurity and if you don't think that's psychologic-
ally addictive you're crazy. Is that what you're saying Casi?"

"I haven't said anything."

"The drunk don't have to weigh their words and calculate their
effect. The drug diminishes their ability to do so and reduces them to
an uncalculating will that externalizes, without censorship, its internal cravings. This freedom is the undervalued effect of intoxication
and it is this effect that proves so attractive. But that's neither here nor
there since the main point is that this drug is employed in overwhelming numbers and without the slightest sense of irony by those
who most recoil from our clients. And yet there's more. Because
when our drug-abusing friend gets home he's greeted apathetically by
his hypermedicated family. The crewcut boy's on Ritalin to combat
his quick-cut-advertising-induced-therefore-overdiagnosed hyperac-
tivity and his twelve-year-old, weight-conscious sister's on Prozac to
take the edge off her classmates and all this with the blessing of both
our drug addict and his anxious, Xanax-popping wife. And the whole
thing's just so depressing that thank God the highly recommended Dr
Upper-West-Side just prescribed him some Lithium to be taken with
his nightly Bordeaux so he can better deal with the whole thing. He
does this from the sofa. The aforementioned chemicals course
through his veins as he watches the news and complains bitterly
about the damn druggies he's supporting with his tax dollars and how
to his liking you can't throw the keys away fast enough. Right?"

"Therefore what?"

"Therefore I say blow this sloppy hypocrite out of the water.
Criminalize the chemical crutches he walks with and watch him
change his tune on the *chemically dependent*; see how quick addiction
becomes a disease when it's him who's been stripped clean. What
would disappear is the distinction these people hide behind, the
distinction that the substances they live by are legally permissible
making their abusers of higher moral worth. Note that every drug I

referred to is perfectly legal in the context described so I'm now really only speaking of the hypocrisy of people who limit their drug use to the non-criminal. I'm saying nothing for the moment about those who use illegal drugs but rationalize that the particular drug they use is harmless and really shouldn't be illegal so in the end it's O.K. because they're not *really* drug users. Or others who currently limit their use to the respectable drugs but secretly couldn't be prouder of their past *real* drug use, which they think makes them interesting, and which they will take any opportunity to divulge but only in hushed mock regretful tones. They're too obvious a target. Our law-abiding user is not so obvious, however, and he profits from this distinction while being a supreme weakling. Here's a person who can't get through a single day without chemical assistance. This despite the fact that his day consists of wearing an Italian suit and tapping keys from an ergonomically designed chair in an airtight, temperature-controlled office then after work stopping by Citarella to pick up some freshly baked peasant bread to complement his dinner overlooking the arboreal serenity visible from his apartment on Central Park West. That's the life he leads yet he can't abstain but he's perfectly willing to judge harshly people who share their beds with rats, use their ovens to heat their apartments, and so turn to admittedly stronger chemical distractions. What do you say about people like that? What do you say about a situation where the Citarella people control the fate of the oven-heated people and use that power to cage them for behavior they themselves engage in? What do you say about these drug addicts Casi?"

"Which ones?"

"The fiscally blessed ones who have pushers with waiting rooms and think of the P.D.R. as The Good Book. Do you think this is a good situation where they cast their votes to send the three-eared Hurds of the world off to rot for their shared crime? Is it *just*?"

"No."

"More than that right. Someone like you should think it's a fucking abomination."

"O.K."

"So what are you going to do?"

"What did you have in mind?"

"This isn't multiple choice. What response can you generate to this? Now that I've pointed this societal mutation out to you, at length and in mindnumbing, intentionally yawn-inducing detail meant to replicate the utter inanity of such societal questions, what do you think you're going to do?"

"I guess nothing more than what I'm already doing, although not for much longer since I'm already tiring of it."

"Is that enough? And do you do it for the right reasons?"

"You mean as opposed to the immense prestige and monetary compensation?"

"Fine, let me concede that you do what you can, do it well, and for the right reasons. You know, I trust, that in the vast ocean of Injustice there are certainly bigger fish to fry than Hurd. Accordingly, there's a philosophical argument that goes something like this. Imagine yourself gaily reposing in your lavishly landscaped backyard. Suddenly you're drawn, in reaction to some plaintive moaning, to look over the fence and into your neighbor's yard where you see a young girl with dirt-caked hair literally starving to death. Can you envision a scenario under which you would not immediately drop everything and come to her aid? My strong guess is you would do so regardless of any resulting personal detriment, economic or otherwise. Indulge me with patience Casi and allow me to once again tell you something you already know. At this very moment while you and I pick at this fried calamari, which incidentally has inexplicably not been properly breaded or fried and is therefore unforgivably rubbery, there exists just such a girl slowly starving to death but out of our sight, her belly bloated by empty want, her lips scarred with thirsty lesions. This girl

222

starves while people like us throw away turkey sandwiches because the sweaty guy behind the counter put mayo on it. Now the only difference between these two girls as they relate to you is proximity yet one spurs you to action and the other you callously disregard. You know, I again trust, that proximity is not a legitimate basis for favoring one over the other. So why don't you obey this moral imperative, drop everything, and devote yourself to rescuing this girl and the many others like her? Or perhaps you think these people should starve to death while you and I gorge on fatted calves by candlelight. I mean please. This philosopher, through me, has lifted your veil of ignorance and laid bare your inconsistent behavior and I can see from the vertical nodding of your head that you agree there is simply no justification for your inaction. Can you really just keep your head buried in the sand while only ineffectually addressing the unjustly caged? What say you to all this? Speaketh."

"Well as I tried to say earlier," I said now. "I'm getting tired of dealing with the caged but I think you might be on to something with this other dilemma."

"How so?"

"Because even though I am an exceedingly happy person, well, that may be pushing it. Even though I'm quite happy. Not really happy, I mean, content let's say. I'm not miserable that's for sure. Not *that* miserable. Let's say I wasn't a happy person even though I am. Let's say I was a fucked-up, confused person. Or sad, that's it, kind of weirdly sad. Just take this premise at face value. Imagine this persistent drizzle between my ears that maybe threatens to turn into a full-blown mental tempest. The real question would be why this is so and how to fix it. Well I'm aware, in the troublingly peripheral way I'm aware of so much suspect data and concepts, of the psych notion that says I'm better off viewing my difficulties as externally based and therefore transient and capable of being borne rather than as internally based, with its suggestion of intractability and concomitant depression. Of course even as I say that I'm also vaguely recalling the seemingly opposite notion that those who view the world as acting on them in a manner outside of their control are more fucked than those who view themselves as agents of their own destiny and maybe these kinds of epistemological vagaries are part of the problem. Not that I don't have things I could point to. Like say a pain in my ear where every sound received feels like a tiny dagger finding its mark and none of the daggers come from a gorgeous minuscule girl who used to yap but now only practices an inexplicable silence. And imagine she had an aunt who always brings up ancient incidents freighted with significance, with Beethoven and loss, or a weird kid who asks simple questions that go unanswered, questions about bumpy old men who approach you all shirtless in icy air and maybe try to hug you and imagine I looked for that nut this morning, the way you might look for a misplaced pair of gloves, outside on the street on my way to work, but didn't see him or an ambulance or anything. Where do these people go anyway? Where do they disappear to? The babies outside of pubby restaurants and the preternaturally old? Do they all fly hastily off of overpasses or step gingerly in front of trains? What about ten-year-olds with perfect uppercut swings and severely overweight bus drivers with big plans and their demented, agoraphobic Prometheus? Imagine I was the kind of person who thought about things like that all the time and imagine I had placed myself in an obscene amount of debt so that I could get yelled at by insane immoral people and deal with criminal defendants too and even when I sleep – sleep for Chrissakes! – a time when all should be placid and good, even then there are leeches in lab coats sawing my skull open and bleeding my brain to their desired effect. Imagine I was that fucked up is what I'm saying."

"Done."

"Even then I think I would feel that the sadness wasn't entirely a function of those things. Because what you've just said makes me

224

think that the genesis of the human problem, at least as instantiated in me, might just boil down to something akin to user error. Because I agree with you that I'm supposed to be a greater remedial source regarding such an extreme malfunction of justice. It's a strange kind of agreement though because it doesn't stem solely from reason. When I agree with a proposition after exercising my ability to reason I do something like accept a series of earlier related propositions as true. Then if these propositions tie together in such a way that they syllogistically lead to a conclusion, I accept that conclusion. Now there's some of that going on here with this philosophical argument but I think there's more to it as well. When you say I should help the starving girl who is thirty yards away I agree but I don't agree the way I would with the statements that one plus two equals three or that bachelors are unmarried. As with all questions of ethics it seems to ultimately come down to a visceral feeling, either obeyed or disobeyed, that impels me to certain conduct. It's not any amount of intellectual reasoning that tells me I shouldn't simply walk away from this girl, it's more like a feeling or emotion and it's one that for some reason I feel certain anyone else would experience under the same or similar circumstances. I simply can't imagine the opposite, can't imagine someone sane not feeling compelled to help and moreover not feeling they've done something wrong if they ignore that compulsion."

"Disagree."

"The question then becomes where this feeling comes from and why it's so universal? Some would say it's instilled in us through a combination of physiological and social conditioning designed to perpetuate the species while others would credit something like God and say He instills it in us. Whatever the source, what if this imperative represents a kind of blueprint for humans? Maybe by violating the blueprint we invite a host of problems."

"What?"

"Imagine you purchase a new major appliance. You bring the sucker home and immediately start using it, secure in the knowledge that you know everything you need to know about its successful operation. The thing hums along for years but there's a hitch because even at the outset you're aware that the device is somehow operating less than optimally. You ignore this failure because after all it essentially performs its function and repairs can be so expensive. As the years march on the thing deteriorates, to no-one's surprise but at a rate that exceeds the expected. Now imagine that one day you come across the appliance's long-ignored owner's manual and you sit down and read it for the first time. It yields its secrets to you and you realize you've been using the damn thing incorrectly. Armed with this knowledge you begin to use the thing the right way and you discover that it operates beautifully. The problem didn't lie in the device nor was it inherent in its operation, the problem arose because of a misconception by the owner regarding the item's proper operation, how it should be used and what its ultimate and proper purpose should be."

"Ha ha ha ha ha! Please! Stop!" Dane held one hand up while slapping the table with the other. "You surprise me Casi. I didn't take you for such a chump. The basic purpose of human beings is to help each other? And what? To the extent that owners of personhood ignore this mandate they invite misery? Are you kidding? Have you not been paying attention? To life as performed on this stone? This is a fucking competition where your misery constitutes my triumph. It is absolutely incorrect to say that you or I have a responsibility towards anyone else, Jesus! I misspoke actually. The only responsibility anybody has towards anyone else is to crush them like a bug should they get the chance. Have you not read your *Origin of Species*? What are you a goddamn creationist? Man is only being operated correctly when oriented exclusively toward his benefit and survival. Everything else is nonsense designed to create the very misery you're talking about. The misery doesn't come from a failure of benevolence, it stems from its very opposite. What eats at people is their impotence not their selfishness."

"Some people maybe."

"Everybody! You see your neighbor enjoy a success and a piece of you dies. *That* is the universal feeling you should be focusing on, the one that thanks God you're not that starving little girl, for that's the one that reveals your true nature."

"By that reasoning the materially successful should be a great deal happier than those who devote their lives to the service of others for example and yet—"

"Ah yes, wealth corrupts and all that nonsense. To find true happiness seek the ascetic and center on the truly important. This is even more wrong than what you've posited until now. Money and other similar numbers in human life are not a corruption of anything. They are immensely helpful tools that allow you to keep score and therefore partially satisfy this nature of yours I'm talking about. Darwin wasn't the only useful person in that family you know. His cousin Francis Galton may have been even greater. He essentially discovered the intelligence quotient or I.Q."

"You mean invented."

"Oh no, I mean discovered! What notion could be more possessed of verisimilitude or intractability than that of varying abilities among humans? Given that, assigning numbers to what had theretofore been the highly nebulous and abstract concept of intelligence was beautiful in its simplicity and inevitability. With this act the competition was joined. And what timing too. Just as technological development was greatly diminishing the importance of physical proficiency and putting the spotlight on human intelligence, Galton and his progeny started numerically branding and ranking cerebellums. This saved the day because nothing beats a ranking. I.Q. and related concepts tell those who are down to stay right where they are and make no sudden movements please. But don't misunderstand because I come to praise not to damn. I praise because I'm one of the uplifted and my aggrandized self-worth craves constant confirmation."

"A legacy."

"Yes. And as for money it's only mankind's most important invention. With respect to money I think everyone has received fair warning. Money is the reason you have no responsibility to that starving girl. It is simply the single most important entity in the world today. Any discussion of justice, morality, and the like betrays a naïve ignorance of this fact. If you have money none of these ephemera matter. The only people crying for justice and fair play are the poor and therefore weak. Take your guy Hurd for example. Do you have any doubt that if he had an excess of bills his problems would evaporate? Imagine the difference, what was his bail?"

"Five over five."

"Five thousand pathetic dollars, so if he has money he's out instead of in jail. With money he gets his drugs prescribed to him and doesn't have to go out into the treacherous streets. And if he somehow found himself with a little crack difficulty and a criminal case to boot, which is unfathomable since the only reason somebody like Hurd sells is to get the money for his next dose, he wouldn't have to beg some twentysomething D.A. for a drug program because he would get himself into one. And then when he had to come to court somebody from that program, somebody whose salary he would be helping to pay, would come to court to say how well he's doing or at least how willing they remain to work with this guy who is, after all, still committed to treatment for what is, after all, an illness and so not his fault. And with all that going for him you can rest assured that Mr Hurd would *not* be about to embark on a three to six sentence."

"Probably not."

"As for your little girl, I have a solution to her starvation problem. She should get on a phone and make a reservation at *Le Cirque 2000*.

You ever been there? The pastry chef is Jacques Torres and he's a fucking genius. Overall the food is excellent although the portions are a little weak. Once she has her reservation she can sit down to a nice, dimly lit meal that will solve her woes. What's that you say? She doesn't have any money and they won't serve her if she doesn't give them some? And who is this surprising? This is why you needn't have any sympathy for the Hurds of the world. What's his defense? That he didn't know the importance of money? Let's say Life is just one long tedious movie. Do the Hurds of the world think that in that movie money is like a supporting actor just happy to be getting some work? Please! That kind of stupidity *should* be punished. Money is the fucking star of this show we're in. It gets the biggest trailer and its name is at the top of the marquee in largest neon. Hurd and the little girl knew the importance of this eight-hundred-pound gorilla that sits wherever it pleases yet they failed to acquire it. They failed to acquire it even though they knew it would insulate them from all sorts of pains. From *all* pain, in fact, if sufficiently acquired. You tell me that nobody should die from a lack of money? I tell you it happens all the time, that this fact shows that money is a matter of life and death, and that it is therefore all the more inexcusable when someone chooses to ignore this fact and fails to get his hands on some. You're aware of the legal concept that a law to be constitutional must be so written as to give potential offenders clear notice of what conduct is proscribed? Otherwise it's void for vagueness right? Well money has been giving warnings regarding its importance for millennia and those who fail to heed those warnings do so at their own peril and garner no sympathy from me."

"Nice."

"Here's a little story to help illustrate. This is me sharing by the way. A few years back I had a girlfriend. She had the prettiest ears you ever saw. So pretty in fact that you could almost say they bordered on the sexually attractive although I must say that the ear is probably the only part of the female anatomy I've never thought of in a sexual manner. It wasn't so much the lobe that was pretty either."

"What about her?"

"She was from Africa. Well she was born here but she still had a lot of relatives over there including her grandmother. Now it comes to pass that the grandmother takes ill. As is always the case with these things it starts out innocently enough with some nausea and stomach upset. First you have to understand the role of this woman in that family. The fact that she has a messed up belly that keeps getting worse sends every relative living here into borderline mourning. The news only gets worse and I have a front row seat to the grim details. Now the grandmother is vomiting continuously and not really eating much at all. On the bright side her stomach is inexplicably swelling rapidly. All this is reported through hurried overseas calls with the overarching question of what could be responsible hanging in the air. Now the grandmother is receiving the best medical care the village she lives in has to offer. The problem is that in that village the best medical care consists of a guy with a bone through his nose waving a palm tree branch on your belly while trying to chant the evil spirits out of you. I'm no idiot, I can see the writing on the wall so I'm telling my girlfriend to get on the next steel bird over there, drop your grandma in it and bring her back here to the land of the indoor plumbing where she can be seen by a doctor who prescribes some-thing other than prayer and positive thinking. I'm offering to pay for all of this. I don't even care, anything is better than the looks on their faces when the topic would come up and believe me it was the only topic. And the stories too. How the grandmother would do anything for the kids and nothing for herself. How she begged them to come to this country and how it broke the remainder of her heart when they did. And my girlfriend was no slouch in the stories department either having spent every summer between the ages of six and twelve with the grandmother in Africa and now everything reminds her of something special related to those special times spent with this special person. To shorten a long story, the grandmother's stomach continues to swell, the witch doctor keeps chanting, and back here the family is fretting the lack of health insurance, pondering the legal obligations of U.S. hospitals and gathering money for a plane ticket. You heard right, gathering money for a plane ticket! It's like, have you ever heard of fucking credit cards? Anyway while they're busying themselves with that and I'm still offering to pay for every last damn thing, this thing on the African grandmother's stomach keeps swelling, think John Hurt in *Alien*, until one day it bursts and she dies from an infection."

"Fuck, what was it?"

"Diverticulitis. The kind of thing a doctor in this country laughs at. Life and death decided by dollar signs, the way it should be. Remember that. Survival of the fattest . . . wallet. And the fattest aren't complaining because our inherent nature is not to help others but to hinder them and ultimately to win. Hurd's employer doesn't seem torn up by Hurd's three to six does he? Here's a guy who will not only aid and abet Hurd in his chemical destruction but will also exploit him for his benefit. Hurd is on the street taking all the risk with minimal reward while his boss counts his money out of sight of the cops. At least there the exploitation is out in the open unlike other more respectable industries. Anyway my girlfriend broke up with me shortly thereafter. I'm sure she couldn't stand to see my face anymore with its reminder of their unforced inaction. This abominable yet oddly touching song by I believe Spandau Ballet was playing while she told me and the hardest part was pretending I was crushed, which I felt I owed her. A shame. I spent a fortune on earrings let me tell you."

"When I was an intern in Brooklyn I second sat a case where our client was a last-minute lookout for an impromptu robbery committed by two other girls. She was a toothless prostitute with tracks on

231

her arms, a predicate for a Hurd-type sale, and the nicest damaged person you could ever meet. The two codefendants pled and the case against our girl was weak. She was out after a 30.30 release and she would come to court in skirts that looked like belts. At trial, they had shit too until in saunters one of the fucking codefendants to testify and blow our girl out of the fucking water. Bear in mind that this witness was the reason our client was on trial in the first place. The robbery had been completely instigated by this woman and she was the one who threatened the complainants with a razor. Of course she wasn't a predicate and thanks to her cooperation she ultimately got something like a flat year. At sentencing, our client, who during the robbery had essentially stood around looking up and down the street and imploring her friends to hurry up, got the minimum which was goddamn eight. When the verdict came in her husband was in the audience. What hurt most was that as the court officers were putting her in for what would be, at best, eight years her husband was up at the rail trying to get some last words in. I don't know why and I'll never forget this but all he kept asking her was whether she wanted the newspaper he was carrying. Like all insistent too. And I'm looking at this guy, with his Coke-bottle glasses held together by a Band-Aid, and I'm thinking, what could she possibly want with a newspaper where she's going? And I wanted to grab the paper out of his hand to like shut him up except I noticed his eyeballs were floating in tears, bobbing up and down, and the way he was squeezing it. The worst was the meekness of it. He looked as scared as he was sad and all this happened in an empty courtroom at like ten at night."

"You see? And if today that witness robber were told she could get out three days earlier if your client did another two years, your client would do ten. Bet on it."

"Well the singer's out I'm sure."

"You get my point. We're in a kennel where every dog is cannibalistically craving canine sustenance and here you are talking about extending a helping paw. Every Thursday my girlfriend's family would gather to pray for the grandmother. Forget that. When I pray I pray to Mammon – the god of avarice. He would've saved that woman's life with laughable ease. His is true omnipotence while your god hears and ignores heartfelt pleas. The sooner you understand and accept that Casi, the better off you'll be. What are you trying to sell yourself? Are you going to buy into the useless fiction that you operate outside the realm of the marketplace because you're a public defender? What's next? You going to go out and buy the requisite brown corduroy sports coat? Grow a ponytail? Then you can stay here twenty years like those guys you see in A.P. parts waiting for their fucking case to be called. And you can spend those twenty years hoping against hope that none of your favorite people ever need your help. What about your mother? Do you know what she went through? Have you ever been around a pregnant woman? And then when you finally came out what did she do? I'll tell you what she did. She stuck her tit, an intimate part of her fucking body, into your expectant mouth so you could eat and not die. They turned their lives over to you those two people. You think they came here from Colombia to wash dishes and clean offices so you could—"

"How do you—"

"– take a vow of poverty? A person of your abilities? Who do you think you are? One of these trust-fund babies playing lawyer without a care in the world? The day will come when your mother and others will need you. She will need you to reciprocate for the years of sightless devotion. What she will need is for you to exercise power on her behalf; to ensure that no avoidably bad things happen to her. To do that you will need money and lots of it. You should thank me for helping you realize that."

"Against your self-interest no less since there's only so much money to go around."

"You going to finish that?"

"No, I lost my appetite."

"I'll take it."

"By my count, you said one thing that was interesting amidst that whole harangue."

"What's that?"

"Did you say you've smoked crack?"

"That's right."

"What the fuck were you doing smoking crack?"

"It's hard to explain but essentially what I was doing was seeking perfection."

"What does that mean?"

"It's a long story."

"One I want to hear."

"Sure?"

"Yeah."

"Well my entire life I've been enthralled with the concept of perfection. Contrary to common perception, as almost everything that's true is, I believe that it is certainly possible to achieve perfection provided you properly limit the scope of your playing field."

"Uh-huh."

"Are you not attracted by the perfect?"

"The perfect what?"

"Perfection in any form. By way of example let's talk about mathematics. Do you know what a perfect number is?"

"Yes."

"I didn't think so. Well pay attention you might learn something. A perfect number is a number that is the sum of its multiplicative factors."

"I know."

"So for example six is a perfect number. It's perfect because the numbers that can divide six without remainder are three, two and one. These numbers are the multiplicative factors of the number six.

234

Note that if we add these three numbers, if we add three plus two plus one, we also get the number six. Similarly twenty-eight is a perfect number since its multiplicative factors, one, two, four, seven and fourteen also add up to twenty-eight. There you are. Now let's put aside for the moment my belief that although I have only ascertained about thirty-nine of these numbers there are in fact an infinite amount of them with infinity itself being a form of perfection."

"O.K.?"

"What's your reaction when I tell you about these numbers?"

"Um."

"Because my reaction when I heard about these numbers and really whenever I hear about anything that I equate with perfection is best described as something like adulatory love. With respect to perfect numbers, I'm not alone either. In ancient Italy there was a secret society founded by Pythagoras, yes he of the Pythagorean Theorem, devoted to the study of numbers. This Divine Brotherhood of Pythagoras, as they were called, essentially worshipped numbers in general and in particular ascribed mystical and magical qualities to perfect numbers. They felt what I know. Perfection rightfully inspires an awe that is religious in nature. Not coincidentally, there aren't many people left walking around praying to a god they do not think is perfect. Of course they make the stupid mistake of ascribing perfection to a separate entity when it is in fact Perfection itself, as its own entity, that they are worshiping."

"Hold it. Here's the problem, you need to properly define the term *perfection*. The numbers you're talking about aren't perfect any more than a particular Rembrandt is perfect. The word perfect is being used in both instances subjectively. The numbers have a particular quality, arguably an attractive one, and on the basis of that quality some human beings over time came to refer to the numbers as perfect. In reality they're no more perfect than say Fibonacci numbers or prime numbers."

"Incorrect. The numbers aren't being called perfect merely because they have an attractive quality. The numbers have a quality that's attractive, true. But we come across other attractive qualities that don't inspire us to utter the word *perfect*. The whole number 10 for example can be thought of as more attractive than 13.29 because of its roundness. The difference is that the quality perfect numbers have is an approximation, maybe even an example, of Perfection. The quality possesses the symmetry and flawlessness of the perfect, of the concept or entity we refer to when we use the word *perfect*. When we study the number six in light of its multiplicative factors et cetera we see that it really is more perfect than seven. It's not a mere subjective judgment, it's immutably true."

"Maybe, but right now I'm more interested in your crack habit."

"Very well then, my love of the perfect not surprisingly led me to attempt to achieve perfection. Before I came up here from Florida, I routinely represented about a hundred or so clients at any given time. Having grown accustomed to that, when I first got here, before I had a chance to build up a caseload, I found myself with very few cases and a lot of free time on my hands. The amount of time I could devote to each client had grown tremendously. Consequently, the quality of representation I could give my clients also increased greatly and that convinced me to revisit an idea I'd been toying with for years. The idea was I would pick a client at random and proceed to give that person *perfect* legal representation. I would represent him in a manner that was not only flawless and resulted in the best possible result but my representation would also have the beautiful symmetrical quality found in all objects we deem perfect. In the end I'd be Time's first human author of perfection."

"How could you be sure of *that*?"

"I couldn't. This famously not being a perfect world and all that, but I could be highly confident. Anyway I did it."

"You gave a client perfect representation?"

"Patience. The next time I was in arraignments I resolved that the sixth client I picked up would be the beneficiary of my perfection; I couldn't be sure I would do twenty-eight cases so the choice was obvious. Barnes was his name, a big mean-looking guy who was the nicest guy in the world with a voice like the women who spray cologne at you in department stores. Let me tell you something, I was as nervous as some twerpy newbie trying his first case when I went in to interview this guy. Remember we're talking about perfection here. Any slip-up no matter how minor would end my quest. If I tripped as I entered the booth or mispronounced his name that would decrease his confidence in me and be the end of it. My nerves were compounded by two decisions I had made. First, I'd decided this would be my only attempt. If I failed to achieve perfection, no matter how early in the process, I would not try again with a different client. The reason for that was twofold. For one thing, I doubted I would ever be able to achieve perfection if I wasn't motivated by the lack of a safety net. This could lead to countless attempts of varying success each undercut by the knowledge that I could always jump ship and start all over. Also it seemed to me that true perfection involved success on the first attempt and not a gradual building up to it. If I were able to achieve success on my first try that would clearly be more perfect than if it took five tries. Agreed?"

"I guess."

"Good, the other decision I made was that I would not engage in any rationalizations designed to fool myself into the illusion of perfection. If I failed, no matter how minor the failure, I would accept it and not lie to myself like everyone else does. If it turned out I was no better than the average chump, if I was unable to achieve perfection even when every fiber of my being was pointed towards this simple goal, then I would accept it, this soul-robbing mediocrity, like a man. Of course, I fully expected to succeed. As I said earlier, it is absolutely true that perfection *can* be achieved."

237

"Did you achieve it? What happened?"

"Basically it was a burglary case. Dead as they come too. My guy gets caught inside someone's apartment. The tenant screams for her husband while the guy makes a hasty exit. Cops nab him a block away. He's got a screwdriver, an inculpatory ashtray, and makes a statement putting himself in the apartment. He's also a violent predicate. Anyway I do a perfect interview and get him out."

"How do you get him out?"

"I make a perfect bail application as I was required to do."

"What does that entail?"

"Well after interviewing him for about an hour and a half, I didn't put the case up for another four hours."

"What?"

"Now you're starting to get an idea of what I mean by perfect representation. During the dinner break I was able to go to the scene and interview some neighbors of the complainants. I gathered more information in those hours, favorable to my client and unfavorable to the complainants, than I normally would during the entire life of a case. By the end of my application, the judge, who was by no means a softie, had no choice but to say R.O.R. It was beautiful, as if he were acceding to a determination made by a higher power. In short, my bail application was perfect. But I want you to realize the level of attention to detail that was present. It was not merely a question of effort. Blind effort without sufficient aforethought, regardless of how strenuous, is the near-antithesis of perfection. For example, before I even started to put together my bail application I had to internally debate what my goal should be. Instinctively, I obviously wanted to get him out of jail with all the benefits that derive from that in terms of trial preparation and the like, not to mention avoiding the injustice or imperfection of being incarcerated absent any legal determination of guilt. On the other hand getting him out raised the strong possibility that Barnes would not return to court thereby opening himself up to the further charge of bail jumping. There was also the potential issue of plea negotiations. Since he was a predicate, any plea, even a perfect plea, would likely involve jail time and it was less likely that he would accept such a plea, which could prove to be a disastrous mistake, if he was not in jail. So there was a strong argument that if I got Barnes out of jail it could ultimately prove detrimental to him and therefore deny me the perfection I sought. Ultimately I made the perfect decision, reasoning that subsequent perfect representation would overcome these potential difficulties, and strenuously sought and achieved his release. The point is you can imagine how often issues like that would arise. To get Barnes out of jail I had to place allegations on the record but every one I committed to tied me closer to a particular defense strategy at a time when I had heard precious little of the People's case. So fine lines were being straddled left and right but in every case it was done perfectly."

"What about your other cases? What did the other lawyers you were in arraignments with have to say when you took five hours to do one case?"

"I did nothing on my other cases. Well I did the absolute bare minimum I could do while still being considered their attorney. As far as I was concerned I represented one client. Barnes. Every and all day I worked on his case."

"It doesn't seem like there would be enough work on one case to occupy your every professional hour."

"Professional hour? Try every waking and I actually found myself wishing I had more of them. Remember, I had to divide my time between preparing for a possible trial, a trial that in order to be considered perfect would at the very least have to result in a complete acquittal, while simultaneously attempting to procure the best possible plea offer for my client; an equally valid yet completely different, at times even antagonistic, form of perfect representation. I had to involve other people in his defense such as investigators, interns, and

239

social workers yet at the same time I had to strive to do as much of his defense myself in order to be intricately aware of every aspect of his case. I had to win Barnes's trust and affection so he would go to trial if that was the course perfection dictated but perfection simultaneously demanded that I often inform him of objective distasteful truths that might cause him to dislike me. I also had to research every possible legal issue that might arise at trial so I read everything ever written on those areas of law and basically became the foremost, though unacknowledged, expert in them. So, you see, a lot of my time was spent doing the things we do on every case but of course doing them perfectly which takes a great deal more effort. But I also spent a lot of time doing things I'm sure nobody does on their cases or even thinks about doing, but which seemed to me necessary to a perfect defense."

"Such as."

"Well for one thing I was new to the New York system so I had to do research in order to gain the extreme familiarity demanded by perfection. I researched the D.A. I posed as a journalist doing an article on how moral D.A.s are or something and as such I interviewed her colleagues both former and current."

"Are you kidding?"

"I ordered all the minutes of any trial or hearing she had ever done to pick up tendencies in her arguments et cetera. I had long telephone conversations with her which I later transcribed and had analyzed by a prominent psychiatrist whose work I then corrected. I had her handwriting analyzed by a complete clod who was simultaneously the foremost expert in the field. Despite all that, by the time the case went to trial I knew her intimately."

"You don't mean?"

"No, but we were friends and I had her convinced I hated my client, thought he had no chance to win, and would not be putting forth a great deal of effort during the trial. Since people inevitably perform to the level of their competition, and since what most motivates them is the fear of losing to someone they dislike, this tactic led to a predictably subpar performance from her and she was not without talent. I also researched the judge in essentially the same manner. Of course, while I knew the D.A. I was dealing with would be the one to ultimately try the case I couldn't be sure that the judge who was handling the case would eventually keep it when it came time to conduct the trial. As a result I had to research every possible judge the case could get sent to so I could know their relevant tendencies. Under various guises, I interviewed countless judges, attorneys, and all other forms of court personnel such as court reporters and court officers. I got a hold of all the statistics showing which parts were the most amenable to acquittals. I analyzed these statistics endlessly looking for statistically significant differences. I made up color-coded graphs based on respective probabilities."

"You putting me on?"

"During the course of this research, I determined that the judge currently handling the case would not be the best judge for me to try to get an acquittal in front of given my type of case. I analyzed the statistics and profiles and identified who the ideal judge to try the case would be. I then figured out what days one was most likely to get sent to that judge by an expediter. Then I manipulated the current judge into thinking she didn't want to try the case because I would be a pain in the ass. This was difficult to do while maintaining the D.A.'s illusion that I would be a pushover at trial but I did it and after some cajoling of the expediter I got sent to my first choice, Judge Teal.

"You get the idea as to the lengths I went, but let's get to your question regarding the crack. As you know, from a defense standpoint all cases basically fall into one of two categories, *I.D. cases* and *what-happened cases*. Conceivably this case could have been either but given Barnes's statement, the ashtray, which the D.A. and my own investigation led me to conclude would be identified as being from the apartment, and other factors, I decided it was a what-happened case and one where Barnes would have to testify. I had interviewed and taken extensive statements from every witness that would appear on behalf of the State. Yes, the cops talked to me. I had written out, in mind-numbing detail, every possible course the People's evidence could take along with the consequent directions my case would take. However, in a case where the defendant testifies his testimony obviously becomes the single most crucial factor in the trial. I had to prepare Barnes to testify better than any defendant had ever been prepped. I had to prep him perfectly.

"This was probably the most difficult thing I had to do. I wasn't content to surrender to the inherent vagaries of my client's performance. Here was an individual who had never gone to trial, who was facing double digit years in jail, and who was aware that his performance on the witness stand would to a large extent determine his fate. Under this pressure, this unintelligent, uneducated individual would have to testify skillfully. Throw in the overwhelming probability that he would not be telling the truth a substantial portion of the time.

"To prep him I had to know him. I had to know what his life was like, had to know what it was like to go through the world as Barnes. When we prepare somebody to testify we try to eliminate the unknown for them right? We ask a colleague to listen to the client's expected direct then mock cross-examine them. Then we gauge the client's response to this fake cross on the theory that we can thereby predict how they will perform on the stand. Well that's fine for your average case but the limitations of that practice are unacceptable within the context of perfect representation. To be perfect I needed to do more. What this method of preparation can't fully predict is how the individual will respond to the pressures of the real thing. This was the great unknown hanging over the case and threatening to fuck with my perfection. Of course trying to predict how a human will react to a novel situation is always a tricky thing. But in thinking about this problem, which I did constantly, the thought occurred to me that if I had to pick someone and try to predict their future behavior I would pick myself. After all I know myself best. Failing that option I would pick some other person whose conduct, attitudes, and other variables I was very familiar with. I thus set out to know Barnes as well as I could in order to gain insight into what his testimonial performance was likely to be.

"I spent an unhealthy amount of time with Barnes. He was in my office every other day at first. We would talk for hours on the pretext of preparing for the case but in fact I was studying him. I didn't kid myself though. I knew I wasn't interacting with Barnes. I was interacting with the person Barnes creates when he's at his lawyer's office talking about his pending criminal case. This was useful to be sure but to know Barnes the way I wanted to know him I had to be exposed to the Barnes that existed at other times. I went to his home and visited with him there. I surreptitiously followed him around and observed him in other settings interacting with other people.

"I then took it even further. I knew all the objective facts about his life from our extensive conversations. I started keeping a diary from Barnes's point of view like actors sometimes do. I got an apartment in his neighborhood and lived there for a couple of weeks without going to work. To simulate Barnes's existence, I gave myself a meager allowance for those weeks. I would wake up each day in this putrid apartment with like twelve bucks in my pocket. Then I would just drink all day and like hang out. But I knew I had to do more. Barnes smoked crack. He was high on crack the day he went into that apartment. I started smoking crack."

"What do you mean you started smoking crack?"

"What's vague about that?"

"There's nothing vague about it, it's just incredibly bizarre don't you think?"

"No."

"Well where'd you get the crack from?"

"I bought it, on the street. Where I was living there was no short-age of places."

"You could've been arrested! Your career would have been over. Not to mention the embarrassment. Everyone would've thought you were a crackhead."

"As far as my career goes I can scarcely think of anything I attach less importance to, with the possible exception of my concern for how others view me. The very reason I was buying and smoking crack was to prove these same people wrong. They say perfection in human endeavors is impossible. I say they're partly right. It *is* impossible, for them, but not for me or a select few others. Besides the risk is minimal if you take precautions."

"So what happened?"

"I put it in my pipe and smoked it."

"How many times?"

"Several."

"And?"

"And what?"

"What did it feel like?"

"Pleasure. Extreme pleasure in a way that makes everything else irrelevant. At first, it seemed like all other pleasures like sex and good food were merely facets of this larger pleasure."

"Have you smoked any since?"

"No."

"Weren't you worried you might become addicted? Did you at any point feel it becoming addictive, feel it becoming a need?"

"It was more like an objective realization that if I had nothing else going on, if I didn't have sufficient access to other pleasures, I could see myself wanting to do nothing else. It was another challenge because there's a weakness involved with addiction. But please kids, don't try it at home. Anyway, the crack wasn't the point. Perfection

244

was and the drug use was done solely in service of that goal. The end result was that those weeks allowed me to prep Barnes perfectly to testify because I had a special insight into what form this individual's testimony would take."

"So it went to trial?"

"It did, which introduced the most important party to any trial, the jury. I thought a lot about jurors and the expectations and biases they bring to the process. I feel that defense attorneys ignore the role of mass media in shaping juror attitudes to their extreme detriment. As research, I read or watched every single popular depiction of our criminal justice system. This included reading fictional legal thrillers for example. This was no small sacrifice as these books are uniformly and horribly bad. They all have these galactically idiotic names like *Proof of Service* or *Notice of Appeal* too. Nonetheless, they *are* extremely popular so I read them and in the process gained insight into the layman's hack-warped view.

"Knowledge of what jurors bring with them and what they expect when they come into a courtroom to sit on a case is the single most important area of knowledge to have if you're trying to get an acquittal. Jurors are conditioned to expect and want dramatic performances but at the same time, for a particular kind of juror that we encounter often in Manhattan, their ego can't help but be implicated. As a result, although it is probably true that the more smooth and polished you are the more persuasive you'll be, I believe this is only true to a point. If you cross that point you now implicate the juror's ego and he becomes cognizant of not wanting to feel he's been hoodwinked by a silver-tongued salesman. If you think I'm wrong ask yourself this. How many times following an acquittal have you spoken to the jurors? What you find invariably is that a substantial portion of them will be falling all over themselves in their rush to tell you what you did wrong and how it wasn't really your arguments that led them to vote not guilty but rather something that they thought of on their own once they started deliberating. This is a juror who most likely went against every preconception she had when she entered the courtroom and voted to acquit but before she goes home she wants to convince herself that she did so based on objective facts and not your performance. Seems to me it stands to reason that this popular emotion can often be an impediment to acquittals.

"Because of this, a bit of intentional fumbling or display of nerves can be useful in creating the perception in these jurors that to the extent they find an attorney's argument compelling they do so not as a result of any skillful, read deceptive, oratory by that attorney, but rather due to the argument's logical appeal stemming from its relationship to the truth. With that in mind, during the trial I had to skillfully negotiate the line between a *perfect* performance, which one instinctively feels should be highly polished, and a *truly perfect* performance which includes some appearance of imperfection in order to create a more acquittal-friendly atmosphere.

"The trial lasted about a week. My performance was perfect. Perfect pretrial legal arguments and perfect voir dire rounds followed by perfect selections then a perfect opening. Of course those things were under a great deal of my control so I was never really concerned. The people's witnesses were a greater challenge since I was then being asked to achieve the perfect in conjunction with an openly antagonistic party. Well I did it. Perfect crosses of the kind usually reserved for the stupid movies.

"Then Barnes testified. I directed him perfectly and he held up beautifully under cross thanks to the perfect preparation. All that was left was for me to give a perfect summation and then get an acquittal of course. If I did that I would have achieved my goal; a goal I had worked tirelessly at for five months. I had overnight to work on the summation. I had written it months ago and it required little revision. I spent my time the night before reflecting. I had no doubts about the upcoming acquittal. The D.A. was a beaten shell who if given a vote probably would herself have cast it to acquit. The jurors had set aside their poker faces and seemed to be openly rooting for my success. They were in the presence of a progressing perfection and they seemed to recognize this. They seemed to understand that a meaningless criminal case paled in comparison to what was being achieved before their very disbelieving eyes and with their near-compulsory complicity.

"In the morning I would deliver this perfectly reasoned, perfectly argued, and perfectly rhetorically pitched speech. I would do so without notes, which wouldn't be necessary since by that point the summation was as much a part of me as my nose. I would deliver it with the perfect tone for the situation and then I would be done. Perfection would become a part of my being. For the rest of my life I would know what I had always suspected, that I was not bound by the limitations of the average person. I was better, and better in a way that couldn't be quantified. I would stand alone in my perfection. I would be greater than God. God is perfect merely by definition. And it is his tautological perfection, not his own will, that makes his every deed perfect. I on the other hand would have created perfection out of imperfection, an altogether greater achievement.

"The next morning I stood up prepared to take my rightfully lofty place in the universe of mortal achievement. The whole thing would take twenty-two minutes. Twenty-odd minutes and I would float out of that courtroom to compose my resignation and start looking for other fields to conquer. And so it went, with everything proceeding as planned until I neared a dramatic pause I had installed near the end. I'd decided that the pause would go on just a little too long to be comfortable in order to create some of the purposeful imperfection I spoke of earlier. The problem was that when it came time to come out of the pause I couldn't fucking remember what came next! I stood there looking at these fucking jurors knowing that every second that passed my dream – the word dream is woefully inadequate here, it was a fucking obsession, a life and death *need* – was slipping away. When too much time had passed for me to possibly reconcile I felt my actual heart being squeezed and lost my breath. Then I slammed my hand down on the podium screamed damnation and sat the hell down."

"Why? You could've just played it off. Easily too. Someone like you? Nobody would've known the difference."

"Too late, I knew. I knew I had failed. I had to abide by the conditions I'd imposed on myself. I had to be honest or else the whole thing would reduce to mere charade. I knew this particular imperfection hadn't been planned. It was a mistake. An error beyond my control. Imperfection at a time when my every action was geared toward the pursuit of perfection and what could be more demoralizing? I credit myself for not having immediately broken down into tears. I was furious. At myself. At life. At my lot to be no better than anyone else."

"What happened?"

"I just told you."

"I mean the verdict."

"They acquitted him in like nine minutes but who cared at that point? I bailed out of there in record time. The jurors wanted to talk to me, probably to ask what had gotten me so angry. I went into my office and barred the door. I had a dartboard in my office back then and I spent the rest of the afternoon trying to hit the bull's-eye with my eyes closed. When I finally did I went home and drank. A lot."

"Damn, you needed maybe some perspective. You tried a case probably better than anybody else ever has and as a result you got an almost instantaneous acquittal on a dead case."

"Listen don't get me wrong. I'm way over it now. But what happened in that courtroom that morning was nothing short of devastating. I had trouble coping. I looked for ways to atone. I thought about writing a perfect appeal. What I found in my preliminary investigation is that writing is an often unsatisfying process even more fraught with error."

"Fuck yeah."

"The rest of my practice had gone to shit too. My other clients barely knew my name and I somehow felt bad about this. Acting like such a responsible attorney on the Barnes case made me actually feel like the responsible attorney I was emulating. I wasn't able to separate the two. Seemed my actions determined my internal state more than the inverse and this new responsible internal state was devastated by the neglect I had visited on my other clients. I was lost. I hadn't expected to still be doing this job. I spoke to a friend of mine at the time about my predicament. I told her what had happened and why it had me in a tailspin. She was a generally useless person this friend but she said one thing that stuck in my head and which finally allowed me to move on, to set my sights elsewhere. She said I was absolved of all blame because my project stemmed from crime and was therefore doomed to imperfection. In other words, the natural or perfect order of things is law-abidingness and because criminality deviates from this it is inherently imperfect. This imperfection then necessarily taints any attempts at perfection such as mine that stem from crime. Now a greater crock of shit than this is hard to envision but it got me thinking about the nature of crime and for that I am grateful."

"Grateful why?"

"Let me put it this way. Have you ever imagined what your performance would be like if you were suddenly cast in a different role than defense attorney? I *have* lost cases, though thankfully not many. That said, I am certain that if I was a D.A., with the advantages attached to that position, the greatest being the ability to exercise a great deal of control over which cases go to trial, I would never lose a case."

"*Never* might be too strong a word but in general I agree."

"What this means is that being a prosecutor is an easier job when the job is defined as the successful acquisition of legal victories. So if you define perfection in one instance as never losing a trial, having a perfect trial record, the prosecution of criminal cases is more susceptible to perfection, whether attainable or not, than criminal defense. Now turn your attention to our clients whose job, so to speak, is to successfully commit crimes. Success obviously involves evading prosecution so in one sense all of our clients are already imperfect failures. Have you ever envisioned yourself, or a comparable other, seriously engaged in the practice of crime? How difficult is the criminal's job in relation to others in the criminal justice system? Well one thing that seems true about crime as a profession is that you far more often see the types of errors that boggle the mind in their stupidity. So you hear about the bank robber who writes the demanding note on his personal stationery. Or the defendant who wears the proceeds of his larcenous activity, unique lizard-skin boots, to the trial on those charges."

"Or the defendant representing himself who asks the complainant in an identification case whether or not she got a good look *at him!*"

"Or the robber who parks his getaway car in a tow-away zone with predictable results."

"Or the guy who stumbles onto a movie set and surrenders to actors portraying cops only to be held for later arrest by the real thing."

"You get the idea. Is there something about crime that makes not only perfection but simple competence such a challenge? I've done my research and it does appear that crime gives rise to a higher incidence of error than your average process. Nonetheless, I think that the commission of a perfect crime *is* possible and I view crime's imperfect nature as a challenge which can potentially create a higher order of perfection. More importantly, what ultimately proved therapeutic to me and what has taken me to the crossroads I'm at today is the notion that I can kill all of the birds currently fluttering about my head with one large beautiful stone. Incidentally, these birds also circle yours so you'd do well to listen attentively."

"What?"

"What?"

"What do you mean?"

"What?"

"What birds?"

"Oh, these birds. For one, although I'm by no means poor, I have nowhere near the amount of money I want or deserve. That's exacerbated by the fact that in my current condition I need to quit my job soon. Of course, for you matters are far more pressing."

"What do you know about it?"

"Second, there's the matter of my fascination with the Perfect and my consequent need to achieve perfection vis-à-vis becoming Godlike and so forth."

"A fascination I don't share."

"Nonsense. I seem to recall you saying that what makes a caper compelling is the idea that you can execute it without flaw. Sufficient planning and intelligence were I believe referred to."

"That's fantasy."

"How many trials you done?"

"I don't know."

"Come on, how many jury trials have you done alone or as lead attorney?"

"Twelve."

"And how many of those have you won again? How many resulted in acquittals?"

"All of them."

"A perfect record."

"Whenever I've tried a case I wanted desperately to win but—"

"More accurately, you were terrified of losing."

"Maybe. But in every case my effort was directed towards a particular result in that instance and for that individual, not in service of some higher pursuit of overall perfection."

"Lastly, there are my thoughts, which I have previously expressed to you, regarding a legacy and the fact that I simply cannot stand idly by watching all sorts of lesser talents build impressive legacies while I prepare to merely disappear without so much as a whimper."

"So what's your solution?"

"Imagine you and I committed the perfect crime, bearing in mind my definition of Perfect."

"What are you possibly talking about?"

"Hear me out. Imagine this crime involved an astronomical amount of money. Now imagine that aside from being committed perfectly, this crime was of such a compelling nature and committed in such a sensational way that it intrigued our information-saturated world with its perfection. With our pursuit of perfection and avarice satiated we could wait for some suitable time when we could not be prosecuted, for example on our deathbed or after the running of the statute of limitations, and we could confess in painstaking detail thereby ensuring our legacy as History's sole purveyors of perfected crime. What do you think?"

"You don't want to know. I've got to get the hell out of here too Dane. This is like the longest lunch ever and I have work to do."

"Go ahead I'll wait for the waiter, it could be hours."

"Here, this should cover it."

"What about tomorrow?"

"What about it?"

"Lunch."

"No. I've got 180.80s, I'll be swamped all day."

"After work then, drinks."

"Can't, I'm meeting some doctor."

"What's your ailment?"

"No it's like a date deal."

"That word still used?"

"Deal?"

"No, *date*."

"No. But speaking of ailments, what *is* your current condition?"

"What?"

"The one that necessitates you quitting soon?"

"Oh yeah. I'm dying."

"You're what-ing?"

"There's that bastard waiter, fucking guy should tip me. Let me snag him else I stay here all day, later."

"Yeah."

I walked into Conley's office with a rare legitimate purpose that I immediately forgot when beset by its panasonic air. Inside was the usual trio of Conley, Liszt, and Debi. But also there was Julia dangling a shiny pump off her stockinged foot, Toomberg with a frayed Penal Law in his mitts, and Cleary with his white collar. Cleary got to wear the cool collar because in addition to being a barely competent attorney he was also, I fuck with you not, a Catholic priest. Unfortunately for Father Cleary his true favorite spirits assumed liquid form and underneath his shellacked yellow lid of hair, which seemed to hover in suspension above his perfectly circular melon, his face wore burst blood vessels in the shape of spider webs as evidence.

The clamor was due to Debi and Conley being mid-debate. Should the odds change continually to reflect incoming Tula news, with people allowed to wager at any point up and until a definitive settlement of the issue? Or should a deadline be set at which point no further action would be accepted and the odds frozen?

On one of the rose-colored walls, an oaktag chart had been hung with evident care. From this chart a prospective wagerer could see the various odds and their respective predictions as well as who was aligned with what outcome and at what price. Television had been wheeled into the room and was awake in hope it would soon feed the room much-sought-after information. The debate was quickly settled and it was decided that all bets would be on with no cutoff other than the natural one mandated by the situation.

Soon thereafter a quiet broke into the room. Then all eyes, guided by invisible but persistent gravitons, locked on to Television and the subdued press conference being held within. Now they, i.e. the news, cut back to the studio with the faux N.Y.C. skyline background. There the immaculately sculpted head shook no and said, "Again, police are asking for your help. If you know anything at all concerning the whereabouts of baby—"

"I hate that," interrupted Conley. "Police are asking for my help? When did that become legitimate? Do your own job. What would be the reaction if the newscaster said *public defender Garo Conley is asking for your help. He has a really busy day in court tomorrow and he needs somebody to cover a couple of cases in Part 43*? I would be laughed out of the box. Cops do it and people rush to the phone."

"We all have an interest in the successful prosecution of malfeasance," said Cleary. "The hotline number allows the community to vent and feel productive."

"Community? This is New York padre!" a chorus laughed.

"Unfortunately, the hotline also gives some sick people a forum," said Julia. "I heard on the radio this morning that somebody called BAD–BABY with an anonymous tip regarding Tula. Apparently he had everyone's hopes up at first because he seemed to know things that weren't in the papers. He said he had it on good word that baby Tula was fine and unharmed and he was very convincing. Unfortunately, when they pressed him on his source it appears he cited Ralph Kramden as the bearer of the good news."

"Not."

"Yes the fat bus driver with the best friend who works in the sewer!"

"Crazy people," muttered Debi without smiling.

Debi did everything without smiling and there was more than a little speculation as to why that was, speculation I could have ended at any moment but didn't. After hearing several people commenting on the fact that Debi never smiled I had grown curious myself and asked her about it in a roundabout joking way that I hoped would insulate me from charges of rudeness. She mumbled something while motioning to a magazine on her table, her voice trailing off as she left the office. When I went over to the magazine I saw the problem. Under the Basic Beauty section there was an article on smiles. The writer couldn't have been clearer. Smiles were a D.E.E. that should be avoided at all costs. D.E.E. stood for *Devastating Epidermal Event* because it seemed a smile implicated more facial muscles on the average than any other common facial expression. As a result, researchers at Whattsamatta U. or something were prepared to state that excessive smiling could lead to premature wrinkles particularly around the all-important windows to the soul. News taken to heart apparently.

"He was claiming to have spoken to Kramden himself?" asked Liszt. I accidentally looked right at Toomberg. "Got to go," I whispered and split.

"Can I change my pick to the mother killed the baby herself and concocted the entire scenario as a smoke screen?" I heard Liszt ask from the hallway.

"Wait up!" said Toomberg running out of the office after me and foiling my plan to avoid him. Drats! is what I thought.

"Did you get an opportunity to review the death penalty material over the weekend?" he asked.

"No."

"We really have to progress on that."

"Don't worry Toomie, I'm with you. It's just that I was swamped."

"How?"

"Christ Toom. I pulled some kids out of a burning building! Don't you feel guilty for asking now? Obviously that was followed by all sorts of commendations and meetings with the mayor and the like. It's been a real whirlwind."

"Seriously, is it true you're working on Tom's case?"

"Yeah why?"

"It's just that, well, you do have a great deal of cases. Are you going to have the time to devote to this case? I mean there's a brief to write. One of us has to go down to Alabama to meet with both the client and the director of the project. Then we have to prepare for the argument and—"

"Easy Toomie please. Don't get all worked up. I've been doing this for the better part of four decades. When I started in this racket you weren't even a prediction. And we didn't have these fancy computers either. Or books. We had to memorize the laws back then."

"Be serious."

"Don't worry man, shit is that Tom?"

"Indeed."

"Did he see me?" I was trying, turtle-like, to retract my head into my body.

"I think so, he's coming this way."

"Fucking fate, quick tell me everything you know about Tom's case."

"Why?"

"I was supposed to look at that file this weekend and I know he's going to ask me questions."

"The burning child correct?"

"C'mon!"

"Well all I know is what I've read in the papers and of course these daily periodicals are famous, or rather infamous, for their superficial coverage of—"

"The short version Toom! Never mind, just give us a couple seconds then come up with some reason why I have to go with you."

"No I'm terrible at that sort of thing."

"Just . . . hey Tom."

"So what do you think?"

"What a mess."

"Do you think—"

"Hey Casi, we have to get going."

"Where?" demanded Tom.

"Yeah where?" I added along with a silent prayer.

"We have to see about those . . . jelly . . . um . . . beans . . . and stuff."

"Jelly beans? What the hell are you talking about Toomberg? What the hell's he talking about Casi?"

"I have no, the hell you talking about Toom?"

"You know. The appeal and . . . the thing . . . and."

"Oh yeah. I better go Tom. What's your day like tomorrow? Actually I have 180.80s. Can we talk the day after?"

"What's happening with that mandatory tomorrow?"

"I don't know. I called the D.A. (lie) but she hasn't called me back. I'm going to the scene right now actually. I don't think it's going anywhere. Let me go."

. . .

"Jelly beans Toom? What the fuck?"

"I told you I'm terrible when it comes to subterfuge."

"Terrible is one thing but jelly beans?"

"Once I committed to the word *jelly* it was almost as if beans had to follow."

"Fair enough."

"Besides, the whole thing is your doing. If you had just—"

"Very true. Thanks Toom. Don't worry you're still my favorite teammate. See you tomorrow, I have to go on an investigation."

I walked out with Debi who was going home early. She had a sharp gait that made mine feel rounded.

"Where you off to?" she said.

"To a scene to try and interview a complainant."

"You know, you should always bring an investigator or another attorney along. You don't want to become a witness."

"No-one was available but I agree."

"I'd go with you but I have this thing."

"That's O.K. Here's one Deb. A Mexican duck walks into a bar and says *bartender a double of Cuervo and put it on my bill.*"

"That's good," she said stone-faced.

What I was doing wasn't very complicated. I had to find Valerie Grissom and get her to talk to me. She was claiming that Darril Thorton had sexually attacked her. My client's response was that this was a total fabrication an otherworldly force intent on propagating evil had put her up to. I had an address, which was more than we usually have, and therefore optimism. If she'd talk to me it would be a no-lose. I would get some idea as to her potential strength as a witness, possibly even get some impeachment material for a later trial, and most importantly get an early quasi-definitive answer regarding the state of the People's case, particularly whether or not Ms Grissom would be appearing in the grand jury the next day the picture of testimonial eagerness.

But none of that was accomplished because I never found her. 322 West 119th Street barely qualified as a building. It turns out that when you read you don't really take note of each individual letter. Instaed it seems your mind fills in details in service of a greater schematic, namely the words you've read millions of times before. Your mind jumps to conclusions in effect. In only such a way could you see a building when you looked at 322. The windows were made of plywood, the apartment doors secured by rusty combination locks. The concrete steps up to the main door gradually self-destructed outward, culminating in jagged ends without handrails where I sat under the assumption that Valerie Grissom had to appear at some point but she didn't have to and in fact didn't before I decided to leave.

I jumped in a cab I hoped would fly home. The cab driver was a lovely guy who betrayed no evidence of owning a tongue. He decided to take the Manhattan Bridge. Just short of Canal St the cab stopped and I saw the billboard peephole that had been set up as visual portal to Man's Greatest Invention. Currently peering in was a tiny guy with a humongous ass, the black velvet curtain splayed on either side of his neck. The immediate visual impression was of a half-man cut off at the waist, reduced to his lower geography and frozen in front of the sign. Like molecularly bombarded particles engaged in Brownian motion, others in the area loitered in skittish disarray. But as we pulled away they congealed into a rational rhyme. With balletic grace they formed a single file. All together now, lining up behind the ass to look in the hole.

Mirror, mirror on the wall
Who's the fairest of us all?
– Ms White's stepmom

Chapter 8

There I was the following morning sitting at a depressing table in a like room with one of those retro billowy soda machines glowing like a plastic rainbow next to its pal with the rotating steel compartments that separated uniformly rejected white-bread sandwiches from their colleagues; and in my hand, between fingers fore and middle with thumb cradling underneath, in a room where precisely this conduct was explicitly not permitted, a profusely smoking cigarette, the kind where the end responsible for filtering had a joyous cavity, the constant flicking of which produced great pleasure in me, and which had inspired me to determine exactly how long I could abstain from that fucking great activity with the not unexpected result that the burning end with its hollow parasitic ash was now considerably longer than the unburnt rest and was obstinately marching towards absurd Pink-Floyd's-The-Wall length as the painful orange paper embers neared my fingers, C fibers firing like mad, leaving ashen skeletal remains that seemed to defy gravity while desperately clinging to their ancestral filter, when in walked Liszt.

He had previously sworn me to uphold what he termed a sacred obligation, namely an obligation to be of great assistance to him in his quest to quit smoking. I would achieve this by, at the very least, *never* – even under the direst of circumstances and regardless of how much he should solicit, beg, plead, or importune – giving him a cigarette. He looked at me, the bizarre stick giving him pause, and said, "Ooh, can I have one?"

"Sure," I said. "Take the rest, I quit."

"Damn," he said as I walked out.

"Casi, it's me."

"I see that."

"You know me right?"

"Uh, no. Sorry I uh—"

"I'm the new attorney on the sixth floor, Darren Leaves?"

"Oh nice to—"

"You're like famous. I've heard really great things about you."

"Oh."

"The other day in arraignments I picked up one of your old clients."

"Really, who?"

"Well normally I wouldn't expect you to remember but he says you went to trial and won. Ramon DeLeon?"

"Sure, Ramon. Back to his old?"

"Yeah, another drug case."

"He's probably all emboldened and wants to go to trial again huh? Sorry."

"What he really wants is you. He sure remembers you."

"The acquittal he remembers."

"He still has your card and he's certain you'll want to take his case over."

"That's funny."

"So?"

"So?"

"So do you want to take his case?"

"Are you clinically insane? I'm serious, are you part of some sort of pilot program whereby the mentally ill are placed in public defender offices in major cities across this great nation and thereby made to feel useful?"

"I know but really the guy has no use for me and like worships you."

"Look Darren."

"Darryl."

"One trial per customer is I think a good policy, so no."

"Really? Because I would take one of your cases in return. Anything to avoid having to see this guy again. He's so mean to me."

"Mean? Listen Darryl."

"Darren."

"They're all mean, haven't you heard?"

"But this is like a no-win situation."

"So lose."

"Please Casi, I'm prepared to go beyond the lengths of appropriate behavior."

"Jesus, believe this?" I said to no-one. "Fine, leave it on my desk."

"Well, it's on today actually."

"For what?"

"180.80 in F."

"Great, I have a ton already. At least you didn't wait until the last minute. You're going to fit in beautifully here, give."

"Really? Thanks so much! I mean it, give me any case you have. Pick the one you've been dying to get rid of."

"Good, I have a guy who rhymes all the time."

"What do you mean?"

"Never mind, you owe me. And I know where you work."

Persistent fuck. I hated getting cajoled into doing something I'd resisted, an all-too-frequent occurrence for me, and making all worse was the file this unknown chump handed me: an indecipherable abstraction that hemorrhaged red ink all over my innocent hands.

I was walking to court surprised at the ease with which I recalled DeLeon's face, not normally a strength of mine. What I remembered was a round serious face that had trouble breathing as the jury entered to read their verdict. And as close to universal legal truth as you get is this: putting aside potential calamities that threaten to personally and intimately befall you, there is no greater anxiety than the quiet charged moments before the reading of the verdict in a case you've parented. And I want you to know this feeling and want, moreover, to be the reason you know it, hence the following:

First, a case that goes to trial is a hideously deformed corporal appendage that forces you to hunch down in deference to its weight. Always on your mind despite your best efforts but you don't dare kill it for fear that you, the host, will join in its demise. Self-inflicted as well. The realization that this deformity is something you freely chose, something you once strove for and something the overwhelming majority of the population has no relationship with or any true conception of. A deformity you adopt every couple of months then cradle in your arms and measure your breath hoping to be an adequate parent. And everyone in the room hates it, wants to see it lopped off and discarded. But you have to put your arm around it, snuggle up to it and protect it from those that would do it harm. Or you can inhale some of the surrounding air that whispers *we understand if you find it hard to kiss this oozing creature on the lips so instead just blow it a kiss from afar and when, in the end, it lays there gasping for life you can turn to us and say you did your best and the creature bought it upon itself at any rate.* You can do that and be like everyone else because no-one says you have to love deformities. Unless you need to.

But that's the trial, which feels positively splendid compared to the verdict. Because there's an undeniably legitimate response to observers who question a trial attorney's particular decision or action during a trial. The response in distilled form is that things happen a lot faster in the well than they do for someone sitting on their fat ass in the audience. In those charged pre-verdict moments, however, the opposite is true. The note from the jury announcing it has reached a verdict instantly accelerates the well toward the speed of light with a resultant slowing of time for those within. In this slowed universe everyone not you seems to exist solely for your benefit or detriment, their realities not rising to the level of yours so that when, after much anticipatory ritual speech by the clerk, the foreperson of the jury plays with his piece of paper and announces his group's creation you feel a strange dissociation. But even so you stand there and your organs seem to tighten from within and there's an empathy so great you start to sense not much difference than if the case were named after you, the People of your State opposing You, and this ragtag body politic entering to announce their recent past and your lasting future. And now it feels less like a decision on a particular incident and more like a final judgment on your life, that collection of tenuously related decisions made and deferred, yet what truly empowers these people, with their own tainted slates, to so decide?

With DeLeon I rose and lowered my head, tensing every muscle in my body, the pulsing transmissions ending in blood-deprived hands that gripped the table while their owner tried to convey nonchalance. What I was listening for was not really a declaration or even a word. It was a syllable. The coveted *nuh* or the devastating *gih*. I would hear one or the other and it would be over. Now I hadn't slept or eaten in days, not the real kind of sleep with minimal synaptic firing and the sensation of actual temporal passage and not the real kind of eating where the victim doesn't swell to twice its normal size as it approaches your esophagus, so when I heard the *nuh* it was unjustifiably a great surprise and felt like a bullet evaded. What I did then was what I always did when I heard those words. I got the hell out of there before they realized there was some sort of error, or the jury changed its mind, or some new evidence surfaced or you get the picture. I didn't need to talk to the jury either. Once a trial was over I never wanted to see them again and I certainly didn't care what they

264

thought about the case. I didn't care if they thought I was the best lawyer they'd ever seen or more likely the worst. I wasn't interested in the often ridiculous leaps of logic that produced their verdict and conclusively displayed once and for all, to themselves, how intelligent they were in that they were able to go beyond the parameters of the courtroom's four walls, if need be, to decide my client's fate. Thankfully *not guilty* spoke for itself and allowed me to avoid all that maddening bullshit. *Not Guilty* also let me avoid ghosts. I remembered very little of the actual litigation of DeLeon's trial. But had the verdict been different it would, like all traumatic events, have been permanently seared into the canvas of my brain, ready to be recalled and agonized over at the slightest provocation. Once recalled I would have mentally run over the strategic roads not taken and how they might have changed the result. This I would have done over and over, in every conceivable combination, with increasingly pained frustration but always with the same conclusion: I was faulty. The kind of unremitting chorus that can impel the wrong kind of person to the wrong kind of conduct.

Not so with DeLeon and when it was over I watched him exhale a half-hour's breath then, after drinking in a little of the power those moments created, I said goodbye and split. Now DeLeon and I were about to reunite in the pens behind Part F and I knew I had to steel myself to hear all about the horror of his false arrest. An arrest, he would doubtless claim, borne from a desire on the part of law enforcement, as a general entity, to avenge its earlier ignominy.

The way Part F worked was this. The part was a pit stop for wayward felonies. With some exceptions, felonies that had been arraigned in criminal court but not yet presented to a grand jury and indicted were placed on the Part F calendar. Consequently the part had a little suspense to it since essentially everybody – judge, defendant, defense counsel, curious onlooker – was there to hear whether the defendant had been indicted; his case morphing from a mere felony complaint housed in criminal court to an indictment voted by a grand jury and requiring that the case be transferred to Supreme Court. And because of New York Criminal Procedure Law 180.80, which required that a defendant charged with a felony be released without bail should "one hundred forty-four hours" elapse following his arrest without an indictment, this suspense was decidedly greater where the client was incarcerated and in the part waiting to hear his fate. Because if you made your living committing felony crime, being indicted on your 180.80 date (the date this period expired) was the norm and carried the extra sting of keeping you in jail on the last possible day you could be held on a felony complaint. Like everyone else, A.D.A.s loved the last minute, so the 180.80 date was generally not only the day they announced the defendant had been indicted but also the day they did the actual indicting.

Of course the defense attorney's mission was to prevent this whole indictment business. This he attempted to do primarily through begging, begging the D.A. not to present the case and offer his guy a misdemeanor plea or better yet to reduce it to a misdemeanor outright. In addition to these cases, indictments were also avoided, at least temporarily, where the D.A. couldn't get his act together in time, the complainant was uncooperative for example, and the defendant was released and given a court date to return. These latter cases leaned heavily towards eventual dismissal after six months and intermittent trips to the part.

All of this was highly relevant because those cases that *were* indicted and subsequently transferred to Supreme Court were truly bad news for the indictee. The overwhelming majority of those cases ended in convictions. First, very few cases actually went to trial (one percent?) and even fewer were dismissed, for whatever reason, in Supreme Court. The result was that almost every case upstairs ended through plea bargaining: the D.A. or the judge offered the defendant a particular sentence in exchange for a plea of guilty and the defendant, leery of a higher number after trial, accepted the offer and pled guilty. So forget whatever revolving-door bullshit you've been fed up and until this upcoming lucid and edifying moment and remember this: almost every single serious, read indicted, case ended in this manner – with a plea of guilty, a *conviction*. And of the few cases that actually went to trial, well over fifty percent of those also ended in at least some level of conviction. So even armed with just elementary reasoning you can see that when a D.A. stood before a judge in F and announced that the person to your left had been indicted, she was not often signaling the beginning of a battle, she was more likely cueing you to cut your (*pl.*) losses.

And all that hung over that courtroom: would you go upstairs with all that entailed or out the door to freedom?

What I hated about the part was the waiting central to the whole process. When you walked in the first place you headed was the table supporting the approximately ten page calendar listing the hundred and twenty or so cases being heard that day. The cases were listed in ascending order based on their docket numbers. The docket number itself represented what number arrest the case was for that year in that respective borough, with 2000NY100000 meaning the hundred thousandth customer in New York County in the year 2000 and so on. Once you found your case on the list you had to ascertain what number that case was on the calendar. The case's calendar number was listed on the far left. Now you needed to know whether your client had been *produced,* that is whether he had ridden the blue bus touting *New York's Boldest* from Rikers Island to 100 Centre Street and the pens behind the courtroom. The quick way to do this was to check the list the court officers posted identifying by number those cases where the defendant had been produced. Your next stop was a visit to the D.A. clerks who had their own table set up in the well. In case you were not already aware of it they would tell you if the D.A. assigned to the case was making any offers, those coveted misdemeanor dispositions I mentioned earlier that prevented the case from ever being presented to a grand jury. If you served cross grand jury notice at arraignments, indicating your client wished to testify before the grand jury, they would ask if he still intended to testify so they could let the D.A. know and make the necessary arrangements. Apart from all that, what you really needed to know was whether they had *word* on the case. Their response took one of three forms. They might tell you the case had been *indicted* in which case you could have the case called and pick a date, usually exactly two weeks later, in Supreme Court for arraignment on the new indictment. Or they might tell you there would be *no grand jury action* which allowed you to go into the pens and tell your guy the good news that he was going home with a new court date that he would in all likelihood assiduously avoid. That case was as good as over. Finally, there was the dreaded *no word yet*. What that meant was that the D.A. intended to indict the case but hadn't gotten around to it yet. The dread came from the fact that the case would not be called until either the 180.80 time was up or until the D.A. informed the clerk in the part of the case's status. This fact plus the number of cases that had to be indicted every day made for a lot of waiting in F.

So I waited a lot that day. And in between waiting some things occasionally happened. Robert Coomer, the chess-playing, sexually confused, unaided-human-flight-attempting bon vivant received the coveted, and expected by him, *no grand jury action* and was accordingly released on his own recognizance. Terrens Lakes's big concern was whether or not he was getting credit towards his future sentence for the time he was currently spending in jail. He was, and his indictment meant he would be shipped upstairs to work out the particulars.

Like Coomer, Darril Thorton exuded confidence when I first spoke to him in the pens. He was confident Valerie Grissom would not be coming to court and that he would consequently be released. And after I extracted a torturous admission from him that Grissom might

268

appear to testify in the grand jury, as the D.A. was indicating she would, he reiterated his desire to testify before said grand jury, my feelings on which you'll perhaps recall. Reeling, I asked him if it was not logical to deduce that if the expelled angel was powerful enough to compel Ms Grissom to appear before the grand jury and spin a complete fabrication then he would similarly use that same power to ensure that the members of the grand jury would vote to indict him. Otherwise where was the sense right? He goes through the trouble of getting Grissom to lie in the grand jury, an admitted evil of the sort he was required to engender, yet he would then allow the grand jury to see through the lie and fail to indict an innocent man, a greater, more perfect evil? He stared at me all happy that I had finally discerned what the case was truly about then, conceding the power of my sally, indicated that if Grissom appeared to testify before the grand jury, as she later did, he would speedily read the wall's handwriting and exercise his right to remain silent with respect to that process. He was indicted.

Across the hall in Part N, which functioned like F but handled only certain drug cases, the Deeble case continued its slow desolate descent. For some clients, principally those in love with drugs but well past the idealization stage, six days in jail, with attendant meals and a presumed lack of drugs, actually seemed to benefit them. The new client often look cleansed with fresher mind and cushier carriage. Deeble bucked that trend disadmirably. She was the color of urine. Green urine. The whites of her eyes were improperly called as they matched the color of her skin. And they were still. Even when her body would animate the eyes would lay dead. She seemed to inhale a disproportionate amount of the available oxygen as she spoke and I felt a corresponding urgency to accomplish.

I wanted to put her in the grand jury. Not so much for what she would say as for what the grand jurors would see. *No way* was what she said to that thought and the D.A. echoed this sentiment when

I repeatedly tried to get a misdemeanor offer. No was everywhere, slamming my inquiries of Deeble regarding whether or not she could make bail and crippling my appeals to the judge to reduce that bail. There was nobody in the audience for her. Nobody I should call. Nobody needed to know what was happening with her case. And when, after five o'clock, the D.A. announced she had been indicted it happened with such a dawnish quietude that the whole thing felt like a jealously shared secret between Glenda and me.

But before I leave a false impression, those things and my reunion with DeLeon happened between long fits of nothing during which I did much of my day's requirement of biologically mandated day-dreaming, the random thoughts inexplicably triggered to appear only to disappear as quickly as they came.

One of those was Wilfred Benitez. Only it was weird because when I thought about Benitez that day I didn't think of the Benitez who outpointed Cervantes at seventeen to become world champion or even any of the later Benitezes. Instead what I thought about, or more accurately what I imagined, was Benitez at like two or three years old in his Bronx apartment. I wondered if the seeds of physical genius began to sprout that early. Because what I kept imagining was his dad breathlessly calling Wilfred's mother into the room. Look! Watch! ¡Mira! He would say. When I go to poke him in the nose he moves his head away or knocks my hand away before I can do it! Yes I see, *pero* be careful he's just a baby. No I don't think you understand. No matter how fast I try to do it he always moves his head in time. Uh-huh, so? Don't you get it? His reflexes are incredible. Can't you see? Well how do you know that not every kid does that? Are you crazy? Look. Again. See what I mean? It's like he has radar or something.

Of course that's exactly what it was like for the man who later came to be called "*El Radar*". But I wondered, was the radar always waiting to be used and ultimately mastered or was it constructed in a harsh gym where even the walls sweat? Did fellow playground toddlers

270

learn the hard way not to make attempts on Wilfred's toys? And what happened when they tried to hit him back? Did he slip their punches the way he would later, at age twenty-three, slip Roberto Duran's right hand at a New York City press conference announcing their fight? Or did he block them like he would millions others, slightly raising his shoulder to deflect their brunt all the while keeping absurdly serene eye contact?

I could, so did, mentally construct moments like that all day. Non-gym moments where someone might have spotted something. Might have seen something that they, even though non-expert, instantly recognized as out of the ordinary. Special. Then they would transfer that spark they had viewed to its owner, the child Wilfred. They would look at him and maybe see more than just one of countless Bronx *Boricuas*.

I'm sorry Mrs Benitez but this is a nursery school. The kids here are three, four years old. We simply must take steps to ensure that incidents like these do not continue to occur. No, you're right. He's not the only one who fights, but with the others the results aren't nearly as devastating. Well yes. I suppose it is our job to break these things up before they get too bad but how shall I put this? When Wilfred's involved it all seems to happen so fast. Quite fast in fact. Almost like lightning I would say. Beautiful lightning actually. What I mean is that, well you've seen lightning Mrs Benitez I won't elaborate. And so on.

And when Wilfred's parents put the apartment's only fan – the kind that used to make a big deal about its ability to oscillate – in their room, I bet Wilfred and his sibs would go out on the fire escape where the air would at least occasionally move, even if only by accident. I bet this because I remembered fire escapes. And people walking on the streets below or looking on from other escapes might have made a quick mental note of the fact that little Wilfred was out there. Most likely one or more of these people would feel compelled to comment that really it was negligence of the highest order to allow such a wee child out on the fire escape, and if the complainant was a non-Puerto Rican then that would quickly be identified as the root cause of such criminal negligence; and really something should be done but not involving the police who we can all agree should mind their own business when it comes to Hispanic child-rearing lunacy.

But surely nothing approaching that much mind would've been paid to Wilfred Benitez. Unless of course we're talking about a previous witness to his spark. Such a person's eyes might gravitate foreverafter to Wilfred as he entered a room or did a fake escape from a fire or swung a broomstick at a tennis ball or whatever preschool physical geniuses do. And maybe one day that person would approach Mrs Benitez and say that her son was not average. That there was something about him. And maybe just this once, futuristic money would not be mentioned. And with the mounting years the amount of people who would do this, who would talk about her son Wilfred in this way, would increase greatly so that by the time an eleven-year-old Wilfred was a gym regular she could expertly parry their well-intentioned words and emotions, taking care to absorb only what pleased her.

And so like the more thought I gave to Mrs Benitez, the more convinced I became that the oscillating fan in her room was not her idea at all but was like more or less forced on her by Mr Benitez. He would say things like he works hard and the kids have their entire fan-buying future in front of them and she would grudgingly go along but when it got unbearably hot, truly so, she would exert her will and on those nights she would spread a sheet on the sofa and other smaller sheets on the floor of the living room so that every Benitez might share the one fan as it oscillated throughout the night, fro and to each appreciative member.

And it was Good that this woman would later nod and swell as they talked about her son.

But then after a while the voices I imagined weren't about Benitez at all. They were about me. And the voices spoke to *my* mother. *Never seen anything like it before* they would say. *Miles ahead of where so and so, yes him, was at this stage.* And the people saying this weren't chumps like you and me, they were the foremost experts in their respective fields and they exhibited genuine urgency too. Now the greatest beauty of it all was that my Talent, whatever it was, was so immensely profound that it wouldn't require any of that annoying Hollywood-montage-best-song-on-the-soundtrack-type training/nurturing that is invariably led by a recovering alcoholic, formerly great, last-chance-at-redemption guru. Instead *it*, the Talent I mean, would simply squire me around. It would define me with its purpose and occlude the remaining universe of choice so that if someone asked me why I did what I did I could truthfully answer that I had no choice. Ah dreams.

From maybe six on there was a piano in the house, brown and small (the piano). A minuet written by Mozart when he was three. The fingers move in a manner that's technically correct yet somehow not fully right and if you want to come closer to the proper sounds and silences you need Alana to play it.

As a young boy Einstein was taken to see a military parade. He saw the soldiers in strict formation, started crying inconsolably, and had to be taken home.

When he was twelve, this would be like 1635, Blaise Pascal used a lump of coal to figure out Euclid's proofs on his playroom floor. In addition to huge contributions to physics, nascent calculus, and the theory of probability, Pascal invented the first calculating machine. In his *Pensées*, he argued that we should wager that God exists since we have less to lose that way.

Friedrich Nietzsche and Richard Wagner were tight. More than that really, in Dick's music Freddy – who once said that without music life would be a mistake – saw a majestic synthesis of all art. In his essay *Richard Wagner in Bayreuth* he urged the German people to treat the coming Wagner festival as they would a sacrament.

When he was twenty-five, Nietzsche watched a cavalry troop pass through Frankfurt. During the war with France this happened. It was then he had a vision that shaped his entire philosophy for in this collection of armed soldiers he saw a Will to Power.

When, in 1876, the Wagner festival in Bayreuth became a reality, Nietzsche disapproved greatly. Here was the frivolous in-crowd elbowing aside the true devotees and, what was worse, Wagner hamming it up for them. Disgusted by what he called the feminism and dishonest idealism that had infected his friend and his friend's music, he split abruptly. When they ran into each other again in Sorrento, Nietzsche turned to Wagner and said:

"Remember me?"

No, wait. That can't be right. What he actually said was:

"Yo, remember me?"

"What?" I said.

"Remember me? It's me DeLeon! You beat my case remember?"

"Yeah, Ramon. Hi."

"I was just telling everybody what a great lawyer you are man. Look man you have to take over my case from this Leaves guy! You know how to handle a case of mine! I can pay you, he said he would talk to you."

"Hold it, stop. You can end your pitch right there. I already took the case from this Darren—"

"Derrin."

"– character. So what happened?"

"Oh man thank you!"

"What happened?"

"I got caught man."

"Caught doing what?"

"Selling."

"Selling what?"

"Coke, man."

"Really?"

"Yeah."

"So you're guilty."

"Yeah I'm guilty."

"And you were guilty in my case too right?"

"What do you mean?"

"The case where we went to trial and won? Remember that case?"

"Yes."

"You sold in that case too right."

"Alright man I'm going to be straight with you. I did sell."

"And you sold here. You want to go to trial again, is that it?"

"No man. I ain't taking it to trial."

"So what do you need me for? If all you need is a plea, this Leaf guy is perfectly capable of talking to the D.A. and getting you a deal."

"Nah man, this time I'm selling everybody out is what it is. I already talked to them cops."

"Selling who out? And keep your voice down."

"The guys I work with and shit."

"What does that mean?"

"I'm giving them up man. I'll tell them cops whatever I have to tell them to get up out from under this. I'll be a C.O. and whatnot."

"A C.I.?"

"Yeah, a C.I. That's what I meant."

"And you talked to the cops who arrested you about that?"

"Yeah at the precinct. And the D.A. too."

"And?"

"And they know I have good shit to tell them man. They want to work with me."

"Good for you. That means you need me even less and you can keep the attorney you have now."

"No way, this is too big. I don't trust him, I need you."

"Did you tell him about all this."

"No, that's what I mean. I don't trust him."

"What trust? All he has to do is stand there while you tell the cops what you know. A properly trained monkey could do it."

"Nah man, I don't want that guy."

"Fine. You know you're going to be indicted today."

"I know all that. They said I would be going to supreme court and that I should talk to you, to my attorney, to tell you to call the D.A. about setting up a meeting."

"I'll do that."

"Thank you man. I won't forget this. Listen if I give them really great information, you think they could get me up out of here?"

"I don't know. They don't really promise anything until they hear what you have to say but it's a possibility I guess."

"Great. Will you be out there when I see the judge?"

"See you then."

"O.K."

I wasn't surprised when I saw Dane as I left court that day. Somehow it had the feel of a planned meeting. And when he started right in as if continuing following a brief interruption I was similarly unfazed. But it was late and I had to meet someone.

"Where you headed?"

I had told him yesterday. My sister had set me up with some doctor. Well I had done the actual calling and arranging and such but it was only at her urging and she was my brother-in-law's cousin's sister's hairdresser's best friend or something and if I didn't get a cab in like forty seconds I would surely be late and there was the matter of a potential wrong foot to be considered.

"Why are you so intent on making a good first impression? She hot? What does she look like?"

The distinction then discussed was the one between trying to make a good first impression, for example during a job interview, and simply following the mandates of common courtesy of the sort involved in returning a basketball to a successful shooter. And where exactly lay the relevance of her appearance of which I had no clue?

"Funny you should mention a job interview. You're nervous aren't you? Like audition-type nerves right?"

Not in the slightest.

"Naturally, who wouldn't be?"

I wouldn't. And wasn't.

"And they're an ugly kind of nerves too, ones that cut to the quick. I realize that society has long since placed its imprimatur on the activity but you must admit that a date is a deliciously odd thing if you break it down."

Meaning we shouldn't.

"Remember that a person is nothing more than the sum of how he is perceived by others, a truth a date probably reveals better than anything. You might dispute this, you might point to people, maybe yourself included, who seem to not give a rat's ass what others think of them. You might also point out that, at any given moment during a day, the average person does not seem overly or manifestly pre-occupied with what others think of them. However, as a thought experiment, imagine a seemingly secure woman being informed that she is about to be told definitively how every single person she knows truly perceives her. Their incontrovertible, and completely devoid of artifice, opinion of her. Such a person would lose it. She would start to sweat. Mentally, she would try to convince herself that she didn't care what these people thought. But the way she would do this is interesting. She would most likely tell herself something like she doesn't care what *those idiots* think. This need to downgrade the opposition is supremely relevant and gives you an idea of the hostility engendered by the tension of the situation. No matter, because ultimately she will not be able to convince herself that she doesn't care. She will know that she stands on a precipice with a very real danger of an emotional landslide. What she would realize, and what anyone else in her situation would realize, is that the wrong answer can be devastating. And mostly devastating in its ability to create reality. If everybody thinks you're an asshole and you think yourself a gem guess what? You're an asshole! And if you confront one of these asshole people and say to them *hey everybody thinks you're an asshole, what's your response to that?* I bet you he doesn't say *that's O.K. I know I'm not an asshole.* Instead he'll probably say something like *the people who know me best know I'm not an asshole.* Either that or he'll try to convince you that despite appearances he is not, in reality, an asshole. In other words, he instinctively recognizes that you cannot combat an unfavorable perception others have of you with your own self-perception you can only either try to change that perception or combat it with the more favorable perception of others who you will argue are better informed. In short, all that matters is what others think. This is why women stick their fingers down their throat, men lick some fat guy's ass to make more money, and certain eight-year-olds feel genuine terror at the thought of getting on the school bus."

Interrogative expression because what was the relevance of all that to someone who had to get in a cab like that instant?

"The relevance is that the reason you're so nervous is that a date, especially of the blind variety, crystallizes this normally diffused anxiety into a fixed space-time point. The pressure builds to enormous proportions as you realize your place on the display shelf. On the bright side, unlike a job interview, this audition is a mutual one.

Meaning you have two people wanting to be liked, well *liked* is probably not the right terminology. What you have is two people who want the other person to be impressed by them. But there's a self-defense element as well so one of the things they want the other person to be impressed by is how little they need that person's validation. Look at me, they say nonverbally, I am one impressive, self-contained motherfucker who doesn't really need your approval but please agree with this self-assessment or else I might start to doubt this perception of mine which deep down I don't really believe. And therein lies the beautiful irony of it all. The beauty is that while these two people are expending tremendous effort, and considerable subterfuge, to create an impressive veneer they are actually subverting their chances of making a connection, the purported goal of the date."

I really had to go, could he please stop talking so I wouldn't feel rude?

"You see what I'm saying? The more you impress this doctor, which of course you do in part by feigning disinterest, the less likely it is that she'll think you are in turn impressed by her, which of course is her paramount concern, whereas your impressiveness is like tenth on the list of things that matter to her. Notice I say tenth on the list. I don't discount it entirely. The reason for this is that if she thinks you are a completely unimpressive individual then the fact that you are impressed by her is of limited value to her and therefore unlikely to ever sufficiently satisfy her psychic needs to the point that you two will connect. So that's the very predictable equation at work here, one where, by avoiding the extremes, the less impressive you are to her the more impressed by her you better be and vice versa. Of course, remember that deep down she probably doesn't think she's all that impressive so if you mess up the equation and are disproportionately impressed by her then she'll in turn view you as less impressive with all attendant consequences. Got that? We can state the equation and its impetus another way. What matters to the average person, vis-à-vis dating relationships and such, is not any particular quality the contender may or may not possess. What matters is how they feel when they're around that person and whether they get sufficient stroking to offset, for those moments anyway, their insecurities. So you'll hear a woman talk about her boyfriend and it becomes apparent that what most recommends him is his obsequiousness. He buys her flowers every day, tells her how beautiful she is. So even though yeah he's a bit of a schlump, he's just so good to her. And they, meaning she, have a lot of fun when they're together. He's romantic, that's the quality he has if pressed. I know what you're about to say about people seemingly attracted to those who treat them poorly but recall that the equation . . ."

A raised hand near a cab before an apology during an exit and how do you forget to ask someone whether it's true they're dying?

I liked about cabs mainly the abdication of responsibility so I always left it up to the driver to decide how to get somewhere. I suspended all judgment and opinion. That's what I paid the big bucks for, to close my eyes.

If I thought about anything, it was how little I was thinking about things. Well that and how I had wanted to go home to shower and change but now it was too late. The shower I mostly craved, a shower almost always being welcome but especially under these circumstances.

Changing clothes would have been nice too. Instead I would be wearing a suit, which would make me look like the kind of person who has to wear a suit, which of course was exactly the kind of person I was. Still.

I wondered if she would be wearing those cool, light blue almost paper-like pajamas. Scrubs. Then the driver was looking at me like you planning on getting out buddy? Because we can't get any more here than this.

And even though I was late I was early because she wasn't there yet.

Her greater sin wiped out mine and made it as if I'd been on time. But what if she wasn't merely late, this stranger? What if she wasn't coming at all? In that case it would certainly have been a mistake to sit at a table the portrait of expectation; said table being located in the precise 0,0 center of the square dining room with me half expecting a spotlight and a corny announcer. And I hadn't wanted to sit at the table because I was perfectly content in the little waiting area they had, where I could pretend my fabulous companion was merely using the nearby restroom and where there seemed to be a sufficient turnover of customer personnel to keep this charade up for hours if need be. But, inexplicably, the bowtied guy with the burgundy leather portfolio seemed intent on getting me to abdicate this area and, with me all guilt-ridden about my late arrival in relation to the optimistic reservation time, I agreed.

I squirmed in my seat.

And the worst part was the way I now felt. Whereas I most certainly was not nervous when Dane asked me before, and in fact could not even truthfully envision being nervous in the near future, I now found that trying not to be nervous, in light of his confident proc-lamation, was akin to trying to follow someone's directive to avoid thinking of a pink elephant. And like a fulfilled scriptural prophecy I found myself increasingly concerned with the kind of figure I would cut, where before I merely worried about her visage. After all, Marcela had raved about this woman's beauty and Marcela herself looked ultrasharp making it unlikely she was easily impressed. And she was a doctor which at the very least seemed to ensure she would not be a blithering idiot.

What would she think of me? I cursed Dane for the fact I even cared. I started to feel actual dread at the thought of her appearing. But maybe this was misplaced. Was I an impressive individual? The first key would be the way I looked. But I truthfully couldn't remem-ber what I looked like being that my facial recognition weakness applied even to my own face. I could get up and look in the bathroom mirror but I was afraid that if the table was abdicated for even a second it would be immediately cleared by a member of what from all indications looked like an overly eager bus staff. Then I would have to call even greater attention to my plight in trying to retrieve the table from one of the current wait-listers. I pictured a microphone being used to announce that the table was already being used. By a single nervous-looking guy. Who had needed to use the bathroom!

Well I felt reasonably corporeally confident so I resolved to get a look at my face without exposing the table. What I did was take the knife I had been entrusted with, hold it up about eye level, and begin to spy the reflection. This was a bad idea as approximately three to five busboys immediately bum rushed me to replace what they assumed was a soiled utensil. Each seemed determined to be the first and within seconds three to five knives had formed a semicircle around my perfectly still face.

"A mirror sir? I don't understand," one said all confused as I took all the knives in the interest of a speedy resolution. I decided to avoid future sudden movements.

In college you waited a certain period of time and if the professor didn't show you were free to split. The only problem was I couldn't remember what this period of time was. But why was this a problem? Even if I could remember, who's to say that would bear any relevance to my current predicament? Who was entitled to more time?

One of my professors, who often skirted the shit out of this grace period, whatever it was, once said that if she could have dinner with anyone she would pick Goethe because he was the last person on Earth to know everything.

Or was that something someone else said about one of their professors?

Tell you one thing, I wouldn't have picked some tardy quack who makes you feel all insecure.

I would maybe pick CalTech physics professor John Schwarz though. For one, the dude knows his Superstring Theory cold, being perhaps the person most responsible for its development, and it seems likely that said theory may in turn ultimately prove to be the key to the Grand Unified Theory or G.U.T. that physicists since Einstein have been searching for to reconcile Quantum Physics with the Theory of Relativity. Also I'm sure Schwarz, like all these guys, knows his physics history. Given that, at some point during dinner I would turn to him and say: *so John what about this deal whereby God, or Nature, or Fate, or whatever you want to call it seems to replace one ginormous theoretical physicist with another?* He would probably look at me all quizzical then I would remind him that Galileo Galilei died in 1642 only to be replaced by Sir Isaac Newton who was born in 1642, at least according to the Julian calendar used in England at the time. Later, James Clerk Maxwell died in 1879 only to be replaced by Albert Einstein born in 1879. My nephew Timmy would wonder if maybe there wasn't enough room on Earth so that the predecessors died to make room for their successors. Mary might wonder the same thing but would likely remain silent.

Or I could be about to have dinner with Joe Satriani. Satch. We could talk about the palm-muted rhythm section of *Always With Me, Always With You* or we could talk about his former student in San Francisco, Kirk Hammett, and how Hammett gives him partial credit for that vicious interludy chord progression in *Creeping Death*.

Or what about the guy who trained Joe Louis for the second Schmeling fight?

Almost certainly dead I thought.

But why limit myself? Forget those puny living types. I could have dinner with fucking Beethoven! Ludwig van Beethoven my friends. I would ask him about Antonie Brentano, what went down there. Then I would say, between the appetizers and the main course, something like my sister Alana contends you didn't really *create* music.

283

Particularly with the late string quartets, she says, there's no way any mere human could have created that stuff. Instead what you did was more like discover notes that had already been celestially arranged to optimal psyche-rattling effect. In other words, your function was not unlike that of a receiver picking up radio waves that could never be heard with the naked ear. Which theory, I would say, would seem to be belied by the apparent painstaking manner of your compositional process. What say you Lud?

But really these dinners would be no fun because of the pressure involved. A dinner with Beethoven would involve much gaping on my part and precious little coherence. Dinner with Traci on the other hand would be a blast. She wouldn't even have to say much. Just the way I pictured she would dangle on the chair.

Whatever the grace period was, it had to be pretty damn close to expiring. Unless I had mixed up the dates or something – normally inconceivable but with my brain not unprecedented. I would wait just a smidgen longer. Or was it smidge?

In the meantime I would eat bread and think only pleasant thoughts.

Like how when I was a squirt the only thing I would consent to eat at restaurants was fried chicken with orange juice. If they didn't have either I would have pout for dinner.

Or how a deaf Beethoven was completely unaware of the crowd's rousing reaction to the initial performance of his Ninth Symphony until someone made him turn around. On May 7, 1824 in Vienna's Kärnthernor Theater that happened.

I guess another important thing about the talent would have to be its potential profitability. I would want to make enough money so that I never had to think about $$ again. I wouldn't have to screen calls from insistent student loan organizations. I could return their calls and maybe pay off all my debt right over the phone. I thought of what I would do then.

"Disappointed?"

"Huh? Oh hi. Sorry, what'd you say?"

"Disappointed?"

"No, I just. Oh I thought you weren't coming and I guess I just spaced out."

I hadn't even gotten to do that thing where you stand when your guest arrives before she sat down across from me. Only now my brain had belatedly processed the information and I suddenly stood up while she remained seated, making it look like I was about to leave and basically making me feel like an idiot.

I sat back down.

"Just stretching the old legs," I said. Mercifully the waiter came over about then, allowing us to use words whose content we were only marginally responsible for. Then as suddenly as he had appeared he was gone and we were once again on stage. To the extent that silence is somewhat acceptable in the context of the entire exercise it is almost verboten at the outset. The ball had to be set in motion.

On the Restaurant:

"Yeah, it's pretty cool. What do you think?" I said.

"I've been here before," she said.

"They certainly are attentive. The staff I mean."

"Yes, they're great."

"Except it now seems to me that this sort of compulsive attention must be motivated by fear. I wouldn't bet against an evil supervisory presence in this place."

"I know the owner."

"Well, I could be wrong."

On the Weather:

"I hate it," she said.

"Yeah, it's brutal. I can't remember it being this cold before.

285

Makes you want to perpetually hang in front of a fire and have life delivered."

"Hmph."

"What?"

"Nothing."

"Imagine not having a place to stay in this cold?" I said.

"I have a fireplace I never use."

"You should, it's one of the few winter benefits. Do you ever have professional occasion to go to the morgue? Is it full of homeless hypothermiacs when it gets like this?"

"What?"

On Her Job:

"Plastic surgery? Really? That's interesting."

"Very lucrative."

"It seems like a mostly New York/L.A. type thing right?"

"What do you mean?"

"Is actual plastic involved?"

"Sometimes. Why?"

"Well otherwise the term would seem to be a slap in the face at the type of person who becomes a patient."

"I don't think I have any idea what you're talking about."

"You know, like there's surgery for when something is actually wrong and then there would be plastic surgery for plastic, superficial people who can't cope with their nose."

On Misunderstandings:

"No I didn't mean to imply that at all."

"Right."

"I'm serious. What kind of a hostile lunatic would purposely insult their dinner companion? I was just trying to be funny."

On My Job:

"How can you represent someone *you know* is guilty? I could never do that."

On How Late It Had Become:

"Yeah wow I didn't realize how late it was."

"I have to get up early tomorrow."

"Me too."

On Dessert:

"No thanks," I said.

"No way," she added.

She lived close enough for me to walk her home and I was Mr Gentleman doing just that. I wondered why she didn't mention she lived about a block from the restaurant. I guess if it turned out I was some kind of nut (there are many kinds) I could have used that information to stalk her. Assuming I fell in love with her. No danger of that.

But despite the lowlights, it had been nice to have dinner with someone and I thought I should do it more often. With a different co-star of course. It beat cold pizza before flickering Television.

She was clacking her wide heels up the four or five steps to her door and I was staying put on the sidewalk. Platitudes were exchanged, breath visible. Then:

"Oh, one thing before you go," I said meekly.

"Yes?"

"I have this pain in my ear. I know it's not a cosmetic issue but I figured."

"What?"

"My ear."

"What about it?"

"It hurts."

"When does it hurt?"

"Maybe a third of the time."

"No *when*?"

"Oh, I don't know. I guess it hurts when I hear noise."

"Don't hear noise," she said.

Chapter 9

"So we'll do *Queen for a Day* O.K.?"

"Uh-huh."

"You're basically familiar with them?"

"Yup."

"Good. I'm printing it out as we speak, it's the standard one. You can review it with your client when he gets here."

"Which is when?"

"My cops just went over to get him from the twelfth-floor bridge, they should be back with him shortly. You can talk to him in here when they get back."

"Deal."

"Yeah and I'm sorry we had to do this so soon after the 180.80 date."

"The next day."

"I know but supposedly according to my officers your guy had information they need to act on quickly. So I figured if your guy was looking to help himself it was going to have to be sooner rather than later. I was thinking of your guy."

"Thanks. How long you been with Special Narcotics?"

"Let's see, this is my seventh year."

"How do you like it?"

"I like it, I like it a lot. Are you the original attorney on the case? Because I had a Leaves?"

"He transferred the case to me. I'm with a special unit, I only represent rats."

"Really?"

"No, just kidding. DeLeon wanted me."

"Oh right. He mentioned he would ask you to take his case over. Did he tell you I talked to him at the precinct?"

"Yeah, you do that often on these run-of-the-mill B sales?"

"No, not at all. I got this call from the Detective. D'Alessio, he's a good guy, I've had him on a couple of cases. Anyway he calls me saying they've got this guy with great information about spots I've done some work on. I've worked on a couple of long-term investigations, which is what I'm trying to get into as opposed to these street sales where only the low-level dealer gets arrested."

"Well you know he's got a lot of really good information (I guess?) for you guys so I hope you're prepared to let him out with a misdemeanor."

"It's complicated. You know he's a predicate and—"

"That's why we need a misdemeanor, this guy's taking a huge risk."

"No I know, believe me. We're very concerned with his safety and we intend to be very careful. That's part of what we want to discuss here today. As far as the deal, you know we don't make any specific promises until we hear in detail what he has to offer, that's just standard. And also any deal would, of course, have to be approved by my supervisor. But if he has the information we think he has and he's also straight with us—"

"He has excellent information (I guess redux) but I've already discussed this with him (lie) and he's only going to co-operate if it benefits him a lot. And by a lot I'm talking about getting out with a misdemeanor. I mean these guys he's talking about mean business (I bet)."

"The problem is he's out there selling and—"

"Exactly. That's the kind of guy you want. You don't want some unreliable crackhead who's going to disappear never to be heard from again. This guy knows a lot, is willing to talk, and would make an excellent witness. This is a minor case. He has to get a misdemeanor. He has to get out while it's pending and ultimately get a misdemeanor."

"Look we're getting ahead of ourselves here. We don't even know if he has any useful information. And you know we don't make any promises until we hear what he has to say. Once we hear what his information is—"

"That's fine if that's the tack you want to take. But you're not exactly inspiring confidence in me that you're going to give him a walk at the end of this. Given that, I don't see any reason for him to endanger himself by meeting with you now. This isn't an A felony, it's a B sale for Chrissakes."

"Well he's a predicate and if we don't make any offer."

"He'll take 4½ to 9. I'll get that from any judge in two weeks. At least then he doesn't have to worry about his safety."

"That's his right. If that's how you want to advise him. But I have to tell you he's already told my cops a lot and we don't even really need him all that much."

"That's silly. Now you're trying to take advantage of my inexperience I think. First, if you're going to want a search warrant you'll need him to go before the judge. Also you can't tell me with one side of your mouth that you can't make any promises until you hear what he has to offer then with the other tell me he's already given you so much quality information that you don't need him anymore. I know he's given you a lot of information and I know it was good stuff or we wouldn't be here. It seems to me you can come back to me with, if not a promise, then some idea of what you will offer him in exchange for his co-operation. I'm not trying to be difficult (yes I am) but fair's

291

fair (whatever that means) and I have a client to worry about."

"No, I know. I can appreciate that and I haven't said that we wouldn't be inclined to let him out or to give him a misdemeanor. But . . . well, I think the proper . . . give me a minute . . . I'm just going to talk to my supervisor for a minute about this."

"Yeah, tell him fair's fair man. This guy's got excellent information."

"I'll be right back."

Right genius, some detective calls you to the precinct based on what my chump client is blurting out and you then drag me in here all urgency the day after his 180.80 and I'm not supposed to get the distinct idea that you would be extremely pleased were he to cooperate? And given the fact that I couldn't stand doing this kind of confidential informant bullshit, at the very least I was going to walk out of there knowing my client was getting a sweetheart deal that would keep him off my back and make the case a minimal-lifting type deal. And the biggest lie was that the cops would be right back with DeLeon when we both knew that shit always took forever-plus. And this constant checking with the supervisor nonsense prosecutors had to do was annoying too. Though not as annoying as a guy essentially committing himself to cooperating on a case where I could have probably gotten him two to four, maybe even one and a half to three, with that possibility now having flown out the window and me desperately trying to win back some sort of leverage so I didn't feel like an impotent observer.

"No I talked to my supervisor and he says that a misdemeanor is a definite possibility so that's that."

"What about him getting out?"

"Yes, possibly, depending on whether or not the cops feel they could use him out on the street to work on this thing. But basically, like I said, I can't make any promises yet, but if your guy does his part we're prepared to basically walk him at the end."

"Good to know."

"Good, so that's out of the way. Here's the agreement so you can look it over until my officers get back. Um, I'm going to step out for a minute. They should be back any second."

He lingered silently in the threshold just a second before leaving. I didn't really know what to make of this Dacter guy. Alone in his office, which had four desks but no other humans, I shivered as the wind whipped through the many cracks between faceless air conditioner and inconsistently painted window. I lent him some thought. Had he said seven, because why then the nerves? By year seven there ought be decidedly less let's-say-intimacy between attorney and case than the amount he was evincing. So either he was a true incompetent, meaning he possessed more than just the generally accepted level of this trait, or there was something about the info DeLeon was feeding him that had visions of grandeur dancing in this meathead's head of meat. I would have to find out, would have to induce him to reveal things he shouldn't. And I loved getting those guys to talk. Oh yeah, they thought, you seem like you're cool and not really into the adversarial aspect of this job so I'm going to start divulging all sorts of interesting and useful material now – only when you later use that same material against me please do so in a manner that's all apologetic. Oh and references to the fact that you're not trying to be difficult are also appreciated.

But wait because what if I was misjudging the whole thing? After all, chances were nobody could be as smart as I thought I was, and fools are often the last to know their status as such. Maybe this clown's nerves arose from the fact that he was somehow screwing me and my client and was fearful that at any moment I might awaken from my overconfident slumber to say *hey, wait just a second*. And I then thought it possible that the answer hid in the freshly printed Queen for a Day agreement I held in my hand. I read it quickly to see. What I read was this:

DEBRIEFING AGREEMENT

With respect to the meeting of Roger P. Dacter, an assistant District Attorney in the Office of the Special Narcotics Prosecutor for the City of New York ("Office") and/or Detective Adam D'Alessio of the Manhattan North Narcotics Unit with Ramon DeLeon ("Client") to be held on the date of this memorandum, the following understandings exist:

(1) Should any prosecutions be brought against Client by this Office, this Office will not offer as evidence in its case-in-chief any statement made by Client at the meeting, except in a prosecution for false statements or perjury.

(2) Notwithstanding paragraph one, (a) this Office may use information derived directly or indirectly from Client's statements at the meeting for the purpose of obtaining leads to other evidence, and if any such evidence is developed, it may be used in any prosecution of Client; and (b) should any prosecution of Client be undertaken, this Office may use statements made by Client at the meeting and all evidence obtained directly or indirectly therefrom for the purpose of cross-examination should Client testify, or to rebut any evidence offered by or on behalf of Client in connection with the prosecution.

(3) Client agrees to waive his right to have his attorney present on his behalf during the meeting.

(4) This agreement is limited to the statements made by Client at the meeting held on this date, and does not apply to any oral, written or recorded statements, made by Client at any other time. No understandings, promises, agreements, or conditions have been entered into with respect to the meeting other than those set forth in this agreement, and none will be entered into unless in writing and signed by all parties.

DATED: New York, New York

_____

BRENDA F. BARROS
Special Narcotics Prosecutor

By: _____

Roger P. Dacter
Assistant District Attorney

_____

Client

_____

Attorney for Client

Which was like the height of routine and so served to simultaneously sate and inflame my suspicion. And it was into this quizzicality that round-faced DeLeon, his hands cuffed behind his back, entered escorted by a linebackersized collection of muscles topped with obviously dyed and jellied yellow hair that forcefully extended its hairy paw at me.

"Defense attorney?" he wondered.

"Yes."

"Detective D'Alessio. Nice to meet you. Have you seen the D.A.?" He had just walked out, I said, and it was resolved that Mr DeLeon and I would be left alone to discuss whatever was routinely discussed between hopeful soon-to-be-rats and their annoyed attorneys.

"So here you are," I said. "Obviously, they want to talk to you."

"Are they going to let me out?" he whispered

"Depends."

"What do you mean?"

"Depends on how useful you prove to be in their eyes."

"Aw man, forget it then. They have to let me out. This information is that good!"

"Listen I'm not the one who told you to cooperate. I'll be glad to tell this D.A. you have nothing to say and we can both walk out of here."

"And I'll get out?"

"Yeah Ramon, you'll get out. Of course not, what are you talking about?"

"What will they give me if we don't talk to them?"

"Nothing. No offer's my guess."

"No offer? Why no offer?"

"Well, the reason's this. They're obviously interested in what you have to say or else they wouldn't have rushed us in here. If you now turn around and say you don't want to cooperate you can bet they're going to try and squeeze you by not making any offer."

"So what would I get?"

"Four and a half to nine on a plea."

"That's cold man."

"It's at least chilly meaning you should've probably just kept your mouth shut whereby you would've been offered something like two to four. This is a bullshit minor case, you didn't have to introduce this cooperation element. If you don't have the stomach for a trial just take your time like a—"

"I don't want any time at all man. I have to get out of here like right now! I'm sick of this shit man. I'm ready to flip on all their asses. These people ain't done shit for me. It's just that I want to make sure I get out and shit. I have to get out right now man!"

"If the information you provide is good enough I guess that could happen. That said, hear me out a second. Why don't you just forget all this and take—"

"Naw man, I want to talk to them. It's just that these guys I'm going to be talking about are serious shit and I have to like disappear and stuff. This is hardcore shit, man."

"Listen, hold on, because I'm getting my usual sense of impending doom only it's coming quicker than usual."

"What?"

"Now you're talking about putting yourself in danger for what? Even if they gave you a total walk, big deal. It's not like your facing life here where you would actually be getting some bang for your buck."

"*Four and a half to nine?*"

"Listen there are things I can do to get you an offer. It'll just take a little time. Besides what do you think you're contemplating when you say you have to disappear? Information good enough to get you a walk means you would most likely have to testify. You understand what that means? That means you have to remain available, meaning visible. If you take off then you violate your end of the promise having already pled guilty which means you'll eventually be begging for that four and a half to nine that looks so unfair right now."

"I know that man. I'm not talking about skipping out. But what about like witness protection and shit?"

"Witness fucking protection? Are you kidding me? This is the state system. Witness protection means a fake mustache and a move from the Bronx to Brooklyn."

"I have to get out man."

"So pay your bail."

"I can't man. That's twenty-five thousand dollars!"

"What are you talking about?"

"That's what I'm saying man, I'm getting fucked."

"You sure?"

"Yeah man, doesn't it say that on the file?"

"Who knows? Who can read this prick's writing? Taking your word for it, what judge set that ridiculous bail on a B sale?"

"Don't know, some fat guy."

"That narrows it down. Why did he set it?"

"I don't know. My attorney and the D.A. went up there for a bunch conference—"

"Bench."

"— and the judge set that bail."

"Was it the same D.A. you talked to at the precinct?"

"Yeah, they delayed the case until he came."

"Fucker."

"What?"

"Never mind. What do you want to do? They won't guarantee anything until they hear what you have to say but it sounds to me like you'll be getting out."

"What should I do? I trust you man."

"I don't know. This cooperation shit never seems to work out. If this were an A felony with you facing fifteen to life or something I'd be the first to say run with it but this is a case where eventually I can probably get you something reasonable so maybe it's not worth the risk. Of course that's easy for me to say because I'm not serving day one regardless."

"I want to do it man."

"O.K., we'll see what we can do then."

"So what happens now? I've never done this before."

"Read this. In a little while the D.A. and that cop are going to come back in here. They're going to ask you questions about what you know. Some of the questions they already know the answers to and are just checking to make sure you're being straight with them. That agreement you're reading says that whatever you say at this meeting will not be used against you except under certain circumstances."

"Like what circumstances?"

"Like read it. If you testify to something different or if they use what you say here today to develop other information."

"What's this part here?"

"That's where you waive your right to have me present during the meeting."

"Fine but you're going to be here right?"

"No, that's exactly what that means. I'm *not* going to be here."

"Why not?"

"Because they know I have a lot of other clients and they don't want me to be in a position where I might hear something pertaining to one of those clients."

"If you're not going to be here, then forget it. And I mean it too."

"Good."

"O.K. I'll do it. Never mind."

"O.K."

"Now what do I do?"

"Sign it . . . good . . . you ready?"

"Yeah."

"Brilliant. Oh yeah, like I just said, one of the things they claim is that the cop will ask you questions he already knows the answer to so they can judge whether or not you're being straight with them and can be trusted."

"So what should I do?"

"Well if you want to do this then you should tell them the truth so it will work out for you right?"

"Got you."

Except that almost none of those precepts, those truly tried snippets and individually wrapped datum that I thought I *knew* because they'd never previously failed to attach to that fact pattern to the extent that they reflexively exited my mouth promising to reassure with routine, would apply here to DeLeon. And this much should've been clear to me from jump based on the eyes I saw.

Because the four eyes that then entered the room were not dull and surrounded by the usual jaded masticated skin so endemic to that spent system. That skin that practically beseeched the clock to tick with greater speed, skin that announced a vacancy and slouched in its chair to make evening plans at 2:00 p.m. No, the eyes I saw then had causally shed that skin and instead now pierced the room with brilliant beams of light; and cast in this new light was the story of how the world looks to a twenty-year-old and what it becomes to a thirty-five-year-old. How those eyes had once looked upon their owner's chosen arena and could only foresee a future, a life, *as seen on Television*. But how over time they grew weary and diminished. Out of self-defense they did this. The constant assault of mediocrity maybe did this along with the realization that the stupid, highly mediated ideal they were secretly worshiping would in no way be approached. Not by someone who was clearly not a star but at best the supportive best friend or just the girl that establishes the killer's vile m.o.

Then again there *were* those moments. Moments when those two disparate world views seemed to inch towards each other with the promise of sweet confluence. Moments when a person thought that, when all was said and done, maybe they would become that which they had previously envisioned. Or better yet they might see that, in fact, they had been this person all along and had simply been biding their time until this moment arrived eager to sweep them along in its momentum. And it was a sad thing, I thought, to see someone in the throes of what they believed might be one of those moments. Sad but compelling and I wanted mostly to stay and understand the cause.

And I don't think that Assistant District Attorney for the Office of the Special Narcotics Prosecutor, Roger P. Dacter, or Detective Adam D'Alessio of the Manhattan North Narcotics Unit were directing much thought my way because after we all mouthed some pleasantries and I gave them the signed Queen for a Day, they never did ask me to leave but instead Dacter started right in with what seemed like a standard kind of opening to a surprised DeLeon:

"Hello, Mr DeLeon."

"Oh, hello."

"I know you've gone over the *Queen for a Day* with your attorney. Do you feel like you fully understand the terms of that agreement?"

"Yeah."

"Good. It's basically there to protect you and to make you comfortable in discussing matters with us openly. We're not looking to hurt you based on anything you say here today, we're just trying to get an idea of the best way for us to work together on this thing to our mutual benefit."

"I want to get out man because—"

"Well I'm sure your attorney explained to you that we don't make any promises until we hear in detail what it is you have to offer. Now based on what we discussed at the precinct the other day, well we've been able to confirm a lot of what you said that day and in our opinion, and I know Detective D'Alessio agrees with this, it's very useful information and if it all works out you are going to be able to

300

help yourself quite a lot. We wanted to talk to you today to follow up on what we spoke about last week, and this has yet to be decided but we're probably going to want you out on the street working with us and working your time down. After today, if through your attorney we can agree to something, we're going to end up making certain promises to you. First and foremost we're going to promise to do the best of our ability to ensure your safety."

"Can I get a new identity?"

"If we determine that's necessary, yes. Believe me, we understand you're putting yourself at risk by giving us this information. Detective D'Alessio is very familiar with all of the people you will be giving information about and I can assure you that we recognize the highly sensitive nature of this situation. Also you should realize that we have a very vested interest in making sure nothing happens to you in that regard. As I'm sure your attorney will agree, the criminal justice system is a very insular society. What I mean is, well, um. Word travels fast is what I'm saying. People have rabbit ears. I'm sure you know what I'm saying."

"..."

"What I mean is that if something happens to you, if we get a reputation for not being able to protect our informants we're not going to be in the business of getting defendants to cooperate very long. You understand? Good. So that's one of the things we promise you. The other is the one most defendants are principally concerned with and that's leniency with respect to your eventual sentence. If we enter into an agreement, you're ultimately going to be responsible for your sentence in that the more helpful you are to us the better the deal you'll receive. Now all this would be set forth in an agreement much like this one. And that agreement would spell out in detail exactly what is expected of you. Obviously if the time comes where you agree to cooperate with us, you will read that agreement and go over it with your attorney to make sure you wish to enter into it. But

I just wanted to go over briefly, right at the outset, what in general terms would be expected of you so there's no confusion. Again, we're trying to do right by you so we want you to know the ways you can screw this up and end up doing more time than you have to. Believe me we want this to work out as much as you do so I want to make sure you're comfortable with the parameters before we go any further."

"O.K."

"First and foremost you have to be honest with us."

"I know, of course."

"I say that because you may be tempted to try to minimize your involvement in certain activities to protect yourself or even exaggerate your involvement in others in the belief that you will help yourself in that way. I'm here to tell you, don't do that. You'll only hurt yourself. First of all, a lot of the things that we're going to discuss today we already know the answer to. So if we catch you in a lie, we're simply not going to use you. More importantly we may not catch you in a lie now but if we realize later that you lied to us we will terminate our agreement and ask that you be sentenced to a high number. This is absolutely the most important thing you have to realize. Our agreement, if there eventually is one, will be contingent on you providing only truthful information and if necessary testifying truthfully. If you don't live up to that promise then you're not entitled to any break on your sentence. Do you understand?"

"Solutely."

"The reason for that is clear. If you are caught in a lie, and that means by a defense attorney or by anyone else, then your credibility is destroyed and you become useless as a witness. That's why our promise of a sentence is not tied to us achieving any particular result. It's tied to you being truthful. If you do that, and put forth a good faith effort, you will get the promised sentence. Now realize that a good faith effort means meeting with me or the detective whenever

302

you're scheduled to, testifying both in front of the grand jury or at trial if necessary, meeting with us to prepare that testimony, and basically being available to do whatever we deem necessary to the successful prosecution of the individuals we arrest as a result of your information."

"I thought the main thing was the money and the drugs."

"Well, we're going to discuss all that. Certainly this case is unique in that there is the potential for the seizure of well, um, quite a bit of narcotics and money. But we also anticipate that a few people will be arrested hopefully including, but not limited to, Red Bags himself."

"I don't know about testifying against those guys. Will they see my face?"

"Well let's not get ahead of ourselves because that would be a ways down the line. Basically with the cooperation agreement, if we eventually enter into one, if you keep your promise, if you always tell us the truth, and if you appear when we ask you to appear, then we will keep our promise of keeping you safe and giving you a lighter sentence. Do you understand all that?"

"Yes."

"Do you have any questions about anything I've said?"

"No."

"O.K. In that case I'm going to turn you over to the brains of the operation, Detective D'Alessio. As you know from the precinct, he's familiar with that area and the individuals involved so he'll know how to best use your information so that it has the most favorable impact for you. Detective?"

"Hi Ramon."

"Hi."

"Oh here he is. This is my partner, Detective Gans, he's going to sit in as well."

"Hello Ramon, counsel."

"Hey."

"Actually I'm going to step out for a minute and get a soda and maybe a snack. O.K. Adam?"

"Fine. Ramon, the way I want to start is."

"Can I get you something Ramon?"

"Um."

"A soda? You want a soda? A sandwich? What do you want?"

"Soda."

"And what kind of sandwich?"

"No."

"Any kind?"

"No I don't want a sandwich."

"Why not?"

"I'm not hungry."

"It's free you know."

"No thanks."

"O.K. I'll be right back. Anybody else?"

"No." (*pl.*)

"As you know we're looking for information on the operation at 127th."

"What kind?"

"What do you mean?"

"No, I'm talking to Ramon. What kind of soda Ramon?"

"Coke."

"Coke or Pepsi?"

"He said Coke."

"I know but did he say Coke because he thinks that will be easier for me to get or does he really prefer Coke? Because I can probably get Pepsi."

"O.K., Pepsi."

"You like Pepsi better right?"

"Yeah."

"Diet or regular?"

"Regular."

"Caffeine?"

"Huh?"

"You want caffeine with that, because I can get caffeine-free."

"No I hate diet."

"Who said anything about diet?"

"You said caffeine-free Pepsi."

"No I know, but that doesn't mean diet. I can get you regular Pepsi without caffeine."

"Pepsi does that? You sure?"

"Sure they do that."

"I don't think so."

"Yeah, I don't think that's right."

"I think it has to be diet."

"No I'm sure of it, it's the gold can."

"That's the gold can?"

"The gold can's diet."

"That's what I thought."

"No, it means caffeine-free."

"I'll take the gold."

"Great, I'll be right back."

"How do they get the caffeine out?"

"And without making it diet."

"Dude knows his soda."

"Let's not wait for him to return. What I want to do, Ramon, is not ask you a bunch of questions right off the bat but rather have you describe in detail, almost like a resume or whatever, how you came to be involved with Red Bags and his crew selling out of 127th O.K.?"

"O.K."

"Once you're done doing that, we'll get into the specifics and I'll ask you any questions we might have, with an emphasis obviously on the upcoming exchange that's scheduled. Alright?"

"Alright."

"Good. So let's not wait for Gans to come back, let's get started."

DeLeon's lips tightened as he looked around and for a moment I thought he had changed his mind. But then I realized that this was more like a dramatic pause from someone enjoying the minor spotlight and incredibly the stupid pause was working because now even I wanted to hear what he would soon say.

"Well, first of all Red Bags had nothing to do with me getting started," he said. "Nothing at all. Reds is nothing in the scheming of things. He's a piece of shit, understand that. When I met him he took orders from me. I came back here, to this country, because of Escalera. Juan Escalera, he's my cousin, asked me to come back here .from the D.R. to work for him. He was supposedly making mad money over here selling and I wasn't really doing anything good over there so I came. I've known Escalera since I was like five, well he's not really my cousin that's just something we call people we're really tight with and shit. I grew up in this country and didn't move to the D.R. until I was fifteen. That's how come I speak English so good. I'm not like some idiot either, I went to college in Santo Domingo and everything. But over there it's not like here. Here if you go to college and become like a lawyer or doctor or something then you're guaranteed to have some decent money at least. Over there doctors and lawyers drive cabs and work in restaurants washing dishes. Even like Casi here and everything who's like the most best lawyer I know.

"So anyway I came back here and started working for the guy. That was about four years ago and I have to admit that Escalera was good to me at first. He worked mostly out of Queens at the time and I was staying at one of his apartments in Jackson Heights. The Colombians were everywhere in that area. That's Little Colombia basically and they controlled almost all the selling in that area. Anyway, they weren't crazy about E let's put it that way. This was mostly because they knew he wasn't Colombian, but also because of the way we made inroads into their business. O.K. the way it works, I know you know this, is that at the level we were at we have someone getting us our stuff from Santo Domingo whereas the Colombians are obviously getting their stuff from Colombia somewhere and bringing it in through Tijuana. Now we're turning around and selling our stuff at a hundred percent usually to one of these little street guys like Red Bags. Now I don't know how, but E was able to get a great price from his guy in the D.R. So in turn we were able to undercut the Colombians' price and get more and more of the street guys to come to us including even some Colombians. Well this pissed the Colombians off because now they have to either drop their prices or convince us to raise ours. They decided they weren't going to do neither. Instead they kidnap Escalera so they could give him their business proposition: either get the fuck out of Queens or start wearing your tongue through your throat. You know about that right? Well let me say that none of us had ever seen Escalera so freaked out. He was like let's get the hell out of Queens I don't need this shit. Suddenly it was Manhattan all up in his brain and that's where our people are, blazay-blazay, and we needed to get over there and all that.

"So that's what we did and basically I was in charge of setting it all up. I had heard of Red Bags and maybe even met him once or twice. He was famous. Basically you heard about him because he was considered a violent fuck and he was like huge, his physics I mean. Also he was the only black guy you ever saw with fucking red hair and freckles. I thought he was stupid because basically those violent guys are. But I'll say this and I'll give the man credit. For his level of dealer, like those street guys with no foreign connection, he moved more than anyone in Manhattan really. So while some piece-of-shit street guys are buying maybe an eighth a week he would buy at least a kilo maybe two in that time. He could move that much because he controlled a bunch of spots around 127th Street and the reason he controlled all them spots was that people were afraid of him because of shit he had doned in the past. You have to understand that from our end we don't give a fuck how many spots he has or how he got them just like our guy in the D.R. doesn't give a fuck who Red Bags is. All we know is this guy has a lot of spots to constantly re-up and he stays clean, doesn't pick up cases. What that means is if you get him to go with you, you've got a great head start to doing business in Manhattan and shit. And I knew that he was having problems with his guy and was looking for someone else. I also knew from looking into it that his current supplier was low-key and not someone you had to worry would step to us and trip out all violent and shit if we took one of his guys.

"One of the big advantages we had was that we were like new and unknown being we were coming from Queens and whatnot. E was able to portray it like we had stood up to the bad big Colombians and now were looking to branch out to Manhattan when obviously that wasn't the case at all and we were actually running for our lives. I give him credit for that though and we were able to shift to Manhattan and take over Red Bags and a couple other minor guys without any real problems. This was the best time. E knew he wouldn't be where he was if I hadn't had set up the whole Red Bags/Manhattan thing so he gave me a lot of responsibility and I basically answered only to him and this other guy who's no longer around. Everything was peaceful too. On our end anyway. I mean Red Bags is a Blood as you know, he's like a Four Star General and shit. That's where the whole red thing comes from. And the hair too I guess. That and the way he packages his shit obviously. Anyway he's a big Blood so there was always some mad violent shit going on with that between him and other blacks but that didn't really affect us in any way. We stayed out of that shit and all we knew is every Saturday he was at E's buying, like I said, one or two kilos and paying in full and in cash. So because of that it was all good you know what I mean?

"We was making money fist over hand and that should have been the most important thing but fucking E had to be stupid about it. There was this whack girl. O.K. she was amazing. I'm serious man you should have seen this chick. She was all that and then some more let's say. And I took up with her or whatever but the truth is she never had any interest in Escalera from what she tells me. So that was the beef basically and, I don't know, maybe I should have made a better effort to smooth things under but I didn't and things just kept getting worser and worser between us. Next thing I know I'm being knocked down and shit and I'm not making any money. So I admit it. I basically went over his back or behind his head or whatever and went to Santo Domingo to talk to the guy who was getting us our stuff, to see if he would front me if I split from Escalera and whatnot. The truth is I didn't have the money to pull off a move like that so I needed this guy to hook me up. He wouldn't and when it got back to Escalera he flipped out. He got all in my face and shit. Then he also started talking shit about the fact I had used once or twice even though we both knew that was bullshit and he was just using it as an excuse. He was basically saying, well if you're going to use you can't be trusted with anything important and shit and junkies are the ones doing hand to hands on the street so next thing I know he's talking to Red Bags on my behalf and I'm busted down to some bullshit four-hundred-dollar-a-week street seller working for Red Bags, but with supposably special status because I'm supposed to still be with E and whatnot. The whole thing was bullshit because it was really about that girl I'm telling you you should have seen. But the truth was I *had* gone behind his nose so I had to take it like a man. I had made my move and failured you know? The truth also is that even though I had been making sweet money for over a year, I was spending it just as fast as I could get my hands on it, mostly on this girl I'm talking about, and because of that I couldn't really afford to tell E to go to hell and fuck off. I just had to like gargle my pride as they say, kiss his ass, and take whatever crumbs he threw at me.

"So now I'm like the only white guy working for Red and he trains his guys to use crackheads and shit to do a big part of the sales for like a dollar or whatever. I hated that shit but I did it figuring it was just a moment of time before I would be back to where I was before and where I belonged. I knew no-one could a did what I didded for E better than me. As far as Red is concerned he treated me well because everybody knew I was Escalera's cousin or whatever. This went on for like six months or something and I'm doing street sales basically in that entire area of 127th Street until the day I got popped. Some fucking guy, I knew he was a fucking cop. I don't know why I went through with that shit. I'll never forget, I mean what kind of construction worker wears white sneakers? I felt like an idiot. Deep down I think I knew he was a cop but I was so sick of the whole shit I almost didn't care. When I got arrested I kind of figured Escalera would let be-gones be gone and come to my defense. I was broke. I knew the deal. A guy like Red Bags, if one of his guys, someone who works for him, gets arrested, he's not going to lift a finger to help them. I mean nothing, no bail, no paid lawyer, nothing. Everybody knows that. That's just the way it is at that level.

"But at the level that Escalera was at and that I had been at, it's a different story. That shit don't play. When one of those guys gets arrested usually his boss will post the bail and pay for a lawyer. It's known that this is supposed to keep the person who was arrested from snitching on the boss, because of gratitude and also from the influence of the lawyer because that lawyer knows who's paying his bill. I knew it was a little different in this case. First of all, what I just said usually happens on the federal level where the person arrested is charged with something a lot more serious than a dime street sale and is facing a lot more time than I was. Still it wasn't like you guys were offering community service on the shit either. I was a predicate from a gun charge I picked up years ago that had nothing to do with the stuff I'm talking about now. Anyway I'm hearing three to six and shit and I'm freaking out cause I've never done so much as day one anywhere. Here or there. So I got word to E that I was facing real time and whatnot. I expected him to represent and shit, bail me out and get me a lawyer. But he didn't. Nothing. Instead he treated me like some punk-ass bitch bringing people to spots for a dollar. The worsest part is that he like stringed me along and shit. He kept saying he was going to do something but he never did. There was always some excuse. That was it man! I swore Escalera was dead to me from that moment on.

"The only side that was bright in all this, I'm serious the only silver lining that was cloudy, was that I had this man right here as my lawyer. I was even ready to take the three to six believe it or not until I realized this guy meant business. After Casi beat the case at trial and I was released that same night, I flew home and had my first *chuleta* in six months. That's a pork chop and it tasted great, like freedom. The next morning who shows up at my door but fucking Escalera! He was like the guy who never got off the fucking bench and whatnot but was the first to spray champagne in the locker room after the win. All of a sudden all he can say is how he knew all along they had nothing on me and how I was right to take it to trial and all that. I wanted to tell him to go to hell since he had done nothing for me from the time I was arrested. He hadn't even visited me or anything like that. But then I realized he was basically there to kiss my ass. Suddenly I'm his cousin again and I had shown I had true colors and whatnot because I took my case like a man and didn't go snitching on anyone. And I should go back to working with him because he was working on something big and there was going to be a lot of money to be made and he needed my help and so on. I was broke man, I had nothing. What the hell else could I do? Do you know what it's like to not have enough money to buy a token and get on a train? That business was the only thing I knew. So I went back.

"But it was weird. Even though Escalera was kissing my ass like never before, it wasn't like I went back to where I was before our beef. He gave me this long speech and dance about how it would be better if I went back to Red and worked my way back up from the street. I'm like *better for who bitch?* But he was like assuring me. You're my number two man he said but now wasn't a good time for changes. A lot of crazy shit was going on and he needed someone he could trust to be involved in the Red Bags operation, so he could have tabs on what was going on down there. He was working on something huge he said. Something that would make us so much money we wouldn't have to worry about small-timers like Red anymore but for now he didn't want to stir the waves. So now I'm back with Red doing street sales but at the same time I'm also getting a nice cut from Escalera and keeping him informed about what's going down at those spots. I was like a double agent and shit. It was kind of cool actually.

"The reason for all that? Well it took me a little while, but I got to the bottom of it and realized why I was so important to E all of a sudden. Why I was being treated more like a partner than before. What was going on *was* fucked up for sure. Below us and above us it was basically chaostic for sure.

"As far as Red was concerned, his spots were being challenged. He was having Crips trouble. Basically the Crips were trying to extend some of their little, pussy operation into Red's 127th Street spots. I guess their strategy was just to disrupt as much as they could. They were like slashing people who bought or sold red bags of crack at those spots and like trying to instigate a war and shit. This was not the biggest deal in the world, I'm not trying to say that, but it was still something E wanted to keep a close eye on. This was a big difference I noticed after I got out. Escalera seemed to have gotten a lot smarter during the time I was in Rikers. Red Bags was our best customer so anything that was bad for him, anything that disrupted his business, was bad for us. In the worstest scenario case, if Red Bags let those spots go to the Crips for whatever reason he would be moving a lot less shit and buying a lot less from us. The truth is E didn't really have the muscle to back Red Bags up and none of the other dealers on E's level were going to get involved because bottom line is those spots being down for grabs was good for them. This had never been a concern before because of the rep Red Bags had as someone not to be fucked with. That apparently had changed and I guess there was the preconception that Red was weaker. I later found out that this happened because one of Red's most violent guys had been sent upstate for a body and also there was this time where Red backed down from a fight in a park or something. Whatever the reason, all the mayhem down there coincidenced with some crazy shit happening above from us in the D.R. The craziness at 127th had to do with the Bloods and the Crips, in Santo Domingo it was about Fat Felix and Freddy El Flaco.

"Fat Felix was Escalera's guy in the D.R. They was pretty tight I guess and I knew Felix was giving him a good deal on his shit. I should mention that Fat Felix is the guy I went to see when I was exploring whether I could break away from E when our beef first started. He was this really fat guy. His hands looked like balloons with fingers drawn on them. Anyway when he said no to me then told Escalera about it I guess they got closer from that and everything was good for them. Freddy El Flaco was Fat Felix's brother. He was *flaco* obviously. So skinny you could see the bones in his face as if the skin weren't even there. Flaco and me were total boys. He was in the business too but not really. Only like a little involvement, not like his brother who was a big time guy. Flaco and I had been to each other's houses millions of times. I knew his fat brother too but just to like say hi and shit.

"The problem started when Fat Felix was killed outside the post office in Puerto Plata. After he died that whole operation was in disarray. Basically Flaco became the new boss and if you know Flaco you know that's crazy because he don't know much about what's necessary in the biz and all that. To complicate things, it turns out that when Flaco took over he had a ton of some really special product on his hands. What do I mean by special? As it was explained to me, this is new stuff that cuts the edge as they say. Basically there was a guy over there, dead now, who was like a chemist with his own lab and whatnot. Well I don't know if he was really a chemist or not but that's what they called him and shit. Anyway it seems he genetically engineered some crazy mad scientist shit over there for Fat Felix just before they both died. Word is that it's like ten times more potent than the most potent shit to the date. So you can cut this engineered shit a shitload more times than other shit and it's still just as strong if not stronger than that shit, I'm not shitting you. This stuff was going to change everything. Unfortunately, no-one knows how the scientist did it because he brung the secret to his grave so this is like the last stuff of its kind on Earth. Now usually a hundred kilos is worth like thirteen million on the street right? Well a hundred keys of this new stuff is worth like fifty million because of how much more street product you can get out of the same amount. Well Flaco has two hundred keys of the stuff meaning like a hundred million dollars worth. Problem is he has no idea how to pull off such a big deal. So he decided he's just going to get rid of the stuff, get what he can for it, then close the whole operation down and hit the beach. This was no surprise to me because I knew Flaco didn't have the stomach for this business. The problem is a lot of other people knew he didn't have the stomach for it. Security became a big problem for him over there. With Fat Felix it was totally different because nobody fucked with or doubted him. I never heard of him doing anything violent actually but still he got the props. I guess it was like grammar school remember? Nobody was strong or anything so you were just afraid of the fat kid? Same thing with Felix. Flaco didn't have that respect because it looked like the wind could break him in half and shit. The problem this caused is that a lot of guys here, when they heard Flaco was the boss, wouldn't commit to a shipment from him. O.K., when you commit to a shipment you take some of the risk, usually half, if something goes wrong and the shit is seized or whatever. Flaco was having trouble unloading what was a lot of shit. I mean he could, and did, move some of it, little by little, but what he really wanted is to be rid of the whole shit all at once and get out of the racket before he got did like his brother.

"That's how E got involved. Flaco remembered I had gone to see his brother about that deal. He knew he could trust me. He decided he would offer me and E all the stuff he had at a ridiculously good price. How good a price? Well usually to buy 200 keys at our level in New York, not that E could ever afford to buy that much at once but still I know, would cost about five million dollars. Now because this stuff is so pure and revolutionary it should go for like thirty mil at least. Flaco decided to offer it to us, through me, at maybe half that which was a gift. Remember man the stuff is worth at least a hundred mil on the street. Of course not that E would be the one converting it into street money but still, even if he only gets a third of that, it's still the kind of sweetheart deal that could set E up for years. Well Flaco reached out to me here with the offer. The problem is this was during the six months I was in. He was put in touch with Escalera who saw a chance to make a great score that could solve all his problems. It's a little complicated, I'll get into it later, but basically the deal was so good that after it was done E would be in the kind of position, fiscally and muscle-wise, that regardless of how the 127th Street situation turned out, he could dictate the terms of dealing in that area so that only his stuff would be sold there. He saw his opportunity, I give him credit for that, and he proceeded to try and deal with Flaco himself. The problem is that Flaco trusted only me and only involved E because he thought we was tight again. When he started to suspect that there was still little beef between us, he wanted assurances that I was going to be involved. This explained the ass-kissing. For Escalera everything was riding on this. If he could make this deal and get all that shit at that price then he was set. He would be richer and more powerful than ever and could move to another level. On the other hand, if it didn't work out he could be finished. Remember, he had l ost Fat Felix and that good price and he was in danger of 127th blowing up soon. That motherfucker was this close to spending the rest of his life selling weed to N.Y.U. geeks at Washington Square Park!

"He was scared of me and what I might do. He knew I was pissed because he had knocked me down to street level and basically gotten me busted. He was afraid I might tell Flaco to forget him and deal with someone else. So he lied to Flaco and told him I was in jail but that I would be getting out soon and had been advised of everything and was onboard with the whole thing. All bullshit. That's why he didn't bail me out because he figured if I didn't know about the whole Flaco deal I couldn't fuck it up for him. I guess he thought I would eventually go upstate and by then the deal with Flaco would be so far along that it would go through. He didn't count on my man here though and when I got out that threw a big monkey bone into the whole deal. He knew he had to kiss my ass and get me to work closely with him on the Flaco deal. I was pissed but money is the cure of all evil as they say and once I was caught up to speed I realized I was in a position to walk away from this in great shape too. I also realized that I couldn't really do anything about this great offer by myself because I didn't have the money to pull it off. I had this great connection because Flaco was now the man to know but I needed the money Escalera had. Actually, I shouldn't say *the money Escalera had*. The amount and worth of the drugs involved was a lot more than we were used to. So much more that, even at the great price we were paying, E had nowhere near the money needed to make the buy. This is what I mean about Escalera having gotten smarter. He set about getting financing for the deal. It was a U.P.O. I think he called it. An Unidentified Public Offering or something.

"You see, the problem was where do you get the bills? You can't exactly walk into the nearest bank and ask for a loan to buy a huge amount of genetically engineered coke. To cut to the chase, what Escalera eventually did is hook up with this guy Colon who I told you about at the precinct. Colon does the same thing as Escalera but on a bigger level. He moves a lot more shit and has a lot more bread. I don't know much about Colon's operation because E made sure I didn't have too much contact with him, probably out of fear that I would try to squeeze him out of the deal, but basically Colon and Escalera became a partnership. Colon wants the access to this deal that E can give him and E needs the money that Colon can supply. Thank God they both need me because Flaco has said he won't go through with the deal without me being involved.

"Anyway we agreed with Flaco on a price of ten million dollars. Yeah, I know. Serious money but in this case a huge bargain. My guess is that like eighty percent of that money would come from Colon. Even so, at the end of the buy Colon and Flaco would merge the areas they were supplying, get a lot more muscle into their operation, and basically change the way business would be done there. After this deal they would be powerful enough to set it up so that, for example, no crack could be sold at say 128th Street that wasn't bought from them. This way it wouldn't matter which way the war between the Bloods and the Crips ended because either way the winner would have to get their shit from E if they wanted to sell in the area they were fighting over.

"And that was basically the status of the whole thing when I got popped for this shit here. E kept saying I had to keep doing that street shit so Red Bags wouldn't get all suspicious and shit and maybe fuck things up. It was a stupid thing to do. I should have just retired out of that shit. I don't know why I listened to that idiot. Anyway, I must have the worst luck in the world cause I did this hand to hand and here I am. There's more details of course. I don't know how much you want to get into the specifics and whatnot."

"So the deal is still on far as you know?" pleaded D'Alessio who looked like he was about to shine Ramon's shoes.

"It was all set up when this shit happened. Supposably it was going to go down very soon but like I told you if I don't get out soon that shit's going to fall apart because Flaco will not deal if it's not with me, I'm telling you that right now. Right now it's been like seven days since I talked to Flaco and that's not good because this shit was supposed to happen mad soon."

"What has Escalera said since you were arrested?"

"What else? He freaked! He knows the whole thing is on jeopardy. He was going to bail me out the first day and get me a lawyer and shit but I already knew I was going to take his ass down and I don't want to have to deal with one of his lawyers and shit. So I told him I was getting the same lawyer who beat my case before and that he said he was getting me out in a couple of days. If I don't get out soon though I know he'll get suspicious why I don't want a lawyer and shit and he's going to figure it out that I'm cooperating. Also by now I'm sure Flaco is wondering where my ass is and I need to get on that quick to smooth things under and shit. So I'm looking to get out today to make that happen."

"We're certainly going to explore that. We talked about this last time. We need to know exactly when and where this buy is going to happen."

"Am I going to get out?"

"Well you're certainly not going to get out if you don't cooperate with us Ramon."

"You have to tell us where this is going to go down Ramon. Then we can help you out," Gans was back and in between sips of gold soda he'd decided to do some detecting.

"Alright man but I better get out! It's going down a week from Saturday at 368 Riverside Drive between 112th and 113th. At 4:00 a.m. the stuff will be there and so will the money. There. You happy?

318

You putting my life in danger! I better be decompensated for it."

"That's not a spot Ramon."

"Of course not man. That's the whole point. That's just like some guy's private house and shit. You have to understand what's going on in the D.R. with Flaco. That shit can't even be called an operation any more. That's just some free-floating drugs there. Flaco's not a dealer man. He's just some guy who's got a lot of shit on his hands that he's trying to get rid of. There's no infrastructure man! He's getting his shit in through Fatso's old line then some girl, some dumb poor sap mule, is getting a buck fifty to drive the stuff in the trunk of a car into the garage at 368. At the same time E and I will arrive at the garage with the money. The guys at 368 will be under strict orders to only give the keys to the mule's car to me and E personally and only after counting every last dollar. If we're a dollar short, or if we're a minute late, or if someone other than E and me goes to that house, then they are to give the keys right back to the girl, give her another hundred bucks, and tell her to drive it back to where she got it and the whole thing's off. If everything is kosher, we get the keys and drive off with the stuff. The car's a throw-in. That's it man. It's not complicated. If you storm in there at 4:00 a.m. you'll walk out with ten million dollars and shit that's worth ten times that on the street. You'll also pop Escalera and maybe one or two big guys from Santo Domingo. But if I'm not out, none of that is going to happen. Flaco won't even ship the shit from the D.R. if he hasn't heard from me."

"Are you sure about 368 Riverside?"

"Of course I'm sure. That's one of the few places we have with a built-in garage like that so it's perfect."

"It doesn't sound very secure. That's not the way—"

"No kidding. Listen, with undue respect, have you been listening to me at all? Flaco's only using people like me who he can trust. This way of doing things would never fly normally. That's why it's going to be so easy. You guys are going to seize a shitload of shit."

"What about Red Bags?" said A.D.A. Dacter who I had forgotten was in the room.

"What about him? He's shit. He doesn't know anything about this. If he did he'd probably go in there firing guns like the stupid fuck he is."

"What can you tell us about him?"

"What did I just do?"

"Are you familiar with any violent acts by him that you personally observed and can give details about?"

"What the hell's this guy talking about?" DeLeon took an aggrieved look around the room but everyone looked away until he came to my shrug. "Haven't I given you guys enough? You know how much you're going to seize? You're all going to be famous! What does he want to talk about some small-time piece of shit like Red for D'Alessio?"

"I'll tell you what," D'Alessio soothed. "You've just given us a lot of information to think over. I know you want to get out and we want to make sure we don't jeopardize this deal. Why don't Roger and I and Detective Gans go meet with the D.A. supervisor and start exploring our options."

"Can I talk to my attorney?"

"That's perfect. We'll leave you guys in here alone for as long as you need and meanwhile we're going to be discussing all of this. O.K.? We'll be right back. Come on Gans, bring the soda."

"Right if I tell you something you can't tell anyone else unless I want you to? That's the doctor/patient privilege right?"

"Similar but you mean attorney/client right?"

"Yeah, that's it. I don't trust these guys at all man. I'm not giving them shit till I get the fuck out of here."

"Sounds to me like you just gave them quite a bit, no?"

"Look man I know you said tell the truth and shit and I basically did but I lied about where this shit is going to happen."

"Why'd you do that? I mean you either want to cooperate or you don't. If you do then you have to tell them the truth or else how will they benefit and, more importantly, how will you benefit?"

"I know but I don't want them to get what they want then leave me hanging. I don't trust these guys. They're worser than the guys I deal with on the outside."

"Listen I can appreciate your paranoia but what happens when they burst into 368 and find some guy watching *Married With Children* in his underwear? Think you'll get a good deal then?"

"No man, I can't get caught in this lie. This thing really is as quiet as I'm saying. If they do what they're supposed to do and get me out then I'll just tell them the location was changed and give them the real place."

"What if they check out 368 before then?"

"I know 368. If they check it out it will look like I told them basically. It actually could have been the location so it's not that big of a lie."

"What else?"

"It's just like an average house."

"No, what else did you lie about?"

"That's it, everything else is true."

"I don't buy that Ramon."

"It's the truth man!"

"Why wouldn't you just let Escalera bail you out? It would be months before the case went to trial and during that time you could have done the deal with Flaco."

"No man, it's just, nah."

"It's just what? Give me the explanation for why you chose to stay in jail."

"Alright man, you got me there. Remember though, you're not allowed to tell anyone."

"I'll try and remember."

"Alright. Truth is the deal's really far along and it's going to go down whether I get out of here or not. I can't make no twenty-five thousand dollar bail. I have to get the fuck out of here or else I'm not going to get my part of the deal. This is the only way I can figure to get out."

"What are you talking about your cut of the deal? You just said that if they hook you up and you get out you're going to tell the cops the real address."

"I will man!"

"Well at that point there's not going to be any deal right?"

"I don't know."

"No, I'm telling you. There's not going to be any deal. They're going to be there and seize everything. So you're not going to be getting any money right?"

"Oh I see what you mean. No, see, the deal I cut with Escalera is that I get a hundred thousand. I get fifty when we get confirmation the stuff is in the U.S. and another fifty after he's picked up the stuff from the house. Everything I said about me being the key to getting this deal done was true. Believe me, why else would I be getting a hundred thousand for my part knowing what a cheap bastard E is? The lie is that I'm not supposed to be going to the house to pick up the shit and the deal is already set up for ten days from today whether I'm a part of it or not. I know Escalera. If I'm in here when the deal goes down I get nothing, that's why he hasn't offered to get me out."

"I see, unless D'Alessio and these idiots think the deal's only going to be consummated if you're out, in which case you'll be free with your dough and everyone will live unhappily ever after. Of course then you'll have something else to explain besides just the change of location."

"What?"

"Why it is you're not going with Escalera to make the pickup."

"Listen I won't have to explain anything. I'll be out of here and I'll have fifty thousand in my pocket. My days of explaining anything to anyone including those morons Escalera and Red Bags will be over. You understand what I mean?"

"Yes and no. Yes, I think I do but no I'm not interested in discussing it in much detail with you because it would put me in a delicate situation."

"Everybody's going to be happy. I guess I never really thought it would work before, but now I'm like positive it will. They'll get me out. Flaco will get the stuff here. I'll get fifty large and poof. Even if Escalera figures out what happened who cares? He's going to be caught in a house with ten million dollars and ten times that worth of cocaine. By the time he gets out I'll be on Viagra and shit. I told you about Flaco, there's nothing to worry about from there. I'll be out of this fucking mess. Now you see why I had to cooperate. I'm not stupid man, I'm a fucking brainiac. Smart like a fucking fox!"

"What about Red Bags?"

"Now you sound like them man. He's got nothing to do with this at all. From what them guys said at the precinct he's gone have a federal rap soon anyway."

"What do you think about their claim to having confirmed some of what you told them? Do you think someone else is talking?"

"No way," and he pursed his lips in support.

"Because if they have independent information that allows them to catch you in a lie it won't be enough to say you would've eventually told them the truth."

"They don't have shit man. I'm all they have. Everything they know about this comes from me. If I tell them the clouds are made of shit, they'll start expecting it to rain crap!"

"They're not going to let you out until you've pled guilty and left your sentence up in the air. This is how they'll exercise control over you. If you take off or lie or whatever they'll ask the judge to give you a huge number."

"It won't matter. I'll stick around to get my fitty and to make sure them cops get what they want and also to see that E gets what's coming to him for ostrich-sizing me like some piece-of-shit crack-whore. After that they can ask the judge for life and I'll try to care from the beach. Fuck them! I'm going to be opening and closing those little umbrellas they put in your drink. Shit, fitty large over there makes me the brown Bill Gates!"

"You'll be out for about a week and having meetings with these guys. What if they want you to wear a wire?"

"No way. They already talked about that last time and I said there was no way I could do that because Escalera is too paranoid and always frisks anyone he talks to about business."

"Is that true?"

"Sort of."

"Is that it? Any other lies I should know about?"

"There's more money. Yo I'm going to be straight with you B because you're my lawyer and shit. There's going to be more than ten large there for sure."

"What's the reason for that lie exactly?"

"Yo here they come. What do you think of all this? My plan and shit?"

"You've thought about all of this obviously, I hope it works out for you."

"So you think they'll let me out?"

"I do. Maybe they have their doubts about everything you've said I don't know, but right now it looks to me like they have visions of fame and applause heading their way and because of that they're probably not too eager to take an overly critical eye at everything you're telling them. So if your question is whether it'll work in terms of you getting out, my answer is yes I think it will work. I think they'll come in here and say they're going to offer you a deal where you plead guilty and are released with your sentence to be determined at a later date. They'll say that if you do what you're supposed to do, such as testifying whenever they need you, you'll eventually be sentenced to something like a misdemeanor and probation. That's your status from a legal standpoint, which is something I know a lot about. But there's another world at play here, and it's one you know a lot more about than me. Assuming I now have the truth about this whole mess, it seems to me to involve an even greater risk on your part than I previously thought. You're going to be responsible, if you aren't already, for the break-up of a really heavy deal that a lot of people are counting on. In all likelihood, the people involved are going to figure out that you're responsible. After all, they know you've been arrested and no-one else who knows about this deal has been arrested recently right? So fine, Escalera will be in jail but what about Colon? And even if they're both in jail, is everyone who works for them going to be in jail? Flaco's not going to get his money. Will he be happy? Even if he is soft, as you say, can you be sure there won't be some other lunatic over there who might somehow be connected to this deal and who might come after you? Have you thought all those contingencies out thoughtfully enough Ramon? Or are you so focused on getting out of here and your measly fifty-thousand-dollar payday that you're putting your life in danger?"

"My life? What life man? I have nothing. My life is being thrown in and out of here. You want this life?"

"It's the only one you've got."

"No I've thought it all throughout man and I definitely want to do this. It's going to work out for me too, I have a good feeling."

And in short order did the three – D'Alessio, Dacter, and Gans – after pausing to make sure it was O.K., come back into that office to offer precisely what I'd predicted. And even quicker was Ramon's breathless acceptance followed by a consensus that the case would be advanced to the following day in Part 49 for DeLeon to plead guilty in front of McGarrity, be released, and begin his career as de facto law enforcement agent.

Maybe what I should have felt then was dread or whatever comes immediately before it but instead it was relief washing over me, relief because I could finally leave that office where I'd spent my entire morning. But also a strange excitement had dawned in me during this telling and only then was it winding down. I liked hearing DeLeon's story. I had done countless buy and busts without ever thinking of the machinery behind them. Not that it was the most complex or scintillating thing either but still I liked hearing it exposed and laid bare. This wasn't some guy snatching an old lady's chain. There was planning. I liked that. I responded to that.

Of course the planning was shit. I thought about Dane and his ruminations on the nature of crime. What if a truly talented person turned those considerable talents to the successful commission of crime? What did I mean *what if* though? Surely loads of such people were at that very moment devoted to successful criminality and I just never met them because a large part of being successful means not getting caught. DeLeon, and Escalera for that matter, disqualified themselves from that group by risking their share of upwards of ten million dollars by not only doing risky street sales but then getting caught.

I thought all that but mostly I thought about ten million dollars. I thought about each of those dollars all the way back to the office. In the warmth of that office, with Swathmore in front of me all animated and sounding like a Peanuts adult, it was the money I thought of. At my current rate, it would take me a little over two centuries to gross ten million dollars. Patience, it seemed, was all I needed. With ten million dollars I could return all my phone calls and answer all my mail without my heart tightening.

I would never ride the subway again and even if I did it would feel different. I would do very little I didn't want to and lots I did. I would feel joy and relief.

I would have a library.

Well, first a house to put it in, not a glorified closet. And there I would sit, in a crazy regal chair made of fine Corinthian leather smoking a pipe for no good reason while draped in a crushed velvet robe. I would read until my eyes failed and my head overflowed. Any book that sounded even mildly interesting I would buy. And not cheesy paperbacks either, hardcovers only. Leather-bound collector's editions if possible and appropriate. I would read everything of note ever written. Gilgamesh to Grendel, Gibbon and Gass, Goethe and Gödol, Günter Grass and non-G works too. I would devour them all. And when I tired of reading I would swim in my pool, parting the azure blue water like a veloce human knife. Or I would visit the equally lush home of my mother and her others, now swimming in the knowledge that I singly moved them out of their cramped quarters.

I would grow wings and shed the shackles that kept me tethered to this place and day. Thus freed, I would soar up and through the air, above the Earth, to exotic locales where I would be pampered *beyond my wildest dreams*. Venice, Paris, Rome, Sydney, Tokyo, Rio, Athens would be my homes.

No, better yet, I would be homeless. Owning and owing nothing and no-one. I would exist well outside the norms and concerns of society, my only concern my personal advancement and evolution as a human being. As such I would only intake the very finest our tepid species had been able to produce. Only the finest foods in my shell, which shell would be subjected to only the finest medical care. Through my repaired ears and into my melon only the most angelic music would pass, which by now you know would include a healthy dose of live Ludwig. And along with those notes only the finest thoughts, arguments, theories, hypotheses, assessments, deeds, proofs, actions, creeds, kudos, slogans, phrases, sayings, limericks, and memories. O.K. that last one's tricky but beauty in, beauty out, as I would be transformed into a timeless yet evanescent superbeing who didn't know what anything cost.

"Success Casi! Sweet success!"

I recognized Conley's voice but didn't see him. "Remember this date for it is truly a great one! Not this date actually, rather the date success was achieved. Today's just the day I confirmed the findings."

"The hell you talking about?" I said as I entered his jack o' lantern office where he sat alone on his couch waving a newspaper.

"The Human Genome Project, what else?"

"Oh that, right."

"The project has borne the sweetest of fruit my friend who possesses fine feathers and you're one of the few people here who can appreciate the awesome significance of this."

"I know, they've mapped the human genome or whatever."

"Jesus, you say it like you're ordering fries with that. Are you sure you understand exactly what has occurred?"

"I'm quite sure I don't, but I have to get going actually."

"Fine, I'll explain. You were once a single-celled egg. That's right you. A single-celled egg! Did you ever wonder how you were transformed from that into your current condition?"

"Genes?"

"No, genes! Your genes orchestrated the whole thing, cooking you from a raw egg into a fully functional human being. What do you think of that? Genes are the life force! *How* you say? What are genes? Think of genes as little packets of instructions that tell a cell what to do. They're hereditary instructions written in a four-letter code."

"A, G, C, T."

"The letters of this alphabet are A, G, C, and T. Each letter corresponds to one of the chemical constituents of D.N.A. namely Adenine, Guanine, Cytosine, and Thymine. So note that while genes give you life they also serve as a type of prison. By using this language to tell cells how to behave, genes ultimately tell your body what to look like, how impressive to be, what diseases to fall victim to, what infirmities to have and all other sorts of freedom-stultifying limitations.

Scientists looked at this situation and said Fuck You, no way shall human beings be thus treated for long! And so was born the international consortium of scientists known as the Human Genome Project. They set about studying the genome or the entire collection of genes with a goal of identifying and locating all the genes and what they are responsible for. In essence they were looking for the blueprint for making a human. You see genes are made of D.N.A. or rather they are in fact short segments of D.N.A. D.N.A., as you know—"

"Yes."

"– is that long threadlike, double-helix whammy-jammy that's coiled inside our cells. If you look in the cell's nucleus, as I have done, you will see that the D.N.A. is packaged into 23 pairs of chromosomes. If you look inside any of those chromosomes, which I have regrettably not done, you will see up to thousands of genes arranged like beads on a string. Now if we knew what each gene was responsible for we could have all sorts of fun. The problem is there are about a hundred thousand of these slippery suckers and they used to take forever to find and identify. I say used to because we've done it!"

"We?"

"I won't bore you with a detailed description of the amazing machines and computers necessary to do this but realize that through the use of certain genetic markers, such as distinctive pieces of D.N.A. that serve as landmarks, we have created genetic maps that allow us to pinpoint the exact location of a particular gene. So, for example, we now have a detailed map of chromosome 22. We know it contains 545 genes, 298 of which were unknown to science before The Project. Mind you, we haven't gotten to that level of detail with all the chromosomes but we do have a rough map of humanity's genetic makeup and we will relatively soon have a perfectly precise map of the entire genome. I don't have to tell you what that means do I?"

"I suppose *we*, there's that word again, could better treat genetic diseases for one. Although I seem to recall one kid dropping dead from early attempts at gene therapy. I guess you could better identify high risk people for various illnesses and engage in preventative measures. Maybe we could find the gene that causes this guy I know to sometimes double over in ear pain."

"My god! Will you forget medicine? Of course people are talking about those things but they're idiots. I'm thinking big. Because while I'm fascinated by them I also know that genes are evil. They're our enemy because they are fundamentally unjust. They tell us who to be and what to do and there's nothing I hate more than being given orders. But now we've been liberated. Because of the Human Genome Project mankind will soon leapfrog several evolutionary phases. This is how it should be. I'm pissed I was born too soon. I should have been genetically altered in the womb. I want the gene for extreme intelligence not the run-of-the-mill shit I got. I want to look like the guy in the Calvin Klein ad. And throw in the big-dick gene too. We will create superhumans, thereby fulfilling our destiny to replace the God we killed off long ago. I'll even throw you a medical bone. Life spans will triple. We will conquer death, the impediment God threw in our path to keep us in our place. All women will be as beautiful as Greta Garbo, as brilliant as Emily Dickinson, and as charming as Snoopy. Of course all that is secondary to the advances the Project will make possible in the field of human intelligence. We are meant to figure out this whole mess called Life yet we haven't. Intelligence is what's gotten us this far but past intelligence will seem quaint in comparison. Last century belonged to Theoretical Physics but this one and the rest will belong to Biology. All other fields of science will have to defer into a lesser role. This is obvious if you think about it. If advances in biology lead to the creation of a race of superhumans far greater in intellectual ability than the humans that have existed heretofore, then predictable advances in other sciences will follow. This is extremely necessary as we appear to have hit some dead ends. In Physics we still haven't reconciled the very large with the very small. And what of Time? Does it even exist? What in the fuck is it? What about consciousness? What the hell is it? What causes it? With respect to this last question especially, it doesn't just seem a question of needing more effort to answer these questions. Something more radical appears to be required. I agree with this nut Colin McGinn who says that when it comes to the vexing questions about consciousness our brains, as currently constituted, are simply incapable of adequately wrapping themselves around the problem. What is needed are new and improved brains and because of today's news we will soon have them."

"Great, let me know when I can pick mine up."

"Too late for us unfortunately. We'll both be dead. Besides I'm talking about fetal intervention."

"I have to go."

"What's with the face? You concerned about the mother? Don't be. These babies will be formed in artificial wombs. It'll be a transparent encasement so you can stop by and check on its progress, make sure everything's going according to plan. Do you realize the amazing number of uncertainties and potential toxins present in a human uterus? Those kids should get hazard pay."

I was in the hallway heading to my office.

"A natural womb is no place for a baby, Casi!"

In my office I found only Dane, sitting intensely in the chair facing my desk. He was balancing on the back legs of that chair, seesawing back and forth courtesy of his feet on the edge of my desk.

"Make yourself at home," I said.

"Where've you been all day?"

"D.A.'s office, listen to this."

And he did, as I told him all about DeLeon, Escalera, and the others. This was done under guise of the common practice of talking to other attorneys about one of your cases presumably for a fresh perspective or whatever. Thing is Dane didn't really listen. He was looking around the whole time, yawning and stuff, and never saying a word. Normally I would have taken this nonverbal cue and cut short my spiel with minimal embarrassment to both parties. But instead I felt compelled to continue as if ridding myself of unwanted skin. And when finally I was done Dane looked at me as if in pity.

"Your guy's a scumbag."

"Really? I like him."

"No way, take your medicine like a man. Why does he have to go trying to bring everyone else down with him?"

"Normally I'd agree but fuck these other guys for trying to cut him out."

"Listen I didn't get a chance to talk to you and tomorrow's my only good day for the week so I had Rane produced for a counsel visit tomorrow. What's your day look like?"

"Good, I just have DeLeon taking his plea and getting out. But I can't work on Rane anyway. Been meaning to tell you, I'm too busy."

"Nonsense, I'll see you tomorrow."

"Maybe," I said. Dane left.

I sat there. It was getting dark out. My window fought against the wind. I lost at least an object a day and that day I'd lost my hat. I didn't want to go out unarmed into that wind but I wanted dearly to be home and couldn't have one without the other.

Outside I did an almost-comic double take at the fountain near City Hall, the one just off PEOPLE WITH A.I.D.S. PLAZA. It was true. That really was water coursing through the fountain's veins and emerging limply out of its open spouts. And that really was a battered guy under an uneven afro stepping out of the fountain and drying his bare chest and arms with newspaper. He would know the answer I thought. What happens to him and his pals when their newspaper blankets fail?

So I got right up to him and gave him a ten. I felt like the guy in the movies who pays the hooker for her time only he doesn't want sex or anything he just wants to know if she's seen *this girl.* Well he was a nice enough guy and all, and he almost sprained my finger snapping up the ten, but he showed little interest in my halting question.

"God bless you! God bless you my man!" he answered.

While he was saying this some other guy was running my way. He had been a witness and wanted to know if I could repeat my performance, this time with him as the star. The original guy rotated the bill every which way in hands covered with grey cracks. I simultaneously watched this and fished in my wallet for more. But it was empty. My pockets too. I had given him my last cent. He split without answering. Then the new guy looked at my empty hands and split as well.

I looked in my bag for a token or a Metrocard. Anything.
Nothing.

I couldn't go to an A.T.M. because I had a negative number there. I did have credit cards aplenty but I had never activated that precious cash advance feature. You couldn't use plastic to take a cab. Or the subway. Or a car service. This was medieval goddamnit. The only thing I could afford was my legs and I was quickly losing feeling in them. What if I asked one of the many people bouncing about to spot me a couple of bucks? What if I used plastic to buy a lavish dinner with a disproportionately high tip then asked the waiter to spot me? What if I begged the token clerk to let me through? What if I jumped the turnstile like countless former clients? Yes, that was it, I would commit a crime and risk my law license to get out of the cold. Or what if I just shut up, stopped huddling in that icy stone corner, and started walking my indigent ass home?

How could God do this to me after all I've done for him?
– Louis XIV

Chapter 10

Then it got dark, so dark so quickly that all I could think was *when did it get so dark?* That and *whatever happened to dusk, wasn't dusk required anymore?* Not to say there was a perfect absence of light, because it was undeniably a lit bridge, but what light did exist was dim and deferred to the dark. No white light, only orangeish apologetic light that never really infringed on the night's black. And I moved through this frigid, windy black swiftly at first but then slowly and with resignation. Resignation because there was no protection, not from the sides and surely not from above.

And the people who moved in the light while it was still white, the ones who snapped pictures and shot video in strict compliance with a script written by and for the species, those people disappeared with the sun. No, only native freaks came out into that kind of black and that night they were everywhere. I tried to keep my eyes from them and glued to the boardwalk floor, where the occasional car sped in and out of my sightline through the windows of the gaps.

You wouldn't know it to view the situation from afar but crossing the bridge did not involve traversing flat ground. Going from Manhattan to Brooklyn meant you had to climb at first, the Earth rising to catch your foot more suddenly with each halting step and a seeming magnetic pull at your back. You overcame this pull and ascended in this way until you leveled off. And the only thing to do then, because you couldn't turn back, was to begin your descent. My descent that night was a cluttered one. The freaks, the ones I had tried to avoid seeing, swirled about me more and more insistently until I had to look up and face them.

There was a chimp. Or monkey, can't really tell the difference. Or even if there is one. Well I could at one time and quite definitively, at least until Alana caused me to start doubting myself; so let's just say chimp. No ordinary chimp either. This ninety-eight-percent-human had joined hands with *the* Uncle Sam. O.K. not *the* but just a guy in a costume. Only this guy had no business being in an Uncle Sam costume because in place of being tall and gangly he was short and fat and very both. He was more like an Uncle Sam bowling ball rolling towards me with his attached friend. His friend – The Chimp – was not in costume. He was naked. Although I'm not sure the word *naked* is appropriately used here given that the average chimp rarely dresses up. He did have a hat. The chimp I mean. Well of course Uncle Sam did as well. That crazy top hat that nearly doubled his height. But back to the chimp's hat. I liked that damn hat quite a bit. Not so much the hat, which was pretty run-of-the-mill far as these things go. It's just that I dig it when like a chimp wears a hat and things of that sort. Of course, this wasn't *like* a chimp wearing a hat, this was an actual fucking chimp wearing a crazy chimp hat that he kept adjusting with his free chimpy left paw. And it took me a while to figure out why, despite my general predilection, this particular chimp and his hat weren't so great but were instead bugging me a little. The problem was the chimp's hat reminded me of my hat. The one I had just lost and whose heat-trapping qualities I was in dire need of at that very moment. I loved that hat. But I didn't know why the chimp's hat reminded me of it since all I could remember about my hat was that it was black. And it had ear flaps. Maybe. It was cool. I mean warm. Though not as warm as the hat the old man wore when I spied him later that night as I finally reached my shelter.

And this was not just any old man who wore that hat. This was the

335

old-timer who a couple nights earlier had tried to hug me to his bare chest. At least I thought, and maybe wanted to think, it was him. Actually I was a hundred percent sure of it. But I had my doubts. Because now instead of bareboned and shivering he wore a serious Russian papakha with matching fur coat. He looked great in that get-up. But old. Ancient. He was taller too. And fatter. In fact, except for the fact that he was the same old man who had tried to hug me, there was nothing, no physical or other similarity, tying this person to that one. Where did he get the coat and hat? And why didn't *that* hat remind me of my lost hat and make me long as well?

Instead the only envy I felt then was directed towards that chimp's hat. So much so that I seriously considered swiping it off the chimp's head when they passed, since he had all that fur to keep him warm. But I didn't think it would fit anyway because I have like this real fat melon where even nonchimp hats rarely fit nicely. More disconcerting was the fact that Uncle Sam and the chimp seemed to be on a direct collision course with me and did not seem inclined, in the slightest, to alter their course to avoid such a collision. I anticipated one of those moments where the two opposing parties engage in a little side-to-side dance until finally one of them just stops while the other sidesteps and walks by. But it never happened.

Although something similar did happen later that night with Angus, right after I ran away from the old man in fur. I had run away from the old man in the fur coat and hat as fast as I possibly could, which wasn't very fast at all, with the blue air feeling like tiny razor blades going down the inside of my neck, and I continued to run even once I got inside. And it was while I was running up the stairs to the second floor that I almost ran into Angus, who must have at that very moment just jumped out of his apartment and begun running down those same stairs.

"Oh Casi," he said panting. "Looks like we're both in a hurry."

"What's up?"

"Want to come with me to meet the new neighbor?" he said as he ran down after I had stepped aside.

"What neighbor?" I called out to him. Silence was his response before I heard the downstairs door close.

Which was the same reaction I got from Alana on the phone when I told her what the chimp had done.

"Hello? You still there?" I said.

"Yeah, of course."

"You have no reaction to that."

"I just don't know what to make of it. I can't imagine what would possess a monkey to do that."

"Not a monkey, chimp."

"No difference."

"Of course there is."

"Would you feel better if it was a monkey?"

"No."

"Then there's no difference."

Which was disappointing because I'd been hoping for insight. So much so that I saved the chimp story for Alana and did not relay it to Louie and Alyona who were in their apartment when I went in and found out we had a new neighbor.

"Carlos Sanchez," said Alyona. "He's a professional dancer, teaches the Mambo."

"Please don't play along Alyona," said Louie. "It scares me a bit."

"What are you guys talking about? Since when do you care about neighbors?"

"See what I mean? Cut the shit, there is no new neighbor. Ralph has a new neighbor not us. I mean Ralph Kramden the character on Television, who is most definitely not a real person, was in an episode of a show on Television called The Honeymooners where a Mambo dancer named Carlos Sanchez, also not a real person, moved into the building and caused all sorts of trouble by being really attentive towards the wives."

"Oh yeah, I remember that one. But what does that have to do with Angus firing out of here like a human cannonball?"

"He went out to meet Sanchez," said Alyona.

"He's not still using that Casio Carousel is he?"

"Yes," they said in unison.

"That reminds me. Did fucking Angus call a tip in to the Tula hotline?" I wondered aloud.

It was a question that remained unanswered even days later when the Tula mystery had been solved to everyone's satisfaction but had in the process given birth to an even greater mystery.

"What do you mean two seven-year-olds?" said Liszt the same day I would later scream at him and punch a hole in his wall. But Debi had the definitive proof in her hand in the form of a *New York Post* that proclaimed **BABY FACED KILLERS!** Two seven-year-old boys, still bathing in their original sin, had snatched baby Tula from her stroller in front of *Thank God It's Not Monday's*. That much was beyond dispute and it was undisputed because of the Video Vigilantes. The area in midtown that contained the relevant *T.G.I.N.M.'s* was one of the original Vigilante Flashpoints and as such was inundated with cameras long before the Vigilantes even entered the City's consciousness. One of those cameras had witnessed the whole thing and would be available to testify if need be.

This pleased Mayor Toad, who at the press conference held for the heroic camera had one arm around the head vigilante and the other around his grinning lieutenant. Toad was there to announce that, thanks to the Video Vigilantes, seven-year-olds operating within the *lenticular penumbras of influence* were now on notice that their misdeeds would be captured on everlasting videotape and ultimately broadcast with the cooperation of Television. The eyes of the camera were all-seeing and possessed with complete veracity. Here, the eyes

338

had seen the two boys lift that baby like a doll and run.

What happened next was still anybody's guess but the end result was not. The seven-year-olds, with parents in tow, had led police to Tula's lifeless body. In a box. In the boiler room of one of the kid's basement. That was it. You could shut down the 1-800 hotline too because there wasn't anyone who could get on the other end of the phone and explain this.

The case would have nothing to do with us since given the age of the defendants it would undoubtedly be some kind of Family Court deal. But I knew eventually I would have to see that putrid video. I hadn't even gotten the Rane video out from inside my skull yet. Maybe meeting Rane would do it, but I had yet to do so because he failed to appear for his counsel visit days earlier when Dane and I kept calling the Department of Correction counsel area at 100 Centre Street in the futile hope that he had been produced. Until finally Dane grew suspicious of the C.O. on the other end of the phone, went over in person to see for himself, verified that Rane wasn't there, and ended up meeting with DeLeon instead.

"Come again," I said when he told me.

"Yeah, he was there."

"On the twelfth floor?"

"Yeah."

"Why?"

"I guess he was waiting to be released after taking the plea in 49."

"What do you mean you met with him?"

"I heard his name. Someone said *Ramon DeLeon* and a bell went off in my head so I just talked to him a little. I told him I was an attorney in your office and was familiar with his case. He said he wanted to talk to me so I had him brought into the counsel room and met with him there."

"You talked to a client of mine about his case?"

"Yeah. Take it easy, he's basically a client of mine as well."

"About his case?"

"Of course, what else?"

"Why?"

"I don't know, just curious I guess. I had taken that whole annoying trip up there for nothing and you have to admit his story is pretty interesting. It was like entertainment."

"Don't do that again please. If you do that or something similar again, I shall be forced to kill you."

"Be glad I did. I found out a lot of interesting stuff about this deal that's going down and it's given me an idea."

"What are we going to do about Rane?"

"How's about a week from today?"

"Maybe."

"I'll try that then."

And the missed Rane counsel visit was one of the many desperate excuses I attempted to deploy early the next day to avoid getting sent out by Judge Bartee on Juan Hurtado. I wanted Hurtado to take a plea because he had no chance. He wouldn't take the 2 to 4 being offered and was undeterred by the prospect of getting the maximum 3½ to 7 after trial. Failing a plea, I wanted an adjournment to delay my grim task as long as possible. I was destined to get neither.

Which was the reason I was in Conley's office when Debi came in with the Tula papers but was thankfully not included in any of the discussion as I was *on trial* and therefore ineligible for messing with. What I was looking for in that office was a book I had on good authority was there. And I was tearing Conley's office apart looking for it because it represented a last hope at salvation for me and Hurtado. In that book there was supposed to be a lovely paragraph or so. Somewhere in that paragraph there should be a sentence or a string of words in which a judge, a judge known for his commentaries on criminal law and practice, would agree with the premise of the crazy defense I had been concocting since openings and which I

340

would soon be committing to wholeheartedly in my summation. The words had to be in the book I couldn't find because Toomberg said they were and that was amply good enough for me.

Toomberg told me the words and the book were in Conley's office when he came into my office a day earlier to ask if I was serious about not working on the Alabama death penalty case with him. I had called Toomberg at home, and told him I categorically refused to work on Jalen Kingg's case, the same night Uncle Sam and the chimp refused to get out of my way on the Brooklyn Bridge.

We had approached from opposite ends and were now about four feet apart with me in the middle of Sammy and the chimp. Only now instead of the dance I'd expected Uncle Sam and the chimp simply raised their left and right hands respectively creating a little London Bridge-type scenario. I ducked my head to walk under and through the arch leaving its owners behind.

I didn't tell Toomberg about the chimp when I called him that night even though Alana had already proved unhelpful. I didn't tell him how, after taking a few more steps on the bridge, I looked back and saw that Uncle Sam and the chimp had reversed course and were now following me. I did tell Toomberg that I wanted no part of Jalen Kingg. I didn't want to meet him, didn't want to learn about his life or look at that picture of him in the file anymore or try to prevent this regicide or any of that because what the hell is the meaning of this Toomberg? Is this a joke? What kind of volunteer situation is this? Specifically? Where should I start? First of all, isn't it reasonable of me to assume, given the fact that we are trial lawyers and not death penalty appellate experts or whatever, that we are responsible for like an early step in this guy's long, drawn-out appellate process and not his desperate last gasp? What the hell is the meaning of this deal whereby our papers are the only thing between Kingg and an electrode hat? And this file I've just reviewed in my less-than-ideal condition is littered with the word *denied* and are

341

we just supposed to add the final one? He doesn't need a lawyer, he needs an undertaker. Do I look like a stolid undertaker?

After continuing in that vein a bit, I told Toomberg the true reason I couldn't work on Kingg's case. The reason was the rainbow candy. The rainbow candy that Jalen's mom used to *make* for him. The rainbow candy made the whole notion of me working on Kingg's case a pure impossibility. It was no longer a matter of choice or free will once the candy appeared. We were dealing with a genetic makeup, namely mine, that was simply incapable of dealing with matters of this nature. Toomberg understood immediately.

"I haven't the slightest idea what you're talking about," he said sleepily.

"The candy Toom. The fucking candy!"

"What candy?"

"Didn't you read that letter he wrote his attorney along the way?"

"I don't know. I know I read everything. Remind me if you could."

"In one of the letters he writes down what he's going to request as his last meal. Do you remember that?"

"I do, what about it?"

"For dessert he said he wants the rainbow candy his mom used to make for him. Did you see that part Toomie? Did you see that?"

"I don't—"

"He says he knows his mom is no longer around to make it but that he's seen the same candy in the stores."

"O.K."

"Christ Toom! What in the world? This guy's I.Q. is 63. Fucking six three!"

"I know but I would think that would make you want to work on his appeal even more. There's no way we as a society should be executing people like Kingg. Not to mention the fact that his trial lawyer failed to adequately convey this fact to the jury during the penalty phase."

"All that is beside the point my large-brained friend. My whole life

342

I can't deal with this type of thing you understand? You might as well ask me to breathe underwater. I can't do it."

"I think I understand. I'll deal with that aspect of the case. There's plenty more to be done."

"I don't think you do understand Toom. Do you really *feel* what it means for this guy to be asking for rainbow candy? They're fucking Skittles. That's what he's talking about."

"I don't know much about candy."

"Do you know where he's getting the goddamn rainbow description from? The fucking commercial! You've heard it right? *Taste the rainbow*! Those fucking bastards."

"I don't own Television."

"Jalen Kingg did. You can bet your ass on that. His mom did. And somewhere along the line she took to calling the Skittles she gave her son *rainbow candy*. And she told him she had made it special for him. And Jalen believed her because it was his mom and she was all he had. It brought them comfort. This woman and the son she had at fourteen in their one-bedroom dump. And far away in goddamn L.A. or Madison Avenue is the prick who decided that Skittles would sell more quickly if they promised Jalens they would *taste the fucking rainbow* which is like a complete fucking impossibility and even if it wasn't who said a rainbow would even taste good you know? That's the reason I can't work on this case. You want me thinking like this the whole time? Did you see what his face looked like in that picture? You see the eyes? Do you realize I'm going to dream about this?"

"Don't make any rash decisions. Sleep on it."

Advice I ignored that night and the following two as well. In fact, I didn't really sleep until I got a verdict in the Hurtado case. Then I collapsed the minute I hit my bed and had a horrible nightmare involving Skittles.

In the nightmare, Uncle Sam and the chimp were referred to but never actually showed their faces. In real life, they followed me.

343

I think following me was Uncle Sam's idea and not the chimp's. Because whereas before they walked more or less side by side, now it was clearly Uncle Sam leading the way with the chimp following slightly behind in what looked like a malformed race.

"There's not going to be a winner," Debi said. "That much is clear."

"I agree," said Liszt as he consulted the big chart on Conley's wall.

"There has to be a winner," said contrarian Conley. "Just pick whoever got closest."

"There's nothing close to this," she said.

"This is bad," he said.

"What do you mean? A lot of people predicted she'd be dead," said Conley.

"Not like this," she countered.

"Not even close," Liszt added.

Which was what Alana said the night I spoke to her and she had no reaction to the chimp disclosure. I asked her how much of the money she needed she had come up with.

"Not even close," she said, and I looked around in my apartment at strewn letters from collection agencies and feeble pay stubs and felt shame. Later I would feel shame again when I stood up and started picking a jury in *People of the State of New York* vs. *Juan Hurtado*. I was woefully unprepared and it didn't matter a bit. I was so unprepared because I knew, as certainly as I could know anything, that there was nobody crazy enough to go to trial on a case this bad. When confronted with the unimpeachable logic of 2 to 4 years in prison being preferable to 3½ to 7, any reasonably intelligent person would take the 2 to 4.

"I can't take it," said Hurtado.

When explained to them in a dispassionate and methodical manner any and every one would understand the futility of trying to win such a dead case. Especially when that person's attorney virtually guarantees said person the case will be lost.

"I have faith in you. I think you'll win," he said.

And of course even were somebody crazy enough to take it this far, once they saw that we were sent to Judge Arronaugh, saw how hostile she was to everything we attempted in defense, heard her all but promise the max, then heard her call for a jury pool and shortly thereafter heard those prospective jurors congealing outside the walls of the courtroom ready to come in and convict, certainly at that point any person would grasp at their last chance to end it all with a nice 2 to 4. This would be true even of a loony Vietnam vet with a tattoo necklace.

"I'm going all the way," he said. And he did. "But I'll take 1½ to 3," he added.

Good news because no D.A. would willingly conduct a trial on a silly case like this over six months. They would offer the 1½ to 3 and move on with their lives.

"Can't do it," said prick McSlappahan.

We must have picked a jury in record time, at least since the advent of the shot clock.

"How do you like your jury?" Toomberg wondered once they were picked.

"What's to like," I said. "But my problem isn't going to be the jury, it's the fact that the people of this state, excluding me and Hurtado, have an overwhelming case."

"It sure does sound that way. What can you do if your client won't plead you know? At least when you lose—"

"Hold it right there bub. Who said anything about losing? What are you trying to do? Jinx me?" I could afford to talk all tough even though the case was so dead because of my secret weapon, which I was about to unveil. The weapon had come to me when I was staring at the relevant statutes while Arronaugh prattled on to me and the D.A. about the rules of *her* courtroom. What an annoying piece of shit. But the brilliance of it, my God. I was more than an attorney. I was an almost mythological entity whose wings would never melt no matter how close I flew to the sun. I couldn't wait to disclose my brilliant defense to anyone who would listen. Just as I predicted, the response was overwhelmingly positive.

"Hate it," said Swathmore.

"It's a loser," said Debi. "And I don't think it's an adequate or even correct statement of the law."

"This guy needs to take a plea," said Gold. "Why doesn't he? Do you want me to talk to him?"

I did. Somebody needed to talk some sense into this chump before we went down faster than two naked skydivers. They were right. My brilliant defense was a sham. Everybody knew I was screwed.

Except Toomie. Sweet, angelic Toomberg with his convex-lensed glasses. I had forbidden him from talking to me about Kingg until Hurtado was done. On Hurtado I was all ears, and he struck the only somewhat optimistic note of the day when he told me that I just might be on to something because he seemed to recall reading something on the issue in a random practice commentary written by an esteemed judge. In the end he agreed to help me out in exchange for my promise to later reconsider on Kingg. He couldn't be in court to watch the trial but, since I had forged Swathmore's signature on a minutes order form and was getting daily copy, the plan was that Toomberg would review the transcripts as I got them and offer priceless insights. The only thing we had done that day besides pick a jury was open:

SUPREME COURT OF THE STATE OF NEW YORK

COUNTY OF NEW YORK:

CRIMINAL TERM: PART 23

THE PEOPLE OF THE STATE OF NEW YORK,   Ind. No. 2582/xx

– against –

JUAN HURTADO,

Defendant.

TRIAL

111 Centre Street

New York,

New York

BEFORE : HONORABLE POLENTA DWADNUM ARRONAUGH,

Justice.

APPEARANCES :

ROBERT M. MORGENTHAU, ESQ.

DISTRICT ATTORNEY, NEW YORK COUNTY

BY: SEAN McSLAPPAHAN, ESQ.

Assistant District Attorney

CASI_____ , ESQ.

Attorney for Defendant

DIANE S. SALON

Official Court Reporter

THE CLERK: Case on trial, People of the State of New York against Juan Hurtado. The defendant, his defense attorney, the District Attorney and the sworn jurors are all present.

THE COURT: Good afternoon, ladies and gentlemen. We have now completed jury selection. As we indicated to you during voir dire, we anticipate that this will be a very brief trial. I can now be more specific and tell you that we expect that you will hear from all of the witnesses in this case tomorrow morning, with you receiving the case to begin your deliberations probably some time around lunchtime tomorrow.

It's too late in the day now to hear any witnesses since we usually make every effort to end court by five. There is time, however, for you to hear opening statements.

First, a couple of things about opening statements. Opening statements are not evidence. They are a rendition of what the attorney expects the evidence to show. Think of them as the table of contents in the beginning of a book or the previews of a movie.

Now as we discussed often during voir dire, the burden of proof in this case, and indeed in all criminal cases in this country, rests solely on the prosecutor. As a result he is required by law to give an opening statement in which he details what he expects to prove through the evidence presented. Conversely, the defendant and his attorney are not required to prove anything so the defense attorney is not required to give an opening statement although he may choose to do so if he wishes.

That said I now turn you over to Mr McNappashaw for his opening statement. Mr McNappashaw.

MR McNAPPASHAW: Slap a hand.

THE COURT: Excuse me.

MR SLAPAHAND: Slap a hand.

THE COURT: Slap it yourself, let's move on.

348

MR SLAPAHAND: It's McSlappahan Your Honor with all due respect and obsequiousness.

THE COURT: I'm sorry. Go ahead Mr McSlappashee.

MR MCSLAPPASHEE: Thank you. May it please the court, ladies and gentlemen of the jury, defense counsel, Mr Hurtado. This case is about crass opportunism. It's about one man who works very hard and another who prefers to steal for a living.

DEFENSE COUNSEL: Objection.

THE COURT: Overruled.

MR MCSLAPPASHEE: On April 27th of last year, that man seated over there, Juan Hurtado, broke into a van belonging to the Salieri Construction and Remodeling Company. As a result, the grand jury in this case has handed down an indictment charging the defendant with the crime of Burglary in the Third Degree.

DEFENSE COUNSEL: Objection.

THE COURT: Overruled.

MR MCSLAPPASHEE: The way he did it that day was simple.

DEFENSE COUNSEL: Objection.

THE COURT: Overruled. But do confine yourself to what the evidence will show Mr Sharpenhan.

MR SHARPENHAN: You will hear from Mr Jerry Bolo. Mr Bolo will testify that he has worked for the Salieri Construction Company for over nine years. The company does remodeling and restorations and owns a van that it uses for those purposes. Mr Bolo will testify that the van is used for purely commercial purposes such as transporting materials and tools to and from work sites. He will further testify further that at approximately 11:30 p.m. on the night of April 27 of last year he had parked the van outside of a church on 35th Street. In New York. He will testify about New York. Mr Bolo will testify that 35th Street is in the county and state of New York. The 35th Street where this occurred is anyway. You will hear Mr Bolo say that he parked the van outside of that church, which is on

35th Street inside the city and state of New York. The county and state of New York. He parked that van there because he was doing work on the church inside. The inside of the church. He will testify that he was doing this work for nuns. Nuns were in that church.

DEFENSE COUNSEL: Objection.

THE COURT: Overruled. Continue Mr McSlappahan.

MR McSLAPPAHAN: Mr Bolo will testify that during the course of doing work on that church, he went out to his van to retrieve a tool that he needed. He will testify that as he neared that van he noticed that a window had been broken and that the side door had been opened. Imagine for a moment the fear that he must have felt.

DEFENSE COUNSEL: Objection.

THE COURT: Overruled.

MR McSLAPPAHAN: He will testify that he approached the van, looked inside, and saw this defendant inside the van rummaging through its contents. At that point he called the police and he and the defendant waited there until Officer Leary arrived to place the defendant under arrest.

You will hear from Police Officer Parker Leary. Officer Leary will testify that on the night of April 27th he was working an 11:15 p.m. to 7:50 a.m. tour when he received a radio run indicating that someone had broken into a van on 35th Street in the county and state of New York.

DEFENSE COUNSEL: Objection.

THE COURT: Overruled.

MR McSLAPPAHAN: Officer Leary will testify that when he arrived at that location, Mr Bolo and the defendant were there. He will testify that after Mr Bolo had told him what had happened, he placed Mr Hurtado under arrest. Prior to arresting Hurtado, however, he searched him. In the course of that search, he found a screwdriver with a sharpened point. Officer Leary will further testify that such a screwdriver is commonly used to commit burglary related offenses.

DEFENSE COUNSEL: Objection.

THE COURT: Overruled.

MR McSLAPPAHAN: At the end, the Court will instruct you on the law. That is solely the province of the Court and I am in no position to tell you what the law is. Sufficient to say, that the law is clear that if this van is used for commercial purposes then breaking into it is a Burglary in the Third Degree.

DEFENSE COUNSEL: Objection.

THE COURT: Overruled.

MR McSLAPPAHAN: The law says that this is a Burglary in the Third Degree.

DEFENSE COUNSEL: Objection.

THE COURT: Overruled.

MR McSLAPPAHAN: This was a Burglary in the Third Degree.

DEFENSE COUNSEL: Objection.

THE COURT: Overruled.

MR McSLAPPAHAN: At the end of the case I will be asking you to return the only verdict consistent with the evidence, which is not guilty to the only count in the indictment Burglary in the Third Degree. Withdrawn, I misspoke. I will be asking you to return a verdict of guilty to the indictment. To the only count in the indictment of Burglary. Burglary in the Third Degree, which is the only count in the indictment. Thank you.

THE COURT: Thank you Mr McShanahan. Counsel will you be making an opening statement?

DEFENSE COUNSEL: I will but can we approach first?

THE COURT: No.

DEFENSE COUNSEL: Very well, though slightly bizarre. A short while ago every member of this jury stood up, raised their right hand, and took an oath. Like most oaths, what you did can essentially be viewed as a promise. Boiling it down even further what you promised to do was uphold and apply the law as it is explained to you. The law as it applies to hearing a case, to deliberating on a case, and most importantly here, the law as it relates to the criminal statute the defendant is accused of violating.

Why is this kind of oath necessary? Maybe the answer is this. I think that jurors, like all human beings entering a novel situation, enter jury service with the kind of preconceptions that may even amount to a predisposition. One of those is surely the tendency to view guilt or innocence as blanket, either/or concepts not susceptible to degrees or shades of variation. Of course our criminal justice system is, to some extent, founded on the notion of varying levels of culpability as evidenced by the fact that crimes come in differing degrees such as the Third Degree Burglary alleged here.

As we discussed during voir dire, those crimes and their respective degrees are themselves defined in statutes that break the crime down into separate, necessary elements, each of which must be proven beyond a reasonable doubt by the prosecutor if there is to be a conviction.

Why do I mention all of that in an opening statement? Simply because it is precisely that kind of subtle analysis which will be required of you in this case. As I said repeatedly during voir dire, this will not be a dramatic case of the kind you might see on Perry Mason or Matlock. You will not be hearing from the defendant and there will be no surprise witnesses emerging from the last row of the courtroom. Moreover, your primary task will not be to decide what happened on the night of April 27th. Your true obligation is to hold the prosecution to their burden of proof. Specifically, to hold them to the extremely stringent yet highly appropriate standard of proof that is proof beyond all reasonable doubt. And you'll be asked to steadfastly apply that standard to every single element of the crime charged in this indictment. Once you do that you'll see this indictment for what it is, a worthless piece of paper because the D.A. cannot legally prove beyond a reasonable doubt that the defendant committed the crime it alleges. In short, you'll agree with me that the prosecution greatly overreached in charging Mr Hurtado with the very serious crime of Burglary in the Third Degree where the evidence makes out a Petit Larceny at best. In only that way can you properly fulfill the oath you took, a critical oath that often serves as primary protection for the lone individual who finds the full powers of the state arrayed against him. Thank you.

THE COURT: Thank you counsels. As I said ladies and gentlemen that is going to be all for today We have a relatively busy day scheduled for tomorrow, during which I anticipate that you will hear all of the testimony in the case and begin your deliberations. Because of that I'm going to ask that you all be here at 9:30 sharp tomorrow morning. Please remember not to enter the courtroom until you are escorted in by a court officer. Also remember my instructions to you. You have not heard any evidence in this case yet. You are not to discuss this case with any of your fellow jurors or with anyone else for that matter. You are not to form any opinions on this case based on what has transpired here today, namely, jury selection and opening statements. You are not to visit the scene where this incident occurred. I don't anticipate any such coverage, but should there be any, you must avoid any exposure to media coverage of this case. Lastly, I forgot to mention this earlier. During the course of this trial, you may come into contact with some of the parties involved in this litigation, for instance, in the hallways or the elevators. By parties I am referring to the assistant district attorney, Mr McShaughnessy, defense counsel, or even the defendant Richard Hurtado. I instruct you now that should such contact occur they will not speak to you even to say hello. Do not be insulted by that as they are simply following my instruction not to communicate with any of the jurors. As you might expect, this is insisted upon mainly to avoid even the appearance of impropriety.

With that last admonition, I thank you for your service today and we'll see you bright and early tomorrow morning. Thank you.

(Whereupon, jurors leave courtroom.)

THE COURT: See you both at 9:30 sharp.

DEFENSE COUNSEL: I need to make a record.

THE COURT: Make it tomorrow.

DEFENSE COUNSEL: No, I need to make it now.

THE COURT: Regarding what?

DEFENSE COUNSEL: Prior to opening statements, you indicated that we, meaning the attorneys, would not be permitted to state a basis for our objections. I complied with that directive during the prosecutor's wholly improper opening statement when I made many objections, all of which were denied. As I said at the time, I strongly object to this rule, which I feel prevents me from making an adequate appellate record. The First Department is clear in requiring that objections during trial must have a stated basis in order to adequately preserve the issue for appeal.

THE COURT: I am aware of the Appellate Division's feelings on the matter counsel.

DEFENSE COUNSEL: I'm glad to hear that. Although I fear it will be of little consolation to me and my client when he is convicted and is effectively denied his right to appeal.

THE COURT: You will be permitted to make a record outside the hearing of the jury. Otherwise, I feel objections become too disruptive to the proper administration of a trial. As I said, you will be permitted to make your record. You may do so now with respect to the objections you made during the prosecutor's opening. Incidentally, I found your constant interruptions of the prosecutor's opening statement with baseless objections highly unprofessional and I think it speaks very well of Mr McSlapashee that he did not respond in kind during your opening, as he would have been well within his rights to do.

DEFENSE COUNSEL: The reasons for my objections were these in order. The D.A. began by making reference to the complainant's employment status then proceeded to circuitously but unmistakably contrast it with that of my client. This is objectionable for several reasons which include it being an attempt to prejudice the jury against my client by making reference to matters which will not be part of the evidence in this case as I feel confident in assuming, and the D.A. can correct me if I'm somehow wrong, that there will be no attempt to present evidence regarding my client's employment status. Nor would any such evidence even be conceivably admissible of course. That objection was overruled without any comment or limiting instruction.

The D.A. then made improper reference to the fact that the grand jury had handed down an indictment. Besides being prejudicial and highly irrelevant because of, among other things, the vastly different standards of proof involved at trial as opposed to in the grand jury, this comment was in direction contravention of your repeated instructions to the jury that the existence of an indictment is evidence of nothing. That objection was overruled as well without any limiting instruction.

The next objection was based on the fact that the D.A. was essentially testifying during his opening rather than making reference to what he expected the evidence would show. Again that was overruled. The next two objections can both be characterized as attempts by the D.A. to create sympathy on the part of the jurors in the hopes that they will base their verdict on those feelings rather than on the evidence. I'm referring here specifically to the prosecutor's references to nuns and the fear the complainant must have felt upon returning to his van.

The prosecutor then told the jurors the contents of the radio run that resulted in the arresting officer in this case going to the scene. The law is clear that this is hearsay and obviously the D.A. cannot do himself, in an opening statement, what he would not be permitted to do through a witness at trial. For his next trick, Mr

McSlappahan informed the jury that Officer Leary would testify that the screwdriver recovered in this case was of a kind commonly used to commit theft-related offenses. Unless basic evidence law is going to be disregarded in this trial, Officer Leary will not be permitted to offer opinion evidence unless he is first qualified as an expert. He has not been qualified as one and based on the police reports I have received I would be strongly objecting to any such qualification, so the D.A.'s comment was at best objectionable as premature.

Lastly, I objected three times when the D.A., after informing the jury that he could not instruct them on the law, proceeded to repeatedly do just that and do so inaccurately in my view.

All of my objections were firmly rooted in unequivocal New York law. The fact that the D.A. repeatedly resorted to these types of improper comments evinces either a profound ignorance of the law or a malevolent disregard for it. More troubling is the fact that each of these meritorious objections was overruled and the improper comment permitted to stand without any kind of limiting instruction. Moreover, I was then denied the opportunity to approach the court to fully explain these objections at a time when an appropriate remedy could conceivably still be fashioned. Accordingly, the only proper remedy after such an inflammatory and prejudicial opening statement is an immediate mistrial, which is what I am moving for now.

THE COURT: Denied. Anything further?

MR McSLAPPAHAN: Your Honor, if I may respond.

THE COURT: No need. Defense counsel's application is denied. Anything else counsel?

DEFENSE COUNSEL: No.

THE COURT: Then I'll see you both at 9:30 tomorrow.

(DIANE S. SALON)

"Wow," said Toomberg. "It's getting pretty contentious in there isn't it?"

"That obvious?" I said. "Even from just the transcript?"

"Sure."

"You're right, it's a problem."

"Why?"

"It's a screwup on my part Toomie. Pay attention, you might learn something. I need the D.A. to be sleepy and overconfident, which would certainly be justified in this case. I don't need him feeling all challenged and vigilant where he might figure out what I'm trying to do and address it before it's too late."

"Think he's figured it out?"

"No, he seems pretty dumb, but even he has to realize that I can't really raise much of a factual dispute when my guy is caught red-bodied in the fucking van. When he thinks about it I think he'll focus on showing that the van was used for commercial purposes."

"A reasonable deduction."

"Which brings me to my other problem and misstep. So far only you, me, and the mysterious judge in that commentary agree that the defendant has to know the van is used for commercial purposes before he can be found guilty of Burg Three. The problem arises when I have to convince Arronaugh to give me the jury instruction I'm drafting. Aside from her general antagonism towards anyone accused of a crime, I now have to overcome the obvious hatred she feels towards me."

"But isn't that true of most judges? They're almost all predisposed against us, yet their fear of reversal will still occasionally force them to rule in our favor."

"True but this is different. From what I see, Arronaugh doesn't seem to give a rat's ass about being reversed and this is consistent with the scouting report I got on her. Think of the ridiculous way she over-ruled all those objections. Every single one of them was legitimate."

"Arguably."

"Trust me. Forget your fancy law books, the only thing that matters here is how much she likes or dislikes me. I should have been kissing her ass from the outset."

"Why didn't you?"

"I don't know, genetics? Anyway I'm not saying it's impossible to get the instruction from her, just saying it's going to be an uphill battle."

"Why not start feeling her out now to see if she's inclined to give you the instruction before you predicate your entire case on it?"

"And tip the D.A. off to my defense so he can blow me out of the water by eliciting testimony establishing how apparently commercial the van was? Negative. This is the proper course because, fact is, regardless of how the judge ultimately rules this is the only chance I have. Your way I have nothing except I've covered my ass. No, this is the way to go, just need to make sure I get that damn instruction. Sure would help if I could find that fucking judge!"

"What fucking judge you looking for?" said Conley the next day during lunch after Bolo and Leary had testified and just before I had to sum up.

"Toomberg says there's a judge, respected and all, who agrees with me that there is a scienter requirement in my Burg Three with respect to the fact that the van is used for commercial purposes. Do you know where that might be? I've been hunting this damn book obsessively and it's led me here, to this bookshelf. So let's have at it."

"I have no idea but I heard that was your defense. Do you think it's accurate?"

"Who cares what I think? Have you seen the book?"

"You think Arronaugh will instruct the jury that your client had to *know* the van he broke into was used for commercial purposes?"

"No Conley. I don't think she will. In fact I know she won't because she already said she won't! But if I can find this damn green book maybe I can change her mind before I have to sum up in twenty minutes."

"Oh the green book. Why didn't you say so?"

"What have I been saying?"

"It's green?"

"Yes!"

"By that judge?"

"Yes!"

"The practice commentaries right?"

"Yes! Yes! Yes! Where the hell is it?"

"I lent that thing out to Grinn. I don't think he ever gave it back."

"Grinn?"

"Yes, Solomon Grinn. Find Solomon Grinn and you'll find your green book. Come to think of it, you probably don't even have to find Mr Grinn. Just go to Solomon's office and the book should be in there somewhere, regardless of whether or not Grinn himself is in there."

"Casi, what box did you have in the Tula pool?" said Liszt.

"What the fuck you talking about?" I said.

"I'm serious," Dane responded the day before when we spoke near the soda machine after I had opened on Hurtado but before I brought the transcripts to Toomberg for his take. He was picking up on a theme he first sounded shortly after revealing he had met with DeLeon. And this all happened before the D.A. called to tell me DeLeon was missing. "It's not far-fetched at all," he said. "It's just a question of expanding what you think of as conceivable."

"Well I regret to inform you that it is the very definition of far-fetched to think that we, you and I, are going to rip off a bunch of drug dealers. Sorry."

"Just hear me out, don't be so close-minded."

"Normally I would for the entertainment value. But I'm on trial as you know so I have work to do."

"This will only take a minute. Why do you think it's so improbable? What do you view as this great barrier? You heard DeLeon tell the D.A. firsthand that security for this deal is going to be shit. What's so farfetched about the idea that you and I, after proper planning, can just walk in on that day and swipe about fifteen million tax-free dollars? The kind of dollars that would never be reported stolen by anyone. Do you honestly think we are incapable of devising a sufficiently clever plan to go in on that day and extricate that dough?"

"Yes," I said. "I'm sure I'm going to end up kicking myself for humoring you even this far but the answer is yes."

"Why? A lack of intelligence?"

"Intelligence has nothing to do with it. Well, yes, O.K., intelligence of the other kind. Plans require information. This plan would require information we don't have. If you'll recall, Mr DeLeon gave the cops false information about where this is going to occur and plans to give them the real location later. Consequently, I do not know the real location nor am I likely to ever learn it. Are you suggesting I call the D.A. and ask him? Or should I have my client come in for a meeting so I can ask him? How would either look in the aftermath?"

"Hold it right there. You insult me Casi. Do you still not know who you're dealing with? I met with DeLeon yesterday for over two hours. I know the exact date, time, and place where this is going to go down."

"If he told you the truth."

"He did. I have painstakingly detailed information. Still think we can't devise a successful plan?"

"If the information you're referring to was properly acquired and chronicled and most importantly was verifiably true that would be one thing."

"Everything was done perfectly by me and can be relied on unreservedly."

"Then in that case I suppose you and I *could* devise a successful plan but that is completely irrelevant. I'm capable of doing all sorts of things that I don't do for an overwhelming variety of reasons. What you are jokingly suggesting is so far afield of anything I would ever actually *do* that my ability to do it successfully is irrelevant."

"Are you worried about the execution? Because if it's not the planning you're worried about anymore then it must be the execution because there's nothing else to it."

"Exactly then, it's the execution that's the problem."

"So you agree with me that if you and I sat down, during the next ten days or so, and fully put our hearts and minds into devising a plan good enough to enable us to steal that money while avoiding detection and harm, we could accomplish this. What worries you is that we will then somehow fail in trying to execute that plan? Is that right?"

"Yes."

"Why? Because I happen to think we could not only devise a perfect plan but that we could, and would, execute it *perfectly*."

"Not that again."

"A perfect crime Casi."

"Listen, let me save you some time O.K.? I'll start with the conclusion while being as clear as possible. I will, under no circumstances, participate in an attempt to steal the millions of dollars that Ramon DeLeon has talked about. I acknowledge that you and I, if properly armed with the pertinent facts, could devise a plan that would enable us, in theory, to steal this money without detection or harm. However, listen closely here, we absolutely *could not*, regardless of the amount of effort expended, make a plan that was *perfect*. Nor would there be any need to do so, other than your bizarre need to pursue perfection. Moreover, we most definitely could not execute any plan, no matter how meritorious, in a perfect manner. In fact, I have my doubts that we could even execute the plan well enough to be successful but that's a side issue. Lastly, there is no need for debate on the various levels of competence we could possibly achieve in executing a hypothetical plan because fear of failure is not the reason I will not be trying to steal that money."

"It isn't?"

"No."

"So let me review. You agree that we *could* figure out how to steal this money. You also agree that we *could* steal this money."

"I didn't say that."

"You didn't say the opposite and one, the good plan, strongly presumes the other. Yet despite this you're not even going to try and steal the money?"

"Correct. Because I don't want to try and steal it."

"You don't want fifteen million dollars?"

"I do, but I don't want to get shot or go to jail."

"So it *is* fear of failure that's stopping you."

"Among other things."

"What other things? Because the fear of failure can be stifled through proper planning, the kind of planning that reduces the variables that can go wrong and ensures success."

"There are other reasons."

"Are you sure? Let me pose this hypo. Imagine I was in a position to guarantee you success, meaning no apprehension or physical harm and the successful acquisition of about twenty million dollars. Are you saying you still wouldn't do it?"

"So I have a ring I can twist to become invisible, that it?"

"Very good, you're familiar. What then?"

"I still wouldn't do it."

"Why not?"

"Because it would be wrong."

"Really? *Really*? Wow, in this age and day. Anything else?"

"What do you mean?"

"Well we've discussed two possible impediments to this caper I've proposed. One is fear of failure. Since you've already agreed that we can devise a plan that would succeed if properly carried out, then this fear of failure can properly be categorized as the fear that we will fail to correctly execute this plan. The other impediment you've just identified seems to be a moral objection. Is there anything else stopping you besides those two things?"

"Guess not," I said after a long pause during which I actually considered the question.

Neither of us said anything else after that and I didn't see Dane again until after I'd summed up on Hurtado and was awaiting a verdict. When I talked to Dane that next day he spoke about his hypothetical perfect crime again and I listened. I had given up hope I would ever again sleep. Three sleepless nights and counting and I knew what it was doing to me. In college I would calculate my sleep cycles prior to going to sleep, then have my roommates wake me during the dreamy portions thus ensuring I would remember, in vivid detail, those bizarre narratives that played in my skull. And even though I fully expected to never sleep again, I did. After I finally got a verdict on Hurtado and almost punched Liszt I raced home and dropped straight into bed. My machine was blinking furiously, doubtlessly with questions about my hot dog-selling cousin Armando's arrest, but I couldn't deal right then. I closed my eyes for just a second.

"*Go out there!*"

"*Are you nuts?*"

"*People paid good money to see this! You owe it to them to get your ass out there and give it your best!*"

"*Who the hell are you?*"

"*I'm his trainer.*"

"*Whose?*"

"*Benitez.*"

"*Benitez who?*"

"*Not Benitez who, Who Benitez. Wilfred Benitez. Your opponent. I'm his trainer, now get your ass out there. Good money has been paid.*"

"Wilfred Benitez? Are you crazy? First of all, if you're his trainer, what are you talking to me for? Where the fuck is MY trainer? Are you even allowed to talk to me without my trainer here?"

"There she is now."

"No way, no damn way. I remember her. With the eyelid? No, I'm leaving."

"The audience paid, Casi."

"To see what? To see me get killed?"

"To see someone get killed. A fight to the death, that's how it was billed. For a limited time only. Money back guaranteed. They paid to see someone die."

"Yeah, me."

"You don't know that. You don't know which Benitez you're going to be fighting. It could be a seven-year-old Benitez. Or better yet, Benitez today. Why do you assume you'll be fighting the Benitez who fought Sugar Ray Leonard or Hitman Hearns? What an assumption! That Wilfred only lived for about eight years at most. In fact, I have it on fair authority that you will be fighting present-day Benitez."

"Now? The way he is now? That's even worse! Who do you think you're talking to anyway? What do you think I am? I love Benitez. You think I would kick someone while they're down? Do you know what I do for a living? For a dying? And you! You especially stay away from me. You of all people know I wouldn't do this. That's right. I remember you. You sliced open my head to look inside and now you're supposed to be my trainer?"

"Don't worry, it's all been arranged. We have the caskets and everything."

"Caskets?"

"Yes. Well casket actually. You see luckily you and Mr Benitez are almost exactly the same size so we only had to buy one casket to deal with either contingency. You didn't know they came in different sizes did you?"

"Not until . . ."

"Until you saw Tula in her little box right?"

"Fuck you."

"She went from one little box to another. You thought about that didn't you? What'd you watch the funeral for anyway?"

"I mean it, fuck you. Just leave me the fuck alone. I don't even know who you are. I know this is a dream too so cut the shit. You can't hurt me. When I say I don't know who you are I mean exactly that too. You're not an amalgam of people who torture me during waking life or anything. And you're nobody from my past either before you say that. In other words, you're no-one to me."

"I'm not here to take an adversarial stance against you Casi. Look I even brought you Skittles in case you lose. You hear that? You know it's a dream huh? Then wake up and pick up the phone. It's about the hot dog salesman. It's your sister she needs money. So does your mother. Your mother! I've arranged some entertainment for you. See that? It's an artificial womb. We can check its progress right through this glass. What do you think of that? Not entertaining enough? Look I don't want to sound like a name-dropper but I can introduce you to people if you'd like. Interesting people. Do you want to meet the two seven-year-olds who took Tula? Do you want to look in their heads like I looked in yours? I hear Rane didn't show for his counsel visit. I can take you to him now if you want. You can find out what he was thinking and feeling when he shot Superdad in his super neck. How does that sound? What about Swathmore's gal? You know, the one who torched her kid. Want to see how it happened? Are you surprised I know about them?"

"No. You know about them because of me. Without me you're nothing."

"Want to know why that chimp did what he did?

"Listen lady. Look at me. Read my lips with your one good eye. None of those people have anything whatsoever to do with me."

"What about the chimp?"

"Fuck that chimp! I don't care about the chimp."

"There's more I want to show you. Look at this . . ."

I should have stayed awake. When I was awake I knew what I was doing. What I was doing was looking for that damn green book and yelling at anybody who got in my way and didn't know where it was.

"I thought Arronaugh already ruled against you on that?" said Toomberg.

"She did but I'm hoping the green book can change her mind."

"Green? That's right it *was* green."

"Correction *is* green. And, if Conley is to be believed, *is* in Solomon Grinn's office where I'm now going to get it."

"Didn't you have a dispute with him the other day?"

"Irrelevant Toomie, the green book cuts across even the greatest of divides. Don't just stand there, come with and tell what you think of today's transcript."

THE COURT: Are we ready to proceed gentlemen?

MR McSLAPPAHAN: Yes. If I could make a brief record of some further Rosario material. A Copy of the 911 tape in this case, which includes the call to the police from Mr Bolo, has been copied and given to defense counsel. I also have a few exhibits Your Honor. I don't know if Your Honor would rather have me mark them now or not.

THE COURT: You could have had them marked during the last hour that we have been waiting. Fine mark them now. But do it immediately.

THE CLERK: Case on trial, People of the State of New York against Juan Hurtado. The defendant, the defense attorney, the District Attorney and the sworn jurors are all present.

THE COURT: Good morning ladies and gentlemen. Well the best laid plans of mousy men as they say. We've already had a minor delay in the proceedings as you are all aware. I told you all to be here promptly at nine-thirty but of course this is New York City which means traffic. To make a long story short, traffic held up a necessary party and that's why we're getting a late start today. Anyway we're ready to proceed now and we're going to do so. Mr McSlappanee would you call your first witness please?

MR MCSLAPPANEE: The people call Jerry Bolo.

Whereupon, the witness, JERRY BOLO, having been called on behalf of the PEOPLE, having been duly sworn, testifies as follows:

THE CLERK: State your name, spelling your last name, and state your county of residence.

THE WITNESS: My name is Jerry Bolo, B-O-L-O, Hudson County, New Jersey.

DIRECT EXAMINATION BY MR MCSLAPPANEE:

Q Good morning, Mr Bolo.

A Morning.

Q You mentioned that you live in New Jersey?

A No. I work in New York.

Q Which state do you reside in?

A New Jersey.

Q Please tell the members of the grand jury how old you are? I mean the members of the jury.

A Thirty-two.

Q Where are you currently employed?

A Salieri Construction and Remodeling.

THE COURT: Would you spell the name of your employer?

THE WITNESS: S-A-L-I-E-R-I.

THE COURT: Thank you.

Q Can you please describe what type of work that Salieri Construction company does?

A We mostly remodel churches, paint them, plastering, gold leaf, wood graining, marbleizing.

Q How long have you been employed by the Salieri Company?

A Three years.

Q Can you please briefly describe what your duties and responsibilities are within the company?

A I'm a church painter. I'm in charge of supplies, and basically that's about it.

Q Does part of your duties and responsibilities sometimes entail the supervision of others?

A Absolutely.

Q Now approximately how many employees work for the Salieri Construction Company?

A Approximately seven, seven and a half.

Q Where is the company located?

A Manhattan.

Q Now, to what areas does Salieri Construction provide the service of remodeling churches?

A New York, New Jersey, Connecticut, Pennsylvania.

Q Now, you've given us a description of the type of work that Salieri Construction does. What type of equipment is needed to remodel those churches?

A We have a lot of lights, power tools, technical tools for all the wood graining, marbleizing and stuff. A lot of expensive tools.

Q How are the employees and different equipment transported to the different job sites?

A We have a van.

Q What kind of van do you have?

A A Dodge Chrysler.

Q What year is that van?

A Brand new. This year.

Q When you arrive at these job sites throughout basically the tri-state area, are the tools and equipment stored while you're working on the church?

A In the van.

Q Mr Bolo, I want to direct your attention to April 27 of last year. Were you working on that date?

A Yes.

Q Were you working for the Salieri Construction and Remodeling Company?

A Yes.

Q And where was the job site that you were working at on that particular day?

A 35th Street.

Q Was it here in Manhattan?

A Yes.

Q Do you remember the name of the church that you were remodeling?

A No.

Q The church that you were remodeling, what hours were you performing this service?

A We work from night at 6:30 until 3:00 in the morning.

Q You arrived at that location at approximately what time?

A 6, 6:30.

Q How many other people were at that location on Lower Manhattan where you were renovating the church?

A Three of us.

Q How did you arrive there?

A By the van.

Q Can you give us a fuller description of the van that was used to proceed to that location?

A A brand new Dodge Chrysler van, cargo van. It's white. It's got our lettering on it, ladder on the top, filled with tools.

Q Can you describe if there are any windows on the cargo side of the van?

A Two swinging cargo doors on the side and in the back of the van, and they both have windows on it.

Q Can you tell the members of the jury what equipment was being kept in the back of the van on last April 27th?

A On that night we had a spray machine, all the power tools. Lights, light stand. Basically all the tools the company owns are in that van.

Q Prior to arriving at the location on April 27th, was the van damaged in any way?

A No. It was brand new. Three weeks old that van was.

Q Do you remember what direction the street and traffic flowed on that street?

A That was a one-way street that went towards the Hudson River.

Q What side of the street was the van parked on?

A The left side of the street right in front of the rectory of the church.

Q Which side of the street was the rectory on?

A Left side, facing uptown.

Q Mr Bolo, I want to direct your attention to about 11:30 p.m. the night of April 27th. Can you please describe to the Court and the members of the jury what occurred at that time?

A I walked outside and I saw broken glass next to the driver's door window. It's all over the ground. I proceeded to the van. I went around real wide and I looked through the hole where the window was and seen a man inside with a – shoving around all the tools. He was digging through drop cloths and the lights and looking around.

I waited there about a minute and he had grabbed the light in his hand, and that's when I approached the van and I said, "Hey, what are you doing in there?" Immediately he says, "I didn't break the window," and I asked him to step out of the van. I accosted him and brought him into the church. I dialed 911 and the police came.

Q O.K. Do you see the person that you saw inside your van on April 27th, in the courtroom here today?

A It's the gentleman right there. He's cleaned up a little bit.

Q Can you just point to him and describe—

A That gentleman right there. Sitting next to the man in the suit.

MR MCSLAPPANEE: Your Honor, I ask that the record reflect the witness has identified the defendant.

THE COURT: The record will so reflect.

Q Mr Bolo prior to you leaving the church at approximately 11:30 when was the last time that you were at the van before 11:30 on April 27th.

A Ten minutes before that. I had walked out, went to the back of the van, opened the doors to reach in for a drop cloth. The van was totally locked. I made sure all the doors were locked before I went back into the church.

Q When you were out there ten minutes before you observed the defendant there, what was the condition of the van?

A The same way I left it when I pulled up that afternoon, brand new.

Q When you first came out of the church about 11:30, what was the first thing that you observed that alerted your attention that someone was in the van?

A Broken glass all on the ground.

Q Do you know where the glass came from?

A The driver's side window.

Q You looked inside the van?

A Yes.

Q Can you tell the members of the jury and the Court what window you were looking through?

A I approached the van on the driver's side, swung real wide so I would come around and look through the hole where the window was of the van, so I could see totally inside the van.

Q When you looked inside the van and you saw the defendant, what part of his body did you see?

A I saw his back. That's why – I didn't see his hands immediately. That's why I didn't say anything. I don't know if he had a gun or a stick or something.

DEFENSE COUNSEL: Objection. Not responsive.

Q I'm going to ask you to testify to what you saw. Don't speculate.

A I saw his back.

Q Now after you saw – withdrawn. When you exited the church what side of the van is closest to the front of the church?

A The driver's side.

Q Which window was broken?

A The driver's side.

Q When you say it was broken, can you just give us a fuller description of what you mean?

A It was smashed out totally.

Q Was there any other damage to that side of the vehicle?

A No.

Q When you first saw the defendant what part of the van was he in?

A The back part of the van.

Q In the back part of the van there are windows?

A There's two more windows. There's a passenger window, two cargo windows on the side and two more windows of the back door.

Q Are you able to see the equipment that's inside from the cargo window?

A Yes.

Q The equipment that you just described as being in the van. What part of the van was that in?

A Between the cargo doors and the back doors.

Q Is that the same area where you observed the defendant?

A Yes.

Q When you saw the defendant with his back faced to you, what's the first thing you saw him doing?

A He was rustling around in the back of the van.

Q When you say rustling around what was he rustling around with?

A He had a light in one hand. He was moving things with the other hand.

Q Can you describe the light that you saw him holding?

A It's a tripod light with two thousand watt light bulbs on both sides which we had purchased to do that job with.

Q I'm going to be showing you what's previously been marked as Exhibit 1 and 2 for identification. And I'm going to ask Your Honor that two additional photographs be marked as Exhibit 4 and 5 for identification.

(Whereupon, exhibits are marked 4 and 5 for identification.)

Q I'm going to ask you to take a look at 1, 2, 4 and 5 for identification. Do you recognize those photographs?

A Yes.

Q What do you recognize those photographs 1, 2, 4, and 5 to be?

A This is the inside of the work van. On the last two pictures I'm holding here are the cargo side doors where someone had tried to pry open the latch that opens the cargo window of the van.

Q Are those photographs a fair and accurate depiction of what the van looked like and what the outside appearance of the van was on April 27th of last year?

A Yes.

Q Now, after you saw the defendant holding the light you've described you mentioned that you had said something to him?

A Yes.

Q And after you had said something to him, what did he do with the light?

A He had put it down.

Q In addition to the broken driver's side window, did you observe any other damage to the van?

A Yes, I did.

Q And what other damage did you observe to the car, to the van?

A That would be the dents that are shown in the picture. The best one would be number 4.

Q Where are those dents?

A They're right underneath the edge of the window on the crease of the metal of the door.

Q The doors you're referring to, are those the driver and passenger doors?

A No. Those are the cargo doors.

Q The dents, can you give us more specific description of where those dents were located?

A They're on the door – there's a latch, a black latch that you push the window out. The dents are located right underneath where that latch would be if you tried to stick something underneath that window and pry open the window enough to push the latch up. That's where the lock to the door is located there. Right on that door.

Q Can you describe what the condition of the paint surrounding that area was?

A It was all chipped. It was dented and chipped.

Q What color is the van?

A The van is white.

Q After that you testified that you had called the police?

A I went in, brought the gentleman into the church where we had made him sit down in a pew, alerted my boss that this was the gentleman I had pulled out of the van.

Q Did there come a time when the police officer arrived?

A Absolutely.

Q How soon after you had observed the defendant in the back part of the van did you see him?

A Ten minutes.

Q When you saw – when the police arrived did you have an opportunity to see the defendant in the custody of the police?

A Yes.

Q Did you see the police recover anything from the defendant?

A He had a bent screwdriver in his hand.

Q I'm going to be showing you what's been marked as People's

Exhibit 3 for identification. Let the record reflect I'm showing Exhibit 3 to defense counsel. Mr Bolo, do you recognize Exhibit 3?

A Exhibit 3 is the screwdriver.

Q How do you recognize that screwdriver?

A That's the one the officer pulled out of the gentleman's pocket.

Q Is that in the same or substantially the same condition as the one you saw recovered from the defendant on April 27th?

A Yes.

Q Mr Bolo, prior to April 27th had you ever seen the defendant before?

A No.

Q Are you a custodian of the van, the Dodge Chrysler that was parked here in Manhattan on 35th Street on April 27th?

A Yes.

Q Are you entrusted to operate and drive that van?

A Yes.

Q Are you entrusted to possess and load and use the equipment that was inside the van?

A Yes.

Q Now, did the defendant have permission and authority to damage the car?

A No.

Q In any way?

A No.

Q Did he have permission and authority to smash the driver's side window?

A No.

Q Did he have permission and authority to scratch and dent the area near the cargo side, the cargo side windows?

A No.

Q Did he have permission and authority to be in possession of the spotlight that you saw him with?

A No.

Q Now, Mr Bolo, the Dodge van that was parked at that location, is that van used solely for commercial purposes?

A That's it.

Q And is that van used to drive employees from the headquarters to various job sites?

A Yes.

Q Is the equipment that's stored at the back of the van, is that equipment that's stored inside the church to do the remodeling?

A Yes.

Q That's where the supplies and different equipment are kept?

A Yes.

MR McSLAPPAHAN: Your Honor, at this time I would like to move into evidence People's Exhibits 1 through 5, and I have no further questions for this witness.

DEFENSE COUNSEL: I need to voir dire on 1, 2, 4, and 5.

THE COURT: No objection to 3 coming into evidence?

DEFENSE COUNSEL: No objection.

THE COURT: Then it is so received.

    (Whereupon, exhibit is marked People's 3 in evidence.)

VOIR DIRE EXAMINATION BY DEFENSE COUNSEL:

Q People's Exhibits 1 and 2 are pictures of the inside of the van; is that correct?

A Yes.

Q Do you know when those pictures were taken?

A At the police station.

Q That same night?

A That same night.

Q You watched the pictures being taken?

A Yes.

Q Looking at these pictures it appears that some extraneous light was used doesn't it?

A Yes. It's the flash from the camera.

Q When you approached the van and found someone in it that was at 11:30 at night right?

A Yes.

Q So the inside of the van wasn't as bright then as it appears to be in these pictures right?

A Yes, it was. The truck was parked directly underneath the only light in front of the church, the street light. It was pretty bright.

Q So the street light made the inside of the van as bright as it appears in this picture taken with a camera flash?

A No, not as bright as the camera flash.

Q Substantially darker correct?

A Yes.

Q And the same is true of Exhibits 4 and 5 which are pictures of the outside of the van is that correct?

A Yes.

Q So when you say that the pictures fairly and accurately depict what the van looked like on April 27th, you're neglecting to mention that the pictures make the van and the area around the van appear brighter than they were on that night right?

A I said, the pictures are brighter.

DEFENSE COUNSEL: No objection.

THE COURT: 1, 2, 4 and 5 are received.

(Whereupon, Exhibits are marked as People's 1 and 2 and 4 and 5 in evidence.)

DEFENSE COUNSEL: May I inquire?

THE COURT: Yes.

Q The first time you saw Mr Hurtado was inside the van?

A Yes.

Q When you asked him to exit the van did he do so?

A Yes.

Q Prior to that had you seen him outside of the van?

A Before I asked him to get out?

Q Yes.

A No.

Q The light you're saying Mr Hurtado had, did he have that light inside or outside of the van?

A Inside.

DEFENSE COUNSEL: Nothing further

THE COURT: You may step down, sir. Thank you.

Call your next witness please.

MR MCSLAPPAHAN: The People call Police Officer Parker Leary.

Whereupon, the WITNESS, POLICE OFFICER PARKER LEARY, having been called on behalf of the PEOPLE, first having been duly sworn, was examined and testified as follows:

THE CLERK: State your name, spelling your last name. Give your shield and present command for the record.

THE WITNESS: My name is Police Officer Parker Leary. L-E-A-R-Y. Midtown South Precinct New York County. Shield number 36785.

MR MCSLAPPAHAN: May I proceed?

THE COURT: Yes.

DIRECT EXAMINATION BY MR MCSLAPPAHAN:

Q Good morning, Officer.

A Morning.

Q How long have you been assigned to the Midtown South precinct?

A Seven and a half years.

Q Before you were assigned to the precinct where were you before that?

A I was six months in the Police Academy and six months in the N.S.U.-1.

Q How many years in total have you been a Police Officer?

A Eight and a half years.

Q What is your current rank?

A Police Officer.

Q In the Midtown South Precinct what unit are you assigned to? Any specific unit?

A Yes. I'm assigned to the burglary unit.

Q Can you just briefly describe what your duties and responsibilities are?

A I drive around in an unmarked car in plain clothes basically looking for burglars.

DEFENSE COUNSEL: Objection.

THE COURT: Overruled.

Q I want to direct your attention to April 27th of last year. Were you working on that day?

A Yes.

Q Can you tell us what hours you were working?

A I was doing an 11:15 p.m. to 7:50 a.m. tour.

Q Were you working with a partner on that day?

A Yes.

Q What was his name?

A Police Officer Santiago.

Q On that date were you in plain clothes or uniform?

A Plain clothes.

Q Were you in a marked or unmarked police car?

A Unmarked.

Q Did you make an arrest on that day?

A Yes.

Q Who did you arrest?

A Juan Hurtado.

Q Do you see that person in the courtroom here today?

A Yes, I do.

Q Can you please point to him and identify an article of clothing he's wearing?

A He's sitting right there with a yellow T-shirt and striped button down shirt.

MR MCSLAPPAHAN: Let the record reflect he has indicated the de fendant.

THE COURT: The record will reflect the identification.

Q I want to direct your attention to April 27th of last year. At that time did you receive a radio transmission?

A Yes.

Q Where were you when you received that?

A Approximately 38th Street and Sixth Avenue.

Q What did you do following the receipt of that radio transmission?

A I went directly to the location.

Q What location is that?

A 208 West 35th Street.

Q What is at that location?

A It's a church.

Q Do you remember the name of the church?

A Holy Entreaty I believe.

Q What direction does west – what direction does traffic flow?

A Westbound.

Q What side of the street is the church on; the uptown or downtown side?

A Downtown side.

Q When you arrived there where did you park your vehicle?

A I parked my vehicle right in front of the entrance to the church behind the white van.

Q Is that on the downtown or uptown side?

A Downtown side.

Q Who did you see, who was the first person that you saw at that time?

A Jerry Bolo.

Q Did you exit your vehicle at that time?

A Yes.

Q Did you have an opportunity to speak with Mr Bolo?

A Yes, I did.

Q At that time did you notice any damage to any vans in that location?

A Yes. There was broken windows on the van that was parked directly in front of me on the driver's side window.

Q Can you describe that van?

A Yes. It was a Dodge white van. Had two rear windows on – two windows on the passenger side and the window on the driver's side and passenger side front door.

Q Are you able to see inside the cargo area of the van from the window on the sides?

A Yes.

Q Now, after you arrived at that location and had spoken to Mr Bolo, did you have an opportunity to look inside the van?

A Yes, I did.

Q And what did you see inside the van?

A There was – I seen basically construction equipment there was drop cloths, portable lights, closed boxes, a couple five gallon cans.

Q I'm going to ask you to take a look at People's Exhibits 1, 2, 4, and 5. Did you take those photographs?

A Yes, I did.

Q Did you take those photographs on April 27th?

A Yes, I did.

Q Are those photographs fair and accurate depictions of what the van looked like on the inside on April 27th?

A Yes.

Q What was inside the van?

A It was drop cloths, portable lights, five gallon cans, a broom. It looks like some sheet rock.

Q In addition to the broken window on the front driver's side did you notice any damage to the vehicle?

A No.

Q And after that did you have an opportunity to go into the church?

A Yes, I did.

Q And did you have an opportunity – was it at that time that you placed the defendant under arrest?

A Yes, it was.

Q Was Mr Bolo present at that time?

A Yes, he was.

Q What if anything did you recover from the defendant?

A I recovered a yellow-handled screwdriver with a sharpened edge.

Q I'm going to ask you to take a look at People's Exhibit 3. Do you recognize that exhibit Officer Leary?

A Yes, I do.

Q What is that?

A It's the yellow-handled screwdriver.

Q Where did you recover that?

A From the defendant's right front jacket pocket.

Q How do you know that that is the screwdriver that you recovered from the defendant on April 27th?

A It's got my initials on it.

Q From the time you recovered it what did you do after you recovered that?

A I take it into my possession and I take it back to the stationhouse, I do – I prepare a property clerk's invoice. I put it in an envelope, put my initials on the item first. Put it in an envelope and seal it up.

Q Did there come a time when you recovered it from the defendant until you submitted it – until you vouchered it, did that leave your possession?

A No, it didn't.

Q You mentioned that you have your initials on that?

A Yes, I do.

Q Is that in the same or substantially the same condition as when you recovered it on April 27th?

A Yes, it is.

MR MCSLAPPAHAN: I do not have any further questions of this witness at this time.

CROSS EXAMINATION BY DEFENSE COUNSEL:

Q Good morning, or afternoon at this point I guess.

A Good afternoon.

Q Where was Mr Hurtado when you first saw him?

A In the church.

Q Did you ever see him near the van?

A No.

Q Did you take any pictures of the van other than the four you've been shown by the D.A.?

A No.

Q Did you speak to Mr Bolo about what happened?

A Yes.

Q Did you ask him what the van was used for?

A He said the van was used for –

Q Hold on. Not responsive judge.

THE COURT: Listen to the question asked and answer only that question.

THE WITNESS: Yes

Q Did you ask Mr Bolo what the van was used for?

A Yes.

DEFENSE COUNSEL: Nothing further.

THE COURT: Any redirect?

MR McSLAPPAHAN: No, Your Honor.

THE COURT: You may step down, thank you.

Call your next witness please.

MR McSLAPPAHAN: Your Honor, the People do not have any further witnesses in this case, and the People rest at this time.

THE COURT: Counsel, will there be a defense case?

DEFENSE COUNSEL: No, and except for the matter we discussed earlier off the record the defense rests as well.

THE COURT: Very well. Ladies and gentlemen. You have now heard all of the witnesses you are going to hear in this case. The attorneys and I have some matters to take care of before you will hear summations so we are going to break for lunch early. Come back at 2:15 to hear summations. I will then instruct you on the law and the case will be yours to begin deliberations. Remember my admonitions. Do not discuss the case with anyone. Do not form any opinions as it is not yet time to deliberate. Keep an open mind and we'll see you at 2:15.

(Whereupon, jurors leave courtroom.)

THE COURT: Counsel, as we discussed I will hear your motion now as if it were made directly after the end of the People's case and prior to the defense resting.

DEFENSE COUNSEL: Thank you. The People have not presented legally sufficient evidence that the defendant committed the only crime charged in this indictment. Therefore I'm moving for a trial order of dismissal under C.P.L. 300.40. The instant indictment contains the single count of Burglary in the Third Degree, Penal Law section 140.20, a class D nonviolent felony. That statute states that, quote, A PERSON IS GUILTY OF BURGLARY IN THE THIRD DEGREE WHEN HE KNOWINGLY ENTERS OR

REMAINS UNLAWFULLY IN A BUILDING WITH INTENT
TO COMMIT A CRIME THEREIN, end quote.

THE COURT: Counsel, I'm familiar with the Penal Law, perhaps you
can proceed to the gist of your argument.

DEFENSE COUNSEL: I need to proceed in this manner, judge, because
I don't want there to be any future confusion as to precisely what
it is I'm arguing here. The term "building" as used in Penal Law
140.20 is defined in Penal Law section 140.00 subsection 2. The
relevant portion of that definition, since it is the one relied on
by the People in their theory of the case, is quote, ANY VEHICLE
USED BY PERSONS FOR CARRYING ON BUSINESS
THEREIN, end quote.

My argument for why the People have failed to meet their burden
is this: The People have not put forth sufficient evidence that the
defendant knew, at the time he broke into the van, that said van was
used by persons for carrying on business therein, i.e. that it was a
building, a necessary element of Burglary in the Third Degree as it
relates to this case.

THE COURT: Counsel, it's irrelevant whether or not your client knew
when he broke into that van that under New York law a van used
for business is a building.

DEFENSE COUNSEL: I agree that my client's knowledge of New York
law is, as always, irrelevant. That is not my argument.

THE COURT: What is your argument? Because it makes no sense to me.

DEFENSE COUNSEL: The argument is that in this case the People
must prove beyond a reasonable doubt that, at the time he broke
into the van, the defendant knew that the van was used to conduct
business therein.

THE COURT: The People most certainly do not have to prove that,
they simply have to prove that it is a building as that term is defined
in the statute. Whether your client knew that that was the state of
the law at the time is irrelevant.

DEFENSE COUNSEL: Again, I'm not talking about my client's knowledge of the law. I'm simply talking about whether or not he knew that the van he was breaking into was a van used to conduct business. It's clear that 140.20 has just such a mens rea requirement. If you look at Article 15 of the Penal Law, where general principles of culpability are set forth, that fact becomes undeniably evident. Specifically, Penal Law section 15.15, subdivision 1, states that when a statute defining an offense requires a particular culpable mental state, as the instant statute does with the term "knowingly", then that culpable mental state is presumed to apply to every element of the offense unless an attempt to limit its application clearly appears.

Here, there is no such attempt at a limit. So when the term "knowingly" is used in 140.20 it applies to every element of the crime according to 15.15. An element of the crime here is that the van was used for business purposes. The People must prove every element of 140.20 beyond a reasonable doubt. By extension they must prove beyond a reasonable doubt that the defendant knew that the van was used for business purposes.

They have so utterly failed to do so here that the case shouldn't even get to the jury for deliberations but should instead be dismissed. The testimony was that the defendant was found in a van that had been left unattended on a dark street at 11:30 p.m. There was no testimony that the van had commercial plates, or commercial lettering on the side, or anything else that would unequivocally delineate it as a van used for commercial purposes. According to the complainant, he had just checked on the van ten minutes before coming upon the defendant. Therefore, adjusting for the time it takes to break into the van, the evidence strongly suggests that the defendant did not spend a great deal of time in the presence of the van before breaking in. The majority of vans are not used by businesses for commercial purposes so a person is justified in believing that a van they are breaking into belongs to this non-commercial majority. The People must overcome that presumption with proof that the defendant knew the vehicle was used to conduct business therein and they have failed to do so. Accordingly, the case should be dismissed. Thank you.

MR McSLAPPAHAN: Your Honor, may I respond?

THE COURT: Yes.

MR McSLAPPAHAN: Your Honor, as you're well aware, a motion by the defense at this time must be viewed in a light most favorable to the People. And addressing the argument that defense counsel has made as far as the knowledge requirement, Your Honor, the ignorance of the law is no excuse. Whether or not this defendant knew what type of van this was is not enough at this point, or it does prove – we've proved beyond a reasonable doubt that he knowingly and unlawfully entered into a building. That goes to matters of law that Your Honor will instruct the jury, and is not necessary for the defendant to know that the vehicle that he's entered into is carried on for commercial business. Arguably he did know.

Once he got inside there were various forms and types of equipment that were inside, all over the van, which we can see on those photographs. And my position is that for the defendant to commit this crime he has to knowingly and unlawfully enter and remain in a building. As is instructed by Your Honor, it is not necessary for defense – for the defendant to know he's entering into a commercial van necessarily and I ask that defense counsel's motion be denied in its entirety.

DEFENSE COUNSEL: Judge, before you rule on the motion, I need to point out two instances where Mr McSlappahan misstates the law. First, he suggests that the defendant's knowledge that the van is used for commercial purposes can arise after his entry and still satisfy the mens rea requirement of Burg Three by retroactively attaching to the specific time in the past when the defendant entered the van and that is plainly wrong.

THE COURT: Not true.

DEFENSE COUNSEL: There's the case of People versus Gaines.

THE COURT: There may very well be, but you're ignoring the other portion of the statute in doing so.

DEFENSE COUNSEL: The statute?

THE COURT: Yes, sir.

DEFENSE COUNSEL: I assume you're referring to the portion of the statute that proscribes remaining in an area unlawfully. That portion of the statute is inapplicable to these facts. The Court of Appeals in People versus Lacotta, 320 New York 2nd, 53, held that when the statute refers to remaining in an area unlawfully it is referring to instances where someone engages in a lawful initial entry but then proceeds to remain unlawfully, for example, their license or privilege to be in the area runs out, but the person stays there with the intent to commit a crime. The Lacotta court ruled that this portion of the statute refers only to this particular form of burglary, which is inapplicable here where the People allege that the defendant entered the van unlawfully from the outset. So I think it's clear that here the People must prove that the requisite mens rea existed at the time of the defendant's entry into that van.

Secondly, the D.A. did not in any meaningful way respond to the interpretation of the statute that I urge this court to adopt, other than repeatedly referring to the defendant's knowledge of the law, which I have already conceded is irrelevant, and making con-clusory and legally unsupported claims that the defendant does not need to know that the van is used for commercial purposes. This is simply not an accurate statement of the law. The Penal Law is clear in Article 15 that a statute written in this manner, with a reference to knowingly entering a building, does confer upon the People an obligation to prove that my client knew it was a building. Burg Three is not a strict liability crime. The mental state of knowingly applies to all terms of the statute, including any attendant circumstances. The fact that the van was used for commercial purposes is precisely such a circumstance.

THE COURT: Anything further?

MR McSLAPPAHAN: Your Honor, the only thing I would like to add further is that based upon that reasoning and logic it would require each defendant to have intricate knowledge of the law of what a building defines and that is not required to make out the burglary count that the defendant has been indicted for.

THE COURT: This is a motion at the close of the People's case that relies upon some interesting factual misstatements. As I heard the testimony in this case the witness, Mr Bolo, indicated that the truck had lettering identifying the van on the side. So that rather than being just a plain white van, there was undeniably, or at least it was clearly identified as being the van of the business company. And of course he also said there were ladders that were kept on the top of the van as well. But all of that is somewhat irrelevant, as the People are under no obligation to prove that the defendant knew that under the law the van was a building.

DEFENSE COUNSEL: Again, the defense is not that the defendant was ignorant of the law rather that he was ignorant of a necessary circumstance and that said ignorance negated his mental culpability. Also Bolo did not say the van had company lettering he said it had lettering, which every automobile has.

THE COURT: Motion denied. Return at 2:15 to sum up.

DEFENSE COUNSEL: Are we going to have a charge conference?

THE COURT: I suppose if you have it that would be fine.

DEFENSE COUNSEL: I'm asking that you instruct the jury that the People have to prove that at the time he entered the van the defendant knew that it was used to conduct business therein. I'm handing up to the Court, with a copy for the D.A., the specific instruction that I'm requesting.

THE COURT: I will charge the jury with respect to the language of the statute. Is there anything else?

DEFENSE COUNSEL: Are you going to charge them that the term knowingly applies to the status of the van as well?

THE COURT: I will charge them with respect to the language of the statute as precisely as is – as suggested by the C.J.I. instructions. Is there anything further?

DEFENSE COUNSEL: The C.J.I. doesn't—

THE COURT: Yes, I know it doesn't.

DEFENSE COUNSEL: Then I need to make a record as to why I believe that's a necessary charge here.

THE COURT: I think you've been doing that for the past ten minutes. Is there something additional you have to add?

DEFENSE COUNSEL: That was a motion to dismiss.

THE COURT: I understand that.

DEFENSE COUNSEL: With a different applicable standard and other considerations. Then I was asking you to dismiss the case, which is admittedly a severe remedy. Now I'm simply asking you to properly instruct the jury as to the state of the law so they may decide if the People have met their burden.

THE COURT: Is there anything new that you think you—

DEFENSE COUNSEL: Yes.

THE COURT: Counsel is, do you have additional material that you didn't mention before that you have to say now?

DEFENSE COUNSEL: Yes. Under New York law, specifically Penal Law 15.20 subsection 1(a), a factual mistake that negates a culpable mental state is a defense. That is the nature of the defense in this case. If Mr Hurtado broke into a commercial van with the mistaken belief that it was an ordinary automobile then he did not have the requisite mental culpability to be guilty of Burg Three and is instead guilty of Auto Stripping or Petit Larceny. Because those charges are not on the indictment the jury's only option is to acquit if they do not believe the People have proved that the defendant knew the special nature of the van.

For the reasons I stated earlier, I believe there is a reasonable view of the evidence that the defendant did not know the van was used for commercial purposes. For that reason, and the clear state of the law, I believe that the instruction I've requested is necessary if my client is to receive a fair trial.

You indicated earlier that you don't believe my interpretation of the law is correct. I mentioned Article 15 of the Penal Law earlier and a further argument stemming from that section occurs to me now. Specifically, in McKinney's, the practice commentaries to Penal Law 15.15, section 1 refers to Trespassing in the Third Degree, Penal Law 140.15. There, the commentator states that for someone to be guilty of that crime they must not only knowingly enter or remain in a dwelling but they must also know that it is a dwelling. This seems perfectly analogous to our case where the statute for Burg Three is worded identically in its relevant parts.

Why would it be any different here? Why would there be a less rigorous requirement of proof for a felony than for a misdemeanor like Trespass Three? To remove this requirement from Burg Three is to transform it into a strict liability crime, something strongly disfavored by the Penal Law.

THE COURT: Counsel, I have heard your argument and repeating it doesn't make it any better or stronger.

DEFENSE COUNSEL: I agree in that it couldn't possibly be any stronger as it relies solely on the plain language of the applicable statutes.

THE COURT: I will instruct them as per the C.J.I. only. Is there anything else anyone wants me to charge?

MR MCSLAPPAHAN: No. If I may briefly address, not to belabor the point. I object to the instruction that's requested by counsel as far as the knowingly elements, and I believe that his instructions really requires the jurors or – require the defendant to have intricate knowledge of the law. It is the law, the definition as Your Honor instructs it to the jury. Not whether or not the defendant was ignorant of the law. And I think that's what defense counsel is asking you to instruct them on. And I would object to the instruction that would say the defendant must knowingly be aware that a van is defined as a building.

DEFENSE COUNSEL: The D.A. repeatedly betrays no understanding whatsoever of my arguments.

THE COURT: Is there anything else?

MR MCSLAPPAHAN: Nothing further.

DEFENSE COUNSEL: You mentioned the C.J.I., I assume you will omit the discretionary part of the instruction that refers to remaining in the building.

THE COURT: I will instruct them fully.

DEFENSE COUNSEL: That wasn't the People's theory based on their opening. Moreover, under People versus Gaines—

THE COURT: Do you think I didn't listen?

DEFENSE COUNSEL: That's one possible explanation.

THE COURT: Why do you keep repeating?

DEFENSE COUNSEL: I'm hoping you'll understand why—

THE COURT: I understand you have a great many beliefs. You're making an argument. I have heard your argument and have ruled against you. The record is preserved. You don't repeat it four times to preserve it. Once will do it. Is there anything further?

MR MCSLAPPAHAN: Nothing further your Honor.

THE COURT: Good then both counsel return at 2:15 to sum up.

(DIANE S. SALON)

"Thoughts?" I said as we made our way to Grinn's office.

"I think she's wrong," Toom said. "If this truly is a case of first impression, as it appears to be, then it's just pretty straightforward statutory construction. That said, I remain amazed that we haven't been able to find a case or anything else on this issue. If you could cite her appropriate authority that would make a tremendous difference."

"You think Toomie?" I said. "Insight like that I could get from my mother for Chrissakes."

"I know I'm stating the obvious but what are you going to do?"

"What am I going to do? Good question. What is the individual to do in the face of pervasive negligent toxicity? So screwed, I'm so screwed. I just had the only possible defense to this case ripped away from me and I have to sum up in twenty minutes. I need to change her mind and if I can't I need to argue it anyway without the instruction."

"I don't think she'll like that at all after she told you what she thinks the state of the law is."

"She's a true idiot."

"I'm quite certain she'll shut you down if you try jury nullification."

"Yup."

"The other thing is, even if she gave you the instruction you've sought, with the testimony that the van had ladders on top of it and company lettering on the side aren't you nonetheless in a very difficult position. In other words—"

"Those words are fine Toom, I know what you're saying. Fucking court reporter. Bolo never said *our lettering* he said lettering. That's it. I was listening like a bat. I swear the gods are fucking me from every angle Toom. Now where's that hideous book." We were in Grinn's office and he was not. There was no green book. There was nothing in there. I had to check the nameplate outside the door to make sure it was still an occupied office. We were rifling through the office's meager contents when Grinn appeared in the doorway.

"Can I help you gentlemen?"

"Conley says he lent you this book that has commentaries by a judge on criminal matters. Ring a bell? It's green."

"I don't have any book by a Judge Green."

"No the book itself is green. The judge's name no-one remembers. Seen it?"

"There's no such book in here."

"Are you sure?" said Toomberg. "Because it's actually quite urgent that we find this book in the next eight minutes."

"Are you calling me a liar? I assure you there is not a single law book in this office."

"That I can believe. Let's go, Toom," and we split without book and without hope, although Toomberg's genuine concern had temporarily revived my belief in the redeemability of man. He looked glum. "Don't fret Toom," I said. "I'm telling you, when I set out to accomplish something I do it. No excuses, no maybes. I have seven minutes. Mark my words, I will find that book and partake of its glorious jurisprudential fruit."

But I didn't. I went back into that courtroom unarmed and just summed up like a good boy. Hurtado was the picture of confidence the whole time as, despite repeated objections, I used every ounce of talent and ability I had to try and convince The Twelve to vote not guilty because there was insufficient proof the defendant knew the van was used for business purposes. Very unbecoming my desperation. I could feel it all slipping away. I wanted to go back in time, wanted to arraign the case anew. I should've sent investigators out to photograph that van before it was stolen for good so I would know the answers to questions I was later afraid to ask. I should've been looking for that book for six months not thirty-six hours. I should've drafted an entire memo on the issue rather than trust an idiot like Arronaugh to understand an oral application without pictures. Most of all, I should've gotten Hurtado to plead, even if I had to produce him for two weeks straight. Swathmore could've talked to him in furtherance, he was great at that. We had no business being on trial on this dog. Now it was hopeless.

Then the D.A. got up. He sounded like he had learned English an hour earlier. He argued there was ample evidence the defendant was in the van as if that in any way addressed the defense. He was horrible. God they always gave you hope. But even he wasn't stupid enough to forget to repeatedly tell the jurors that the van had company lettering on it. Fucking court reporter.

But thus are miracles sometimes born and I went back to my office feeling better than I had in a while about my chances. I sat at my desk and waited. And waited. Nothing. I went to Conley's office where Television was showing the Tula funeral, paid my respects, and came back. Nothing. Dane came in and we talked forever. Still nothing. Eventually it got to the point that I just wanted to hear something – anything. People were congratulating me on keeping them out so long but I didn't care. I wanted it over with.

I just wanted sleep. Let the Dozen say what they wished, just say it already so I could go home and sleep. I loved sleep then. I was so ready. Although I was a little worried about what I would dream. "*. . . there she is. She's a beauty huh? A replacement for Tula I suppose. See that? That's Grade A cow placenta we're using. Only the best. That's what they paid for, the best. They? The parents who else? You know who the parents are going to be? They're waiting patiently outside the door. An eighty-year-old woman and her genetically engineered grandmother. Do you want to know what was inside that hole on Canal? Want to know why Dom took a header off that overpass?*"

"*That was pretty self-explanatory as I recall.*"

"*Do you want to see the flight though? Won't take long. What else do you want to see? Just give me the word and it shall be yours to view. Do you want to know what's going to happen? I can show you. We can skip ahead. You trust me?*"

"*Leave me alone.*"

"*Mary's sure been quiet lately, huh?*"

"*Shut up.*"

"*How's your ear?*"

"Fine, never better."

"Why lie? Oh I almost forgot. This conversation between us is being taped for quality control purposes. If you'd like we can have the video-tape transferred to D.V.D. Would you prefer that? If so, you must exercise that option within the next 23.2 seconds or have it irretrievably lost. Because here's the future whether you want to hear it or not. Everybody leaves. Everyone. Just be patient as every day the wait becomes shorter. Think it was a good idea to watch that funeral?"

The funeral was held in Conley's office where the pink now seemed more like laundered blood red. Television had broken into its regularly scheduled programming to show the procession of the tiniest casket I had ever seen. There were hundreds in the church including the cameraman. Not camera*men* because one network had secured exclusive rights to the St Patrick's Cathedral service. Atop Television lay a transparent jar with the money for the pool. The cork stopper on top couldn't fasten against the weight of the bills. I could make out a hundred. Everyone was crying. The camera would cut to someone for a close-up then a yellow caption would appear below the weeping face identifying it in relation to the casket's occupant. The whole thing really was a procession. It kept building and growing to a promised crescendo. I turned away from the images but didn't leave the room. I didn't want to look back.

I didn't want to look back that night on the bridge either. I knew Uncle Sam and the chimp were following me and I knew the distance between us was shrinking steadily. I also knew that if I turned around and faced them directly, it would all become aerated and apparent and I was sure I didn't want that so I just kept walking.

But after the chimp did what he did my attitude changed. So when I later came across the old man in fur I didn't take my eyes off him for a second. At least not until he executed a perfect 360° spin that dropped him into a sudden split from which he quickly sprang up and started shuffling towards me in an exaggerated gait. I turned and ran away until I almost ran into Angus.

The way I almost ran into Dane after I left the funeral in Conley's office and returned to my office to keep waiting. He was leaving my office, his back to me.

"Don't split," I said. "Here I am."

"What happened?" he said.

"They're still out," I said.

"How long they been out?"

"Couple hours."

"Very impressive."

"Forget that. What did you mean the other day when you said you were dying?" I said as I closed the door.

"How come your officemates are never here?"

"Julia's around. Greene splits early, right from court if he can swing it. I've got to say, you look good for a dying man."

"Looks deceive, often. You on the other hand look quite horrible."

"Lack of sleep. Will you take over Hurtado's case for me now so I can go get some?"

"Only if you're going to win. I despise losing."

"It's inevitable. Now, are you dying?"

"You really want to know?"

"Only if the news is pleasant. I want to enjoy these last few moments."

"It's not pleasant. I'm dying. Every day and every minute of those days I get closer to my end. The worst part is not knowing what I have. I don't know if I have brain cancer, a gunshot, or an Acme safe to the head, the only thing I know for sure is it's coming."

"I see, you're not dying at all. I think I'm disappointed."

"I can feel it happening too. I feel myself drifting into senescence. Don't you? Every day I wake up against my will, shave my hairy face, put on one of these monkey suits and come in here to exchange language with strangers. What kind of life is that? That's not living. That's dying, slowly I admit, which is even worse. This is a prison."

"No it isn't. You're free. You can effect change. Do something that won't make you feel that way. Go into Swathmore's office right now and quit. Then on Monday you won't have to wear that monkey suit or clip those hairs. You can prepare to climb Mount Everest or whatever your heart desires."

"Do I look like a fucking dilettante to you?"

"Fine, you're a free agent, *accomplish* what you wish."

"Ahhh, thank you, now you're getting it. You see I can recall a time when I didn't feel this way at all, maybe the only time in my life I didn't. It was when I was in the midst of providing that guy perfect representation. The pursuit of perfection Casi. I'm going to pursue it again in the form of a perfect crime and I'm going to convince you to join me in this heist. When I walk into that building to seize that thirty million I guarantee you I won't feel like I'm dying. And when we execute our perfect plan perfectly and walk out of there with said money I further guarantee that you will feel more alive than you ever have. In fact the very notion of *alive* will mean something different to you than it did before you entered that house. You will, for the first time, experience the fact that life is nothing shy of a miracle. Do you feel that way now? Of course not. You're living in a Platonic cave with blinders on to boot. Come with me to the light, Casi. Don't stay in the dark with the sightless others. You genuinely feel you belong with them? I dare say you don't and that you know this viscerally. You're as capable of perfection as I am. Join me in this and learn what it means to truly exhaust a potentiality."

"No, sounds great though. Meaning do it, what do you need me for?"

"Because people like us don't stem from trees. I see it in you. The air encircling you is suffused with the same longing I animate daily, the same contempt that you orbit the sun and not the other way around, making you the perfect person for me to do this with."

"Wrong, because as I've iterated repeatedly I don't believe perfection can be achieved. That pessimism alone should disqualify me.

Find someone who agrees with you, seems that would increase your chances of success."

"You don't think yourself capable of perfection? Search inside yourself for me. I'm talking about if you devoted every fiber of your being to its pursuit."

"Sorry, no. I don't see perfection inside myself, potential or actual."

"You must hate what you see then."

"Not at all but I recognize its limitations. Have to know your limitations. I'm a firm believer in Boyle's Second Law of Thermodynamics and that's what I see when, at your request, I look inside. I see increasing entropy, there and everywhere else. I finish a summation and two minutes later five things jump into my head that would have made it better. In this case I'd have plenty of time to engage in that toxic activity while I sat in prison."

"First of all, forget Boyle. As you know his *law* is not one in a strict sense in that it does not demand a particular result but rather identifies a probability, albeit an admittedly overwhelming one. I readily acknowledge that perfection is highly unlikely, that's what makes its achievement so damn attractive. Moreover he's referring to closed systems, which the two of us and our plan are not. We would export all the necessary error or disorder out to the rest of the world while achieving perfection within our system. As far as prison goes, you've got to be kidding me. Remember, when I failed to achieve perfection it's not like I missed by a mile and invited a total disaster. I didn't lose the case for crying out loud! I wasn't able to achieve what I wanted, true, but I still effectively *guaranteed* myself success from a conventional standpoint. In a worst case scenario the same thing would happen here."

"What if we got caught?"

"Caught? By who?"

"I suppose by those whose job it is to catch criminals who steal money, which is what we would be."

"Are you kidding? We know these people. They couldn't catch a cold if they slept in a meat freezer wearing wet sponge pajamas. You're not listening. When you fail to achieve perfection you don't create disaster you achieve, at worst, flawed success. If you're right and we just miss out on perfection we're still walking out of there with thirty-five million dollars. Even you don't think we would fail so miserably as to be apprehended by law enforcement in a situation where it's highly unlikely they will ever even become involved, do you?"

"They're already involved."

"But they don't know the truth. Believe me, the attempt at perfection is what makes this a no-lose situation. When I failed last time, all I could do was sit on my sofa in my underwear and space out. This time even failure would bring a nice consolation prize in the form of forty million dollars. Sure beats a year's supply of fucking Turtle Wax."

"I can't figure out if you're serious or not."

"I am *one hundred percent* serious. You know what I did with that perfect case. Why would you think I'm joking? Just like then, the chance of error can be made infinitesimal. You would essentially be saying no to fifty million dollars for no good reason other than inertia."

"That and the fact that it's wrong to steal ill-gotten drug money."

"What difference does it make where the money came from? If the State seizes it you think they'll have a problem using it to pay for government nonsense?"

"Yeah, they'll use it to pay for schools, we'll be shopping for Porsches."

"Not at all. They'll use it to throw a parade for people who swing sticks at balls for a living, while you'll use it to help people dear to you, whom you love and owe, and who look to you for protection. You'll use the money as you see fit. You can say you'll use it to rectify some of the horrible inequities of our society. You can pick hundreds of people at random, people this society ignores and shuns, and use the money to help them lift themselves out of the morass that binds them. Those people can, in turn, later do the same and as a result you can end up helping literally thousands of people with money that would otherwise be used to pick up confetti. You can help rebalance the scales. Isn't that the right thing to do?"

"The act itself would still be wrong."

"Would it? What vestigial notions of morality are you clinging to? In this dystopian cauldron? I worry about you Casi. You need to wake up. Your naïveté will get you slaughtered otherwise. You're in a war zone and hesitant to jaywalk. You're the driver at the Indianapolis 500 worried about getting a speeding ticket."

"What shape would we be in if everyone took that approach and acted accordingly?"

"A Kantian objection? Are you kidding? Where would we be? You're seeing it! This is what would happen. How much worse can it get? What were you just watching on Television?"

"Whatever. Maybe you have a point, what do I know, but that doesn't change the extremity of what you're proposing."

"It's only extreme because you're comfortable in your numbness, but that very numbness will undo you if you don't heed me. Let me ask you this. Imagine for a moment your sister was kidnapped while in Colombia visiting relatives. Not inconceivable by the way considering you have family there that she has visited and kidnappings are about as common there as assaults are here."

"I'm very tired."

"Just a minute, what would you do?"

"Die."

"You would kill yourself?"

"I wouldn't have to. I think I would just wither and die when I heard the news."

"Then what would you do?"

"I'd go get her."

"What do you mean? How would you possibly do that?"

"I would do research. I would find out as much as I could about what happened. Then I would buy a ticket and fly to Colombia where I would do more research and I would go get her."

"You know who does kidnappings right?"

"Yes, but I wouldn't care I would still go get her. I would get a group of people together. Pay them."

"Would you kill someone if you had to?"

"Yes."

"Would you pay a ransom if you had to?"

"Yes, but I'd rather kill them."

"Now, what if you were falsely arrested for a serious crime you didn't commit and it went to trial? If the opportunity arose to pay off a juror, to ensure you avoid a conviction that would send you to jail for a minimum of ten years, would you do it?"

"Yes."

"What if the juror couldn't be bought but could be intimidated. Would you do it?"

"I don't know, maybe. If it was a man, and he didn't have kids or anything and he wasn't going to be permanently harmed. I guess."

"What if all that failed, you were convicted and sent away for ten years? Would you participate in a plan to break out?"

"Fuck yeah, the cage hasn't been built can hold me."

"Pretty extreme behavior you're copping to don't you think?"

"I'm really tired."

"Why would you do those things?"

"Those would be questions of survival. I'm not going to jail for ten years for something I didn't do. I'm not letting some scumbags take Alana. I'm not going out looking for these situations but I'm also not the type to just sit back without a pulse and accept having hell imposed on me. My life would be at stake."

402

"Exactly. Well your life is at stake right now whether you concede it or not."

"I'm doing fine, thank you."

"You have no money. How is that fine?"

"I'm twenty-four!"

"You're dying. It should serve as not the slightest consolation that your disease is currently in a temporary remission if it has not yet been cured."

"What disease is that?"

"Poverty is the medical term, also known as Slavery."

"Slavery now?"

"Yes, that's right. Because in this life, you either have money or else money has you, and we both know which category you fall into. I mean look at you, you are not vigorous and free, you're diseased and captive. You're a slave. A slave to gold, it calls and you come running, and if your master commands you to rise, your knees straighten reflexively," he stood with a mock military rigidity that managed to exude subservience. He stared at me and I looked away. Then I absently tapped the spacebar on my keyboard as he walked towards me.

"It's not even that exalted actually since there's nothing golden about it," he continued. "No, you take orders from green paper, think about that sometime." He sat back down only now he tried to look sad. "And this is your reaction to that state of affairs? What are you going to do, wait until you truly and desperately need your master, for example when you need to hire the group that's going to get your sister? What if it's too late then and it gives you the back of its hand? Do you think these opportunities at liberation come along every day?"

My belt vibrated. I was being paged. "23" it said, meaning there was a note from the jury, probably a verdict.

"I have to split Dane, that's the part."

"If luck had anything to do with anything I would wish you the good variety."

"Thanks, I think, see you later."

"I have to go too, here's my number."

"Yup," I said going out the door as he handed me the number I would later use after waking from seventeen hours of the deepest of sleeps. Walking to court then I was happy. It would soon be over.

Once there it all happened so fast. It was like a Marx brothers routine. In a foreign language. What I needed in retrospect was a standing eight count to get my bearings.

It all started with the jury's note asking for read-back of all testimony regarding commercial lettering on the van. This was quickly followed by the D.A.'s sheepish admission that he had discovered, over the break during a conversation with Bolo, that the van in question did not have any commercial lettering. I reminded Arronaugh that McSlappahan had relied extensively during his summation on the fact that the van had such lettering. The obvious remedy given the centrality this question had assumed was to inform the jury that no testimony need be read back since it had come to our attention that the van did not in fact have any commercial lettering. The jury would then be free to decide what weight to give this fact. Arronaugh did what stupid people do when they can't understand. She got mad. The jury would not be so informed. The truth would be damned. Instead she ordered the false testimony read back to the jury. The testimony where Bolo said the van had *our lettering*. Fucking court reporter! My mistrial motion was denied. The hell was going on? The jury took all of two minutes after the read-back to return and say words I had never, in that context, heard before. They were thanked and dispatched. A now *Guilty* Hurtado turned to me with complete incomprehension.

"You came in second," I said.

He had gone to trial with me because I was Hispanic he said. He knew that was a sign from God.

There's a manner of speaking you use while lawyering. A manner as affected and rife with artifice as your average campaign speech, with a similar fear of offending. Once the verdict sank in, I began tossing out applications like a desperate quarterback in a two-minute drill. And as they were denied one by one I began to lose that lawyerly artifice and sounded more and more like the pissed off intense motherfucker I was:

THE IDIOT: I don't know why you feel you have to keep repeating the same arguments.

ME: You should be grateful I keep giving you the opportunity to correct your ridiculous rulings.

THE IDIOT: Well what you are saying at this point is going in one ear and out the other.

ME: I don't doubt it. What would prevent it?

Two statements I would later especially regret when contempt proceedings got rolling in earnest.

I don't even know why I went back to the office. It was late and there didn't seem to be anybody there. I had two voicemail messages: a disappearance and a reappearance. A.D.A. Dacter wanted me to know that DeLeon had disappeared so he would be requesting a bench warrant from the judge on Monday. DeLeon was not returning calls, had missed the last two meetings and when police went to his house today his family said they hadn't seen him in three days. As if in his stead, Raul Soldera was back. He was involuntarily returned on a warrant according to the clerk for Cymbeline's part and I should go there on Monday for predictable further proceedings.

As I was leaving, Liszt saw me and called out. I went into his office. "What happened Casi?"

"We went down."

"Damn, sorry. Listen it was an impossible case, you did what you could."

"Uh-huh."

"Hey look at it this way. You finally lost. Everyone has to lose eventually. You no longer have that burden. You're just like the rest of us now. Win some, lose some."

"Wrong. I don't win some, lose some. I win them all and lost one, and the one I lost is because some criminally stupid judge couldn't get her head out of her ass long enough to do her job right. Fuck!" Then I did a stupid thing. I punched a hole in Liszt's wall. I needed sleep. I got the hell out of there.

They were gaining on me. The chimp-toting Uncle Sam was picking up speed. I would have to do something. I was almost off the bridge when I turned to face them. That's when Uncle Sam came up to me and said:

"I want you man! That's right. I know you don't look like Ward Cleaver but your Uncle wants you!"

While he was saying this, I noticed the chimp was slowly swinging his left paw in an exaggerated bolo punch. I was listening to my Uncle who seemed to want a response but I had both eyes firmly planted on his hairy pal. Suddenly the chimp jumped up until our eyes almost met and took a swipe at me with his right chimp fist.

I leaned my head back just in time and he missed, the hair on his paw barely scraping the tip of my chin.

Once to every man and nation comes the moment to decide.
In the strife of Truth with Falsehood, for the good or evil side.
– James Russell Lowell

Chapter 11

"I need to forget all this. I need to feel a sense of accomplishment, of forward momentum. Need to feel that a discrete, meaningful segment is behind me. That this person who squeezes into the subway in the morning and waits for orders isn't the real me. I'm in a hurry to feel this too," and I was in this hurry sitting on the bare floor of my room, the side of my bed completing the makeshift chair.

"Uh-huh," the phone said.

"So . . ." I didn't want to impel things, just wanted them to happen.

"So let's do what I've proposed."

"Yes. Let us. Yes"

"Excellent. I love witnessing, even just auditorily, moments like these."

I was alone there, in a spot near an echoing corner. "Moments like what?" I emitted and the waves bounded off selfsame corner and joined on their regress the still-faintly-existing Yes to envelop me in multilayered sound.

"A moment like this, when you make this kind of decision, when you decide you will not simply accept what the world is trying to force down your throat, that you will instead forcibly take that which is rightfully yours no matter the means. This moment."

"Oh," I said and began to hang up but then there was that thing where you hear the phone's voice just before you bury it into its holder:

...*minds me* the voice said so I stilled my hand and bent my head down to the receiver.

"I say it reminds me."

"Heard you, bye."

"Reminds me of the moment man ceased merely gazing skyward with sidereal awe and in its stead resolved to one day inherit those stars."

Part Two

Revolutions are ambiguous things. Their success is generally proportionate to their power of adaptation and to the reabsorption within them of what they rebelled against. A thousand reforms have left the world as corrupt as ever, for each successful reform has founded a new institution, and this institution has bred its new and congenial abuses.

– George Santayana

Power is the first good.
— Ralph Waldo Emerson

Chapter 12

"You look different."

"No."

"What do you mean no? You can't just verbally negate a perception of mine. I'm looking at your fat face and I say it looks different."

"No. I look the same."

"Are you looking at a mirror right now and I'm somehow missing it? Because you should be watching the road the way you're swerving."

"I don't have to look at a mirror. I know I look the same because I refuse to look different. I refuse to accept change in any of its myriad forms and incarnations."

"What about what I see when I look at you?"

"It's wrong, a misperception."

"You look like you're suffering from a lack of sleep."

"See what I mean? I slept seventeen hours straight last night."

"Exactly as I intuited. You overslept in the truest sense of the word. You overdosed on eye movement that's rapid. What'd you dream?"

"Nothing."

"Fine, don't tell me. You old people are all the same."

"O.K. I'm less than three years older than you."

"How's work?"

"Who cares?"

"Look at this, see that?"

"No."

"Look!"

"Can't, place it right in front of my face."

"Here, watch the road though."

"What is it?"

"You like it?"

"It is what?"

"Why do you choose to answer a question with a question?"

"When?"

"Huh?"

"Who?"

"How?"

"Where?"

"Why?"

"What?"

"Whatever. Seriously, Casi, you like?"

"It's very pleasing but also disturbing in a way."

"I knew it."

"*Now* can I know what it is?"

"It's an announcement. Eight weeks from tomorrow. My first show. Well, me along with other artists actually."

"Get out, superb."

"Yes superb, very."

"Why didn't you say?"

"In Aikido, did you know that the idea is often to use your opponent's own weight and momentum against them? Did you know that?"

"I did, you know I know that stuff."

"Right."

"Have you told anyone?"

"No, most people don't give a shit about Aikido."

"I meant about the show."

"Who would I tell?"

"There's no shortage."

"How does that own-weight-used-against-you deal work anyway? I'm going to tell everyone when we get there. Hey what made you want to do this anyway? I was shocked."

"Is there a thread somewhere to the Aikido comment?"

"You just got the urge to pick up and go over?"

"Pretty much."

"You sure it was a chimp?"

"I am, but I thought it was irrelevant?"

"I was wrong, it's highly relevant. It would've been far worse were it a monkey. I mention Aikido because I hope to use a similar technique to get you to talk about what's going on in your life. That's why I held my success story till now. Although you are, of course, the first of similar blood to know."

"That's funny. But why the subterfuge? Just ask me what's going on, as any sane human would."

"I know from experience that such a revolutionary method fails against you in these instances."

"What do you want to know? Why we're going to mom's?"

"I want to know how you managed to sleep seventeen hours straight? You might be the smartest person ever to sleep that long at once. Normally only the simple can achieve that kind of slumber. When I lie in bed at night, sleep is the last thing I can possibly hope to create."

"Still?"

"Yeah," quiet consideration, "you must have dreamt some freaky things too," more consideration, "why'd you need all those hours?"

"What kind of instance is this?"

"Kind of instance?"

"Yeah, that necessitates an Aikido technique to get me to talk?"

"Oh right, I think you're in a state. You get in these states and you're in one now. I can see it in your eyes. And now you tell me about the seventeen hours and I'm thinking that those hours must have been preceded by a lot of mental pacing back and forth. So some*thing* has certainly happened and that's why you look different I bet. Is it the monkey?"

"Chimp."

"Was it a Reese's monkey? Is that the problem?"

"It's rhesus."

"It was? I knew it."

"No I mean it's rhesus not Reese's."

"Yeah recess, that's what I said."

"It's not that either. It's not Reese's or recess, it's rhesus."

"So you admit it was a monkey and not a chimp, which incidentally makes all the difference in the world?"

"It was, without question, a chimpanzee. I just thought it was important that someone who shares my surname know that Reese's doesn't make a monkey, they only make peanut butter cups and pieces far as I know."

"Maybe. This is cool isn't it, the two of us here talking."

"Cool? I guess."

"No I mean principally the fact that we're two, that number."

"Two?"

"Yeah I like the number Two because if you have two of something then there's no middle, each is equivalent to the other."

"I don't—"

"Because of the day I mean. What a great coincidence is all I'm saying. You've looked at a calendar today right? It's twos everywhere and now there's two of us in this car. We two fit the day."

"Or maybe we're the two zeros."

"How many zeros?"

"Ha ha."

"Well here we are, you going to tell ma about the monkey?"

"No."

414

"You going to tell Marcela?"

"No."

"Are you going to tell—"

"Look I'm not going to tell anyone about the fucking money, I mean monkey, I mean chimp! I'm never going to discuss, or otherwise mention, that primate again, to you or anyone else."

"Hey guys!" walking towards our car, incredibly unencumbered and hugging her shoulders, was Marcela.

"Yay," said Alana.

"Hey kid, alone?" I wondered from inside a hug.

"That's funny, inside with mom." She stared from a smile. "This is so great, you guys here. Casi, you look different. What did you do?"

"See?" exulting.

"What?" Marcela said. She looked at me, then Alana, then back at me.

"Nothing, let's go inside it's freezing," I countered.

Inside.

"Mom turn the heat on, what the heck? I can see my breath."

– ¿*Ay, quiere un* sweater?

"No, *quiero* heat."

"*Sí* mami, it's cold," offered Marcela.

"Remember when we were little, we weren't allowed to touch the thermostat?" said Alana.

"Yeah well those days are over," I said. "Out of my way."

"Where are Buela and Buelo ma?"

"Probably huddling near the oven," I said.

– ¡*Ay tan lengui-largo*!

"You do have a long tongue at times," said Marcela.

"Open up, let me see."

"Ithere vood?"

"I'm sure, but stop flapping your tongue so I can measure it," said

415

Alana.

"My tongue is normal length, now let's get some food on it." We went into the dining room. "There's my little girl. Hi beauty. How about a smoocheroo Mary? Go ahead, plant one right there . . . make it a strong one. Thank you cutie. What do you say?"

". . ."

"Still not yapping huh?"

". . ."

"Love you quiet girl."

". . ."

– ¡*Ay que dicha*! Thas great – came from the adjacent living room.

"That *is* great Alana. Casi, did you hear this?"

"Yeah, show them the announcements," I yelled into the living room as Timmy entered the dining room where I sat salivating. "Hello terrible Tim, what do you have to say for yourself?"

"Why is there so much consistency in near-death experiences Casi?"

"Oh boy."

"Why?"

"Exactly what consistency we talking about here Timothy?"

"You know, there are those things everybody says happen. The white light, the tunnel, the rising above the body. There was more but I can't remember it all right now."

"Ah right. The long-gone relatives, the blissful peace, the peaceful bliss. Tell me Timmy, do you save these questions for me or can anybody play?"

"Right it must be true if so many people say it happened?"

"No."

"How come no?"

"First of all, how come *what* must be true?"

"Right those things they say, must happen?"

"Hold on Timmy. Let's take it step by tortured step, can't believe this.

O.K., it *is* beyond dispute that people have previously been declared dead only to later revive and continue life. It is also beyond dispute, I believe, that the interval between these two events has been as long as several minutes. Do you know why those things are beyond meaningful dispute? Because medical personnel, who can be considered reliable under these circumstances, have attested to those facts. It is also true, and beyond dispute, that some of those same people have subsequently been interviewed and have given accounts of what they experienced during the interval between life and death. What is not so clear, my chubby little friend, is that those accounts have been entirely, or even overly, consistent. It may be you recently read a book, or more likely watched a program on Television, where a group of these people was paraded about and they proceeded to recount basically similar tales that included some or all of the elements we just mentioned. This does not, however, necessarily mean that people who die and then retract their death have similar experiences, or even that their accounts of those experiences are similar. It may be, for example, that one of the people interviewed reported feeling like a crouton in a bowl of split pea soup. You're not likely to ever hear that person's account because it's so damn weird and outside the thematic scope of the program or book, understand? You see before you, the recipient, ever even enters the picture, the collector of the accounts has already parsed them into what she feels is the meaningful from among the meaningless. But let's start towards your real question. I will grant you that it seems the collectors are able to collect more than their share of white-light, dead-relatives stories. You want to know what that means right? Well if there's one thing experience has taught us, my little sawed-off partner, is that some of them are full of it – it being shit. Those people include those who are intentionally lying, for whatever bizarre reason, and those who are merely suffering from a wishful confusion. But put those people aside for the moment because, in all likelihood, they do not account for all the witnesses. If someone comes back after being

417

declared dead and says that, during the time they were supposedly dead, they felt themselves rising above their body, then connecting with long-lost relatives and approaching a white light feeling all peaceful, would that mean they truly had this experience? Sure, why not? Unless they're lying, they did have this experience. But so what right? People have all sorts of odd experiences. You may dream tonight that you've been selected to become the new Underdog, why would, or *should*, anyone care? Similarly why should anyone care what these people experienced while dead? I suppose we now come to your real question. You want to know if the fact these people had these experiences, the specifics of which they allegedly share with many others, means that the experience has relevance and applicability to the population as a whole, since as we discussed the other day it appears we are all going to die. First, note that these experiences at best tell you what it's like to die for a short while and then return, they arguably tell us nothing about what it's like to die when the death takes. You might say the experiences are proof that what we call death is in fact not final but more like a passage to this other life and reality, the one with the white light et cetera, and you may be right and you certainly wouldn't be alone in that belief since it seems to me that at least a clear majority still believe in some kind of afterlife. But bear in mind that, as usual, there is a physiological, non-mystical explanation that is, at the very least, highly plausible. You see it turns out the human brain produces chemicals. It also turns out there's a drug called Ketamine. Well, behold and lo, seems this drug, when properly administered, will make the recipient feel like they are elevating, will make them feel bliss, will make them see a white light, in short, will make them have most of the experiences we're talking about here. So I can imagine you're starting to get the picture. It may be that our brains produce a Ketamine-like chemical as we near death or that a relevant portion of our brain is otherwise somehow stimulated. Get it? Now the possible reasons for this might be interesting but we'll have to discuss that at some other

418

point because right now I'm starving. The bottom line is this, my plump and inquisitive nephew. You will never get a satisfactory answer, no matter how much effort or reason you expend, to these types of questions. You probably can't even hope to acquire even mildly strong evidence either way. You will never know, beyond doubt, in advance, what is going to happen to you when you die. Never! And really why should you care? Why do you give a rat's ass? You're five years old. Don't worry about what happens when you die, worry about what happens when you live for crying out loud! Christ, if I was your age I'd be out living it up, hitting on chicks, getting drunk, c'mon. You with me kid?"

"Casi, stop scaring my son," Marcela said, entering with glorious food.

"I don't even want to know what you're telling him now. Go play *gordito*," she said and *gordito* did.

"Me scare him? You should be telling him to stop scaring me. What kind of parental supervision is this?"

"I'm serious. You think he doesn't understand the things you say, but days later he's quoting you and asking me some bizarre question."

"Yeah Casi, play nice," Alana laughed slightly.

"He started it," I said. The food was on the table: round clay-colored bowls, yellow rice with strips of red pepper and dots of green peas, salted *tostones* of green plantains and various overdone forms of meat. "Oh man this looks good, I haven't eaten in like two days."

– ¡Ugh! – gasped my mom. – ¿*Como asi*? You have to eat *hijo*. That's not good *papi*.

"Harumph."

– ¿*Por qué* you didn't eat Casi?

"Because, mom, I got nobody to take care of me. I'm all alone. What am I supposed to eat? Pizza? I can't get good food like this over there, so what's the point in eating?"

"Oh please, don't make me laugh," said Marcela.

"Something wrong with your kitchen? Because you can come by and use mine anytime," said Alana.

"You see mom? No love."

– I'm serious *hijo*. You have to take better care of yourself. That's why you look so different.

"I look the same."

"Something happened, he won't say what," added the ever helpful Alana.

"What happened Casi?" said Marcela as my mom looked on all interest.

"Nothing happened, nothing at all. Did I miss something, who listens to Alana? Are we going to eat or just yammer? What about Mary and Timmy?" I said trying to change the subject.

"They ate already," said Marcela.

– *Ay*, I'm worry.

"Mom, what are you talking about? What's there to worry about? I eat like a pig. The only thing is I was on trial this week, that's why I wasn't eating or sleeping or anything."

"Why didn't you say so?" said Alana. "What happened?"

"I was on trial."

"I mean what was the result?"

– No, I'm worry about Armando – came the reprieve.

"Yeah, what's going to happen with that Casi?" said Marcela.

"Don't worry about that either mami. I'm already on it. I called over there. He's not going to be coming through for a little while yet. I'll head over there in a bit and make sure everything works out fine."

"Why was he arrested?" said Marcela.

"He told mom it was for selling hot dogs without a license, right ma?" I said.

– Aha.

"Total bullshit," I said, "no big deal."

"Can they do that Casi?" said Marcela with a look on her face.

"Yes, they can, but it's not a big deal. I'll take care of it."

"Yeah ma, don't worry," said Alana. "This is Casi's bread and butter. This is why we plucked him out of that orphanage and plopped him into that fancy law school."

– *Ay sí,* plees Casi. *Que pena con* those in Colombia. They send him here and we were supposed to take care of him. *Ahora* look where he is.

"He'll be fine, he's a big boy. He'll be chugging *aguardiente* tonight."

– *Miren tan buena esta remolacha.*

"Ill . . . beets?"

"No way."

"Nobody wants *remolacha* ma."

"I don't understand why they would arrest some kid selling hot dogs out of a van," said Marcela. "He was so happy with his hot dog van too."

"He's probably going to want to hightail it right back to Colombia after this kind of hospitality," said Alana.

"Doubt it," I said.

"I think he'll still want to stay," said Marcela. "At least I hope so."

"What do you mean you hope so?" said Alana and Marcela did a thing with her lips that Alana saw but ignored. "I mean I don't get it," she continued. "Over there, Armando was a computer programmer. Yet he's willing to come over here to sell hot dogs out of a hot dog shaped van. And for what? What's his reward? He's doing this in a country where they arrest him for doing it. They basically arrested him for working. I guess he's only supposed to come here to take pictures of the Statue of Liberty and buy his share of miniature souvenirs. These guys come here for what exactly? To line up outside in the freezing cold waiting for somebody to come by in a pickup and give them work for the day so they can do the shit nobody else would do, for money nobody else would take, and in appreciation get used as scapegoats by fat rednecks who keep their trailer's fridge full of

Meister Bräu?"

"Easy now."

– *Ah sí, asi es* sometime.

"*Pero* why ma? Why do they still do it? Can't we explain to them that it's not worth it?"

– They do it because dey think ees worth et.

"Well they're wrong."

– Alana *allá* there are no jobs. And *aunque* you have a job is no mean you're going to get paid. *La hermana de* Armando works for the university en Cali and they haven't paid her in two mons.

No-one spoke and in the silence I tried to remember which one was Armando's sister. Hearing nothing my mom seemingly felt an elaborative tug.

– *Y* the job *que* Armando had anyway it finished when they killed his boss walking into the office one morning. *Pero* even if he still had that job it doesn't matter because he know he could do better here. *Yo no digo que* our family is starving over there. ¡*Tampoco*! *Pero* even the people who are doing O.K. over there know it would be better here and they want to do better. *No todos, porque* some can assept et, *pero otros* can't assept et. Being held down by somesing you no control like jour country where jour born. At the same time, *mientras otros* can do whatever they want because of the lucky of where they born. ¿Because of *lineas en un mapa* like your father would say? Juss luck? (She kept talking here but I was thinking how much I disliked maps while others can't finish entering whatever turnstile-enclosed entertainment before they're running to the illustrated vertical square that tells them they're standing on a red dot.) Right now maybe ees harder for Armando than over there. *Pero*, he's just *un* kid. One day he marry, have keeds *y* those keeds will be born here. They will speak *el inglés* perfectly and they will know what to do. He does it for them. So *allá* I wore suits and here I cleaned hotel rooms but today look at my three kids. If we don't leave, Casi *por ejemplo*, would be like

Armando right now. Instead Marcela has a house and keeds, Alana es *un* artist *con* her first show, *y* Casi is an avocado.

We shut up and ate. She looked kind of sad as if saying things you'd only thought was somehow wrong. We all looked at each other but no-one had the heart to tell her how unimpressive these things seemed to us from the inside looking out or that the correct translation for *abogado* was attorney. No-one made any move towards the *remolacha* either which might have helped matters.

Who would break the silence?

"You guys feel that?" said Alana. "Do you feel it hanging in the air? It's the four of us. The exact four who would have sat at this very table ten years ago. Don't you get it?"

"Get what?" I said. "We get together quite often."

"More often than any other family I know," added Marcela.

"I know but I'm not talking about the four of us being together, I'm talking about the four us being together *exclusively*. When was the last time you can recall that?"

"I'm sure it was very recently," said Marcela.

"Not so fast. Think about it. You've been married nine years."

"Seven."

"Timmy's four."

"Five."

"Buela and Buelo moved in six years ago."

"Three years ago."

"Exactly, see what I'm saying? Look at this table, it's the four of us. We're even sitting where we used to sit."

"What's your point?" I said.

"That don't you feel the electricity of this moment? Here we are, it's like a reunion. This used to be us. There was no-one else. I would come home from school and head right to my room to sulk and paint and just try to feel interesting. Then one by one each of you would appear. Marcela would start dinner and ma would show up to finish.

Then remember the rule? If you were going to eat it had to be at this table with the Fantastic Four. A good rule I think ma. There are things the four of us have lived and shared that others could never understand and that will always be the case even though we're so much different now and so little the same. And that thing, that feeling, is in this room right now and I like it. The four. Us four."

"We were five."

"Yeah we were, I know, but then we were four and we've been four almost as long as we were five and that's fine because what are you going to do?"

. . .

"I've been thinking a lot about who the real me is. Who the real any of us is."

"Goood," said Marcela in a way that I was sure betrayed more of her enthusiasm than she intended.

"You see I know I act differently when I'm in this house. I feel like a kid again and so I find myself falling involuntarily into my old role. Basically I act different than I do when I'm with my Pratt pals for example and that got me thinking that maybe you guys don't know the real me. Maybe you just know the way I act when I'm cast in my familial role. Don't say you've seen me with my friends either because I'll just respond that what you're seeing then isn't the real me either but just the person I am when I'm with friends but being watched by family. Then again maybe the opposite is true and everyone out there doesn't know the real me, the one that only comes out when I'm in this foursome. The problem is that I now spend a great deal more time out there than I do in here. I'm happy right here right now, and maybe that's because I don't have to act as much or if I do the performance doesn't have to be as good, as expertly mannered you know?"

" . . . "

" . . . "

424

"..."

"The real problem is I'm greedy. I want complete, utter, unceasing bliss. But I don't want to fall into it either. If happiness were money I wouldn't want to win the lottery. I want to accomplish it, *urn* it as John Houseman would say. I want it to be an achievement because I want to be in control of my life. I don't want things to happen *to* me, I want them to happen *because* of me. Power I want. I want to feel the way I do when I stretch a new canvas and I want to feel that way all the time. The blank canvas fills me with the power of imminent creation. I'm its god and it always bends to my will and when I'm done I know, inside, that it's markedly better than what almost all of my similarly engaged others can achieve. That's happiness."

"Good," said Marcela again but this time sounding the perfect pitch.

"You know how I came to know all this? I'm currently undergoing self-psychoanalysis, which is all the rage. Actually, I invented it myself because I'm certainly not going to pay some idiot my hard-borrowed money to be my rented friend and tell me it's not my fault. Anyway, the result of sitting on my couch and listening to my crap is this conclusion. To the extent that I have good qualities, they are the product of fortunate genetics and brilliant rearing, thank you cute Mom (responsorial smile). On the other hand, any undesirable qualities or circumstances that I face are solely the function of my own individual and self-generated neglect, sloth, insecurity, avarice, pettiness, selfishness, insincerity, jealousy and other embarrassing causes too numerous to mention. Isn't that great? This realization is the key to my newfound happiness because of the amazing power it invests in me and remember that power is happiness. What's misery on the other hand? Well, lack of freedom and its resulting absence of power."

"Like in jail," said Marcela. "Where Armando is right now."

– *Ay*, don't remine me. Casi if we have to pay bail, we can collect from everyone to get the money. Or if we have to pay *un abogado*.

425

"I don't think that's going to be necessary mom. Like I said, not a big deal."

"O.K. *hijo*. I juss hope they don't take *el* hot dog car. He bought eh all the way from Texas."

"Don't worry they won't." I ate. "Texas? What do you mean Texas?

– *Sí*, Texas.

"When was he in Texas?"

– Thas where he came in.

"What are you talking about? He flew into LaGuardia, I picked him up myself."

– He flew to LaGuardia from Texas.

"What the hell was he doing in Texas? Wait are you telling me he came in illegally?"

– *Sí*, he's here illegally.

"I know *that*, but you're saying he didn't originally fly in on a tourist visa?"

– No, he came in through Mexico.

– *¿Entiendes bien lo que te estoy preguntando verdad?*

– *Sí, claro.*

"Jesus fucking Christ."

– *¡Casi por Dios!*

"I have to go like right now."

– *Pero* finish your food.

"Can't, have to get to Armando right away."

You suppose anyone mighty is on their way,
like, to save the day and shit?

Chapter 13

I got there just in time. Just in time to realize there was absolutely nothing I could do but watch. I watched as a court officer announced to the court that an I.N.S. detainer had been filed against my cousin Armando meaning he wouldn't be going anywhere. He wouldn't be drinking *aguardiente* that night as I had smugly predicted. The case itself wasn't the problem anymore as it was dismissed in deference to Armando's greater legal thicket. And it wasn't until then, when the officer made his announcement and their prey, my cousin, was escorted into the back, that I realized how small Armando was. He turned and smiled at me just before disappearing into the doorway and he seemed to be shrinking by the second. By contrast everyone else in that room seemed large and still growing. Even the women were giant and their words came fully equipped with echo and resonance in that corny suburban excuse for a courtroom. It was an inside joke the whole thing and from my seat on the outside looking in I felt nothing but contempt for those hideous people who in reality were just doing their jobs and so had no real responsibility; and I hate people who just do their job when their job consists of trapping my cousin.

I sat there stunned for longer than made any sense. Then I spoke to the attorney who had handled the case. Amidst his constant defensive reminders that his involvement with the case was over because the criminal charges had been dropped, I gathered the pertinent information I would need then left.

I went to Armando's apartment, which was not far from the court-room. He had rented this basement apartment, the kind with black bars on the windows, from an apostrophe-shaped elderly woman with severely thinning hair that formed a faint blue aureole around her deeply creased face. She remembered me from when I helped Armando find the place and she let me in but only after assuring me forcefully that she never used the key otherwise. Except for Television the place looked oddly unlived in. I turned it on and sat on the couch. The couch I sat in was essentially a giant bean bag. It enveloped me, sealing me tight to its bosom. It was going to take a Herculean effort to get out of there so what was the rush? I lay there and thought about what needed to be done. Something had drawn me to that place. I looked at everything but Television. From where I sat, you could see the entire place. I didn't see any papers, the kind of things I would gather for him. Nothing seemed urgent in that apartment and I wanted urgency.

Then I saw a plant, in a lonely corner and browning in its dirt-colored pot. I peeled myself off the couch and went to it but somehow did nothing. Instead I went around gathering Armando's meager belongings in a nylon bag I had found near the couch. When I was done the place was a true shell but there was still the matter of the plant.

I didn't know when, if ever, it would get water again. I grabbed a huge Scooby Doo cup from the sink and filled it up. Then I went over to the plant and poured the water in. It felt as if old Scoob would never run out of water as I kept pouring and pouring, slaking the plant's thirst. Then before I had a chance to adjust, the water swelled the soil over the lip of the pot and onto the floor. And I should have cleaned up but I didn't, I just grabbed the bag and split.

I went to the landlady's side door to return the keys. After opening the door only slightly the visible portion of her face registered surprise, as if we hadn't just spoken, but then it all seemed to click and she extended a withered hand to accept the return. I told her Armando might not be around for a while and not to worry. I wondered when the rent was next due. As for the hot dog, I would be back to get it later if necessary but frankly I had no way of driving that furter just then. All this made her want to know things but I was done sharing and blew her off. Before leaving I told her there was a plant in the apartment. Would she mind going in there once in a while and feeding it water; even if it was just enough to ensure its continued life? There was a Scooby Dooby Doo cup in the sink she could use for that purpose.

I didn't sleep another seventeen hours that night it just felt that way. On my old bed in my mother's house like the squirt I used to be but covered with a guilt I never felt back then.

The next afternoon I was back in Brooklyn Heights and all that remained of the day was a dull orange sliver peeking out over the horizon. I sat in my apartment but it was that annoying time of the day where it's too early to just tune out until you fall asleep but it's also too late to commit to any real activity.

In place of activity I went downstairs to Angus's; maybe hopeful that Traci would be there. She wasn't, but the apartment's usual three inhabitants were. Angus was watching Television, his mouth drooping slightly and his eyes darting sideways.

TELEVISION: . . . *hardy, har, har. That's funny Alice. I hope they like those jokes on the moon cuz that's where you're going!*

Louie and Alyona were working on a pizza from opposite ends and threatening to meet in the middle.

"Casi, what's up?" one of them said. "Come on in."

"Hope I'm not interrupting," I said.

"Interrupting what?" Alyona said. "Just having pizza man, have some."

"No thanks, I was actually concerned I might be interrupting Angus who I can see is still engaged in his Honeymooners quest."

"Not at all," said Angus. "We're well past the stage where outsiders can in any way interfere."

"We?" I said and turned towards the pizza, "You two are involved in this now I gather?"

"No, *we* meaning me and Ralph," answered Angus.

"I see."

"You see I no longer have to pay constant attention to Ralph to make him real. Just as Louie, for example, doesn't need my undivided attention in order to continue living. I'm not saying we're there yet, I'm just saying that far less effort is required on my part at this stage."

"Uh huh," I looked at Louie and Alyona for some clue but neither would meet my eyes.

Zzzzzt!

"What—"

"Did you hear about Tula?"

"Yeah, of course."

"What's going to happen to those kids?" said Louie. "Can they fry them that young?"

"No, there'll be no frying. You have to be eighteen here."

"Jesus, Lou," said Alyona, "even if that wasn't the case, what are you talking about? Are you nuts? They're seven-year-olds!"

"Weren't too young to kill that baby's all I know," said Louie.

"It's not their fault. Blame the parents," said Alyona.

"Blame someone," said Louie. "That's all I'm saying. Tula's mother's going to want someone to pay, that's for sure."

"What does Traci think about it?" I said.

"Non sequitur anyone?" Angus said.

"Just gathering opinions," I said.

"Traci? I don't know what she thinks about it because she dropped my ass after I didn't show that time."

"Really? You crushed?"

"Not at all. I mean she was cool and everything but we never really connected or anything if you catch my drift. No biggie, her loss. There are a lot of Tracis in the sea man. I'm currently looking into a two-for-one type deal actually. She wasn't even that hot to be perfectly honest."

"Good. I'm going to call her."

"Call her? What for?"

"For talk."

"Didn't you hear what I just said? She dumped me."

"Exactly, think I'd call her if you two were still together?"

"Are you fucking with me? How'd you get her number?"

"I didn't, you're going to give it to me."

"No can do dude. Man, you would call her? I thought we were friends."

"You just got done saying how she means nothing to you. Reference to the fact that there exists a multitude of Tracis was, I believe, explicitly made."

"That's different, you're talking about going behind my back to hook up with a girl I'm still in the process of getting over."

"Where's the behind your back part? I'm asking *you* for the number. Listen, just say that you were full of shit before. That there is only one Traci, and that her exit was a loss. Say that it would hurt you if I called her and I'll say I won't call her."

"It would hurt me if you called her."

"Then I won't call her."

"Meanwhile what are you laughing at?" Louie said looking at Angus; "because it's five minutes after seven and the deal was you would put something different on at seven."

"Oh yeah right. How's this? Acceptable?"

"Perfectly so."

"Thought you might say that."

TELEVISION: *All advertising, all the time.*

"Yeah baby" said Louie shining bright.

"What is this now?" I said.

"Great new channel dude!" His enthusiasm and smile meaning to tell me that our little moment of tension was already well-forgotten. "*AD*.T.V. it's called. Alls it is is all commercials all the time, no other programming. They've cut out the middle man. Isn't it great?"

"Whose commercials run on the channel?"

"Everyone's dude. Every company or precept you can think of. Every commercial, current, past, even future!"

"Why would anybody watch?"

"Are you kidding?"

"Well, O.K. Why would anyone *besides you* ever watch?"

"I watch," said Angus. "I enjoy it, but I also feel I have a moral obligation to watch."

"You have a moral obligation to hear a sales pitch?"

"Absolutely. After everything Television's done for you? When I walk into a store and plunk down hundreds for Nikes do you really think I've been snookered? Someone as sapient as me? I don't buy the Nikes because I've been deluded into thinking they're going to make me jump higher or make me look cooler. I haven't been duped into an acquisitive desire at all. I buy them to express my gratitude to Television. I buy all those things shown on the screen to allay the guilt I feel over not repaying a dear friend who has given me so much. After the endless hours of entertainment and love Television has given me, the least I can do is buy the little products it wants me to buy. That's how I show my support. And watching *AD*.T.V., when I'm

432

not busy with the Honeymooners, is more by way of support."

"Forget that," said Louie. "Look here's a true classic from the middle ages! See that? First the problem has to be established. This poor dumb sap is wearing a shirt that has not been appropriately laundered and is therefore soiled in a visible area. Here comes the penalty. See how he's being rightfully ostracized by those who would otherwise be dear friends? Now the problem has to be given a name, but not just any name, a name catchy enough to stick in the head of the human wallet that's watching. There it is: *Ring Around the Collar.* You have to love it. It doesn't get any more lyrical than that. Now comes the rescue. Back then, the rescuer was always another person but even so the rescue always came in the form of the true hero, the product. See? She's telling his wife about Wisk. Now they show the product at work as a celestial voice, in this case the great Bob McFadden, takes over the narration. Finally, we get the closing shot of heaven. You see? Collars don't come any cleaner than that. Look at the expression of joy on the wearer and the unconditional acceptance from his peers. Then a final shot of Wisk. Forty-five seconds tops. Beautiful seconds. That, my friends, is true art."

"What did you mean when you said it was an ad from the middle ages?"

"Beautiful right Casi? Art right?"

"Yeah beautiful, what did you mean?"

"Huh?"

"Middle ages?"

"Yeah, that was an ad in the seventies."

"How's that middle ages?"

"Oh right. I should explain."

"No, not again. I'm actively begging," said a seemingly pained Alyona.

"I know you've heard it before but he hasn't. He also deserves exposure to my wisdom does he not? It's simple Casi. Television advertising can be broken down into three separate stages. The early years, which consisted of really straightforward stuff like Jack Paar saying he uses Right Guard or whatever and it's good for such and such reasons, spans from the invention of Television to maybe the mid-sixties. Note that in this era it was still considered important to at least pay lip service to logic by, for example, listing positive features the product allegedly had. The middle ages, from which we just saw probably *the* classic example, takes us from there to the eighties and mostly features adherents to these mini-narratives. What we have now, of course, is nothing short of a golden age where man has achieved near-transcendental technique and skill that bypasses altogether the need to supply information. It may even seem, as some have argued, that there's no more development to be had. But most are confident that a few pioneers will emerge to develop the field even further. I of course plan to be one of them."

"You plan to be one of the people who's confident that pioneers will emerge?"

"No, wiseguy, I plan to be one of the pioneers."

TELEVISION: . . . *call 1-800-PLASTIC for a free consultation.*

"Hey I know her," I said. "I went out to dinner with her about a week ago."

"She's hot."

"She better be, she's selling good looks," said Angus.

"Good point," said Louie.

"That's a lot of noses," said Angus.

"Sure is," said Louie.

"Some of these before-noses don't look so bad. In fact, a lot of them seem perfectly fine," said Angus.

"Beautiful," said Louie.

"I don't know that I would go so far as to say they're beautiful but they do look fine."

434

"No, the noses aren't beautiful. The advertising technique is beautiful. This is what I mean about how far we've come. Here is a commercial which is clearly a low-rent piece of crap not even worthy of being on this channel. Nonetheless, even this pedestrian effort obeys established advertising stratagems that would have seemed amazingly nuanced as little as ten years ago. Of course the before-noses look fine. If they didn't, if they were obviously flawed, you the viewer might be able to distance yourself from the patients. Instead, the idea is that you, the viewer, will look at your nose differently after seeing this ad. In other words, you thought your nose was fine, never gave it a second thought, until you saw this ad and saw all these noses that look similar to yours, maybe even better, being labeled before-noses in need of repair. The advertising doesn't address a need, it creates it. It is self-sustaining."

Zzzzt!

"What the—"

"You must have fallen in love with her, she's gorgeous."

"No."

"She's not?"

"I didn't fall in love with her. Didn't even fall in like."

"You going to see her again?" asked Louie.

"No. You're free to call her, want her number?"

"Funny."

"She's famous now too," added Angus.

"Yes, among the literally hundreds of *AD*.T.V. viewers."

"It's something. Though nowhere near the level of fame I will soon achieve."

"Uh-huh."

"I say nowhere near the level of fame."

"I heard you," I said.

"I will soon achieve."

"O.K."

"Don't you want to know—"

"No."

"– how?"

"No."

"Really?"

"What, because of Kramden?"

"No, in my chosen field of psychology."

"Fine, how?"

"Should we tell him Louie?"

"Sure go ahead, it's Casi."

"Phobophobia."

"Phobiwhat?

"Phobophobia, the fear of becoming phobic."

"No such thing right?"

"That's right not yet. That's where I come in."

"You're going to discover, diagnose, and categorize it?"

"No, I'm not going to discover it. That involves far too many variables. I'm going to create or invent it. With Louie's help of course. Louie here will hypnotize the subjects."

"Yeah, I'm getting good from studying Dullen."

"Anyway once hypnotized, the subjects, in their highly suggestible states, will be taught to fear, beyond all rationality, the prospect that they will become phobic. This will not be very difficult to do by the way because it turns out that there are about a million phobias. Take Triskadekaphobia, the fear of the number thirteen or Sciophobia, the fear of shadows. Maybe our subject is pentheraphobic and irrationally fears his mother-in-law, or is hobophobic and therefore fears bums or beggars. Maybe he suffers from Ostraconophobia, the fear of shellfish. Or maybe he suffers from Enissophobia, the fear of having committed an unpardonable sin. You get the point right? By the time I finish cataloguing and detailing all the possible phobias to my subjects, they will fear that phobias are lurking around every corner ready to invade their system. I will foster this feeling, and augment their fear, to the extent that they will become phobic about this fear. They will be phobophobic. Get it? Don't you just love the irony?"

"Love," said Louie.

"What's the name for the fear of being drawn into bizarre and ultimately irrelevant conversations?" I wondered.

"So they'll be afraid of everything?" said Alyona.

"No, not at all. They won't be afraid of anything specific like snakes or the dark, instead the only thing they'll fear is fear itself! Nothing specific will scare them but they'll nonetheless be deathly afraid that something specific will irrationally scare them in the future. The sheer number of phobias out there will serve to convince the subjects that they will assuredly succumb to one of them in the near future. But they won't, instead they'll just create their own phobia. With my help of course."

"Where does the fame come in? Because I cannot name a single person who once classified even legitimate phobias."

"That's the easy part. I'll use the best results anecdotally, meet the bare requirements of my field, which are a joke, and turn the whole thing into a study for publication in the prestigious Journal of Psychology. The study will become an emblem for our anxious times. The media, led by high-school-level newsweeklies, will jump all over the study and mindlessly trumpet my conclusion in lieu of analysis. The national gaze will finally be on me. Just like that. Fame. Finally."

"When are you going to do this?"

"As soon as we get suitable subjects. We had one but he died."

"What?"

"No, not because of anything we did. He died of hair cancer."

"What?"

"Hair."

"Hair what?"

"Hair cancer."

"The hell are you talking about? No such thing."

"And yet it killed him. Tragically."

"What killed him? And don't say hair cancer because no such thing exists."

"Louie?"

"Cancer of the hair dude, I got it first hand."

"There's no such thing."

"Tell that to his mortician, man. Meanwhile the guy's dead of hair cancer is all I know."

"How do you die from hair cancer exactly?"

"I don't know. They wanted to do a follectomy but he wouldn't agree so he died."

Zzzzzt!

"What the fuck is that noise? That's like the third time I've heard it."

"Don't ask, you don't want to know," said Alyona.

"Don't want to know what?"

"You hate them man. Trust me, just let it go."

"Now I have to know, seems like it's coming from behind the sofa."

"O.K. man, take a look but just remember I warned you."

Behind the sofa was a plastic, transparent box. Inside the box a dark raccoon or something was trailed by an extensive tail. At one end of the box were two levers ending in round buttons, one green and one red. A tube extending from above and into the box contained blue pellets that I assumed constituted food. Even from where I was, and I was in no hurry to get any closer, I could see that the floor appeared to be electrified. A memory clicked in and these various elements started to fall into place.

"Is that a—"

"Rat," said Angus.

Zzzzt! The rat jumped I think hitting the top of the box with his head.

"I thought so, what the hell are you guys doing?"

"It's complicated," said Angus. "It's sort of an experiment."

"I mean what are you doing?"

"The idea behind the device."

"What are you *doing*?"

"What, it's just a rat."

"Those shocks look vicious."

"And?"

"And you're responsible for them, you're creating suffering. Alyona, you on board with this?"

"What are you worried about?" said Angus. "You hate rats, it's a fucking rat."

"You're right I do hate them. That's the biggest rat I've ever seen too."

"Isn't it?"

"And it's black."

"Practically, yeah."

"Where the hell did you get it?"

"Fucker broke in," Louie said. "We had to trap the bastard."

"In here?"

"Yup."

"Where?"

"In the kitchen."

"What the fuck Alyona? Talk to your uncle, we can't have this. Let's get a fucking panther in here or something, my goddamn skin's crawling."

Zzzzt!

"Look man I hate rats fully, it's true, but can't you get that fucking box to stop shocking it like that?"

"It's all in the name of science dude. Besides aren't you the same person who ripped that whole animal rights bullshit when we saw that clip of a celeb in fur being splashed with paint?"

"You did rip it," added Louie.

"I believe your exact words were that if a chimp had to be tortured in order for mankind to figure out a way to make your gloves one degree warmer then let the torture begin."

"I said that?"

"You don't remember?"

"I remember it generally but you sure I said chimp?"

"Yup."

"And not monkey or some other animal?"

"Chimp," they said together.

"Whatever, I wasn't going to witness the chimp torture. Why are you shocking it?"

"Angus?"

"Well this is the last stage of the experiment, during which the rat is receiving random electrical shocks of random intensities. You see, initially the rat was in control of its environment. By pressing the green lever it could supply itself with food pellets. If it pressed the red lever it was shocked. Once the rat learned this setup, we switched the levers so that red became food and green the shocks. As I said, now the shocks are random and so is the food. We are essentially teaching the rat the inescapable truth that life is beyond his control. Reward and recrimination are distributed randomly and completely independent of his conduct. Do you know what the result should be on the rat?"

"Learned helplessness or depression I would guess."

"Wrong, the rat will become depressed and engage in extreme inaction otherwise known as learned helplessness. Alyona and Louie will I'm sure attest that we can already see this happening with our rat friend here. A similar experiment was done with dogs and it worked."

"What do you mean it worked? Presumably the experiment, which I remember vaguely, was conducted in order to discover or learn something not to create something. The experimenters were curious to see what differences would emerge between the dogs that could terminate their shocks, those that couldn't, and those that were never shocked. The key difference is the comparison component. This here is not an experiment, you know that Angus. There's no control group here. You're not trying to *learn* anything. You're basically just torturing a rat. Like I said before, you're needlessly creating suffering and that seems, no *is* wrong."

Zzzzt! The rat twitched violently and I saw maybe a little blood coming from its nose.

"Creating suffering?" said Louie. "Talk about your proverbial drop in the bucket."

"Seriously," said Angus without eyeshift. "Who's the bastard in charge of *our* glass box? What about Siamese twins?"

"Conjoined," said Alyona.

"That's right Siamese fucking twins," Angus continued. "You thought I forgot about them didn't you? You've seen them right Casi? You come into the world all happy only to find that you're permanently attached to your sibling. That must be real fun for the parents right? And probably one of them has to die for them to be separated. That's good huh?"

"Television has shown me babies born with two heads," said Louie. "Two damn heads! What's up with that? Somebody up there is taking a perverse pleasure in this shit."

"Much like Lucy Ricardo often did, God has some 'splaining to do Alyona," said Angus. "What would he say? And don't tell me about free will. I'm talking about babies born hideously disfigured solely for the purpose of experiencing extreme suffering prior to being extinguished for good. And don't forget their parents, devoured from within by psychic Ichneumonidae as a result and don't even get me started on *that*. Realize that this is clearly outside the scope of free will, since there is nothing any human being has conceivably done to

441

cause the situation. This is a huge distinction so don't forget it; I'm not asking how God could allow some dude to walk into McDonald's and spray the place with bullets, since I'm sure you'll say God has to give that dude autonomy for morality and even life to have any meaning. Fine. Bullshit but fine. What about the kid born with two heads though? Explain why God so loved the world he gave it twins of the Siamese variety that an infernal boiling agony should suffer unto their parents the length and breadth of their interminable days."

"Fine, I'll play devil's advocate if that's the role you want to cast me in," said Alyona. "God might say that suffering is a necessary component of life, at least the kind of life that's desirable. Suffering tests people in ways nothing else can. By passing these tests people evolve and develop, they become better people. The alternative, a world free of suffering, is heaven and nobody ever said this was heaven. But there *is* a heaven don't forget that. Maybe you think this right here is hell. Fine. But what if I told you that to get to heaven you need to pass through hell, that such a layover is the only way you can arrive at that glorious place? Would you still want to go? Would you endure the price? Would it be worth it?"

"I wonder, Alyona, what you would say about a father who mercilessly tortured his children day after day then when confronted by law enforcement put forth the defense that he was torturing the kids for their own good so that years later when they had moved away, and were free of his torturing ways, they would better be able to appreciate the beauty that is life as a non-torturee. I think you would undoubtedly label such a person a lunatic and call for a severe jail sentence. Are we similarly at the whim of a lunatic?"

"I didn't say, Angus, that our current hell is the only way to later appreciate heaven. I posited that it was the only way to *access* heaven."

"The distinction eludes me. Besides, maybe I don't want heaven regardless of the price. Maybe I have Ouranophobia and am consequently scared shitless by the very mention of heaven."

"You can argue and joke all you want but the one thing you can't do is deny that all of this nonsense fed to Casi, Traci, and the like *might* be true almost despite itself. You must acknowledge, if you're being honest, that these concepts may offer an entirely accurate and true depiction of the world you live in. There may be a God who presides over literally everything. There may be a heaven of love and a hell of hate. Centuries of human attempts at using reason to resolve these questions have, without fail, been for naught. True, all philosophical attempts to prove that God exists, like the famous Cartesian attempt to prove that God's existence is evident from the fact we even have such a notion, have failed miserably. But, conversely, where has someone *disproved* the existence of God? Where have legitimate attempts even been made? Isn't that troubling? Where is the slightest proof, after those same centuries, that there is no God? And don't say Nietzsche because I'm talking about proof here, valid premises leading to a logical conclusion."

"Fine, if you define proof stringently enough, I suppose I can't really prove that unicorns *don't* exist, yet I think I'm perfectly reasonable in not believing in them. But all that is beside the point as it relates to our rat friend. Because whether God exists or not, there is still such a thing as justice. Justice exists, and this rat is getting what it deserves under its mandates. This rat is evil."

"Evil?" I said.

"Yes, very aggressive."

"He was," said Louie. "It's true."

"He *was* very violent from what we observed," said Alyona completing the consensus.

"Even assuming your observations were correct, that doesn't necessarily make the rat evil right? How do you know that rat wasn't doing its fucking rat best? Maybe that rat has the natural temperament of a serial killer rat. Maybe the rat does nothing to foster, or in any way supplement, this temperament. In fact, what if it does the opposite?

What if that rat does everything it can to combat and diminish this temperament it was saddled with from day one through no fault of its own? Perhaps the rat is able, only through a tremendous exercise of rat will and sheer rat determination, to control those extreme impulses to the extent that they manifest themselves only as extraordinary combativeness. Such a rat should be commended and admired not tortured. Who are you all to judge? Do you know the rat's inner state? You know only your own yet you're loath to judge yourselves."

"Casi?" Angus said as I walked to the door.

"Let the rat go," I said.

"Yeah I now think we should let the rat out too," said Alyona.

"I don't care," said Angus. "Let him out."

"No way, fuck that rat bastard," said Louie. "If he doesn't want to be shocked let him get his rat ass out of that box."

"Goodbye," I said. "Stop shocking that rat, you rat-torturing bastards. Not just that, let it out of that box too, that's almost as bad. Oh and Louie?"

"Yeah?"

"I'm calling Traci."

No more things should be presumed to exist than are absolutely necessary.
– William Occam

Chapter 14

What was I supposed to do then I wondered. Was there even a supposed-to for this kind of situation? A situation where when I looked at my receding past everything seemed retrospectively marked by an extreme order and predictability yet all moments since seemed to obey, and promised to continue obeying, their own set of stochastic, undisclosed, and undiscoverable laws. Where I was fully aware of the pitfalls and folly of a finely tuned narcissism but still the known universe seemed to bend and bend inexorably inward and towards me where it awaited my next move, supremely ready to react accordingly. And how I knew that decisions I would soon make or defer would have near-Sophoclean import and yet nonetheless it all seemed oddly irrelevant.

I wondered then what the first true doubters must have felt. How simultaneously freeing and paralyzing to untether the moorings of the previously unquestioned Known. They must have emerged about the same time as the first knowers these doubters; their ability to frighten and unsettle commensurate with the plausibility of their particular doubt.

To acquire true certainty, one doubter thought, you first had to subject everything, all your lovingly held beliefs no matter how basic, to the penetrating, white-light glare of true doubt. And I was game and had no problem going along with Descartes, those bygone days, as the physical world we held so dear melted away like the ball of wax in his hand by the fire. And when he said that dreams were often only identified as such once they'd been safely tucked away in the past by the awake dreamer, I inaudibly screamed my assent. And that meant of course that even *right now* could be nothing more than a mere dream, a chimerical illusion of a physical body in a physical world. Could you imagine? *This* not really happening? It was true visceral doubt I felt and I liked it so much, could feel myself bathing in it so thoroughly, that even after my guide had long discarded his doubt, and achieved his version of certainty, I still clung stubbornly to mine. I was unpersuaded by his return and could not be so easily talked back from the ledge. For days people would talk to me and I wouldn't know what to make of it, how to respond to them, what level of reality to assign them or our whole exchange. The logical climb back into certainty never approached the allure of this illogical descent into doubt; the echoes of which I then felt stirring in me again.

But like this renowned doubter, I too had my first principles I embraced in order to keep from drowning whenever the mental seas got too choppy. I had to go to work, even if that building was the last place on the globe I wanted to enter. I had mouths to feed. O.K. I had no kids so it was really *mouth* to feed. Mine. Maybe I had to put food on the table, even if there was no room in my apartment for a table and there was no expression for putting food directly into your stomach. What was needed was an expression for just going to work out of force of habit.

At least I knew better than to go underground in my condition. Nor did I want to be a pedestrian in that unremitting, percussive cold. I had newfound, temporary wealth because my check had gone in that morning so I drove in and parked in a nearby lot. I had left early to avoid traffic on the two-mile trip and was so successful that I ended up looking for ways to kill time before entering the building I didn't want to enter.

446

I sat down to coffee nearby, relentlessly spinning the post-recycled paper sleeve around the cup and drinking little. At the counter near the cash register was a selection of candy where two guys were arguing. "No way motherfucker," the one said, "Almond Joy's got the nuts, Mounds don't!"

Sometimes I felt like a nut. The kind of nut who could go up to those guys, bang their heads together Stooges style, and walk away before the police arrived; never to be heard from again.

The Post had a Special Exclusive Fold-Out Commemorative Collector's Edition Section on Tula. Sponsored by the good folks at Sony who not incidentally brought you The Casio Carousel. It contained a Tale of the Tape comparing the two seven-year-old killers. Everything but their names because of their ages: instead they were Killer 1 and Killer 2. Tula's was compared to previous horrors and it was strongly hinted that Tula was the victor. Psychologists were interviewed and they responded by spitting out, without the slightest hesitation, capsule psychological profiles, color-coded, for One and Two. The defense lawyers were interviewed and their vital information – phone numbers, addresses, websites – was given. The President, of the country, had a statement. The neighbors, in deference to one of the norms mandated by these situations, were heard from. The police told the reader what had happened, what would happen, and how.

The footage is what everybody really wanted, when could they see it?

But the Video Vigilantes were suddenly shy. Mayor Toad seemed to have become at least an honorary vigilante and he explained that negotiations for the release of the video were ongoing. The Post had exclusive rights. Not to the video or to any of its images, but rather to the announcement of when and where the video and images would be released, and through what venue. You were urged to stay tuned. Only *tuned* couldn't be right I thought. Once released, Julie Stole reported, the footage could be played on an endless loop thanks to an ingenious new device called The Casio Carousel and the story went off in that direction but without me.

The reason I didn't want to go into that building was the rotten timing. Except for Soldera's return I had no cases on. Usually good but then meant that for the majority of the day I'd be sitting target for anyone interested in discovering what happened the Friday before, not the sort of thing I enjoyed.

Like seeing Liszt walking towards me in the hall and thankfully not noticing me, which reminded me of maybe punching a hole in his wall. I quickly ducked into the first office to my left before he could spot me.

"Yes?" It was Debi, her office I had leapt into and what the hell was she doing there so early?

"Oh hi."

"Hello Casi. What is it?"

"Oh I . . . just wanted to ask you something."

"What?"

"What's what?"

"Your question?"

"Question?"

"You said question."

"Right."

"So?"

"So what?"

"So what is it?"

"I was wondering if you could . . . tell me what . . . the . . . temperature . . . is today."

"The temperature?"

"Yeah, the weather."

"Believe I heard say it was nine degrees."

"Wind chill?"

448

"No, regular."

"Celsius?"

"No, Fahrenheit."

"Kelvin?"

"Once again, Fahrenheit."

"Wow."

"Yes."

In situations like that I'm often perfectly willing to let my opponent think me possibly insane rather than expend the social effort necessary to rehabilitate my good name so I split.

I sat in my office and waited but nothing happened. Not at first and not later. Julia and Leon didn't arrive and I discerned they wouldn't. Outside, the swirl of activity increased steadily and I picked up bits and pieces of information. It seemed Swathmore would be on vacation all week and that accounted for the looseness in the air. An attorney was in big trouble too. What would they do to him? Assault is what it was. She had heard forgery. Contempt. A new guy. Had he heard about the nine degrees? Because that was *without* the wind chill factor having been factored in, and said factoring was reportedly required by law; meaning meteorological law. And even though there was surprising agreement that seemingly little by way of wind was present out there, it was also universally agreed that a post-factor negative number could be expected. Yes.

It was then, at that height of auditory receptiveness, that I decided I would not leave my office that day, for any reason, until it was time to feed my mouth around one o'clock. Soldera could wait until the afternoon, he wasn't going anywhere with Cymbeline in charge anyway.

Everything I would need could be piped in. The room would function as a makeshift womb. Bobbing and awash in amniotic fluid, I would ingest its silent emptiness and reflect upon both my last near-quarter-century and my next move.

Once I made this decision, the outside noise, as if in direct response, seemed to die down then disappear.

I *knew* so little.

But I knew that the stillness of that moment, the solemn sanctity I had managed to create out of pure silence and inaction, would never *ever* be disturbed.

"What say you Casi?" said Dane loudly. "I tried you all weekend. What's going on? Don't you talk to your answering machine? So you lost. Big deal. That entitles you to turn into a recluse? Did you forget we have work to do? You call Saturday morning to give the green light then fall off the face of the Earth? Notice the interrogatory lilt at the end of these sentences by the way. You need to put this behind you, the sooner the better. Throw yourself into your work. Your work, and mine of course, is extracting those millions from that building."

"You sure you don't want to use our P.A. system when you say that? Because I'm not sure the guy who sells papers in the lobby heard it."

"Now you're working with me. Get angry. A little anger is good I always say. Of course, a lot of anger is even better but I usually leave that part out. One thing we can all agree on is the clear enemy: complacency. So when do you want to start planning?"

"Look I hadn't slept in days."

"The human body, regrettably, needs sleep."

"Right."

"The effects of extreme sleep deprivation have been likened, by those who do that kind of likening, to the use of hallucinogenic drugs."

"Exactly. I know, and when I talked to you that morning I hadn't slept in some days. Well actually when I spoke to you I had just slept seventeen hours."

"Straight?"

"Yeah, but before that I hadn't slept in several days and I think it affected, I mean I *know* it affected, my brain and what I was thinking."

"I haven't read anything talking about the effects of too much sleep."

"No it's still sleep deprivation if looked at from the perspective of several days."

"Maybe, but seventeen hours? Sheesh."

"What I'm trying to say is that I wasn't really thinking straight when we talked."

"Straight?"

"Right. Not straight. Crooked maybe. I was thinking crooked."

"Like a crook."

I laughed. "You get where this is going right? I'm not going to be partaking in any desperate heist."

"Me either don't worry. I would never participate in a *desperate* heist. This heist is going to be methodically thought out and planned, as well as expertly executed. But not if we don't get going soon on our preparations. I'll come get you for lunch and we'll start. Bye."

I sat there trying to cultivate the reborn silence, but this one lasted even less time than the previous one.

"So?"

"Toomie! Where were you yesterday? I called you every hour on the hour."

"I didn't get any message."

"I don't leave messages."

"So what happened?"

"When?"

"With the case."

"Ah the case. What do you think happened? I lost because of that ridiculous defense you made me put forth."

"*I* made you?"

"Actually the crazy thing would've worked if not for damn Arronaugh."

"What happened?"

"Well the jury comes in wanting to hear testimony about company lettering on the van. Fine, except that while the court reporter is looking for the testimony the D.A. pipes in saying he spoke to the complainant over the break and it seems there was no lettering on the van whatsoever."

"No."

"Yeah."

"Yes!"

"Right. Except Arronaugh rules that the jury doesn't have to hear this little bit of information and directs the court reporter to read back the part about the van having *our lettering* to the jury."

"No."

"Yes."

"Really?"

"Yup."

"So they convict?"

"Soon as they hear the testimony."

"So it worked, they based their decision on whether the defendant had reason to know that the van was commercial. The problem is their verdict appears to be based on a factual misstatement."

"Which the judge was aware of and refused to remedy in any way. Worse than that, which the judge was aware of and allowed to be repeated!"

"What a strong appeal, I believe the leading case is—"

"Appeal. Guys like you get all excited about the appeal. Don't you see that I view the very existence of an appeal as a disastrous failure? No much worse, a personal affront of the highest order for which I blame you."

"What about a 330.30 motion?"

"I know, I have to do one."

"A motion to set aside the verdict."

"Yes."

"The relevant question under such a motion is—"

"I know all about them Toom. I just never thought I'd have occasion to do one and I blame you."

"I think you have a great argument that—"

"Don't you want to know why I blame you?"

"You don't blame me."

"You're right, I don't, but someone has to take the blame for this fiasco and I'm telling you right now, it's not going to be me. I wash my hands of this whole affair is what I do."

"Perhaps—"

"Let's not talk about that trial anymore Toomie, agreed?"

"O.K.," he said then looked around sheepishly only finally meeting my eyes when I conspicuously stared at his swiveling head. "Last week you said that once you had completed the trial, you would be available to fully discuss Jalen Kingg's appeal. I believe the agreement was that I would assist you with Hurtado in return for a promise to reconsider your refusal to work on Kingg because of the Skittles."

"Right, an agreement I fully complied with. You helped me and I gave you a promise. What more do you want from me? I held up my end."

"Fine, I misspoke. My help was in exchange not just for a mere promise but for the actual reconsideration."

"All I can go by is the language you used. Precision in language is the most critical of human endeavors. If I were to ignore your plain language and provide actual reconsideration in exchange for your help I would be indirectly encouraging future sloppiness in your language, greater sin of which I am not aware. I consider you my portly friend and I could never do that to such a friend, meaning one who's portly."

"Well then, aside from our agreement, you did in fact make a promise. If you did not now actually reconsider you would be breaking that promise. What are your feelings on that?"

"Well, putting aside for the moment my admitted sophistry, what is the status of my promise in light of your dismal performance on Hurtado?"

"Dismal? The current state of the law is such that—"

"Don't worry Toom, I just like to see your facial and other non-verbal reactions. You really think I would abandon you the way that Ledo bastard abandoned us? After everything we've been through together? Don't ever forget that promise I made to you decades ago in the sweaty jungles of Vietnam as you lay dying from V.C. lead in your gut. Remember it?"

"No, but as I recall you placed it there in a friendly fire mishap."

"I don't think that's accurate but truthfully that whole period was a drug-induced haze for me so you may be right. Anyway the reason I was calling you yesterday was my cousin."

"Cousin?"

"Yeah I have this cousin who came here from Colombia about a year ago. Only I recently found out he came in illegally from Mexico and into Texas. Anyway he dressed some van up like a giant hot dog and started selling them."

"He was selling vans that had been decorated to look like oversized frankfurters?"

"No he was selling hot dogs out of the van, its wiener-like appearance serving as a kind of automotive advertisement."

"Got it."

"Anyway he got arrested for selling them without a license."

"Uh-oh."

"Exactly."

"I.N.S.?"

"Yup, there anything I can do?"

"He entered illegally?"

"Apparently."

"I don't know much about this area of the law, but my guess is there's not much you can do, they just remand them and initiate deportation proceedings right?"

"Yeah but the question is can you fight it in any way?"

"I doubt it because the bottom line is he has no arguable right to be here."

"I know but c'mon there has to be something."

"Most just come back, I believe, although re-entry does constitute a federal crime."

"And he'll certainly never be granted legal entry."

"Correct."

"So now what?"

"Well unless you're going to break him out of the facility where he's being held."

"Great idea, there's no other choice. You in?"

"In what?"

"I can't do it alone for Chrissakes there's bound to be *some* security. How about a deal? You help me break my cousin out and I'll promise to help you spring any relatives of yours who may be incarcerated in the future."

"You'll promise or you'll actually help?"

"Now you're thinking Toom, maybe you are smart after all."

"I'll check on this I.N.S. thing for you but I'm fairly certain there's nothing one can do."

"How about more than *one*?"

"I'll check. As for Kingg there's a bit of a problem."

"What is it?"

"Twenty days."

"How many?"

"Twenty."

"Good Lord."

"How far along on your point are you?"

"I can get it done Toom. It's just going to be brutal. How about you?"

"I'll be fine. But one of us has to go down there very soon, this weekend at the latest."

"Not one of us, me, right? It's my point."

"I suppose."

"You're right too, it has to be this weekend in case something comes up."

"There's a flight out of Newark Friday morning, I checked. We can set up attorney visits for both Saturday and Sunday and you can catch an early Monday morning flight back. I talked to Pat Haggerty, she's in charge of finance and she says they'll pay for it all."

"Anything else?"

"That's pretty much everything."

"I commend you for your thoroughness. Why can't we both go?"

"I have a wedding this weekend."

"Congratulations but you don't invite me?"

"I'm not getting married, I'm a guest."

"Good point."

"So you'll go?"

"Well I won't really know anybody except you, but sure I'll go."

"Not to the wedding, to Alabama."

"Oh, sure, always wanted to see the resplendent beaches of Alabama."

"You're going to Atmore, no beaches."

"You always screw me Toomie. Man I've got a lot to do before I get on that plane, expect a lot of late night calls."

"That's fine. I believe I'm in the mood for some coffee, would you like to join me?"

"No, I'm never again leaving this office."

"Well I'm going to get some, would you like me to bring you back some form of beverage?"

"Yes."

"Coffee?"

"Yes."

"How?"

"I'm easy, just get me one of those I think it's called a fatslap-pushpush-in-the-bush-consigliere-capillary-freezy-supremicious or something, extra non-decaf please. Now when the guy pours the espresso into the foamy milk please make sure that he pierces the smallest possible area of the upper foam. The result should be akin to a brown pin prick on a sea of white. Moreover, when he pours the espresso in he should do so at such a deliberate rate that the espresso and the milk, which incidentally should be foamed to no more than a seventy-five percent congealment status, will not mix but rather will form two distinct levels featuring two different colors, with a great deal of wavy quantum action taking place at the border where they conjoin. Once that's done I shall like a fair amount of cinnamon sprinkled atop of the now pierced milk. Now when I say a fair amount of cinnamon I do not mean that the entire surface area should be covered. Rather the appearance of the cinnamon should be not unlike that of a distant nebula, such appearance with which I'm sure you're familiar. Remember, a cinnamon nebula is the goal. A cinnebula if you will. As for sugar, enough should be added to combat the inherent bitterness of espresso coffee but not so much added that it overpowers all the other competing flavors the beverage brings to the table. Also do not stir the beverage, as such a stirring would undoubtedly compromise the dual-level system I just mentioned. Instead add the sugar at a rate where each individual sugar granule will have its component molecules sufficiently bombarded by surrounding molecules, traveling at a high rate of speed due to the extreme heat of the beverage, as to occasion the dissolving of the granule before it reaches the bottom of the cup. Lastly, please take care to walk the drink over with minimal bipedal concussion so as to not disrupt the dual-level system. Thanks man."

"I'm just going downstairs to the gentleman with the newsstand so do you want from the orange-lidded dispenser or the brown?"

"Brown."

Sweet silence.

"Hey remember me?"

"Sure, Derrin."

"Darius."

"You sure?"

"Yes."

"O.K., what's up?"

"Sorry about your case, I heard what happened. That's bullshit man."

"Happens."

"Anyway, everything turn out O.K. with DeLeon?"

"Not unless you know where he is."

"What do you mean? Isn't he still in?"

"No I got him out so he could be a C.I. but then he disappeared."

"Disappeared how?"

"How do you disappear? I guess you stop returning the D.A.'s phone calls, miss a couple of meetings, then are not home when they come looking for you."

"So he's going to get—"

"Screwed he's going to get, if they ever find him."

"I heard, just a rumor, that you tried to punch Troie Liszt in the face."

"You did?"

"Yeah."

"And what happened?"

"He ducked just in time and you made a hole in his wall."

"Amazing."

"Is it true?"

"Somewhat."

458

"What happened?"

"Actually he came after me, throwing punches with the worst of intentions after learning I was unwittingly sleeping with his wife."

"Wife? I didn't even know Liszt was married."

"You're surprised? Imagine mine."

"But the hole."

"Sure, that was made by me trying to get away from him. Notice how the shape of the hole conforms perfectly with the shape of my head."

"Really?"

"I have to go to court now."

"O.K. I'll get going."

"Thanks. Listen tell anyone you want about what Liszt did, but leave out the part about his wife, that's touchy stuff."

"Sure."

He left.

"Here you go."

Coffee.

"Thanks, Toom."

"I heard the strangest thing coming up here."

"What's that?"

"Did you swing a bat at Liszt's head, miss him, and make a hole in his wall?"

"That's generally true but it's being taken out of context."

"What possible context could justify trying to hit Liszt in the head with a bat?"

"Well what you're not being told is that, at the time I swung that bat, Liszt was coming at me with a beer bottle he had just broken over his desk."

"What?"

"Don't look at me. Something about the Yankees' third starter being better than the ace of the Mets' staff, I don't know. You'll agree I had to defend myself right?"

"Be serious Casi, what happened?"

"No, this is horrible!"

"What?"

"You don't bring me a little snack to go with this coffee?"

"Sorry, should we get together tonight to discuss Kingg?"

"We should and shall."

"Six?"

"Yes."

"Here?"

"Yes."

"O.K., I'll see you then."

"Yes."

And he left.

And I stayed and nothing happened.

Until Dane came back and just sat there. Minutes passed.

"You going to say anything?" I finally asked.

"I heard you pulled a knife on Liszt. That's good. It's good for you to practice violence, which will be a necessary component of our heist."

"I never *pulled*, as you say, a knife on Liszt."

"Gun?"

"No for Christ, what are you possibly talking about?"

"That's disappointing."

"Besides, whether violence is or is not a necessary component of this fictional heist we've talked about is personally irrelevant because, as I've already indicated to you today, I am not going to be a participant."

"I'll tell you Casi, this constant vacillation is entirely unbecoming and frankly beneath you. You have to decide, this instant, who and what you are. Are you saint, sinner, or something in between, because nothing's worse than in between. To disappear into the lumpy, undefined center when the lure is so clearly found at the edges. No-one *aspires* to mediocrity. Mediocrity withers and dies with nary a notice; its practitioners rendered mute by their race to the middle. Sinner or Saint, that is your question. Although, to be fair, the question is so easily and intuitively answerable that it should hold little of your interest. Here's what I mean. What do you see, what do you feel, when you look inside yourself? Is burgeoning Sainthood in there as best you can tell? Do you sense a placid patience, a humble acceptance of your inherent unworthiness? Do you feel a serene resignation that your base wants will go unquenched? And a gratitude that it is so? Do you somehow *just know* that your life was meant to unfold solely in the service of God and others, to the neglect, even detriment, of your own well-being? If these saintly elements don't reveal themselves to you in response to your inward gaze don't despair, at least not yet. This doesn't necessarily mean your relegation to a brief life of anonymous toil. Because I'll bet when you peer inside you see something else. I bet you see an impatient anger that threatens to engulf your very being. Anger that the stupid can rise, covering the talented in their wake, with only negligible dissenting cries. Anger that the sons and daughters of Dionysus are allowed to continually gorge on the blood and flesh of the cowering weak. Anger that some can drape their hearts in black robes as they toss another human away like a cumbersome bag of bones, can lock your cousin, your own blood, in a cage like a laboratory chimp. Anger that all this occurs against the unforgiving backdrop of never relenting time, the passage of which slowly robs you of your power to wield a remedy, shrinking you before every watchful eye. You feel that incipient rage right? Good because the first step is not some bullshit, new-agey acceptance that the anger exists. The first step is to bypass that altogether, pinch your nose, shut your eyes, and jump into a pool of that simmering fury. The frigid jolt on your skin will shake you alive and impel you towards action. It's this very action I now offer you and what do

461

I get in return? Indecision."

"These observations might carry a scintilla of weight if you were proposing we rob an armored car, a bank, or a police evidence room. Instead you propose we rip off people who are themselves outlaws, maybe even subscribing to the same ethos you now extol."

"The money we're going to take is generated by the War on Drugs – that hypocritical, mass-produced mindfuck currently lining everybody's pockets but ours. Besides this is just a first step. We didn't choose this setup, it fell in our laps. Nonetheless, while planning this heist we're going to be able to forget everything else through the thrill that comes from exhausting our abilities. When we do it, our bodies will be electrified by our naked displays of will. And when we've succeeded, you will not only *know* that you are one badass fuck, but you will finally and truly be free. The money will liberate you and give you power. Use that power however you wish. At the moment I'm weighing taking my share, going to Washington Heights, and using this tennis machine I have to shoot hundred dollar bills into the midday sky. The human roaches will have to flood the streets and scavenge for green paper, exposing the rotting foundation beneath society's crumbling facade. How entertaining. Can you picture it, the beauty, the statement? What can you say about art where the medium is human bodies and their inanimate captors? But I do get your point. Armored cars and banks would be better. That can come later, after this first step. Meanwhile what do *you* plan to do afterwards? Because you said you were in."

"And you said you were going to come back at lunchtime, yet here you are well before."

"True."

"I have work to do."

"I'll be back."

"I'm sure."

*

I didn't say that just to get rid of Dane, although I did want to get rid of him. I wanted to do some work, didn't want to fritter away the morning in chatter. I wanted to make lists. So I did. Lists like this one:

1. make list;
2. experience the reduction of stress that comes from the mere creation of a list;
3. come to the realization that this reduction in stress is illusory as it fails to be based on any tangible accomplishment;
4. armed with this realization, accomplish actual, necessary tasks, but first;
5. so as to avoid scattershot activity, and maximize productivity, think of what needs to be done and make a list.

I wrote furiously as lists spun off into sublists that were listed in various sensible orders. It worked, all this writing, and served to ebb my recent dark past. I couldn't stop. I would finish a page only to push it off my desk and onto the waiting floor to begin a new one. My dwindling volition was in those pages. When I was done you couldn't see carpet for the pages.

"What's all this?" asked Conley.

"Lists."

"Of what?"

"Of everything. For example, that's a list of all the lists I was going to make. Here's a list of my favorite all time lists. There's a list of all the trials I've done. A list of all the hearings. I made a list of everybody I knew who later died. Conversely, I listed everybody who started living within my awareness. I listed every single person I know. I listed all the people I don't know in ascending order of knowledge and descending order of ignorance. A list of people I wish I knew and those I wish I didn't. Things I wish had happened and those I wish hadn't. The former list is divided into those things I could have made happen, and which therefore require self-flagellation, and those beyond my control. Some of the lists are rankings. Everything is ranked. Artists and works of art. Scientists and works of science. Pugilists and works of Pugilism. Theologians and works of Theology. All the ologies, for that matter, are ranked. The aforementioned Theology along with Biology, Geology, Endocrinology, it's all there. The greatest of all time are in those pages. And the worst."

"Why?"

"Because everything is susceptible to discrete, unproblematic listing. Anything can be ranked. Subjectivity has nothing to do with it. If something is ranked higher it simply *is* higher. Better. Understand?"

"I do and I agree. In the future, we'll rank all humans according to the quality of their particular genome. A numerical value will be assessed and tattooed between the individual's right and left ass cheek. A job interview, for example, would simply consist of looking into someone's ass."

"I thought everyone was going to look and be substantially the same?"

"I'm describing an intervening step. Anyway I need to talk to you."

"I don't know enough about that stuff."

"No this is a work-related conversation."

"Really? We ever had one?"

"Doubt it. Anyway as I'm sure you know."

"Don't be so sure, this is me you're talking to, and I can't talk right now either."

"Why not?"

"I'm busy."

"Doing what?"

"Working, what else?"

"Because it looks like you're just writing reams of these lists."

"That's the thing about looks, they have the power to deceive and all that. Anyway I'm hard at work and as a supervisor in this place

I believe your primary function is to maximize my productivity. In accordance with that, I shall now ask you to quit me to my work. In exchange for my promise to discuss the matter with you later of course."

"Very well."

"Thanks Con."

Only I didn't do any work after he left or at all before I met up with Dane for lunch.

We were back at Deleterie's for like the third time in ten days even sitting at the same table. I decided I would eat like never before. Maybe not go back in the afternoon either.

It was called a mozzarella caprese salad. Perfect slices of fresh mozzarella, made on the premises, without even a hint of a salty presence, as it should be. The slices were arranged circularly and flanked by similar slices of fresh plum tomatoes, which although unmistakably red, veered towards the orange as I liked. Atop sat razor-thin slices of angelically lean and pink prosciutto ham. Completed by the occasional sprig of romaine lettuce and topped by extra virgin olive oil and balsamic vinegar, and all in conjunction with fresh warm semolina bread. The blessed concoction was perfect and it was only the beginning.

"Have you thought about what I said Casi?"

"You said something?"

"Man you looked pissed Friday."

"Friday?"

"When you got that verdict."

"How do you know?"

"I was there."

"Where?"

"In the courtroom."

"Why didn't you say anything?"

"What was there to say?"

"What were you doing there?"

"Did you know studies indicate that 94.3 percent of the time an individual changes his or her mind he or she later comes to regret that change. Did you know that figure jumps to 99.9 percent when the mind-change involves participation in a heist or caper?"

"I'd need to see the underlying figures. When is this thing anyway? Ten days you said? Ten days from last Wednesday is this weekend and I'm going to be in Alabama anyway so I guess we can forget all this."

"Here's why what I'm proposing is just."

"Will you forget all that, deal with my logistical objection first."

"O.K. when are you coming back? Who cares anyway, it's simple, cancel the trip."

"Can't."

"Why in the world are you going to Alabama?"

"To meet with my death penalty client."

"Send the other guy."

"He can't, he's getting married or something."

"Easy then, just bail out. I see attorneys do it all the time when they realize the extent of the time commitment. I mean it's not part of your employment here, you have no responsibility or debt to anyone."

"Bail on the project? You nuts? You actually think I would dick Toomberg in that manner? No way, Toom's the only friend I have hence I'm not dicking him. I'm going, I leave Friday and don't return until Monday so it's not happening, sorry."

"Fine I'll go with you and we can keep planning and practicing there. I can always say I'm joining the project."

"I see and I guess we'll just have to contact Escalera and ask him to move the whole drop to Alabama so we can rip him off right?"

"The exact date of the delivery is three o'clock Wednesday morning. The Wednesday after you get back."

"I see. This you know how?"

"It's all in this packet. Here."

"What the hell is this?"

"Information. All the information relevant to the heist. The exact date, time, and place, along with a blueprint of the place and other relevant documents. I anticipated questions of the sort you just asked, so every piece of information has a cited source."

"This thing's like . . ."

"358 pages."

"When did you?"

"What do you think I've been doing the last five days? Research, what else?"

"Where does your research tell you DeLeon is?"

"Not sure."

"Why not?"

"Well I know he got his $50,000. Where he went with it I don't know definitively but my guess is Santo Domingo."

"How do you know he got his money?"

"It's in the packet. Read it later."

"So you've been busy."

"Beaverlike, aside from acquiring the necessary facts—"

"Facts? What facts? You mean this?"

"Right. Aside from that, I've taken some time to ponder the moral objections you raised earlier."

"Forget all that will you. I don't want to talk about that anymore. So your painstaking analysis leads you to think it would be a good idea to come to Alabama with me?"

"Yes."

"Why?"

"Because we need all the time we can get. Time for us to formulate the plan together and time to practice its execution."

"You mean there's no plan in this packet?"

"No. I can acquire info of the sort in that packet on my own, but the actual plan has to be a cooperative effort between the two of us in order to be perfect and in order to maximize its chances of success."

"Why did you set about acquiring all this info since I had said no? Some of this was acquired before I said yes on Saturday right?"

"A lot of it but we don't have unlimited time here so I had to take the chance. Besides I knew you'd come around."

"Were you going to do it alone otherwise?"

"No, it can't be done alone."

"Were you going to go with someone else?"

"No, it was the two of us or not at all."

"Look at me."

"What?"

"Were you going to go with someone else?"

"No."

"So who else have you told?"

"No-one."

"I can't imagine you did all this work on the off chance I would change my mind."

"I sleep like three hours a day. What else would I do? Besides I put a lot of stock in my ability to read people. That said, your concern is understandable and only serves to bolster my belief that you are the only person I could do this with."

"My belief in you, on the other hand, is taking a hit."

"How so?"

"You propose that you and I, like two members of the Legion of Doom, join forces to engage in a lucrative heist. By way of convincing me to participate you've continually pointed to your thoroughness as a primary factor that all but ensures our success. Well I like thoroughness and precision, I really do, but I also recognize that there's a potential downside to their pursuit. It seems to me that success in a heist involves two major components. One is getting the goods, in this case money, the other is not getting caught. Of these two the second is by far the more important. Meaning if we try to do this and for whatever reason are thwarted and never get the money but ultimately nobody is ever the wiser then I can live with that. On the other hand, if we go in there and walk out with tens of millions of dollars, but a year later I'm in jail getting a head start on twenty to life guess what? I won't consider that a success.

"Here's why I mention this: The way I see it, any thorough effort expended towards the goal of getting the money has the potential for increasing the chance we get caught. You say you should come to Alabama with me because that will enhance our preparation. I say it will also increase the chances of us getting caught by creating a hard record, a paper trail of airplane tickets, hotel reservations and the like that will tie the two of us together and at the very least increase the chance that if one of us gets caught the other will get caught. You see what I'm getting at? I see this blueprint to the building and I think that's great and certainly useful. But immediately I also think, how did you get it? And how could you later explain getting a blueprint to the very building where a crime occurred days later? You see every action you take in support of a crime, and that can theoretically be proven later, has to have a compelling innocent explanation."

"Are you done?"

"You want more examples? You say DeLeon got his money. How do you know that? To learn that you probably tied yourself to this group of people in at least some form and moreover in a manner that was likely unique for them and therefore likely to be recalled by them. Just as I'm tied to the whole thing, for better or worse, by virtue of the fact that I am DeLeon's attorney and attended that meeting. So this pamphlet is not an unqualified good in my view. For example, how was it generated? This thing would be People's Exhibit 1 in any, God forbid, trial. Is there a record of it anywhere? On a disk? A hard drive? I need to know that all of this has been part of your focus."

"May I respond?"

"Please. But first a warning. Don't respond by saying that I'm giving law enforcement too much credit and that the things I point out would never conceivably become relevant. If you said something like that I concede you would probably be right, at least under the usual definition of right, but I don't care for that kind of right because in this situation I'm not interested in probabilities. I want the thoroughness to cut both ways and be at least as concerned with the contrapuntal aim of avoiding detection. Of course someone honestly claiming to pursue perfection would never resort to such an argument anyway, right?"

"Is it possible to be proud and chagrined simultaneously? What an astounding lack of faith in me you continually display. If you'll look closely at the print on the pamphlet that has generated such controversy, you will see that it was generated via a typewriter, with no computer involved in any aspect of the process. Also if you'll read the last paragraph on the last page you will learn that the typewriter used to create the pamphlet has been destroyed and no longer exists. In fact, when you read the pamphlet closely you will see that every single nugget of information included therein, in addition to identifying its source, is followed by a little section describing the precautions taken during its acquisition. So you'll see that the thoroughness absolutely does cut both ways and consequently your fears are unfounded.

"As for my suggestion that I accompany you to Alabama, you have a legitimate point; although it is not one that should cause you to lose even the slightest amount of faith in me. It has always been my contention, from the very beginning of our discussions, that in order to achieve the perfect crime the input and insight of both of us would be required. This is different from my previous pursuit of perfection which essentially required only my action. The other interesting difference is the one you've now pointed out where there is this byplay and tension between learning as much as we possibly can about this transaction while being careful not to needlessly tie ourselves to this upcoming event that is likely to gain some measure of notoriety at least in its limited community. That's why you and I are ideally suited to teaming on this. Because you are right to detect a possible slight recklessness on my part as it relates to the possibility of getting caught. Just as I was correct in detecting personality traits in you that would serve to counteract this undesirable element. So rather than shake your confidence in me the preceding should only serve to heighten your confidence in my abilities as evidenced by my choice of you as a partner. In other words, the system I've created worked beautifully. I proposed something that was less-than-ideal and you vetoed it. If this is indicative of the skill we will cumulatively bring to this endeavor then you can start reserving those Concorde tickets. I'll bring the Hydrogen, you bring the Oxygen and we'll never thirst again."

"Or we'll drown."

Next was the fried calamari. I could tell the guy had fried the rings the exactly proper amount of time. What I mean is that, prior to dumping in the squid, he must have heated the oil to the correct temperature of about 350° so that the calamari would fry quickly enough to avoid excessively absorbing oil and fat. The result was beautiful, golden-brown rings of calamari that were neither over-cooked nor overly chewy and which were covered with thin breading that clung to the rings even as I dunked them into the moderately spicy cup of marinara sauce provided on the side. Superb.

"Let's let today be the last day of inaction," said Dane. "Take the thing home, read it, and tomorrow we can start to plan in earnest. I think any major objections you might have will be addressed in there."

"Tell me what you think is going to happen."

"O.K., next Wednesday—"

"A week from this Wednesday?"

"Yes, Wednesday morning."

"You mean like Tuesday night slash Wednesday morning?"

"Right. At exactly three in the morning a woman will drive an old

Chevy Nova into the garage of 410 East 123rd Street between 1st and 2nd Avenue. In the trunk of the car will be cocaine with a street value of nearly one hundred million dollars."

"Where'd you get that address from?"

"From DeLeon."

"When?"

"Last week, when I spoke to him at the twelfth floor bridge."

"How many times total did you speak with him?"

"Just that once."

"For how long?"

"Slightly over two hours."

"What reason did you give him for that level of interest?"

"He loves to talk and I told him I needed the information because I would be working on his case, which was extraordinary."

"Other lawyers and clients were there?"

"Sure. They came and went. None of them was there for the entire conversation. No-one we know either."

"It's not exactly soundproof there. Who's to say some guy who's in didn't hear the whole thing?"

"No way. C'mon we were careful. Remember he's a C.I., no different than others. We made sure nobody heard."

"Did you take notes?"

"No."

"Two hours plus and no notes?"

"No need. I recorded the entire conversation. A transcript of the complete audio recording is in there and is largely responsible for the packet's bulk."

"How?"

"Simple. I snuck a little tape recorder in there without anyone knowing. Don't worry the only tape was destroyed along with the typewriter used to transcribe its contents."

"What makes you think he was telling you the truth about the date and location?"

"I went to the location and I also have the blueprint and 410 is exactly as he described it."

"What about the location he gave the cops at our meeting?"

"Similar but clear across town on the West Side."

"Did he tell you if he ever gave the cops a specific date?"

"Yes. He said he met with them the Tuesday morning before we talked and told them it would be this Saturday at four a.m. A complete lie."

"How complete? What kind of place is that?"

"The place has no connection to anything."

"It must have some connection, DeLeon didn't just create a place similar to the actual location out of thin air."

"Fine, you want the whole story. The actual place, 410 East 123rd, belongs to Escalera's second cousin. The guy's totally legit, a union electrician and everything, and in no way connected to selling. Anyway Escalera loves the guy's place and thinks it's ideal for this kind of thing so about a year ago he starts shopping with help from DeLeon for a similar place to buy. One of the places Escalera looks at is 368 Riverside. It's a lot like 410 with precisely the kind of garage Escalera likes and everything. Well it never goes much further than that and Escalera ends up buying nothing. So when DeLeon is sitting there and decides to give the cops a fake address he remembers 368 Riverside, which of course has the benefit of being both architecturally plausible yet pretty far from the true location."

"And that's where the cops will be this Saturday at four a.m.?"

"Exactly."

"And when they find nothing they'll create some excuse to arrest everyone in there then squeeze them for info."

"Fine, they'll get nothing. I checked, the people living there are all squeaky clean. No records, which is rare for that area."

"And if the cops say to them *do you know someone named Escalera* will they say *hey isn't that the guy who almost bought our house?*"

"Very good but no. The house was sold but not to Escalera. It was sold to these clean people who had no contact with Escalera whatsoever."

"So what *will* the cops think on Saturday?"

"I hope they'll think that DeLeon pulled a fast one on them and invented the whole scenario to get out."

"Doubtful. But what about 410? What's the deal with that joint?"

"Clean. I ran the address in all the appropriate databases and as far as I can tell the place has never been the subject of any law enforcement activity at all. The owner is Escalera's cousin and his wife, both fully clean. Obviously all of that is part of the location's appeal from Escalera's standpoint."

"Why would this upstanding electrician suddenly agree to transform his home into a stash house?"

"He doesn't know. You see, as I said, Escalera loves the place and thinks it would be perfect for this but he knows his cousin would never go for it. Well as luck would have it, the couple has a tenth wedding anniversary coming up. So here comes Escalera with their anniversary present, an all-expenses-paid trip to Paradise. Paradise Island in the Bahamas for, you guessed it, the week of the exchange."

"Sure about all that? Because DeLeon made it sound like a neutral third party would be there and would be counting the money before giving Escalera the keys to the car with the drugs in it."

"All bullshit designed to draw attention away from the real location."

"Have you verified any of this?"

"It depends what you mean by verified."

"Ah."

"No listen. In addition to verifying that 410 is precisely the kind of place described by DeLeon, I have verified that it is indeed owned by a union electrician and his wife and that the electrician is in fact Escalera's cousin although he does not share his last name. I have also established that, aside from these two childless individuals, no-one else calls that address home. Most importantly, I have verified that these two individuals have booked a flight to sunny Paradise Island for next week. And guess who paid for the tickets? The plastic of one Antonio Escalera. All strong evidence that Mr DeLeon was telling me the truth don't you think?"

"I do. How did you do all that?"

"Not hard. Deeds, tax returns, Escalera was so proud of the deal he got that he made DeLeon drunk talking about the airline. So I trust you see the unlikelihood that DeLeon invented all of this or even that he referred to this factual backdrop in a fictional way. Correct or should I go into it?"

"No."

"No you don't see or no don't go into it because you do see?"

"Fine, he told you what he thought was the truth."

"No he knows the truth. The airplane tickets, for example, are not a product of DeLeon's mind."

"So he told you what was true at the time but that was two weeks before the exchange and we have no source for further information. DeLeon's gone with the wind. The info he gave you was very specific. Next Wednesday at precisely three in the morning. If that changes, for any one of a million possible reasons, we have no way of knowing."

"I suppose it could change but it's unlikely."

"Why? They have the house for the whole week. It could be anytime that week."

"No, you'll see, when you read the transcript, that I covered this exact thing with DeLeon. I wondered how he could be so sure of the exact time and that it wouldn't be changed. I masked this by saying I was concerned that the deal had already gone off depriving him of a legal benefit. He said it would never be changed because Escalera is a very superstitious man who loves the middle."

"Middle?"

"Yeah, all middles."

"Middles of what?"

"Middle of anything."

"What does that mean?"

"It means, for example, that if you gave him the choice between the numbers one, two, and three he will always choose two because it is the middle number. In high school he played nose tackle in a 3–4 and in college, when he was no longer comparatively big enough to play the line, he switched to middle linebacker in a 4–3. If he's in a car's back seat he sits on the middle hump. If he's playing checkers—"

"I get the picture but shouldn't this then be on a Thursday?"

"No because the couple flies on a Sunday and returns on a Saturday. That means that the house will be completely empty for five days, Monday through Friday with Wednesday being the middle day. Escalera would never change the day."

"Why three then?"

"His lucky number. I told you, superstitious."

"Of course it could still be changed due to circumstances beyond Escalera's control."

"I suppose but so what? It should be pretty easy to tell on that date if something is going down or not. Remember we know about the plane tickets. The house should be empty. If we detect any activity whatsoever, especially a car driving into the garage at three a.m., then we know it's on. If nothing happens, then we turn around and go home with nothing lost."

"True. Now let's say it happens precisely as DeLeon said it would. What has already happened and what will happen?"

"Can we get some more bread with that too pal? Thanks."

My main course was in front of me now, steaming and calling. Beautiful breasts of free-range-on-weekends chicken pounded out then stuffed with fresh spinach and a touch of prosciutto in a sweet Marsala wine and mushroom sauce with caramelized onions.

476

"Well?"

"Well what?"

"Are you going to answer my question?"

"Our food's here," he said his upturned palms cradling his dish in visual support.

"Yeah?"

"I certainly can't eat and talk at the same time."

"Try."

"How can you eat and listen at the same time?"

"I'll manage."

"Fine, it's all in the packet. DeLeon got out the same day I talked to him. I'm not sure if it was a necessary prerequisite or not, but about thirty-six hours later Freddy's shipment arrived in the U.S. The shipment represents everything Freddy has and signals his exit from the drug trade. He used his brother's old line to get the stuff in, with none of them knowing there's anything particularly special about this shipment regarding size or anything else. Remember Freddy has dismantled his brother's entire crew both in the D.R. and the little he had here. So what he did is have the stuff delivered to his nephew's house in the U.S. The nephew's not connected in any way and the extent of his involvement is just keeping the stuff in his house for a week or so. I know what you're thinking but nobody, not DeLeon, not Escalera, not anyone, knows who this guy is or where he lives."

"Well he's Freddy's nephew right?"

"Yeah but that's a dead end, trust me. Anyway there the stuff will stay until the mule goes and gets it that day."

"That day?"

"No, you're right. Not necessarily *that day* since that would imply that the current stash location is within a day's driving distance of 410 and although that is almost certainly the case, since nobody knows where the stuff currently is then no-one can say that with complete confidence."

"What's your guess?"

"I think the stuff's nearby in the outskirts of the city but we won't be able to determine where."

"Who's the mule?"

"No-one knows except Freddy. The only thing Escalera and DeLeon know is that at 3:00 on the dot *someone,* acting alone, will drive a car into the garage at 410."

"What car?"

"Her own car, connected to no-one."

"A Nova."

"Right but it could be any woman who owns a Nova in the whole damn country and that's assuming she's the registered owner, and I can't think of a way to narrow it down much more than that."

"Me either, yet."

"Anyway she takes all the risk. She picks up an antique Tansu trunk at the house of the nephew. A locked trunk to which she does not have the key. The key to the trunk was previously mailed to Escalera from Freddy. In return Escalera used a mailing service to mail Freddy a garage door opener that opens the garage to 410 and a key. Presumably, Freddy then turned around and mailed the opener to his mule here. Next Wednesday morning the mule will drive the Nova, with the locked Tansu in the trunk of the car, to 410. She will use the garage door opener to open the door and enter the garage at exactly 3:00 a.m. She cannot be late. If at 3:01 she's still not there, Escalera and his minions will assume something is wrong, they will deactivate the garage door opener, and she will be denied entry. She cannot be early either for the same reason. In the garage will be two of Escalera's guys. Everything I know about them, which isn't much, is in the packet. They will pop the trunk to the car, take the chest and one of them will bring it into the house which connects to the garage from the kitchen. Using the key they will open the chest then weigh and test the stuff inside. The mule will stay in the garage with one of the

478

guys. If everything is cool, a locked red duffel bag, which Freddy was previously given the key to, will be placed in the trunk of the car. If the third floor watchers give the go ahead in terms of police presence, the lady will get in her car and drive off, the transaction complete. Bottom line is about eight men in that house and the mule. The mule is required to come alone but we can't unequivocally foreclose the possibility that others will be lingering in the vicinity when she leaves ready to take possession of the bag. And that's the deal in a nutshell, though there are of course a lot of details that you need to learn."

"So."

"So I want that red bag. More specifically, I want the fifteen to twenty million dollars in untraceable cash that's going to be in that bag. Cash that cannot be reported stolen. In my mind that bag already belongs to me, I just need to go and pick it up. I want that bag."

"Me too, I guess, but how do we get it?"

"That is the question."

"How are you leaning?"

"The money will be inside 410 some time before 3:00. The mule only complicates things. We can go in and get the bag before she even shows up."

"No."

"Why not?"

"What happens to the woman when she shows up?"

"What concern is that of ours?"

"No."

"We'll talk about it, in your packet is a description of the kind of guns we'll need."

"No."

"It's in there, trust me, you just haven't looked closely enough."

"No, I mean no guns."

"What do you mean no guns? What the hell are you talking about?"

"I'm talking about neither of us having guns on that day."

"You crazy? You know the eight people I was telling you about? I hate to break the news to you but they *will* have guns. And they will be jumpy and tense because they know security sucks."

"Or they'll be complacent, thinking there must be no danger if security is so lax."

"That's quite a gamble, don't you think?"

"No, because even if you're right and they're super-jumpy I still won't bring a gun or even go with you if you bring a gun."

"You're serious."

"Of course."

"We need guns."

"I won't do it."

"We'll be killed."

"Doubt it, who would kill me?"

"Who? Someone who has a gun and isn't keen on you taking their millions."

"I can live with that risk Dane. After all we're the ones creating this contentious situation right? It seems only right that we should take the brunt of the risk."

"What exactly is your objection to the guns? You prefer a grave risk of death? I personally don't fear death in the slightest, but the overwhelming majority do so I'm rather curious."

"Guns are for the stupid Dane. A well-trained monkey can go in and fire a gun, big fucking deal."

"You propose we just ask nicely for the money?"

"Violence is the language of the simple. You initially proposed that we formulate a plan using our intellects and execute it using our wills, but now you propose we go in with guns like a couple of high-school-dropout-liquor-store-robbers. That's your idea of perfection? If you think we will fail without guns, if you think we'll be killed, then let's not do it. *You* wanted *me* to do it remember? Not the other way around. Did you think I would just be a passenger on your train to criminality? I bring my own beliefs about what constitutes a proper plan. That's why you wanted me remember?"

"Is there anything else I should know about?"

"The chest."

"Whose chest?"

"The Tansu with the drugs in it."

"What about it?"

"I want it."

"I see. Greed. How do you propose we turn it into cash while still paying extreme attention to avoiding apprehension as you have mandated?"

"I don't want to turn it into cash I want to destroy it."

"Destroy it? Why's that?"

"You're insane if you think I'm going to be even peripherally responsible for some two-month-old girl being left unattended and gasping around in search of a tit in some ratty apartment while her mother goes out looking for crack."

"I see. But you're not willing to bring a gun into that house lest one of these people, who *does* actively contribute to the creation of gasping, unattended babies, gets hurt."

"Right."

"Do I have it all now?"

"More or less."

"Great, let's review. You're willing to come along on the heist but only if we go into an apartment where an extremely high-level drug deal is about to go down, completely unarmed, at precisely the moment the deal is to be consummated, so that the mule, who we don't know, can't be blamed, and take about fifteen million dollars and drugs worth seven times that from these undoubtedly heavily armed fellows. We then destroy the drugs, in the process ensuring we've made mortal enemies of numerous violent people both here

481

and in Santo Domingo. Do I present the general picture?"

"Yes."

"I like it."

Dessert was an espresso – is there a greater beverage? – which I willingly imbibed despite the fact it never failed to later create in me an inordinate anxiety, and a piece of cheesecake. The cheesecake was perfect, not that shitty New York crap, but Italian ricotta cheesecake. Light and grainy, barely sweet with the edges nice and brown at just the right thickness and topped with a sweet but natural tasting strawberry sauce swirl. Bliss.

"That was a brilliant meal my good man," said Dane addressing the serious waiter. "I can't speak for my tight-lipped friend here but I think everything was highly delicious. You work in proximity to a near-genius kitchen and by extension I'm prepared to label you, whether warranted or not, a man of extraordinary culinary gifts."

"Oh good, I'm glad you likeh. You come again no?"

"If I came any more I'd have to don an apron."

"Hah, hah, hah! And you signor?"

"I also thought everything was superb, thank you."

"Let's go," said Dane a bit later.

"Yeah," I said and we split.

Outside, in the cold, was all the reality you could bear. I still had to go to Cymbeline to hear Soldera's fate. Dane said he was going home to think so we parted ways somewhat abruptly. I looked up at the sky without real cause. It was true that the temperatures had unmistakably belonged to winter for quite some time but now the sky was finally reflecting true winter as well. And not early festive winter or dwindling late-stage winter either. This was exact midpoint winter, in appearance and fact, topped by a perfectly white firmament. Perfectly and uniformly White in a way that made me think Star Trek et alii had it all wrong when they portrayed the vast outer reaches of space as occasionally interrupted black. It wasn't black out there, it was white, and this was being revealed to me all at once without intervening gradations. You could climb high as you might and look all around but all you would see is missing color. Absence in every direction. Isotropic and sad White, nothing else and nothing more. And how could I have failed to notice until just then such an achromatic expanse? Such a vapid emptiness that precluded all matter and meaning. But those days it was true that a great many critical things were hidden from my view by their very prevalence.

There was a little girl
Who had a little curl
Right in the middle of her forehead,
When she was good
She was very, very good,
But . . .
    — Henry Wadsworth Longfellow

Chapter 15

Waiting for them to bring Raul Soldera down, and for Cymbeline to deign to return to the bench after the lunch break, I thought, surmised, conjectured, discovered, remembered, wished, guessed, intuited, researched, hoped, prayed, feared, speculated, theorized, recalled, learned, posited, and deduced that although Wilfred Benitez *was* born in the Bronx, as I said earlier, he actually lived most of his life in Puerto Rico.

His father Gregorio, or "Goyo", was in agreement with Dick Van Patten that eight was enough. Enough children and probably not too difficult to get Clara Benitez to agree. Wilfred Benitez was eighth and last. Of Wilfred's seven sibs, three were brothers and the three were Gregory, Alfonso, and Frankie. They weren't just brothers either they were colleagues, because Goyo didn't have sons, he had boxers. Boxers he managed and trained. His favorite boxer was his namesake Gregory. Gregory started boxing when he was eleven and if you've never heard of him, or of Wilfred's other two brothers and their boxing careers, rest assured that, outside of this, you likely never will. Wilfred Benitez, about whom you *will* hear a lot, first began boxing, that is, first had his skull repositioned around his brain, when he was seven years old.

He did this in a ring located in the backyard of the Benitez home in San Just, Puerto Rico, a *barrio* hidden a couple miles east of the capital, San Juan. The Benitez family was split, some in San Just, some in New York, and it was Gregory Benitez's misfortune to be in Puerto Rico, in that makeshift ring, in that sweltering backyard, across from his younger brother with the immense talent who repeatedly kicked his ass – a curious expression that rarely if ever involves an actual ass being actually kicked but which does seem to accurately reflect what it must feel like.

But Gregory was good too. Good enough that Goyo, whatever his level of ability at talent evaluation, could almost taste the distinct flavor of success nearby and so pursued it with his entire spirit. He threw himself into this. You've seen Goyos before. He was the mother teetering back and forth on her heels, at an angle from the stage, mouthing from memory all the lines her daughter will soon spit out to a receptive sea of docile heads wearing video cameras at the school play. He was that sagging father yelling at his son to pick up the back elbow as the little league ball approaches the vicinity of the plate, then reducing that batter to tears when, after being verbally paralyzed into inaction, he looks at a called third strike. He was them *in extremis.* And what was the result of that? If all the Benitez boys were given the Goyo treatment why did Wilfred become who he did and the others just his brothers?

I think Wilfred Benitez liked that backyard ring more than his brothers. But he wasn't better than them *because* he liked the ring more, rather he liked the ring more because he was better. The ring gave him something it couldn't give the others. And not because of Goyo or because of Wilfred's overwhelming effort. Not in this case.

The ability to hit and avoid being hit swirls around in the air, unattached and looking for a home. A little lands here, a little there.

More here, less there, and an in-between amount elsewhere, all in an unpredictable dance of musical chairs. For whatever reason, a whole damn lot landed on Wilfred Benitez and beginning in 1965 you could see for yourself, and over the years many did, in that San Just yard. Those who saw, *knew*, and more gratifyingly Wilfred knew.

In the ring he knew what you were going to throw, from where and at what angle, seemingly before you did. A brilliant counterpuncher, he also knew you were going to pay for that punch. And after a while you knew it too and so became reluctant to expose yourself by throwing any more punches, a bad reluctance to have in boxing.

Outside of the ring he knew far less. When he wasn't inhaling boxing, Wilfred exhaled it. School was only a mandatory respite from boxing so he stopped going after junior high. Later, multiple observers would comment on the childlike behavior that emanated from this unmistakably adult body and the difficulty he seemed to have emoting and processing complex thoughts. It was better those days when his mind matched his number and best when it was on that canvas, between those ropes, making instantaneous decisions that were never wrong.

Wilfred boxed every day. Every day of his life he threw punches. A left jab should shoot straight out from a rapid shoulder twitch. The straighter and stiffer the better. A good left hook, the kind any self-respecting Hispanic boxer aspires to throw, and the kind that serves as a perfectly appropriate counter to failed lead rights, ideally involves, whenever possible, a violently sudden hip twist. Uppercuts with each hand had to be learned in order to build the brilliant infighter. Overhand rights, right crosses, proper footwork, cutting off the ring and leaving it expansive. Fighting off the ropes, a future specialty, and in the lonely, contested middle. Every day for hour upon hour until the muscles remembered on their own. All this and the only real injury he received during this time occurred when he got his face tangled in barbed wire while chasing another boy near his house; the jagged scar raising from his nose to his jaw and always visible throughout his later career. He fought and learned: learned to fight. That was everything.

And Wilfred still only fifteen.

So there are finally those things that can only be learned by facing other lunatics who started boxing at seven or so years old. After 111 amateur bouts, Wilfred turned pro and had his first official fight on November 22, 1973, seventy days after his fifteenth birthday.

His first opponent owned the unlikely name of Hiram Santiago. The fight took place in Puerto Rico and was a junior-lightweight contest, meaning neither fighter weighed more than 130 pounds. The 130 pounds belonging to Santiago heard the bell signaling the start of the fight but never heard one declaring the end of the first round. Before that second bell could sound, Benitez, who would not later be known for his punching power, separated Santiago from his senses, from his ability to stand upright. The first-round knockout was not a contest; it was not a test in any meaningful way nor really any kind of learning experience. What it was was a confirmation. Hiram Santiago started to confirm what others thought they had seen in that backyard ring. Further confirmation came a mere eight days later in St Martin against Jesse Torres. Torres lasted until the second round before getting knocked out.

After knocking out his next three opponents in a total of ten rounds, the fifteen-year-old must have felt as if his hands were made of stone. Then Benitez fought Victor Mangual in Puerto Rico. On April Fool's Day 1974, Victor Mangual, despite being thoroughly outclassed and losing every round, became the first opponent to go the distance against Benitez. The eight-round fight was a necessary learning experience for a fighter who would later establish his greatness principally by outboxing his opponents not stopping them; although there *were* still plenty more knockouts to follow including one in the third round against Juan Disla later that month.

Enter the inimitable "Easy Boy" Lake. Benitez easily knocked out Lake in the first round on May 11, 1974, but it must have been the most compelling, competitive first-round knockout in boxing history because the public apparently clamored for a rematch and three months later, after three more Benitez knockout victories, they got one. "Easy Boy" entered the rematch an enthused fighter. He vowed not to repeat the pugilistic mistakes made three months earlier. This time, he thought, he was armed with valuable insight he had gained on his back. What's more, he was a quantifiably better fighter now. Five times better it turns out, as he lasted until the fifth round this time before again being knocked out. (The Easy Boy Lake career would not be a stellar one, not helped, surely, by the fact that three of his first four fights were against Benitez.)

Goyo kept Benitez busy. After Lake, he fought three more times in 1974 for a total of twelve fights that year, all wins. The following year was almost as busy with Benitez adding eleven more victories in as many fights. After beating Marcelino Alicia on September 1, 1975, by second-round knockout, Benitez's professional record stood at 23-0 with 19 knockouts. He was every minute of sixteen years old.

What was it like to oppose Benitez those days? Benitez was the worst kind of opponent because he made you feel primarily the futility of your effort. His nickname was the "Bible of Boxing" because all his punches were technically perfect. His other nickname was "Radar" and that was the real problem for his opponents. Getting punched in the face makes you want to punch the person back. Problem was you couldn't hit Benitez. His reflexes were otherworldly and he was a heavenly counterpuncher. When you miss a punch you leave yourself open. Against Benitez all you did was miss punches and all he did was tag you in response. He had tremendous hand speed with scientific accuracy. Along with his reflexes, he was equipped with other tremendous defensive skills, even at sixteen. You wanted to think, in the ring and elsewhere, that the more effort you expend the more successful you'll be, that hard work rewards itself. But against Benitez the opposite was true. The more punches you threw the more you got hit with nothing to show for it. You were prepared to give a great effort and you did, but here was this sixteen-year-old punk calmly channeling inexplicable ability to severely punish your effort. Except for a nagging tendency to skimp a bit in training and a lack of overwhelming power, an expected consequence of that kind of slick hand speed, Wilfred Benitez appeared to be a boxer without weakness.

Of course the deck was stacked. Benitez may have been only sixteen but he was a future Hall of Fame boxer. His opponents through 1975 were just that, opponents. The question was no longer whether Benitez was a special boxer. At any given time there are about a hundred boxers in the world who fit that description. The relevant question was whether Benitez was special even when viewed within that pool of humans. Goyo and Wilfred decided to find out.

Benitez had gotten physically bigger during his two-year career. He was now fighting at junior-welterweight with its weight limit of 140 pounds, ten pounds heavier than when he started. That weight division was ruled by one man. The Junior Welterweight Champion of the World was a Colombian fighter named Antonio "Pambele" Cervantes. Cervantes was a dominant champion and a national hero to Colombians. After becoming champion in 1972, he had made fifteen successful title defenses scoring twelve knockouts. Champions want, principally, to remain champion, but the great ones also want to be challenged. Cervantes decided that his next defense would come against Benitez on March 6, 1976, in San Juan's Hiram Bithorn Baseball Stadium.

The announcement of this fight was received less than enthusiastically by some of Boxing's cognoscenti. It was negligent mismanagement, they said, to put a seventeen-year-old boy, even one with that record (25-0 20 K.O.s), in the ring with an accomplished thirty-year-old champion who had fought 86 times. Regardless of

Wilfred's innate ability, the highly skilled Cervantes represented a tremendous jump up in class from the guys Benitez had fought to that point. Specifically, of the five opponents Benitez fought leading up to the Cervantes fight, three of them were fighting their first professional fight and the other two were a combined 13-20-1. Based on that alone, it was highly doubtful that any seventeen-year-old could ably adjust to this suddenly far higher level of competition and perform admirably, never mind win the fight. Perhaps Cervantes agreed and reasoned that fighting Benitez in his homeland would generate decent interest, and money, with minimal risk.

Back then there was a belief, the vestiges of it still occasionally heard today, that in order to take a champion's title by decision, especially one who had reigned as long as Pambele, you had to clearly outperform him. If it was close, the champ got the benefit of the judges' doubt.

When the day finally came to fight, it must have dawned on Pambele fairly early what was happening. He must have realized that nothing external would help him overcome this challenger. Factors like experience, will, heart, determination, the aforementioned champion's scoring advantage, those things count most when the talent level between the two fighters is close. Pambele had lost fights before, though not in five years, but he had certainly never been on the wrong end of a talent gap like this. It didn't matter how much Pambele wanted to remain champion or even how much Benitez wanted to ascend to the throne. It was all about the talent gap and it was astounding this gap. Astounding not only because of Benitez's age but also because of the immense quality of his opponent. Pambele was no washed-up fighter ready to be taken. After losing a split decision to Benitez that night, Cervantes would go on to win his next thirteen fights over the next four years. He would regain the championship, once Benitez vacated it to move up to welterweight, and defend the crown seven more times until finally coming across, at age thirty-four, another all-time great in Aaron Pryor who would stop him in the fourth and essentially end his career as a championship-caliber fighter.

Against Benitez, Pambele couldn't do anything while his opponent did as he pleased. Benitez's hand speed and impenetrable defense controlled the fight from the opening bell. It was a brilliant performance. After fifteen relentless rounds of this, Wilfred Benitez became the youngest world champion in the history of Professional Boxing.

How could it have happened? How could a seventeen-year-old have done this? Wilfred Benitez was among a small handful of the greatest boxers ever to step into a ring. This did not become true because of what he accomplished on March 6, 1976, rather he accomplished what he did because the above was true. Comparisons to Sugar Ray Robinson and Willie Pep poured in for the kid with the ear-to-ear smile who boxed with balletic artistry.

After successfully defending his title two months later with another work of art, Benitez took the summer off to enjoy his new status. Getting Wilfred to train properly for fights became increasingly difficult for Goyo. The Cervantes fight, for which he did train semi-diligently, had only confirmed what Wilfred believed from the start: the usual rules didn't apply to him, to someone who had what he had.

That summer, the United States sent probably its best Olympic Boxing team ever to Montreal for the summer games. The 1976 team, which included two future heavyweight champions in the Spinks brothers, Michael and Leon, won five gold medals but had one unquestioned star – Ray Leonard. Sugar Ray Leonard won one of the five golds and the camera loved his face, his name, and his relative articulateness. After the games, Leonard retired saying he would never box professionally. He would almost immediately change his mind and fight.

Meanwhile Benitez would only fight when it counted, with minimal training in between. But these were big-time fighters he was fighting now and not surprisingly the performances became shaky. A draw against Harold Weston in New York, for example, during which a seemingly disinterested Benitez was clowning to the crowd, what the hell was that? It was time to right the ship, so the Benitez camp went back to old reliable "Easy Boy" Lake for a third encounter. Predictably, Lake was again the picture of ease; he regressed and went out in the first round. (This loss sent Lake into a nine-year retirement with a record of 0-4, all the losses by knockout.)

Now Benitez was hardly training at all for his fights.

He was a welterweight now, fighting at 147 pounds. The welterweight division was a glamour division steeped in history. The former home of true greats like Henry Armstrong and Sugar Ray Robinson, the division was about to experience a dramatic resurgence with brilliant boxer after brilliant boxer passing through its doors. These guys could hit but Benitez wouldn't train, wouldn't properly prepare to face them. Before fighting Bruce Curry, a very good undefeated (15-0) fighter for whom Benitez should have trained a minimum of four weeks, Benitez trained for seven days. It showed. Despite winning a close ten-round decision, Benitez was knocked down for the first time in his career. His innocence thus lost, he then tasted the canvas twice more that night. No flash knockdowns either these visits to the canvas; Benitez, the defensive genius, was *thisclose* to being taken out by goddamn Bruce Curry! But he wasn't. He survived and won and in the process showed the kind of courage any great boxer must have. Solely because of his heart and talent he had lived to fight another day, with the relevant *other day* occurring three months later when he fought an immediate rematch with Curry. Despite training only ten days this time for a guy who had given him all sorts of trouble, Benitez won a ten-round decision handily. Then, after a six-month layoff caused by his contraction of Hepatitis, Benitez utterly dismantled the very good Randy Shields

492

in six rounds and just like that he was back on track.

But in this new division he was not the champ, he was one of many welterweight contenders. The Welterweight Champion of the World was Mexican great Carlos Palomino. Palomino had been champ for about three years after knocking out John Stracy in England. During that time he had successfully defended his title seven times, five times by K.O. Overall, the twenty-nine-year-old's career record stood at 27-1-3 and he had not lost a fight in nearly five years. His next defense would come on January 13, 1979, against Benitez. Palomino was favored.

At nineteen years of age, Benitez was attempting to win his second world title. He had willingly ceded control of the junior welterweights back to Cervantes in ambitious recognition of his growing body. The increased weight limit made proper training even less of a priority. For the Palomino fight, a monumental career-defining contest, Benitez trained fifteen days.

Despite this negligence, when January 13, 1979, arrived Benitez easily dominated Palomino to appropriate his title. It happened over and over; as the presumably naturally larger man, Palomino repeatedly did what he was supposed to do by backing Benitez into the ropes. What happened on those ropes, however, would forever change the way Benitez was viewed in boxing circles. Because it was there, his back on the ropes and Palomino firing punches, that Benitez destroyed the champ. It wasn't a case of him leaning on the ropes so as to induce Palomino to punch himself out à la Ali's rope-a-dope against Foreman. Such a strategy would only ever work against a 230-pound fighter anyway and would be lunacy against a welterweight who could throw punches forever. No, what Benitez did in this fight was lean on the ropes while somehow avoiding getting hit and countering Palomino to death. It was one thing to be unable to hit an opponent whose constant movement in the ring makes him an elusive moving target. It was quite another, and a special kind of evil torture for Palomino, to be unable to hit someone who is standing in one spot and has nowhere to go. For fifteen rounds Palomino rarely laid a glove on the preternaturally calm Benitez, also k.a. the *New* Welterweight Champion of the World.

Benitez's performance against Palomino shook the boxing world. For the second time in his career, Benitez had destroyed a highly respected champion who hadn't lost in years. More significantly, it was evident during both fights that he was markedly better than these accomplished champions. Some started calling him already the greatest defensive fighter in the history of Boxing. Moreover, even in a sport where the premier athletes were often in their early to mid-twenties, the fact that Benitez was only nineteen years old was not lost on boxing observers who felt he could get even better.

After defending his title two months later with a unanimous decision victory over the Harold Weston who had earlier fought him to a draw, Benitez was firmly entrenched as the best welterweight in the world and a strong argument could be made that he was the best boxer in the world *period*. In 1979, Muhammad Ali, perhaps the greatest heavyweight of all time, had retired and while the new champion, Larry Holmes, was clearly the best heavyweight in the world, no-one was willing to call him the best fighter in the world *pound for pound*. Carlos Monzon, the great middleweight champion (160 lbs.) who ruled seemingly forever (record 14 title defenses), had also retired two years earlier. Alexis Arguello was undoubtedly a great fighter at that time. The current junior-lightweight champion (130 lbs.) was, like Benitez, a two-time champion, having earlier vacated his featherweight crown (126 lbs.) to move up. Unlike Benitez, however, Arguello *had* lost fights (4) and had even been stopped. Nor was Arguello, who admittedly had scintillating, explosive power in either hand, casting into doubt the basic tenets of the sport.

But, in truth, any discussion of the world's best fighters at the time must necessarily center on the welterweight division Benitez now ruled and the dark spectre of Roberto Duran was the new looming presence in that division. Duran was a maniacal, intensely malevolent fighter who won the lightweight crown (135 lbs.) in 1972 then mercilessly ruled that division for seven long years. During those years he held the crown without interruption while fighting a remarkable 38 times. Overall his record was 67-1 with 53 knockouts. His only defeat was a close non-title decision loss to Puerto Rico's Esteban DeJesus, a loss that so enraged Duran that he later fought DeJesus twice more and knocked him out cold each time. He was a vicious ruler too; after dismantling one opponent and sending him to the hospital he promised to not stop there and send him to the morgue if they fought again. The Panamanian's "hands of stone" had terrorized the division to the point of boredom, so a couple of weeks after Benitez ascended to the throne, the twenty-seven-year-old Duran vacated the lightweight crown, skipped the junior-welterweight division altogether, and became a welterweight.

Also in the division was a twenty-year-old kid named Thomas "Hitman" Hearns. Hearns had won his first seventeen fights, all by knockout. Two months after Benitez beat Harold Weston by decision, Hearns fought Weston and iced him in the sixth round detaching Weston's retina in the process and thereby ending its career.

But really the public had already decided on its favorite welterweight. Ray Leonard, with his Olympic background and telegenic smile, was seen as the miniature but logical successor to Muhammad Ali. This anticipated succession drew strength from the fact that Leonard was trained by Angelo Dundee, the man who had trained Ali throughout his brilliant career. Another Ali was probably too much to ask for, but with The Greatest gone Sugar Ray was clearly the most popular fighter in the sport. Moreover, his 25-0 record against good competition suggested there was ample substance behind the compelling style although many still stubbornly insisted he was a mere creation of Television. Whatever the truth, because of his star quality, Leonard was an attractive opponent. His appeal would draw the interest of that portion of the public not normally interested in Boxing and would therefore mean more money for the person across from him.

Benitez agreed to make his second title defense against Sugar Ray Leonard and the bout was scheduled for November 30, 1979, in Las Vegas, Nevada.

When the court officers finally brought Soldera out, before the judge had even arrived, he looked like partially inflated skin. He smiled at me when our eyes met which made no sense. Was it just that they were the first friendly ones he'd seen in a while? Did he think their owner could help him, that deluded?

I played my role and asked what had happened that day when he stepped out for a purported second then vanished. He tried. He said he'd gotten sudden sick then attempted to call but . . . a-series-of-unrelated-words-that-could-never-combine-to-form-exculpatory-sense. Then he stopped and just shrugged his shoulders as we both seemed to implicitly acknowledge the futility of him breathing more lonely falsities into the air.

I tried to get him out, tried to reverse a force no more forgiving than gravity. I told Cymbeline what had happened, why it wasn't faultless Soldera's fault. Why he should be released and restored to what he was before that day, that is, a collection of crooked bones tortured and punished by her whenever its physical condition improved. I expressed remorse on behalf of another which it then occurred to me was probably not strictly possible.

Nonetheless I continued, afraid to stop. She mostly said nothing but when she did utter something, I would seize on the slightest word, the slightest hope, and run off in that direction. She never stopped me. She would look at her watch then through me. The court reporter kept up her soundless typing and I kept going. The court officers rolled their eyes, they wanted to go home and I was the only thing stopping them. Even when I thought I was done, I found I could keep going. I knew I was making a fool of myself and should just shut up but I couldn't. I was mentally pretending I was trying to talk myself out of going to jail and operating under this hypothetical there was nothing I wouldn't say. Nothing too stupid. Until at longest last there was nothing more I could think of, damn limited brain, and I stopped speaking.

Cymbeline summed up. The defendant had been given a break by a previous judge. Because of his medical condition he'd been allowed to remain out, following his plea of guilty and pending his sentence, provided he produced intermittent medical updates, stayed out of trouble, and continually returned to court. Despite this opportunity, the defendant had failed to return to court and no reasonable and believable excuse had been provided. Moreover, there was ample reason to believe that the defendant's physical condition was not as bleak as had been painted by defense counsel. Consequently, there was no reason why the defendant could not be sentenced in accordance with the statutory sentencing requirements relevant to Criminal Sale of a Controlled Substance in the Fourth Degree a class C felony with a mandatory minimum sentence, under these circumstances, of 3 to 6. The defendant was remanded. The case was adjourned for exactly four weeks for the Department of Probation to prepare a pre-sentencing report and for the defendant to be sentenced. Take charge court officers.

Soldera gone, Cymbeline then looked at me intently. She had the appearance of someone who had handled a minor detail and was now ready to get to the fun part. "Now that that's out of the way," she said, "the only thing left to consider, as I'm sure you've been made aware by your supervisors, is your conduct counselor."

My conduct I wondered? Was I now being accused of possessing stolen property as well?

"Very good. Keep it up counselor, it's remarks like that that have gotten you into this situation. I'm sure Judge Arronaugh will be interested to hear that you're continuing the conduct that serves as the basis for her complaint."

Arronaugh? Complaint? I didn't understand.

"I assure you counselor that a contempt proceeding is a very serious matter especially for a young attorney such as yourself. Made all the more serious in this instance by the fact that I will be joining Judge Arronaugh as a highly esteemed co-complainant based on what Mr Soldera told this court here on Friday."

Co-complainants? Never heard such a term. She must've simply invented it. It wasn't one of those invented terms I liked either. Co-complainants sounded bad. Bad for me. Like double the trouble or something.

"Do you know what Mr Soldera told this courtroom before you arrived counselor?"

I didn't and I was hesitant to hazard a guess.

"Put succinctly he claims that you told him to leave this courtroom on his last court date when a warrant was ordered. Now don't say anything. You of course have the right to an attorney and the like. I will simply say that it is a very grave matter when an attorney, an officer of the court, counsels an individual to break the law, the law in this case being the proscription against bail jumping. If that were the only allegation of course it would be a different matter. I don't have to tell you that Judge Arronaugh alleges you made some tremendously disrespectful and disruptive comments on Friday that constituted contempt of court. All of this will, of course, be detailed in the forthcoming complaint counselor. If I were you I would stay in close contact with my supervisors as they will be the first to be informed of the formal charges. Good day counselor."

That mouthful said, she left.

I felt shame for some reason but it didn't last. The court officers made little inviting, faux-supportive comments trying to get me to talk about what the judge had said and I almost did, but then I changed my mind and went in the back to see Soldera.

"What's going to happen next time?" he said.

"She's going to pick a number and sentence you."

"No more doctor's letters?"

"No more."

"It's O.K. man. You tried so hard, you fight so hard for me man. If not for you I wouldn't a been out all these months man, if not for you, and it was good this time I was out. I didn't use any stuff, even out you know? No poison. Anyway I know I don't got long left but in the time I do got I'm going to remember what you didded for me."

Soldera was crying now . . . slowly.

I looked at him crying. I kind of wished I could cry too but I couldn't. I don't mean that I couldn't allow myself to cry. I mean that even if I had tried my damndest to cry I would have been unable to. I said "did you tell the judge I told you to split last time you were in court?"

"I don't recollect what anything I said man. She was like screaming at me and shit and I was just responding in defense and whatnot. I think I did say that maybe. For sure actually. Why? That going to get you in trouble?"

"Doubt it."

"Because I can tell her the truth next time."

"No, she's evil, she'd just take it out on you at sentencing."

"You in trouble?"

"Cares."

"You're in trouble?"

"How could I ever be in trouble?"

"O.K."

"Settled then."

*

When I went back into the courtroom to get my bag all the court officers were gone and the door was locked. I went through the sneaky door judges use to enter the courtroom. Beyond that door was a maze of hallways leading to a slew of doors but no magic EXIT sign in sight.

I moved briskly with a determined gait as if I knew perfectly well where I was going. After making a couple of ill-advised turns, I was now irredeemably lost and couldn't have retraced my steps had I fervently desired. I started opening doors at random without succor. Twice I opened the door to courtrooms where jurors were hearing evidence. The doors were supposed to have goddamn plaques detailing what was inside but they didn't. When I came across the plaques they were bunched up on the ground, in a corner, next to a dropcloth and a can of paint. What evil genius had created these catacombs? And for what nefarious purpose?

Near defeat, I tried a green door fully expecting another judge's glare. Instead I saw stairs, stairs I took all the way down for what seemed like a lot more than seven floors. At the rock bottom were two more doors, side by side and identical. I tried the left one for a change and it opened. The cold felt good but I was below street level in a pit-like enclosure without visible egress. I threw my bag up and out of the pit. Then I scaled the cement wall, did a gymnasticy flip over the rail at the top, and landed on the sidewalk. My bag had opened upon landing, spilling everything everywhere. I fell to my knees to gather the detritus.

I'd never exited that way before. I doubted anyone else had either.

I'm no stranger (meaning than before).

Chapter 16

My memory knew no middle ground. Brilliantly exact, to the point of absurdity, on some matters while negligently absent on others, with neither rhyme nor reason a guide to determining which when. After collecting my things from the sidewalk, I was overcome by a powerful desire to go home, and to avoid Conley now that I knew what he wanted to talk about, so I did. But no sooner had friendly Casper let me in, and my body dropped on the sofa, when I remembered that I had agreed to meet Toomberg in my office that night to work on Kingg. My apartment felt transient now and seemed to tease me for my stupidity.

But I had an idea.

I picked up my phone, a device that had to be held at a precise 53° angle from the user's face in order to work properly, and called Toomberg. He wasn't there and I was whisked to his voicemail. Because of the distance created between mouthpiece and mouth, you had to yell on this end to be audible on the other. I left a message:

Toom! It's Casi! I had to come home because of a thing! I was wondering if we could do it here at my place so I wouldn't have to go back to the office! There's a library a couple blocks away! I love that library too, it would be a great place to work! I don't mean to suggest it's an overly special library or anything! It's your basic library! You got your newspapers on wooden sticks if you like that sort of thing! They've got their share of books too! Though incredibly The Magic Mountain isn't one of them! You believe that?! No Magic Mountain! Thomas Mann they keep out but they've got all sorts of other Toms in there. All the Toms and Thomases your soul could desire! Not Tommy Mann though! Anyway call me back! It's Casi!

I hung up and hit redial.

Toom! Me again! I didn't give you my number and I'm not sure you have it with you at work! Also I lied before and I feel guilty! Not about the library, it's as I described it! When I said I had to come home because of a thing, the thing I came home because of was my pathetic memory! I completely forgot about our meeting! Why do people say completely forgot?! If I only partially forgot then that's called remembering and I wouldn't be leaving this message which I never do! Call me!

I rehit redial.

It occurs to me now that I might have given you the wrong impression before about Thomas Mann like I'm some big reader of his work and was thus outraged that I couldn't find Magic Mountain! Truth is I've never read Magic Mountain or Buddenbrooks either for that matter! And the reason for that has nothing to do with the availability of those books in my local library! I have a dog-eared Magic Mountain and though I have picked it up countless times over the years it never takes me very long to put it down for good or at least until the next time! And before you get all worked up I assure you that I have other equal and even far greater holes in my education! Just wanted to come clean . . . an expression that as I think about it right this minute either makes perfect sense or no sense at all!

The moment I hung up, the door knocked. Well someone knocked on my door and it's hard to screen such a thing when you've just been screaming into the phone loud enough for the entire tri-state area to hear. I never asked who it was before opening either as I liked to be surprised. Accordingly, I abstained from looking through the peephole. If I had, I would have been ready for what I saw when I opened: Traci smiling and possessing a high degree of delectability.

It seemed there was a pendant. Traci had left this pendant in Louie's apartment and wanted it back. It had been arranged that she would stop by then, when Angus would be there, and get it from him. Louie and Alyona were not supposed to be there, and they weren't, but neither was Angus. "I think I hear him in there, I hear voices anyway, but he doesn't answer the door," she said. Did I know where he was? She heard voices. When I told her that Angus never turned Television off, even when nobody was home, she said she knew that but this was different. Different because, "the voices didn't sound like Television but it was weird because they also didn't sound like they emanated from real people. They sounded like something in between those two things, in the middle." But since they also didn't sound like Angus she was now convinced I was probably right and nobody was home. She could wait inside I thought aloud. We could leave the door open so we would hear if one of the three stooges showed up ready to rescue her pendant. No, I didn't mind.

The pendant had hung on her grandmother. The grandmother was now dead and didn't need pendants. She should've never worn it outside her house. Traci.

The sofa was comfortable.

"It better be, it takes up about eighty percent of the room's surface area."

"I was going to say, this is a very small—"

"*Cozy* was, I think, the term used by the real estate agent."

"Yes, this is a very *cozy* apartment."

"I wish it was fucking *airy*."

Laughter.

"How come Alyona and those guys' apartment is so much . . . less cozy?"

Because it was a weird building. I lived in the only brownstone in Brooklyn Heights that wasn't a box or rectangle. It was a bottleneck. The pressure fizzled and bubbled below in the fat part of the bottle.

There it compressed and mounted as it rose up and into the narrow mouth of the bottle. That's where we were, the escape.

"So you feel pressure?"

"No, but because it sounds sort of cool when you say it that way that's my story and I'm sticking with it."

I didn't sit on the sofa with her. I sat on this crazy, wobbly stool with my feet on the arm of the sofa. Against the other arm lay Traci. She had slipped out of her shoes and sat on her folded legs, her hands clasped together atop her knees. I'm going to say she had flaxen hair, even though she didn't, because I like that word. Flaxen. Her eyes I have no good single word for but how could I have previously failed to notice their emerald luminescence? The face was all cheekbones but not too sharp, just right. The entire time I made these observations Traci had been speaking. I had listened not at all, and now she was unmistakably waiting for a response.

"Yeah," I said plaintively like all *whattya gunna do*?

"So you think I should?"

"Hard to say," especially when you haven't the faintest idea what the discussion is about.

"I figured you would be the person to ask."

"Sure, you'd think."

"Being that you obviously went to law school."

"Law school, right. Law school yeah."

". . ."

"Yeah, it's just a tough question you know? Maybe it would help if you restated the problem. In the plainest language possible."

"Should I go to law school?"

"That's as plain as it gets."

Suddenly Traci didn't look so great anymore, asking me if she should go to law school. Who cared? Go or don't go. What, really, was the difference? Who took career advice from the likes of me? And I hated people who used the word *career* in referring to themselves. Not

504

that she had used that word far as I could tell. Like people who wore fancy hats. Just expose your dopey skull, do your time on this rock, then go wherever it is we go when all's been said. Of course I should point out, in fairness, that if a woman wore a hat I practically melted. That, and the fact that the black, bowler-type hat Traci wore then was highly scrumptious, made me forget my annoyance almost as soon as it had arisen. While thinking these thoughts it seems I had managed to keep my mouth moving and somehow satisfactorily answer Traci's question. We could move on.

"So you and Louie?"

"Finished. If we ever even got started."

I was smitten now. She had smote me. I loved her voice. It was gravelly and weak like it had recently been overtaxed. What a revelation being there then, with her. I needed only play this situation just right. The mutuality of our interest was in the air, hanging and waiting. Even the simplest dullard would have no trouble converting the current situation into a long-running, torrid interaction. Even so, the utmost precision and care was called for. Every word would have to be measured. Every nonverbal cue refined to shiny perfection. Just this once I could personate normalcy, do the things everybody else does without spending a second thought. I could pretend. I'd seen it done before and had no doubt about my ability to mimic. Above all, I had to be conventional. Had to play it cool.

"We should fall in love," I said.

"Love?"

"Yeah."

"I'm not sure I get what you mean."

"You've heard the expression *falling in love*?"

"Yes."

"You know generally what it refers to?"

"Yes."

"So let's do it, let's fall in love with each other."

"You're crazy."

"Why? Doesn't it look like fun?"

"What look like fun?"

"Love. I mean look at all the breath expended on the subject. The movies, the books, poems, songs. That many people can't be wrong. Love!"

"Yes, love. But what is it and what does it mean to fall in it?"

"You don't know what it is? You've never felt it?"

"Probably not the kind you're talking about. You? Well, obviously . . ."

"What?"

"You're telling me you're in love with me yet we hardly know each other, practically strangers."

"First of all, I never said I was in love with you. Secondly, the amount of time we've known each other is irrelevant. I know a wacky Italian poet who scarcely knew the woman he adored and who would later guide him through Paradise."

"You didn't just say you love me?"

"No, I proposed that we fall in love with each other since all indications are it would impact favorably on our lives, make us happier."

"How romantic, too bad you can't *choose* to fall in love."

"No?"

"No, you either feel it or you don't."

"How would you know?"

"It's obvious, there's a loss of control there that precludes choice."

"So you're saying no?"

"Right, no."

"Because?"

Laughs.

"Because you can't *decide* to fall in love. It either happens or it doesn't Casi."

"Guess you're right, but you sure have strong feelings on something you couldn't even define a minute ago."

"What do you mean?"

"What *is* love?"

"Love is like a . . . feeling . . . where . . . you just love."

"Uh-huh."

"Look we all know what love is even if I can't put it into words just this moment."

"You'll know it when you feel it right?"

"Right."

"And you don't feel it now."

"No."

"Me either but I think I wish I did."

Traci looked out the window then placed her palm on the pane. "It's freezing out again," she said. "I can't ever remember anything like this. Can you? I mean it used to be, O.K., a cold day here and there, the kind you would take notice of, but this is every day, day after day."

"Relentless," I said. "There's no relent," I added.

"Exactly. I read today that the temperature hasn't reached double digits in like two weeks, I mean where are we? Not to mention the wind, my God." Traci was drawing on my window. With her finger on the condensation. "The thing about this kind of sustained cold," she said after a fairly long while, "is that after a while it almost fails to register, know what I mean? It becomes like just another part of us, our world, no more noticeable than the sky or the trees."

"The sky is white."

"Right."

"I mean uniformly white though. That can't be good right?"

Just then, Traci sprang up out of the couch. She had heard something I hadn't. "Someone's downstairs," she said. "Maybe I can get my pendant." She jumped out promising to return. I turned to watch her go out and almost fell off my stool. I left the stool on the floor and moved to the sofa which was still warm with her heat. I looked at the window and tried to identify her drawing. I couldn't.

Traci came back in to say "false alarm."

"Who was it?"

"I don't know but he looks lost."

"Besides lost, what else does he look like?"

"Like professorial, meaning eggheady."

"Toom!" I shouted out the door and I was right. "Up here!"

My master plan had worked, I was pleased.

Traci was leaving. We said goodbye. First her then me.

She disappeared out the door and Toomberg appeared. "I did have your number," he said. "And I've been trying to call you for the last hour but have received only constant busy signals."

"I guess my phone's finally had it, sorry."

"They now manufacture phones of the cellular variety by the way."

"Never."

"Anyway I procured your address from Denise but no apartment number was listed."

"I see."

"So I was kind of lost."

"Understood, thank you."

"I think someone is calling you, out the window. Is not someone calling your name?"

I looked out the window and saw Traci looking up. When I opened the window to hear what she had to say, the cold stayed outside at first. But nanoseconds later it came in, riding an invisible tidal wave and causing me to shake, my teeth chattering, and turn to the side to avoid a direct hit.

"Casi?"

"Traci."

"Just saying. If I did do what you proposed? If it was possible?"

"Yes?"

"It would be with you."

She smiled. I smiled back. Then she turned, hugged herself, and walked down the block. I watched her the whole time. When she reached the end of the block she turned right at the corner and out of my sight. I never saw her again.

"Was that the woman I passed on my ascent?"

"Wasn't she absolutely, transcendentally, achingly beautiful?"

"She was fairly attractive."

"Keep your shirt on Toom, don't go overboard."

"I'm sorry, are you in love with her? I'm not familiar with the conventions."

"Relax, I'm talking about her attractiveness on a purely physical level. I didn't make my statement in any amatory way. I'm simply asking for your opinion as to her level of beauty."

"I'm a married man."

"You are? And you're getting married again this weekend? Isn't that illegal you polygamous bastard?"

"I am not getting married this weekend, I am merely *attending* a wedding."

"Guess that's your story, may as well stick with it. But what of that woman's heart-delaying beauty?"

"I said, she's attractive."

"I pity you Toomie, using that word to describe the situation. Don't you realize how intoxicating women are? How amazing life is? You know, there didn't have to be women, and they certainly didn't have to be this compelling."

"There had to be women for life to continue."

"Exactly, I for one would certainly kill myself."

"I meant from a reproductive standpoint."

"I suppose that's true too, if you want to get all technical."

"You believe life to be amazing Casi? As in amazingly good?"

"As in, yes. Amazingly good. How else can you describe a state of affairs where I can be sitting in this lonely apartment one minute only to answer the door the next to find *that* woman standing before me?

Where she will later stop in bone-piercing cold to tell me that, if she could, she would fall in love with me."

"Where two seven-year-olds will snatch an infant and beat her to death?"

"There's that."

"Just pray nothing similar ever happens to you or yours."

"I'm in control here Toom. Things don't happen *to* me. They happen *because* of me. Do you have any kids Mr Melvyn Toomberg?"

"No but did Hurtado conclude the way you wished?"

"Ow. Agony. Stop. That's different though."

"What happens more often? An attractive woman appears in your doorway or you deal with someone like Arronaugh or Cymbeline?"

"You know about Cymbeline?"

"Naturally, everyone does."

"Who's everyone and what do they know? Specifics."

"Fine, everyone at work knows that you are going to be charged with contempt because of Arronaugh and Cymbeline."

"Oh."

"What did you say to Arronaugh anyway?"

"I don't know but it was probably contemptible."

"Did you urge a client to leave Cymbeline's courtroom because she was going to put him in?"

"Of course not. But I should have."

"Aren't you concerned?"

"Why should I be? Somebody'll smooth it over for me. Maybe Gold, he's great at that sort of thing."

"I don't think that's going to happen here."

"So I'll fight it. Isn't Tom supposed to be like the greatest lawyer in the Western Hemisphere or something? You think he's going to let me get convicted?"

"Now you sound like a client."

"That *was* stupid. The point is that our psuedo law firm will expend, if necessary, all of its limitless resources on my defense."

"I don't think so."

"You're right, you can't expend all of something that has no limit."

"Also, from what I'm hearing, the people you're counting on to help, you may end up viewing as additional enemies."

"How so?"

"Well the rumor, and it's just that for now, is that along with the contempt proceeding there's going to be a contemporaneous in-house investigation."

"Regarding what?" I was laughing, near-hysterically, I think at the phrase *in-house*.

"Well, several things."

"Like what?"

"Like that you might have forged Tom's signature to get some minutes."

"Of course, they should investigate me if I hadn't!"

"That you verbally assaulted Solomon Grinn."

"Verbally?"

"Assaulted."

"Assaulted?"

"Verbally."

"Which time?"

"On more than one occasion."

"That's all? It'll never stick."

"That you physically assaulted Liszt."

"Liszt?"

"Physically."

"His wall?"

"No his person."

"Whose person?"

"Liszt's person."

"Liszt has a person now?"

"The allegation, I surmise, is that you tried to punch him."

"That's crazy. That should be an easy one to fight. Just ask Liszt, he'll say it was his wall, not him, that I took offense with. Ask him."

"I can't because he's out."

"Out where?"

"Out of work, out on Disability."

"Why, what happened?"

"You happened it seems."

"Me? He can't be saying I hit him."

"Emotional distress, I gather, from the near miss. That's my impression although he may be saying you did in fact hit him, that sort of thing being notoriously difficult to ascertain. At any rate, he's on indefinite Disability Leave as a result of your encounter with him."

"Good Lord."

"Yes."

"Man, this is like a multiple count indictment they're working on against me."

"It would appear so."

"And Tom's out for like another week?"

"At least. And even when he returns, Tom's influence may be waning."

"Really?"

"Yes, in fact—"

"Anyway on Kingg we're basically preparing to throw a Hail Mary pass aren't we?"

"I must warn you, if that's a sports metaphor those invariably escape me."

"And if we fail they take him out like a week later right?"

"They execute him yes, if we fail."

"What do you suppose Kingg will be thinking then?"

"When they execute him?"

"Well, before. Just before for example."

"I don't know, I don't really know him."

"You don't have to know him do you?"

"What do you mean, Casi?"

"They executed a federal prisoner last year didn't they?"

"Yes, they did."

"An unrepentant killer right?"

"I don't know."

"Well, hundreds dead right?"

"Right."

"At his hands."

"Yes."

"And no stated remorse."

"True but that assumes his public proclamations matched his internal state."

"Right, in fact that's sort of what I'm getting at. You know what I heard this guy did just before he was killed? This unrepentant killer and avowed atheist?"

"What?"

"He was offered and received a sacrament, Extreme Unction."

"Isn't that like Last Rites?"

"Yes, especially in this context."

"O.K., why is that meaningful to you?"

"Because Extreme Unction is a sacrament, one of the seven, whereby the recipient is essentially prepared for death and the ensuing afterlife through repentance, forgiveness et cetera. Don't you find it amazingly anomalous and all sorts of suggestive that this individual, who killed hundreds without apology, and who maintained all along that he did not believe in God, at the last moment basically asked for forgiveness and prepared for an afterlife?"

"Maybe it's true what they say regarding the dearth of atheists in foxholes."

"Yes! Let's talk about that statement. Can we determine whether or not it's true and what the consequences would be accordingly? Is that even the type of thing we can discover Toom?"

"Yes, of course."

"How?"

"Through reason."

"Fine, well, the statement is there are no atheists in foxholes. Is it true?"

"Literally?"

"No, let's take the alleged truth the statement is trying to express, which is, I think, that people who are faced with their imminent mortality invariably turn to a belief in God and all attendant beliefs. What do you say?"

"First I suppose we need to address what it even means for a statement like that to be true."

"I guess does the statement accurately reflect the physical world we live in and the people we share it with? In other words, is it true that human beings, when faced with the very real possibility of impending death, invariably turn to a belief in God regardless of their prior level of piety."

"Phrased that way, I think the answer is simple. The answer would be that the statement, if it means what you just said, is almost certainly *not* true, so few things being true of *all* people."

"Now we're getting somewhere Toom, I agree. So let's modify slightly what we think the statement purports to allege. Imagine we have the individual who coined this phrase before us presently. She says, look, the world is divided into those who believe in God and an afterlife and those who don't. Of those who don't, I believe the overwhelming majority of them will in some form adopt such a belief when they believe they are about to die. Do we agree with her?"

"I really wouldn't know where to begin examining her statement. The little experience I've had with people who were aware they were dying was with people who had a belief in God and an afterlife to

514

begin with, although it did seem that the belief was if anything strengthened and not weakened by their circumstances."

"I knew a woman who worked as a nurse at an intensive care unit. Now as you know nurses are basically saints making a pit stop on earth; dealing with the nastiest shit you can imagine without any of the prestige or compensations doctors get. So, unlike you, she dealt with an endless procession of people facing imminent death and according to her, in all her years, not one, *not one* patient who knew he was about to die persisted in an atheistic or even agnostic belief. Now if you know anything about the extreme laxity of my data-gathering standards then you'll know that this nurse's statement, along with my own admittedly limited experience of the near-dead, and along with our Extreme Unction friend is enough to convince me of the general truth of the foxhole statement."

"So if it is true, a rather large proviso but one which I'm willing to forgo challenging for the moment, what do we take from that?"

"That's the interesting question of course. Why do human beings engage in this behavior Toom?"

"Maybe they're seeking comfort. The person is about to have something bad happen to them, as bad as they can envision. Under those circumstances, the person is looking for a consolation, so he latches on to the belief that the imminent end isn't really an end."

"A belief he never had before right?"

"Presumably."

"Well no, I only want to deal with people who truly never believed not those who just said they didn't but deep down did."

"O.K."

"If one of those people is going to adopt a belief purely for psychological comfort, and despite the fact that they believed the proposition to be a complete fiction prior to their predicament, why not adopt a different belief that might offer even more hope without any possible downside? Why not suddenly choose to believe that human beings, despite all evidence to the contrary, are in fact immortal and death is nothing more than an elaborate ruse? Or better yet that human beings are in fact mortal but I myself am not. I am immortal. Why not choose to believe any of those things? Note that those beliefs, if believed in the absence of a God, would arguably offer more comfort to the atheist since they would not involve any apologetic explanation to a higher being both for the disbelief and for any other wrong actions or inactions. So why not?"

"Because those would be the beliefs of a madman. Nothing speaks in their favor, there's no proof."

"And where is the *proof* of an afterlife? Of a God? Surely someone who was previously an avowed atheist would be the first to say there is no actual proof right?"

"Maybe there is no proof *per se* but there's a certain safety in numbers and a lot of other people believe in God and an afterlife whereas seemingly no sane person believes in their own corporeal immortality."

"Why is that the case? Why is it that countless seemingly sane people believe these things in the absence of proof?"

"One possible reason is that these beliefs are endemic to human culture and therefore predispose us to their adoption."

"So that someone who has truly resisted these cultural impetuses their entire life is suddenly incapable of resisting them at a time when, near death, you would expect them to be less affected by societal pressures than at any other time in their life?"

"Desperate times call for desperate measures."

"You make it sound as if these beliefs can never fail to provide comfort but what about our Extreme Unction recipient? You think he wanted to confront what he had done? Wouldn't such a person be better comforted by the belief that what follows death is a complete nothing? *Nothing* by nature entailing no need to confront one's senseless slaughter of children?"

516

"People are petrified of nothingness. Repentance and groveling they can deal with more easily I think. Maybe this fear of a complete nothing, not true belief, was his motivation. Besides, the papers said that although an atheist, he was raised Catholic meaning his last-minute belief may have been nothing more than him reverting, in his darkest hour, to an emblem of his simpler youth and drawing comfort from that. So I'm not ready to concede that he experienced true belief, though of course he may have."

"What do *you* believe?"

"As I just said, I have no way of knowing what he was truly experiencing."

"No, I mean what do you believe on the general subject?"

"I leave work early on Fridays to avoid sundown and this isn't a hat."

"Right, so you're just being devil's advocatey when you say these things. You would say that, if true, the atheist in the foxhole doesn't so much adopt these beliefs as his eyes are pried open to the truth when spurred on by the extreme circumstances. You would say that the reason so many humans have this belief in God or an afterlife, and not other unsupported beliefs, is that their belief is justified by objective, even if unknowable, *truth*, which they somehow feel or know on some level. Of course, someone would answer that the belief is so popular and widely accepted not because it contains any truth but rather because it is an excellent source of comfort in a cruel world. You might, in turn, answer, as I've hinted, that all sorts of beliefs offer or would offer similar or even greater comfort yet they are not adopted with a fraction of the frequency as this belief. You might also add that the belief is often held by those to whom it is unlikely to offer any comfort and by still others whom you would expect the belief to actively discomfort. You could argue from these facts that this type of belief is therefore to some extent ingrained in humans. And to this, someone might respond that even if the belief was ingrained in us, that would not serve as the slightest assurance that the belief is grounded in or otherwise reveals *truth*. Moreover, this person might say, the things you proffer in support of the idea's ingrained nature constitute mere circumstantial evidence. It may very well be, as you said, that a God belief et cetera is such a major part of our cultural structure and history that it predisposes us to its adoption in such a strong way that it makes the belief seem native and inborn. Which naturally raises the chicken/egg question of why the belief holds such a prominent place in human cultural history. Which place your opponent might grant but only before pointing out that as humans and their culture have evolved, the belief has rightly weakened. Adding that a seemingly strong majority of recent great thinkers have been atheists, or at least agnostics. That the scientific method currently reigns supreme and unchallenged and that one must never forget that there is, after all, no credible proof in support of the belief. To this last objection you could respond that the seeming lack of proof is, in and of itself, a form of proof of the belief's truth value. After all, can your opponent name another belief that has persisted for so long and so consistently in the absence of any empirical support? At which point your opponent may very well get fed up and ask if you're one of those creeps that doesn't want schools teaching evolution. Evolution, he would say, proves definitively that no single entity created man, discrediting any and all opposing fairy tales like the one found in Genesis. The obvious response being that if there was a supreme being, a being who possessed consummate omnipotence, perfection, and beauty, we would expect him to operate in a certain way. We would, for example, expect that if such a being was to create a race of something called humans it would be done in a celestially and appropriately complex way such as the method described by Darwin. We would also expect that the universe containing those humans would not function in a mechanistic Newtonian fashion but would instead be the bizarrely complex and counterintuitive Einsteinian slash Heisenbergian maelstrom we've discovered. In other words, the discovery of increasing complexity in any form is evidence of God not its opposite, not least of all because it makes the accident called life seem even less likely without a guiding force and all those other intelligent-design-type notions. All that you would surely say, and all that your opponent would respond. Back and forth, forth and back, with seemingly no legitimate means for choosing between the two opposing worldviews. Isn't that the situation we now find ourselves in Toomie, my high-I.Q. compatriot? Is the situation hopeless or can we, by employing reason, determine which is the better view? I cannot imagine two people such as you and I failing at this. Thus am I prepared to stay in this room, for weeks if necessary and with the occasional delivered cheesesteak, in order to, with your help, definitively answer this most important question once and for all. You with me?"

"First things first."

"Meaning?"

"Meaning some day I may be willing to sit down with you and hash all this out but right now it is far more important that we discuss Jalen Kingg's case and formulate a successful strategy for saving his life. *That* first thing has to come first."

"First? What could be prior to this question? Can we truly know anything before answering this question?"

"Yes, because this ultimate question you're talking about is meaningless at the moment. Not to mention that I and countless others have already answered it."

"Not the way I'm talking about."

"Maybe not, but to our satisfaction, and that's the only truly important aspect of the question."

"You find this kind of activity and these kinds of questions unimportant? You?"

"To a large extent yes. Intellectual discourse and investigation are admittedly great fun but only truly meaningful when conducted in the service of others. In a few days, a bungled mess of a person, a child's brain in an adult, who has from birth been mercilessly tortured by circumstance will be killed unless you and I use our minds, and all other advantages that were given to us by mere accident, to stop the killers. In service of this goal I'm more than willing to spend the days of thought you're talking about. But I would no sooner, under these circumstances, engage in what you propose than I would in endless games of tic tac toe."

"Ah but what about tic tac *dough*?"

"Same answer."

"Fine, I'll assume there's no God for now and accordingly devote all my intellectual energy to our project."

"Good, but I fail to see the connection."

"Well if I were to conclude that there *is* a benevolent God who reigns over a blissful afterlife then why would I possibly put so much effort into trying to keep Kingg here with the living, where he has experienced nothing but abject misery and where if we are successful he can expect a whole lot more of the same in his rancid cage. That would be like an attorney pleading with a parole board to keep his client incarcerated. Better he should be released to take flight with an angelic brain in place of his current, faulty instrument."

"I'm not sure how to respond to that but if it gets us started I'll take it."

"But one last thing."

"What?"

"How did you come to the conclusion, whenever you did, that it would be wrong for the state to execute an individual like Kingg? I assume you know that a strong majority of this country's population disagrees with you on that point?"

"How?"

"Yes, how."

"I guess I thought about it."

It was settled and we got to work. We worked long, hard, and well. That Toomberg was a smart fuck. He could grasp things instantly but without mentally simplifying their complexity like most. When we were done I felt I knew Kingg. I certainly knew the situation he was in as well as I could. And despite some huge problems I felt in control of the case now and my trip out there would, I was sure, cement that control. It was late.

On his way out, Toomberg stopped near my door and looked at some articles and books I had on the semicircle table there. "What's all this boxing stuff?" he said.

"Boxing stuff."

"I find Boxing fascinating," he said. "I don't mean to say that I watch individual matches and am fascinated. Rather I find the very existence of Boxing fascinating. Aren't you ever surprised that human beings are still willing to admit they derive pleasure from seeing others hit and harm each other?"

"No, I guess I'm too busy being one of the pleasure-receptors."

"I mean the sport should probably be banned don't you think?"

"I don't know."

"You *don't*?"

"I guess, it's complicated."

Toomberg left and moments later it wasn't so much that Dane knocked on the door as it seemed to open on its own with him in the doorway.

"We have to talk," he said. "I have an idea."

"How did?" I wondered.

"Secretary gave me your address, you really should provide an apartment number you know."

"You must've just passed Toomberg on the way in."

"Must have, may I come in?"

"It's late man, I'm beat."

"It's about our plan, and your conditions."

"I figured, but besides it being late I just spent quite a few hours working so can't we talk tomorrow?"

"Allow me to say one word. Then if you still want me to leave I will."

"One word?"

"One."

"Fine, just one word and no tricks."

"Course not, tricks are for kids."

"What's the word?"

"Swords!"

"Swords?"

"Swords."

We looked at each other silently for like ten seconds.

"Come in," I said. He sat on the treacherous stool and I lay on the sofa. "What about swords?" I exhaled.

"My new favorite channel's this goddamn Beastly Burden Channel. I can watch a predatory cheetah chase down a hapless antelope all fucking day. The best part is when they're sitting around waiting on a victim. These cats will do things like stretch their jaws revealing their honed instruments of death. I don't have to tell you what they look like when they spot dinner either. They uncoil like a spring, every muscle rippling and taut in service of a single objective; to kill and eat. There's no deliberation, no contemplative thought. Instead their entire being, their very existence, is nothing beyond desire. A desire that must be fed. It's glorious and beautiful and I love it.

"Of course it can also be quite sad. As a matter of fact just before coming here I was home crying it was so damn sad. It seems a pride, has there ever been a more apt word, of these gorgeous cats had fallen on hard gastronomical times. Anyway one of these famished felines has managed to secure a tasty meal, but is eating alone without catty support. Suddenly it's surrounded by goddamn hyenas, those mangy mutts. Turns out they want the cat to share. Share! Can you imagine?

This majestic, sexy, sleek beast giving even the slightest bit of its lion's share to those ratty mouth-breathing pieces of shit. Now if you know anything at all about the situation, you know there's not a lioness in the world that is going to lose to a fucking single hyena, is going to let a hyena take even a morsel of its food. And don't kid yourself, the pussy hyenas know this as well. Of course we're not dealing with a single hyena here, we're dealing with like twenty of the bastards and, as I said, one cat. They surround the cat, these filthy dogs. But the cat, like the viewer, knows that twenty dogs can kill it if they need to. It takes one last bite of its zebra dinner, a zebra it fucking acquired when no-one else could, through its feline will and sense of self, a zebra rightfully bestowed on it by the cosmos, then leaves it to the mutts. Well if that doesn't make you cry then you're just an unfeeling bastard and I take my leave of you. The cameraman had the gall to stand there and film these lowly furry rats stuffing their faces, knowing that not one of these weasels would've had the balls to so much as look at our cat crossly if not for their overwhelming numbers."

I closed my eyes.

"What can we say about a world that permits such nonsense Casi? Nature should stop worrying about vacuums, which nobody gives a rat's ass about, and abhor hyenas emboldened by packs. Watching the horrid display, I imagined I was that cat surrounded by those hyenas. I thought about it of course because of what we're going to do. Know what I concluded? That if I was surrounded by those hyenas, even if they numbered in the hundreds, they would pay a blood-soaked price for that zebra. Especially the first one. You see one of them would have to be first in trying to take some of my zebra burger and I would make sure that presumptuous fuck got it worst of all. I would kill him with the extremest of prejudices. But not just him, I would take a violent chunk out of as many of those pricks as possible. If they chewed one of my paws off, I would keep using the other one to fuck up as many as I could. I would take the bloody stump back from them

523

then beat them to death with it like Samson with that jawbone. Basically they would have to kill me before I would allow them to so much as *lick* a single zebra bone and even then my final suspiration would be a defiant bite. I would die it's true, but I would sooner die than know that I, an august, resplendent, regal lion had surrendered anything to that lowly riffraff."

"What about swords?"

"Swords? Are you high or something? What's a lion to do with a sword?"

"You said swords. You got in here by saying the word remember?"

"Oh right. I thought about our plan in light of the things you said at lunch. You say you won't go in with guns and I don't want to go in unarmed."

"You're not suggesting."

"Of course I am. If I don't who will?"

"True, but I don't know, it seems so."

"Cool? Intense?"

"Bizarre."

"We're going in with swords Casi, serious flesh-emulsifying swords. If you think about it, it's perfect."

"What if I don't think about it?"

"Then it's still perfect. I mean you're wary of a violent accident right? You don't want to do harm. Well a sword is a far more precise instrument than a gun. A sword can circumscribe movement in a way a gun can't. If you put a sword to someone's neck or stomach and tell them they can't move, they *know* they can't move without cutting themselves. You're absolved of all responsibility. With a gun, you end up having to shoot the idiot, which you don't want to do, or worse you run the risk that your opponent will discern your reluctance to do same and that can be a big problem. Lastly, I like the element of surprise involved with swords. I believe that there is less of a chance of retributive violence if we use swords because they'll be taken

524

aback, think we're insane or something. I mean who walks in there with fucking swords? I think the use of swords should also satisfy any aesthetic impulses you may wish to appease. Of course you know how to expertly handle a sword right?"

"Dane, the only thing more ridiculous than your assumption is the fact that I *do* know how to use a sword."

"Then it's settled, swords it is. I'll go procure them."

Leaning over the banister just outside my door, I watched Dane go down the stairs and out the door. Then there was noise below, a lot, from Alyona's. I was tired but I wanted to see what was going on, maybe grab that pendant so I could later get it to Traci. I changed my mind when I got halfway down the stairs. I went back up and inside. What I saw from those stairs changed my mind. A hulking blue figure flashing into that apartment and sealing the door behind it.

Back inside I visually drifted to the picture Traci had drawn on the window with her lovely digit. Because I had opened the window the once-sharp condensation lines had blurred, although they continued to exist in a way that made an identification at least theoretically possible. I looked at them but nothing came forward. Just meaning-less lines without apparent form.

I stared.

Then it clicked. I saw precisely the image Traci intended. How strange. And then that thing happened where it became impossible for me to look at that window and see a different image or even no image at all.

For there was never yet philosopher
That could endure the toothache patiently.
– William Shakespeare

Chapter 17

"Christ Cleary, that's precisely what I'm saying. Why doesn't your pleasant fiction of a religion account for the Saturday between Easter and Good Friday? This is our life!"

"How do you mean, Deborah?"

"Well, as I understand it, Good Friday is a big deal right? A very sad day where you Christians reflect upon the crucifixion, death, and all other sorts of maudlin subjects. Two days later you have Easter, a joyous, bright day. Misery followed by bliss but what about the Saturday in between? Nothing. No fancy name."

"Holy Saturday."

"No fancy name that stuck, no reflections, no feel whatsoever. No meaningful commemoration of any kind and yet this Saturday is the day that most accurately reflects what our lives are like. After all, the majority of our days are spent in neither splendid bliss nor abject misery but rather in a state between those two extremes. A boring state where nothing much seems to happen but which is life's bread and butter. If you want to look at why your religion engages less and less people every year, ask yourself why this critical day is essentially ignored. I say celebrate and name the day, make *it* the celebratory centerpiece, and you'll take a significant step towards addressing our real concerns. Maybe get some people to come back."

"I completely disagree."

"What a surprise Conley."

"I'm serious. One of the painfully few things Cleary and his sort get right is ignoring that day. I kind of agree that the Saturday between Good Friday and Easter reflects the majority of our lives but it does that by being completely meaningless and thus *should* be entirely ignored. Take Casi here as an example. You've all heard that he's gotten himself into a bit of a pickle here. So what? I bet he'll never even remember any of this when all is written and done. How old are you Casi?"

"Twenty-four."

"Exactly. He's middle-aged, a meaningless stage of life that nobody remembers."

"What are you talking about middle-aged? He's a kid. Middle-aged is like you, fifty or so."

"Really? Let's say the average male in this country lives to seventy-two. If that's the case then ages 0 to 23 represent youth, 24 to 47 are your middle ages, and 48 to 72 your senescent decline into death."

"That's absurd. But fine, even if we allow you to define the term middle-aged in that way, why would it follow that whatever happens during this time period is meaningless?"

"Good God! Must I forever be the world's instructor? Do the terms Primacy and Recency mean anything to you? The human brain processes information a certain way. The things that come first, i.e. primacy, and the things that come last, i.e. recency, are the things that will stick in the human head. The rest is part of the forgotten middle. In a brief, where do you put the damaging admissions? In the middle! If placed in a lineup and given the choice of where to stand where should you stand? In the middle! These are not my usual unsupported ramblings, these are well-settled principles. In sum, Cleary is right to ignore that Saturday. Where he errs is when he tries to tell us that the Friday and Sunday *are* meaningful. No way. This, our world, is just a giant theater, showing Life, a poor play written by a middling playwright featuring repellent and insipid actors that will close within the week. Friday doesn't matter because Sunday is a scam and because of that, Saturday, id est our lives, couldn't possibly mean less. You're also wrong Debi when you try to paint our lives as this boring but ultimately benign even pleasant endeavor. Life, even at its best, is a tedious chore. For the overwhelming majority it's Good Friday every day. If you disagree chances are you're the sort who doesn't pay attention, because life is hideous if you do. The things you have to see and otherwise experience will sap the joy right out of you. You start out shitting in a diaper, dependent on random lunatics to cart your shit away and fill your belly. You have no control over anything, can't even speak! Then at the end, where I am, you feel like a giant bruise that won't heal, your knees make more noise than your mouth, family members become strangers far as your memory can tell, and you resume shitting in a diaper. And in between? Well I already told you what I think about that. Life isn't sweet, it's sour, and that's what keeps Cleary in business. Those are your choices, boredom or agony. Life is nasty, malevolent, toxic, evil, and brutish. And you know the worst part? The part that really sticks in my craw, whatever a craw is."

"What?"

"It's too short."

But it does move.

     – Galileo Galilei on Earth

Chapter 18

"Forgive me dude cause I'm a sinner."

"Well forgive *me* but I highly doubt the word dude is involved."

"Seriously."

"Fine. Forgive me padre because—"

"Father."

"Forgive me Father because I'm a sinner, something along those lines."

"I'm a sinner?"

"Yeah."

"I don't think so, that doesn't sound right."

"What doesn't sound right?"

"Sinner, that word. Don't think that's the right word."

"I think she's right. I don't think you have to make a blanket generalization like that about being a sinner and all. I think you just have to indicate that you are going to sin dude, I mean Father."

"Going to sin? You mean that you've previously sinned right?"

"Right."

"What if you haven't?"

"Haven't what?"

"Haven't sinned."

"If you haven't sinned then what the fuck are you doing there?"

"Exactly."

"See I don't think that's right. I think the point, or at least one of the points, is that you can always go because you're always sinning whether you know it or not."

"What kind of insane crap is that?"

"Yeah, what kind?"

"I'm just saying, I didn't make it up."

"Just ask Cleary, he'll know for sure. It's his job."

"Yeah ask Cleary."

"Forget Cleary, we don't need his help."

"Yeah forget him."

"Fine so you say something like *look I've sinned eighteen or whatever times and I'm here to confess.*"

"Wait, what are you talking about?"

"Yeah what's with the numerical reference?"

"I distinctly remember you had to provide a number. I think you had to tabulate and disclose exactly how many sins you had committed."

"No way. The number you're thinking of is the number of times you've confessed. You have to tell the dude how many times you've confessed in your life. That way they can gauge your progress and shit."

"No . . . no way. Hold it just a minute. The number you're thinking of is, I think, how long it's been since you last confessed."

"Yes! Now we're getting somewhere. That's exactly right. You have to state when the last time you confessed was. You don't have to give a specific date or anything though; I think you say something like *it's been blankety blank since my last confession.*"

"O.K. so something like, my name is—"

"No names."

"No?"

"Anonymity."

"O.K. So cutting right to the chase you say something like, forgive me for being a sinner and I haven't confessed in a year then you get into it."

"I have sinned."

"You have? When?"

"No, *I have sinned* is what you say. You say *forgive me for I have sinned it has been five years since my last confession.*"

"She's right. I remember it perfectly now and she got it almost completely correct. The precise wording is this: *Forgive me Father for I have sinned. It has been a decade since my last confession.*"

"Yes."

"Agreed."

"That's exactly right."

"So what?"

"Yeah, who cares?"

"I don't."

"Me either."

"Yeah, why *do* you ask Casi?"

The church on 35th Street, the church where that prick nosy civilian Bolo was working that night the previous spring when meathead Hurtado made a brief stop into that van on his way to state prison; the church where they held him, seated in a pew, a guard at each side, until the police arrived to bring him to me, the white one named Peter and claiming Catholic, the church where I arrived well after dark that night; That Church was closed.

I went back to the illuminated Bingo-type board. The weathered plastic letters, alternately red or black with no seeming pattern, did in fact spell what I thought they had so why the barred door?

Maybe there was a tricky side door or doors. It made sense that they couldn't just go and keep the front door open, the world being the world, but just as assuredly there would have to be a side door of some sort. A way to get in.

There *was* such a door, just one, but it was closed with such prejudice as to be nearly indistinguishable from the surrounding stone walls. What about a rectory? Every one of these things had a corresponding rectory right? Probably not in the city though. Rectories were probably just a leafy suburban thing. Wait, what was I thinking? There had to be a rectory. Where else would the priests and their confederates hang out when they weren't performing mass and sacraments and stuff? I knew they didn't live in the church, that was for sure. Except maybe now they did live there and that's why they had to lock the doors since you have to lock the doors to where you live if you're going to get any kind of meaningful sleep. The whole thing was very confusing so I wandered around the perimeter of that artful boulder kicking little pebbles and looking down.

While doing that I wandered into this garden-type enclosure in the back where I had no business being. There were these cool stone benches back there and I was about to go sit on one when I heard a soft, collared voice.

"Can I help you?"

"Oh yeah . . . I was . . . are you . . . open? Like for business."

"Business?"

"The doors were locked."

"When it gets dark we lock the doors. Masses daily at ten a.m. and noon."

"No, I'm an attorney."

"Same schedule for attorneys."

"No what I mean is I'm here investigating a case, not for any other reason."

"I wasn't even aware a lawsuit had been filed."

"No, a criminal case."

"Criminal?"

"Yes, it was several months ago. I just want to talk to someone. I need to. Someone who was here."

"Come in young man."

Those words were a soothing balm to me. My shoulders relaxed and fell. We walked to the door together. He turned a giant key that looked like it belonged to a dungeon. Two opposing metal bars rushed past each other towards the middle and the entry yawned open as a result.

He was young and strong. For a priest anyway. He had short, suspiciously black hair that formed a proceeding hairline less than an inch above his eyebrows, eyebrows that looked like little islands just off a continent. There was no warmth at all coming from my host, but still, once inside I felt good, safe. I also felt guilty though because I'd never been in there before. Not when it mattered and could have made a difference. It was a virtual reality in there. The painted expanse inside didn't seem like it could be supported and enclosed by what I had seen outside.

"I'm Father Mulcahey," he said and he surprised me by sitting on the steps going up to the altar. Or were they coming down from there?

"Really? That's funny."

"Funny?"

"I mean Mulcahey. Father Mulcahey you know?"

"No."

"Never mind. It was stupid. I'm totally way off. I thought for a moment that it was the same name as the . . . just forget it."

"Oh right. It is, you're right. I get that a lot."

"Get what?"

"Never mind."

"Right."

"So you say someone broke into our humble church?"

"No what happened, this was last April, was that someone was working on renovations here and my client broke into his van while he was here."

"Allegedly right?"

"Well we're well past that unfortunately. Anyway the contractor nabbed him and they held him here until the police came."

"Yes, I do now recall hearing about that incident."

"Oh good, I'm looking to talk to someone who witnessed that."

"You need to talk to Father Irizzarry."

"Irizzarry?"

"Yes, as I recall he was the priest on duty that night."

"Duty? You guys have that? Like shifts?"

"Well someone is always available. That night it was Father Irizzarry, I'm certain."

"That's what I thought, I mean in terms of the availability thing you're talking about. But seeing as you guys were closed just now it seems a strange kind of availability."

"Closed?"

"The doors."

"What about the doors?"

"No it's just that they were locked. The doors. I thought, I mean a long time ago, that they were never locked, you know, as a matter of course, all things being equal, in the course of human events. I'm not sure exactly what that just meant even. So you say Father Irizzarry was here that night?"

"Yes, you'll want to talk to Father Irizzarry."

"Great, can I?"

"Can you what?"

"Can I talk to him?"

"No."

"Why not?"

"He can't speak to you."

"Really? Is it like a vow of silence situation because I have a niece that—"

"No, he's not here. He's gone."

"When do you expect him back? I can wait around or just come back later."

"No, he's gone for good."

"He quit? Do you know where he went?"

"He was a very good man so I feel very confident about his new location."

"You're saying he died?"

"I am."

"I'm sorry."

"It's not your fault."

"Right . . . yet I feel oddly responsible."

"I hope his absence isn't going to adversely affect your case. I don't think anybody else was here that night that could help you."

"Thanks, that's alright. The case is basically over anyway. I was just looking into a final thing really."

"Confession?"

"No, there was no confession. That's about the only thing they didn't have but really there's not much need for a confession when they catch you in the van."

"No, I was referring to your situation. Would you like to take confession?"

"Confession?"

"Yes, Penance or Reconciliation, it's a sacrament, you are Catholic aren't you?"

"Yes, I mean no, I don't really believe, I mean, I don't think that—"

"Well there's no harm in talking right? You look like you might want to talk."

"No, I hate talking."

"Well I'm here for the next hour if you change your mind."

"You mean you're here for just that purpose?"

"Yes, we offer the sacrament twice a week for a two-hour period."

"I see. But isn't there some kind of specially designed booth? I seem to recall a little bootheroo."

"There is, over there."

"Truth is I don't even remember the, like, preamble you say just before you disclose the sins and all that. I mean there's a thing you say right?"

"There is, but you can also just go in and talk about whatever you'd like to talk about."

"Alright," I said, and the words had barely escaped my mouth, and my instant regret registered, when he got up and walked towards the booth. I followed him but when he went into his little curtained portion I contemplated making a break for it. After all, I thought, I hadn't even given him my name and chances were overwhelming I would never see him again. Instead I pulled the curtain to the side, heard a whirring sound, and gingerly entered the enclosure. I knelt on the little ledge they had there for that purpose and planted my chin on my right hand. There was a pleasant because only slightly translucent little screen separating us that I was highly grateful for. But then the priest slid that screen over revealing a lesser, far thinner, screen in its place. I guess it was better than nothing but I was tempted to slide the other one right back. He didn't say anything so I figured I had to start.

"Hi Father?" I wondered. "As you know, I have sinned since my last confession, which was a few months ago." That was a lie. "Actually that's not true. I made a mistake. It's been more than a few months. A lot longer."

". . ."

"Also I didn't really make a mistake. When I said it had been a few months just now? That wasn't so much a mistake as it was an out and out lie. Both were lies in fact. You understand? When I said it had been a few months since my last confession, that was a lie. It wasn't true. Therefore when I later said I had made a mistake, you know when I said it had only been a few months, that was also a lie. Of course, the one lie led me to tell the second lie out of sheer embarrassment so I suppose the argument could be made that it's all just

536

one lie with maybe two subcomponents although I will not now make that argument. Anyway now that I got that out of the way I suppose I'll start listing my sins, which as I recall is the way I'm supposed to proceed."

" . . . "

"I think I'm going to proceed in chronological order since that seems the best way to achieve completeness and I want to cover everything. Of course it's unlikely that I will remember everything, human memory being what it is. The question, I guess, then becomes whether something that I did in the past but cannot now remember is even relevant in this context. Whether it can even be said to have been done by me actually. You see what I'm driving at right? Locke?"

" . . . "

"I mean, taking the extreme example, imagine I previously slaughtered someone in cold blood but now have no recollection of it whatsoever. It doesn't seem that that action can then do me any harm now. I mean in terms of weighing on my conscience and guilt and all that, you know? What the hell is a conscience anyway? Sorry I mean heck. Why do I know, with seeming certainty, that I would feel like absolute crap if I did slaughter that dude yet I also know with similar certainty that the social conditioning explanation that will almost certainly be offered up fails to apply in my case in many other situations where you would expect it to? I mean that makes perfect sense doesn't it?"

" . . . "

"Listen I'm no expert at this but aren't you supposed to have a speaking part?"

"Perhaps, son, you should begin by simply listing your sins."

"Right, what constitutes a sin though? Never mind, I'll just start. I *am* going to go in chronological order. Reverse chronological actually so I can get the ball rolling with sins that are like still fresh in my mind. I was going to talk about something that happened this morning but I now realize that lying is a sin. I mean that's pretty well established right? After all lying is one of the ten commandments isn't it? Not lying of course being the requirement. Thou mustn't bear false witness and all that. Well if lying is a sin then I guess my most recent sin was the lie I told at the outset of this confession. The one I've admitted to. All of which might make me the first person ever to commit a sin in the very process of seeking forgiveness for earlier sins. Or not, who knows?"

". . ."

"Strange kind of sin lying though. Let's say a lie is a declaration the declarant knows is not true, why is the creation of one a sin exactly? What the hell, heck, is so sinful about telling a lie? Take my earlier lie as an example. So I said something that didn't accurately reflect truth, whatever that is. So what? How exactly is morality implicated? So these words that were uttered didn't happen to correspond with truth. Big deal. Is truth so paramount that a violation of it in any form is a *sin*? If that's the case then what is it about truth that makes this so? If it's a sin because God says so then why is God so hung up on truth? Is truth so important because without it, and without reliance on basic conformance with it, human interaction becomes hopelessly complicated and unsatisfying? Well that seems a concern more apt to contract law or social utilitarianism than to the lofty realm of morality. On the subject of the lofty, does God always expound the truth in its purest form? If so, and there's never artifice or ambiguity of any kind involved, then we need only look around to see what God thinks of us and it isn't good. Or maybe truth itself is God or a major aspect of God and therefore a violation of truth is the equivalent of a direct slap to God's face? Frankly I find those kind of anthropomorphic views of God to be the most annoying kind of bullshit, I mean bullcrap, and basically highly silly and arbitrary. And that's how I view your proscription against lying. I can't get too worked up about it is what I'm saying. Especially when, as here, it's

538

clear no-one was hurt by the declaration. And while I can certainly mentally concoct a situation where a lie would be grossly wrong I can also easily envision the opposite. The result is that the whole thing ends up seeming almost pedantic and superstitious you know?"

". . ."

"Which I guess brings me to the heart of the matter namely this. You could argue that when I do finally get around to it and recount my sins, that the telling itself will be a form of lying. You see the problem is I'm not really a true believer, I don't think. I don't truly believe in the things you're offering me right now. Don't believe they truly and accurately represent the world we live in. Not that I've given it an overwhelming amount of thought either. But I also didn't give it much thought earlier in my far younger life when I did believe in all you expound. That didn't seem like much of a conscious decision either. My environment back then just seemed to actively gravitate me towards those beliefs just as I now find myself pulled towards the opposite belief. The belief that there is no God et cetera and that this is all just a somewhat unhappy accident that lends itself to people seeking solace in things like a belief in God. But I can't stress enough what a gradual undramatic process this has been. It's not like I *did* have a strong belief in God until the day my best buddy had his balls blown off in Korea and died in my arms and I decided that such a thing would never occur in a world ruled by God, it's nothing like that. It's also not a case where I'm making a conscious decision that I'm going to attempt to define myself by this belief or non-belief. It's more like a continual weakening that turns into a disappearance."

"I understand."

"Thing is I don't think my disbelief has ever quite risen to the level of certainty of my previous belief, I know it hasn't. I may not believe that God exists but I also recognize I could be wrong. I know this because I have previously been wrong about other things that I was far more certain about. I also recognize that this is not the kind of area where an error is impossible or even unlikely. What that means is that if I *am* wrong and everything that you, Father Mulcahey, believe accurately represents the state of the universe then engaging in this process in a state of disbelief could be just the kind of slap in the face we spoke of earlier. At best it seems to be a kind of cynical attempt to cover all my bases in the absence of true contrition. On the other hand, since I recognize that your worldview might be correct shouldn't I attempt to remedy my failings and redeem myself in conformance with that possibility? In other words it's the lack of certainty that gives me pause. If I knew with certainty that this was all just a pleasant fiction, which if you were honest you would admit is at least a possibility as I have done with the converse, then there'd be no reason to be here at all. Anything would be permissible. Certainly there wouldn't be any reason to worry about something as silly as whether or not your words conformed with amorphous truth and we could dispense with a lot of the ill feelings we experience in this and similar areas. Quality of life would improve dramatically for everyone. No guilt, conscience, or restrictions. Which of course raises the possibility that my desire for such an existence influences my lack of belief in those things that would make such an existence impossible. See what I'm driving at?"

"..."

"Well, let me start. It was a small thing. I guess the idea was you would push the little red button at the top and that would set into furious motion these little wheels or whatever. The whole thing was probably two by three inches at most. Looking back I guess it was some kind of miniature slot machine although that was not a comparison I could have made back then. I was just a little squirt there at our Lady of Perpetual Remorse or whatever and severely limited in what I knew of the world outside. I did know that I liked that little thing when my man Marlon showed it to me. He showed it to me in the bathroom and I got to try it out a couple times. I liked everything about it for whatever reason. Well everything except the fact that it belonged to Marlon and not me.

"Anyway don't ask me why but I thought it was just about the coolest thing in the world at the time. Of course once I had it in my grubby mitts it didn't seem like such a big deal at all. The worst part is I think I had to stand there mute like the little prick I was as he told me he had lost it. As I recall I lost it myself later that day and felt a profound sense of loss. What a mangy twerp. I feel nothing but disgust when I look back at that. That place is full of all kinds of things like that for me. Like there was this dopey kid there that everybody ragged on including peripherally me. Poor sap. I once told this other kid to put a carton of milk on his chair just before he sat on it and he did. Do you see the immensely weasely aspect of this? I didn't put the milk there myself where I would be sticking my neck out and risking getting in trouble. I gave some other kid the idea and watched him get in trouble while not ratting me out. God, what a dick! I think of that all the time. I think of this kid, barely old enough to watch cable, sitting on that carton of milk and what that must have felt like, physically and mentally. They made us wear these hideous polyester pants then and this would have been lunchtime so I'm sure he was wet the rest of that day. More than once that day he probably wondered what he had done to merit the constant abuse he endured. I think of that kid. I think of being at a party years later where these lowly vermin were fucking with this girl who had passed out from too much drinking, drinking she probably did to get over some kind of social anxiety because she wasn't the type of girl who could just drop into any party and expect to receive favorable attention. What I think about is how I just stood there doing and saying nothing like some damn wooden pole. How instead of mentally telling myself the countless, sickening ways they were wrong, I instead chose to rationalize and diminish the actions of these worthless fucks. Whatever. I don't like remembering those things but every once in a while you know? I fantasize about living those moments again, avoiding those acts I regret and taking stands I should have. Can you offer me that? Can you arrange for me to *travel back in time* as they say in sci-fi? That would be something useful you could give me instead of whatever you have planned for me at the end of this. What do you anticipate that's going to be by the way?"

"..."

"Well, whatever. Maybe you'll rule that I have to recite seven penitential psalms once a week for the next three years, I don't know. Of course someone could question the legitimacy of your role in all of this. I mean what do you have to do with anything? You didn't sit on that carton of milk. Forget it, I know what you're going to say. Go ahead say it."

"..."

"Besides that stuff was a long time ago and I'm sure I covered it in a previous session. After all it's been a long time but this isn't the first time I've been in here either. Here's something I know I haven't covered. I stole some money. Well stole is probably too strong a word. I took some money that wasn't mine but also really didn't rightfully belong to the people I took it from, which makes it probably a technical violation at most and likely not that big of a deal. Although it was a lot of money I should add."

"How much?"

"Well, a lot. Like ten million dollars or so."

"How much?"

"Exactly. But don't jump to any conclusions, I plan to use the money to do a lot of good whereas if I hadn't taken the dough it would have been used for entirely nefarious purposes. Overall, society will benefit. That's the only reason I'm going to do it. I know that sounds like a rationalization but you have to realize that the people we took the money from are pretty bad characters and I'm essentially a good person. My real problem is . . ."

"Yes?"

"Well what if someone got hurt? I mean really hurt. What if someone died? Isn't that as bad as it gets?"

"Are you telling me someone died?"

"Yes, someone did, I think. What's the situation in that case? You know what, forget it, it's not relevant. What I really want to talk about is a little tricky. This was a couple of years ago. I don't want to talk about that either actually. Isn't there some kind of general dispensation you can give. God, I hate this!" As I said that I kind of slapped my hand down on the ledge in front of me. At first nothing happened. Then there was a loud cracking noise and it felt as if the entire booth was collapsing on us. Mulcahey booked out of there in nanoseconds. I stayed seated, curious to see what would happen next. The booth didn't collapse but the dividing wall did crack and fall forward into the space the priest had just vacated. I got out.

"Look what you've done," he said pointing.

I looked at what I had done then back at him. "Look what you've done," he repeated.

I looked down at what I had done and saw that it was bad.

"Look what you've done."

"I can pay," I said.

"Look what you've done."

"I can pay for it. I'll leave you a blank check and as long as you wait a week or so you can make it out for whatever you need. I can also just probably fix it myself."

"That's not necessary."

"Well here's my card. I can pay if you change your mind, but right now I have to go," I began a near-sprint out of there.

"Wait son!" he was running after me flapping some paper up and down.

"I really have to go," I said.

"I just need you to sign this release."

"Release?"

"Yes, a release is a—"

"I know what one is, release for what?"

"It's standard, it just says you agree to appear on the program described therein."

"*Clerical Confessions*? What is this?"

"Yes, that's the program. You see there was a hidden camera in the booth. They recorded everything we said and if the producers think it's interesting enough they may decide to use it. On the program. It's going to be a new show on H.B.O."

"You want me to agree to put what I just said on Television."

"No it's not T.V., it's H.B.O."

"I'm sorry, I don't think—"

"No you don't understand. This is a legitimate program on H.B.O. called *Clerical Confessions*. You can see it's on the up and up. You see the letterhead on the form? I'm assured the program itself is going to be quite tasteful yet compelling."

"Are you a real priest?"

"Yes, absolutely son. It's designed as an educational tool."

"No, sorry. Sorry, no. I have to go."

"But the release, no-one has refused."

"I'm sorry I just don't want to be on Television."

"It's not T.V., it's H.B.O.!"

Outside I slowed from sprint to jog then brisk walk. I ended up walking the whole way home. Miles in the dark cold. Many times I thought of diving underground into the tubes but I never did. I didn't think of that nutty priest either.

Instead I thought how there is no height you can reach that ensures you won't then fall. To fight Sugar Ray Leonard in Las Vegas on November 30, 1979, Wilfred Benitez was guaranteed 1.2 million to Leonard's even million. It would be the only time the magnetic Leonard would make less than his opponent in the ring and was evidence of Benitez's higher standing, at the time, in the boxing community. The greatness of the undefeated two-time champion Benitez was already beyond dispute so the most intriguing element of the fight was the expected verdict on Leonard's worth. Although at twenty-three he was two years older than Benitez, Leonard had less ring experience, particularly at the championship level where this would be his first such fight. Leonard's talent was evident. He had tremendous hand speed and, while probably not quite as difficult to hit as Benitez, he was no defensive slouch. The question was whether *inside* he was a real fighter or just a flashy media creation in a sport that missed the sensational presence of Muhammad Ali.

Of course while the general public understandably viewed the up-coming fight through Leonard's eyes, the fight was no less critical for Benitez. If he could become the first man to defeat the biggest star in the sport he would at least partially ascend towards his celebrity, money, et cetera. The fight was a crucial challenge.

Benitez responded to the challenge by becoming San Juan's fore-most discotheque inspector and not beginning rigorous training until he arrived in Vegas on November nineteenth, eleven days before the fight. Eleven days. Eleven days to prepare for something you've spent the sum of your twenty-one years preparing for. The first two days were occupied just adjusting to the shock of the physical torture that is boxing activity. The next nine days were insufficient and troubling. During sparring sessions those days Benitez's nose was broken, which means a sparring partner hit him hard enough and cleanly enough to do that. That was not a good sign. Goyo was upset and worried, predicting his son would lose to Leonard.

Benitez himself made no such prediction. He was confident going in. He always was when inside ropes. So inside the ropes of that Caesars Palace ring on November 30, 1979, he knew he would be better than his opponent because he always, every single time, had been. Except this time the other guy felt the same way.

Three separate times, while waiting in the ring for the announcer to attend to various details (*exempli gratia*: Benitez 36-0-1 [23 K.O.s]; Leonard 25-0 [16 K.O.s]), Benitez and Leonard engaged in staredowns – those ritualistic exercises peculiar to Boxing where the two opponents will stare at each other from a negligible distance with neither man willing to optically cede an inch. (On those occasions, although both men were listed at five-foot-ten and about one hundred and forty-six pounds, Benitez appeared to be the bigger man). The sight of these staredowns must have seemed an odd one to an audience fully aware that neither man was known for his punching power or aggressiveness in the ring. What it was was more like a staredown of abilities. And the whole thing the height of silliness in a sport where you could legally punch your opponent in the face if he bugged you so much.

But all that was beside the point; the unmistakable one being that when two truly great fighters get in the ring then the fight can't help but be great on at least some level. On these occasions, and on that night, several elements hang in the air. There's nowhere to look, that's the first thing you notice. Any fight is lucky if it contains one great fighter. If it does, you watch that fighter. You watch him because it's hard to watch both and the great fighter's ability pulls your eyes. You watch his superior ability allow him to do as he pleases. But what happens when both fighters draw your eyes equally? What happens when all you've ever seen each do is dominate? When you can't picture either fighter being overtaken but you know one of them will be? Well you get what they had there in that ring on that night. You get those charged moments just before the bell rings and the fighters' world begins to decide which of the universe's infinite possibilities will be actualized.

I think Benitez was lonely in those moments before the opening bell. The kind of loneliness that can normally only be attained through extreme solitude. There can be no more alone.

Boxing gets called an individual sport and that, I think, gets it wrong. It's individual, true enough, but unlike say tennis where you are promised, regardless of your comparative skill, a minimum period of survival, that is, some success, Boxing offers no such quarter; the whole thing can be over at any second, embarrassment always peering around the corner. It's that potential for embarrassment that makes Boxing less a sport and more like concentrated life; a life where you accept that you're going to have to be hit on the head, and it's going to hurt and harm you, in order to accomplish what you wish.

Often the greatest art is inaccessible to all but a few. After the bell rang to start the fight, Benitez and Leonard met in the middle of the ring and did little that was obvious. Warily they circled each other, each channeling from above their half-share of the pulsating energy in the surrounding atmosphere. Both missing, nothing landing, neither willing to open up, wary of the other's counterpunching ability. Leonard in particular seemed cautiously mindful of what had consistently happened to previous Benitez opponents who had rushed forward to attack only to miss everything while providing ready targets for vicious Benitez counters. So he stayed back. Nor did Benitez go against his nature and rush forward. Instead the audience was given an ebb and flow dance in the middle where true knowledge would be needed to discern any slight advantage that might emerge.

Those looking saw that while he wasn't coming close to landing it, Leonard's left jab was extremely quick and sharp, certainly the best Benitez had ever faced. Midway through the first round Leonard shot out a right that Benitez easily made miss; but as Benitez raised his head back into position, Leonard landed a left hook to the head, the first effective punch of the fight. Leonard sought to press his momentary advantage. He fired multiple punches in perfect combination and each with steam. They all missed. Benitez effortlessly slid his upper body side to side, to and from, here to there. Leonard didn't land again that round. At the end of the round they stared each other down again but it was Leonard who had to be a little unnerved at the realization that sometimes hype matches reality and is more like unadorned truth and maybe the person across from him did have radar and was impossible to hit other than incidentally and intermittently.

At that moment Benitez must have felt that this fight would not differ in any meaningful way from his previous ones. To lose he would have to get hit and he didn't get hit ergo et cetera; he would win. Except that in the next two rounds he did get hit. The quickness and speed of Leonard's left jab was a problem that wasn't going to go away. In the second, before another intermissionary staredown, a jab by Leonard landed clean and visibly knocked Benitez off balance. That was slightly embarrassing. More embarrassing was the jab near the end of the third that actually dropped Wilfred to the canvas. He jumped right up then smiled and shook his head. He wasn't hurt and dodged everything the rest of the round but the point was made. Getting dropped by a jab is never a good sign for what it says about either a fighter's balance or his ability to absorb his opponent's power.

Wilfred had given away some early rounds and even been down. Leonard had growing confidence and early momentum. Benitez needed to wake up soon. In the fourth he did, never getting hit significantly and landing some good left hooks. Nothing happened in the fifth save for Leonard employing the lame Angelo Dundee strategy of trying to steal a close round by impressing the judges with a meaningless feather-fisted flurry in the last ten seconds. In the sixth, both fighters, neither of whom ever took their eyes off their opponent, leaned forward, eyes up, at the precise same moment, causing their foreheads to clash angrily. Benitez was cut, Leonard wasn't. A bad situation had just gotten worse. Benitez seemed to realize this and it spurred him to his best moments of the fight to that point as he doubled and tripled up on his left hook showing his inhuman hand speed. At the end of the round he smiled with blood streaming down his face.

The next few rounds were close with neither man establishing a clear advantage. For Wilfred it wasn't going badly but it wasn't going overly well either. Leonard just seemed slightly stronger, like he had to be less careful. In the ninth, Wilfred's mouthpiece became visible. His mouth was open, he was tired. Leonard wasn't. In the tenth, Wilfred's tired hands were down when he wasn't throwing wild, amateurish punches that further betrayed his fatigue. In the eleventh, he stuck his tongue out at Leonard in seeming recognition of what was happening. In belated response Wilfred caught a hard left hook that hurt him and sent him to the ropes where he stayed waiting for Leonard. A wary Leonard, perhaps remembering Palomino's futility in a similar situation, hesitated repeatedly and failed to follow up with anything significant. Nevertheless, Benitez was now clearly losing a fight that was more than two/thirds over. He was tired but if he had trained properly he wouldn't have been since the action to that point didn't justify a twenty-one-year-old being that tired after eleven rounds. Fortunately for Benitez, the terms *second wind* refer to a true physiological phenomenon and in the twelfth he got his. He fought better, landed more punches with greater accuracy and showed more energy. The fight was closer.

Going into the fifteenth, Wilfred and his corner knew he needed at least a big final round to remain champion. There had to be a palpable urgency. The man across from him was trying to steal a piece of him and make him less of a person. With the end of the fight quickly approaching, stamina and pacing would no longer be a concern for either fighter. They could leave it all in the ring as they say. In that last round, Wilfred approached his true ability level and had his best moments of the fight. He landed serious punches in combination that snapped Leonard's head back and he did this without opening himself up too much. A determined Leonard responded in kind and the alight crowd bubbled over as the two men traded sizzling punches in the middle of the ring.

With about twenty-five seconds remaining, Benitez got caught flush with a compact left hook to the top of his head. His upper body jerked back and then forward and he dropped to one knee. He got up, shook his head, and went to a corner. The cut on his forehead sent blood down his face slicing it into perfect halves. He smiled beneath it. He bled. To the referee he nodded yes meaning more. When the action resumed he stayed in the corner. Leonard rushed in and threw punches almost wildly, most missing. Wilfred moved his head as he had a thousand times before.

More punches but not many. Suddenly, the ref steps between them and stops the fight. Leonard jumps up on the ropes. He is the New Champion. The old champion walks around the ring smiling. He is walking towards the jubilant Leonard who has been lifted up by his corner.

He extends his arms as if to hug but is ignored.

This space intentionally left blank.

Chapter 19

"You realize of course that once we get this money none of what you just said will matter right?"

"I know."

"No you sure? Because you maybe don't sound like you mean it."

"No I understand."

"For example, you're going to quit right?"

"Yes."

"Sure?"

"Hell so, what am I the janitor who goes back to work the day after the Lotto press conference where they hand you the oversized novelty check? Of course I'm going to quit. I'm going to move too. I'm not going to see anything that reminds me of anything else ever again."

"Interesting."

"Whatever."

We were sitting in my living room and it was noisy. The unpainted radiator in the corner that constituted the sole barrier in my life between clammy continued existence and rigorous mortis hissed furiously, its metal top hat on the side undulating wildly. The two front windows swelled inward barely barring the whistling wind. Spread out on a table between us was a lot of wrestling paper along with photographs and blueprints. Dane surveyed the scene then looked up at me.

"That's a lot of stuff isn't it?" he said.

"More than you would think could be generated in less than a week."

"And now we're another less-than-a-week away. After tonight just six full days remain before we go in and, if I understand you correctly, you will be in Alabama for at least a part of four of those days."

"Yes."

"So how do you feel about it?"

"Still concerned about DeLeon."

"I don't think you need to be."

"Well, where is he then?"

"We know where he is, he's in Santo Domingo enjoying his big fifty."

"We don't *know* that. You assume it."

"Fine, but it's a strong assumption."

"I'm not sure it really rises to that level."

"Oh stop."

"I'm serious, I must not be as willing as you are to make assumptions when my life is on the line."

Dane exhaled a smile. "Listen, let's review what we do know beyond doubt and why I feel it justifies me in making my assumption. First, we know DeLeon got out right? We know he's not in jail anymore?"

"Yes we know that."

"You've read the packet right, so we also know the drugs have arrived in this country, correct?"

"Correct."

"And we know from DeLeon that he was to make $100,000 total, fifty when the stuff got in the country and another fifty after the deal was done."

"That's what he said."

"We also know that his plan was to take that first fifty and split before the deal came to fruition, agreed?"

"Yes."

"So isn't it highly reasonable to assume that after he got out he played his role in getting the stuff in the country, got his fifty, then split as he said he would?"

"So how come we haven't been able to confirm his presence there?"

"Well that's not all that surprising is it? We have limited time right now and one would certainly expect DeLeon to be laying low over there for many reasons, not the least of which is the necessity of staying clear of Flaco until at least next Wednesday."

"That's part of the problem, part of what holds me up. You've only set forth that part of DeLeon's plan that supports your theory. For example, you assume a correlation between DeLeon's release from jail and the arrival of the drugs about thirty-six hours later."

"Of course."

"However, as you know, DeLeon told me he lied when he told the cops the deal would not go off without his liberty when the truth was it would in fact go off with or without him."

"True and I believe that was the case. If he had stayed in jail, the deal would nevertheless have gone through without him. That's why, as he also told us, he was in such a hurry to get out so he wouldn't lose his fifty. That said, once he did get out I think Escalera astutely knew that here was the one guy who could call an untimely halt to the proceedings. I think at that point, at Escalera's urging, DeLeon reached out to Flaco, helped seal the deal, and got his fifty in return. After that it was all according to plan and he split."

"Well there was more to the plan though, right? As he explained it to me, and I know what your response is going to be, he was then going to give the police the real information thereby ensuring that Escalera would be arrested and therefore unable to retaliate. This is not a minor issue. If he in fact did give the police the right information then we're going to be in for a nasty surprise next Wednesday."

"I know what he told you but remember what he told me. Through my help, DeLeon came to realize the moral illegitimacy of vengeance.

553

He realized that the best way to be free from the fear of retaliation was to avoid creating the need for it in the first place by allowing the deal to go through. Obviously to do that he couldn't give the police the real information. Nor could he stick around here, not with the police looking for him. The best solution was for him to get his money and disappear immediately. Now he didn't come to this conclusion accidentally. I, of course, led him to it by the nose every step of the way, but in a manner which allowed him to ardently believe he had come to it all by his lonesome. That's how come I know he took his money and split without ever talking to the police again. Because when I left that day that's what he was going to do."

"Except that when he left me he was going to do something entirely different. So we know he's capable of changing his mind on this matter and we can't foreclose the possibility that he did so again."

"But we also know that he has in fact disappeared and the police are looking for him, making it unlikely that he's hanging around risking jail or that he in any way cooperated further after we parted."

"So we've gone from perfect to unlikely?"

"No, remember what I said before. There's a very simple way to test my theory. We know what the false information DeLeon gave to the cops was. All we have to do, and by *we* I mean *I* since you will be in Alabama, is go to the fake location at the fake time and see if there is any police activity. If there is that pretty much confirms my theory and we can proceed in calm."

"Obviously extreme care has to be taken Saturday right?"

"Certain things go without saying."

"Don't overstate what we can determine on Saturday either."

"I know, I know. The police could be in possession of two dates, including the correct one, and be checking out the Saturday one out of sheer thoroughness, but even you have to admit how unlikely that is."

"Yes."

"Bottom line is we'll know quasi-definitively on Saturday, so let's get to the actual plan."

"Fine," I said. "Given the scarcity of time remaining I think we need to start by mentally eliminating those potential avenues we've been ruminating on but which, for whatever reasons, are not practical. Tonight we need to at least substantially narrow the universe of possible plans."

"I agree. On that note, as I said before, I think it's going to be very difficult to locate the nephew for example."

"Yeah I don't think we should waste any more time on that because even if we could discover that location and get the trunk before Wednesday there's still the problem of how to turn it into money while also destroying its contents so that's a dead end in my view."

"Well we need to talk about that last part but yes I agree that perfection requires we abandon that avenue. Likewise I feel that any further attempts to identify and possibly intercept the mule are similarly doomed."

"Yes."

"Which means we have to do this sometime around three a.m. next Wednesday."

"Right."

"You've studied up, right Casi?"

"Extensively."

"So you'll know everything I'm about to say, but here goes anyway. We know that at three there will be ten people in that building, nine of whom are profiled in the packet."

"Right."

"Three in the garage to start, one will stay with the mule, the other two will carry the chest up to the first floor. Waiting there will be Escalera, his financial partner Colon, and Grullon who will weigh and test the drugs. If Grullon gives the go-ahead, they'll signal Ballena who will come down from the second floor with the duffel bag of money. The two will go back to the garage with the bag and give it to the mule consummating the deal."

"That's eight."

"Right, plus the two lookouts on the roof make ten."

"That we know of."

"Well that's all there is from that end, I'm sure of it. But I think you make a good point when you say it's likely that people from Flaco's end will be in the area to at least quickly snag the mule and get the money."

"You would think. Otherwise that's a lot of money to entrust to someone getting a hundred and fifty dollars."

"At any rate, what is obvious is that the purchase money is going to have to arrive at 410, assuming it's not already there, a strong assumption given that the house is still occupied by civilians, sometime before three. The idea therefore is that—"

"No."

"What? You don't even know what I'm going to say."

"Look I know what you're going to say. Here's the problem. Several problems actually. First and foremost, if things get fucked up from their perspective, that is, we steal their money, before the mule arrives, then you can be sure they will hold her, torture her, and probably kill her, on the off chance she was involved. And even putting aside the considerable moral difficulty inherent in causing that to happen to someone who is getting a hundred and fifty dollars, a woman no less, there is the practical problem that the only time we can be sure the money will be there is at precisely three a.m. not two-thirty or some other time sufficiently in advance of the exchange to avoid complication."

"That's your better argument."

"Fine, but this is certain, whatever the plan is it must encompass the mule's safe exit."

"O.K. I'll give you that you stubborn fuck. And I gave you the crazy swords that are in this bag."

"The swords were your idea."

"Only after you proscribed guns, which any self-respecting malfeasant will tell you is a vital element of almost any successful heist."

"Almost, but who wants to be part of the murky middle right?"

"I gave you all that, understand, but now is the time to concede that your proposed destruction of the drugs must promptly go out the window."

"No way."

"It's so fucking impractical! It will be the death of this thing too."

"We just need to think of something."

"Listen, hear me out will you? There are going to be at least ten people, probably more, in the area of that money."

"The area is irrelevant because we have to do this inside the building."

"Fine, ten people then."

"Only nine of which will be interested in thwarting us."

"Nine and we are two. The only way, it seems to me, we can ever hope to overcome that discrepancy is to divide the house into its four zones: the basement, the two floors, and the roof. The best thing we have going for us is that seventy percent of their force is in the bottom half of the house and that the relevant zone, the third floor, has only one person."

"Ballena."

"Right."

"A single person entrusted with providing security for all that money and who not incidentally happens to be referred to solely by the Spanish word for Whale despite the fact that everyone agrees he is not obese."

"True, he's no doubt large but he is nevertheless only one person whereas we are two highly motivated individuals carrying swords. Anyway you see where I'm going with this right? The drugs that you want to destroy—"

"Have to."

"Those drugs are on the second floor surrounded by five people. Understand my concern now? See, you haven't thought about it in terms of zones."

I reached into a folder on the table and handed Dane a sheet of paper. It was a copy of the blueprint he had included in his packet. On it, the house had been divided into four zones just as Dane had suggested with illustrations depicting the number of people in each zone and the approximate times of their presence. He looked at it, first smiling then concerned.

"Well I see you *have* thought about it in those terms," he said. "Which would only make it all the more baffling should you insist on entering the most heavily fortified zone in the house to destroy the drugs."

"I know it's tight," I said rubbing my chin, laying back, and just generally trying to affect an air of genuine empathic concern for his plight. "But there must be a way and besides I'm not convinced we could even pull this off without implicating the two lower zones anyway."

"I think we can if we forget about the drugs."

"So you're saying come in and leave from the top so we only have to deal with three guys?"

"Exactly."

"But they're in communication with each other."

"That's O.K., we can disrupt that pretty easily."

"I agree we probably have to go in from above for several reasons." I thought in silence. "The other major option is the garage."

"That's tough."

"Yeah, they'll be too vigilant there. What if we get inside before

Wednesday and are already there when the money arrives," I said.

"I thought of that but when? You don't get back until Monday afternoon and by then Escalera and his guys will already be there."

"So let's do it Monday afternoon, which is enough time to ensure that the Wednesday morning exchange will be canceled and the mule will be safe."

"We're not sure the money will be there remember?"

"Right, sorry."

"C'mon stay with me."

"Tired," I said. I closed my eyes and lay on the sofa. For minutes there were no words until Dane spoke:

"I think that coming in from the top, either from the roof or the third-floor fire escape is our best option. It gives us the most time in the house and in proximity of the money without the entire crew knowing what's going on."

"Assuming the entirety will ever know."

"Right, our job is to minimize the people who are aware of our presence and in that way attempt to deal with the disparity in numbers."

"Yes, and as a backup I think we should explore ways in which we might be able to create the illusion of greater numbers on our part."

"Nice, now you're awake," he lit a cigarette and exhaled as if an important segment was behind us. "So correct me if I'm wrong but it seems we've agreed we have to go in around three from either the roof or the fire escape."

"Yes," I said.

"And we agree we'll leave the drugs alone."

I said nothing.

"We agree we'll leave that heavy, impractical chest, whose contents will be spread all over a room containing five armed protectors on a floor we don't even have to enter to acquire our money, alone. Alone."

I looked away and at the window, only I couldn't see through the window and to the outside for the condensation. Visibility was poor.

"Forget the drugs right?"

". . ."

"Right?"

"Let's go on with the plan, we don't have to decide everything all at once."

"Fair enough."

"And I don't think the fire escape is going to work either," I said. "For one thing, it's on the front of the building where anybody on the street can see. If it was on the back facing that little yard they have, that would be a different story. Also it leads into the main room of the floor where The Whale is likely to be waiting or at the very least where you would expect him to spot us immediately, not good. Again if it led into some minor forgotten part of the floor it would be a far more attractive option."

"Which takes us to the roof entrance."

"Exactly."

"Which gives every indication of leading into precisely the kind of minor, hidden area you're talking about."

"Yes," I said. "At least judging from the video." (Dane had obtained, from what he assured me was an untraceable computer source, a video of a virtual tour of 410 from when it was briefly on the market six months earlier.)

"So consequently you say roof."

"Yes, I think we can come down and out that door into that little alcove and gather there before Ballena or The Whale or whatever has the slightest idea what's about to hit him."

"I agree. It's a strange kind of roof access for a residence, lucky for us."

"Yeah if it was the kind of thing where we had to drop one of those crazy attic ladders or something that would make it a lot more difficult that's for sure."

"So there you have it. This will actually be easy the more I think about it."

"Whoa, I wouldn't go that far. There's still the problem of getting past the two roof guys before we even get to that alcove right?"

"Right and twice since we'll likely plan on leaving through the roof as well."

"So?" I said.

"So, Casi, I think it's a reasonable assumption to make that of the two guys on the roof one will be watching the front, the other the rear. And we know they will have point to point radios to communicate with the other guys if necessary, should they see police or anything else suspicious. Now as an initial matter it would seem we have to get on that roof from one of the two adjacent roofs."

"There's no gap right?"

"No gap on either side but there is one critical difference. 410 faces north right? Well the building on its east side is taller than 410 while the building to the immediate west is shorter. I think we need to come over from the taller building to the east for two reasons. First, we're going to have to be on one of the adjacent rooftops sometime before three and obviously we don't want to be seen. Well it's going to be a lot easier to avoid being seen by people who are below us than by those above us looking down. Second, we're going to want to have as easy a journey from rooftop to rooftop as possible and from the rooftop to the east we will have the help of our friend gravity. So I think we need to come from the east, from 408 specifically. Now as luck would have it, there's an abandoned building three doors down from 408 at 402 East 123rd Street."

"Really?"

"I'm telling you it's fate. The building is all boarded up and is fairly impenetrable save for a side door to the basement that takes you up to what used to be the kitchen and if you keep going up from there you can get to the roof in a manner similar to 410."

"There's no gap between 408 and 410, what about between 402 and 408?"

"One gap, between 406 and 408. Maybe eight feet, we can deal with it."

"How?"

"Obviously we still need to create a lot of details but before we do that let me give you, in general, what I propose."

"Go ahead."

"I will make a key to that door at 402. Sometime prior to next Wednesday, I will use that key to go into that building and leave everything we need to do the heist. I'll leave the swords, the radios, the clothing, everything so it's waiting for us that night. On that night we go to 402. We take the swords. We go up to the roof. We cross, cross, cross until we get to 408."

"What about the gap?"

"A ladder, pole vault whatever."

"What-vault?"

"Pole."

"I don't even know what that could possibly mean."

"Like I said, we'll get to the details later. To continue, when the time is right we jump down to the roof of 410 from 408. We go down the staircase and out to the second floor. We deal with Ballena and take the bag without allowing him to notify the others. We go back up to the roof, all the way across back to 402, back down to the basement, out the side door and home with our money. Any questions?"

"Many. Are all of the buildings from 402 to 408 the same height?"

"Yes."

"Good."

"Except for the gap we can practically fly between 410 and 402."

"I hate the gap."

"Fuck the gap, no big deal."

"So how do we get to 402? How do we get out of there when we're done?"

"We have to decide that."

"How do we get past those two guys on the roof twice?"

"We have to figure that out as well but what do you think about the plan in general?"

"I think it's good, or at least our best bet, but our success seems really contingent on the accuracy of DeLeon's information, to a degree I'm not entirely comfortable with."

"How so?"

"Well for example, how do we know that Ballena will be the only guy on the second floor? That's a huge issue too. It seems to me you would want more than one person protecting that kind of money."

"We know because you heard DeLeon. Escalera does it the same way every time and he's not about to change now. Ballena is always alone in a separate, nearby location or room until they weigh and test the drugs. Then they radio him and he brings the money over."

"But this is a big deal."

"But not a risky one from their perspective. The last thing they expect is a move on that money. From who? A guy about to get it anyway?"

"Maybe you're right."

"I am right, DeLeon's right."

"So how do we get by the roof guys?

"I think we might need to create a distraction."

"That's the last thing I think we should do," I said. "Any distraction we create artificially might have the opposite of the intended effect. If I'm sitting there all complacency and suddenly something out of the ordinary happens, the first thing I'm going to do is safeguard what's at risk."

"That's a risk, no doubt."

"On the other hand, we might have the perfect built-in distraction."

"What's that?"

"Well what's that house going to look like at exactly three a.m.? Think about it. At exactly that time the Nova will pull up to the garage. The north side roof guy at least will be watching the car from the roof to assure that it arrives alone and with only one occupant. The three guys in the basement will be watching the door open, checking the car, unloading the chest. The three on the second floor will first be looking out the window then waiting in anticipation for their cohorts to come up. In short, that seems as good a time as we're going to get to go in there undetected."

"Not bad and what I like is that since we know Escalera is a stickler for time we can time it to a tee."

"Exactly. If we do it right, the first time Escalera will discover something has gone wrong is when he asks Ballena to bring down the dough. When do you think that will be?"

"Well let's think it through. Three o'clock she gets there. Couple of minutes to get the trunk out and bring it up the stairs. Now they unlock it, spread out its contents and begin the weighing and testing. Remember this is a lot of shit. It's going to take a while to test it all. Remember also what DeLeon says about Escalera and testing. Escalera is thorough to the point of paranoia. He tests and weighs extensively from every portion of the shipment. This stems from an incident when he got beat, on a minor deal, because he only tested the top and bottom of the stuff and not the middle."

"What happened to his fascination with the middle?"

"Maybe that was the genesis of it I don't know."

"So lots of testing."

"Yes and Ballena will not be summoned until it is all complete."

"Bottom line?"

"I'll say fifteen to twenty-five minutes."

"Those field tests are pretty quick."

"Yeah but it all has to be weighed and remember that every single portion is being tested. The unknown factor is how the stuff will be

564

packaged. The more individual packages there are the longer the testing."

"Is there any way it could be less than fifteen minutes?"

"No I don't see how."

"So let's assume the worst case scenario and say we have fifteen minutes to get in there, get the dough and get the hell out of that area before those guys flood the street looking for us."

"I think that's right."

"So what have we established so far Dane?"

"We've established that we're going to use swords, that we're going to begin at 402, that we're going to enter 410 through the roof, that we're going to exit through that same roof and go back to 402. Most importantly, I think we've also established that we are two avaricious, insane fucks who refuse to be marginalized by a society that exalts the acquisition of wealth above all else."

"O.K., I'll take your word on that last one. That still leaves a lot left to decide. I'm thinking of these things. I made a list while you were talking:

When do we get to 402?
How do we get there?
How do we leave the scene with the dough?
How exactly do we get past the rooftop watchers?
How do we deal with Ballena?
How do we keep him from notifying the others in the house?
Exactly how big is this guy that he warrants being called Whale yet isn't fat?

There it is off the top of my head. I'm flying Friday morning so between tonight and tomorrow we need to decide these questions to a high degree of certainty."

"No, to a perfect degree."

"So?"

"So did you watch The Beastly Burden Channel at all today? They had this Kodiac bear—"

"I don't have cable."

"This fucking bear—"

"As I've been saying, I think one of the keys is to minimize greatly the amount of time we're engaged in clearly culpable conduct. For that reason, I think we should arrive at 402 as close to three a.m. as possible."

"Fine but given that the three o'clock time is a strict go time we don't want to cut it too close either."

"Let's say 2:30 at 402 meaning that an hour later we should be well on our way home with the dough."

"I like it Casi."

"How do we get there?"

"How do you get anywhere in this city? Subway I guess."

"Subway might be O.K. for getting there but leaving there is still a getaway right? We're going to make our getaway on the subway where any flatfoot can decide to ask us what's in the bag?"

"On what basis?"

"So we're going to rely on their understanding of and respect for the U.S. Constitution now?"

"You should've seen this bear man."

"The getaway please."

"So we'll drive, we'll leave the car a couple blocks away."

"What car? Not mine obviously."

"Why not? You've said repeatedly that you want to minimize the length of innocently inexplicable conduct. What's more explicable than being in your own car?"

"Let's table it for now."

"Fine."

"Here's the main thing. Focus on the time between when we're on the roof of 408, say 2:58 a.m., until we get out of the side door of 402. How do we do that?"

"Listen we do have a week. I don't think too much of the plan should come together all at once. That seems dangerous to me, sloppy and precipitate. I mean we've got all day tomorrow. You're not going to work tomorrow right?"

"I'm not but we don't have all day because I'm also meeting with Toomberg."

"I thought you were meeting with him tonight."

"Yes and tomorrow night as well."

"Man alive, you need to be entirely focused on this."

"I am. This isn't brain surgery, I can do other things simultaneously. Besides you're the one who wants to stop tonight, I want to keep going."

"That's because I've given it a lot of thought and I think the planning stage of this, to be optimal, has to proceed at a certain pace. Perfection is never a matter of indiscriminately spending copious time. I'm fully confident that everything we've decided to this point is unequivocally correct but I would lose that confidence if we proceed too quickly. That's so because once we decide something I never want to have to revisit it. That would not be a perfect allocation of time or mental resources. In these situations, things must develop at their proper rate, a delicate balance must be achieved, so that the participants, you and I, have just the right relationship to the plan."

My relationship to the plan was dysfunctional. Dane evinced so little doubt about its eventual efficacy, about its perfection and our ability and need to properly carry it out, that the whole thing became something more than real yet somehow still distant. If reality is sometimes so intense and bizarre that it feels like bad, unpersuasive fiction, then this was a fiction so powerful it outrealized reality. The whole thing scared me in a way that made me involuntarily cognizant of my every cardiopulmonary move; the ways a body keeps itself alive. I

567

resolved to take two possibly wholly incompatible steps in response. I wanted to throw every cell of my being into the formation of the plan but I thought I would eventually back out, maybe by intentionally creating some impediment. I had too much doubt, I thought, to successfully carry it out.

"I think I need to keep working on this," I said. "I don't feel comfortable yet and Toom won't be here for a while."

"Alright we'll break it down. It's 2:59 a.m. and we're on the roof of 408 immediately adjacent and above the roof to 410. Any problems to that point Casi?"

"No there shouldn't be any problem. By the time I get back from Alabama you'll have left the stuff in 402 right?"

"Right."

"And you'll be very careful doing so right?"

"Naturally."

"What if some crackheads go in there to smoke or something and find our swords et cetera?"

"I thought of that but no. The key I'm going to make is really the only easy way in there and I think that easy-way-ins are the only thing we have to worry about in this context."

"Are there any imminent plans, by the city or others, to deal with that abandoned building?"

"No, six months and counting with no plans."

I had to give this to him. I don't think Dane had ever answered *I don't know* to any question that involved the acquisition of information.

"And I never will," he said. "Because all the homework is already done. The only thing left to do is some reasoning by our two brains and of course any factual research that may arise as a result."

"O.K. so 2:59 now what?"

"Seemingly two major options. We can allow Heckle and Jeckle on the roof to see us but somehow incapacitate them in such a way that they can neither stop us nor use their radios to notify the others of

568

our presence or we can get on the roof and under without them detecting us. I don't see any other option, do you?"

"No."

"So what's it going to be then, eh?"

"You're saying, Toom, that you saw no-one as you were coming up?"

"No-one, why?"

"Never mind."

"Have you been working?"

"Yes."

"And you think?"

"I think I remember the day Gold was walking around looking for volunteers trumpeting *unprecedented autonomy* and *priceless experience*. Remember? He said there was this organization in Alabama that devoted itself to assisting death row prisoners and they were looking for attorneys willing to work pro bono. I think about how I really should have stayed seated in my swiveling chair but how instead I tracked him down and signed up on that little clipboard he was carrying. I think about how even though that happened months ago, it wasn't until last week, with the literal *deadline* approaching, that I truly understood the enormity of what I'd agreed to."

"A man's life."

"That but also the paucity of actions taken on the kid's behalf to this point."

"It *would* seem that quite a few mistakes, of both commission and omission, were made before we became involved."

"The trial was a joke."

"Yes."

"Look at this transcript. I've done fucking hearings on sales that were longer than this!"

"I know but—"

"Not to mention the excruciatingly long list of things I would not have thought could possibly happen here, at this time, but that nonetheless somehow all manage to exist in this case, which was assigned to us allegedly at random."

"I know."

"I'm talking, in order, about the fact that Alabama does not have a fucking public defender's office. So that Kingg's lawyer at trial, this prick Bennigan, was assigned at random by the judge on the case, a judge whose concern with the efficacy of defense counsel we can surmise from his later actions."

"Good point."

"How this worthless shithead Bennigan was a solo practitioner whose practice consisted almost entirely of exchanging bank checks for deeds with the occasional petit larceny thrown in. How he was paid roughly the amount that a well-situated soda machine takes in in a week. How this grossly unqualified individual proceeded to put on the single most somnambulant, almost apologetic, performance I have ever had the misfortune of being exposed to. How even the slightest contact between Bennigan and his client should've sufficed to convince him he was representing a near-vegetable cloaked in a human epidermis costume yet he failed miserably to adequately convey this to the jury. How despite all this, God amazingly took time off from his busy schedule, as if to say that here *finally* was something that offended even his sensibilities, reached into that jury room and, like a master of puppets saddled with a group of particularly inexpressive marionettes, returned a verdict of life in prison rather than death. How at that point that empty, hollowed-out, prick of a trial judge Pearson overruled the jury and sentenced Kingg to death without so much as suggesting a reason. How this is perfectly permissible under Alabama's death penalty statute but is impermissible in all but one other state and has never been done there."

"All true."

"How, and this is a great one, how this same Bennigan, who I wouldn't trust to properly water my lawn, is then incredibly assigned to perfect Kingg's appeal where the most meritorious issue, thanks in no small part to Bennigan's own failure to preserve a single legal issue for appeal, was the ineffective performance of Bennigan himself. And in such a way is the guard entrusted to keep himself prisoner so that predictably Bennigan files this aptly named brief, a more turgid and unpersuasive collection of prose being difficult to envision. And since then what? Since this awe-inspiring series of events what action has been taken on Kingg's behalf? Nothing."

"Us."

"Nothing! Because of course Alabama would have to be one of only two states where once the direct appeal is complete, a death row inmate like Kingg is no longer entitled to an attorney despite the fact that there are about a zillion further legal actions that can be taken to try to prevent him from being zapped. But Mrs Kingg is in her fancy subterrestrial box and with her so interred there's no-one left who can picture Jalen's face except those who wouldn't want to. So without a lawyer the deadline to petition for state remedies passes."

"Yes."

"The two-year deadline to petition for federal habeas relief passes."

"Yes."

"Enter us to mop up."

"Well I like to think we can do more than that."

"Really? That's nice, and I like to think there's a brotherhood of man except every time I let my hands down I get belted in the face. Has anything that's been attempted on Kingg's behalf so far worked? The Governor, who has one eye on November and has sole authority to commute Kingg's sentence, has proven to be an obvious dead end."

"True."

"The State Supremes said there was nothing interesting here."

"True."

"Leaving us, you and I, alone and abandoned by our sponsor organization, to do what exactly?"

"District court."

"Right. To file a three-point brief with a judge from the appropriate district court urging sweet relief. Three points, one for each of us. Only that fuck Ledo did less than zero on his Yellow Mama electric chair point before heading out to the dopey place where they plant giant letters on hillsides and the sea swallows the sun each nightfall."

"True but we knew what Ledo was when we gave him the least meritorious point, a point that has already been decided by the Supreme Court. And besides I like what we have on that issue now anyway."

"Fine but the worst thing about Ledo is I'm filled with this overwhelming desire to take the next flight headed left, find him at whatever Melrose Place sidewalk joint he's sitting in discussing the use of light in Rohmer's films, snatch the tofu burger out of his mouth, and rap him in the face with a fork. Only that desire is tempered by my realization that, if not for the last week or so, I wouldn't have done any more work than he did. Everywhere I look I see Ledos and I fear I may be no better than them. Isn't that frightening? Shouldn't somebody as good as me be appreciably better than a Joe Ledo?"

"Is this the point?"

"At the moment."

"Can I read it?"

"Sure, it's no secret."

"So what's it going to be then, eh?"

"Heard you the first time."

"And?"

"And I'm thinking."

"Well don't think too long. Remember the balancing act I spoke of. The balancing act Casi."

"O.K., Dane."

"Well?"

"Well I think we need to get by the roof guys undetected."

"Twice?"

"Yes, I mean, at least the first time for sure."

"Because?"

"I know that incapacitating them, and by that I assume you mean tying them up or something, has the advantage of facilitating our exit as well."

"Exactly."

"However, the downside of that method is the difficulty it would present for our stated goal of keeping Escalera in the dark as long as possible."

"How does it do that?"

"Say these guys are tied up at 3:00, what happens at 3:05 when Escalera radios up to them to make sure everything looks good? When he gets no response he's going to panic and investigate and he's going to do that at a time when we're still dancing with The Whale on the second floor."

"Good point."

"On the other hand, if we sneak by them at 3:00 and again at say 3:10, then the first time Escalera will sense that something is wrong is when he asks Ballena to bring down the money at about 3:15 or 3:20, and incidentally we should look into possible methods for further delaying that time of discovery. Anyway, by then we should be back in the car."

"Seemingly the problem then becomes The Whale. Him we have to incapacitate because he's specifically guarding the bag we want. What happens when Escalera radios Whale while we're two feet away and gets no answer?"

"First, Escalera's far less likely to radio Ballena, other than to call for the money, because he's not a lookout. Second, I think you're right when you say we'll have to physically confront The Whale because it's highly unlikely that said creature will peel its eyes off that bag for even a second. So unlike with Heckle and Jeckle on the roof, with The Whale we seemingly have no viable choice."

"So sneak past the roof guys, harpoon The Whale with our swords, and sneak back out, all in ten minutes or so?"

"Absolutely not."

"Less than ten minutes is going to be tough."

"No harpooning."

"What's this now?"

"No harpooning."

"Did you not read the profile? The Whale is an inveterate savage."

"I'm serious Dane, no."

"Amazing. Fine, sneak in, *incapacitate* The Whale, and sneak back out with the bag."

"Right."

"So really all that's left to decide is how exactly we sneak in then out and the precise way we deal with Ballena."

"If you want to oversimplify, yes."

"I want to, tomorrow?"

"See you then."

"I read your draft last night Casi."

"Ditto."

"I don't know how you did that in less than a week."

"Paid good money for that point."

"Do you agree with me that the electric chair point is as good as it's going to get?"

"Yes, as good as, given the directly contrary and controlling legal authority from the highest court in the land."

"Well put, and *my* draft?"

"Haven't read it yet."

"You just said you had."

"Never."

"You said ditto."

"Right, ditto. You said you read my draft last night and I indicated that I also read my draft last night. Had I wanted to quickly yet artfully convey to you that I had in turn read *your* draft I might have said *vice versa* or something similarly pithy."

"How precise."

"Thank you."

"It wasn't a compliment."

"Oh."

"Don't you think you should have read it by now."

"I will do so imminently don't worry Toom. Meanwhile I encourage you to view my inaction as a token of my immense trust in your abilities."

"I'll do that then. My only question about your draft is right here where you wrote this."

"You mean, I bet, where I wrote in gargantuan font GAPING HOLE."

"How did you guess?"

"I think we have two big problems and not a lot of time to remedy them. The one Gaping Hole refers to is the one whereby probably our best argument is that Jalen's trial counsel was remiss, and consequently that his performance was ineffective to a degree that is constitutionally impermissible, primarily because he did not during the penalty phase present sufficient evidence to the jury, and by extension to the court, of Kingg's mental impairment; the theory being that an adjudicator well-informed in that area would not have chosen to fry a dim Kingg."

"Right."

"Well is it just me or is it not true that in making that argument it would be the very definition of advisable to present the court with unimpeachable and specific proof of exactly what Kingg's condition is, i.e. a psych exam of some sort? I mean, yes, it's obvious to us from his letters and these meager school records that there's some serious synaptic interference here but that does nothing for us, we need the court to understand that. Where are the experts lining up to say this kid is more like a human clam with the idea being that, although Alabama of course permits the frying of the mentally infirm, and putting aside for the moment the pending Supreme Court action on the issue, the more mentally messed up Kingg is the graver his attorney's omission in failing to adequately establish that mitigating fact and therefore the more likely that Kingg was denied his Sixth Amendment right to the effective assistance of counsel?"

"I agree but we don't have any of that."

"Hence the fucking gaping fucking hole in our case right?"

"Perhaps but seemingly not one we can remedy."

"Why not? I know these people, they're all idiots. It's just a question of getting the right idiots to wax idiotic on our behalf."

"Any potential evaluator will want money to make an evaluation and write a report. We don't have any money to give said evaluator thus we don't have any resulting evaluation."

"How do we not have money? This is a country of organizations. Everywhere you look people are organizing themselves into groups, one joining many and many morphing into one. They have money, let's have at some of it. What's up with our little parent organization there in Alabama?"

"I tried but they're over-budget for the year."

"Over *what*? The year just fucking started."

"He also said they have to allocate resources where they feel they will do the most good. I believe the terms lost and cause were used in conjunction."

"They're lost alright. That's O.K., there's more where that came from. I'm sure there's a Humans for the Ethical Treatment of Retards somewhere or something isn't there?"

"Sorry, I looked."

"I bet if we were raising money to prevent an endangered condor from flying over a municipally funded, baseball-only stadium dressed in a banner advertising Joe Camel to impressionable twerps we'd have considerably better luck."

"Maybe."

"Wait a minute Toom how stupid are we? We work for one of these very organizations. Let them pony up the dough. After all, they got us into this mess."

"I tried but they say they can't for this kind of thing."

"Christ. Well let's get one of these chumps anyway, I'll pay for it."

"You're going to do what?"

"What am I supposed to do?"

"You have that kind of money lying around? Those experts charge considerable fees."

"No, but I'll get it. I'll have it by the time they bill us anyway."

"Remarkable."

"I know but what am I supposed to do? I'm aware that it's probably not going to make a difference but what about the small but discernible chance that it will, or already has?"

"Already has?"

"I'm not prepared to live with that unexplored chance, not here with this."

"Already has?"

"Yeah, never mind."

"No, what did you mean because I get the feeling you meant something."

"Look I don't want to spend a ton of time on this but that's the thing about chance."

"Chance?"

"Correct, chance. I have something like a chance theory if you'll just give me a chance to give it to you."

"Proceed."

"Here goes: I say there's a *chance* that retaining a psych expert will prevent Kingg from being executed right? What I seem to be saying is that if I take a certain action, create a certain event, then a later desirable event may occur as a result. We say these kinds of things all the time and the statements are primarily a function of how we experience Time, that is, in a linear fashion. But of course as many have shown we have no legitimate basis for believing that how we experience the world, including things like Time, corresponds perfectly to ultimate reality, that is, the things causing, in a manner of speaking, the experiences. In fact we can provide many examples of verifiable phenomena, such as the particle/wave duality of certain entities, that seem to contradict the manner in which experience tells us the world works. Similarly, with Time the fact that we experience it as a linear procession of events does not mean that's what Time truly is; or that it even exists for that matter. So let's posit a possible description of true Time. Basically, imagine a vantage point with respect to Time whereby you can see all events at once. When you observe it from this vantage point, Time is not linear. Instead, from this view, you see that events that exist in spacetime do not really precede or follow each other and therefore probably cannot be said to cause each other either. They exist all at once so to speak. Now what if within that matrix of spacetime events you're observing there exists both the acquisition of a psychiatric expert and consequent psych report on Kingg as well as the court granting a stay and Kingg surviving? Now what if more than one of these matrices exist on some level, with one representing me spending money and Kingg living and another the converse?"

"This is basically possible worlds as a way of explaining possibilia right?"

"Kind of but slightly different. We don't have the time to delve thoroughly but I'm not really talking about possibility so much as I'm talking about this weird view of Time. Bottom line is I'm intrigued by what goes on when I come to recognize that there is a *chance* an action by me might result in something I want. If Time is actually configured the way I set forth but our limited minds are unable to grasp this true nature of it, then my palpable experience of this chance may be more than just a purely mental exercise and may actually be my admittedly limited experience – since I don't have the omniscienty vantage point I spoke of earlier – of the actual existence of these two events; the retaining of the expert and the subsequent, so to speak, saving by the bell. In that sense, the reason I perceive, on a weak level, that the chance exists that retaining an expert will be relevant is that it really is relevant and *actual* as I will later discover. Of course it only seems *later* to me, someone who is trapped into a myopic view of the whole of Time. The point being that this feeling I now have, the feeling that there's a chance that might be actualized but only if I pay that expert, may actually be a glimpse into, and evidence of, this matrix where the two events exist. Who am I to fuck with the order of the universe? You get it? It's like a workable chance theory. There's a chance here that I can't now ignore. Chance."

"Fat chance maybe."

"Exactly, it might, unbeknownst to us, be a fat chance, so we have to give it a try."

"No, fat chance as in *fat chance*, as in little or no chance. Understand?"

"No, a fat chance is good. The fatter the chance the more of it there is and obviously the more chance of something good, in this case a legal victory, the better. You want your chance to be fat, a slim chance would be bad."

"You can't modify our language to suit your needs Casi. Fat chance is bad and always has been. And, by the way, I think that your true and inapposite bottom line is this. If one *could* step back out of Time so to speak and learn the truth as you claim to intuit it, that is, that events don't really precede or follow or *cause* each other but rather they exist as it were simultaneously and independently, then there would be even less reason for you to retain a psych expert since such acquisition or failure of same bears no relation to Kingg's ultimate fate and in fact such decision, the decision whether or not to retain an expert, already exists, and is in some sense predetermined, on some real if unknowable level. So your theory, and I use the term generously here, of Time and Chance actually ends up putting everything under the auspices of chance in the strict sense of the word and thus you should save your money. If you're right about chance I mean."

"True, but what are the chances of that?"

"I come bearing gifts and it's all gold too, none of that corny myrrh or frankincense whatever that is."

"Frankincense is like a gummy substance you get from trees, presumably prized back then."

"You got any lying around Casi?"

"No."

"Want any?"

"No."

"My point exactly. This stuff here is golden gold, unalloyed and pure."

"What do you got?"

"Everything we determined was necessary. Three gifts I bring. First, here's the key, literal and figurative, fashioned solely out of gold and beautiful in its import."

"It does look like gold."

"It better, it's nothing but. Twenty-eight carats of Au with nothing to dilute."

"You made a key out of gold?"

"Of course, pray tell of what substance I should've made a key that will gain us access to 402 and by extension to the riches of 410?"

"I don't know but the question seemingly becomes why, if you have the ability to make keys out of pure gold, you are—"

"Gift number two. *State of the Art* the salesman said without a hint of irony and I couldn't believe people like that still exist. Two cameras and this here gold-plated remote control/monitor."

"They're tiny."

"They don't come any smaller. I figure each of us will be responsible for placing one of the cameras on one of the western corners of the adjacent roof then we'll meet back in the middle, on a direct line to the roof entrance, where we can observe the monitor and decide the best time to make a break for it, probably one at a time."

"What do you mean by remote control?"

"That's the beauty of it. Not only can we see what the cameras see but we can maneuver said cameras through the use of these rather dainty joysticks. What say you to that?"

"I say two things: good purchase and practice with the device while I'm in Alabama so you become proficient."

"Yes. Lastly, I give you the Gold Series Positron 3000. Again a different salesman said something similarly lame that I cannot now recall."

"These are stun guns?"

"Stun batons, mini-batons really. Eight inches with the whole baton proper, excluding the handle, electrified so you don't have to worry as much about making precise contact."

"And this will take down a huge guy?"

"500,000 volts. It'll definitely take him down but it's going to take a few seconds it's not like instantaneous. I figure one of us will immobilize Whale with one of the swords and the other will shock him and take him down."

"Take him down for how long?"

"If we zap him good then tape his mouth, it'll be a good ten, fifteen minutes before he can get up and walk down. How do you like the gold-plated handles?"

"You sure it's going to be hundreds right? The money?"

"That's what he said, why?"

"Because I'm concerned about the weight of the dough. You say you tested hundred dollar bills and fifteen million is about 210 pounds. That's bad enough in the context of us trying to get out of there with high tails while sneaking by two guys, but what if it's twenties and weighs a 1000 pounds or fifties and weighs 420?"

"It won't be. It's going to be hundreds and weigh between two and three hundred pounds. We'll bring bags, split it up into manageable amounts and divide the toil. I can see what you're thinking: here's another thing that can go wrong. Not really though. Look it's our money and it pisses me off to no end that these hyenas are currently holding it but if worse comes to worst and it's a thousand pounds of twenties, which I highly doubt, then we'll take what we can manage and that's that."

"True."

"And so it is done no? The bulk of the planning and preparation."

"I suppose."

"There's no suppose about it. It's as done as done gets done. Next Wednesday morning your car will be parked in that spot on 122nd Street."

"Assuming it's open."

"No, no assuming. It has to be that spot."

"I know that spot is ideal but there are others nearly as good."

"No there's no ideal and near-ideal. There's only two choices, perfect or deeply flawed. That spot is perfect for the two reasons we've discussed. One, it's immediately before a driveway so you can pull out quickly and two, it's almost directly behind 402 so we can leave through the backyard with minimal exposure."

"Fine but what if it's taken?"

"You're just going to have to get there with sufficient advance time to ensure you get it, even if it takes a couple of hours."

"A couple hours means 1:00 a.m. If a spot is taken at midnight, for example, chances are strong it will still be taken at 3:00 a.m., sleep being generally predictable."

"So you'll go the night before and have no problem. Parking around there is actually great. I've gone by there five times the last couple of days and that spot's been vacant about ninety percent of the time. You'll go, park, go home, then come back later."

"Fine."

"To continue, at 2:15 we meet at the 24 hour bodega. We have a Yoo-hoo."

"What?"

"Or similar beverage. At 2:30 we go to 402. We use this gold key to get in. On the top floor we change. We get our swords. By the way did you decide which sword you want?"

The night before Dane had, at my request, left the two swords for me to inspect. One was an excellent curved Japanese Katana the other a brilliant medieval Gladius that while maybe slightly wider than I would have liked was considerably easier to use one-handed. Both were beautiful, well-proportioned and sleek, almost swinging themselves the instant you broke your wrists. Light. And savagely sharp. So I stood in front of my mirror in varied feral poses of aggression trying to determine with which I looked cooler and coming to the conclusion that I wouldn't mind terribly walking around with a sword in my hands at all times.

"I'll take the Gladius," I said.

"Is that a beauty or what? Good choice. The batons'll be there, the cameras, the bags, the rope. We'll go out the roof of 402. We cross two roofs to 406. That takes us to the 8 foot gap."

"You mean the 8 foot gap that's more like 12 feet?"

"And which I nevertheless think we can merely jump? The very same."

"*Jump*, you're nuts Beamon."

"Anyway I take the rope I've already procured, lasso-throw it across the gap and onto that hydrant-like structure on the roof of 408, attach the gold pulley wheel slash hook that I'm going to fashion, tie it off on our 406 structure and slide across one by one."

"Where's the rope?"

"Home."

"And it's thick?"

"It's a wharf rope, like three inches thick. At the critical moment don't be surprised to hear it laugh at our weight."

"Even with the bags appended on the way back?"

"Even with, although I still think we should just throw the bags over."

"No because they'll make noise on landing and might awaken nosy guilty bystanders. I think the bags should be like backpacky so we can wear them during our slide back."

"O.K. after we slide over to 408—"

"And you're sure you're going to be able to lasso 408 like you say?"

"Positive."

"Good grief."

"On 408 we each place a camera where it can observe one of the guys on the 410 roof. Then we watch the monitor for the perfect moment and sneak by them."

"Sounds so easy."

"We go down to the second floor. One of us puts a sword to Ballena and the other zaps him. He drops. We tape his mouth. We take his radio. If anyone radios him you answer in barely intelligible Spanish buying us time. We open the bag and divide its contents into ours. We go back up. We check the monitor and sneak by again. We take the cameras. Back to the gap. We use the pulleyed rope again, this time weighted down with the green. I detach the rope from 406, remove the pulley wheel, and throw it over to 408. Then back to 402. We clear everything out of there, go out the door and out the back, through that alley and to the car. Put all the bags in the trunk of the car and we're off. Escalera and his others discover what has happened but have no clue who did it and can't call the police. The only evidence that anyone was ever there is the rope on 408. The only person who sees us is The Whale and he never sees our eyes."

"Or hears our true voices right? You're going to pick up those things?"

"Yeah I'll get them. And that's that. Presto extracto. Agreed?"

"Yes. I guess the mental aspect *is* pretty much done. It's all physical from here on out but it's regrettably more physically demanding than I thought it would be."

"How so?"

"Well as example there's the lassoing of the 408 structure, that's not easy."

"I can do it."

"The lugging of a hundred or so pounds each with speed essential, the swords."

"All eminently doable. Eventually everything intellectual becomes physical. The plan is there. I look at it and see that it's good. Now it's time to execute it without remorse or restraint."

"Why don't we go through it again in like more detail and make sure we're not overlooking anything?"

". . ."

"No I know we've talked about everything an extreme amount of time but I don't think it can hurt."

"I had an acquaintance who was a big guitar player. I mean like ten hours of practice a day, every day, lacking fail. He said that on those rare occasions where something such as a minor injury would prevent him from practicing for a few days when he returned to the instrument he found paradoxically that he played better than ever."

"I understand."

"Seems the unexpected jolt away from his practice routine, a routine he followed piously for untold years, served to refresh his creativity and allowed him, in some sense, to view his instrument anew."

"Got it."

"I think a similar thing may happen here where we've spent the better part of three days poring over the least and last of our plan's relevant minutiae."

"Point taken."

"Perhaps this forced abstention that begins tomorrow morning with your trip to Alabama will serve a similar purpose."

"No need to continue."

"You see the analogy?"

"Yes."

"Whereas he was playing the guitar we are—"

"I urge you to abandon this point."

"I need a number where I can reach you."

"Yes but don't call."

"Right, you return?"

"Monday morning. You're going to 402?"

"Tomorrow."

"You'll practice the physical things we talked about?"

"All weekend. When are you going to the scene Casi?"

"Monday night I guess. Anything else?"

"Just one."

"What?"

"This might be the smallest apartment I've ever been in. Meaning square-footage-wise."

"And what's the other problem?"

"No problems, it's all good."

"You said, Casi, that there were two major problems, one of which you identified as our failure thus far to retain a psychiatric expert to evaluate Kingg and his mental impairment. The other?"

"So many others."

"The main other?"

"Well I read the amazingly thorough compendium you put together detailing every case in which that court granted a petition similar to ours. You know what I saw? What unifying thread emerged?"

"What?"

"Innocence. Invariably, on some level, the court feared the defendant might be innocent right?"

"I suppose."

"No suppositions, just yes. Their defendant lungs shouted their innocence for any and all to hear. Where's our protestation of innocence?"

"None."

"Instead we get unremitting and unsolicited declarations of guilt. I've been doing this for a quarter of a century and I can count on one hand the number of clients who didn't proclaim their innocence if the case was even semi-serious."

"True."

"Now when it counts I get this guy who won't even service the notion with his lips, what the hell?"

"I know and unless we have a good-faith basis for arguing his innocence we can't ethically do it."

"And practically speaking unless we argue, or at least suggest, that this guy didn't do it, we have no real chance."

"Strictly speaking, none of our points depend on a lack of culpability."

"No *real* chance."

"You're right, but maybe that's why you're going to Atmore."

"Why?"

"Well perhaps to extract something akin to a reverse-confession out of Kingg."

"You mean to get him to confess his innocence?"

"Well if he tells you he's innocent then we can argue it right? And if we can argue it, armed with a good-faith basis in spite of the overwhelming evidence, then it can't hurt our chances right?"

"Too weird."

"Innocent people do confess Casi."

"Yes."

"Just as the guilty often deny to the end."

"The bitter one. So my job is to turn him from one kind of liar into the other?"

"You mean from truth-teller to liar."

"Unless he really is innocent."

"He does *look* innocent."

"Which probably means he's guilty."

"He says he's guilty."

"But that could be an innocent mistake."

"What if you can't reverse him?"

"I'll feel guilty, full of guilt."

"How guilty can Kingg be anyway in light of his mental apparatus?"

"And how innocent given same? And can he go from one to the other and even back again?"

"With your help, maybe."

"And you at a fancy wedding where the game hens are Cornish and the liquid spirits flow without pause."

And so later that night when I slept it felt more like a newly invented process only slightly suggestive of sleep. And I arose later weighted down with two big questions: one on Kingg and one on Whale. But I decided I only had the energy to deal with one of them that morning; I would call Dane or Toomberg in that pre-airport interval not both. And in my skull each side argued vociferously on its behalf and I vacillated between the two, forth and back repeatedly until I resolved to abstain entirely.

And when I suddenly decided, really *knew*, which call to make, it surprised me a bit. Now the other option seemed laughably unviable and the proper course so nakedly visible. But when I eagerly picked up the phone I found that the infernal machine didn't work and so called neither.

If you could live forever, would you and why?

I would not live forever because we should not live forever, because if we were supposed to live forever then we would live forever, but we cannot live forever, which is why I would not live forever.
– Miss Alabama in the 1994 Miss Universe contest

Chapter 20

To judge from the sparse attendance on the plane no-one wanted to go to Alabama that morning. I didn't either but there I was, going. And those pills you take to combat expected nausea I suspected worked solely by making you so drug-addict needful of sleep that all other states of existence (i.e. nausea v. non-nausea) ceased to exist in any meaningful way. And so when one of the unburdened stewardesses, a decidedly matronly sort who in my compromised state I somehow managed to convert into an object of semi-sexual longing, came by to offer first cinematic headphones then a compartmentalized meal the most I could muster was a dismissive, narcotized wave of the hand, or like two fingers. Which gesture I later came to regret when, empty stomach grumbling and between bouts of deep but intermittent sleep, I became transfixed with the attractive happenings on the square screen before me. And instead of a nice miniature meal on the tray in front of me I had this like glossy packet insane Toomberg had put together and given me to read. The packet contained answers to everything you were afraid to ask concerning not only the particular judge who would decide our petition but really about Alabama as a whole, past and present. For some reason Toom felt that the greater my knowledge about this parcel, the greater our chance of success. So I read what he'd included there when I wasn't looking at the screen. But now the sight of assorted beautiful people speaking without voice filled me with an ineffable sadness and so I found myself inventing and supplying dialogue for these representational humans. And also the captain was the loquacious type who would probably one day, in true frustrated-incorporeal-spirit form, continue talking from beyond the grave and thus he kept taking advantage of us, his captive audience, via the microphone they give those guys:

On that square I saw a smallish girl sitting on the floor using her twin bed as backrest. Her lips moved without effect and in the direction of a freakish purple toy. We were meant, no doubt, to feel we were experiencing the inner life of a child.

This is Inda Cipherable, your Captain, speaking.

My captain?

We were getting closer to the girl's face, although it was happening slowly, and maybe imperceptibly if not for the greater concentration possible in the absence of sound, and I would have bet on the presence of swelling violins.

I've just turned off the seat belt sign, that was the slight ding you heard. You are free to walk around. We'll be cruising at an altitude of about thirty-five thousand feet.

Now we were almost there, inches away, and I could see that the girl's eyes were tearing, her lips moving slower.

We'll be in the air several hours, long enough so you'll feel as if the walls are closing in but not long enough that you can just go to sleep and get some real shut-eye.

The girl wasn't saying anything now, putting me on equal footing with my fellow headphone-clad passengers. She lifted the freakish toy, which I now saw was an elephant of some sort and not purple so much as black.

Yes, beautiful Alabama, and I have some good news for our passengers who may represent components of a potential interracial marriage. Because in the two thousandth year since the birth of our Lord, Alabama became the last state to overturn its anti-miscegenation law. That's right folks, blacks may now legally marry whites in Alabama and whites may do the same, to blacks of course.

Three more little girls entered the room carrying nothing and bringing the total to four.

I'm one of those pilots who likes to pepper his passengers with little interesting facts about their destination.

The three new girls sat with the old one and they joined hands. Then they all stood and went towards the door and out; the camera slowly tracking in futile pursuit.

In 1963, in Birmingham, a bomb went off, note the use of the passive voice, in the basement of the Sixteenth Street Baptist Church. The bomb, well the people behind it, killed eleven-year-old Denise McNair and three of her friends.

In an unjustifiably immense three-walled kitchen, where not everything was in its place but only in a contrived orderly way, and where this kitchen was located in one of those semi-hermetic, uniformly colored constructions meant to convey neither affluence nor abject poverty but rather the presence of a *working class*, with the work referred to being precisely the type assiduously avoided by those in the classes above and below; in that kitchen stood a startlingly beautiful woman in the midst of a half-hearted attempt at looking not-beautiful. Also in that kitchen was an unmenacingly tall man patiently absorbing his enforced inactivity while the beauty-in-disguise was allowed to deliver what seemed to me like an at-least-somewhat-critical little speech in the shadow of the man's back.

"Just tell me one thing Trevor," she said. "Just answer me one thing after all these years, you owe me that. One damn thing."

"What's that?" he said, although all we continued to see of him was his back.

"Exactly what connection do we have to those four little girls just depicted in a different room in an obviously different house?"

"I don't know and don't call me Trevor."

"Why not?"

"Because Trevor is one of those names given to Hollywood characters in meager attempt to depict the inanity of our world but is never actually the name given to such a character."

"Fair enough but what about the girls?"

Trevor thought about the girls. It was impossible, at that point, to say with even the slightest certainty what connection, if any, he might have to those girls. This was so because the writer/director, in one of those either inspired or insipid moves that usually only first-time low-budgeters make, had refused to allow any of the thespian participants to see the entire script. Instead each actor was limited to his lines and those spoken in his or her presence. And the reasoning behind this was endearing enough given that such full scripts exist nowhere else in life – that is, you do not normally know what little girls, no matter how intimate the relationship you share with them, say or experience in your absence – and so, the thinking went, the lack of such a script-knowledge in that limited environment could only serve to enhance the projected apparent reality of the resulting depiction. Although, of course, it took no more than a couple seconds of thought to conclude that laser-beam-accurate depictions of reality might not be the ultimate goal of these two hour slices of images paired with chatter, as evidenced *inter alia* by the facts that: (1) all sorts of necessary activities that undeniably occur in reality and that in fact comprise a large percentage of that environment's time, such as eating, sleeping, using the bathroom, and watching Television are almost never cinematically depicted at all, let alone in anything remotely resembling accurate time intervals; (2) there exists, in this cinematic world, an abundance of unexplained violations of the laws of physics, such as where an individual will pick up a ringing phone then respond verbally after one

593

second in a manner that cannot possibly be justified by the quantum of information that can be conveyed in that second or when two people are practically screaming but cannot be heard by someone three feet away simply because the person is technically in a different room or the way bedrooms where lights have just been turned off never get entirely dark despite the absence of any visible light sources; and (3) the cinematic depictions feature an almost unfathomable incidence of heart-palpitatingly attractive women and the concomitant, almost complete, absence of the truly slovenly and unattractive.

And it took only a little more thought than that to wonder why anyone would so greatly value a high degree of verisimilitude in these situations in the first place since at least part of the idea in fictions like these was presumably to entertain on some level and yet so very few people seem enthralled by the quotidian happenings of Life itself, which of course represents the ultimate realism. But still, this and the fact that the film was shot entirely in strict sequence, another not-unheard-of-but-extremely rare deal, certainly created, on the set anyway, the at-least-illusory notion that here was the unmitigated, unfiltered, and unadulterated procession of again Life itself and this somehow energized and pleased the cast in a way their non-set hours never did. All of which meant that when Trevor and Jackie (not coincidentally the true names of the actors as well as of the characters they portrayed) stood in that implausible kitchen they maybe weren't so sure where exactly created artifice ceded to stark reality.

And maybe it was this indecision that was evident on Jackie's face as she spoke. She pushed her fingers through her hair, which she tended to do in these situations, and turned away. Her eyes landed on a picture she had long ago placed on an uncrowded shelf. One she'd looked at countless times. A picture of her, alone. And though the picture had been there for years, as much a part of the room's background as the wallpaper, she was able, as sometimes happens in these instances, to look at the picture as if for the first time. She saw that it

594

was her in the picture but not really. She remembered why the picture was there. The picture was not taken with anything resembling a good camera or by anyone resembling a good photographer. But when she opened the Ste-D-Mart envelope that night, still dressed in whatever uniform was being imposed on her at the time, it positively jumped out at her and away from its neighbors. This was before everything this picture. It jumped because of the way she looked in it. She hadn't kidded herself about its accuracy. She knew she was not an overly attractive woman although she certainly didn't skew too far in the other direction either. But in the picture she was effortlessly beautiful in a Madison Avenue way. She explained this to herself, to the extent she did that sort of thing, by saying that in life there are angles and the picture just happened to capture a fortuitous one for her. And she respected that happenstance enough to put the picture up, giving it a prominent place and maybe two further thoughts since. Until that moment, when muffled language was being directed at her in futile attempt and her trembling hand was looking to stop on the kitchen's center island. The face in the picture just seemed so much fresher, as if better lit. And though not immediately visible, he had been a part of that picture in the same way he'd somehow managed to be a part of everything about her for as long as she could remember.

And so even though he could see she was not looking at him, and could hear that she wasn't saying anything, he was not prepared to make the leap to the conclusion that she wasn't listening to a solitary word springing from his lips and certainly he had not the slightest clue regarding the import of the photograph she appeared to be staring at, that sort of thing generally being lost on him. But he'd also decided that today was the day they were going to discuss the Thing that happened. Today. And he had hoped to do it somewhere else. Because in there, the place he'd been forced to leave if only by chivalry, he always felt diminished by the memory.

"Are you listening to me?" he finally said. "Jack?"

"Yes. Fine, take it and go."

"No, I think we need to discuss this."

"What?"

"Because Donna says this isn't healthy."

"What?!"

"I know you don't want to hear this but . . . about Petey."

"No, stop."

"We need—"

"Stop it Trevor, you promised. We agreed we would never talk about this again."

"No you agreed. *You* agreed. I had no choice. You said you would leave and I'd never see you again at a time when I could not have dealt with that. You forced me into it Jackie, and I said O.K. but now I want to talk about it, we need to."

"No I don't *need* to do anything, get away."

"Donna says it's not healthy, that you need to talk about it. That human beings need to talk. It's like the way you didn't go to the cemetery that day."

"Shut up will you? Will you please just shut up? Please? Maybe promises mean nothing to you but they mean something to me and you promised we would not talk about this."

"I just want to know that you're O.K. about this."

"O.K.? Yes, I'm O.K. So O.K. that you should leave me alone. And fine I'll go ahead and say what I'm supposed to say. Here it is: I'm happy for you and Donna O.K.? And, of course, yes, I particularly know how happy that moment will be for her and all that. Is that enough, are we done? Because there's only so much I can take Tre."

"Nobody grieves forever Donna says."

"I wouldn't know, I don't know anything about grief. Whatever grief is, I haven't felt it."

"You're grieving."

"No I'm not. A word has to be invented for what I'm doing. For what I felt then and still feel now, even years later. *Grief* won't cut the mustard here bub, maybe *torment* or *agony* try."

"I understand."

"Maybe those words begin to describe what it feels like in a world that can one day contain a three-foot-high giggle named Peter and the next day not. At night, like a prisoner in solitary, I mentally cross the date off my imaginary calendar as one less day I have to endure. Do you understand? What I look forward to more than anything is death because it can't be any worse than this here. Are you beginning to get the picture? How little resemblance my status bears to yours? And someone needs to explain to me why I feel dirty all the time. How I can shower then bathe then dress in freshly laundered garments yet still feel unclean and troubled in my own body. And the worms. Tiny flesh-colored worms made of some unspeakable fungus that writhe and crawl just beneath my skin and out of view. I feel them all the time too. And I'll claw and tear at my flesh to get them out but all I get in return are these marks. Also what about this empty blackness that starts in my stomach and instantly spreads outward whenever I acknowledge it, and the longest I can manage to ignore it is like a couple hours and even those hours are spent in subconscious fear of the black? And I hate how much more intelligent I've become, how much more I know now. Because one of the things they tell you is that time is your friend, the only thing that has the power to heal your gaping wounds. More than that really, that it *will* heal them. And maybe before, when I had no need for these kinds of notions, I would've been impressed by this thought. But now I know that the people who make these statements can call themselves scientists all they want in a vain attempt to secure the imprimatur of legitimacy the term would afford them but they cannot change the fact that they are not so in even the loosest sense of the word. You see, armed with my greater intelligence, I know that if a true scientist says with certainty that a molecule, for example, will definitely do X, then it

597

will do X. See? Yet when these pretenders tell me that something will have a certain effect on me they're basing that prediction on some self-help section of the bookstore they themselves circularly created. And they're talking about those wildly unpredictable entities called humans so that whatever the percentages in their favor may be, they still tell me nothing about *me* and what *I* can do to get out of this infernal cell. And worse still, I can now say from experience that this *Time* they're all so fond of is nothing but an illusion. People say *years* like it means something, like it represents some vast expanse. Well I'm now on the other side of those years and I can report that they do nothing, they're no different than days, weeks, months, or even hours. Every day I wake up and feel no better, every day it happens again, his hand slips out of mine and doesn't return leaving me grasping at empty air. Each day a freshly opened lesion. I want this pain to end even though it no longer really hurts if that makes any sense. There's no substance, no drug, no activity or person that can help me. I see life now as it truly is, its atavistic savagery, and so feel nothing but contempt for those innocents able to view it as I once did. It's as if everyone else is in a beer commercial and I'm the designated driver and do you realize how profane this all looks to someone who's had their eyes wrested open to the truth? I'm afraid to move for fear of getting some of the world on me," she slumped to the floor. "I want to be left alone. There is no *help* and even if there was I wouldn't want any of it. I don't need anything other than to be alone so I can hug my knees and cry in solitary peace without affectation or shame. I want to cry until everything inside of me is expelled, especially that which I need to live. The very blood and plasma that sustain me I want to cry right out of my body. I want to die from this loss of tears, die from a rended heart. And no I don't need or even want someone to talk to because I don't want to talk. What I want now is just to sit and *feel* this. To exercise every day the last option I have, the last thing I can do that gives me a small sense of accomplishment, a sense I might be something more than just mindless animate material; to find a way each day to avoid killing myself."

". . ."

"Can you give me that? Go on. Can you at least do that you worthless, lummoxy bastard? You useless piece of shit. You shithead. That's right, a shit head. A person whose head is composed solely or at least mostly out of actual shit."

We are now flying over Alabaman airspace. We will soon begin our descent. Just thought y'all should know that.

So I knew I had inhaled too many of those pills when hours later I didn't have the strongest recollection of things like picking up my bag from those cool baggage carousels airports have or getting the rent-a-car paperwork done. And either the directions I had weren't great or their reader a true dope because I found myself basically driving around aimlessly as if touring Alabamian Highway Food & Fuel installations. After about the third or fourth time I passed the same giant overalled farmer with a burger in his hand I finally spotted a sign that said Atmore something-or-other with a picture of a tiny jail cell. I knew the hotel I was slated for wasn't far from the prison so I took that exit in hopeful expectation I could feel my way there without the directions I'd thrown out the window in frustration.

My big break came when I saw the giant banana. And I don't mean to suggest that I knew immediately it was a banana I was looking at when, from a considerable distance, I saw the yellow tumescent structure that menaced the clouds and partially occluded the bottom of the orange sun. While thinking about how an establishment that sells bananas could afford such a structure I remembered that my hotel was called The Orchard and that reference had been made somewhere, maybe a brochure or something, to some kind of cognizable fruit theme. That was enough for me and I accelerated towards the banana. And as I neared the banana I saw it had friends, an apple and a peach at first and later an orange. This *was* The Orchard and each

599

oversized rooftop fruit represented a different wing of this colossal hotel.

Of course the roads leading into The Orchard couldn't be simple and direct so it took me quite some time and frustration to properly negotiate their labyrinthine excess. When I finally did park the car it felt like an upset victory. I got out with my corny little bag and my box of Kingg stuff, then entered a large room that was far more arboretum than hotel lobby. Everywhere I looked, keeping with the theme, was an indoor tree, rising towards the high ceiling and often warping towards another. And the fruit was everywhere, set out on tableclothed rectangles and inviting you to grab and ingest it. Limitless, perfectly ripe and healthy with encyclopedic variation, the fruit that was continually offered, almost pushed, by The Orchard would become one of the two entities that dominated my stay there. The other being B.M. Santangelo.

B.M. stood for Big Mac he declared as he introduced himself and I questioned, to his face, the legitimacy of using initials to shorten what, in Big Mac, amounted to a nickname itself; to which he responded that he had not the slightest idea what I was talking about since Big Mac was his true, parentally bestowed, on-the-birth-certificate name. This exchange occurred just a few feet from the front desk, which desk was mere feet from B.M.'s little workstation, a station that reminded me of some kind of kissing booth and where B.M. was positioned to perform his duties as The Orchard's concierge and from which I never saw him absent despite the fact that I passed said booth at all sorts of varied and unseemly hours, leading me to the near-inescapable conclusion that B.M. Santangelo worked twenty-four-hour shifts one after the other without cease or even interruption. He had shot out of that booth after hearing me give my name and other particulars – a ruddy, fit, and wide exclamation point who jutted his hand out and smiled.

"You're the feller from New York are you not?" he said after the above exchange.

"I guess, I am from New York."

"Well I've set you up in one of our premier rooms. If you'll allow me to show you to it, I'll take the opportunity to display to you some of the more interesting aspects of our little hotel."

"Little? Can I ask? The size of this place, I mean what's around here that feeds a hotel of this size?"

"We are the largest hotel on the eastern seaboard even though we are not technically on that seaboard, we don't board that sea."

"Huh?"

"As I'm sure you've noticed, our hotel is partitioned into separate areas we call gardens, each named after a particular fruit. Now the best of our nine gardens, and the one we're currently headed to because it contains your room, is the aptly named banana garden. In addition we have apple, strawberry, peach, pear, mango, watermelon, orange, and kiwi gardens. Any questions?"

"Yes, is Mac like a middle name with Big being the first or is Big Mac like Peggy Sue or Billy Joe, that kind of deal?"

"Hah hah! I like this character," he said and slapped me on the left shoulder so hard he possibly tore my rotator cuff. "From New York," he added. Then, "You O.K. pal?"

"Yes," I said swinging my arm slowly like a windmill.

"Good because I want your stay at The Orchard to constitute nothing but unmitigated pleasure." He went on to list the many services offered by The Orchard, pausing occasionally to point and gauge my facial reactions. These services included foremost the extreme availability of superb fruit, pieces of which I joyously sampled as we strolled along on the tour. And I could, B.M. said, have my run of the place and its fruit at nothing approaching extra cost. There were massages, herbal rubs, detoxifying ointments, and many other skin-tingling possibilities. In essence, if you weren't in her lap you were at least getting one of those hugs that's all arms from Lady Luxury. This tour went on for a while.

Finally, at the room, B.M. activated, via portable device, my pliably plastic room key then used it to let me in, placing my bag on the little tray they had near the bed for that purpose. At that moment, my guilt got the better of me and I said "look I didn't say anything earlier because truth is I was enjoying the little tour but I think you must have me confused with someone else."

"No, I know who you are."

"I say that because I can't imagine you're this solicitous of all your guests so I can only assume you've mistaken me for some guy who's threatening to buy the hotel or something."

"I assure you, The Orchard would never be offered for sale. Furthermore, I know precisely who you are. You're from New York. It's not that difficult really. Fact is we don't get many unaffiliated singles such as yourself. This weekend, for example, you're our only guest who's not with Serpent."

"With who?"

"Serpent. The Society of Egalitarian Reptile Protectors Entitled to New Technology for long, S.E.R.P.E.N.T. for short. You'll see S.E.R.P.E.N.T. members everywhere this weekend. They're having their annual convention in one of our state-of-the-art convention halls and they've effectively commandeered our gardens for their lodging."

"You're kidding right? Serpent in the gardens? Is this some kind of put-on? Where's the hidden camera? Next you'll tell me I'm not allowed in the Apple wing."

"As a matter of fact no guest is, we're renovating."

". . ."

"At any rate enjoy your stay and if you need anything, and I mean anything at all, see me right away," he said leaving abruptly.

And B.M. hadn't exaggerated when he raved about the room because it *was* great. There was, of course, a wicker basket full of excellent spotless fruit. There was a tremendous incarnation of

Television with something called a PlasmaTronic screen. Atop sat a black box that offered guests like me a seemingly limitless panoply of entertainment options that included almost every feature movie, made-for-Television movie, or music video ever created along with every episode of classics like B.J. and the Bear and Happy Days (including one where The Big Ragu transcends time slots to considerable studio squeals). The bed was the size of an airport tarmac, something called Regal Resplendency Size. The workstation was great. The Internet was instantaneous almost anticipating your next move, the phone was transparent affording you an intimate look at its inner hardware, and the fax machine was somehow smaller than the average sheet of paper. The bathroom was larger than my New York living room with a perfectly round Jacuzzi tub containing all sorts of odd arm and foot rests.

It was early afternoon when I started to examine and sample these and the many other amenities the room had to offer. Each bought me successively less joy and despite the obvious potency of the vaunted but inaptly named Tele-Communications Port I was unable to execute a simple phone call to any number in the New York metropolitan area. It had gotten real dark in the room by then so I went around igniting each of the many bulbs in the room until I felt like I was being interrogated. I grabbed a handful of perfect, dark-red strawberries and lay in the middle of the bed. From there, I would hold each individual berry up by its green hat then devour its underlying corpse in one or two bites. Then I would toss, without exceptional miss, the green remnants into the garbage can a few feet away. When I was done the room felt larger than when I had started. And because the entire ceiling of the room was actually made of mirror I could see that it wasn't just a matter of perception. I was very small on that bed – alone in that room. I stared at the reflection above me. The garishness of the bed and its coverings. The consistency of the fruit theme. I felt so lonesome.

Outside my door, in the hall, no-one felt lonely. They frolicked, trading laughs and audio jabs, striving to outnoise each other. Then someone knocked on my door. I was sure it was a mistake that knocking. When I opened the door I saw a smiling woman with a drink in her hand.

"I saw you in the hall before," she said. "Aren't you coming to the orientation? There's going to be food and drink and I hear both will be quite good."

"Huh?"

"Oh I'm sorry, you are with Serpent right?"

"Oh. Yeah I'm with Serpent."

"Thank God, I would've felt so stupid. The way you looked at me I was like, this guy has no idea what I'm talking about."

"No I'm a reptilian protestor."

"You mean a reptile protector."

"Exactly."

"Wow your room is so much better than ours, can I see?" She started to walk in and I was thinking I hadn't really told such an egregious lie as I probably had a greater affinity for reptiles than the average person and, if forced to commit, could see myself agreeing that they deserved as much protection and access to new technology as any other vertebrates, although from the phrasing, I then thought, it was probably the protectors themselves who were claiming to be entitled to new technology. And I loved the way she walked as if a light string she wished to avoid snapping was tied between her dainty ankles.

"Jacqueline c'mon, we'll be late!" said a disembodied female voice from the hall with the urgency common to the realization that the party being called may be about to engage in exclusionary diversion.

"I gotta go," she said spinning around to face me. "But I'll see you down there O.K.?"

"O.K."

"Yes."

She left. I stood near the door until I had done so for a longer period of time than I had interacted with her. Then I went back to the bed and lay in it. I closed my eyes and dreamt they kicked me, quite literally, out of the hotel because I wasn't with Serpent. Once so expelled I slept on the street.

The next morning I got that thing where you're not sure where you are when you first open your eyes. The clock on the table was blinking 12:00 and my watch, wherever it sat, was not easily accessible. The position of the sun against the sky was hidden from me by the manically effective drapes. I had no idea if it was early or late, had ample time or none. I could've found out but I didn't. Instead I slid further under the vacuum-sealed blanket and returned to sleep. When I woke from that sleep, purposeful ignorance was no longer an option. I got up, found my watch, and saw that I would have to hustle. I got ready and went downstairs.

"I can tell you where it is, I can even show you how to get there, but I also have to tell you that I don't think you should go there." So said B.M. Santangelo that morning in B.M.'s concierge booth as Big Mac Santangelo tapped on the keyboard in front of him using his index fingers only and pausing often to click his mouse. He was getting me directions, directions that would take me from The Orchard to Holman Prison's Death Row. He indicated verbal satisfaction and the printer began to spit out paper. Surprisingly, the printer was one of those old kind that made a racket and took its time syllable by syllable. When it was done B.M. Santangelo snatched the paper, removed the perforated edges, then extended the result towards me while staring as if to say *have you no reaction to what I just said?*

"You don't want me to go there?"

"I recommend you do not go there, that's correct."

"Why not?"

"What do you want to be going to that place for?"

"I don't know that it's a want situation, I have to go there."

"Nobody *has* to go there."

"Well I do. It's the reason I came here, the reason I'm staying at The Orchard and everything, you understand?"

"I think it's entirely probable that you feel that way but I have a responsibility to my guests. I consider it an almost sacred responsibility to ensure their well-being, and that responsibility now requires that I advise you not to go there, not to take the approximately forty mile trip to that place."

"Thanks for your concern B.M. and thanks for the directions but I'm going now."

Surrounding Holman Prison in Atmore, Alabama was nothing that warranted a specific name. And it wasn't so much that I entered that facility as it was that I just found myself inside. And little of inanimate physical essence that I saw there on either day made any lasting impression on me or even seemed to minimally register at the time.

What I can't help but recall is Jalen Kingg and The Guard.

To get to see Kingg I had to constantly show an extreme amount of paperwork. The last person I showed this paperwork to was The Guard who was hirsute and lean but commanding in a way that made the many bars in the vicinity seem extraneous. And I thought, in the many minutes I spent waiting for him and his friends to establish that I did not bring a cake with a file in it, that Death Row was so named not in reference to the future that awaited its inhabitants but rather in reference to the inert quality of the life found within. The still, mute air.

The Guard came back and told me that Kingg was on his way. He said there were rules I would have to observe and I nodded. He pointed:

NO Cell Phones

NO Beepers

NO Paging Devices Of Any Kind
NO Smoking
NO Eating
NO Drinking
NO Shouting
NO Yelling
NO Screaming
NO Spitting

I nodded again, thinking we were done, but there was more so he pointed elsewhere:

DO NOT Touch The Inmate
DO NOT Give Anything To The Inmate Except For Legal Material
DO NOT Accept Anything From The Inmate Except For Above
DO NOT EVER Allow The Inmate To Touch You

I said *O.K.* and he said *good* then we just stood there, he and I, alone and waiting.

"You know you're the first right?" The Guard said.

"Yeah," I replied. "No, I mean, no, the first? First what?"

"You're the first visitor Mr Kingg has had."

"Today?"

"Ever."

"No."

"Yup."

"What are you talking about? I'm sure his mother came out before she died."

"Never."

"Other family he has?"

"None."

"Really?"

"Yes."

"Sure?"

"Yes."

"What about his lawyer, I'm not his first. Didn't his lawyer on the direct appeal meet with him?"

"No."

"What about someone from the project or whatever it's called, the people that got me involved in this?"

"No-one."

"I'm sure you're wrong. I think they meet with everyone whose case they take. Maybe you were off that day."

"I work every day there are visits."

"Maybe you called in sick."

"Twenty-three years on the job, never called in sick or taken vacation."

"Your wife must love you."

"Single."

"Oh."

"Twenty-three years on death row partner, I've seen them all come then go."

"Hm."

"Not many want to work this post you know."

"I didn't."

"Not an easy post, I'll admit that right up front. See I don't know if you know how it's done here, because I've never seen you here before, but we use the chair here."

"Yes, I know."

"So you know about Yellow Mama, that's what we call her."

"I do."

"Well then you probably know about her, shall we say, fickle nature."

"Hm."

"I know about it first hand because I'm the one who literally pulls the switch as they say."

"Oh."

"That's right, no-one else would do it when I first got here. Which is an odd thing in and of itself don't you think?"

"Um."

"I mean the fact that nobody wanted to be the one to do it. The thing is, around here support for the death penalty runs about ninety percent and among people who do what I do for a living that figure is probably even higher so you wouldn't think there would be this great reluctance to be the one who actually carries out the sentence. People out there think of a judge or the governor as being the one who seals a man's fate but really it's me who does it right? So in that sense I do understand the reluctance. It *is* technically killing. Don't get me wrong I know it's completely different but still there's also a sense in which it's also just killing. I once crunched the numbers and figured this out, it was strange when I first said it out loud, at a party I think it was, but I've killed more people then the next ten people scheduled to be executed combined. Well that was true at the time, God knows if it's still true. Some of these guys have put up some serious figures. You get the point. I'm a killer. Killing is killing. One day I'll shave your kid's head. I don't like it, he's a decent kid the few times he talks, but that's what it'll probably come to regardless. I'll shave his head and then I'll massage the conducting gel they give us into his scalp and just pray he's not another John Evans. You know John Evans?"

"Evans."

"Well I was here for that just like I've been here for all of them. It's the smell that people don't realize. Burning human flesh is unlike anything you've ever smelled, I can guarantee you that. You don't want to smell that and you don't want to see the eyes either when that thing's not working like it's supposed to, let me tell you. Like I said, I was here with Evans when it took fourteen minutes and three separate jolts to finish the job. They kept hearing a heartbeat the doctors.

I was there when he caught on fire after the first one and some of the sparks that came out from under the hood landed on me. When it was finally over he looked like the charred piece of meat at the end of the barbeque, the one that falls through the grating? Those things happen is what I'm saying, that's a fact. People don't want to hear it but they do happen and it could, God forbid, happen to your kid for example. And you know what counselor? I remember Evans all the time, I do, but fact is at least with Evans it was difficult you know? Maybe it should be difficult to end someone. The ones that really stick in your mind are the ones that seem to have nothing to them, like just turning off a light. That's just my feeling but maybe that explains it I don't know. Know what I mean?"

"Definitely, explains what?"

"Like I said, people are in favor of the death penalty and all but when they find out what I do for a living it's not like they get all happy or anything, I get the feeling they kind of think I must be weird for doing what I do you know? Like it's somehow wrong for me to do what I do even though it's my job. Look who I'm talking to, you probably get the same thing. O.K. here he comes. You can have a seat in there and wait for him it should only be a couple of minutes. A pleasure meeting you young man, I can tell from the way you speak that you're quite intelligent, your client is in good hands, I'll tell him too."

When they bought Kingg in to me he wouldn't look me in the eye. I think he thought he was in trouble. I looked at his face and saw that he looked no older than in those pictures taken years earlier. Like the twin in the rocket, in that still air Jalen had aged slower than the rest of us. I introduced myself and told him I was the same person who'd written him those letters. His attorney, lawyer. We traded words. It wasn't really like talking to a compromised adult, more like talking to a fully realized eight-year-old who displayed occasional flashes of comparative near-brilliance.

"You knew I was coming today right? I told you in the last letter remember?"

"you melvyn?"

"No, that's good though. You're right Melvyn Toomberg is your attorney too. You have two attorneys right now. Melvyn's one of them and I work with Melvyn. I'm your other attorney, Casi."

"oh, they let me have two?"

"Yes, you can have even more, it's O.K."

"what about mister joe?"

"You mean Joe Tellem Bennigan?"

"yes."

"You're right he was your lawyer at trial and on the first appeal but when cases go further than that, like yours has, you get different lawyers, understand?"

"but I never said anything bad about mister bennigan or nothing."

"I know. This is just the way it's done Jalen it doesn't mean you didn't like Mr Joe or anything, it's just that the case has become more serious and Mr Joe, uh Mr Bennigan, doesn't deal with cases when they get to this point."

"oh."

"Just like him though my job is to protect you, do you understand?"

"yes, like mister joe."

"Right, Melvyn and I are going to do everything we can to protect you."

"to keep me here right?"

"Well actually what we want is to get you moved to where people with less serious sentences are held."

"or to get me out of jail?"

"That would be great."

"but where would i go?"

"We'd think of something, it would be a nice problem to have."

"where? my mother died."

"I know."

"where will i go?"

"Jalen, the chances of you getting out aren't very good. Melvyn and I are much more concerned with—"

"but i don't want you to get me out unless there's a place for me to go, can you just tell me where i would go if i got out even though i know i'm probably not going to."

"I don't . . . you would . . . you could stay with . . . Mable . . . Jalen."

"maple?"

"Yes."

"is she nice?"

"Yes, very nice."

"what does she look like?"

"She looks like Maple, she's very nice."

"but how does she look like?"

"Well she's big, but soft and chubby, and she has a mansion with lots of room for you."

"a big house? like big with land?"

"Yes and behind it is a river of the clearest water you ever saw to swim in or drink. You swim in it and it cleans you, drink it and it fills you."

"and trees?"

"Trees everywhere, trees that fruit just jumps off of. But that's it Jalen. I shouldn't even tell you that. That's just for you to know where you would go, O.K.? Promise we won't discuss it more than this because, like I said, it's very unlikely I can get you there. Promise?"

"promise but you promise to try to get me out to go there right?"

"I promise."

"then i promise too."

"Good then, it's settled. Now do you have any questions about your case?"

He didn't because to have some would've required at least a minimal understanding of the course his case had taken to that point and there seemed to be no danger of him acquiring that any time soon. But in that doleful vacuum I saw the chance for true accomplishment. I vowed that, at the very least, over the next two days I would achieve what countless letters had failed to achieve. By the time I left, Jalen Kingg would have a true understanding of everything that had happened to him in his past and what his future could or would contain. What small laurels I contented myself to seek.

"Jalen," I said. "I want to start by making sure you fully understand everything that has happened in your case and where we go from here. I know you'll already know a lot of what I'm about to say but based on the things you just said and your letters and stuff I think your understanding of your situation could probably be better. O.K.?"

"o.k. but i'm not going to miss recess right?"

"Recess? What's recess?"

"you don't know what recess is? oh my god, recess is only the bestest part of the day."

"You mean like at school?"

"recess! we go outside. it's the only time we can go outside."

"Oh I understand, you have recess every day?"

"of course, they have to give recess every day."

"What time is recess?"

"it depends on the day, what day is today?"

"Today's Saturday."

"saturday?"

"Yes."

"saturday is 1:15. saturday is 1:15 to 1:45. every saturday is the same."

"Well it's almost one o'clock now."

"almost one?"

"Right. So I think that, yes, you are going to miss recess today only."

"i can't miss recess, they have to give recess every day, half-hour every day."

"I'm sure they do but because of our meeting today I think you're going to miss it."

"that's what allan hale said but i didn't believe him, but he said that's what happens when you have a visit and that i didn't know that because i ain't never had one was all." Kingg looked up at the fluorescent bulb above us then back at me. He put his face in his hands.

"I'm sorry but this is very important and it's just one day O.K.?"

"o.k."

"I want you to listen carefully to what I'm about to tell you because it's very important that you be informed O.K.? O.K.?"

"yes."

And he did sort of. And I didn't look at my notes once because I knew everything about his case cold. And it took a long time but he seemed to understand. And I felt good and he looked sad and scared and then I felt bad too. And we were both tired and there wasn't much time left and The Guard was hovering but in a nice apologetic way.

"We'll talk more tomorrow."

"tomorrow?"

"Yes I'm going to come back tomorrow to talk to you again."

"every day?"

"Tomorrow for sure."

"monday?"

"Not Monday?"

"tuesday?"

"No."

"when next?"

"I'm not sure but tomorrow for sure."

"o.k."

"We're running out of time today Jalen so I want to cover one last thing. Remember I told you about your statement to the police and how that was bad evidence against you at trial?"

"bad?"

"Yeah, how it hurt you, your chances of winning the trial?"

"i remember you said that, yes."

"Well earlier you seemed concerned about Mr Joe, your first lawyer, that he would think you said something bad about him or didn't want him to be your lawyer."

"no, I never said mister joe was bad mister casi."

"No I know, because it would bother you if he thought you had right?"

"yes."

"O.K. now remember Detective Irisland?"

"the detective?"

"Yes, the one you gave the statement to."

"yes."

"He told you you should make a statement right?"

"he said to tell what happened so i did. i wrote it down. he helped me. i told the truth like he said."

"Are you sure it was the truth what you wrote?"

"yes."

"Or were you trying to make the detective happy so he wouldn't be upset with you? I won't get mad, you won't get in trouble, if you tell me the statement wasn't the truth."

"it was the truth, i wrote the truth."

"And you understand that if it wasn't true, what you wrote, you can tell me that now and nothing bad will happen right?"

"yes."

"O.K. we'll talk more about that tomorrow."

"o.k."

"And we'll talk about what happened that night you were arrested O.K.?"

"yes."

"Maybe we'll talk about your life before that night too."

"before?"

"Yes."

"o.k."

"Goodbye Jalen."

"bye."

And you had to sit there until they had taken Kingg off the floor. The Guard would get the O.K. on his radio then escort me out. Walking down the hall after he got the signal The Guard told me things about Jalen, how he interacted with the prison staff and the other *guests* as he called them. We got to the log where I would schedule the next day's visit.

"What time is recess tomorrow?" I said.

"Recess? What?"

"Does he ever go outside?"

"Rec is one half-hour every day for each guest, counselor."

"What time is that tomorrow in Jalen's case?"

He told me and even though it severely curtailed the amount of time we could meet, I scheduled the next day's visit so Jalen wouldn't miss recess.

In less than an hour I was back at The Orchard, which stood lonely against only dull remnants of sun. Everywhere I looked I saw nothing but hurried human activity. In the lobby, through a crowd's noise, I saw B.M. Santangelo. He acknowledged me with a nod of his head and came right over.

"I hope you like bananas," he said when he was about five feet away.

"They're O.K."

"Trust me these exceed O.K. I just left a bunch of beautiful bananas outside your door. These bananas were on a tree in a remote part of Honduras this very morning. They will be perfectly ripe in exactly one hour, which is when I recommend you eat the first one for a fruitful experience you will not soon forget."

"O.K., thank you."

"You're of course welcome."

"What's going on Big Mac? What's with all the people?"

"These people are here for the party tonight."

"What party?"

"Tonight is S.E.R.P.E.N.T.'s twice-yearly annual gala."

"Wait—"

"Undoubtedly the social event of the year around these parts."

"Really?"

"Oh yes."

"What's so good about it?"

"Well I'm not at liberty to disclose too many specifics but suffice it to say that quite a number of highly prominent people will be in attendance tonight."

"Really? Prominent? Highly?"

"Yes and the food for example will be superb, prepared only by the finest chefs in the world. We provide all the fruit of course. Everyone will be dressed in the finest garments pieced together by the finest designers. The entertainment will be provided, again I'm not at liberty to disclose, by this country's most popular and in-demand entertainers. I'm talking about music, comedy, performance art you name it. It's all very exclusive, Serpent members and their invited guests only, security is impenetrable. You get the picture."

"So it's for Serpent people?"

"Right. Well as I told you before almost everyone staying at the hotel this weekend is with Serpent. So it's for them during the convention."

"Oh good because I was meaning to ask you about that. When you said yesterday that I was the only person staying in the hotel who wasn't a Serpent you were exaggerating right?"

"No, not at all. You are in fact the only person currently in the hotel who's not affiliated with Serpent. Well except for my staff of course, but you get the idea."

"Yes I think I do. You're saying that tonight at this very hotel will occur the greatest party known to man, an event of such decadent delight that to merely witness its opulence would provide untold pleasure. In essence, tonight The Orchard is one big party and I'm literally the only person not invited."

"Well in a manner of speaking, I suppose, but remember you're speaking with one B.M. Santangelo. There are strings that can be pulled, even yanked if need be. I will get you into that party young man."

"No thanks B.M. I was only curious . . . and kidding."

"Are you sure? It's really not a problem."

"Thanks but no. Good night Herr Santangelo."

"Good night young Master."

I went upstairs, fell asleep earlier than I had in years, slept uninterruptedly through the night entire, and dreamt nothing I could remember.

"Want to see his cell?" asked The Guard as he inexplicably looked me up and down the next day.

"I don't have much time with him today."

"That's just it. It's going to take some time to get him from medical so I was just thinking of your entertainment."

He took me to the cell. It resembled a box. A small one.

"Eight feet long by five feet wide," said The Guard.

Built into the cell's door was a hole.

"Four and a half inches high by eleven inches wide," said The Guard.

Through that hole was where Jalen got his meals. Fresh fruit was never included. Inmates were allowed out of their cell only a short time.

"Forty-five minutes to an hour a day," said The Guard. The only personal items permitted in the cell were books and pictures not to exceed six in combination. Far as I could tell Jalen had nothing other than the letters Toomberg and I had sent him, a spongy marble notebook, and three poorly lit photos of his mother none depicting a smile.

"That's basically it counselor. I thought about your kid last night. I know his date's coming up and everything, well unless you can do something about that of course. I don't mean to suggest that I know how that's going to ultimately turn out. I thought about you meeting him for the first time. That must have been tough. I've seen them all come and go is what I'm saying and I think I've gained some insight into the type of things you might be feeling right about now. Anyway your kid's date is coming up and I think I can help you if you'll see me after you meet with him today. I'll give you something that I think will help you with his case is what I'm saying. Quietly though, I wouldn't want people around here to know that I was helping the enemy so to speak. So *after* you meet with him we'll talk. Let's go back, it shouldn't be much longer."

In the same space I had met with Jalen the day before, I sat and waited and pictured him in that cell. Then I pictured myself in that cell and how I would probably pace and pace in the available space looking for a way to end it. When Jalen came in he smiled and was happy.

"Hey," I said.

"you came back," he said.

"Yes, I told you I'd be back today."

"i know but everybody said you probably wouldn't."

"Oh."

"but you did."

"Yes, did you think about the things we talked about yesterday?"

"how did you know? i even wrote some of the things down that you had said on this paper they let us have."

"Good and now you probably have a better understanding of what's happening with your case right?"

"i had never had anybody visit me before."

"I know."

"i told everybody that i had gotten a visit from an important lawyer, that's you."

"You're my most important client Jalen. If I lived around here I would come every week."

"is today the last day you're going to come visit?"

"Probably, but remember I told you yesterday that you were going to be getting another visit this time from a doctor, a psychiatrist."

"yes, i remember."

"And remember I told you he was going to be interviewing you on more than one occasion so he can help us convince the judge to change your sentence, remember?"

"yes, the doctor. he's going to come more than once right?"

"Yes exactly. You're going to keep getting visits."

"and you're going to come back again after the doctor?"

"I think today is probably the last time I'll ever see you Jalen."

". . ."

"That's alright. Other people are going to come and help you too, I'll make sure of it."

"who's going to take me to maple?"

"We talked about that remember?"

"i know but if there's no-one to take me then—"

"We talked about not discussing Maple anymore remember? I only told you that so you could know how good it will be if you get out but it's kind of like a secret, understand?"

"but who would take me is all i want to know."

"I'll come and take you if you're going to get out don't worry."

". . ."

"We don't have a lot of time so let's talk about the things we need to talk about so I can help you."

"o.k. i want you to help me now that i know, and can you bring me fruit next time?"

"What?"

"can you bring me fruit? they don't give fruit here. the food is good i'm not complaining but they do not give fruit. another guy here says i haven't had fruit since the day i got here."

"What's your favorite fruit? Never mind. If I come pick you up that day I'll bring a whole damn basket O.K.?"

"yes, and there'll be fruit where i'm going right?"

"A ton."

"like the rainbow?"

"The what?"

"the rainbow fruit. my mother used to make it. it's in the stores too though, i seen it. do you know what it is?"

"Yes."

"you do?"

"Yes."

"my mother would make it better than anyone. it's my favorite. right it's in the stores?"

"Yes."

"it's called rainbow right?"

"It's called Skittles?"

"that's right that's the other name! right that's real fruit?"

"I, I think so, yes."

"i knew it, that's what i said, your eyes are funny now."

"Who else lived in your house besides you and your mom?"

"usually it was just me and her but then sometimes i would have a different dad like for a while."

"Would one of them be around more often than the others?"

"yes that was gary, he was my real dad but then he would drink and he would have to leave, so someone else would come and stay until they left, like that."

"You have no brothers or sisters right?"

"i had a big brother but he's an angel now, he was always an angel, even before i was born. my mother said he was only here for three weeks before he had to go to heaven because he couldn't breathe right. he was one of the people in prayers at night."

"I see, did you always live in the red brick place?"

"yes in the red brick always. that's where i was when the police came to rest me that night. i was hiding in a closet but my mother said i had to come out."

"In school why weren't you in special classes?"

"the teachers would say i should be in a different room but then my mother would go and yell at them and they would keep me where i was. the teachers really wouldn't mind because i was quiet. and when i was old enough i quitted."

"You were quiet?"

"yes . . . i . . . had a stutter then."

"Did you get into fights at school?"

"no never."

"Never?"

"no."

"Did you used to get in trouble in school at all?"

"no."

"Why did you quit school?

"i wasn't graduating and then the sizers started coming."

"What do you mean?"

"sizers i started having."

"Seizures? Is that what you're saying? You started having seizures?"

He did, every few weeks even though there was no indication of them in any of the meager medical and school records I had. And he said they only started after the Big Bike Headache, which I gathered was an ugly unaddressed head injury that resulted from a school prank involving Jalen's bicycle. From what I gathered that bicycle must have been quite a sight. It was called a Rose Lady, it was his mom's, and it had one of those absurd banana seats and those exaggerated fenders that curl around the top of the tires. It was Jalen's daily means to and from school and it was the kind of thing other kids tend to notice. One of the kids who noticed it took a wrench and completely loosened then removed the screws that attached the bike's body to its front tire. When the bell rang ending that school day, a larger crowd than usual gathered around Jalen's bike, and though they took extra care to avoid his eyes a nervous laughter seemed to course through them as Jalen got on. And those bikes are designed fairly well because, though wobbly, it actually managed to ride forward a short while. But only a short while because the parking lot Jalen rode in was covered with things like shattered glass and spent cans and when that front tire met its first resistance it immediately quit while the rest of the bicycle continued forward. The quickly ascending rear wheel pitched Jalen past the handlebars and drove him face-first into the choppy pavement. Jalen said that against the crowd's laughter he just picked the glass out, wiped the tears and blood off, and pulled the bicycle home, the body with his hands, the amputated wheel over his shoulder. He told no-one what had happened and the seizures started coming a short while later. We spoke about other things like that.

"What about that night, the night you were arrested?"

"i did it."

"Why?"

"for money."

"There was no money, why'd you do it?"

"i don't know."

"Maybe you didn't really do it but you've convinced yourself you did, is that possible?"

"no i did it."

"Maybe for some reason you think you should say you did it, maybe to protect someone, but you didn't really do it."

"no i think i should say i did it because i did do it and it's wrong to lie my momma say, right it's wrong to lie?"

And many other similar, only slightly varied, and increasingly desperate exchanges between us until I accepted that I would fail miserably at the most critical aim of my visit. And time was running out.

The Guard came in. He told me what I already knew then left.

"why are you mad?"

"I'm not mad at you kid."

"you look mad."

"But not at you, just at things. I'm almost always mad, you understand?"

"i think so."

"You heard kid, I have to go soon."

"i know."

"But the last two days have helped I think. I discovered a lot that's going to help your case."

"really?"

"Really, we're going to do everything we can."

"why?"

"Why?"

"because you have to?"

"No because we want to. We're your friends, I'm your friend."

"why?"

"Why? Because I like you Jalen and because I didn't have any friends before coming here and I needed at least one."

"oh."

"Anyway remember that even though you may not see me again that doesn't mean I've forgotten about you, or that I'm not working on your case, or that I'm not still your friend O.K.?"

"i understand."

"I'll write you more letters. Everything is going to be alright Jalen."

"sometimes i get scared or really sad but when you were here i didn't feel that way as much."

"When you feel that way think about something nice. You have nice things too. Think about that football game you went to that time or that flower dress your mom wore for your kindergarten graduation or that valentine you got in second grade or think about maybe getting out."

"maple?"

"Sure, when you feel bad think of Maple."

After I signed out The Guard handed me a folder.

"This was what I was talking about before," he said.

"What is it?"

"It's an A.S.P., an anti-sympathy packet."

"A what?"

"Right, well I've been doing this for many years as you know and, despite the way I earn a living, I am not a monster. I realize that people who actually come in direct contact with our guests will as a result almost always begin to feel a great deal of sympathy for the condemned man. I myself am not immune to this by the way. Anyway I have a lot of contacts in the Alabama criminal justice system so with their help I took to putting together these packets if you will. Basically they consist of graphic evidence, the more graphic the better, of the misdeeds that landed the sympathy-receiving guest here in the first place."

I opened the folder, saw some colorful photos and reflexively turned away from them.

"See? Never forget that counselor. The ultimate punishment administered here is severe, that's true, but it's also only meted out to the ultimate offenders. Look at this picture for example. You see that in the upper right hand corner? Those are teeth. Human teeth blasted off a face like so many Tic Tacs. See how her jawbone hangs from the skin?"

There were other pictures too, showing more open-eyed matter in crimson puddles.

"It's not just pictures either counselor. Read those reports if you want to know more about the people in the photos, like their names, how they lived, what their relatives thought and felt when they heard the news, what they said in court. People who never did anything to your kid other than exist in his vicinity. I'm not trying to be an asshole son, just maybe reminding you that there *is* another side to this. I think if you focus on that from time to time when you need to it might help."

That last night at The Orchard it got quieter with every passing minute. The previous evening's party was well over now and the whole of S.E.R.P.E.N.T. was in rapid exodus from the hotel. No-one seemed to be replacing them either as a sepulchral calm filled the empty gardens.

Whenever I stepped out of my room for even a second, five maids would be waiting by the door with nothing to do, waiting to possibly clean my room. That night I went to sleep very early again and my dream picked up where the one two nights before had left off. I was on the street and hungry. Strangers would give me tasty morsels of food but whenever I went to sink my choppers into them, that I might gulp them down into my vacant waiting belly, they would turn into assorted Battlestar Galactica action figures. What hunger too. And when I woke up I saw why the hunger because the room-service dinner I had ordered the previous night lay uneaten on the tray near my bed. And I liked the things on the tray, the way everything was small and toylike. The tiny ketchup bottle with the typewriter-size 57 and the shrunken cans of drinks that were soft. The food was still there but now congealed and inedible.

Checking out in the lobby, I saw Santangelo as he entered the corner of my eye.

"Have you given any thought to extending your stay with us young man?"

"Hello B.M."

"Actually I just received the formal paperwork this morning. My legal name change finally came through. I am now Mr Big Mac Wideload Santangeleeskees."

"Big Mac Wideload?"

"B.M.W. for short. B.M.W. Santangeleeskees."

"O.K. B.M.W. thanks for everything."

"Not so fast. Can I convince you to stay longer, at no charge of course."

"No charge?"

"Yes, we have plenty of vacancies at least until the next convention, which isn't for several weeks."

"Thank you B.M.W. but—"

"Just a minute now, I'm prepared to offer you a veritable protective cocoon here at our facility. I will use every resource at my disposal to ensure it. You will be like a pink, plump infant who wants for nothing and of whom nothing is expected. What do you say? Your womb, I mean room, is upstairs waiting for you. I can recharge the key right here. No need for words, I can see the answer forming on your face as we speak. I'll go ahead and charge it up."

"No, no B.M.W. I have to go. Right now."

"If you're worried about the plane tickets they're not a problem I can take care of that with a couple of clicks or even one double-click."

"Thank you but no, I better go."

"If you insist then, but if you ever again need anything round these parts let me know lickety split. Remember the name, B.M.W. San-tangeleeskees."

On the flight back I avoided all pills, it seemed wrong to take them. I wanted to experience whatever the flight would give me without any decrease in sensation or awareness. So this time when the stewardess came by with the headphones I snagged them violently, hoping for distraction from my mounting sickness. But someone at the airline must have screwed up because when the movie came on I saw with dread that it was the same flick from the earlier flight, the Story of Jackie and Trevor. Except that now, fully awake and armed with audio, I saw that the movie was entitled Terms of Bereavement and it was actually a comedy. But not a good comedy where witty people trip and wear funny outfits either, rather one that relied principally on the smug knowingness of its audience. A comedy in name only, neither divine nor vulgar. A comedy in error, full of irony and self-reference and signifying an empty nil.

If a man will begin with certainties, he shall end in doubt, but if
he will be content to begin with doubts, he shall end in certainties.
– Francis Bacon

Chapter 21

When Alana and I were but squirts, a trip to the airport was as good
as it got. To begin with, such trips almost always occurred late on
Friday nights, an already magical time of the week where what passed
for pressure and responsibility was drained from our little lives. Then
there was the airport itself with its tiny coin-operated Televisions,
beeping golf carts, and revolving luggage carousels. We liked pretty
much everything about it, especially the end result because a trip
to the airport almost always meant someone was coming from
Colombia and they would be staying with us, which would mean
chaos in our home; chaos being almost universally welcomed by
squirts growing up in highly stable homes like ours and probably
loathed by our opposites. I for one would have to sleep on the sofa if,
for example, my twin bed and Alana's had been joined and tied
together at the legs for Buela and Buelo to sleep in. And I loved sleeping on that sofa because whatever inexplicable material it was covered
in managed to maintain itself at a temperature ten to twenty degrees
cooler than room temperature and what could be better than that for
sleeping?

And no-one in our family ever, for any reason, did something like
take a cab home from the airport or stay in a hotel while visiting
family. So expensive and wasteful. Other people permitted those

things when their families visited but they were the wrong kind of people. Quiet, unemotional people who at all times thought of nothing but their self-interest. People unwilling to make even temporary sacrifices. People who viewed things like trips to the airport and overnight guests as extreme impositions and so declined or threw money at the problem.

When I told Alana about my travel plans for that Monday she said she feared I was beginning the not-terribly-long process of becoming one of those cab and hotel people. She said she would come to the airport, in my car, and pick me up; thereby avoiding, or at least delaying, my probably ineluctable descent into that unfeeling frost.

All of which sounded nice and helpful until I found myself sitting in the precise area we had agreed to meet and there was nobody around who even resembled Alana. I began to lose even the scant hope I initially had that the great many number of things that could go wrong with an endeavor like ours would not go wrong on this occasion. For one thing, Alana could quite easily have forgotten our arrangement entirely as I was unable to make the customary night-before-reminder phone call and in fact during my three-plus days in Alabama, despite repeated attempts, I was never able to execute a simple phone call to a location outside The Orchard. Then there was the matter of the airport itself with its many gates, flights, and screens with changing numbers and letters, none of which represented great Alana strengths. I could be there all day.

I knew what I was going to do in now less than two days and I wanted to go in there with the right mindset. I wanted to think positive thoughts so I thought about Benitez and what happened after he lost to Leonard. The problem with the loss to Leonard, well one of them anyway, was Wilfred's reaction. The great boxer hates to lose. More than that really, he fears and despises it down to the final gasp of his soul's air. In fact he can so little accept loss that even obvious losses are followed by inevitable, sometimes insane, excuses. And this is not a generalization about a group of people called *Great Boxers*. Rather this is a partial definition of that term: a concept that has great intuitive appeal when correctly considered. Losing a boxing match is not at all like discovering that another person is better than you at a particular skill. Remember that Boxing is basically fighting. If someone outfights you then you have to come to grips with all that entails. Being outfought, or worse knocked out, means you have been emasculated and are subsequently less of a man than your opponent. In other words, if the world consisted of just you and him, he would get what he wanted and you wouldn't. You have to understand that notion to be a great boxer because there is nothing that will motivate you to continue taking an obvious beating, not love of money or fame, not enjoyment of athletic competition, other than the fear inspired by this realization. The great fighter's arrogance will not allow him to concede that another person is better than him and this refusal *makes* him perform better. The problem with Benitez in the loss to Leonard was how easily he seemed to accept defeat. When the referee stopped the fight handing Wilfred his first loss, a T.K.O. loss no less, Benitez didn't argue with him even though only seconds remained in the fight and he didn't seem badly hurt. Instead he smiled as if *no big deal* then exerted almost as much effort trying to congratulate Leonard as he had the previous fourteen rounds. It was almost as if he was relieved he had finally lost and more than one observer thought they saw this.

But every fighter eventually loses if he fights long enough and takes anything resembling appropriate risk and all the Leonard fight proved was that Benitez was no different. What truly matters is what happens after that first loss. After Wilfred's first loss he climbed back into the ring on March 9, 1980 in Florida against someone named Johnny Turner. Benitez knocked Turner out in the ninth round and followed that victory, five months later, with another knockout win, this time over Tony Chiaverini.

In between those two Benitez fights, a new Welterweight Champion was crowned. After successfully defending the title he had taken from Benitez with a fourth-round knockout of Dave Green, Sugar Ray Leonard then defended his title against former lightweight champion Roberto Duran. Duran basically disliked everyone, especially opponents, but he seemed to reserve a special malice for the pretty boy Leonard. During the press tour leading up to the fight he did charming things like give Leonard's wife the finger (meaning his middle one) and essentially questioned Leonard's manhood at every opportunity. Many later characterized Duran's actions as an attempt, ultimately successful, to draw the slick Leonard into the kind of chest-to-chest fight he could not win, but more likely they were simply evidence of a genuine hatred and arrogance from an insanely intense Man. The fight took place on June 20, 1980 in Montreal, the site of Leonard's Olympic triumph four years earlier, and, whatever the motivation, Leonard *did* principally stand toe to toe with Duran and he *did* get outfought and lose; a loss that featured Leonard absorbing a short right/left hook combination from Duran midway through the second that almost dropped him on his face and that had him in serious trouble. Toward the end of the fifteenth round Duran taunted Leonard by pointing at his own chin, a chin that had proven surprisingly difficult for Leonard to hit. When the fight was over Leonard extended a glove toward Duran as peace offering but Duran dismissively waved him off. Then when Leonard raised his arms in the universal boxing sign for *I think I won* Duran pushed him away, a look of complete disdain on his volcanic bearded face. When the close majority decision was announced, Duran was the new champion, there was no longer any dispute over who the best pound-for-pound fighter in the world was, and Duran had gone a long way toward securing his spot as one of the ten greatest boxers of all time. Leonard, who would later show a distinct aversion to granting rematches to vanquished foes, requested and was given an immediate rematch. The fight was scheduled for November 25, 1980 in New Orleans.

Before Leonard/Duran II took place, Thomas "Hitman" Hearns fought long-time welterweight titleist Jose "Pipino" Cuevas on August 2, 1980 in Hearns's hometown Detroit. The Mexican Cuevas was making the twelfth defense of his title against the undefeated Hearns (28-0 [26 knockouts]). In the second round Hearns, who would prove to be one of the most devastating punchers in boxing history, caught the normally iron-chinned Cuevas with a right cross to the jaw. Cuevas's legs did a funny dance, his hips swiveled until he stood there, barely suspended, defenseless and waiting. Hearns moved forward, repeated what he had done with another evil right cross, this time to the head, and Cuevas pitched face first onto the canvas. He got up at the count of eight but he looked like a hollow shell and the referee rightly stopped the fight giving Hearns the title and setting off a raucous Detroit celebration for their favorite son, the undefeated and seemingly undefeatable Motor City Cobra.

In the November rematch with Duran, Leonard did fight far more slickly and consequently he was winning. So much so that he even took to clowning in the ring, embarrassing Duran by doing things like winding up exaggeratedly or sticking his face out in invitation then slipping the punch. Then incredibly, in the eighth round, Duran turned away from Leonard and uttered the two most famous words in boxing history. Duran's *no mas* meant he had quit in the ring, a huge no-no and an incalculable shock given the type of fighter Duran had been to that point, and Leonard was again the champ. No-one knew exactly what had happened and that probably remains true today.

Elsewhere, the new Middleweight Champion of the World was Marvelous Marvin Hagler who two months earlier had gone to England to knock out their Alan Minter in the third round and become champ. With Leonard, Duran, Hearns, and to a lesser extent Hagler all over the boxing news, Benitez was in danger of becoming a decided afterthought.

Although not in the class of those fighters, Maurice Hope *was* the

Junior Middleweight Champion. Hope agreed to defend his title against Benitez on May 23, 1981 in Las Vegas. Benitez would be attempting to secure his third world title in as many weight classes; an achievement that had been substantially devalued by the proliferation of weight classes and world titles but one that would nonetheless represent a significant fistic claim that none of his contemporaries could make. (Perhaps not for long, however, as Alexis Arguello would be attempting the same thing a mere month later when he would challenge Jim Watt for the Lightweight Championship.) Hope was a nice fighter with a stiff jab that was one of Boxing's best and an awkward southpaw style but this was still Wilfred Benitez. Benitez dominated Hope from the start putting on a truly beautiful performance. Maurice Hope, it turns out, had none because he possessed nowhere near the quickness or speed of Leonard and so, with Wilfred's defense as tight as ever, was unable to land even isolated clean punches let alone put multiple punches together. This was Benitez as the brilliant boxer who looked like he had been born and would die in a ring. He won every round, occasionally fighting as a southpaw and often backing Hope up with vicious combinations and dropping him in the tenth with a straight right. Then in the twelfth, as Hope retreated into a corner, Benitez feinted with his left, shifted his weight perfectly, then threw probably the best punch he would ever throw, an overhand right that landed flush and completely eviscerated Hope. Hope lay perfectly flat on the canvas and if they didn't have to close the arena that night he might still be there. Benitez was the new Junior Middleweight Champion and he joined Henry Armstrong and Bob Fitzsimmons as one of only three triple crown champions in boxing history. Benitez left the ring to celebrate, the hangers-on literally doing just that. Maurice Hope went to the hospital. He was released the next day and less than four hours later got married in Vegas's *We've Only Just Begun* wedding chapel. In the wedding pictures Hope doesn't smile because Benitez has knocked two of his teeth out.

The Hope fight placed Benitez back at the forefront of Boxing. A devastating one-punch K.O. of a respected fighter, by a man whose boxing skills were beyond dispute and one who had just shown he could also fight effectively from a southpaw stance, (Benitez was in fact a converted southpaw and in previous fights like the one with Bruce Curry had shown a tendency to involuntarily regress to that earliest incarnation when in deep trouble; however, in the Hope fight Benitez quite intentionally used the stance solely to better deal with Hope's own lefty stance), spoke to a maturity and completeness as a fighter aspired to by only the very greatest. The twenty-two-year-old Benitez was on top again. When he returned to Puerto Rico he was greeted by hundreds of fans at the airport and the island's newscasts led with his victory. His prominence was restored to pre-Leonard levels and, from a general Boxing standpoint, the slew of other truly great fighters between Welterweight (147 lb. limit) and Middleweight (160 lbs.) guaranteed that an unprecedented number of so-called Superfights would take place between them with enormous money and a higher order of immortality at stake.

Boxing's public sat around devising and imagining more matchups between these five physical geniuses and by and large they would ultimately have their wishes granted. Benitez longed for a rematch against Leonard while, as the first of the welters to move up to junior-middle, many wanted to see him move up once more to challenge Hagler and attempt to win an unprecedented fourth world title. Instead Benitez signed to make the second defense of his title against Roberto Duran who was hoping to begin the removal of that inexplicable black mark on his resume by winning a third title and beating a fellow great. The fight, which was scheduled for January 30, 1982 in Caesars Palace, carried an even greater significance, and thus greater pressure for the fighters, in the rabid Latin American boxing community because it featured two of its all-time premier boxers.

At a New York City prefight press conference held to hype the

635

upcoming bout, Duran began the intimidations that had unnerved Leonard before their first fight. As the two men approached each other for that corny publicity staredown, Duran fired a right hand at Benitez's face. Benitez, who in those days could probably avoid a punch while sleeping and dreaming he was dead, slipped the blow and responded with his own right that landed and raised a welt above Duran's eye. The exchange showed, at a minimum, that Benitez would be more comfortable than Leonard in the unique Duran milieu and also that, as was usual with Duran, the upcoming fight would be personal.

Before Benitez/Duran took place, Sugar Ray Leonard and Thomas Hearns squared off. The fight, which was an immense event featuring two extremely popular fighters, took place on September 16, 1981. The fight was billed as boxer (Leonard) versus puncher (Hearns) but actually ended up featuring an intriguing flip-flop in styles by the two fighters. Early on Leonard warily avoided Hearns's already legendary power and as a result did little. Then suddenly, in the sixth, Leonard connected with a left and badly hurt Hearns almost taking him out. Hearns reacted by getting on his bicycle and outboxing Leonard from a distance using his substantial reach advantage to pile up a significant lead on the cards and badly swell Leonard's eye. Finally in the last stage of the fight a desperate Leonard, who'd been exhorted by his trainer Angelo Dundee with his famous *you're blowin it now son*, rallied to hurt and finally stop Hearns in the fourteenth round of a close fight. The victory put Leonard on an even higher stratosphere and all interested eyes turned towards a potential megafight with Hagler.

When Benitez and Duran finally did meet in the ring Duran found that it was not much easier to hit Benitez than it had been at the press conference. Benitez was even better than he had been against Hope considering that Duran for all his insanity had *never* been handled like this. (Duran's only two losses at the time were the close non-title

636

loss to DeJesus and the bizarre quit against Leonard.) The fight started a lot like Benitez/Leonard with a great deal of feints and respect and little action, but by the middle rounds Benitez had taken over, cutting Duran and pasting him with impunity. Duran never solved Benitez's defense and actually looked outclassed, which was almost inconceivable. In the end, to no-one's surprise, Duran wasn't even slightly chastened but, his insolence aside, Benitez had won convincingly in another legendary performance.

Regardless of what his future would hold, after the Duran fight Wilfred Benitez had assured himself an extremely lofty place in boxing history. He felt invincible, suprahuman. He had just out-toughed the original tough guy and obviously no-one was slicker. He was what any human should ultimately aspire to. He was beautiful and ugly simultaneously. The beauty was evident from the beginning and the ugliness was supplied by the very nature of his profession. Now the Leonard fight must have seemed like a hiccup, one that would be avenged at that. Then he would move up to middleweight and fight Hagler. And once Hagler had been befuddled, if he could retire without another loss, Benitez would get more than a few votes as the greatest boxer ever, period.

Everything was that good. In Puerto Rico he was almost deified. He was healthy, good-looking, and charming with a smile and childlike nature anyone he met loved. His bank account was swollen and await-ing more. Everyone wanted to be around him, happy just to be near him. He was as good at what he did as anyone in the world and he was twenty-three years old.

I was like that Benitez. I had maybe not always put the appropriate work in and had therefore messed up. I too had lost. But likewise I would rise again. Everyone I saw around me looked like they were in my way and I was sick of walking around these people and would start to go through them if need be to get what I wanted, needed.

I thought all this as I sat on my suitcase waiting. Then I noticed a woman walking right at me. I averted my eyes but when I looked back at her she was still staring. She was getting closer and I was wondering what the hell she was looking at. She walked right up to me, never for a second taking her eyes off me, then stared. I stared back and she smiled. Then I jumped back out of genuine fear.

"What is it?" she said.

"I didn't recognize you until this very moment."

"What are you talking about? You've been looking right at my face for like a minute."

"Yeah I was like *who is this chick and why is she staring at me?*"

"You are so weird, your own beloved sister."

"I was looking but not looking."

"Either way it doesn't explain you getting scared, what's that about?"

"It's kind of scary when you suddenly realize someone you've been looking at is someone else you know? I mean not the person you thought you were looking at even though you had no idea who you were looking at or why they were looking at you, it scares you is what I'm saying."

"Apparently. Anyway, here I am."

"I see that. I hope you didn't hurt yourself rushing over here to arrive a full hour and a half late. Hope you didn't pull a hamstring or anything."

"You said 2:30."

"Never."

"Someone said 2:30."

"No-one."

"You should see the traffic."

"Then I guess we'll see it on the way home."

"Not so much the traffic as your car."

"What about it?"

"Just the car."

"Yes but what about the car? What specifically is wrong with it?"

"Fine the car's fine, a tremendous automotive machine destined to give you years of faithful service."

"So?"

"I forgot."

"Ah."

"But it's not my fault. Who doesn't call the night before to remind? Especially knowing how I am."

"I tried."

"What happened?"

"Never mind, let's split. I love you, thanks for getting me."

"Seriously, it's quite an imposition. They have cabs you know."

On the way home, in the car, Alana and I spoke. I told her briefly about Alabama, leaving out any mention of The Orchard. She asked about Armando. I told her it was a damn near hopeless situation, a situation that lacked hope. She said there must be something that could be done and I said no there mustn't. Then she told me some bad things. She said Marcela had kind of reached then passed her breaking point with respect to little Mary's silence. She described a bit of imploring screaming that was met by more silence and that was then believed, principally by those who had no medical basis for holding such beliefs, to have resulted in Marcela not feeling so great, which in turn resulted in her being taken to a hospital where she stayed overnight out of precaution and concern for her due-any-day child. And I was further informed that during that brief hospital stay Marcela's mother, the mother Alana and I shared with her, took the opportunity to disclose that she had some rather mysterious lumps in some rather troublesome areas and that she had not disclosed this fact earlier out of a fear that she would be forced to have them inspected by those making their living in the medical profession, a profession said mother held in decidedly low esteem and from which she never again expected to hear anything resembling good news. The result being that certain tests were in fact done and all that was left to do now was await the results, which waiting it was understood could be done simultaneously with the wait for Mary to talk and Marcela to give birth to another human whose presence would no doubt some day give rise to feelings similar to the ones we were currently enjoying. And I was not to mention the whole lumps thing to anyone because Alana had been sworn to secrecy, a secrecy she placed the highest importance on.

"Yet you're telling me."

"Telling you what?"

"You're telling me about the lumps."

"What's your point?"

"My point is that despite being sworn to secrecy and despite claiming to take that responsibility very seriously you have nonetheless just given me the information thereby violating your pledge."

"Yes but only because I am in turn swearing you to secrecy not only with respect to the lumps but also with respect to my telling you about the lumps, comprende?"

"I think so, you're saying that being sworn to secrecy doesn't really mean that in a literal sense it just means that if you do disclose the information you must in turn swear the new illicit hearer to secrecy. So I can tell anyone I want to about the lumps as long as I swear them to secrecy."

"God no, swear you won't tell anyone."

"I swear."

And unlike her I didn't, although I later thought about it a lot and every time I did it halted my breath a bit. There was more too, none of it secret but all of it unsettling, with terms you hear in campaign speeches made from behind podiums or late at night from gesticulating men eager to tell you they dropped out of college: terms like *job security* and *health care coverage*. Terms I can barely stand in those

640

contexts and positively despise when the subject is my family, people
for whom I should have long ago made those terms irrelevant. And
as Alana said these things she began to fade from view and hearing
until she disappeared entirely and I sat alone in the moving car. It was
one of those times when you sense that something critical but inde-
finable that relates to your life and how it's lived has ended
irrevocably and so you feel an anxious loss. Out of this solemn
desinence I felt various incunabula threaten to emerge none of which
promised anything of even slight appeal.

Then Alana returned and spoke more of the same and though we
were in the car and thus could have gone to the people she spoke of
relatively easily instead I just nodded and dropped her off at her
apartment. After that I drove around a bit, not really knowing where
to go or how. Until finally I went home, threw my bags on the couch,
erased all my messages without listening to them and went right back
out the door. On my way down I heard a loud, vaguely familiar voice
in Angus's apartment. The noise from in there swelled at an accelerating rate until I knocked on the door and heard in response a flurry
of activity followed by a cricket-exposing-type-silence. Then Angus
opened the door looking artificially animated and wary. I saw that
there was no-one but him. But before I could investigate he grabbed
me by the shirt and pulled me in screwball-comedy-style. It felt odd
in there.

"Remember what I said yesterday?" he said.

"We didn't talk yesterday."

"You sure?"

"I just got back a few hours ago."

"That's right you were in Arkansas."

"Alabama."

"Two states? How long were you gone? I saw you the other day
didn't I? The day before the day before yesterday no?"

"No, never mind."

"Well you've nevertheless heard this I'm sure," he leaned over and dropped something on my lap. It was that day's New York Post and it was so proud of itself. The Post was exercising its exclusive right to announce the exact time and place where the Tula video, the Video Vigilantes footage of the baby-killing seven-year-olds, would be premiered. That very Monday at 6:08 p.m. was what it said using large numbers. In The City Hall Press Room it added with the haughtiness that comes from exclusivity. "And look at that," Angus added pointing to the triangular mirror clock on the wall that digitally reported 6:06 p.m. I looked at Angus who had dropped onto his sofa, elbows on knees, chin on hands.

"I'm going to go," I said.

"Excuse me?"

"I don't want to see it."

"Have you lost control of your faculties?"

"Why? I'm not interested."

"I don't see where you have a choice. Look this is my favorite part, see the solemn look on the mayor as if his mere presence at such a distasteful event requires an almost superhuman effort on his part? See the face?"

"You look pretty run down yourself Angus."

"I'm excited."

"You don't look excited. You look almost saggy really."

"Well now's not really the time to discuss it but it has been a strange couple days to say the least."

"Where are Alyona and Louie?"

"Shhh here it is."

Television seemed bigger than I remembered and might even have been new and improved as Angus routinely replaced perfectly functional sets if he believed he could detect any diminution whatsoever in their representational performance. At any rate, the result was that the people inside it didn't seem much smaller than the two of us watching. The Casio Carousel on top announced in yellow its IDLE status.

Then the room was suddenly bathed in a surreal silence and the reason for that was the people depicted on the screen. Those people appeared to not know what to do next. There seemed to be no-one there who was in charge. Someone like a mayor is never really in charge in a situation like that and that was evident from the way he looked around waiting for instruction. Our silence persisted with neither of us thinking of moving or otherwise disturbing it. Then, at the exact moment that Angus's triangle changed its numbers to 6:08, the mayor acknowledged some unseen person with his chin, rose from the row of folding chairs that had been carefully arranged on a stage to face a quiet invited audience, and walked to the podium. The podium bowed under the weight of its multi-microphone hat; each microphone clearly identified by its owner while vying to hear the mayor best. Toad spoke, haltingly at first but then with growing confidence when a Television with a built-in V.C.R. (or was that a built-in Carousel?) was wheeled into the room and rushed to his side. The mayor spoke with what he thought was the appropriate solemnity. He pointed toward the people he had just sat with, one of whom was identified as a Video Vigilantes bigwig by the crawl at the bottom of the screen, and clapped his hands without sound. Then he held up an odd-looking tubular device as a foreign head suddenly appeared behind the microphones to inform the invisible audience that there would be no questions until the footage had been completely aired. This new guy thanked The Post and in response the camera cut back to the row of chairs. There one of the guys nodded gravely while the previously helpful crawl stood mute. The mayor was at Television now where he proceeded to insert his tube. The whole event had such a high-tech sheen to it that I was surprised by the third-rate letters that appeared on the screen to announce we would soon be viewing The Tula Kidnapping Etc. and that the so-titled footage was A Video

Vigilantes Production. What next appeared on the screen in no way resembled a dispassionate frills-lacking recording though. Instead we saw an active camera zooming in and out and panning from side to side. Different angles were tried and rejected. Black and white rejected in favor of color and various filters used before settling on a slightly blue one. Those preliminary matters determined, the picture revealed a green, old-fashioned baby stroller appearing from the left of the screen as the audience gasped. Now the people on the stage seemed to bend toward their screen as across from them Angus did the same. I wished I had left.

I looked away then back again. I felt no suspense, only horror then relief when the screen emitted a ghastly pulse of yellow light before going black. I wasn't sure at first what exactly we'd just seen. The producer had done that thing where your screen at home is the equivalent of the external screen at the location so it wasn't until seconds later when the camera panned back to reveal a stunned but noisy group at the press conference (the mayor had literally thrown his hands up) that we understood the fault lay in our city's hall and not in that living room. A guy there took charge and began to fiddle with the appliance and even the mayor finally got up and gave it a respectful whack to the side but it was fruitless. Then the overhead bulbs that provided the only remaining light in the press room also went out. This last failure led to a complete surrender, one that took us back to the news studio then to regularly scheduled programming.

"Well that's quite the letdown. How's that for timing huh?"

"Yeah," I said. "I have to go."

"O.K., I have a legal question before you split though."

"Shoot."

"Do you think The Post now gets to announce the rescheduled date for the footage? I mean is this blackout, brownout, or whatever it is, a contingency they prepared for?" I shrugged and left. I heard the door close behind me as I went down the stairs and before I could

644

even hit the street I heard that strangely familiar voice start up again. I got back in my car and drove to the area of 410. Exactly thirty-one hours remained before the relevant 3:00 a.m. I looked around at this scene of a future crime and was struck by how absurd the whole idea was. I left my life for a few days, returned, and that made the whole thing seem impossible, almost comic. I felt intense doubt. I envied the people I saw walking around me. People who would not for a moment consider what I had considered and would never have reason to. It was important, I thought and everyone thought, when you get to a certain age and point in life, to have created a specific conception of who you were, the things you did and didn't do. I decided that the planning with Dane had been fun and thrilling in a weird way but it never really corresponded to any potential truth. Its subject matter never concerned something I would ever actually attempt. And that realization seemed to fill the area with a bother-some defeatism.

The next day I would go to work and Dane would want to know why the ignored calls et cetera. I would tell him that as far as the caper went I was out, was never truly in. I would add that he was of course free to do as he wished with no interference from me, each man being famously the agent of his own victory or defeat. I would speak those words, the whole thing would be over, and I would enjoy a peace I had not felt in weeks.

I got out of the car. It was maybe not as cold as I remembered it pre-Alabama. People were everywhere on that street too, small clouds shooting from their mouths as they milled around flat-tire repair shops and fried chicken places with bulletproof glass. And I remem-ber how all those people looked around and laughed in unison when a sound like a record being played backwards was suddenly heard throughout followed by the sight of every light on the street suddenly dimming rapidly until reaching complete darkness. The many stores that seconds earlier had the streets surrounded and seemed so intractable now vanished. In this sudden black it was difficult to make out any object or take a certain step. Then as abruptly as the blackness had come the lights were resurrected; creeping up in intensity until they shone even brighter than before, omnipresent and ready again to illume the way.

*But if I were the author of my own
being, I would doubt nothing, I would
experience no desires, and finally I
would lack no perfection.*
— René Descartes

Chapter 22

David Hume was his favorite Alyona once said. This was during one
of our first real conversations, at the end of which I think we
exchanged keys to our respective apartments although I almost
immediately misplaced his. I said I guessed there was nothing wrong
with Hume provided it was acknowledged that Descartes was The
Man. At the end of the conversation I went home and made this list:

1. Descartes
2. Kant
3. Wittgenstein
4. Kripke
5. Lewis
6. Hume

A list with which I would now strenuously disagree but I am merely
reporting what it was at the time.

Anyway it was Hume who observed that everything we say we
know about what he called matters of fact (e.g. that the sun will rise
and set every day) we learn through our understanding of cause and
effect. We see one event always follow another and as a result come to

the conclusion that the preceding event *caused* the other and that in the future the events will continue to share this causal relationship. We extrapolate too so that, for example, we don't have to have ever actually seen an unsupported bowling ball to know it will fall. We know this from having seen other similar objects behave. Nor do we have to be familiar with the natural laws that cause the ball to drop as evidenced by the fact that even young unschooled children know what will happen.

This was interesting enough at a time when many philosophers occupied themselves, at least partly, with these kinds of purported classifications of different types of knowledge and mental operations: such as what is known *a priori*, meaning instinctually and without reliance on our senses including, for example, the fact that I exist or that $1 + 1 = 2$, and what we know merely as a function of language (e.g. that the proposition *bachelors are unmarried* is always true); but the nicer part was where Hume, while acknowledging that we are of course justified in drawing conclusions like the above one about the sun, indicated that he was unable to provide any real reason why we should draw such conclusions. Specifically, it is certainly not *necessarily* true that the sun will rise each morning (contrast *I exist* or *bachelors are single* which are necessarily true) as we can imagine a contrary state of affairs without internal contradiction. Moreover, the fact that the sun will rise or that a ball in a certain state will fall cannot be demonstrably and conclusively proven for the simple reason that no matter how many times or how consistently one event follows another there is simply no *proof* that it will do so the next time nor by extension any good reason for claiming to *know* that it will. In other words, we can in some sense imagine a situation where the ten-thousandth time a bowling ball is released it does not drop. Therefore we can never conclusively prove that a ball will drop merely by repeatedly dropping one and this is true regardless of the number of times we do so. So in skeptical sum, we have this whole body of knowledge that we can directly attribute to the field of cause and effect but when closely examined it appears that the human perception of a causal relationship is a mere psychological phenomenon and as such not built on the strongest of foundations and certainly not on anything resembling indisputable knowledge.

I thought of this Hume bastard that night when I got in my car and turned the key, an action I had taken countless times and which action had not once failed to be followed by the sound and feel of the attached car starting. But this time, when it finally counted, I heard and felt nothing in response no matter how often and desperately I made the violent twisting motion. I called Dane:

"What's up?" he said.

"Fucking car won't start, the fuck," I said.

"Where are you?" he said.

"At a phone a block from it," I said.

"Well O.K. this is why we gave ourselves several extra hours. Find some other way to get there," he said.

"Like?" I said.

"Like this is New York. Subway? Cab? Need I continue?" he said.

"Oh yeah? And when we walk out of there with hundred pound bags?" I said.

"Right. Can you get another car? Borrow one?" he said.

"Who has a car but me? This is goddamn New York remember?" I said.

"Can you get the irredeemable prick started?" he said.

"Probably but that's beside the point," I said.

"How's that?" he said.

"Well if this whole thing was about removing the element of chance do you think it's advisable to at a critical juncture rely on a car that a mere hours before failed to deliver," I said.

"I hear you but we might have no choice. What do you think's the problem with that piece of shit anyway?" he said.

"I think it's bad," I said. "The battery's completely dead but there's no external explanation I can point to, I didn't leave the lights on or anything. That means probably something like the starter or the alternator, which means I can fix or re-juice the battery right now, shit I can buy a brand new one and install it in the seven hours we have, but that won't mean that when we jump in this bastard at three-twenty it'll definitely start and that's a fucking frightening state of affairs because what do we do then?"

"It's not ideal I'll admit that, but the important thing is this: there's nothing we could have done differently. We addressed this issue. The car had never done this before, all systems were go in that area. What could we have done differently? We didn't have limitless time, we had to spend our time where it was most likely to be needed. I think everything to this point has still been done perfectly. Things like this just happen sometimes and are beyond the control of mere mortals. There's a reason *chance* is a word, it describes an actual phenomena that's all. Get the thing started and we'll take our chances. We will not fail just because of this," he said.

"What the fuck are you talking about? I know I'm not to blame for this worthless motherfucker not starting and that consoles me not a bit. The question is what do we do about it. Taking our chances as you call it is not high on my list of responses," I said.

"So what do you want to do? You've thought about it," he said.

"I think we have to at least consider canceling the whole thing," I said.

"No this is a minor thing," he said.

"How is it minor?" I said. "If those guys are looking for us when we get to the car and it won't start what do you suggest we do then?"

"I'm not sure but we have several hours to decide, we can leave the bags in the locked trunk and leave by subway then return tomorrow with a new battery," he said. "I don't know but I do know that canceling is extreme and unwarranted."

"O.K. I have to go," I said.

"Where?" he said.

"There's a twenty-four-hour garage near here, I'll call you when I'm done," I said.

"How long?" he said.

"Hour, hour-and-a-half," I said.

"This might fuck with the parking situation too," he said.

"It might, I'll call you," I said.

I pulled the battery out, stripping my hands raw in the process. I locked each of the car's four doors then slammed mine closed. I kicked the rear bumper of the car as I walked by and when a lady tried to look at my face I looked away. I felt the cold for the first time that night and it got inside me shaking me involuntarily. I put the battery down then pulled my arms out of their sleeves and hugged my chest. I was shaking and sweating. When I stopped I put my arms back in my sleeves grabbed the battery and went towards the subway. There was no-one at the station. The guy who ran the newsstand had already pulled down the metal door. I took the elevator down by myself. It was dark and quiet.

I was the only one in the subway car. After two stops I got out. At that station there was no elevator. You had to walk. As I neared the top of the stairs I made sure to fasten every last button I had. Then I pulled my hands up into the sleeves and cradled the battery in my hands using the ends of the sleeves as makeshift gloves.

When I crossed the threshold of the garage a soft bell sounded and a guy slid out from under a car just like the cliché. He wanted to know what the problem was and I told him. He hooked the battery up to that machine they have and it barely registered. He said it would take an hour to get it fully juiced. I told him I didn't have an hour and did he have any new batteries he could sell me.

"I do. Well I have basically new ones I could sell you," he said. "Of course do you know it's not your starter or your alternator? Because for a battery to be this dead."

"Give me a new one," I said.

He pulled one off a shelf

"I know it doesn't look new," he said. "But it is, it's never been in a car."

"Do you have any that look new in addition to being new?" I said.

"No, but look I'll hook it up and show you." He quickly clasped a clamp on each of the batteries terminals then pointed to the display as the needle shot up. "See?" he said.

"You have any others?" I said.

"This is the only new one," he said.

"How much?" I said.

He looked up at the ceiling and told me.

"How much if I leave you this one?" I said.

"I'll give you five for that one," he said.

"No," I said. "Charge it up I'll get it tomorrow, and give me the other one too."

I put my hands back into my sleeves and cradled the *new* battery. I walked out. When a long blue car with a miniature regal headdress on the dash approached and our eyes met I yelled at him to stop. He did and I got in. I told him where I was going and asked him how much. I knew he couldn't answer.

"Whatever you usually pay," he said looking at the rearview mirror.

The car took longer than the subway had. I gave him a ten and got out five feet from my car.

I popped the hood. No-one was around. There was little light where I stood. I dropped the battery into place. The connecting cables were loose and with some effort I was able to pop them into place with just my hands. I got in the car and put the key in the ignition. I lay my forehead on the steering wheel and tapped its sides with my hands. I looked up and turned the key forward. After a brief hesitation, the car started. I called Dane:

"O.K. it started," I said.

"They charged it?" he said.

"No," I said.

"You got a new one," he said.

"Sort of," I said.

"You feel confident we can rely on the car?" he asked.

"No," I said.

"It's getting late and we need a parking spot," he said.

"I know," I said.

"So we'll proceed with the plan as if this never happened?" he said.

"Yes," I said.

"See you there," he said.

"Yes," I said.

I took the Brooklyn Bridge to the F.D.R. Wherever I went I hit traffic. It was almost eleven on a Tuesday night. I screamed that out.

I got off at the 96th Street exit and headed westbound. I made a right onto Second Avenue and traveled the twenty-six blocks north-bound to 122nd Street where I made a right. As I drove up to the spot, I saw what I thought were a lot of the same people from the night before. They would look at me as my car passed then look right back at the people they were with.

The parking spot I wanted was taken as were the ones directly in front and behind it. It was almost midnight. From the car I could see the back of 402 where we would enter.

I took a spot on the other side of the street about twenty yards back and waited for the good spot to open up. I turned on the radio and put in a C.D. The Kreutzer Sonata. The presto first movement filled the car. I breathed in and the warm air entered my lungs then somehow spread out through my veins to pulsate just under my skin and raise it into bumps. I had to change discs. The twenty-four caprices of Niccolo Paganini as performed by Alexander Markov. The volume knob was as high as it could go. My heart slowed. I reached down with my left hand and pulled the lever. The seat reclined and I closed my eyes.

When the C.D. ended it went right to the radio and an ad for something called Relaxacil. The sudden noise startled me and I sat up. The parking spot was open. It was after one. I turned off the radio and pulled out. There were less people on the street then. I pulled into the spot and heard a loud car horn. Then a giant car with fins pulled up alongside mine. The driver was yelling at me. The passenger leaned forward and yelled too. He balled his hand into a fist and pointed. The driver threw something in my direction and wondered why I didn't get out of the car.

I got out of the car and walked toward them. It was almost one-thirty. There was no-one else around. I told them that if we got into a fight, the three of us, it was *possible* the two of them would emerge victorious and maybe even kill me but that it was *certain* that one of them would lose an eye. I explained to them that if we engaged in a fight I would dedicate myself almost exclusively to achieving the removal of one of their eyeballs. I said that I would do this with little consideration for my own safety or the ultimate result of our battle and I added that once I took that tack I would almost certainly achieve my goal because that was the type of person I was. I told them I thought that whichever of them lost an eye would later feel the whole thing had been a bad idea regardless of my condition. Neither of them got out of the car. They drove away yelling.

I was finished with the car. I put the key in my front pocket where it couldn't be misplaced and walked to a nearby supermarket. Except for the people working I was the only one there. I walked down every aisle grabbing things and stacking them in my hands because I had not taken a basket from the front. I went to the cashier and paid for a large bag of candy and a magazine. I put everything else back.

I bought a one dollar scratch-off lottery ticket at the register and scratched it off with a dime I had received as change. I won a free ticket. When I scratched the free ticket I won five dollars. I started to leave then went back and bought five more tickets with my winnings. The last one of the five made me a two dollar winner so I bought two more. I only opened one of these and it too was a winner entitling me to another free ticket. I placed the winning ticket on the counter told the girl to keep it and split.

I sat on a bus stop bench and read my magazine. I threw the candy away. The bus schedule was taped to a post. Every time it said a bus would appear one did, precisely as predicted. Then the bus would open its mouth and release someone in sibilant exhale. Four times this happened then I saw it was two-twenty. I got up and went to the bodega. A half a block from the bodega I saw Dane walking towards me. He was the same distance to the store but from the opposite end. We met at the door. We spoke then walked in. It was two-thirty.

Dane went right over to the fridge on the side. He slid the door open and pulled out a can. He turned towards me, spun the can in his hands and showed me its face. It was a yellow can with brown letters. A Yoo-hoo.

"I thought you were kidding about that," I said.

"Fuck no," he said. "I love Yoo-hoo, reminds me of being a kid. The key is to not shake the bottle or in any way disturb the chocolate sediment contained therein. What are you getting?"

I didn't get anything. I had rolled the magazine into a tube and was smacking it against my right thigh. We walked out.

On the corner of 1st Avenue and 123rd Street we made a left and walked toward the front of 402 from the same side of the street. Dane looked skyward as we walked.

"What are you looking for?" I said.

"Just making sure nobody's watching us from up there," he said.

"Did you not do what we said?" I asked.

"I did," he said.

"Exactly like we said?" I asked.

"Yes, exactly. I went on the roof of the tallest building in the area and looked down on these roofs. I did not see anyone anywhere until sixteen minutes ago when Heckle and Jeckle took their places on top of 410," he said.

"Good," I said.

"But it doesn't hurt to make sure one last time," he said then he took the gold key out of his pocket and held it up for me to see.

"So they're on the roof?" I said.

"Yes," he said.

"So it's definitely happening then," I said.

"Happening," he said.

"And the cops went to the other place on Saturday right?" I said.

"They were there," he said. He gave me the gold key. "How do you feel?" he said.

"Anxious," I said.

"Like sportscaster anxious meaning eager?" he said.

"No," I said. "Like O.E.D. anxious meaning apprehensive." I went down the outdoor steps on the side of 402. I turned the key and opened the door. We went inside the basement. Nobody saw us.

It was very dark. Dane switched on the light but it immediately sparked and went off. The bulb was dead. I felt my way to the staircase that led up and out of the basement. The light on the first floor worked.

We went to the top floor. I wore tight black leather gloves. I put on black overalls over my clothes. I put on a transmitter. I grabbed my sword with one hand and hung the stun baton from my belt with the other. I checked the time. It was 2:38. I slid the sword into my bag then strapped the bag to my back diagonally like a guitar. I told Dane the time and we sat down.

Dane looked at me and spoke. His lips moved. I had earphones on. I was listening to music. The obvious thing by who else with Fate knocking on my door. I stared back.

Later Dane pointed at his watch and stood up. I took the music off and stuck it in the bag on the floor. I stood up.

"Let's go," he said.

I pulled a black mask down over my face then tapped the exposed sword handle, driving the sword further into the bag. Dane went up the stairs. I followed him.

On the roof we stayed low. I left the door open. We crossed quickly to 404 then 406. I looked around and saw no-one. Dane said he saw no-one either. It was 2:51.

On the roof of 406 near the ledge was a rope. Dane took the rope and slung it over his shoulder. Then he took a black cowboy hat out of his bag and dropped it on his head. He looked at me.

"Ready pardner?" he said. I shook my head in disbelief.

He started swinging the rope in a circular motion above his head. He threw the rope across the alley towards a pole on the roof of 408. The end of the rope bounced off the top of the pole then fell bouncing off the ledge of 408 and swinging down until it crashed into a window of 406.

"No," Dane said.

"Fuck," I said. Dane looked at me and pulled the rope up. We said nothing.

"No-one's home," he said. "Perfect," he added. Dane swung the rope again then threw it. It stuck barely to the top of the pole then quickly came off when Dane pulled on it. I looked at my watch. It was 2:54.

I looked at Dane and started slowly walking back towards 404. He had pulled the rope back up again. I motioned to him to follow me.

A third time he swung the rope over his head. Then he closed his eyes and threw it again. The hoop at the end of the rope perfectly encircled the top of the pole then quickly descended to the base of its three feet.

Dane pulled hard on the rope securing it tightly to the pole. Then he tied the other end to our pole at about eye level. The taut rope extended from our pole about four feet from the ledge to the slightly higher pole located atop a block structure on the roof of 408.

Dane looked at me. I went over to the rope. I lifted myself off the ground by pulling on the rope and it held. I dropped down.

Dane took a gold pulley-type hook out of his bag and attached it to the rope. He walked backwards to where the rope was tied, a hand on each of the hook's handles. He took a breath. Then he ran to the ledge and jumped off towards 408. He covered about two thirds of the distance between the buildings without really implicating the rope. Then the hook pulled violently on the rope momentarily warping it. The hook's two handles were separated by ball bearings in the middle. Dane slid towards 408. Just before hitting the ledge he lifted his lower body forward and up becoming almost perfectly parallel to the ground below. He cleared the ledge and landed softly on 408. He slid the handle back to me and I caught it.

I grabbed each handle tightly and walked to the ledge. I stood on the ledge looking at the street below. I rocked my weight back then forwards. I slid across the rope quickly at first then slowly. I stopped just short of the ledge of 408 and started sliding back towards 406. I quickly swung my feet forward and managed to just catch the ledge. Dane lunged forward and grabbed my ankles pinning them to the outer side of the ledge. My left foot slipped off. My mask had twisted and covered my eyes. I let go with my right hand and tried to adjust the mask. It fell out of my hand and landed in the alley below. I grabbed the handle again. I slowly bent my right leg until I slid to 408 and sat on the ledge.

I dropped off the ledge onto the roof and, not thinking, let go of the hook. It slid away from me before I could grab it. Slowly it slid away from me and beyond my reach stopping just past the ledge of 406.

"Oh shit," I said.

"Why didn't you jump like we said?" Dane said.

"Oh fuck," I said.

"We said jump because of the incline remember?" Dane said.

"We said jump," I said.

"Jump we decided," Dane said.

"I lost my damn mask too," I said.

"That's alright," Dane said.

"If it's so alright why don't you give me yours? Wait . . . where the hell's your mask?"

"I decided against it," he said. "I don't like anonymity."

"What are you talking about? We're going to let these guys see our faces?" I said.

"Yeah fuck them I don't care what they see, I just want my money," Dane said.

"That's insane," I said.

"There's nothing insane about it," he said. "Even with the masks only one guy was supposed to see us anyway and he doesn't know us from a hole in the wall and will be in no position to remember anything at any rate."

"I guess," I said. "But—"

"There's no guess about it," he said. "C'mon let's go."

"Go where?" I said. "Besides the masks, how are we supposed to get back across?"

"I have an extra hook in the bag," Dane said. "I planned for this contingency."

"What are you fucking smart?" I said.

"Let's go," he said.

"I don't know without the masks," I said. "But connect the hook now anyway to save time later."

"True," Dane said. He started connecting the replacement gold hook to the rope then he stopped.

"What's up?" I said.

"Can you believe I needed three attempts to lasso this shit?" he said.

"You got it though," I said.

"I know but I still haven't sorted out what that means. And like just now when you almost didn't make it across and then we lost the hook. It's like what in the holy hell is going on?" Dane punched the pole. He looked down then up.

"It's 2:57," I said.

"I'm furious as I've ever been," he said.

"It's late Dane. Let's go," I said.

"Fucking life Casi," Dane said.

"Let's go Dane," I said. "Look you missed twice but then you got it. A fucking impossible million to one shot and you made it with your goddamn eyes closed. And I almost didn't make it but I did. I should've jumped like you said. That was my fault. And I lose the fucking hook and you have a crazy backup? Who thinks of this shit? It's 2:57. Three minutes."

"Fuck it," Dane said. "Let's go get our money. I'll think about this later. But I'm in no mood I'll tell you. Someone's going to pay for what I'm going through right now."

I taped the new hook to the pole to keep it from sliding away and we walked toward 410 together. I put my camera on the northwest corner of 408's ledge and Dane put his on the southwest one. We met in the middle and sat on the roof with our backs against the ledge separating 408 from 410. I looked at my monitor. I saw no-one. I used the joystick to scan the area with the camera. There was no-one.

"You see anyone?" I said.

"No," he said.

"What the hell?" I said.

"Well that makes it easy," he said.

"Except where are they? You said they were there before," I said.

"They were," he said.

"So where the fuck are they? Because we have the whole roof covered and I don't see shit," I said.

"They must be inside somewhere," he said.

"Yeah and with our luck they're probably flanking Whale as we speak staring at the money," I said. "Or better yet they're right inside the door making sure no-one comes in from the roof. Let's abort this whole thing. Nothing's going the way it was supposed to. Remember what we said about if things weren't going well?"

"They're going fine, here they are," said Dane. "They must've gotten called down for something now they're going back to their posts. It's 2:57:53. Plenty of time. Look there they go, positioned exactly as we expected. Heckle on the North, Jeckle on the South. 2:58."

I looked at Dane's monitor.

"Oh man," I said.

"What?" Dane said.

"I know these guys," I said.

"Who?" said Dane.

"Heckle and Jeckle," I said.

"What do you mean you know them?" he said.

"We got into it like an hour ago," I said.

"Why?" he said.

"Parking," I said.

"What?" he said.

"A parking space," I said. "We were arguing. It was the kind of thing they would remember. I'm sure of it."

"Let me think about this," he said. "I don't think it matters. They're not going to see you anyway."

"If they do they'll know where I'm parked," I said.

"Now you're giving them way too much credit," he said.

"A mask would sure come in handy right about now," I said.

"Then you shouldn't have thrown yours into the alley," he said.

"I was trying to keep from plunging to my death," I said.

"If you had jumped like we agreed," he said.

"And if you had bought a mask like you said you would I could use that one since they haven't seen your face," I said.

"I have no response to that," he said.

I laughed.

"2:58:32," Dane said. "Almost showtime."

"I'm not sure," I said.

"What do you mean you're not sure? In less than a minute and a half I'm going in. Are you coming?" he said.

"Let me think," I said.

"You know David Lewis?" he said.

"Who?" I said.

"David Lewis," he said.

"Yeah, I think, isn't he a D.A. or a court reporter or something?" I said.

"D.A.?" said Dane. "I'm talking about Professor David Lewis formerly of Princeton and recently admitted to the Great Nothing. Philosophy. Know him?"

"Yes," I said.

"Didn't think so," he said. "But surely you know Leibniz and his concept of possible worlds at least as continually and disrespectfully alluded to in Voltaire's Candide?"

"Yes and I know Lewis too. What's your point?"

"2:59 even," he said. "The point is that if we accept his form of modal realism as true, which we should, then since we both admit that it is possible we will turn around from here and abandon the plan, we acknowledge that there exists a world where you and I do in fact turn around from here and go home."

"And?" I said.

"And there is of course likewise a world where we go forward and get that money," he said.

"And?" I said.

"And I have nothing but contempt for these people, if you can call them that, who will turn around at this point," he said. "And when I think that one of them looks just like me and has the audacity to go around calling himself Dane it makes me want to draw blood from the anger. Remember that because right now it is certainly at least *possible* that you and I will go get that money, that means at least two of our counterparts will in fact get it. Don't we need to be those two? Of course we do, it absolutely *must* be us. I don't care what it entails. You have total power and control here. You just have to decide who you want to be and that's who you'll become." He looked at me. "2:59:41 and it looks good," he said holding up his monitor. "Ready?"

I looked at the monitor. Each of the guys was standing at his ledge looking up and down the block. Then Heckle in the front said something like *here we go* and spoke into his radio.

"Fine, let's go," I said.

"Good," Dane said.

I spun over the ledge and landed softly on the roof of 410. I placed my monitor near my face staring at Jeckle on the screen as he patrolled the back of the roof. With my naked eyes I stared at the back of Heckle as he bent over the ledge looking down on the street and the surely approaching Nova. I took three long steps and stopped behind a heating duct. When I was sure neither had seen me I took another five steps then slid past the door and into the entryway to the top floor. I looked at the monitor and Jeckle hadn't moved. I looked at Dane still at the ledge and he signaled that Heckle hadn't seen me either. I waited.

Thirty seconds later Dane was in the entryway. "We good?" he whispered. I looked at the screens. "Yes," I said. We walked down the six stairs to a landing. I positioned myself so I could see the second floor while not being seen. I saw the dorsal portion of a malicious entity as it stared out the front window. It was Ballena.

"Damn," I said.

"What?" Dane said.

"I can see it," I said.

"What?" he said.

"The Whale, I see it," I said.

"So is it big?" he said.

"I wouldn't say big. I think the word doesn't yet exist for what it is," I said.

"Let me see," Dane said. I moved out of the way and he looked. Then we switched places back.

"What the fuck *is* that?" I said.

"He's large," Dane said.

"I didn't know they made humans that big," I said.

Ballena walked away from the window. I didn't see any bag.

"What's the matter?" Dane said. "Let's go."

"I don't think it's going to want us to take its bag," I said.

"I don't care what it wants," Dane said. "It gives us our bag or we carve it up into so many blubber compartments."

"I think there's a disconnect here," I said. "You don't seem to be seeing or acknowledging what I am."

"I see some shithead with our money and I want to go get it," Dane said. "Now."

"First of all I don't see the money," I said. "Second of all, what exactly is it we're looking at? I'm not exaggerating for effect, it doesn't look human."

"He's a human being," Dane said. "Just like you. Made of flesh that pierces and bones that break. Our swords can cut him and our batons will drop him. Do you look forward to engaging him? Maybe not, but if it was just you and him locked in a room and only one of you could emerge alive would you let him kill you? Is that what you're saying? Because I want to be clear on what it is you're admitting."

"But what is that on its arms?" I said. "It doesn't look like any skin I've ever seen."

"I don't know," Dane said. "Let's go get a closer look."

I didn't say anything.

"I can't do it alone," he said. "Are you really going to hang me out to dry at this stage of the game?"

"Relax, I was just looking at the fucking guy," I said. "No need to get all exercised every time I display the slightest hesitation."

"So we're good then?" he said.

"We're good," I said.

We started to go out, me first, then Ballena said something and someone on the second floor answered. I turned and looked at Dane. He nodded no.

"Who was that?" he said.

"I don't know," I said.

"Was he on the second floor?" he said.

"Yeah," I said.

"Fuck," he said.

"Yup," I said.

"Fine," he said. "I'll take Whale and you take this other fuck."

"Wait," I said. The other voice came out of a room and into the hall where Whale stood. It was Ramon DeLeon.

"Jesus," I said.

"What?" Dane said.

"It's DeLeon," I said.

"*What?*"

"It's fucking DeLeon. He's here," I said.

"You sure," he said.

"Positive," I said.

"What the fuck's he doing here?" he said.

"What else?" I said. "Stupidity and greed. He wants the other fifty that comes once the deal is done."

"Dumb fuck," Dane said.

"He knows us," I said.

"Idiot," Dane said.

"Now what?" I said.

"He knows us," Dane said.

"We need to think," I said.

"The fucking clock is ticking," Dane said. "3:07 these guys aren't going to take much longer to test that shit."

"Where's the bag anyway?" I said. "Shouldn't it be right next to Whale?"

Dane looked up at the door at the top of the stairs. I heard a noise come from that direction. I took the monitor out of my pocket and looked at the screen. Heckle and Jeckle were sitting on the roof with their backs against the door to the stairs. Dane looked at the screen.

"Things are going real well wouldn't you say Dane?" I said.

"It's going to get pretty interesting in here soon," he said. "These fuckers are leaving us no choice. We can't go backwards I guess we better go forward."

"What about DeLeon?" I said.

"Fuck him," Dane said. "I like him too but fuck him. That's what he gets for being greedy. He should have done what he said he was going to do." I looked at Dane. He was pulling his gloves tighter onto his hands.

"Chill out," I said. "Maybe he'll go downstairs and leave Whale alone with the money, assuming the damn money is even up here."

"Maybe," Dane said. "But we can't wait much longer. We were supposed to be out of here by now."

"Just give him a minute," I said. "We can't leave yet anyway. Not with those two fucks up there sitting right by the door."

"One minute then," Dane said. We waited.

Then Dane said we should go if we were going to go and I agreed. But before I ran out Dane put his hand on my shoulder. "Wait," he said. "Our first break." I looked back and saw DeLeon disappear down the stairs to the first floor. There was laughing on the first floor.

I took three quick steps forward. The Whale's back was to me. It turned around. I put the point of my sword to its neck and it stopped.

"Easy, Ballena," I said. "Don't be stupid, it's not your money." It got angry when I said that. Its lips curled. I waited for Dane but he wasn't there. Then he came out of one of the rooms. "I don't see the bag," he said. "Where's the bag you?" he said.

"Fuck you," The Whale said. Dane went into the other room. The Whale pushed his neck forward onto the sword and smiled. "Don't be stupid," I said. "You're not too big to bleed." It smiled. With my left hand I grabbed my baton. Dane came out.

"Not there," he said.

"Handle this first," I said. "Then we'll look for it."

"No we need him to tell us where it is first," Dane said. "While he still has a tongue, which won't be for very long if I don't get an answer soon." The Whale said nothing. "Fine, cut his throat," Dane said. "better yet I'll open this fuck up since it's me he's defying." I turned between Whale and Dane. "Come on man just tell us where it is and you'll be fine," I said.

The Whale took his left hand and grabbed the blade of my sword pulling it away from his neck. The blood flowed down my sword and onto my gloves. With his right hand he grabbed my throat and started squeezing. Dane came forward and swung his sword across the back of Whale's leg. It dropped to one knee then sat on the floor in its own blood. It held on to my neck. The sword fell. It pulled me forward. I fell to my knees. There was blood around us. I wasn't breathing.

Dane cut at the hand around my neck but it didn't loosen. I took my baton and plunged into The Whale's chest. It shook but held on. I felt some of the current pass to me. The Whale's eyes were wide open and I was staring into them. I saw Dane take his baton and push it into The Whale's neck. I felt the current more then. The Whale squeezed tighter. I plunged the baton deeper into The Whale and his grip finally loosened a bit. Dane kicked at the wrist. The hand came off and I fell back. I took exaggerated breaths that wouldn't synchronize. Dane dropped his sword and grabbed my baton then he added it to The Whale's neck. The Whale shook. I could smell burning flesh. Its hair rose. It reached for my sword on the floor. I crawled over to it and slid it just past his reach. Dane pushed harder with the batons. The Whale's eyes bulged. It bared its teeth. Then it stopped moving and its head hit the floor. The Whale's blood was everywhere. On the floor and on Dane and me. On my hands and chest. On my face.

"We should kill this fuck for what he just put us through," Dane said.

I couldn't speak. I looked at Dane like I didn't understand.

"He's not dead," Dane said. "He's breathing see? Truth is I couldn't do it. Not to him. I just liked him too much you know? He's pretty damn cool don't you think? Did you see his face when you said it wasn't his money? It was like he was insulted."

I tried to speak but still couldn't. A voice filled the room. It came from The Whale's point to point radio on the floor. Dane picked it up and started to hand it to me. I pointed to my throat and nodded no. The speaker wanted to know if everything was alright. What was that noise? Dane pressed the button on the side of the radio. He held it to his mouth and spoke.

"Toedoh bien," he said. He looked at me. I waited quietly. "He was admirable that prick wasn't he? The fucking will on that beast, the talent."

I felt I could croak out words then. "When were you most impressed?" I said. "As he did his best to join his thumb to his pinky with my neck in between?"

"Hey bottom line is I got him off you right?" he said. "And I just bought us a little time too with that bilingual display."

"That was the worst attempt at a Spanish accent possibly ever," I said. "It's a miracle this room isn't being stormed as we speak."

"Well it worked and we somehow managed to stay pretty quiet throughout this violent drama," Dane said. "In fact, that was another thing that was pretty admirable about this gargantuan fuck. Did you

668

notice how he refused to call for help even though he had multiple opportunities? I think that's a guy used to handling things on his own wouldn't you say? Anyway they're distracted down there right now, they're not focusing on my accent. Another thing about this fucking Whale I just thought of."

"Can we just look for the fucking money please?" I said. "It's goddamn 3:17 you lunatic."

"O.K. here," he said. He handed me the radio. "If they check again you answer it. You don't look so hot right now by the way, I'll look for the dough while you recuperate."

I sat there with the radio in my hand. Dane went into the first room. He came out and said the bag definitely wasn't in there. I looked at my roof monitor. Heckle and Jeckle hadn't moved.

I got on all fours to breathe better. Dane went into the other room. I crawled to where the stairs were so I could see the first floor. I brought the radio with me. I saw men down there. They walked around each other. Escalera sat at a table. DeLeon stood next to him.

I saw a woman. I saw a beautiful woman with light brown skin and green eyes. I saw her looking at Escalera. The only thing I saw in the room then was her face. She looked scared. She walked away from the table and the men watched her. I could see her stomach. She was pregnant.

Dane came out and said he couldn't find the bag with the money. "The damn money's not here," he said. "These fuckers don't plan on paying. They're just going to rip Flaco off knowing there's nothing he can do about it."

"I don't think so," I said.

"So where's the dough?" he said. "I've looked everywhere, I know it's not here."

I shrugged.

"C'mon Casi stand up," Dane said. "This is serious, where's the fucking money?"

I looked downstairs. I saw Escalera signal to DeLeon. DeLeon brought him a radio. The woman was in the corner. She was beautiful. Escalera spoke to the radio. His voice filled the second floor. I looked at Dane. He gestured. The Whale started to stir. I put the radio to my mouth. I spoke in a low clipped voice.

"¿Bajo?" I said.

Not yet Escalera answered in Spanish. But soon he said. I let go of the button and looked down. Escalera was looking at DeLeon in a strange way. He signaled to someone. That person grabbed the woman by the shoulder. He sat her down on a chair and stood over her.

"We better go," I said.

"Not without the money," Dane said.

"Whale was looking out the window before," I said. "Look out there."

Dane looked out the window. Downstairs I saw Escalera tell DeLeon to go up and check on The Whale because he didn't sound right. DeLeon walked toward the stairs.

Dane said he had good news and bad news. I said DeLeon was coming back up. We had to go.

"The good news is you're a genius," Dane said. He turned around holding a red duffle bag. He lowered it on the floor and opened it. It was filled with money. A lot of money. "This thing's heavier than a motherfucker though," Dane said. "Let's split it up quickly."

I asked what the bad news was. I reminded him that DeLeon was coming up.

"The bad news is I felt a lot of eyes on this place just now," Dane said.

"Cops?" I said.

"No," Dane said. "More like the people we talked about as a possibility, here to make sure the money gets delivered as promised. You get me? I think it's going to get pretty hot in here soon."

I heard DeLeon start up the steps. The money was spread out on the floor.

"Let's go," I said. I looked at the monitor. Heckle and Jeckle were still sitting right by the door.

"It's too late," Dane said. He grabbed his sword and ran to the doorway. I moved to the side. A man walked in. It wasn't DeLeon. It was Landro. He looked at Whale and turned around quickly. Dane put his sword to Landro's neck and told him to be quiet. "Or I'll remove your neck," he said.

"Tell them everything's O.K. up here," I said.

"Everything's cool," Landro said toward the first floor.

"Anybody else coming up?" Dane said.

"No," Landro said.

"What about DeLeon?" I said.

"He's the one told me to come up," Landro said.

Dane pressed his sword in a bit. "Is Escalera going to pay?" Dane said.

"I'm not sure. I don't think so," Landro said.

"What about the girl?" I said. The Whale was moving. We had forgotten to tape its mouth.

"What channel are the guys on the roof on?" Dane said.

"Three I think," Landro said.

"What's supposed to happen with the girl?" I said.

"Don't think, *know*," Dane said. "What fucking channel?"

"Three, Three," Landro said.

Dane looked at me. "Give me the radio," he said. I tossed it at him and he caught it with his free hand. I put the money in the bags. The Whale opened its eyes and looked at me.

Dane put the radio to Landro's mouth and pulled the sword back a bit. "Tell them to get back to their posts. That Escalera's pissed. Like they missed something," Dane said. Landro spoke into the radio. I looked at the monitor. Heckle and Jeckle scurried back to their respective ledges. I nodded at Dane.

Then Landro tensed up and fell. Dane caught him before he hit the floor and set him down. I saw the baton in Dane's left hand.

The money was in the bags. The Whale was looking at me. Dane grabbed one of the bags. I grabbed the other. We went up the stairs. Dane went first. At the top of the stairs we looked at the monitors. Heckle and Jeckle hadn't moved from the ledges. Their backs were to us.

"She's pregnant," I said.

"Who?" Dane said.

"The woman, the girl, the mule," I said. "They have her."

"She'll be fine," Dane said.

"Let's go back and make sure," I said.

"When?" Dane said.

"Now," I said. "Let's make sure."

"Make sure of what?" Dane said. "Make sure we die? They have guns. We have these and that fucking Whale's waking up."

"I'll just go get her," I said.

"What?" Dane said.

"She's beautiful," I said. "Take both bags and wait for me."

"Casi stop fucking around," Dane said. "We're almost there. Take your bag."

"Take them both," I said. "I'll be back."

"Fuck," Dane said. "You crazy fuck. This is the last time I rip drug dealers off with you."

I went down the stairs. Landro and The Whale were on the second floor. The Whale was trying to sit up. Landro lay motionless on the floor. His eyes were closed. His belly rose and fell with each breath.

I heard a loud noise downstairs. I heard screaming. Near me The Whale sat up. I looked down. Men had burst into the first floor. Guns were drawn. The woman backed into a corner. She slid to a window. No-one looked at her. There was screaming. Someone fired his gun. More shots were fired. I watched the woman go out through the fire escape. Her head was down.

DeLeon put his hands around his head and ran to the back wall. He looked up and saw me. He looked right into my eyes.

I closed the door and locked it. I heard people moving up the stairs. I heard more shots. I heard more screaming. I ran to the roof stairs. My leg got caught on something. I looked down. The Whale had grabbed my ankle. It was on the floor. I swung my sword down on its arm. The sword carved into the scaly skin on its arm, bounced back and fell out of my hands. The Whale didn't let go. It pulled my leg and I fell. From the floor, with my other leg, I kicked the sword out of its reach. It slid away and stopped near Landro.

The Whale slid along the floor toward the sword. It dragged me along by the leg. People were kicking the door. The Whale stopped sliding. It was tired. It opened its mouth and went to bite my face. I stuck the baton in its mouth at the last instant. It bit down hard on it and fell back. My ankle was free. I moved to the stairs. I pulled myself up the stairs, to the landing just before the door to the roof. I heard the second floor door break open.

I opened the door to the roof. Jeckle was in the doorway. He took a step back. He looked at my hands. I looked at his. He punched me on the chin. His fist bounced down and into my neck. I saw black. My left foot dropped two steps. I held on to the rail. He punched me again somewhere. With my left hand I grabbed him by the shirt. My neck felt like it was trying to swallow my head. I pulled him forward and drove my right hand palm first into his nose. He grabbed my throat. I plunged my fingers into his eyes. He let go. I threw him down the stairs. He landed in the doorway on DeLeon and the others as they entered.

I moved out onto the roof. Dane wasn't there. I saw Heckle on the floor of the roof. He was open from chest to waist. His insides formed a lumpy pool around him. I looked away exhaling.

I ran to the ledge. I barely managed to climb over it to 408. I was hurt. I moved toward 406. I heard Dane call out to me. I heard people behind me. I ran to the ledge and the pole that had the rope. The hook was waiting for me there. I grabbed it. My arms burned. I slid across. Gravity pulled me right to Dane. I saw the two bags at his feet. I heard voices coming. Dane took out a serrated hunting knife. With three back and forth motions he cut the rope that connected 406 to 408. We each grabbed a bag and ran to 404. When we got to 402 I looked back.

I saw two men on 408. One of them ran and jumped toward 406. I saw his body and his head disappear before reaching the ledge. I heard a truncated scream. DeLeon was the other man. He turned around and ran back.

We went inside 402. We went downstairs. We got undressed. There was blood on us. All over us. Everything except the money went into a third bag. I saw the music. We went to the basement.

"I have to get my mask," I said. "From that alley."

"Tomorrow," Dane said. "It's too hot right now."

"Too late then," I said. "There's going to be cops all over here in a few."

"Fuck," Dane said. "Let me think."

"My acid's all over that mask," I said.

"I know," Dane said.

"Bring the money to the car and wait for me there," I said. "These transmitters still working?" We checked and they were. "I'll tell you where to pick me up or whether to split or whatever," I said. "I have to go get it right now."

"Let's go together," Dane said. "There'll be guys there."

"No get the car ready," I said.

"What about the girl you crazy fuck?" Dane said.

"She got away," I said.

We went out the back of 402. Dane went to the car. I went through the backyards to the alley between 408 and 406.

The man who had jumped was there. I moved slowly. He didn't move. I saw that it was Jeckle. He was on a car fender. The fender's end had gone deeply into his back. His eyes were open.

I didn't see the mask. I looked for it. I heard screaming. A woman. I saw my mask hanging from a pole on the side of 408. I couldn't reach it. I found a stick. I used it to knock the mask off and I caught it. I stuck it in my pocket. The woman screamed again.

I went to the street and stuck my head out. I looked toward the scream. I saw four people down the street by 402. Escalera had a gun in his hand. The Whale was next to him. DeLeon was in front of them talking. In Escalera's other hand was hair. A woman's hair. The beautiful woman was being pulled by the hair. She was screaming. She was pregnant.

DeLeon spoke to Escalera. Escalera nodded. Escalera raised his gun and squeezed a round into DeLeon's face. Ramon fell to the street, a copper mist where his head had been. The woman swallowed her voice. Escalera spun her around towards me. I pulled my head back in. The streets were quiet. I put my mask back on.

I looked at Jeckle in the alley again. His radio stuck out of his pocket. I went over and took it. It looked fine. I stuck my head back out. They hadn't moved. Escalera still had the beautiful hair in his hands. The Whale was looking around in a circle. I put the radio to my mouth.

"That's no way to get your money back," I said.

"Who the fuck is that?" Escalera screamed. He pulled his radio out. "Who is it?" he said and I heard The Whale say "that's him."

"He's right it's me," I said. "Let the girl go and we can discuss how you go about getting your money back."

"There's that. Or I can shoot her in the neck if I don't see your face in the next five seconds," Escalera said.

"Well I'm two blocks away so that's not going to happen," I said. "Meaning you can't see me but I can certainly see you you worthless fuck and if you so much as leave a bruise on her from here on out you'll never hear from me or your money again. Well I shouldn't say never. Just that the next time you do see me will be the day I kill you."

I saw Escalera put down the radio. He looked around. The Whale paced.

"What do you want?" he said.

"I want the girl," I said.

"Come get her," he said. "Bring the money and I'll turn her over to you you thief."

"No let's do it my way I think," I said.

"What way is that?" he said.

"Let her go and I'll tell you where to go to get your money," I said.

"Fuck you," he said.

"O.K. goodbye," I said.

"No wait," he said.

"Let her go right now," I said.

"How do I know you'll give me the money?" he said.

"I guess you don't," I said. "But you know exactly what will happen if you don't let her go don't you?"

"Her blood will be on your hands if you don't bring that money here immediately my friend," he said.

"I'm not your friend," I said. "As for blood, I'm already covered in it and I'm going to let all yours next if you hurt her."

"You fucking threatening me?" he said. "Do you have any idea who I am? Who this person standing next to me is? All your friends who came running in are dead do you understand that? Do you want to join them because that was just the beginning? Do you think there won't be retribution for some of the people back there? Angel Colon is dead do you understand that? That's a heavy fuck. You think that shit's going to go unanswered?"

"You have a choice," I said. "Make it. I don't want your money any-more. You can let her go and take it. Or you can hurt her, never see the money again and die tonight or soon thereafter. It seems an easy choice. Make it."

676

"Answer my question you fuck!" he said. "Do you know who we are?"

"Yeah I know who your friend is because he was lying unconscious at my feet twenty minutes ago," I said. "I *allowed* him to live. And I know who you are and we both know you're nothing close to your big friend there. No, you're the coward who threatens women and shoots an unarmed friend in the face. So I will not extend you the same courtesy I did your humpback friend, decide now."

Escalera pushed the woman away by the head. She ran away down First Avenue. I called to Dane on the transmitter.

"Where are you?" I said.

"Sitting in the car," Dane said.

"See the woman?" I said.

"Yeah she just ran past," he said.

"She being followed?" I said.

"No she's good," he said. "I hear cops though."

"Yeah come get me," I said.

"Did you get the mask?" he said.

"Yes," I said. "Northwest corner of 122nd and Second Avenue, right now."

I used the radio to Escalera. "Good," I said. "Go two blocks east with Ballena. I'll leave the bag in front of 312. I'm watching you too. If you do anything other than what I just said the bag won't be there." They went. I left. I went to the corner and seconds later Dane pulled up. I got in and he drove Westbound.

"Money's in the trunk," Dane said. "We good? We're clean right?"

I looked at Dane.

"Well?" he said. "We good?"

"We're something."

"Good."

"Fucking Dane man."

"You alright?"

"No," I said. "I'm all wrong."

"This is it, what we wanted, we got the money."

"Fuck. God."

"Easy."

"The fuck happened?"

"A true mess is what it was. Take the mask off man. What happened when you went back?"

"You were right. Some fuckers walked in there and started demanding the money. Then just like that they started shooting each other up."

"It was taking too long they lost their cool and I don't think Escalera was sure he wanted to part with the money. I could tell it was going to get bad out there. Why'd you go back? I fucking told you not to go back."

". . ."

"What did you do when it exploded?"

"I tried to split. DeLeon saw me. Then The Whale grabbed me."

"Fucking Whale. You were right, I should have killed it when I had the chance."

"I never said kill it."

"You should have."

"I'm not sure it's fully vincible anyway."

"Wait DeLeon saw you? Your face?"

"DeLeon's dead."

"What?"

"Escalera just shot him in the face on the street."

"What?"

"That."

"You sure?"

"I am."

"That fuck, he'll regret that."

"Colon's dead too."

"Really?"

"Jeckle's dead, he fell trying to jump across."

"You saw him?"

"Up close."

"Fuck."

"What happened with Heckle, Dane?"

"Oh he's gone."

"What happened?"

"He died."

"How?"

"Who lived Casi? Let's put it that way."

"Escalera and The Whale, maybe Landro. That's it."

"A disaster. Except for the money a perfect disaster. Fucking human endeavors. God damn it. Almost nothing was where it was supposed to be. Stupid fucks, look at them now."

I gave Dane the radio to put in the bag with the other things to be destroyed. The pain in my neck rose to the top of my head and out to my ears. Dane stopped the car and got out.

"Take the money too," I said.

"You take the money for now remember?"

"Take it."

"Why?"

"Just get it out."

"What's up?"

"Nothing's up, I just don't want that stuff in the car in case I get stopped."

Dane popped the trunk and took the bags with the money. He carried the three bags to my window where I sat. "Like I said before," he said. "These bags will soften the blow." He left.

I drove home. Over the bridge, the streets were empty. Everything was empty. I parked the car and went inside. I heard laughter coming from Angus's apartment as I approached. I sped up to get away from it. I went inside my place and sat on the floor with my back to the wall.

I had a message. Alana said I should call her back regardless of the time. Marcela had had the baby, a fat boy, and Mary had spoken again. Now no-one could shut her up.

For some reason my alarm clock went on then. The radio said I could have the world provided I gave them twenty-two minutes in return. The woman said that *a man was shot in the face and killed on 123rd Street while horrified witnesses looked on from their windows. Police responding have made the grisly discovery of several more bodies in a nearby apartment as well as in the surrounding area. No word yet on a possible motive for the killing but police are urging anyone with information to call the N.Y.P.D.'s tips hotline.* The woman then added that a car must have its oil changed every three thousand miles in order to operate optimally but that nothing prevented one from doing so more often than that. She then identified what she felt was the best place to go for that purpose.

The radio kept getting louder and louder until it died abruptly. The lights went off. The blinking red light on the answering machine disappeared. The little blue clock on the V.C.R. was gone. I felt my way to my apartment door and opened it. The lights in the hall were extinguished. I went to my front window. The street lights were dead, the traffic signals blank. I looked at the Promenade. Nothing.

Across the river, the city was completely black. There was no bridge anymore, no buildings or structures of any kind. The colors of the rainbow no longer shone there; only monochromatic, primordial black everywhere. The deep blackness of the evening waters surrounding Manhattan had risen, engulfing what they once supported and submerging the newly benighted island of lights.

I looked up just in time to witness a celestial transfiguration. The new terrestrial darkness allowed the heretofore invisible above to emerge, as the sky, now cleansed of all mortal light, became dotted with astral pinpoints. I went out and wandered the streets; for the first time in that hyperkinetic place, walking beneath the stars.

Part Three

I cannot believe that God plays dice.
– Albert Einstein

The world of the happy is quite another
than the world of the unhappy.
– Ludwig Wittgenstein

Chapter 23

Today's Citibank temperature is absolute zero. Once again the current
Citibank temperature in Central Park is absolute zero. That temperature
is bought to you by Citibank. Citibank. If you bank in the city, bank on
Citibank to do your city banking. Citibank. You can bank on them. Back
to you Dave.

Jim I thought the Third Law of Thermodynamics pretty much forbade
that temperature from ever being reached.

I have no idea what you're talking about Dave. I just report the number,
I don't get involved with the legalities of the situation or any of those
other extracurricular shenanigans.

O.K., well I wonder, Jim, if there are any special precautions our listen-
ers should take given that the temperature is absolute zero. Absolute zero
is rather cold is it not?

Good question Dave and yes absolute zero is indeed cold as in the
generally accepted value of minus 273.15 degrees Celsius and I don't even
want to get into what that means on a Fahrenheit or even Kelvin scale.

The precautions Jim.

Right, well in terms of precautions there really are none adequate to the
situation. I suppose I would counsel people to stay indoors for one. If you go
outdoors you will die. The cold will stop your heart in its very tracks, petri-
fy your flesh, and freeze your blood so that it ceases to circulate. You will die.

What about the homeless Jim?

They're not listening to this Dave, they're already dead.

Like my dream in The Orchard where I was scrounging desperately for food, this dream borrowed heavily from present reality because when I woke up the cold in the room made my eyeballs recoil from the lack of eyelid protection. And as cold as it was in that bed, even beneath multiple covers, I didn't even want to imagine coming out from under them and onto the bare hardwood floors. But there was a definite knocking. And waking up into that cold in that way made me think of being a squirt and awakening in our tiny cold apartment where the only heat was in the very immediate vicinity of the unpainted radiators and how my mother would take the polyester uniforms we would wear to hear nuns yell at us and place them on top of those radiators so that when we were ready to slip them onto our chubby little bodies they would be nice and toasty and in large measure combat the frost of that place. And I looked for the radiator in my current bedroom, so I could put my prospective clothes on it, but couldn't find it. I heard more knocking on my door. The radiator wasn't anywhere. I looked in the rest of the apartment. No wonder it was so cold, there wasn't the slightest hint of a radiator anywhere. How had I ever been warm in that place? I felt reasonably certain that the apartment had contained, at some past point, multiple radiators, but at that moment it was undeniable that no such contraption existed in that forsaken place and also that there was still that persistent knocking on my door that would need attending.

When I said *wait* to the knocking door I saw my breath escape taking most of my valuable inner warmth with it. I walked to the door with my comforter wrapped all over me and three separate times almost fell on my face. It was Alyona.

"Hi Casi, sorry, it's almost eleven-thirty I didn't think you'd still be sleeping."

"Me either."

"Anyway, I'm sure you've noticed there's no heat."

"Noticed."

"Well, I'm sure you know about the blackout."

". . ."

"The whole damn city practically, no electricity. Seven hours and counting too and since we're among the unfortunate few around here to use electric baseboard for heat I guess we're shit out of luck. I told my uncle to leave those damn radiators alone but he was adamant that it would save money. Can you believe the timing? Wait, it occurs to me you've been sleeping, do you even know there's been a blackout?"

"The radiators?"

"I know, they're gone."

"But when?"

"While you were in Anchorage remember? Ridiculous timing too. So you knew about the blackout?"

"Yeah but you're saying they still haven't gotten power back?"

"Exactly, all of Manhattan and parts of Brooklyn have no power whatsoever."

"Are like major riots and shit going on?"

"Good instincts but no. Everyone thinks the combination of the late hour of the blackout, which meant it was fairly quickly followed by the emergence of the sun, along with the ridiculous cold, is keeping people from flouting the law, against their base instincts of course. Nonetheless, there's a great deal of worry about what will happen in about six hours if power isn't restored given that people will have had time to digest and plan."

"Oh."

"Bottom line is this is a time we'll probably never forget. You should see the Promenade. Anyway I just came up to tell you the deal with the heat and to offer you my cousin's apartment in Staten Island where we will be sleeping tonight if the heat's not restored."

"Thanks, nice of you, but I'd probably just go to my mom's or something."

"Right, didn't think of that. You get used to dealing with these guys like Angus and Louie who have no family for miles and you forget you know?"

"What do they say about it?" I said pointing at the paper in Alyona's hand.

"Who Angus and Louie?"

"No, The Post."

"Oh they got screwed big time. You know they're the only paper actually printed in Manhattan so they lost all their power too and had to go with what they already had. So while everybody else has some cool variation on Darkness Falls or some such nonsense, they're stuck with this. See for yourself."

I looked at the front of the paper where it said **MASSACRE!** above a split picture of the sidewalk of 123rd Street and the inside of 410. I gave the paper back.

"You believe it?" Alyona said.

"Yeah."

"So where were you last night? Angus was trying to introduce you to someone."

"I was here."

"No cause we thought we heard you like really late but then when we knocked no answer."

"I was sleeping, deep sleep. I'm sick."

"Telling you man, got to get that ear checked out."

"It's not my ear, my ear actually feels pretty good come to think of it."

"So?"

"Just sick."

"Well whatever it is, this cold won't help."

"No."

"Well Louie and I are going to get some food. Want to come? There'll be heat."

No thanks I said and he left.

I remembered the baby so tried the phone, it didn't work.

I wanted to go home. I wanted to meet my new nephew. I knew my entire family was in noisy, celebratory congregation, most likely in my mother's house, even on a Wednesday morning, and I wanted to be there for that. Alana and I were the only ones who lived in New York and I knew from her message that she was already there. If I wanted any information I would have to go home.

I looked out the window. I didn't see any chaos but the immanent stillness was possibly worse. Suddenly I was really hungry and regretted saying no to Alyona's invitation. My initial reaction was almost always to say no to that kind of thing then, almost as often, to nearly immediately regret it. The apartment was so cold it made me feel hollow. I decided to go down and try to catch them before they left. Then I would get in my car, go home, and see everyone.

Angus answered the door and I saw that I'd already missed the others and Angus didn't know where they'd gone only that they'd gone to get food and he had not gone with them because he was sure that at any moment everything was going to be alright and power would return and everything that was *off* in his apartment would go *on* again and he wanted to be there at the precise moment that happened just as he'd been there and fully cognizant at the precise moment everything went dead; he wondered, he said, if it wasn't warmer in my apartment given that science tells us that heat rises.

"Who tells us that?"

"Science."

"Oh. Well I don't think my apartment is any warmer. I think the heat has to exist first before it can rise."

"There's always heat."

"Not if its absolute zero."

"True, but it isn't, so there's heat."

"Alright then, where is it?"

"It's around, I'm sure, it's just not having any effect."

I went inside when he asked. I watched him as he returned to the middle of his sofa then I looked at the black screen as it reflected my face back at me. He wore a hat, I had never found mine, and one of those ridiculous coats that's all bubbly and doubles your girth. His face was drained of all color, his visible hair shone with grease. He chewed at the skin on his fingertips.

"You O.K. Angus?"

"In what sense?"

"Do you feel alright, in that sense, because you don't look great."

"I've been better, no question about that. But be that as it may, I'm still perfectly sanguine about the fact that we are going to get through this little problem in a matter of a few more minutes. This too shall pass Casi."

"This blackout?"

"Yes. I have faith, you know why?"

"Why?"

"Because I am twenty-three years old and in those twenty-three years science has never let me down. And it's not going to let me down now. Two years before I was born was the last time we had one of these, at least on this scale, and you cannot seriously expect me to believe that for the duration of my entire life Father Science has not adequately investigated and prospectively remedied the deficiencies that occasionally cause us to become cloaked in unnatural darkness."

"Forgive me but isn't the strongest proof there's been no prospective remedy what you currently see when you look out the window?"

"But I have faith, faith in science."

"O.K."

"Faith."

"You still going to school? I mean figuratively, of course, from your computer and everything."

"School?"

"Yeah Columbia, Psychology, that school?"

"Oh."

"So?"

"Columbia yes, Psychology no."

"Meaning?"

"Meaning I've seen the light and now realize that terms like *social science* are devoid of meaning. Psychology is no more a science than astrology and here I was studying it like some hairy caveman magically transported centuries forward in time and oblivious to the news; the news being that in Science man has found his long-sought panacea to all that ails us. Really, how did you keep from laughing when I would tell you I was a psych major?"

"So what's your new major?"

"Physics, what else?"

"I see. So at this rate you should be getting your bachelors around the time you hit, what, thirty-five?"

"See now you're talking about time and I have a lot to say about that but I'm not really prepared at this moment to take a hard position on it, not at this time."

"Why not finish Psychology, which you've spent years on, then pursue Physics? That way you have *something*."

"Finish Psychology? What do you think I've done? Finish it is exactly what I did to it. I *finished* Psychology the way no-one before had ever finished a discipline."

"What are you talking about?"

"I created a malady and as if that weren't enough I created a human being Casi! That's what I'm talking about."

"What? Who?"

"Kramden that's who."

"Ah man you still on that?"

"Of course I'm on it."

"What are you doing to yourself Angus?"

"You don't understand."

"I'm serious man you weren't always like this, you're losing it. I thought I was in bad shape until I came in here. It's that fucking carousel, you need to stop with that thing. This blackout might be the best thing ever happened to you. Come with, let's go outside. We'll look for those guys, get something to eat."

"I'm going to forget you said that about the carousel because we're friends, you and me I mean. Although the carousel and I are friends as well."

"Fine, I'm sorry then, but let's go find those guys. Let's go *outside*, it'll be good. Besides it's just as cold in here maybe colder if that's possible."

"Everything's going to come back on any minute."

"I think you should go outside. I think you should develop a stronger relationship with reality and going outside would assist you in that."

"Funny you should mention reality because that's exactly what I'm trying to get to the bottom of. The problem with Psychology was it was too nebulous, there was no certitude, it was like trying to predict what the weather was going to be in two months with all those damn butterflies constantly getting in the way. Like with Kramden—"

"Please Angus no more Kramden."

"O.K. I won't mention him again but that doesn't change what I'm after though. I want answers; answers to the deepest questions and when I get them I want them to be indisputable and to constitute true *knowledge* not probabilities or conjecture. This is what Physics, a true science, is going to give me and now that I've aligned myself with the true king I can take my place at the right hand of the throne armed with a perfect understanding of the ultimate reality, what it precisely is and what it means. That's the reality I'm going to be developing a relationship with."

"O.K."

"Proof! Indisputable *proof* without qualifications or gradations of any kind. Proof of the kind that simply doesn't exist in Psychology. Physics can be verified, Psychology can't, therefore one is a science while the other was an extreme waste of my time."

"I understand."

"So what's with the face?"

"No face."

"Yes face. What is it? What are you thinking?"

"No just that, well I hate to say it but you know there's no real proof in science either right?"

"What? Have you lost the little remaining sanity you possessed? Have you not heard of a little guy named Einstein? Well he *proved* that Newton was full of it when that apple fell on his head and shit. $E = MC^2$ and all that other crap was proof, simple as that."

"Well what he did was propose a theory and all subsequent experiments and observations have conformed to the results one would expect to get if that theory was true."

"Sounds suspiciously like proof to me."

"Except the same was true of Newton's work for many years and under your criteria he was allegedly proven wrong."

"No you're looking at it the wrong way."

"More importantly we can never really *verify* any of science's claims in the sense of proving them to be indubitably true. They just aren't susceptible to that kind of an operation. Hume showed this, ask Alyona he can explain it. As for what makes something a science it's not the fact that its statements can be verified, it's that, unlike in Psychology, they can be falsified, that is, found to be untrue. Read your Popper on that."

"My *popper*? The only Physics my dad cares about is the shortest

691

possible path his beer can travel to his lips."

"Not your popper, Karl Popper."

"As for this Hume character, what does he know? When did he write? The fucking thirteen-hundreds? What did he write on? Fucking papyrus? Fuck him, he's just bitter that science has completely co-opted his cheesy field. Let him keep speaking ill of science and I'll shove my new terabyte iPod up his ass, see how he likes that."

"Alright, I'm going to get some food, you coming?"

No thanks, he said, and I left.

Outside there was a slight but palpable energy in the air. It was one of those moments when strangers talk to each other and speak principally of when they discovered the situation and its resemblance to entertainment. People, many of them wearing foreheads stained with dirt, were reduced to long-obsolete forms of communication. Those with battery-operated radios would use them to intercept radio waves carrying a stray datum here or there and then relay it to others using their mouths. They did this with such force that even non-participants like me could, through mere presence, become informed. In this manner, I learned that because of the darkened traffic lights no cars would be allowed on the roads until power had been restored. I would not be going home. People were stuck on elevators, people in subway cars, in buildings with electronic doors. Police were everywhere. The diner wasn't open but a person, probably the owner, was standing outside the door with a baseball bat looking everyone in the eye. A woman handed me a leaflet. It said that if the blackout affected my *thermal status* there was a place I could stay and it identified that place and it listed the symptoms of hypothermia and I wondered how they, the organization, managed to get the leaflet printed. I wandered about. Nothing was open. I had no idea where Alyona and Louie could have gone. A couple of blocks away I found an open store lit only by the sun. A lot of people gathered near the open door of this place as if cheered by the proprietor's defiance. They spoke and planned and in general behaved like a community. I said nothing. I bought some things to eat then left.

My apartment didn't feel as cold when I got back.

Then the sun left and it started getting colder.

I put gloves on.

It got dark.

I went under blankets.

I pulled the sofa away from the windows to the center of the room, the last place in the apartment it would fit. I sat on the middle of the sofa fully dressed with every blanket I owned on top of me. I curled up into a ball. My knees were to my chest and my arms around them, my chin was between my knees. I rocked back and forth under the blankets. The only noise was my breathing. I ducked my head under the blanket and breathed my own exhaust for a while. I started feeling sick so I popped my head out. I didn't know what time it was but it was completely dark in there. I tried to burrow inside my own body to find the body heat I was told would be there but found nothing. I got a little scared.

I started to have strange doubts. I allowed myself to think that maybe I really was the only existing person in the world. After all, I could never truly *know* that anyone else existed, at least not the way I *knew*, at that very moment, that *I* existed and was shaking uncontrollably. Maybe I was just a brain in a vat with some alien clown going overboard while stimulating the area for unfathomably cold.

So that's where I was; the quiet I had longed for for such a long time had finally come and I found that more than anything it caused me to doubt the very material world that had left me hugging only myself. I wondered where the survival pamphlet was. I wondered really . . . if maybe . . . well . . .

Chapter 24

um . . . if it was actually possible to die just like that, in an apartment in historic Brooklyn Heights, with every blanket I owned draped all over me and no-one there to witness or document it.

I hadn't heard a noise in hours but I decided I would check downstairs on the slight chance they hadn't gone to Alyona's cousin's after all. And I didn't so much knock as I just allowed my body to fall against the door. I heard some movement inside and relaxed so much as a result that I almost slumped to the ground. The door opened. I moved closer to make out the face and saw Angus, looking considerably worse but managing a weak smile.

"What time is it?" I said.

"No idea but God it's cold. It's inside me, is it inside you yet?"

"Yeah, I can't stop shaking. Where are the others?"

"Some cousin or something, with heat."

"How'd they get there?"

"I don't know."

"There's a place with heat. A pamphlet. Let's go there."

"A pamphlet with heat?"

"A pamphlet identifying heat."

"Where exactly?"

"I don't know."

"It's cold."

"So cold."

"Come in. Let's burn something. In the sink or tub. Books. Let's start with this Hume sonuvabitch." I went in. "Alyona comes back before leaving. I ask him to tell me about Hume before he goes and he hands me this book. I read it and you may be fucking right and here's the weird part: I'm sure, sure as I can fucking be, that if I had not read this Hume individual the power would have come back by now. God I miss power so much."

"I miss warmth . . . but can't burn books."

I sat in a big chair and pressed into one of its corners. I needed to stop moving and losing the benefit of whatever heat I had managed to build up in a particular spot. The candle that provided what little light the room had was flickering towards its end. I heard Angus' breathing on the sofa across from me but saw his features less and less. We didn't burn anything.

"Look outside," Angus said. "Yesterday wherever you looked was a star so bright you couldn't believe it was real. Tonight we get nothing." The candle went out and I lost his face along with everything else in the room. There was nothing to look at; all we had left was our voices and the words they caused. In that dark it was as if we could see those words; they were our only reality. "Which is fitting as I see it, this sudden lack of galactic light, because make no mistake but that we have been abandoned by the very universe that contains us."

"And that you seek to understand to completion."

"Yes."

. . .

. . .

"See the thing about that Jetsons lyric is there's no conceivable way that *eep op ork ah ah* can translate into I love you. First there's the fact that the alien language uses four different words whereas the alleged

English translation famously uses only three. Then there is the matter of the repeated ah at the end of the alien phrase which would seem to mandate that, at a minimum, an accurate translation would be something like I love you *you* making the correct lyric something along the lines of *eep op ork ah ah and that means I love you you.* Casi?"

". . ."

We sat in the dark and said nothing and it kept getting colder and it kept feeling darker and we didn't know what time it was and there was no noise in the streets. I had stopped shaking, instead the room shook while I sat there, frozen still.

"Look we're obviously going to die tonight."

"Yes," I said.

"So I guess the only thing left to determine is who the greatest man ever lived was. Because ultimately greatness is the only thing that matters, the only thing that endures."

"We're not *all* going to die. Just you and me . . . freeze to death . . . us."

"So what? Far as we're concerned the world ends tonight. Mankind ends tonight because tonight we're mankind. Tonight ends."

It was hard to both think and speak well, you had to choose.

"Plato, how's that for a start Casi?"

"Yes, O.K."

"I mean that stuff's brought untold entertainment to untold kids."

"Huh?"

"Play-Doh, the dude who invented Play-Doh."

"No, no."

"What then? What inventor?"

"No, no inventor, no."

"Scientist?"

"Maybe."

"What else is there?"

"..."

"Fine I'll throw some names out to roll the ball getting . . . um . . . yeah roll the ball getting . . . I mean the get balling. I'll see your Plato and raise you an Aristotle how's that? Galileo, Copernicus, Kepler, Christopher Marlowe—"

"You mean Shakespeare."

"Never heard of him. Newton, Einstein, the guy with the cat, the uncertainty dude. The guy . . . Richard . . . um."

"Dawson."

"Yes, Richard Dawson. No wait, he hosted Survey Says that's true but I don't even think he ever produced it so no, not greatest man ever, but maybe Chuck Barris who both hosted *and* produced The Gong Show along with other seminal programs. So Chuck Barris is in there . . . and Chuck Berry too since they sound so much alike that it seems unfair to leave one out. That pretty much covers it don't you think? Good, now let's review our list and make sure we didn't miss anyone. We have Homer . . . um . . . Simpson, Virgil. Aeneid. Who else did we say? Milton . . . Bradley. Bach, all the three B's in fact, Bach, Leonard Bernstein and the other B. Hume, Kant, all the guys in that book, Descartes, Leibniz, Berkeley, anybody who *went* to Berkeley. In fact anybody who went to any institution named after a dead philosopher including naturally Georgetown and Stanford, which are of course named after Phyllis George and Stanford Marsalis respectively. Gutenberg who conducted the Gutenberg trial. Nureyev Rudolph. Rudolph Valentino. Engelbert Humperdink for that matter. The guy who invented the Gouldberg variations, T. S. Eliot Gould. Oppenheimer and Manhattan, you know, of the Oppenheimer project. Eric's son Leif, meaning Leif Garrett, who discovered Earth but watched Columbo get all the credit and even though he played for the Vikings was too much of a pussy to do anything about it. Hannibal. American Vespucci. Verdi. Vendredi. Veni, Vidi, Vici, all three of them. The Marx brothers, Karl *and* Groucho. The guys they worked with, Engels and Harpo. Socrates and the guy who poisoned him then put him in a hemlock. Darwin and the first guy who coined the term Darwinian. Don Quixote and his sidekick . . . Tonto . . . Villa I think. The guy who discovered the nap. The guy who founded the Freudian slip. Pasteur, the inventor of milk. The guy who unearthed the tango, the guy who discovered cash. The guy who wrote Tango and Cash. Locke along with Stock . . . even Barrel. Angelo meaning Michael Angelo. Who else Casi?"

" . . . "

"Well there you have it then, I think that's everyone. Who do we pick?"

" . . . "

"Then we'll do the women."

" . . . "

"Bottom line is I'm going to keep talking because if I'm talking then I'm not dying. No dead man has ever talked so *cogito ergo some*one who is talking, in this case me, cannot die, at least not insofar as they are talking per se ad infinitum. Understand? Anyway I'm ready to vote and I vote for Gilligan Glass, father of Angus Glass and lover of beef. I'm sorry what I said before about the beer. It weren't true father! He's a good man, a real man. Not like I was. He woke up every morning and did something he didn't want to do. Now as my life ebbs away I realize I did something I didn't want to do about three percent of the time. The other ninety-three percent of the time I *watched* people do what I wanted them to do. What I accomplished the last couple of days was great, no question about that, and don't think it hasn't occurred to me that finally achieving this achievement has led to my imminent death by in effect giving me the green light to expire now that I've achieved greatness, but the truth remains that what I've done is essentially simulate my own life. And now it's over. I guess the only consolation is that I will not experience death since death is by definition something that cannot be experienced. It's coming though . . . I can't keep talking . . . there's simply nothing left to say. Goodbye."

"Bye."

"Although I certainly didn't think it would end with this kind of feeble whimper that's for sure," he sighed and sank lower. "No I always thought it would be like the end of Scarface whereby a veritable army would be required to take me out. I thought I would be raging against death with all my final breath. I certainly didn't think my final demise would come because Alyona's uncle read in Landlord Magazine that he could save money by installing electric heat. I didn't think *that* . . . father please . . . help me . . . Gilligan Glass . . . that's who I vote for."

Angus stopped talking. He was asleep. I knew this because his breathing changed. I was in the chair.

I stayed awake, diving further and further into the chair and always conscious of my eyes being peeled. So I know I was awake when I saw DeLeon come to me, from out of the darkness and into a new slight light, one without independent basis, to show me that his face had been shattered open, its skin barely clinging to the flesh it once covered; the lower cheeks swollen outward in a parody of a smile. I looked away but he wanted me to see. I called to Angus. DeLeon said his face hurt. He said it hurt more with every passing minute. That the hurt didn't go away, that I should know it continued to exist even after everything else had ceased to. That it was true pain. That I could try to imagine what it was like and still not truly *know* and that wanting it to go away meant next to nothing because it was a given. He said all that, the bloody remnants of his lips moving up and down exaggeratedly, and I looked away from him and into the black frigidity knowing that Angus was right and I was going to die that night. I pushed DeLeon away and fell forward out of the chair.

When I looked up from the floor I found I could see Everything. I saw the fundaments of the universe; quarks and neutrinos in visible ubiquity, jittering and bouncing, off each other and onto me. I saw Time itself, the fourth dimension, naked and enormous in its full horror, neither flowing nor frozen, and beside it the relativistic Elsewhere, lifeless and defunct. I saw Music, not the notes or the sounds but what it verily was. I saw incomplete but beautiful Math, its integers and the rules they obeyed, and I understood it all.

I saw minds. I saw thoughts, disembodied but clear. I stared at consciousness itself, saw what it looked like, and became frightened. Concepts were visible; I saw Justice and Cowardice, Enmity and Envy. I saw leprous bodies piled high, discarded by what had animated them and seemingly congealing into a single mass of fibrous muscle and cartilage. I saw the unborn and the dead as they clawed at the living. And the living weren't healthy. They were diseased and deformed, with arms where legs should be and skin peeling to expose ambiguity where distinction was needed. I watched flesh devour flesh and heard bones crack from weight and from that moment on I started hearing everything as well. I heard colors and circles, trees and triangles. I heard Fear lick the face of Hate accompanied by a final whispered scream. Then I heard, felt, and saw the world begin to crack open to admit, little by little, the return of Light. The light dispersed everything else as I watched it grow and fill the room.

I saw Angus on the sofa and watched the breath leave his nose. I stood up. The sun rose and the room shone. Then the artificial light began to return as if responding to its father. One by one its sources came to life casting a plastic brightness on what had hid in the dark. The heat began clicking furiously and I dropped to its level inches away. Television came on and Angus opened his eyes.

"We're going to be alright," he said.

"No," I said. "But we're going to live."

Angus stood and walked to a basket. He took out a control of the remote variety and began to reprogram his H.D.V.D.C.R. I couldn't move yet.

"I had a dream," he said. The heat began to fill the room. "Our thoughts during dreams are often more lucid, I feel good." For the first time in over a day I took off my jacket. Angus saw this and took his off. "And I don't give a cow's dick what Hume said, science rules! Smell that heat? That's what science smells like, that's science baby."

"Cows don't have dicks."

"What?"

"Bull."

"Exactly, that's bull!"

"No, bulls have dicks."

"Fine, have it your way; but I still don't give a bull's vulva about Hume."

My car wouldn't start. Everyone was everywhere. I took the A to Times Square. Toad's response to the blackout had been to decree that every light in the square had to be placed on T.I.T.S. (or the non-acronymic *Temporarily Illuminatorily Trebled Status*) even during daylight and it was hard to make out people or structures in that brightness. Giant digital soda cans poured their would-be liquids near skeletal human underwear holders and a morning news program aired on the giant screen turning the area into the world's largest living room and us into passive viewers. Arrows illuminated in succession toward neon women and Disney characters handed out free previews to their parents' movies. I looked around confused. I needed a bus. I was desperate and lost. A guy in a van said he went where I needed to go provided I had the two dollars he needed. Everyone in the van talked about the blackout except me. The van dropped me off two blocks from my mother. I walked and found that the unmitigated cold of the last two days had made me more suscep-tible to losing my warmth so that by the time I got to the house I was shaking again.

There were no cars in the driveway and I feared I would be alone. The door was locked but I thought I heard voices inside. I climbed in through the window. I walked into the living room. My mother was there with others. Alana was there, Timmy and Mary. Flames cracked in the fireplace. They said Marcela was still in the hospital but doing well along with the baby and both would be coming home any minute. I walked to the fire as my face stung from the new heat. No-one talked about the blackout and Mary filled the room with words.

Will you read this to me? Please?
– Mary

Chapter 25

THE STORY

Garrapata Nahyuv-McDunnit
A New Translation by Nestor del Tobón

The agèd Queen two princes begat; her newer half-young
As Elder was old. Until, as mothers wont do,
She urged the younger where travel and likewise what bring.

Thusly did it come to pass that this younger of two
Did alight onto our world from the openest sky
Feebly armed and with only sense slight of where he'd go,

What he would do once there and why.
The sky he quit was soft and warm
Yet the low land he saw draw nigh,

Growing steadily in his eyes, seemed frigid and hard,
With poorer air than the home he'd departed and less
Room where he might hope to safely ensconce his heart.

For where he then landed was densely forest
Where aught the tallest trees were small
And truly the roundest circles seemed square.

Of this forest he deemed study all.
Looking first up before down
Then side to side with scant awe.

But not without adding to his face a mounting fearful frown
For well he understood he was not rightly of that place
And also did he perceive an encroaching darkness then.

One that would blind him to leafy trees,
The slight creatures extant and home,
And the very ground that supported his

Weight and pushed up against his own
Feet ensuring he could not take flight
To ascend from that darkening globe

And return whence he left.
Thus did his princely mind
Resolve that ere Day went

He would endeavor, through sight,
To find his way out of that
Tangled brush and unchecked grime

Which had entwined his heart,
Rooted him to heavy Earth,
And obscured his purpose from the start.

To begin, the resolute prince first
Traveled eastward where he found
The forestry slighter yet thicker,

The pull greater from the ground,
And a harshly disfigured beast,
Enormous in both sight and sound,

Blocking any passage he might attempt
While addressing him thusly:
"Only one who is truly lost,"

Spake the beast, "would dare appear before me
In such a manner wholly unarmed
So that thy certain and grievous defeat

Would occur in and of slightest momentum
And in every possible event
With greatest attendant harm."

Only when the young man spoke naught
Did the creature hastily quod,
"Or is yet my speech intemperate?

For could not the sight of thou naked
Yet calm portend the terrible truth
Of a strength and power greater for being well-hid?"

Nor to this either did speaketh
The young prince, well aware
He of his dearth of strength

Both hidden or evidently clear.
Choosing instead sudden flight
So eager he to abscond from there.

And with expanding black night
Cloaking the fearsome still beast
Did the young prince then decide

To travel farthermost west
In ardent search of method
For retrieving what he'd lost.

So he traveled toward the sinking sun
The horrors of the eastern creature
No dimmer by virtue of being done,

The approaching horizon as if afire
But aglow with the promise
That the answer somehow lay near,

Visible to all, yet in expectant wait only for his
Discovery. Thereat went the young man
Hopeful that second would be last of his voyages.

But his hope did dim much when
Arriving at length at the New
He found a chasm, widened without end

By long sad years, into which the sun now
Disappeared entire taking what meager light
And warmth the new world had theretofore known.

Descending into that hole complete
He found others in appearance as him
Tearing at each other in scattered effort

To raise themselves and sowise climb
(Supported by the massive weight
Of others) but undone by a fall each time.

And the heaven-descended prince eyed the replacement
Moon seeing what he thought the lovely face
Of his mother and entreating it to reveal his fate.

But while the moon's light did soothe his eyes
Not far had th'orb truly bade
To answer his doubtful sighs.

And presently from the moon's appearance did fade
The reassuring visage of his mother
So that the young prince was in solitude forced

To seek his means of homeward return,
Out of that world of empty dread
And once again to that of his noble mother,

Through the use of Thought, for surely it had
Been the greatest of the intentionally few
Gifts with which he had obediently traveled.

So quickly did he move away
From that yawning earth
To let his troubled mind weigh

Thoughts of how he might at last depart
That ruinous place. Upon themselves
Those learned thoughts did build, the true

Of them supporting novel ones
And emerging from those
The strongest for corners.

Building through such means
A ladder, ethereal but true,
And able to support his corpse

Thought he. Yet learning instead too
That as he would attempt to elevate
The insubstance of the ladder would

Rebel against his body's weight,
Keeping him lower than he wished
With dreams of Mother still frustrate.

And though the ladder grew its best
With success eventual
Still imbued with promise,

The young prince grew so impatient with it all,
The progress so deliberately slow,
So often seeing the moon rise then fall,

That he soon sought a newly improved route,
One that would re-wed him to the heavens
With rungs that ought repel his feet until home.

Accordingly did he construct magic vines
Which vines he tied to each step
Of the ladder as up he would steadily rise.

And not until he felt a slight drop
In his climb did he look below
To see the wroth eastern beast rising up

In pursuit, alternating each ascending paw,
Baring its many demonic teeth,
Intent fully on reaching its prey.

The young prince did then raise his speed
Only, in his hurried frantic haste,
To see distance shrink twixt him and beast.

Until, from mere distance at last,
He saw in approach the cloud
That segued to the world of his past.

And in a final leap conducted in the highest above
Did the young prince presently and safely land
Beyond the portal cloud past which the beast dared not run.

Content instead on the ladder to stand
And wait, in vain if need be,
For the return of the princely man.

Who now searched in that safety
For the mother he did not see
Unaware that her end had been deadly,

Just the shortest of measured time since,
At the sullied hands of a brother jealous
That the younger's journey did not include he.

And now did that elder brother seize in his hands
The limp body of their heavenly mother
To pull on her head by the lifeless hairs

Until only the severed head of her
Remained in his bloodied grasp,
The better with which to deceive his brother.

For into that head he reached to scoop
What in life her skull had cradled,
Creating thusly of the skull a masking top

That forcibly he placed over his head
To in such manner then falsely greet
His brother in guise of the recent dead.

"O my journey 'twas long and full of fright,"
The now becalmed prince spoke,
"Yet the fragrant peace I have only hither felt

Makes my adventures seem far less dark."
Then adding, hearing no response,
"Your son, the other, does he not hark

To my just now resurrected presence?"
To which came the misprize reply:
"Gone not long from this celestial place

At my request and in search of thee.
Whom I now in turn urge
To return and search well for he."

A great shiver the young man felt at those words,
His mind's sight of the beast still unextinguished
Despite his recent and most beneficent turn.

Until the dead woman's grief and shame
Did bubble over from a rapid swell
Causing fresh blood from her neck's wound to shed,

Forming rivulets of liquid crimson that fell
Downward and across her debased killer's chest
Exposing his sin and inducing his brother's knell.

And at skin and flesh the brothers tore without rest
Their bodies mingled then forever fused
As twain fell into the porous cloud then past;

Wherefore the wretch his spoilt meal swallowed
Ingested whole but in an utmost violent way.
Mother's voided head left to lie on the cloud's floor . . . abandoned.

Where it remains to this day
In the centralmost cloud
Of our modern sky.

But when Mother's pain becomes too great to be borne
Witness how her aggrieved blood will resume its flow
To flood the earth awash in dull arrows of rain

And set to swim and tread our doleful land of woe.

THE END

"Why'd you want me to read *that*?"
"Because it's a story."

Now comes the mystery.
— Henry Ward Beecher's last words

Chapter 26

"I see you employed vacation time all week only to come in on Friday, not sure I see the logic in that."

"You kidding? Doing so was a stroke of genius on my part if I may be so bold."

"You may, but how so?"

"Well you'll agree, I assume, that Friday has the best feel of any day, certainly of any weekday."

"I suppose."

"So by effectively reducing the week to this one day I have success-fully, albeit temporarily, combated the enduring agony that is my every waking minute."

"Agony?"

"Augh."

"So how bad is the kid's impairment in your opinion?"

"What do I know? *Kid* is exactly right. It's like talking to someone who's a lot younger than they look. The eyes are the way they are in the picture and the way he talks gives it away a bit too."

"Well that psychiatrist we retained just faxed us this. It seems he wants some sort of assurance of payment before he'll go out and see Kingg."

"Like what? What assurances are there in this world Toom?"

"I guess he'll settle for someone signing this."

"Give," I said. I took the paper and signed it without reading it. We were in a conference room and, like every Friday afternoon in that place, it was eerily desolate. I looked at him when he took the paper back. "I have to save this kid's life," I said.

"I know."

"No I mean *have to* like life-depending-on-it-type shit, my life."

"O.K."

"What a mess I've made."

"I'm optimistic about this supreme court thing quite frankly."

"I mean saving someone's life is an indisputably good thing right?"

"I believe so, yes. Especially in this case."

"A poor little sap who sees the world through those eyes, who got laughed at in school, and who lives in a tiny cinderblock square no-one ever visits."

"Saving him would be good I agree."

"An unequivocally *good* act. And by extension someone creating such an unambiguous good would therefore be a good person."

"I'm not sure about that."

"And that would of course be true regardless of what had come *before* the good act. Using the term *before* of course only in its common sense since I believe I have already expressed to you my belief in the nonlinearity of actual true time; which nonlinearity, incidentally, I just recently confirmed through direct observation."

"When exactly did you express this belief of yours to me?"

"Before, so to speak."

"I don't recall that."

"So you see my problem."

"Not really."

"Leaving open only the question of *how* we can achieve this unproblematic good, the achievement of which I have just demonstrated is critically necessary else I forfeit my continued viability as a being."

"As I said, I believe there are many good signs, and other close observers agree, in the court's latest actions, although we'll know more on Wednesday of course. And I think these signs, if they bear fruit, will hold the key to saving Jalen's life."

"I wish I could share your belief in that group of people but I can't. I simply can't bring myself to expect anything non-toxic to emerge from them or anyone similar to them. On the other hand there are still things I *can* control."

"Such as?"

"I can control what comes out of me. I can write something. I can write something so compelling and persuasive that even the scum that read these things for a living will, upon reading it, do what I need them to do. What do you think of that?"

"I think that's certainly the correct approach."

"Toomie. Young, large-brained yet fundamentally naïve Toomie. You don't have to humor me in an effort to get me to hand in the best possible product. Haven't you been listening? I'm determined to create a document so achingly beautiful and effective and important that should I drop dead as the final draft is being printed it would matter not the least. And I have already begun this process incidentally. All I do is work on this thing. I'm writing all the time. If you see me staring out a window, I'm writing. As I speak with you now, I'm writing. It's as simple as that. Nothing else matters to me the way this thing I'm writing does. This job for example is nothing more than a distraction. I should come in on Monday and quit so I can spend my every waking moment and some sleeping ones writing the thing, honing it and perfecting it until it cannot properly be said to have come from me at all."

"Speaking of distractions, I understand that with respect to your pending contempt charge they will be conducting, what, some form of hearing in a couple of weeks?"

"Yeah the fourth, I meant to ask you about that. Can they do that?

I mean I'm a dangerous person I admit as much but it's not like I'm posing an imminent threat to the stability or decorum of a particular courtroom, which is what contempt power of the kind being invoked here is purportedly designed to address. What justifies them in holding this kind of hearing weeks later, and adjudicated by the very aggrieved party no less? It seems like the most they could do in this after-the-fact manner is put me before some kind of disciplinary committee and I would like my chances in that setting a lot better because I could do something like fly the brother of one of the committee members in from Italy to sit next to me so they discern I mean business. I mean I'm no lawyer but I know my rights."

"Sounds right but that's Cymbeline for you. I wouldn't put it past her to have spoken to the committee and set up some special procedure just for you."

"Cymbeline? Who listens to her?"

"Many, she *is* the administrative judge after all."

"She is?"

"Of course, you didn't know that?"

"No."

"You may be the only person in our entire circle who didn't know that."

"Fine, she's the administrative judge but so what if she is?"

"Well that means she wields a certain power, not to mention that in addition to holding that post she's also very highly and politically connected."

"Stop, this sounds like a joke of some sort."

"Unfortunately I'm not joking."

"See you know these things, that's exactly why I'm going to ask you what I'm about to ask you."

"What's that?"

"I get to have an attorney at this thing. Apparently they don't want to violate every single rule established through centuries of American jurisprudence. So what do you say?"

"Sure."

"Of course some type of barteristic transaction will have to be worked out to satisfy your justifiably outlandish fee."

"Of course."

"But aside from that I'm a dream client for this reason. I will not bother you with any annoying protestations of innocence. Instead, I acknowledge my guilt. And not a technical, spurious guilt that comes with an explanation either. This is like a pure guilt-concentrate that courses through my very veins like substitute blood. All I ask is that you somehow make it so I can avoid the rightful consequences of this guilt. Fair is fair and I want unfair. I want to admit to wrongdoing, admit I do little else, yet have it lead to nothing punitive. Can you get me that counselor?"

"I'll try."

"Thank you then, it's settled."

"I do feel compelled to insert something at this point."

"Insert away."

"You can't joke your way out of this one young man."

"You haven't seen me joking at my best."

"You also have the in-house charges remember?"

"Still with the in-house?"

"Yes and on the fourth as well if I heard correctly?"

"On the fourth?"

"Yes, and Deborah Podurk is heading the panel that will be questioning you."

"How do you know all this and shouldn't *I* know this stuff?"

"You certainly should, hence my reference to the advisability of you decreasing the mirth factor and maybe paying more attention to these two events that threaten to derail your career."

"No can do Toomster. I'm a writer now, nothing more. I have to save Kingg with my prose. The rest is meaningless. Did you say the fourth?"

"That's what I heard."

"So you're talking basically a twi-night doubleheader of legal disciplinary proceedings."

"It seems, why?"

"Well if you know your baseball you know it's very difficult to sweep a doubleheader. The almost default result is a split, but a split on the fourth might do me little good."

"I see."

"Never mind, we'll sweep."

"I can't help you on the in-house thing."

"Where's Tom anyway? Can't he just issue some hastily worded executive fiat instantaneously clearing me of all charges. I mean, isn't he in charge here?"

"He's still on vacation."

"What kind of vacation is this?"

"Exactly, you may have hit on the problem. The vacation may be a euphemistic one."

"Good grief."

"I don't know."

"What's it like being married anyway? You're never really alone, not the way I am. Do you even remember being alone?"

"Sure."

"If I were you I wouldn't remember it, not for a minute. Anyway it's all about the Kingg right now. All Kingg all the time, you think it would help if I took some kind of formal vow?"

"Vow?"

"Yeah you know, if I *vowed* to save Kingg's life, don't you think that might help? I mean a vow is a serious thing isn't it? More serious than a pledge right? Has a vow ever been broken? Has one ever been disavowed?"

"Sure otherwise we wouldn't need the term."

"I'm not sure that's true but I'm not going to be vowing anything anyway so it doesn't matter. Thanks for representing me though."

"You're welcome."

"I'm going home to work on Kingg."

"O.K. but by the way, what are those marks on your neck? Are those bruises?"

"Don't be silly. What would I have to gain from having bruises on my neck? See you Monday Toom. And remember; it's all about the Kingg!"

"Elvis Presley? That king?"

"No Conley, not the fucking king of rock and fucking roll."

"Who then? The king of pop? Of all media?"

"No, the king of nothing, meaning not the king of anything. Kingg. Jalen Kingg. Of death row. My client."

"I see."

I turned, semi-waved, then walked away meaning the conversation was unequivocally over and I would not have to discuss anything odd or far-reaching. It meant I was alone, all the doors I passed closed but an incredibly open window somewhere excreting a plaintive whistle, walking but sensing that the air immediately behind me was being disturbed.

"Where you headed?" Conley confirmed. I turned to face him, looking him in the eye but feeling detached.

"Home to save Kingg," I said.

"I'll walk with you, where do you live?"

"Not sure," I resumed walking. "You part of this committee I have to go before?"

"No, I hate anything committee-like. I believe strongly in tyranny and capricious rulings."

"You know anything about it?"

"Just that Debi's heading it and she's determined to take you down."

"Why?"

"No idea but it's definitely personal."

"What makes you say that?"

"What else could it be? Business? Aren't those the only two choices?"

"Personal how though? What have I done to her?"

"Did you make her laugh?"

"What?"

"Did you make her laugh because she hates to laugh."

"Don't think so, but I *have* tried."

"There you go."

"No, that can't be it."

"Fine don't benefit from my hard-earned wisdom."

"When did Debi get all this juice anyway? Where the hell's Tom?"

"Vacation."

"When's he coming back?"

"That's classified."

"Classified what?"

"What do you mean?"

"What's it been classified, that's what."

"I miss your meaning."

"Well you just said the information is classified, so classified what? What classification has it been given?"

"No no no. *Classified* speaks for itself. It's a *res ipsa* that *loquiturs* or I suppose more accurately a *res* that *ipsa loquiturs*. Bottom line is if something's classified then no-one can know it."

"That's silly. Someone has to know it otherwise how could the determination have been made that it should be classified? Aside from that, just saying that something has been classified without more is almost senseless or at least highly unhelpful. Now if you tell me that something has been classified top secret, for example, now you've told me something meaningful, namely that only those with clearance to disseminate top secret material can be provided the information. Is that what you're telling me? That the date of Tom's return has been classified top secret?"

"That's classified as well."

"Never mind."

"Besides, what are you worried about that toothless committee for? What are they going to do to you regardless of Debi's designs? Fire probably the best young attorney to come through here since me? The only part of your body you have to worry about is your wrist because that's what's going to get slapped. On the other wrist, what you *should* be concerned about is Cymbeline, since by all accounts her animus towards you is both personal *and* business and that's the worst kind."

"How's it business?"

"How? You do know Cymbeline's the administrative judge don't you?"

"Of course, everybody knows that. But how does that make it business?"

"Poor Casi, don't you know this thing stretches all the way to Albany?"

"Albany? Stretches? What are you talking about?"

"What Albany? Did I say Albany?"

"Look, truth is I don't give a fuck about either committee or whatever you want to call them. All I care about is writing. Writing this Kingg thing and saving his life with it. That's all. The rest is bullshit and meaningless."

"Now you're on to something unmitigatedly true. You're right to peg all this stuff as meaningless and that includes by the way, and forgive me for saying this, your deposed king on death row."

"Wrong."

"Actually the only thing that matters at this moment in time is Dark Energy."

". . ."

"Did you hear me? Dark Energy."

"I heard you."

"You heard me, sure, but do you know what it means?"

"What about the genome project? It no longer matters?"

"That matters too of course but in a slightly different realm of human activity. You know about Dark Energy right?"

"What about it?"

"You know how Einstein when he checked his relativity math saw that it described a universe that was expanding and since he firmly believed it was not actually expanding he then created and threw in his cosmological constant to make the equations work and the universe they describe stable? You know how when it was later confirmed, by Hubble and others, that the universe was in fact expanding Einstein called the cosmological constant his biggest blunder? Well I guess it's the mark of some people's genius that even when they think they're wrong they're actually right as we now have Dark Energy, which certainly appears to exist and which functions very much like the constant."

"I know all this, now tell me why Dark Energy is the only thing that currently matters."

"You see we now know that the universe is not only expanding but it's expanding *at an accelerating rate*. Think about that for a moment. The old picture was of a Big Bang followed by expansion until, impelled by gravity, all of the matter in the universe begins to attract itself at a rate greater than the rate of expansion causing the universe to contract and contract until it ends in the Big Crunch. Of course when cosmologists looked at the universe and took out their calculators they saw that there had to be a lot more mass and matter than they could account for, meaning the universe was full of not only what we could see but also an invisible Dark Matter that fills over ninety percent of it."

"I have to go Con."

"O.K. let's stay with Dark Energy then. Perhaps I have not adequately conveyed the sheer enormity of the accelerating expansion. The acceleration suggests there's not going to be any big crunch after all. The universe will continue to expand infinitely! The universe is basically immortal and it is so thanks to Dark Energy which overcomes the attractive force of gravity with its own repellent force that drives the universe's expansion. Do you follow me?"

"You're being followed but maybe you can accelerate *the story* a bit."

"I'll cut to the chase. Man has created these new wide-field telescopes. We are going to look through these, both from the ground and in space, and we are going to figure out once and for all what this Dark Energy shit is. We cannot be expected to master that which we do not fully comprehend so once we *know*, with the help of these scopes, what Dark Energy and Dark Matter truly are then we will be ready to master the universe. There's no question this is going to happen, it's just a question of when. Don't you see? The universe is going to keep on expanding forever and expansion is just another word for progress. When a chain of stores expands for example that's good, that's progress. Like the universe, Man is expanding at an accelerating rate and he's doing this through technology. Do you doubt this? Because no-one of the slightest mental competence does. The growth of technology and knowledge has not recently been steady, it's been exponential. If you magically transported a man from 500 A.D. to 1500 A.D. he would eventually adjust to the intervening changes. But take a man from as recent as 1800 and put him in our world with handheld computers and planes and particle accelerators and satellites and space exploration and A.T.M.s and cell phones and nuclear power plants and he would lose his limited mind in about five hours! The same is true of us if we could travel into the future. After all the guy in 1800 didn't think there was a lot left to invent and discover did he? He couldn't have conceived of *this* right? So obviously things are going to happen in the next centuries that we cannot now even conceive of. The future world will be more unrecognizable to us than our present one would be to the 1800 guy. I used to say that in five hundred years we will not recognize human beings or society because of things like the Human Genome Project but now I see that it's going to come a lot sooner than that. And that, my friend, is why Dark Energy is all that matters right now. Because we are going to solve the ultimate riddles of the universe and ensure that this remarkable force that ensures universal progress and immortality is bent to our will. Men and women don't matter, only Man does. Man right now, armed with his technology, just feels like such an unstoppable force. Man is on the precipice of conquering the universe and at a time like that men like Kingg are sadly irrelevant."

"Take it easy. Just two days ago Man, that near-deity that wields technology like an irresistible sword, forgot to pay the electric bill and the lights were turned off."

"Hmm."

"I'm taking this cab."

"Take."

. . .

"Brooklyn Heights. Columbia Heights and Orange."

"I can leave you on Orange and Columbia Heights, is that O.K.?"

"Orange and Columbia Heights?"

"Right."

"As opposed to Columbia Heights and Orange?"

"Indeed."

"Fine."

. . .

"Some blackout huh?"

"Uh-huh."

"I was here for the last one. Now that was a real blackout. Makes this one look like a brownout really. I even told my wife, this should've been classified a brownout. And I really saw no need for Times Square to have been placed on the T.I.T.S. either. Not for nothing but it's very hard to drive, let me tell you, when it's that bright. It's like drifting towards the sun or something. Like when a ship comes off its orbit in those science fiction movies, ha ha!"

"Yeah."

. . .

"Here we go."

"Thanks, keep the change."

"Consider it kept pal."

Humana, humana aya . . .
    – Portly fellow standing outside Angus's door

Chapter 27

Step on a crack break your mother's back. That is, if you step on a crack on the sidewalk, either the planned ones that result from those cement squares they create or the ones that stem from elemental corrosion, then your mother will, as a result, sustain that rather severe back injury. So not wanting that to happen I walked in the stilted manner required, my steps sometimes long, sometimes short, without pattern, and my head always down and looking; so that I was incidentally able to spot immediately the half-globe paperweight that contained a miniature Manhattan island, which island one could create snow on through mere inversion. The thing lay unattended on the sidewalk, which allowed me to invoke a further adage: the one that states that finders may keep while losers only weep. I snatched it up and continued walking home. Only I then decided that I should instead strive to step on every crack and the achievement of that slowed me down considerably.

The storm door to my apartment building had this compulsively effective spring that resisted with all its might any effort to open said door so when I absentmindedly let go of the knob while standing in the doorway the door came flying back to slam me in the shoulder, spinning me towards the street and freeing the globe of my hand's grip that I may watch it land on the edge of the top step, triggering the globe's sudden explosion, its protective dome of glass instantly dividing into countless dull diamonds that accelerated away from each other, the flakes of synthetic snow dropping without life onto the cement, the water expanding in thin waves to mark the step in astral-shaped black, and the now exposed plastic skyline limply descending the three steps aboard its solid base until hitting bottom. I didn't clean up or anything, I just went in.

And although I heard nothing as I walked up the stairs to the second floor I distinctly felt that some one or thing was in the area. What I in fact saw on the second floor was, I gathered, a man. A portly fellow standing outside Angus's door. He stayed in the shadow of the corner, a corner I would have to pass to go up to my apartment. He spoke:

"Hey pal," he said in a way that made me think he knew me and I was supposed to know him, making more than a terse greeting expected. I said something in return and he took a step forward and out of the dark. He was big. He had short black hair and white clean-shaven skin. He passed his hand by his mouth and raised his cheek up and down with the corner of his mouth. He wore what looked like a uniform – dark gray or blue or even faded black, I couldn't tell – with a white shirt and a dark tie held in by a zipper that ended chest high at two significant lapels. He was absolutely familiar and I'm using that word in its strict sense, meaning he was like family, but I also knew I had never seen him before. That or I had seen him so many times that the sight of him had lost all meaning. I struggled to speak, which I wouldn't have even tried to do but for the fact that he seemed to expect me to.

"Do I? Do we know each other? I'm sorry."

"C'mon pal, you know that I know that you know that we don't know each other."

"Oh." I looked away and went to knock on the door.

"Never mind that," he said. "Angus isn't home. And I don't know the names of those other two nuts but they ain't home neither."

"Oh, you know Angus?"

"Sure I know him. How else would he know me?"

"Makes sense."

"Humana, humana aya uh, would you do me a favor there pal?"

"What's that?"

"Do you have a kern?"

"A what?"

"A kern. I understand you can make a phone call if you have a kern, I'm not from here."

"Oh a coin? Where you from?"

"Bensonhoist, 328 Chauncey Street. Or 728 I'm not sure."

"Yeah, Bensonhurst's Brooklyn. Pretty much the same rules apply throughout here with regards to pay phones and the like."

"I had a phone once but I got rid of it, you married kid?"

"No."

"Good thinking, keep it that way ho! Now what about that kern? Don't think of it as a loan, think of it as an investment in the corporation of me. I have big ideas."

"I might have one," I said. "Let me see." I started digging into my many pockets but found nothing. I took my time and felt my fat companion losing patience until:

"Come on!!" he said shooting his open hands out from his body and bending his knees slightly.

"Take it easy," I said. "I don't have one."

"Sorry," he said and did that cheek thing.

"Alright . . . but I have to go." I started up the stairs then turned back. "I didn't catch your name," I said.

"I didn't throw it wo ho!"

I laughed.

"Just kidding," he said.

"So?" I said surprised at my apprehension.

"Herbert. Herbert John."

Thank God I thought. "Well nice to meet you Herbert," I said. "I'm Casi."

"Oh you're Casi huh? I have a message for you."

"What is it?" I said.

"A detective came by looking for you."

"I'm sorry, a what-tective?"

"A detective, N.Y.P.D. I suppose. He said your name pal, wanted to talk to you."

"Said my name? You sure?"

"Yup, said Casi, remember it clear as a bell."

"What was his name?"

"Detective ass? Andro? Something with an A I think."

"D'Alessio?"

"Yes! No. It's either that or it isn't, I'm not sure. But if I was you I would definitely maybe be uhscared."

"Thanks Herb."

"Call me Jackie," he said.

Fuck I thought.

Inside my apartment, sitting on my couch, his feet on my stool, reading my newspaper, was Dane.

"What the?"

"You should lock your door," he said.

"I did."

"I didn't say you didn't."

"You implied it."

"Don't put words in my mouth."

"I didn't, now you're putting some in mine."

"Maybe."

"I thought you were gone."

"Gone? From where? How?"

"Gone. You know as in took the money and ran, as in haven't heard from you in a couple of days when I would certainly have expected to."

"*That* gone? You think that little of me? How beneath my dignity would such a move be? No, your well-gotten gains are safe. Come with me now and we'll get it."

"Get what exactly?"

"Eleven million dollars for now."

"For now?"

"It changes every time I count, it goes up."

"Eleven total."

"Eleven each, but you can have mine if you wish. Let's go."

"No, there's a problem."

"A what? I'm sorry I don't think I heard you correctly."

"A problem."

"There's no problem. I told you, over and over I told you, that we would, at a minimum, get that money and if you come with me now I'll show it to you, you can smell it then start spending it. The only question, not a problem, is what our next project should be."

"Another question might be what to do about the N.Y.P.D. detective currently looking for me."

"Detective?"

"Yes."

"Ha ha, that's the problem? Please."

"That's the one."

"Detective who?"

"Not sure but I'm thinking D'Alessio who was at the meeting."

"How do you know?"

"I don't, I said I *think* it's D'Alessio."

"No, how do you know *any* detective is looking for you at all?"

"Some guy just told me downstairs."

"Some guy? Downstairs? Fuck him, what does he know?"

"I trust him, he's a good man."

"How long you known him?"

"Seconds."

"I see," he said. He turned the newspaper he was reading so I could see the front. "You saving this for a reason?"

"Yeah that's another problem."

"What, the press? Now you're worried about them? Law enforcement and the press. Could you pick more feeble entities to be spooked by?"

"I'm sorry I can't share your confidence but things seem pretty messed up to me right now. The plan certainly wasn't for what happened back there to happen. The plan wasn't for that picture to be splashed, as they say, all over the front page of the next day's paper and the plan most definitely didn't involve a detective coming to my home, *my home*, where I do my most sacred breathing, to question me. None of that was part of the plan and none of that is good in any conceivable way."

"You jest, surely, this is a time for exultation not concern. This newspaper and its relatives have the attention span of a six-month-old. Where's my thanks for the blackout that effectively ended what little fascination the public would've had for our events? This detective? He sounds like he couldn't detect a frog if it landed on his head and took a shit. He keeps nosing around and the only thing he's going to detect is my foot up his ass."

"What about that picture? What about what it depicts? Can you change that? Because that was fucked up and fucked up because of us."

"*Because of us*? Did we tell those fuckers to come in there and start shooting up the place? Because I don't remember doing that."

"True. You're right right? That was going to happen whether we were there or not."

"Now you're thinking."

"Fuck Escalera for trying to avoid paying too. He's the one fucked up the whole thing if you think about it."

"Even if you don't."

"Fuck that, I'm the one that went back for the girl. She would've been killed right?"

"Who knows?"

"But she wasn't. DeLeon just wasn't supposed to be there, DeLeon."

"Escalera."

"That piece of . . ."

"He'll get his, everyone does."

"I can see it so vividly though. Whenever I want and at times I don't."

"And that, as they say, as you say, is that."

"Except you in no way addressed this detective other than to disparage his abilities without any possible basis in fact and in contravention of the available evidence, which shows that he is at least competent enough to have appeared at my doorstep, a move you and I know is entirely warranted."

"He knows what then?"

"I don't know but he knows something, otherwise why look for me?"

"He knows you're DeLeon's attorney and he knows DeLeon was one of the bodies, that's all he knows. He knows how to read a notice of appearance, hooray for him."

"I don't think so. Are you slipping, is that the problem?"

"More like I find this scenario wholly uninteresting but go ahead. What makes you think it's more than that?"

"Two things. First, it's only been a little over two days since the investigation presumably began and already this detective has found his way to interview me? That would seem to belie your claim that interviewing the attorney of one of the victims is just a pro forma charade without any specific basis. Second, as I believe I've mentioned, this prick came to my home! He didn't seek me out at the office or at court or through the D.A. This was an act of aggression. He wants to unsettle me, show me he knows things about me and there's no safe haven. And so I'm unsettled."

"You surprise me. You allow this maggoty louse to do that? This lousy maggot? If you're right and this *was* an act of aggression, then there's only one response to things of that nature. You meet even the slightest aggression with a disproportionately evil response. Look at you. A double-digit millionaire cowering at the implied sight of a civil servant. How tacky, and worse, how boring. Who cares what this cop thinks or even knows? And it's not a failure of empathy on my part either. I wouldn't care if I found that fuck sitting on my couch when I got home. The whole thing simply holds no interest for me, intellectual or otherwise."

"The prospect of a new involuntary address in upstate New York doesn't get your attention?"

"Please, now you're invoking the truly impossible but fine I'll humor you. Let's go through the situation. Who saw us at 410 or better yet to save time who saw us that is still alive?"

"Saw us?"

"Yeah *saw*, as in with their own two eyes."

"Still alive I guess just The Whale since the paper says Landro was shot dead."

"And who, if anyone, knows we were there through other means, again, limiting ourselves to the living."

"Just Escalera I guess, who DeLeon could have told of my presence before being shot."

"And who was probably shot for that very reason in fact."

"No. What? No."

"You don't see that happening?"

"I don't—"

"DeLeon says, in that chaos, something like *I just saw my lawyer* and Escalera takes his frustration out on him because he consequently blames him for things getting fucked up."

"I don't . . . who cares? Does it matter? The point is Escalera could know I was there."

"So Escalera and The Whale. You think they'll be visiting their local precinct any time soon or offering to pick us out of a lineup? Of course not. All the factors that made the involvement of law enforcement so unlikely before Wednesday still exist as far as I can see."

"Except we now know a detective *is* involved. A fact that seems to strongly suggest that somewhere, somehow, things got fucked up with respect to avoiding detection."

"Nonsense, no way. You got the mask right?"

"What do you mean I got the mask? You burned it didn't you?"

"I burned everything you gave me."

"So you burned the mask."

"And we certainly left no prints."

"No but the struggle with Whale. What if I left blood or hair?"

"Now who's not thinking? Analysis of something like that would take weeks, it's been hours."

"True. So what then? Give me a plausible explanation for the detective at my door."

"Could be a P.B.A. fund raiser for all you know. You'll know soon enough I suppose, so what's the point in expending any more mental activity on it?"

"That's a reach."

"Anyway I've been thinking about what we should do next and it occurs to me that true perfection—"

"Next? Are you mental? I have a detective up my ass and you want me to plan the next insanity?"

"Relax will you? Besides if you want to worry about something shouldn't you worry about the two individuals who we *are* certain, without speculation, *do know* we were involved. Especially when one of those two individuals saw our faces quite well and appears to be the sort of entity that has no regard for life or limb, its own or others, and respects no laws, natural or otherwise?"

"At least those two can't put me in prison."

"Which brings me to a question. Why are you still working? Did you not hear what I said about the eleven million, twenty-two if you accept my share?"

"I heard you but it's not that easy. I have certain responsibilities, as do you, which I cannot just drop like a hat."

"Like what?"

"Like a hat."

"No like what responsibilities?"

"Like a yellow-eyed pregnant woman, a rhyming fool, and a guy who thinks the devil is the detail keeping him in jail. Not to mention my kid on death row. Should I twirl tiny umbrellas between thumb and forefinger while watching the sun sink into the ocean and forget these people?"

"Precisely, are you the only attorney left in New York? If you leave will those people get plumbers assigned to represent them?"

"So put my faith in the competence of unknown others? I do that about as often as you express doubt."

"Well put perhaps, and probably justified. You're staying you're saying."

"Yes, until that stuff's done I'm staying."

"And in the meantime you'll be picking up more stuff."

"I'm not in arraignments for a while as fate would have it."

"So you don't want to come get your money? Don't want to at least see it? It's truly beautiful when completely laid out before you."

"No I'm too busy, I'm writing. I'm a writer now."

"Writing what?"

"A brief."

"Writing? Told you I tried that when I first failed at perfection didn't I? It doesn't work, but find out for yourself if you must."

"My writing has nothing to do with a failed attempt at perfection because remember that I never made one."

"Fine but what's the harm in coming with me now to look at your money? What's the most you've ever eyeballed at once?"

"Not until this detective thing is settled."

"As you wish, I'm leaving now. If you change your mind about seeing it let me know. I'll be hanging around a bit longer, truth is I'm rather enjoying the idleness. Also get that detective's name when you can and we'll take care of that. Escalera and The Whale? We'll just see what happens, goodbye Casi."

"Yes, good."

He closed the door behind him and I sat on the floor. I had this hand-me-down (multiple times) area rug covering the hardwood floors and I picked and pulled at its stray threads. It was so quiet. I lived alone. I wondered how I could have come to live alone. I thought how if I stayed in that space a full week, for example, and didn't press any buttons I could conceivably go that entire time without hearing another human voice. That in a city with more people than many countries. I tried, concentrating, to *hear* something, anything, but there was no sound anywhere. The walls that normally felt like they were so close to themselves they might kiss now seemed to recede from me and each other. The place felt immense, in both size and spirit, and I was alone and adrift in it, searching in vain for any sound that might reassure me, betrayed by a silent emptiness that grew out into the stillness. I started talking:

"It's true," I said. "I should be exulting."

I said it was certainly the case that many things I had to worry about before 410 were no longer concerns. I have a lot of money I said.

"Of course, now I have a whole new set of worries," I said. "Like what do I do with that money? Where do I keep it? How do I convert it into a spendable resource? *Laundering* the money is the term you're looking for," I added.

736

I stood and walked to the mirror.

"Launder as in to make clean what was once dirty. But what if there are things that once sullied cannot be fully cleansed? That notion may be true. True as it is indisputably true that you have done things that cannot be erased or taken back."

I looked away.

"Then there's the matter of possibly getting caught with all that entails," I concluded and silently decided that this last worry was the greatest of all and rendered the others meaningless. I resolved not to think about the future and what it might bring.

Instead I would enjoy that moment, a moment when someone not overly concerned with accuracy could say I was contentedly sitting on top of the world.

The same place Benitez sat after beating Duran in January of 1982.

The natural next move for Benitez was a rematch against Sugar Ray Leonard but barring that – and Leonard showed no inclination to grant Wilfred that rematch – another logical move was a fight with either of the two remaining members of The Quintet (Benitez, Duran, Hagler, Hearns, Leonard) Benitez had yet to face. Rather than move up another weight class to fight Hagler, Benitez decided to make the first defense of his WBC junior-middleweight title against Thomas Hearns. The fight was scheduled for December 3, 1982, marking the longest stretch between fights for Benitez to that point. Hearns was moving up in weight but at over six feet he had always been exceedingly tall for a welterweight and the move was expected to only benefit him. Coming off his loss to Leonard he promised to be highly motivated for the critical championship fight and his two knockouts of admittedly nondescript opponents leading into the fight with Benitez seemed to indicate that the devastating defeat to Leonard had not caused him any irreparable damage or robbed him of his crippling power. The fight would feature these two brilliant fighters at their peak and predictions were pretty much split down the middle.

Developments leading up to the fight only increased the signifi-cance of the matchup. After losing to Benitez, Duran returned to the ring on September 4th in Hearns's Detroit against some Brit named Kirkland Laing. He looked old and meek and, whether he decided to retire or not following the well-earned ten-round decision defeat to a barely capable retread, the fight surely signaled, everyone agreed, the end of Duran's career as a premier fighter.

After defending his World Welterweight Championship with a third-round knockout of Bruce Finch in Reno, Sugar Ray Leonard began to complain of vision problems or *floaters*. He was diagnosed with a detached retina in his left eye (the one that had swollen to gory proportions against Hearns) and three months after the fight had surgery to repair the problem. He was warned of the danger of losing his eyesight if he continued to box. On November 9, 1982, during an odd press conference for some reason held in and around the boxing ring where he made his professional debut, Leonard announced his retirement from Boxing, lamenting that he would not be fighting Marvin Hagler in the fight the universe most longed to see.

The loss of Leonard and the perceived elimination of Duran meant the upcoming Benitez/Hearns fight would create a clear challenger to Hagler and make whoever of the three managed to ultimately emerge the biggest star in Boxing. Along with the bout's significance there was considerable interest in seeing Boxing's most skilled boxer against its most fearsome puncher; the fight would feature one of the great-est defensive fighters ever against one of the best offensive ones and it wasn't entirely clear how it would unfold. On a personal level for Benitez, who had accomplished more than Hearns to that point, a decisive victory would all but erase the negative impact of his only loss. Benitez seemed to recognize the importance of the fight as well as the unique threat Hearns presented because he trained as much as he ever did. And good because on December 3, 1982, in New Orleans, in the ring just before the opening bell, Thomas Hearns looked scary.

The extra seven pounds he was allowed at junior-middleweight appeared to consist entirely of sinewy but granite muscle. Whereas at welterweight he had looked freakishly thin, against Benitez he looked very much like the human cobra his nickname implied he was. Benitez looked good too, solid, but next to Hearns maybe small.

From the outset, Benitez, like every single human who would ever step into the ring with Hearns, was wary of his opponent's power, especially from the right cross. As a result he moved a lot and Hearns established a good jab and crisp punches while stalking Benitez and wisely eschewing punches to his elusive head for solid body punches. In that manner Benitez ceded the first three rounds as it became apparent he would have significant trouble getting inside Hearns's long punches to land his own. In the fourth he seemed to solve Hearns a bit, fighting more effectively to win the round and also benefiting from a point deduction by the ref. He appeared to have weathered the storm that was the early rounds against Hearns and seemed ready to begin winning rounds and imposing his skillful will.

But Hearns was too good and in the fifth he bounced a right cross off the top of Benitez's head so powerfully that Wilfred seemed to lose his legs for a moment until he fell forward, his gloves landing on the canvas for an official knockdown. He survived, but in the sixth he caught another right cross flush at the end of the round and after bending exaggeratedly at the waist he fell back against the ropes in deep trouble until the bell saved him. After a seventh and eighth round that featured more, albeit less dramatic, Hearns dominance, Benitez had a decision to make.

He was clearly losing the fight. Hearns looked simply awesome that night. He was bigger and stronger. He had hand speed that was at least equal to that of Benitez. In Emanuel Steward he had an all-time great trainer and in accordance with his instructions he was executing a perfect game plan. Worst of all was the inhuman power. Benitez felt all the punches, even the ones he blocked. A Hearns punch that landed on his arm, for example, would deaden that spot for minutes.

On the other hand, as the Leonard fight had shown, if Hearns had any weakness it was his chin and stamina. To have any chance to win Benitez would have to go against his nature by forcing his way inside the reach of The Hitman to try and land the bomb that would change the fight. And that was the decision that needed to be made because the fact was that as great as Hearns was offensively, if Benitez dedicated his efforts principally to avoiding being hit he would not be hit. It was that simple and that certain. It was an option. He could go into a defensive shell and circle the ring. He would lose a decision, true, but he would avoid embarrassment and avoid needless pain. Then he could simply say that Hearns's particular style was too difficult for him and people would agree and no-one would fault him too much.

The other option meant getting inside no matter the cost. It meant throwing punches once inside, which meant by necessity getting hit hard and often by punches that Benitez already knew from most recent experience would hurt and possibly knock him unconscious. And either tomorrow or years from now, thousands or millions, when Time has ground our bones into an ashy mist and the very Earth we now inhabit has drifted into its third-generation sun, let the record reflect that Wilfred Benitez, who had more money than a thousand people needed, who'd been bred since infancy to fight at the expense of all else, who seemed like a perpetual child who did not take his career seriously, understood his responsibilities and chose to fight. Let it reflect that he bounced a left hook off the top of The Hitman's head and that head fell to the canvas as a result. That he came forward winging his fists like he had done since he was seven and that, as expected, he took ugly shots to the head in return. That some of those shots momentarily disrupted communication from his brain to his legs but he never fell again. That he would take two to land one but that he kept taking them, kept trying to win. That he did not relinquish greatness easily but that it had to be forcefully wrested from his grip by overwhelming superior force.

When the fight was over Benitez smiled as always and hugged Hearns. One judge had it a draw but the other two were decidedly for Hearns. The announcers reminded their audience that Benitez was still only twenty-four. They said you could still expect great things from him in his future. If told what that future would hold they would not likely have believed it.

I said nothing the whole time I thought about that and now the silence was bugging me again so I released some music into the room. What was I thinking protesting the quiet? Silence was a gift. You needed it to listen to real music and my ear was mysteriously better to boot. I closed my eyes. It was rapturous.

But I wondered if there wasn't something wrong with my C.D. because I heard a faint percussive knocking I didn't recognize, although I mentally acknowledged I could've simply failed to notice it before since, healthy or not, I didn't have the best ear.

Or a simpler explanation could be that there was someone knocking on my door, which there was. When I opened the door I saw Herbert. He was wearing a light-colored, possibly white, satiny jacket and holding what appeared to be a bowling bag.

"Hi Herbert," I said.

"Call me Herb," said Herb.

"Done."

"The music."

"I'm sorry was it too loud?"

"No pal o'mine, I just noticed you went right to the second movement."

"Oh, yeah, uh."

"Well, as I'm sure you know, the second movement of the Eroica is a funeral march. A *funeral* march, y'unnerstand?" his eyebrows rising in wait.

"O.K., and?"

"Well it's just that when someone goes right to the funeral like that I start thinking maybe something's wrong you know buddy?"

"Nothing's wrong."

"That's right pal. Nothing *is* wrong. You keep listening to that music is what you should do. There didn't have to be music you know. Anyway I hope this isn't about what I told you with the detective and all. Because that's nothing to concern yourself about."

"Why do you say that Herb?"

"Call me Jackie," said Jackie.

"Fine Jackie but why do you say I shouldn't be concerned? Not that I am mind you."

"It's like this letter I once got saying the government was investigating my taxes. You shoulda seen how I got myself all worked up over it, hoo ho! I had myself convinced I was being investigated for not reporting a clock with a horse in its stomach, I mean a horse with a clock in its stomach ha ha!"

"So what happened?"

"Oh my friend calmed me down. Anyway pal, wanna go bowling?"

"Bowling?"

"Yeah, you do bowl don't you?"

"Sure all the time. Well I mean I bowl quite a bit. Actually, well, I have bowled in the past, once or twice, maybe, I think."

"Let's go then."

"No I better stay, I have a lot of work to do."

"Oh yeah? Whattya do?"

"I write."

"O.K., suit yourself pal."

"Before you go Jackie."

"Yeah?"

"How did your friend calm you down that time with the tax investigation?"

"Oh I see. Well think of it this way. This detective that's investigating you."

"I'm not sure I'd call it that but what about him?"

"Can he put you up in front of a firing squad?"

"No."

"Can he push you over a cliff?"

"No."

"Can he string you up there on the end of a rope?"

"No I guess not," I laughed slightly. I felt better. Jackie was right. "Thanks Jackie, I feel better, you're right," I said.

"Never mind that Jackie business," he said walking to the door and turning his considerable back to me. "Call me Ralph."

"Ralph," I muttered.

Ralph opened the door and started to walk out. Then he popped his head back in. "The worst he can do to you is send you to the federal pen!" he said and immediately left.

I sat back down. The federal pen. Ralph was right. Well it wouldn't be a *federal* pen but at that moment it seemed almost probable that I would end in state prison. It was true that the press had already lost interest in the 123rd Street Massacre but that was only because the monster wasn't being fed anything new. The arrest of a public defender with a weird name for any involvement in the deaths, however peripheral, would certainly qualify as a press case.

Given that, and the D.A.'s office usual reaction to those types of cases, I thought I'd be fortunate to get something like five years determinate on a plea. Five years in lonely prison, I would do six/sevenths of that.

I wouldn't talk to anyone the whole time I was there. I would pull what that guy who accepted Chekhov's Bet did where he read everything under the sun while voluntarily imprisoned for fifteen years. I would read everything ever published; I would learn a few more languages, learn all day and every day. It would actually be a great deal of fun in that sense. I would have some time to think. I could write. Not briefs or anything boring like that, majestic stuff. No less a supernova than *El Ingenioso Hidalgo Don Quixote de la Mancha* was detonated from prison. I could write about what happened to me, what I did, nah.

"I should just pipe down is what I should do," I said. "I have too much to do to sit around here thinking of this bullshit. The only thing I should be thinking about is the writing I have to do. I'm going to go outside and get some fresh air then come back and write until I drop, how's that?"

I left the door open and went outside. Ralph was gone. It was less cold that day. I walked half a block and felt someone following me, first just with their eyes then with their entire body. I stopped and waited. He came up to me.

"Casi?" he said.

"What?"

"Are you Casi?"

"Never heard of him."

"I happen to know you're Casi."

"Oh Casi you said?"

"Correct."

"Never heard of him."

"Can I have a moment of your time?"

"No."

"I think you'll want to talk to me."

"You do? Why's that?"

"Because I know what you did."

Chapter 14 + 7 + 4 + 2 + 1

How disconcerting really. Imagine looking someone directly in the face and seeing only your doubled image looking back at you. He wore those ridiculous mirror sunglasses that usually only state troopers are oblivious enough to wear. Against the skin of my chest I could feel my heart press. My entire body tightened into itself trying in vain to disappear.

"What, who are you?" I said.

"Detective Mondongo Assado," he said extending his hand. I started to put my hand forward then pulled it right back when he again said "I know what you did."

"Are you having some kind of mental difficulty Detective?" I said.

He smiled and seemed to think better of his approach. "I'm sorry," he said, "I didn't mean to be confusing or to sound adversarial either," and that's when I knew I was in trouble and needed to get my head out of my ass quickly.

"What do you want? I'm in a hurry."

"It's about a former client of yours, Ramon DeLeon."

"Oh so you're one of the geniuses helped get him killed?"

"So you know what happened?"

"Yeah I know what happened. He was cooperating with you guys and next thing I know he's on the front page of The Post. Good work. I'll be sure to steer some more clients your collective way."

"Just curious, how do you know what happened?"

"How could I not?"

"What I mean is that you certainly couldn't have told from the picture in the Post and I'm sure there are several Ramon DeLeons, so how did you know?"

"This might be difficult for a New York City detective to comprehend but most people can put two and two together and get four."

"I see, so you had no inside information, just what you read in the papers?"

"Is this what you came to see me about? How I could know that the DeLeon killed was my DeLeon or should I say *your* DeLeon since he was cooperating with you guys and signed an agreement in which you collectively promised to protect him."

"I had nothing to do with his cooperation as you know. I'm a homicide detective. And besides, from what I understand, he stopped cooperating well prior to his murder."

"I see, can you blame him?"

"I'm more interested in what happened the night he and the others were killed."

"O.K., well, good luck with that."

"I thought maybe you could help me."

"I'm sure I could."

"Really? So you admit you have information?"

"None at all. But based on what I perceive to be the quality of you and your colleagues' work, if put in charge of the case, I'm quite sure I could do better, meaning I *could* help you. That said, as you might have heard, I'm kind of on the other side of you guys so I don't do much crime-solving."

"Except that, as I said, based on my investigation, I think you happen to know a lot about this incident."

"I think your exact words, twice, were that you knew what I had done. So what exactly is it you think I *did*."

"I misspoke if I said that. Although it does occur to me that perhaps you better hope you're right about my ability to solve crimes."

"There's no *if you said that*, that's what you said. As far as what I know about what happened, I certainly don't know anything that the D.A. and the detectives who were there for the meeting don't know, so just talk to them. After that if you still want to talk to me, get me at work or through the D.A."

"Strange."

". . ."

"Strange I said."

"What is?"

"Just that if a client of mine was brutally killed I like to think I would want to assist in the investigation as much as possible. I don't know how to interpret your reluctance, unless you have something to hide that is."

"Or unless, as is the case, I simply know I have nothing to say that could help your investigation."

"Well, with all due respect, you couldn't possibly know that without talking to me about it."

"So talk, you're right, tell me what you know and I'll try to be of assistance."

He looked at me with those mirrors and said nothing. I felt better. I thought he would leave. That I would never see him again. That everything would still be good. Then he asked if I was hungry and when I shrugged added that we should get something to eat and discuss what happened, that it would be better than him going through the courts and compelling me to talk and that it would be a means of clearing myself of any suspicion, not that there was any he was quick to add. I felt a form of violence well up in me at the sound of those last words. I wanted to seize his face with my bare hands and tear it off his head. I smiled and said sure.

We went to a nearby diner no-one ever went to where even the limited staff seemed surprised to see us and maybe unsure of what to do in response. We ordered and started getting food in record speed. I felt anger mixed with mounting fear.

"So you knew about this big deal that was going to happen Wednesday morning right?"

"What big deal?"

"Yes, this big exchange on 123rd Street that resulted in DeLeon being killed in the street."

"No."

"You're saying you weren't at the meeting with DeLeon and the D.A.?"

"No I'm not saying that, but that's not what you asked me."

"Well wasn't the deal discussed at this meeting, a meeting that was attended by only you and four others?"

"Not to my recollection."

"You're saying the deal wasn't discussed?"

"A deal was discussed as I recall. But it wasn't for any Wednesday morning and it wasn't at 123rd Street either."

"I see, when was it for?"

"A Saturday I believe."

"Where?"

"Not sure but on the West Side somewhere, Riverside Drive maybe, but not on 123rd that I'm sure of."

"Why did you stay for the meeting?"

"Why wouldn't I? I was Mr DeLeon's attorney as you pointed out."

"So you had inside information about this high-level deal that would be going down right? With all that money involved."

"I guess not."

"What do you mean? You just said you were there didn't you?"

"I was there, that's true, but apparently I didn't possess any true information since it appears that Mr DeLeon was either lying to the D.A. or the upcoming meeting he was talking about was subsequently cancelled. Or are you saying it in fact went off in the manner he said it would?"

"I can't discuss that."

"Thought you wanted my help?"

"Did you know he was giving the D.A. false information?"

"So it was false? Intentionally so?"

"Yes, it was. Did you know?"

"No, how could I given that neither the D.A. nor the detectives apparently knew and they were certainly a great deal more familiar with the subject than I was."

"Of course DeLeon could have confided in you that what he was giving them was untrue and it follows that he could have gone so far as to give you the true information."

"That's funny, you think our clients tell us the truth huh? They don't do it when it would benefit them, what would've been the reason for doing so here? What exactly is your theory Assado? That I knew when the meeting was really taking place and went there and killed DeLeon so I would have one less case to worry about?"

"When was the last time you saw DeLeon?"

"I guess the day he was sentenced, the day after the meeting with the D.A. as I recall."

"Did you ever talk to him after that?"

"No, next I heard about it was the D.A. telling me he had lost him and would be asking for a warrant."

"Did you tell the D.A. you had reason to doubt the information DeLeon gave?"

"No, that would assume I *had* a reason to doubt it."

"So you believed it to be true?"

"I guess but I also didn't give it much thought. It didn't carry much importance to me either way. I just handled the cooperation, what happened after that was not really any of my concern. You sure you're a detective?"

"Why do you say that?"

"Just that some of your questions betray an almost complete lack of understanding of a defense attorney's role in representing a C.I."

He shut up and ate. I mentally debated plunging my fork into his face. I ate but not really. I stared at him. He was older with gray facial hair that made his face look like a baseball glove that had been left out in the rain. Thin too. The skin under his black eyes sagged and every vein on his hands bulged like rivers on a relief map. After an interminable time . . . he looked back at me.

"You asked before about my theory," he said. "I think that somebody knew about that meeting Wednesday, knew a lot of money would be there. Somebody not directly involved, someone neither of the parties gave much thought to, and somebody they certainly didn't expect to see on the night of the exchange. I think that this person or persons broke into 410 123rd Street at the time of the meeting with the intention of stealing the money and that as a result things got a little violent leading to the death of DeLeon and pretty much everybody else there. I think they got the money. I think they killed some people. That's my theory."

"O.K."

"Now I have to go soon and thank you for meeting with me but I do have one last question for you, which is what do *you* think about what I just said?"

"What *I* think? Well obviously I have no way of knowing whether or not yours is a good theory since I don't really know any of the facts you're basing it on."

"True I guess. Tell you what. I'll keep working this thing up, then we'll talk some more. How's that sound?"

"Annoying."

"Maybe I'll bring you some of the photos of DeLeon. You couldn't see the face in the papers. As you probably know, he was shot in the face."

"No, how would I know that?"

"Point blank range too. You can make out the face, that's what people don't get. Really half the face was almost unaffected. The other half of course looks like ground meat with occasional skin mixed in. His mother's really counting on me to find the person who did this. His mother."

". . ."

"I'll bring you the pictures. Know what I think when I look at them?"

". . ."

"Do you know?"

"What?"

"I'm just grateful I had nothing to do with what happened to him or the other people inside that apartment you know? I'll bring you the pictures of all of them. I think you should see them. What I mean by saying I'm grateful is this. For whatever reason I think we all carry around with us the results of our actions. They trail us like the train on a wedding dress. Trust me on this, I'm a lot older than you. I wouldn't want that face, the one I saw in the pictures, following me is alls I'm saying."

". . ."

"Is there anything you want to tell me?"

"Yes I better."

"Go ahead."

"Thanks for the food."

". . ."

"I mean it, thanks."

"O.K., we'll talk soon. I'll be back, we're not done yet Casi."

He stood up but didn't leave. There seemed to be no reason to say anything anymore, to keep up any appearances.

It was quiet. Then a waitress started laughing.

He looked at me some more. I looked down and after a while heard him walk away.

I was the only person left in the diner who didn't work there. I drank more coffee then left, walking home as slow as possible and avoiding the sidewalk cracks.

Back in my apartment I couldn't remember the reason I had gone out. The only person I wanted to talk to was Dane but my phone was still broken. Now I realized what was going to happen to me in the very near future so I knew I had to hurry.

I put on slight music I could ignore and started to write. The type of this music I most favored they no longer made. Turns out they asked around one day and I was the only one enjoying it so they decided to just stop making it. Most of the bands that were making the music when this decision was made simply disappeared and got real jobs, the ones that survived made different music that appealed to more people. The result was that when I listened to that music it felt a bit like traveling to the past or visiting ghosts, and this despite the undeniable fact that a very healthy portion of the music I listened to otherwise was created a far longer time ago, by people long departed, yet produced no similar feelings.

I wrote all weekend. I never left the house. I ate whatever was in the fridge and slept on the sofa when I was tired. Monday I went in real late so I spent almost three full days in that condition.

I wrote about how preteens had fixed it so that Kingg would fall on his head. How they did this because he looked and acted differently than them. I wrote that he began to have seizures following this head injury then attached and referred to the meager medical records we had in support. I wrote how Kingg hadn't been in the greatest mental shape even before that and attached those records as well.

I included information about Kingg's home life. How you couldn't find his father if you combed the earth. How his mother never stopped working for a minute but never made more than legislative minimums her whole life before dying in wait for a new kidney. I described where they lived and how, and reminded the court of the kind of schooling the young Kingg received. I told them about the various live-in boyfriends of Ms Kingg and the impressions they chose to leave on Jalen.

I cited cases, all asserted as persuasive not binding authority, for the proposition that we should not execute someone like Kingg. Aside from that I reminded them of what Jalen's attorney had done. How he had sat there like a constitutionally ineffective potted plant. A plant that couldn't be troubled to have Kingg examined or to present the slightest evidence of an impairment that should have been obvious and this during a phase of the trial that amounts to nothing more than an invitation for precisely that information. I just kept writing and watched the thing grow to absurd proportions.

The day I had to return to work I woke up early and started writing again. Only at that early hour, working on very little sleep, I kind of lost my mind a bit. I wrote that certain things were leaving me nauseated. I said that judges made me feel that way. Not most of them but all of them. I said that you for example, the judge I'm writing this to, made me feel nauseated. The nausea came from understanding that people produced by every conceivable advantage got to decide whether someone like Jalen lived or died and what was worse was they never fucking seemed to decide that the person should live, that a person's life, any person, was more important than whether some fat fuck at a country club thought you were hard enough on crime or whether you continue to get sufficient reelection campaign contributions you worthless retarded piece of shit. Why should you be allowed to decide anything beyond what you have for lunch you mental infant?

Nausea-inducing things like that I put in the actual brief. My fingers moved and the words appeared in the document. I felt sick. My head hurt so much. The room spun. I knew everything was going badly for me but felt powerless to change anything. I tried to vomit

753

but couldn't because I hadn't eaten in so long, instead my empty stomach would dryly convulse, tearing my eyes and leaving a painful burning reminder in my throat.

I walked into the nearest suit and stumbled out the door. I knew then why my ear had stopped hurting. Whatever had previously haunted it had obviously moved to my brain. There it surely lay, causing severe pain to the surrounding head and slowly spreading its dendritic margins until it would ultimately occlude the organ and my life entire. The steps I took down the stairs were wobbly and unsure and when I opened the door and stepped outside the cold made me feel sicker. At the bottom of the steps stood a man looking directly at my face. It was Detective Assado.

"Hello," he said.

I walked down the steps and stood across from him.

"Are you alright?" he said. "You don't look good at all."

I looked at him but said nothing.

"I got those pictures you wanted to see."

"I never said I wanted to see any pictures," I said. "You were the one with the pictures."

He started to take them out. I began retching again with nothing produced except more pain. Then I coughed a lot and when I spit out the results it looked like blood. I wiped my mouth with my sleeve. I was bent over, my hands on my knees. I looked up at him, raising my head only slightly.

"Well I went through a lot of trouble to get these so I'm sure you won't want to be rude."

I stood up. Through the tears in my eyes he looked stroboscopic. He held the picture up for me to see the way limo drivers hold their signs up at airports. "What are those marks on your neck by the way? I meant to ask you last time." When I ignored him he went on yapping like it was the most natural thing in the world to be so treated.

"I have to go," I said.

"I need to talk to you some more actually. Let's talk right here and get it over with."

"It's cold."

"It's not bad. I think it's starting to warm up." I sat on a step and put my face in my hands. What could I do, he kept talking. "See I think someone went in there that night and took the money."

"What money?"

"The records we found indicate the presence of quite a bit of money. Money to pay for the considerable amount of drugs involved. Only while we found the drugs, mixed in among the bodies, we never found any money."

"So?"

"So someone took the money. And it was a third party not directly involved in the transaction."

"Why do you say that?"

"Well the people in the house already owned the money they were going to use to buy the drugs so they wouldn't steal their own money right? And if the people who brought the drugs stole the money then why even bring the drugs like they did?"

"Who says it was stolen at all? Looks to me like the deal went off as planned. The drugs are where you say they're supposed to be and the money is gone, taken by the people who sold the drugs. Why do you need a third party?"

"Except that clearly the plan was not followed, something went wrong. I saw the bodies to prove it."

"Fine, the buyers didn't want to pay so the sellers took the money forcibly, hence the bodies. I still don't see a third party Detective. More importantly what exactly does any of this have to do with me?"

"Do you recognize this guy?" he said handing me a picture. I recognized the person pictured as one of the lookouts. Heckle. He was on the same roof where I last saw him, in a drowning pool of his viscera with police tape circling him.

"Of course not," I said. Then I looked closer. "Wait a minute, wait a minute during which cotton is picked," I said. "Yep, that's him. He sold me a pair of shoes once the prick. Really bad but expensive shoes." I handed the picture back to him. "If you ask me, he got what was coming to him. I'd look at disgruntled shoe shoppers Detective."

He stared at me. I stood up straight and stared back.

"The third party we're looking for came in from the roof and killed that individual. As always the person left traces behind that we will eventually use to catch him. I felt sure you would recognize the person in that picture. From the roof. But I guess not right? That's what you're saying?"

"It is."

"Anyway I been doing this for twenty-eight years and my experience is that when we do catch you, I mean this guy, he'll be almost relieved. He'll be able to unburden himself, know what I mean?"

"No."

"It's not easy to kill."

"Lucky for you."

"Sure there's the insane. But whoever did this wasn't insane. This took careful, almost morally responsible, planning."

"I have to go I'm late."

"The person will be relieved," he said and I thought I saw a sneer.

Alone in my office I started writing again, this time in longhand. I didn't have to go to court that day so Jalen was everything then. When I took a break Mr Melvyn Toomberg Esq. came in.

"What are you doing?" he said.

"Writing Jalen a letter."

"Really?"

"Yeah I've been writing him more letters since I got back."

"And he writes you back?"

"He does."

"Just keeping him posted?"

"Exactly."

"And your progress?"

"Believe it or otherwise I think I'm almost done, look." I handed him the stack of paper.

"What's this?"

"My point."

"You're kidding."

"I never kid, you know that."

"When did you . . . it's huge . . . it's . . ."

"I know. Would you mind editing it to fit the page limit and all that when I'm done? I'm just no good at concision."

"Actually there's no page limit."

"No page limit? Yahoo, I'm just getting started then."

"There's no statutory page limit but I have to think there's a practical one to how much these judges or more accurately their clerks will read attentively. I don't understand how it could be that long though."

"It's not really that long if you look at it from a certain perspective, provided of course that perspective is one from which things that are very lengthy nonetheless appear to be quite short either due to Lorentz contraction or some other as yet undiscovered phenomenon. I'm sure you know what I mean."

"Are you O.K. Casi? I mean physically."

"Physically?"

"Yes."

"Meaning you take it as a given I'm not O.K. otherwise."

"No it's just that, well, you look quite bad, no offense. Again, physically."

"Well I've been *working* man. How do you want me to look? Isn't work what you wanted? I haven't eaten or slept and I've seriously cut down on my breathing too. Also there's this detective, never mind."

"Your neck, I asked you before, what are those marks?"

"Oh those."

"What are they?"

"Liszt did that."

"Liszt?"

"Yeah I promised I wouldn't tell anyone but he tried to strangle me in retaliation for what I did to his wall. Notice how the bruises perfectly match his paws?"

"Be serious."

"Don't worry about it, how's your point going?"

"Up until a few minutes ago I thought well. Then I saw this, it's quite imposing."

"But there's no limit right?"

"Right."

"And you'll be ready to argue it?"

"Me? I always assumed you would argue it. I feel confident in asserting you are better at that sort of thing."

"Not really Toom, you're smarter. That's all that counts. Besides I may not be around, I don't think I'll be around."

"Where are you going?"

"No just that, you know with the hearings and, just be prepared to argue it is what I'm saying. I'm just concentrating on this you know. When I finish this I'll know I did something and whatever happens after that I can live with, know what I mean?"

"No, not really."

"Let's just save this kid that's all. Save the kid. Everything else is getting fucked up. I fucked it all up. But this is good, no doubt. Come by tomorrow and I'll have the finished product waiting for you. Well, in need of your editing touch of course, but for all intents and purposes finished."

758

"Look if this is about the hearing in a couple of weeks I just want to assure you that I'm going to handle it to the best of my abilities and I'm optimistic."

"I know, thank you. Come by tomorrow and get the brief."

"Wednesday's the big day you know. The Supreme Court hears argument in Atkins versus Virginia, in which they will decide whether states can continue to execute the mentally retarded."

"That's Wednesday?"

"Yes it is. Of course even a good ruling would probably instigate a great deal of litigation on who fits into that classification and would take our representation of Jalen into yet another direction but nonetheless I am cautiously optimistic."

"We'll see what happens."

"I think it's going to be a good result."

"I know, come by tomorrow and get that O.K.?"

"Yes."

Later that day I got a page from Denise saying someone in the reception area wanted to talk to me. I knew it would be Assado but still found it somehow shocking when I stepped out and saw him.

"You said I could come talk to you here so I thought I'd share my latest thoughts with you."

"I'm busy."

"Won't take long."

"What are they?" eyes closed, forehead in hand.

"Just that it occurs to me that I still haven't asked you the clichéd question you've probably been expecting."

"Which is?"

"Where were you on Wednesday? Isn't that how they show it on T.V. and then at the end I tell you not to leave town?"

"I wouldn't know."

"So where were you last Wednesday counselor?"

"Like everyone else I guess I was shopping for candles."

"You're right, I should be more specific. Where were you early Wednesday morning before the blackout? Say three in the morning."

"Three in the morning?"

"Yes."

"Sleeping like always."

"You sure?"

"Quite."

"Strange."

". . ."

"That's strange."

"What is?"

"No because I talked to your neighbors. You know the four guys that live below you? And they said that on that Wednesday morning, at that time, you weren't home."

"I'm curious how they would know. They're neighbors not room-mates."

"True but they said, one of them in particular, that they were knocking on your door at that time and got no answer. Something about wanting to introduce you to a new friend."

"They're mistaken."

"Normally I might agree except that as you know this was just prior to the blackout, which was certainly the kind of memorable event that would stick in someone's mind you know?"

"I don't understand. Are they saying that when I didn't respond to the knocks they broke down the door and conducted a thorough search of my bed and my entire apartment and established that I wasn't there?"

"No."

"Because otherwise I fail to see how not answering a knock on your door at three in the morning is evidence of anything other than maybe sanity."

"So you didn't hear any knocking."

"In my bed sleeping, I failed to hear it that's right."

"I see and you're sure you were in bed?"

"Where else would I be? I have to get my sleep don't I?"

"O.K., but one other thing."

"Uh-huh."

"Could you get me a picture of yourself?"

"Why?"

"Well it seems there were eyewitnesses to the incident we've been talking about. I just want to show them a picture of you so we can maybe rule you out and we can stop meeting like this. Of course I could get just get your O.C.A. picture but this would be quicker and I'm sure you want to be cooperative right?"

"We done? That all?"

"There is one last thing actually."

"What's that?"

"Don't leave town."

I went home shortly after that. Everywhere I stepped I looked around for Assado. On the way up to my apartment I stopped at Alyona's and banged on the door. No answer. I banged harder and Ralph answered the door. He was wearing the same bluish uniform from the other day.

"Hey pal," he said.

"Ralph?"

"That's my name, don't wear it out, ho ho!"

"Is Angus home, or any of the others?"

"Just me pal."

"You live here now?"

"Soytenly, for now anyways."

"So where are those guys, I haven't seen them in a good while. I think since the end of the blackout really, almost a week."

"Beats me."

"No idea?"

"No, you must be just missing them, what's the big deal?"

"Just real weird is all. I've lived here over a year and during that period I don't think I remember a time when all of them were out of this apartment at the same time like this and now suddenly I haven't seen any of them in like a week."

"What are you inferring?"

"Nothing I—"

"No I know what you're inferring! You're saying I had something to do with their disappearance!"

"Their what?"

"Pins and needles, needles and pins, it's a happy man that grins," he said. Then he forced a small smile with his lips pressed tightly together. "Now what am I angry about?" he said serenely. "I know what I'm angry about! *You* accused me of moyder!"

"Take it easy Ralph. I did no such thing. I just wondered if you knew where they were since you said you live here now."

"Alright pal, you're right. I just get steamed. When I'm in the right, I'm in the right."

"O.K. I'll be seeing you."

"Oh someone came by to see you but you weren't in. Tori, Tara, Terry something like that."

"Traci?"

"Yeah that's it."

"Came by to see *me*? Or came here?"

"No she never came here. She was coming down from your door, she asked if I knew where you were. Everyone's always asking me if I know where someone is in this place."

"Amazing. Did she leave a number, an address, anything?"

"No. Quite a comely young lady at that pal. If I weren't married."

"You're married?"

"Sure, how else would I have a wife?"

"What's her name?"

"Whose?"

"Your wife."

"Why Alice of course."

"Got to go," I said.

The news about Traci was beyond thrilling. I could think of little else even though I was supposed to be writing. Instead I paced around my apartment wondering how I could possibly contact her in the absence of a surname. I did feel much better. I shaved and showered and got dressed in case she came back. Then I practiced spontaneously greeting her and rehearsed some ad-libs. I longed to see her, maybe she would be wearing a hat, and it wasn't as cold as before so she might even be wearing a skirt or something.

The next morning I jumped out of bed with actual energy. I had eaten. I showered again put on my sharpest suit and, after looking out my window to make sure no-one was out there waiting for me, whistled various happy tunes as I walked out the door. It was liberating to think how I would never see Assado again, had all the money I would ever need, and would soon connect with the very yummy Traci. And that's the way I felt, relieved and calm, until the very moment I stepped outside and saw Assado staring at me from the sidewalk.

"Goddamnit," I said.

"Oh great," Assado said. "What a fortunate coincidence, I need to talk to you."

"I'm late for work."

"This won't take long, you have that picture?"

"No."

"I thought you wanted to cooperate?"

". . ."

"Never mind I'll get the O.C.A. What I wanted to ask you was whether you've heard of the Video Vigilantes."

"Go ahead."

"O.K., have you heard of the Video Vigilantes?"

"Yes."

"Good, so you know what they do. Well as luck would have it, seems that night they had a camera, or actually several cameras, trained on 410 and the surrounding areas, including the roof."

I literally felt blood rush to my face but said nothing.

"Are you O.K.?"

". . ."

"Well of course we're still waiting to get the actual tape. It has to be located among the thousands the Vigilantes have. But within a few days we should have it and I guess then we'll know for sure if my theory about the roof is right."

"Good for you, good luck with that."

"What do you think I'll see on that tape?"

"I have no idea."

"Really? None?"

"None. Why, what do you think you'll see?"

"Well no point in speculating, won't be long now. Guess I'll be seeing you once I get the tape."

"I don't see why."

"Remember what I said about town."

"What? About it not being big enough for the both of us?"

"Funny. No about not leaving it."

"Where would I go? I love New York. You know I've been thinking about it and really the best way to put it is that this city never sleeps."

He nodded his head up and down. "Goodbye counselor," he said and left.

I went back upstairs, called the office to say I wouldn't be in until

764

the afternoon, and resumed writing. For the next several hours I lost myself in what I was doing and I don't think stopped typing for more than twenty seconds at a time. When I finished I was done. I printed the brief, stuck it in a box, and went to the office.

Toomberg wasn't in his office when I stopped by with the box late that afternoon. I left it on his desk with a hastily composed note and looked around. There were all sorts of diplomas and plaudits and seemingly any tome ever created with The Law as justification. As I walked out he came in:

"I finished it," I said. "Left it on your desk."

"Really? Great I'll bring it home tonight. I'll probably finish reading it tomorrow on the long train ride."

"Train?"

"Yes I'm going to D.C. tomorrow, to watch the argument on *Atkins.*"

"You're going to the Supreme Court?"

"First thing in the morning. Listen, I think it's going to go really well from what I'm hearing."

"Why do you say that?"

"Just from what I'm hearing. You know, the word on the street."

"I'm sorry the what? The street?"

"You know what I mean."

"Listen, don't get your hopes up Toom."

"No it's not just me, I have a friend who clerks for one of the justices and when I talked to him this morning he seemed to maybe agree with me."

"He did?"

"He's a bit tight-lipped so it's hard to say definitively but I thought so"

"That's something I guess."

"Darn tootin."

"What's that with the tootin?"

"I'm sorry I'm just excited. Everything just seems to point to them ruling that you cannot execute the mentally retarded without violating the Eighth Amendment's prohibition against cruel and unusual punishment."

"Just be careful you don't cruelly and unusually punish yourself by getting too excited. Remember until they rule anything's possible. Speaking of, when would they rule?"

"Not for a few months but that's the other great news. Until the Supreme Court rules Alabama can't do anything to Jalen."

"So this thing isn't actually due?"

"No we still need to comply with the time limit to preserve everything but at the very least, regardless of how the court ultimately rules, Jalen has a few more months. Like I said I think the court's going to ultimately save this kid's life. I'm optimistic."

"You really think those nine fucks would do that?"

"Oh, show some respect. That's the Supreme Court of the United States of America and yes I do. Maybe."

"I hope you're right and I've never known you to be otherwise Toomie."

"What's the matter?"

"Just tired, from writing."

"You should go home and rest, you haven't looked good for a while."

"Is Tom back?"

"Vacation."

"Still?"

"That's what I heard."

"This is like the longest vacation ever. What about his case? The woman torched her kid. I'm supposed to be working on it with him and he hasn't talked to me in weeks."

"He got relieved on that."

"What?"

"Sure, a while back. You didn't know?"

"Why?"

"It was right before he went on vacation as I recall."

"Not when, why?"

"No-one knows really."

"What the fuck is going on here exactly?"

No-one knew, I went home.

I did feel better when I thought of Jalen being safe for at least a few more months, couldn't wait to write him with the good news. I supposed Toomberg was right about the respect thing too, especially if the nine were going to rule the way he thought they would.

When I saw Assado sitting in the hallway just to the side of my apartment door it took all my restraint to keep from kicking him in the face. "Who are you?" I said. "Can I help you?"

"I thought you might want to let me take a look around your apartment," he said and he pointed at my door.

"Why would you think that exactly?"

"Well I know you want to cooperate so I thought you would save me the trouble of getting a warrant."

"A warrant, really? A warrant based on what Assado?"

"Detective."

"I'm curious Mondongo, what evidence, if any, you would present in support of that warrant."

"Are you saying I *cannot* enter your apartment?"

"That's right. Now I've answered all your questions, answer my single one. What would you say to get that warrant?"

"Remember before, I told you how I think most of the people I arrest actually feel relief? For whatever the reason, I *have* observed a need to confess among the guilty, a need to purge so to speak. What do you think about that?"

"I think this is as good a time as any to end this conversation as well as any future contact."

"You think? Because frankly I feel like we're just getting started. Have you ever been to confession?"

"No."

"You sure? Because I'm told the person confessing really does feel a lot better afterwards. More to the point, have you heard of a show called *Clerical Confessions*?"

"A show?"

"Yeah on T.V. Well actually it's not T.V it's H.B.O. Heard of it?"

"No."

"You sure? Anyway I guess what happens is they secretly videotape people confessing. As in to a priest, you understand?"

"I think so."

"When I first heard about the show, it's in pre-production now, I didn't give it much thought. But now I picture all sorts of law enforcement possibilities attaching to it. Are you catching my drift? I mean can't you imagine a videotape showing an individual confessing his sensational crime to a priest? Sure there's all sorts of clergy privilege issues but imagine the priest willingly providing the tape apparently in some sort of retaliation for the confessor having destroyed his little cubicle or whatever they call it. Can you imagine all that? What would you make of it?"

"Once again I haven't the slightest idea what you're talking about?"

"Not the slightest?"

"Not."

"O.K. well since you won't let me in I guess I'll be leaving. Of course if you haven't figured it out by now we'll probably be seeing each other fairly soon. Unless there's something you want to say to me now."

"There is."

"Shoot."

"You have change for a dollar?"

He did and after he left I went outside and used it to call Dane from a pay phone.

Quid rides? Mutato nomine de te fibula narrator.
– Horace

Chapter 29

The Benitez/Hearns fight would not be the last between members of The Quintet. Incredibly, the year 1983 would belong to Roberto Duran. The same fighter everyone wrote off as washed-up following his loss to Laing was reborn that year, cementing his status as one of history's truly great fighters in the process.

First, in January of that year, Duran fought Pipino Cuevas. The fight featured two former welterweight champions each trying to register a much-needed significant win. At twenty-six, Cuevas was five years younger than Duran and, having followed the Hearns disaster with two impressive knockout victories and a close decision loss, certainly appeared to have more left than the seemingly spent Duran who had lost two of his last three fights and who had failed to score a knockout victory in eight fights and almost three years. Cuevas appeared to have the clear advantage is what I'm saying. Instead, Duran began his latest series of surprises by stopping Cuevas in the fourth round.

The impressive victory removed some of the taint of the Laing loss and as a result Duran was given a shot at the W.B.A. junior middleweight title held by Davey Moore. Moore, a good fighter with impeccable amateur credentials, was one of Boxing's rising young stars having won his title in just his ninth professional fight and having made three defenses, two of which were highly impressive knockouts of very good fighters. He was far bigger than Duran with a sculpted body and legitimate punching power and he was favored by a clear most. The fight was held on June 16 in Madison Square Garden before a decidedly pro-Duran crowd.

The stage was set for the young champion to finish what Laing had started by convincingly defeating Duran and thereby hastening the end of his career. Of course by the time the fight was stopped by his corner in the eighth round, Moore had lost every round, his eye was grotesquely swollen, he had visited the canvas ass first, his mother had fainted in the audience, and he lay against the ropes with seemingly little clue to where he was or what he should do next. Improbably, Roberto Duran was again a Champion of the World. The arrogant Duran surveyed the boxing landscape and saw no-one he wouldn't fight.

That included Undisputed Middleweight Champion Marvelous Marvin Hagler who had gone to court to make the part starting with Marvelous his legal name. Hagler had all the looks of a dominant champion and I'm not just referring to the bald head, chiseled body, and menacing beard. During his three-year reign he had made seven successful defenses all by impressive knockout and overall he hadn't lost a fight in eight years. As a natural middleweight he was another opponent who was considerably bigger than the five-foot-seven Duran and, unlike Duran, he was in his prime as a fighter. Duran signed to fight him on November 10, 1983, in Vegas, in what would be Hagler's first superfight. Given the extreme unlikelihood that Duran would fight cautiously by either grabbing or moving and Hagler's obvious punching power, the potential for Duran's first conclusive knockout loss loomed large.

But once again the greatness of Duran was undeniable. Although he lost a close decision there was no question who the more impressive fighter in that ring was. Against a far bigger and stronger opponent who many suspected, correctly it turns out, would ultimately prove to be one of the greatest middleweights in history, Duran, years removed from his prime and fighting a full twenty-five pounds higher than his ideal weight, was very effective, as expected rarely taking a backwards step but more importantly also boxing brilliantly at times and never really being in trouble. In many ways the loss was his most impressive fight. Throughout the Hispanic community Duran was back, the disgrace against Leonard forgotten based on the way he had engaged and defanged the perceived monster Hagler. Everywhere, that community's Boxing-mad fathers bought their sons a *papa rellena* and told them Roberto Duran was our greatest fighter and again a true Man.

Boxing being a zero-sum deal, Duran's gain in prestige was Hagler's loss. For all the reasons stated, his failure to stop the older, smaller man reflected poorly on him. While Hagler waited for his chance at redemption, Duran decided to keep making big money and signed to fight Thomas Hearns for his W.B.C. junior-middleweight title.

Meanwhile Sugar Ray Leonard watched the Duran/Hagler fight, saw Hagler's apparent vulnerability, and decided he should unretire and fight Hagler after all, despite the risk to his eye. The plan called for him to first fight a tune-up bout against someone named Kevin Howard. On May 11, 1984, Leonard fought Howard and he didn't look good, even hitting the canvas for the first time in his career before winning by ninth-round knockout. Discouraged by his performance and what it seemingly bode for a fight against Hagler, Leonard immediately retired again.

The Hearns/Duran fight took place about one month later on June 15, 1984 and it was one of those rare boxing events that actually inspires nothing short of awe-filled fear. With thirty seconds left in the first round Hearns landed a clean right cross (what else?) to Duran's jaw and Duran went straight down. He got up, not overly well, and survived the following flurry as the bell sounded. This is where the fear part came in because between rounds Duran, who had over seventy professional fights at the time, mistakenly went to a

771

neutral corner where his trainers had to go and fetch him. In other words, this was a punch he wouldn't be recovering from but you also knew his corner wouldn't stop the fight. At the start of the second Hearns swarmed Duran against the ropes, mostly missing, until he seemed to step back to give himself room to throw his signature punch. The right landed squarely to the side of Duran's face and his reaction was instantaneous. His gloved hands dropped like an abandoned marionette's and he slowly crashed face-first to the canvas, unable to break his fall in any way. The referee immediately stopped the fight, probably thinking a casket needed to be ordered. Duran's cornermen rushed into the ring to stand him up. After some time Duran pushed them away and seemed to ask what was happening.

Hearns's scary victory and Leonard's latest retirement made the next big fight an obvious one. After posting two more knockout victories each, Marvelous Marvin Hagler and Thomas "Hitman" Hearns fought on April 15, 1985. It was one of the greatest, most violent fights in boxing history and it lasted only three rounds.

The first round, which usually involves little action and is almost always characterized by a cautious feeling out process, was especially extreme. Hagler, perhaps still stinging from criticism that he was too passive against Duran and probably also realizing that, despite his considerable boxing skills, he could not outbox from a distance the man who had outboxed Leonard and Benitez, came out intent on creating the kind of war that would negate Hearns' height and reach advantage. Hearns reacted to Hagler's aggressive bombs in the only manner befitting his greatness. He didn't hold Hagler or move away in the hopes of weathering the early storm until he could follow his gameplan that called for sticking and moving. No, he planted his feet and unleashed hell right back on Hagler. One of the very greatest offensive fighters ever let loose with everything at his disposal in service of attempted murder.

The first savage right cross went practically *through* Hagler's hairless pate. The same punch that had iced so many, that had paralyzed Cuevas and Duran, now tested one of history's greatest shock-absorbing chins. Hagler was hurt like never before or since but he didn't go down. The force of the punch went through to his legs and straightened them but he took it and covered up. He recovered and started throwing again prompting a still more furious response from Hearns and so on. They traded punches like in no first round ever seen and somewhere in there Hagler adjusted to the inhuman power of Hearns, Hearns broke his right hand on Hagler's head, and Hagler's punches started to increasingly affect Hearns. At the end of the round the crowd seemed to be in a state of delirious exhaustion.

In the second round, Hearns began to box from the outside at his corner's urging but now his legs didn't look so great and despite guarded success in that round the option of doing that for an entire fight seemed irretrievably lost. In the third, Hearns cut Hagler above the eye, an angry cut that the ref had the ring doctor look at. A desperate Hagler, fearful that the fight would be stopped on cuts, began waging full-scale war again. Shortly thereafter he landed a looping right that wasn't particularly vicious but that functioned like the final drop of water that causes a flood. Hearns's legs were now completely gone. He stumbled across the ring with Hagler in pursuit. The ensuing punches from Hagler were really window dressing and Hearns slumped to the canvas giving Hagler his greatest victory and leaving Hearns to rebuild from another devastating defeat.

Blood streaming down his face, his heavily muscled arms raised, Hagler looked invincibly evil. Leonard gave no indication that he would end his latest retirement. But the following year, when Hagler again looked beatable in defending his title with an eleventh-round knockout of John "The Beast" Mugabi, Leonard announced he would again unretire for the purpose of fighting Hagler, this time without any tune-up fights beforehand. The boxing world would finally get the fight it had longed for.

On April 6, 1987, the fight took place in Las Vegas. Both in their thirties, neither fighter was what he once was and the fight, though highly dramatic, was truthfully only a slightly-above-average affair. Hagler started slowly, showing his age and giving away a lot of early rounds. Then Leonard tired and Hagler came on strong. In the end, Leonard received a disputed decision. Hagler sought an immediate rematch but about a month after the fight Leonard announced he was again retiring. Seeing that the Leonard rematch would never happen, Hagler retired as well and never fought again. He was rich and healthy and wherever he goes today someone tells him he won the fight, that he was robbed. The retirement of Leonard, who had shown little interest in defending any of his newly won middleweight titles, created multiple championship vacancies in that storied division. One of the vacancies was filled when, in October of 1987, Hearns smoked the Argentinian Juan Roldan to take one of the middleweight titles and become the first boxer to win titles in four different weight classes. Leonard then announced he was ending his latest retirement with the goal of winning his fourth and fifth titles; no-one really mentioned the eye anymore. He accomplished his goal on November 7, 1988, when he knocked out someone named Donnie Lalonde to somehow simultaneously win titles in both the super-middleweight and light-heavyweight divisions, bringing his career total to five. (The thing with the titles was becoming more ridiculous with each passing day as seemingly every other second a new weight class was created complete with about thirteen different organizations ready to declare their "champion".)

In the meantime Hearns was slipping fast. Defending his middleweight title against Iran Barkley on June 6, 1988, he was of course dominating when suddenly, in the third round, he got hit with a wild right hand that left him out on his feet and barely upright; upright, that is, until Barkley landed another right that finished the job, knocking Hearns down and out. When in his next fight he again visited the canvas in posting an unimpressive decision victory over James Kinchen, the consensus was that the shopworn Hearns was truly finished. On the bright side, Sugar Ray was, not coincidentally, finally willing to give Hearns that rematch he had ached for for so long. The fight was scheduled for June 12, 1989, and Leonard was the heavy favorite.

Roberto Duran meanwhile had fought no-one of note following his loss to Hearns, winning seven fights but also losing a decision to someone named Robbie Sims. Yet so electric was the Duran name that he nevertheless received a title shot against the new champion Iran Barkley. Duran was thirty-seven, hadn't fought a significant fight in five years, and was fighting a strong middleweight in his prime who was coming off an impressive knockout victory over an all-time great. Naturally Duran dominated Barkley, dropping him in the eleventh round and winning his fourth title by decision.

When Leonard/Hearns II took place four months later it was billed as The War. From the very start it became apparent that Hearns wasn't the only one who had lost a lot as Leonard looked slow and hesitant to pull the trigger on his punches. That said, both men appeared to be at similar stages in their deterioration making for an exciting evenly matched fight. But whereas their first fight eight years earlier had featured consummate skill, this one was more about two great men unwilling to surrender their ghosts. Hearns in particular – after admitting he was so haunted by the 1981 defeat that he thought more about Leonard than his woman – fought like he would rather die than lose again. He also fought better than he had in years, twice dropping Leonard with rights and generally controlling the fight throughout despite ultimately settling for a controversial draw in what was a scintillating, dramatic, *great* fight that featured ringside commentator Marvelous Marvin Hagler openly rooting for "Tommy".

That should've been it really if there was any kind of warm rhythm to these things. Instead Leonard and Duran inexplicably mixed it up a third time on December 7, 1989, a mere nine years after the infamous *no mas* fight. The predictably tepid fight went to Leonard and a few weeks later the boxing decade these five men had dominated came to a close. Except for Hagler, they would all fight in the nineties but never against each other and never with anything like the former hoopla attaching.

On the decided periphery of all this interstitial fistic mayhem that characterized the mid-to-late-eighties stood Wilfred Benitez. Five months after losing to Hearns, Benitez fought Tony Cerda. Cerda was not a bad little fighter and an expert at kissing his cousin, having fought to a draw in four of his last five bouts. Benitez won an easy ten-round decision. It was his forty-eighth professional fight of which he had lost only two and each of those to a fellow great. There was no shame in that. He was twenty-four and still a premier fighter.

But insensate Time is nothing if not cruel and heartless. It corrodes then destroys, so that the man you literally and figuratively looked up to with your chubby face, who scooped you up to cross the street and patted you on the head to laughter, will later look *through* you from a crooked hospital bed then blindly up at you while wearing makeup in a bargain casket. The people who now surround you generating warmth will disappear leaving only an empty chill; the body you own and the brain it houses will malfunction. And sometimes, especially in Boxing, even a twenty-four-year-old can become an old man overnight.

Benitez next fought Mustafa Hamsho. Hamsho was a capable fighter, as evidenced by the trouble he had given Hagler two years earlier before being stopped in the eleventh on cuts, but Benitez had every reason to be confident he would post a meaningful win that would reinstall him at the forefront of his sport. Instead Benitez lost a clear decision, his first unjustifiable loss. (Just how unjustifiable became clear a year later when Hagler stopped Hamsho in the third in a rematch granted to Hamsho primarily on the strength of his victory over Benitez. *That* was what all-time greats did to people like Hamsho.) Now Wilfred's career needed repairing but Duran had shown that you could suffer a bad loss and still come back to later post big wins for big money. After all, Benitez reasoned, Hamsho was better than fucking Kirkland Laing. So after posting a decision victory against a nondescript opponent in February of 1984, Benitez signed to fight Davey Moore, the same opponent Duran had used to rocket himself back to stardom.

Only now the reasons for the Hamsho loss started to maybe slowly reveal themselves. In the gym, training for Moore, he noticed that palookas who'd always managed to come down with mysterious ailments whenever he was looking for sparring partners were suddenly rearranging their schedules to be available. They wanted something to brag about, wanted to say they once held their own against the great Benitez. People were saying things too, louder and louder. That he seemed off in the way he acted towards people, well, more off than before anyway. When the Moore fight occurred, the latent, the whispered, became apparent and undeniable as Wilfred was knocked out by a right hand in the second round from the same fighter who could do nothing against a thirty-two-year-old Duran. Something was definitely wrong.

Wilfred had broken his ankle in three places while crumbling to the canvas so, with the necessarily idle recovery time, he didn't fight again for almost a year. This, of course, would have been a good time to retire, even at twenty-four, but that kind of thing never happens so we'll move on. The truth was he needed the money. Tax problems, bad investments, all those things people always say when they've somehow managed to squander absurd sums of money. If he retired he would have no hope of getting back what he had lost. So instead he did what he'd done since he was seven. He fought.

He fought the decent Mauricio Bravo in Aruba on March 30, 1985, and knocked him out in the second round. Maybe the layoff had been the best thing for him he thought and this notion gained credence when he followed that victory with a seventh-round knockout of Danny Chapman in July. Now he could step it up again, the thinking went, and his next fight would be against the undefeated (22-0 19 K.O.s) Kevin Moley in Madison Square Garden.

Moley was a pretty good fighter who had been carefully nursed by his management team to an undefeated record. What happens in Boxing though is that eventually the protected kid with the stellar record has to fight someone legitimate. When that point is first reached, as it had been with Moley, what customarily happens is the fighter will fight someone who still has a recognizable and respected name but who is far enough along on his decline as to pose no real threat. Moley's team identified Wilfred as that individual. They reasoned that he was nothing more than the shell of a once-great fighter and as such would represent an easy yet superficially impressive victory for their fighter. They were both right and wrong. They were right that he was a shell. What they failed to realize is that even the shell of a great fighter can often beat a merely good one. They got what they deserved those fucks. After being dropped by a right fifteen seconds into the fight, Benitez got up, made the sign of the cross, and proceeded to give Moley a thorough ten-round pasting. There were actual flashes of the old Benitez as he lay against the ropes impervious to his opponent's attack, doubled and tripled up on his jab, and repeatedly bounced short straight punches off Moley's melon. Maybe he was back all the way Benitez thought. Those other incidents weren't signs after all, just a temporary lull. Damn he was still only twenty-six.

In the ring, after the fight, Benitez was excited. He grabbed the microphone that had been used to announce his victory and addressed what had been a supportive Garden crowd in broken, halting English. At times he seemed to have trouble speaking, it was one of those uncomfortable situations. But he managed to thank the crowd for coming to watch him fight *at the stadium of Madison of Madison*

Square Garden. He told them he was born in New York but added that he was raised in Puerto Rico. He said he liked fighting in New York. He finished by yelling *God bless you all because God has made me winner again! God bless you!* to loud cheers. Off that he would not be retiring.

Coming off the Moley victory, Benitez signed for a similar fight against Matthew Hilton. Hilton was a highly marketable, white($$), Canadian, twenty-year-old with a serious left hook who was being groomed as one of Boxing's next big stars. He was undefeated (18-0 13 K.O.s) and coming off one of those impressive-in-name-only victories against former middleweight champion Vito Antuofermo. Benitez actually trained properly for this fight and came into the ring in shape knowing that a victory over the high-profile Hilton in a nationally televised fight would likely gain him the Hagler title shot and big payday he had blown with his loss to Hamsho. He would be back in the Greatness conversation, still with a chance to make more history.

Early on it was one of those good news/bad news deals for Benitez. The bad news was that Hilton had really heavy hands, or I should say *hand* – the left one. He showed this by dropping Benitez in the first with a good body shot. The good news was that he was slow as an hourglass and somewhat amateurish in the way he set up to throw punches, telegraphing everything that was coming. He was the kind of guy a prime Benitez ate for lunch, frustrating to no end with his defense before winning a decision. This was where the further bad news came in, however, because Benitez looked awful. Every punch that landed solidly, and there were more of these than ever before, seemed to at least stagger Benitez. He took a beating from this chump who in a just universe would have been honored to hold Wilfred's spit bucket. He got hit clean, hard, and often while the Montreal crowd chanted for *Matthew, Matthew.* In the sixth he got caught with a severe left hook to the head, the kind of punch he never got hit with before. He must have wondered what was going on. He must have wondered this as he stumbled back against the ropes and the twenty-year-old came in firing more punches he couldn't get out of the way of. It should have ended there but it didn't. On the basis of some now-remembered, long-ago-installed instinct Benitez moved his head just enough and Hilton got tired just enough that soon Wilfred was firing back and, whenever the ref intervened, shaking his legs in the hopes they would return.

If Benitez was in a ring he was trying to win. It didn't matter that he couldn't or even that he knew he couldn't. If he fell and shattered his ankle he tried to stand on it and continue. If a twenty-year-old was hitting him with punches he had easily avoided in the past there was nothing you could do about it. You certainly couldn't stop fighting, you couldn't quit. No, you took the punches best you could and fired your own back in the general direction they were coming from. You made movements that had been ingrained in you since before puberty and for some reason you hoped the ref wouldn't stop the fight. And in the eighth Benitez got hit with so many consecutive solid punches that the referee came very close to the fighters and appeared to be on the verge of stopping the fight. Except that when he looked closely at Wilfred's eyes to see what was there he saw him shaking his head no and grinning in the universal boxing sign for *this guy can't hurt me.* But he could. The ref didn't stop the fight then but in the ninth it didn't matter. Against the ropes as Hilton threw everything he had, Benitez was only barely surviving when he got hit with a particularly savage left hook. The punch shot Wilfred's chin to the left and the top of his head in the opposite direction. He slumped to the canvas, his left arm becoming entangled in the ropes so that he fell on his chest, his left shoulder suspended by those ropes and the left side of his face at the referee's feet. He raised his head and looked up at the ref. He slowly shook his head and blinked his watery eyes. He wanted to stand up and keep fighting. He wanted to clear his head and last the round. Then he could recuperate between rounds and even though he had lost every round to that point, had been down twice, he would come back and win the fight, give Hilton the type of beating that would make his people regret they ever considered putting their guy in the ring with him. He would win because he was WILFRED BENITEZ and that was reason enough. So he tried to stand and put himself in a position where Hilton could legally throw more punches at his head. Where you would have covered up and cried, he tried to stand. He couldn't, didn't come close, and when the count was over the ring doctor rushed into the ring as the announcers openly feared for his safety.

It was over. All of it. Everyone could see it except the eyes that mattered. What Wilfred saw in the ring with those eyes was the same thing he had always seen. He saw openings and opponent mistakes; opportunities to hit and moving gloves to avoid being hit with. The difference was that by the time his damaged brain would send the signal to his body it would be too late. Too late to expose the opening and, what was worse, too late to avoid the incoming punches the way he had done so easily for so long. And when those punches would land the same brain that since age seven had absorbed the shock of incoming skull had had enough and that brain would rebel by starting to partially shut down.

Everyone saw this and Wilfred felt it. It hurt him more than just physically but he kept fighting because ultimately it was what he *was*, the one thing he had made himself into, and everyone who's like Wilfred wants to be something whatever the cost. He fought three more times in 1986. He fought even though he didn't feel great, didn't sound great, and was acting more erratic and childlike every day. He fought and posted two decision victories, even including a win over the decent Paul Whittaker who was undefeated at the time.

But then the first end came and it was a vicious one.

Fighting Carlos Herrera on November 28, 1986, in an unnoticed fight held in Salta, Argentina, Wilfred Benitez was knocked out in the seventh round. Forget Hearns and Leonard, this guy couldn't be said to be on the same level as Hamsho or Moore or even a rising Hilton as was evident in Herrera's next and last fight when he was knocked out by fellow-Argentinean Juan Roldan in the second. The brutal, ignominious loss to a guy like Herrera was finally a hint even Wilfred could take. He retired and hoped he would start feeling better.

I had banged the payphone receiver into its holder out of the frustration I felt when no-one answered and now I held the phone's exposed innards in my hands and tried again. When it somehow worked and Dane answered he wanted to know whether I was crazy and what I was talking about confession.

"Are you crazy?" he said. "And what are you talking about *confession*?"

"I confessed."

"To who? That detective?"

"No not that kind of confession, the sacrament."

"The what?"

"The sacrament of confession. I participated in it, sort of."

"When?"

"I don't know, a couple of weeks ago maybe."

"O.K. so what's the problem?"

"Well, what Assado said for one."

"But if it was a couple of weeks ago."

"It's hard to explain but—"

"Just come over, come over and we'll talk about all this."

Which I did. And this happened at an obscenely opulent suite at The Plaza.

"The hell you doing *here*?"

"Where else should a man of my means live?"

"You live here now?"

"Sure, for now. Like it?"

What wasn't to like in a suite the size of an auditorium with carpet so thick we grew six inches, multiple silver trays of food rolling about and square vents blowing perfect temperature in? And Dane walked around in a slow semicircle occasionally dragging from a fat cigar from you know where and also sipping from a foot-long champagne flute while wearing a ridiculously shiny, almost mirrorly reflective, black robe.

"Have some Cristal, relax. You look a mess," he said.

"No."

"Fine have some Maine lobster tails, right there. Pulled up this very morning and still warm. I haven't laid a fork on them either."

"No thanks."

"What then? You want to go get your money now don't you?"

"No, I don't."

"Why not?"

"I just have more pressing things right now."

He inhaled deeply, flaring up the end of the brown log pointing out from his mouth. "So what's the big problem?" he said. "Because as I see it it's that you've let this flatfoot tie you all up inside and for what? You haven't enjoyed minute one of this victory and for no good reason."

"This fucker knows man, you know he knows."

"So what he knows? You sound like a fucking client. Who cares what he knows? What can he *prove*? I'll tell you what. Nothing! So he's fucking with you. I told you, fuck him up right back. It's not like you don't have the materials or the tools to do that."

"What do you mean?"

"Unbelievable. It's as if, having established that you're the kind of person capable of doing what you did, you now suddenly want to regress into being the kind of person who worries about things like cops."

"I never stopped being that person. I told you from the outset what my principal concern was. And as it turns out it appears I was wholly justified because whatever happened back there we seem to have screwed up in such a fundamental manner that the unthinkable, law enforcement involvement, is currently all I can think about."

"Not true, that's not the way it happened, you're wrong about that. But before I even get to that there's a more basic issue to consider here. As I've said, I find the whole avoiding-apprehension-after-the-fact deal supremely boring but since you obviously don't then it would seem you need to do something about the situation. Something decisive even extreme if necessary but something that will finally put this all to bed for good so you can fill your pockets with treasure in peace. Now what's this about a confession?"

"What did you mean when you said I could fuck with him back? How?"

"See that's where you surprise me because it seems that the stress or whatever of this situation has messed with your brain in a way that is completely unacceptable."

"*What*?"

"Well the way you apparently hear this fucker's declarations and are either unable or unwilling to look past the limited question of how they potentially imperil or otherwise affect you to what they say about their speaker."

"I see."

"Not yet but you will."

And we talked about Detective Assado and what Dane thought about it but I didn't tell him about Clerical Confessions and truth is when I walked out of there, having reconsidered and imbibed a substantial amount of the champagne, having ordered and received a therapeutic massage, having likewise ordered a ton of room service and sampled one of the Cubans, I did feel a whole lot better. Better that is until I stepped out into the artificial brightness of the circular area where rich people give strangers their car keys and heard that infernal voice again.

"The Plaza wow. Not bad for a public defender," Assado said. "I'm serious, where you getting that kind of scratch exactly?"

"They don't charge you to visit their guests."

"Oh who are you visiting? Are you at liberty to tell me?"

"No."

"Funny I chose that phrase huh? I mean who knows how much longer you'll be *at liberty* right?"

"Can I help you with something? In other words, is there a reason you're following me?"

"Just a couple of things I want to discuss with you. Maybe we could grab something to eat."

"I just ate."

"Really? Here? That's like a fortune. What'd you have?"

"I forget."

"And I suppose you forget who you just met with as well?"

"That's right, I do."

"O.K. so you're full. Let's go get a drink instead then. I'm told there's a couple of good bars around here."

"I don't drink."

"You don't? Because you look like you've had a couple tonight."

"I did."

"So what did you mean?"

"I didn't say I've never had a drink. I said I don't drink and I don't. But I used to drink."

"A couple hours ago."

"Right."

"Well come watch me drink then. That can be entertaining in its own right."

"Thanks for the offer but no."

"So what *do* you want to do?"

"What do I want to do? I want to go home."

"What about me?"

"What about you?"

"What do you want me to do?"

"Since you ask, I want you to crawl back under whatever rock you crawled out from under a few days ago and never show me your face again."

"We both know that's not going to happen though don't we? I'm nothing if not persistent. Persistent Peter my friends used to call me in high school."

"Really?"

"That's what they called me."

"No I mean you had friends?"

"Well I was using the term loosely to describe the people who attended my high school at the same time I did."

"Oh, and your name was Peter back then?"

"No, it's always been Mondongo."

"I guess in those instances alliteration tends to be viewed as more important than accuracy."

"So you'll come? It won't take long."

And on the way there Assado would periodically giggle to himself like something was the most amusing notion he'd ever had. But he looked older than when I first met him, less colorful.

"I just have questions," he said when we sat down at the empty-save-for-one-drowsy-woman bar. "Questions I know you'll want to answer. I sit around thinking about this case, that's all I do, and I get these questions. And I get these questions and I think, *who can help me answer them*? And I always come back to you, because you know so much about what happened that night."

"You're wrong."

"I think, for example, about how much money was taken that night. Millions, lots of them, and all in cash like that. People don't realize that money like that invites its own problems you know? I mean what do you do with it? You can't walk into a bank and deposit it into your account right? What do you do, put it under your mattress? We're talking about *millions*. I mean this presents problems even for people who are engaged in long-standing and consistent criminal activity, criminals. I'm sure you know that they devise all sorts of fake businesses and everything to convert the money into the kind that can be deposited into bank accounts. You're wondering where I'm going with this. Well if my theory's right and the person or persons who took this money are not really practiced criminals but more like ordinary people who found themselves with some inside information and did this on the spur of the moment so to speak, then it stands to reason that they will have even more problems than the average criminal in laundering this money no? So that's one of my questions. You know, where's the money and what kind of problems is it causing the holder, how will they try to legitimize it? Which of the two of them has it?"

". . ."

"Yeah I guess I should mention that. I know now that two men did it. I can't tell you how I know that or anything, it's a pending criminal investigation, and no matter how close we are to making the arrests I can't compromise the integrity of that in any way, I'm sure you understand. Anyway I bet only one of the two currently has the money and that's got to make the other one uncomfortable you know what I mean? So that's another question I have. By the way did you remember yet who you were just visiting at The Plaza?"

". . ."

"The other thing is this with regard to the two guys we now know were involved. If I was one of them how would I know that my partner wasn't in some way cooperating with the police in return for leniency? And since I couldn't know that wouldn't I be tempted to beat him to the punch so to speak by talking to the police or specifically a detective that I knew was working on the case so I could get that leniency for myself? I mean there comes a time when a person should be able to see the handwriting on the wall as it were and start thinking seriously about cutting their losses don't you think? You have to wonder why I'm so interested in speaking with you. How I've been able to progress and proceed in this manner. Don't you?"

Assado kept talking without pause and somewhere in there I decided to give up, that all was lost. I wasn't even listening to what he was saying anymore but he was looking at me and smiling and I can't really say I hated him anymore just that I was tired and wanted it all to be over. Then he laughed.

"What?" I said.

"No just that some people really aren't cut out for prison you know? You're a very good-looking guy actually. I know this guy in state corrections and the truth is that the sexual assault problem in New York State prisons is largely a thing of the past. But, you know, do you even want to have that like in the back of your mind and whatnot? Have you thought about that? By the way what are you, Italian? You a paisan?"

I looked away and he kept talking, on and on. I could hear him now. He started talking about money.

"What?" I said.

"I'm trying to help you, the money."

"I don't understand, *what*?"

"The money. If we were to locate it, that could be a great help to you. Of course I'd have to talk to my supervisor you understand? Don't you?"

"Yeah I think I do. I understand now, thank you."

"So?"

"And I am Italian."

"Really? I thought so, where from?"

"Italy."

"Where in Italy."

"A little village by the heel. Tiramisu di Bosco I think it was called.

I came over by myself when I was a couple of weeks old."

"I see, you're pulling my leg."

"I have a couple of questions myself that maybe you can answer Assado. Is that alright?"

He sat up.

"Like I was wondering why you're even working on this case since it didn't occur in your precinct."

"Well I'm not going to discuss that."

"Oh, because when I called your precinct a short while ago with an offer of information they didn't seem to know what I was talking about."

"Well they wouldn't."

"So is it like one of those Hollywood-type things where you're like suspended but you're so used to administering your own brand of street justice that you pursue the truth on your free time? Is that what it's like?"

"Maybe."

"Well what is it exactly?"

"There are parallels."

"Because I also know that neither of the detectives that met with DeLeon has talked to you about this case."

"How I conduct this investigation is really none of your business."

"Just questions Assado, don't get so bent out of shape."

"Uh-huh."

"Also I noticed that when you showed me those pictures from the scene they were like copies of copies and I would've just expected better access to the evidence from the lead detective on the case. Then there's all the times you mentioned specifics about what happened at 410 but since you never spoke with either of those narcotics detectives and the investigation doesn't even properly belong to your precinct then your source for that information can only be . . . but that can't be right . . . can it?"

There was a long pause here where Assado would smile and take long drinks from his glass then look around and murmur. Finally he looked directly at me.

"So you want to do it this way huh? I tried to be nice but I guess you prefer this."

"What you said about your friend in corrections was nice I suppose, I didn't like that."

"You know what? You have no idea who you're fucking with. No idea at all."

"I think I know exactly whom. I'm just not overly impressed, there's a difference."

"I could disappear you if I wanted. It just so happens you know where something valuable is. And I got news for you, the wrong people know that you know where it is. I was offering to help you. I could do you myself, say you reached for my gun."

"I'm right here."

Assado pointed to his glass then raised two fingers. When the glass was empty he turned to face me and I sensed he was shedding a character he had created.

"You have no idea what you've gotten yourself into do you? Let me give you some free advice then do whatever you want because personally I don't give a fuck if you live or die. You like playing bad guy? Well the guy you're fucking with, and no I don't mean Escalera, *isn't* playing and I think you know that. He isn't playing and he's immense and he's got you in his cross hairs. You got your little reprieve. That's what this has been the last few days, an opportunity. If you had availed yourself of it, told me where the money was, I maybe, *maybe*, could've convinced that animal not to hunt you down and end you, to just take back his boss's money and leave the matter at that. Now? Well that was your chance but you didn't take it and now I have no sympathy for you. What you did was wrong and you know it."

"Said the cop on the drug dealer's payroll, who I'm sure would've rushed right over to said drug dealer with the money instead of taking it for himself and never being heard from again."

"See that's what I mean about you not comprehending fully, how you fail to understand the severity of the situation you're in. What you're about to learn is there are certain things in life that cannot be controlled or even contained. A certain violence gets unbound and there's nothing in our godless universe to slow it. All the world's malevolence and evil concentrated into one creature. That's the thought occurred to me when I first saw Ballena and since 410 he's grown worse, everyone sees it. So when you say I would keep the money I laugh because I would no sooner make an enemy of that than I would try to obliterate the Sun. You simply don't defy Ballena in that way, no sane person would. So I'm giving you one last chance. You know me now and I surely know you. Tell me what I want to hear and you'll never see me again. More importantly, you won't see that thing I hesitate to even call a man. You get to choose, speak to end this or suffer greatly for your silence. Live, or die the kind of protracted death you least want, which is it?"

He stared and I looked down at my drink.

"I have no idea what you're talking about," I said with barely sufficient air.

"I tried to be your friend."

"You threatened my life, stop patting yourself on the back."

"Tell me who the other guy is, we'll deal with him and I'll put in a good word for you. Nobody has to know."

"I can't."

"Then you'll get what you deserve."

"We all will."

He said something else then left. I was shaking and looking around. The nearby woman raised her face to reveal a coaster stuck to her check. I downed a copper-colored shot and left. I felt not entirely sure what had just happened but confident I was finally rid of Assado who had bleakened my every move for days. As I saw it there wasn't prison to worry about anymore, I was maybe even happy.

Though not as happy as Toomberg was the day the Supreme Court heard argument in <u>Atkins</u> v. <u>Virginia</u> because that day, late in the afternoon, Toomberg walked into my office with a silly smile plastered on his lumpy face and optimistic hope for mankind in his heart.

"Well I'm back," he said. "Don't you want to know how it went?"

"Back from where?" I said.

"I told you, D.C., the Supreme Court, remember? To watch the oral argument on Atkins versus Virginia?"

"Oh right, sorry. So what happened?"

"What happened, I'm happy to report, is that all indications are that we are finally prepared to declare unequivocally that a certain state-sponsored activity, namely the execution of mentally retarded individuals, is unconscionable and cannot continue. We have evolved to that point and that makes me happy."

"Who's we?"

"Society, more specifically this country, and even more specifically the Supreme Court of this country as one of the bodies we've entrusted with making these determinations."

"Good grief."

"Surely you grasp the significance don't you? Jalen Kingg's going to be alright."

"Hold on will you? Start at the beginning. First, what makes you so sure they're going to rule in our favor?"

"Well I observed the argument and the questioning was definitely in our favor."

"O.K., that's the first bad sign. What else?"

"Also I have a good friend from law school."

"Harvard."

"Yes."

"Wow, that was just a stab in the dark. Aren't you impressed?"

"And he clerks for one of the justices."

"Souter."

"No."

"Scalia."

"No. Anyway I spoke to him after the argument."

"Ginsberg."

"I'm really not at liberty to say."

"So it's Ginsberg, what's she like?"

"It's not Ginsberg and I'd rather not say."

"There's only nine, give me a second."

"I spoke to him and he said that his justice, who represents a critical vote, is leaning in our favor, strongly leaning."

"Ah-hah."

"What?"

"So it's one of the swing guys, you just all but revealed your source my friend."

"Really? Who are the swing justices?"

"No idea."

"More importantly, he said he has it on good authority that another critical vote will go our way. There you have it, actual progress."

"So we just wait then?"

"Correct, once the decision comes down we'll have some legal maneuvering to do but I feel very confident that victory will be ours. What are those?"

"Letters."

"What kind?"

"To and from Jalen."

"Might I see?"

"If you must."

He grabbed them and his smile grew, which growth I had not thought possible.

"You know, you like to pretend you're this off-the-cuff guy who couldn't be bothered with procedure and rules but look at you you're meticulous!" he said. "Every letter you've ever sent him or received from him copied and filed in chronological order, and nothing is even slightly out of place on your desk, ha ha!"

"Look at me? Look at you, you're positively giddy."

"I am indeed."

"That's kind of rude Toom, don't you think, to act all happy like that when the rest of us are miserable?"

"Who's happy?" asked Conley walking in.

"Toom here," I said. "He's all happy because the Supreme Court will allegedly soon rule it unconstitutional to execute the mentally retarded."

"Says who?"

"Says he and he's never wrong."

"But how do you know?"

"Just leave it at that please I don't want to hear the whole account again."

"So why does it make you happy? How does it affect you? Is he allowed to answer those Casi?"

"He may."

"I'm happy because of the progress it represents or will represent."

"How do you mean that?"

"Simply this, I believe it is wrong to kill a person as punishment for their actions when that person is mentally challenged. I believe all sorts of similar things and often find that society at large disagrees with me. Consequently on those rare occasions where society comes into agreement with me on an ethical issue such as this one I become hopeful and happy in a sense and consider it progress."

"You call that progress? Progress will be when there are no more retards. Then we won't have to worry about whether or not they're getting fried."

"I don't understand."

"Besides you're describing progress as society agreeing with you on a position you hold but what if you're wrong in holding that position? In that case you wouldn't be looking at societal progress but rather more like a regression."

"But if I thought that adopting the position would constitute a societal regression then I wouldn't personally hold the position either."

"But you could be mistaken."

"In which case I wouldn't know I was mistaken since part of being mistaken is believing you're right so I would still be justified in being happy. And what did you mean no more re—, no more mentally challenged individuals."

"Oh boy," I said.

"There's a project," Conley said.

"No please no," I said.

"Look there's no such thing as human progress Melvyn. At least not of the kind you're describing. What I'm saying is don't celebrate when people are nicer to retards, instead be impatient for the time when endeavors like the Human Genome Project make retards a thing of the past. Because the great injustice is not that these people are occasionally being executed. The inexcusable injustice is that they exist at all. Why should someone be born with a brain that doesn't function properly? Is the ability of your brain an important thing? Do you want to be one of those people? Of course not. So why do we stand for other people having that misfortune? Because it's not us and we're selfish and that's unacceptable."

"So what do you propose? Until then this is still progress."

"No, no no no no no and no. The first sign of progress will come when we give up."

"Give up?"

"Exactly. Imagine yourself father to two boys. For years they trade punches in their common room while you try in vain to get them to get along. Finally one day you give up and just separate them, put them in different rooms. Problem solved, no more fighting. That's where we are. So you say people are slaughtering each other unabated because they don't like their opponent's skin? Well I say stop trying to educate these lice and just make everyone's skin the same. That'll end the slaughter. Do you doubt it? Only when we give up in that manner will you start to see genuine progress."

"Wait a minute," said Toomberg but just then Conley was paged to reception and not often have I felt such relief. After he left Toom turned to me.

"By the way, there's another reason I've been feeling so sanguine about humanity of late and that's your brief."

"Huh?"

"I just finished reading it and don't really know what word to use to describe it."

"The word *finished* I most covet."

"Well I certainly don't think it could be filed exactly as is."

"No I told you, you'll fix it."

"It would almost certainly get you disbarred or something but it's nonetheless an astonishing document and as such it filled me with optimism. That someone was capable of that. That someone wanted to do that, someone I know no less. It had qualities of art. In fact I discussed it extensively with my wife and even though we ultimately concluded it was not art we gave it more than passing consideration. I think what ultimately denied it that lofty status was the work's selfish prescriptivism if that makes any sense, its innervating desire for a specific result. True art, by contrast, seems marked by a generous susceptibility to extrapolation. Your work, understandably, is not sufficiently oriented in that direction to constitute art and has more in common with something like advertising. Advertising of course, despite the activities it often subsumes, is not art and neither, regrettably, is your document."

"I wasn't aiming for art Toom."

"Oh I know of course. I was just so shocked and affected by it that I felt I had to share that with you."

". . ."

"I'll make the necessary edits and we'll file it. Well I should say I doubt, based on today, that we will actually end up filing it. And all that work for nothing. I hate to say it but you may have poured your very soul, as you obviously did, into the creation of this work and it may never be read by anyone, it may never so much as influence a single person's actions. I just came to that realization, how awful."

"Wait a minute, maybe it is art."

"Well that's the only downside to today's events I suppose. I'm still thrilled. Can I be the one to tell Jalen the good news, well to write him about it."

"I don't know."

"Please, up until now you've basically had all the personal contact with him and I'm very grateful for that but I would love to do this. I think I could do it with appropriate concern for the fact that he and I do not have the relationship you have with him."

"It's not that, and I'm not doubting your reading of the situation, it's just that . . . if you're wrong."

"I see, I'll couch it appropriately don't worry. It's not just that it would give me pleasure to write the letter either. I also believe that writing a letter like that with potential good news fulfills an important obligation of ours."

"There's nothing really that *must* be disclosed."

"Not that kind of obligation. I'm talking about an obligation I think we have to not only seek legal success but also to provide our client with the occasional ray of light and hope so to speak. Especially now that he's in that outrageous enforced isolation. In a manner of speaking, we're his only friends."

"Alright but don't go overboard."

"I won't," he said getting up to leave. "And don't worry I'll be sure to give you a copy of the letter for the file, ha ha!"

I laughed too but not then, later, when I saw Ralph and the way he was dressed.

"What's the meaning of this Ralphie boy?" I said when I could. Like an overstuffed sausage, Ralph was encased in a tight crewneck sweater. Atop his head sat a beret-type lid and his similarly tight white pants ended a good six inches above his ankles. In his hands was a titanium Big Bertha golf club that he swung slightly between his parted legs in the hallway outside his door.

"Hey pal," he said. "Whattya say we try and get nine in before supper."

I laughed again.

"So? Whattya say pal?"

"Oh you were serious? What are you talking about?"

"What am I talking about? What am I talking about? Golf! Nine holes. Let's go pal."

"It's like ten degrees out."

"I don't care what degrees out it is. Somehow Mr Monahan got the impression I'm this great golfer and now we're playing on Sunday. You have any idea what this could mean to my future? I got two days to learn how to play golf. Surely you're going to help me pal."

"How did Monahan get that idea?"

"Uh humana, well never mind that! You gunna help me out or not?"

"First of all, I've never played golf in my life. So there's that. Second of all, even if I was an avid golfer, the current temperature is I think seven degrees. Seven."

"It's just as well. I can't learn to play golf in two days. It would take at least a week. Me and my biiig mouth!"

"Guess you're just going to have to tell the truth."

"The truth? Have you gone cuckoo? I'm serious, I'm calling Bellevue cuz you're nuts!"

"What then?"

"Simple, I'll just have to feign some sort of injury. Do you have any of those fake plaster casts around?"

"No but good luck, let me know how it works out." As I reached the top of the stairs to my apartment Ralph called out to me but so lowly that I debated whether to pretend deafness. When instead I answered he said someone had been there looking for me. My insides tightened and I sat on the top stair.

"He didn't give his name or anything but he seemed really interested in finding you that's for sure."

"What did he look like?"

"Hard to say."

"It was that detective who once before talked to you about looking for me right?"

"Oh no it soytainly wasn't him."

"I'm pretty sure it probably was."

"Oh no it definitely wasn't him."

"How can you be so sure?"

"Oh I'm sure pal," he said. "Wait here." He went inside then came back out with a newspaper, The Post. I came down and took it from his hand. "See?" he said. "It wasn't him."

On the front page of the paper was a picture of Assado's head. I don't mean to say that the photographer only captured Assado's head within the frame of the picture. I mean that Assado's head was now its own separate entity. I turned quickly to page three. It said what I already knew, that the head and its nearby body belonged to Homicide Detective Mondongo Qualtagh Assado and that it had been found, along with another *decapitatee*, at an uptown apartment known to function as a drug stash house. It said the other head belonged to *known minor drug kingpin* Juan Escalera and that the preliminary available evidence pointed to a dispute over drug money and that Assado was a *dirty cop*. And someone from the medical

799

examiner's office said there were no signs of *serration* meaning most likely that *the excisions were achieved solely through extreme pull combined with torque* or as another put it *them heads was simply ripped off* which led the police to conclude that *either a machine of some sort or a great many individuals were involved as no single human could generate that kind of force.* I put down the paper and dropped my wet face into my hands.

"See what I mean," Ralph said. "That's how I'm sure it wasn't him. Besides the guy was looking for you this time was bigger than the cop, much bigger. He was probably the biggest fella I've ever seen he was. No I take that back, he was *definitely* the biggest fella I've ever seen. He had arms like long fire hydrants pal. I once knew a guy named Harvey who we thought was pretty big but this fella today makes Harvey look like my friend Shirley, ha ha! Anyway I told him I didn't know where you were but that you definitely lived here and should be back relatively soon. I don't know, he didn't seem to want to wait. He had strange skin too pal, in some areas."

I thanked Ralph and left. From a payphone I tried Dane at The Plaza but they said he wasn't there. I tried him at his old apartment but a new tenant answered and I wondered why you would keep the same phone number as the previous tenant. And I got similar results the days thereafter and checked myself into a miserable hotel, the kind that still advertises Color T.V. as an attraction, and went to work only sparingly and then only to answer Jalen's letters, letters I saved up and until the day Toomberg came into my office to start preparing for my hearing in Cymbeline; only we never did prepare because I left shortly after he entered my office, went to get my stuff from that dump, and moved back into my apartment for good. That day, the last day I saw Toomberg, I had been told multiple times, in the usual locations, that someone was looking for me and usually the person telling me this would have a strangely troubled look on their face. I was in my office alone with all the Kingg letters and after I read the newest ones several times I wrote Jalen a final letter and made a phone call. Then I hung up the phone ripped it off the jack and flung it across the room. Some people looked in and left without saying anything then a minute later Toomberg appeared smilingly unaware.

"You'll be glad to see I took your advice to heart," he said. "I truly tried to contain my optimism in this letter even though every ensuing event since we first spoke has only served to increase it. Here's the copy I promised you for your files. Oh I see you already have the Kingg letters out, perfect. Want to know why I'm even more optimistic now?"

". . ."

"O.K., well I was thinking about what Conley said the other day regarding what I guess he would call the inherent unfairness of the mere existence of individuals who are mentally impaired. First, what are your views on the subject?"

". . ."

"Because I know Conley has this reputation as a bit of a strange bird but . . . go ahead get that . . . well? . . . aren't you going to answer that? Casi!"

"Huh?"

"Aren't you going to answer that?"

"Answer what?"

"The phone, you're being paged from reception."

"Oh," I clicked the red button. "Yeah Denise."

"There's someone here to see you," she was whispering. "He was here this morning too but he won't give his name."

"Uh-huh."

"What do you want to do?"

"O.K."

"What?"

"What did you say?"

"There's someone here to see you."

"Oh."

"What do you want me to do?"

"I'll come out."

"Casi?"

"Yeah."

"I don't know how to say this but he's really big and kind of scary looking and he seems really upset. Do you want me to call security?"

"We have security? Since when?"

"Well the building does."

"Oh, security? No that's O.K."

"He's very big."

"So?"

"He's very angry, I don't know."

"Who is he?"

"I don't know."

"Well what's his name?"

"He won't give one. You want me to ask again? He's upset."

"Never mind, I know who it is."

"You want me to say you're gone for the day? He can't hear me behind the glass."

"Right."

"Casi?"

"Coming."

I stared straight ahead. Then I stood up and walked out on Toom, down the hall and out to the reception area. But the person waiting there for me was someone I had never seen before and after the slightest investigation it turned out he wasn't even looking for me but rather some other attorney whose name was only slightly similar to mine. And he wasn't scary looking at all, at least he didn't scare me. Nor was he all that big either.

Who, if I cried, would hear me from among the Angelic Dominions?
– Rainer Maria Rilke

Chapter 30

#Z311
Jalen Kingg
Cell 9C-03
Holman Unit
3700 Holman
Atmore, Alabama 36503

Dear Mr Kingg:

I am writing to introduce myself to you. Enclosed with this letter is one of my business cards with all of my contact information.

As you can see I am a New York City public defender and I, along with Melvyn Toomberg and Joseph Ledo, two other attorneys in this office, will be representing you *pro bono* during this stage of your appeal in the hopes of ultimately securing a vacatur of the death sentence you received.

I will, of course, keep you informed of all relevant proceedings in your case but feel free to contact me at any time with any questions or concerns. Thank you.

Sincerely yours,

#Z311
Jalen Kingg
Cell 9C-03
Holman Unit
3700 Holman
Atmore, Alabama 36503

Dear Mr Kingg:

I hope that you are doing well. With respect to the status of your appeal we are currently still awaiting delivery of the entire file on your case.

Once we have received and fully reviewed these remaining documents I will contact you with information as to what legal issues we expect to raise and how we will proceed from a procedural standpoint. We expect that to occur relatively soon.

Until then, feel free to contact me if you wish to discuss your case. Thank you.

Sincerely yours,

#Z311
Jalen Kingg
Cell 9C-03
Holman Unit
3700 Holman
Atmore, Alabama 36503

Dear Mr Kingg:

I hope you are doing well. I have made repeated attempts to contact you by phone but I have been unsuccessful so I will continue to write you these letters and hope you will respond to them.

We have completed our review of the file on your case and have identified three issues that we anticipate raising in the district court. Having not heard from you, I don't know what level of detail regarding our representation you're comfortable with so I've just included with this letter various cases and other legal materials relevant to those three issues so that you might familiarize yourself with our expected arguments.

Please call me, or if that's not possible write me with any issues or facts you believe might be relevant to your appeal and that either relate to the events leading up to your arrest or to the circumstances of your trial and direct appeal. I look forward to hearing from you soon. Thank you.

Sincerely yours,

#Z311
Jalen Kingg
Cell 9C-03
Holman Unit
3700 Holman
Atmore, Alabama 36503

Dear Mr Kingg:

I am writing to inform you that Joseph Ledo has left our office and will no longer be working on your case.

However, Melvyn Toomberg and I continue to work long hours on your appeal and I assure you that we will capably and vigorously pursue every possible avenue to success.

I again urge you to contact me to discuss your appeal in general and any specific information that you feel might prove helpful to us. Thank you.

Sincerely yours,

_____

Jalen Kingg #Z311
Cell 9C-03
Holman Unit
3700 Holman
Atmore, Alabama 36503

Dear Mr Kingg:

I'm sorry I haven't written to you in a while but everything is going real well with your appeal and we're working very hard every day to write the best possible brief for you so that the judge will remove the death sentence from your case.

I'm writing to tell you that I will soon be going to Alabama to visit you so we can talk about your case. Also Mr Toomberg and I have decided that you should be interviewed by a psychiatrist so he can assess whether or not there is something about your medical condition that could prove beneficial to your case. I will let you know exactly when that is going to happen.

Do you have any questions? If you do, please write me a letter and put it in the addressed envelope I'm including and I will write you back immediately. We will do everything possible to succeed on your behalf, I promise. I hope to hear from you soon. Thank you.

Sincerely yours,

Jalen Kingg
#Z311
Cell 9C-03
Holman Unit
3700 Holman
Atmore, Alabama 36503

Dear Mr Kingg:

This upcoming weekend I will be visiting you on both Saturday and Sunday. While I'm there we can discuss your case and what happened and what Mr Toomberg and I hope to do to help you.

The visits are already officially and firmly scheduled for those two days so please make sure you are available as it is very important for your case.

I look forward to meeting you soon Jalen.

Sincerely yours,

Mr Jalen Kingg
#Z311
Cell 9C-03
Holman Unit
3700 Holman
Atmore, Alabama 36503

Dear Jalen:

How are you doing? You should save these letters and answer them. It was very nice to meet you and I would enjoy receiving letters from you.

And you can write me whenever you want to talk about anything, whether it has to do with your case or not.

The next step is for Melvyn Toomberg and I to retain a doctor who will meet with you and evaluate you as we discussed during my visit. I will let you know who that will be and when you will meet him as soon as I know for sure.

In the meantime, Melvyn and I continue to work hard on the brief that we will soon file on your behalf. We're doing everything we can Jalen and we hope to have some good news to report to you soon.

Until then, stay hopeful.

Your friend,

lawyer Mr Casi
2330 Broadway
Floor number nine
New York, new York

Casi;

Thanks to you four visiting me because everyone hear says thas whut good lawyers do to to prupare a case for the litegation of trial testymony.

i also agreee about the Maples house because i have never have the oppurtunity to live somewhere like that and i will show the same and simular respect for your doctor or you're assisstant Mr Melvyn Toomberg if or when they come to visit me.

So thanks to you agin and i too think the news will be good because of you now been my lawyer.

P.S. "i WiLL KNoW ANSER THE LETTERS YoU RiTE To ME BECAUSE i HAVE MET YoU AND KNoW THAT YoU HAVE MY BESTS iNTERST iN MIND AT ALL TiMES AS BECAME EViDENCE WHEN YoU ViSiTiED ME iN JAiL oN BoTH oF THE DAYS YoU CoME"

Mr Jalen Kingg
#Z311
Cell 9C-03
Holman Unit
3700 Holman
Atmore, Alabama 36503

Dear Jalen:

I was very pleased to receive your letter and I look forward to more of them in the future. I hope you are doing well or at least as well as is possible under the circumstances.

The latest news is that Melvyn Toomberg and I have retained Dr Wendell Pegnapper to perform the psychiatric evaluation we discussed. He should be coming out to visit you in the next few days and I will inform you as soon as possible of what he says.

In the meantime the brief that Melvyn and I will file on your behalf is slowly taking shape and should be completed relatively soon. I will give you a copy of it when it is finished.

Lastly, as you may have heard, the United States Supreme Court has agreed to hear a case to decide whether it is legal to execute people who are impaired in the manner we think you're impaired. This decision could have a great impact on your case and Mr Toomberg, who knows a lot about that court, is optimistic that the news will be good. I'll let you know what happens.

Stay good Jalen. We're doing everything we can and there's reason to believe that things will work out for the best in the end. Write me with any questions or anything else you want to talk about.

Your friend,

Mr Casi – Atturney at Law
2330 Broadway
Floor number nine
New York, new York

Dear sir(s);

Thank you for you're fine letters to me which i have saved all of them even though i chose not to response to the first ones And I will now anser ALL oF THEM iN THE FUTURE TiME.

Thank you also agin for the news of the Supreme Court Hearing my case and I too am sure that they will see the case in you're favors as your the best lawyer i know and everyone hear agrees.

P.S. "CAN YoU TELL ME MoRE ABoUT WHERE i WILL Go WHEN i GET oUT BECAUSE i HAVE NoT ToLD ANYoNE PER YoUR WiSHES BUT i THiNK oF GoiNG THERE ALL THE TiME AND i HAVE MULTiPLY QUESTioNS BUT FoRGoT To ASK THEM Too YoU WHEN YoU WERE HERE?"

Mr Jalen Kingg
#Z311
Cell 9C-03
Holman Unit
3700 Holman
Atmore, Alabama 36503

Dear Jalen:

I hope you are doing well. I apologize since it appears that my last letter to you was confusing.

The Supreme Court has *not* agreed to hear *your* case. They have, however, agreed to hear a case called <u>Atkins</u> v. <u>Virginia</u>. and their ruling on that case could have a major effect on your case because the defendant on that case is similar to you (or so Melvyn and I would argue) meaning that if the court eventually rules that it is unconstitutional to execute him we would be in a great position to argue that you cannot be executed either since all courts in the U.S. have to agree with the Supreme Court.

Of course even if we get the ruling we want on that case we would still have to show that you meet the criteria of people who cannot be executed. Based on the report from Dr Pegnapper we feel reasonably confident that we would be able to do that.

I hope that clears up the situation. First we need a good ruling from the court on that case, then we would rely on the doctor to show that you are like Atkins. Do you understand?

Write me with any other questions you might have and I'll keep you posted on any further developments in your case.

Your friend,

Mr Casi – Atturney at Law
2330 Broadway
Floor number nine
New York, new York

Dear Mr Casi,

i must advice you that i have been moved too a diferrent unit because of an incidence that happend in deth row generel pop and now in this unit I do not get resess and i am not allowed to recieve visits or letters accept from you because of the constipation of the U S and your my lawyer.

So please right me as many letters as you many as you can because the guy who bringes me the letters is nice and talks to me with jokes but he's only aloud to come if he has a letter from you to bring and if he doesn't come then i dont see anyboidy the hole day.

P.S. "i UNDERSTAND NoW ABoUT THE SC BECAUSE BEFoUR i WAS PUT HERE MR HENK EXPLAiNED iT To ME AND HE NoSE A LoT ABoUT THE LAW BEiNG THAT HE iS oN "7 CoNSECKUTiVE LiFE BiDS"

Mr Jalen Kingg
#Z311
Punitive Isolation Cell #17
Holman Unit 3700
Holman Atmore, Alabama 36503

Dear Jalen:

Please write me as soon as possible explaining the events that led to you being placed in the unit you're in. I have not been given, despite repeated attempts, any explanation for why you have been placed in isolation from Holman Prison nor any information as to how we can appeal or seek to amend that decision.

I would like to do everything I can to get you placed back in the cell you were in before, with the recreational breaks you had and the contact with people.

What happened? Write me soon and include as much as possible.

As for your brief, everything is proceeding well and we should be done soon. Also the Supreme Court will soon hear argument from the lawyers on that case we spoke of then they'll make a decision a couple months later. Depending on the court's decision we will then file any necessary further papers on your case.

Stay positive despite this negative development because everything can certainly still come out in your favor.

Your friend,

Mr Casi – Atturney at Law
2330 Broadway
Floor number nine
New York, new York

Dear Sir;

i do not think i am aloud to discuss what happened in a letter to you but i dont now for sure because theres no-one i can ask here. i don't know what you could do to get me back to my other cell but please do it if you can because there i had pictures of people {like my mo}m and i had a notebook that i could right in and look at to drawe pikchurs of things.

Here I do not see anyboidy all day. This is tru every day and it is dark as well. If the superior court rules in my favor can i get back to my cell and my things? Can I get resess?

p.s. "iF YoU Do NoT NoW THE ANSERS PLEASE RiGHT ANYWAY BECAUSE THEN SUMoNE HAS To BRiNG ME THE LETTERS iN PoERSoN"

Mr Jalen Kingg
#Z311
Punitive Isolation Cell #17
Holman Unit
3700 Holman
Atmore, Alabama 36503

Dear Jalen:

I checked and you can of course write me a letter with an account of what happened that resulted in you being placed in isolation by prison officials. Please do so as soon as possible so I can try to help you.

In several days, the Supreme Court will hear argument on <u>Atkins</u> v. <u>Virginia</u>. The brief in your case is basically completed as well, with just some final editing left to do.

Hang in there, I know this is a difficult time. Everything can still work out, both with this disciplinary thing and with your case in general.

Your good friend,

_____

Mister. Casi / Pleese rite me sum more letters fast please. You

don't have to tell me about the case because i just want

thje letters four the reason i stated before.

P.S. i am only aloud to get leterrs from you.

Mr Jalen Kingg
#Z311
Punitive Isolation Cell #17
Holman Unit
3700 Holman
Atmore, Alabama 36503

Dear Jalen:

I am sending you ten different copies of this letter in ten different envelopes for the reasons you stated. I will send you multiple copies of every letter from here on out as well.

I have tried everything possible to get you transferred back to your old cell but it appears I will not be successful. I am assured, however, that at the end of this month you will be transferred out of isolation.

In my next letter to you I will include a copy of the brief that we will be filing on your behalf. I will also update you with any news we might have regarding the Supreme Court case we've discussed. In sum, we have reason for optimism at this point and I want you to remember that at all times.

But no matter what happens on your case you will soon be going back to your old cell. So stay strong until then and things will get better Jalen.

Your friend,

casi i have to get out of here because it is dark and there is no-one else accept me and i have not seen the pictures that i have in my old room and thosae are' my pictures by rite right?

i want for you to come and get me and take me to maple's house. Please comeas oon as possible becuase i want to get out really bad and i am sorry for allthe rong that i have done and the chaplan befour says that if one is sorry then one hath be forgiven so please come get me.

P.S. "please come get me"

P.P.S.S. "i am goin to write othur letters and put them in this same enveloap when I rite them the next days"

casi you do not have to send all those many leters any more because they changed the procedures when i got a lot of leters last time and now they just put it thru the hole with my food and the guy with jokes doesn't bring me personly the letters anymore

i want to get out now more than before! when are you coming? The guy who pushes the food thru the hole says I am not going back to my cell when this month is over and that you are lying\

When you come please bring me frute like you promised and please bring me the rainbow candee that they sell in stores too and when I go to live in Maple's big house I am going to help ebryone who lives in a smaller house then me.

P.S. "no matter what anywon says i WILL NoT BELIVE THAT YoU ARE LYING To ME" i do NoT care any more if i get out of hear realy

i now i am not going back to my cell when the munth ends and they said my picktures are gone too any way

i knowe you cannot come and get me You cant come now and you cant come never no matter what the virginya court says and i know i will never get to see the house you said

becase the candy in the stores isn't the same as my mother made becuas it comes in a plastic bag and mines was in a bowl with flowers and my moms made it hesself and she says to thank you because you was the only person whoever visitied me here

if i cant get out i don't care what happens in here or anywhere else AND YoU Cannot TELL ME WHY i SHOULD

i'm not sorry anymoar neether and i think noone else is sorry neither probly

Jalen Kingg
#Z311
Punitive Isolation Cell #17
Holman Unit
3700
Holman
Atmore, Alabama 36503

Dear Jalen:

Enclosed with this letter is a copy of the brief we will soon file on your behalf. Also I just received your last three letters and you are wrong. At the end of this month you *will* be transferred to your old cell and your pictures will be there just as they were before you left.

I cannot just come and get you out, that's true. But we can, and will, make it so you cannot be executed. You will get a life sentence instead. You have by now probably received a letter from Melvyn explaining why we are so optimistic that this is what will ultimately happen.

This would be a major legal victory and something very good that would have happened to you, there's no denying that. It will be proof that good things can happen to you too, that someone or something is protecting you. That Melvyn and I are truly your friends. Do you understand?

I guess you have to care what happens, even in there, just because no-one is allowed to quit, no matter where they are or what happens to them.

When I finish this letter I am going to make a phone call to your facility. Do not be offended but as a result of that phone call you will probably be receiving psychiatric attention and will be watched even more closely. Good news is coming you just have to wait a little longer for it and then it will be hard to remember the bad or if you do remember it the memory will almost make you feel good if that makes any sense. I'm going to arrange for Melvyn and I to come out for another legal visit so be on the lookout for that Jalen. Be good kid.

Your very good friend,

P.S. Why no postscript (P.S.) on your last letter? I look forward to them.

TO WHOM IT MAY CONCERN:

This letter should serve to inform you as the:
mother / father / next of kin / friend / domestic partner / significant
other / legal counsel of

Mr / Ms / Mrs   Jalen Kingg

that the aforementioned individual: Has been duly executed according to the bylaws and strictures of the great State of Alabama and of
the United States of America of which it is a part / Has had his death
sentence altered to one of life imprisonment without the possibility
of parole / Has absconded from the facility and is currently at large;

Other: (explain) Inmate has taken his own life thereby avoiding the
judicial justice previously meted out by the People of the State of
Alabama.

Consequently, said inmate's residency at Holman Prison is considered
terminated effective immediately. You have the right to appeal this
decision but to do so you must notify the above office within fifteen
business days of your intention to do so.

Yours, etc.

William T. Grennan President and Principal Stockholder

Chapter 31

Making me feel like even more of a client was the fact I kept swiveling my head back to eye the faded-black doors to Cymbeline's
courtroom whenever they would part to permit an intruder. I was
hoping for Toomberg but every time I looked it was someone else,
someone not there to help me. And this was the same day Raul
Soldera's case was on for sentencing so they brought him out crying
from behind a walker and he would periodically wipe his tears with
his bare palms but then his skeletal wet hands would keep slipping off
the handles so that he almost fell several times before finally reaching
the defense table. Where he sat down next to me and in front of
Cymbeline and I told him to *take it easy* because *it'll be alright.* Which
it sort of was for a change because Cymbeline was soon saying that
no updated probation report had been completed meaning Soldera
could not yet be sentenced. The case would have to be adjourned.

"To the first of next month," said Cymbeline. "By which date I
assume your office will have assigned Mr Soldera a different attorney."

"Why's that?"

"Well let me place on the record the following. This same attorney
who currently represents Mr Soldera will, immediately following the
calendar call in this case, be the subject of an extensive hearing
regarding multiple charges of contempt of court. Moreover, this court
will not only preside over said hearing but is one of the principal

824

complainants, so to speak, against this attorney. I should add as well, by the way, that Mr Soldera himself is expected to be a witness in this hearing and it is anticipated that he will provide rather damaging testimony to the effect that this attorney improperly counseled him to attempt the crime of bail jumping."

As Cymbeline said this Soldera was vigorously shaking his head *no* right next to me as Cymbeline's law secretary went up to the bench and whispered in her ear.

"Well I'm now informed," she continued, "that Mr Soldera has recanted that testimony and therefore will not be called as a witness against this attorney. And I will not now place on the record my personal views about the legitimacy of that recantation but suffice it to say that Mr Soldera will be dealt with in the appropriate manner at the appropriate time. Notwithstanding this latest development, however, the fact remains that a substantial conflict of interest exists in this situation that can only be remedied by the assignment of a different attorney to Mr Soldera's case."

"Or by this court recusing itself."

"Excuse me counselor?"

"This court should recuse itself thereby eliminating any potential conflict of interest. And since it's obvious that you have some type of personal animosity towards me that could unfairly prejudice my client I am making that request at this time."

"Application denied. I believe the more appropriate remedy is for your office to assign a different attorney."

"How is interfering with my client's Sixth Amendment right to counsel preferable to a different judge sentencing my client, which happens all the time in this building?"

"Because I took the plea and I will do the sentencing."

"You did not take the plea," I said, and Cymbeline's law secretary did some more whispering into his boss's ear.

"Application for this court to recuse itself is denied. Case is adjourned to the first of next month for an updated probation report and sentencing. Put him back in. Now, counsel, are you ready to proceed with the hearing?"

"No."

"Why not?"

"Because I'm still waiting for my attorney to appear."

"Is that the only reason?"

"Yes."

"Good, because he just walked in. I'll give you a minute and forty-five seconds to consult with him then we'll get started."

I turned around, this crazy-looking character with a green bow tie and a silver briefcase was coming into the well and extending his hand toward me. "Devin Quackmire," he said. "But you can call me Mr Quackmire, I'm not a big believer in formality." Now Quackmire looked about fifteen so the chances of me calling him mister were not great. But more importantly who the fuck was this fuck?

"I'll be representing you at this here proceeding," he said.

"What are you talking about? Where's Toomberg?"

"I'm not familiar."

"Toomberg! Melvyn Toomberg. That's who's supposed to represent me today, not you. I've never met you before, you look like my paperboy. No offense kid but what kind of lawyer are you? How old are you?"

"Hey I never said I was a lawyer, at least I'm honest right? As far as my age, my understanding is you're prevented from asking me that under the A.D.E.A."

"What? Read my lips Doogie, where's Melvyn Toomberg?"

"Oh Marvin Toomberg? The guy who was going to represent you?"

"Melvyn."

"The guy who was going to represent you?"

"Precisely."

"Marvin withdrew."

"What does that mean? Melvyn's my friend he wouldn't withdraw."

"I spoke to him by phone, I think he was in Burma or something. He said to tell you he was sorry but that he couldn't do it after what happened with The King. Now I've never been a big Presley fan myself so I didn't really pursue it further but that's what he said, something about letters too. Have you seen him since the letters?"

"Fuck." I sank into my seat.

"Hey look at that," Quackmire said. "Above the judge between the two flags. Ha! They got to get that fixed huh? Or maybe they should leave it ha ha! Just kidding, no pun intended."

"Or created far as I can tell."

"O.K. let's get started," said Cymbeline. "Mr Quackmire, your appearance for the record." Everybody introduced themselves except me and a line of witnesses sat in the front row. I stood up and interrupted.

"I don't want this individual to represent me," I said. "I certainly never agreed to have him serve as my attorney and I understand he's not even a lawyer. I'll represent myself is the bottom line."

"Well I can't permit that."

"Why not?"

"Don't play ignorant. You're as aware as I am of the rule that the man who represents himself has a fool for a client."

"O.K. that's a saying not a rule. And so what?"

"That saying has been around a lot longer than you young man and I will abide by it! Are you denying its truth?"

"I'm pointing out that it's merely a saying and as such represents no binding authority. A saying, like *early bird gets the worm*. No, worse actually, because at least that particular saying calls for a certain result, if you have a worm and you're deciding who gets it, the saying dictates you give it to the bird that's earliest. On the other hand, the saying you're invoking doesn't even call for any particular result. Where does it say a person *can't* represent himself?"

"It's a proverb, a maxim if you will, and as such it certainly may serve as legal precedent. I will therefore uphold that statute as I took an oath to do."

"Now it's a statute?"

"Mr Quackmire, who I have known since he was thirteen—"

"When was that? Last year?"

"– will continue as your representative. And you, counselor, will sit down and be quiet or I will enter a summary adverse finding against you immediately. People?"

"Yes your honor?"

"Call your first witness."

I sat down as Judge Arronaugh strode to the witness stand. Suddenly Cymbeline ducked her head behind the bench as if she'd just remembered something. When her head popped back up she was wearing one of those exaggerated white-curl wigs that actors are always wearing when they sign the Declaration of Independence or something. And now she had this extreme gavel the size of a tricycle in her hand too.

"Don't worry Casi," Quackmire leaned over to tell me via the left side of his mouth. "We're going insanity."

"What are you talking about?"

"Insanity is a complete defense."

"Maybe so but I'm not insane."

"How would you know? You're insane. That'll be the day, when I let someone who's criminally insane run the show."

The testimony itself was not that damaging although Quackmire's crosses often bore little relation to any conceivable issue and seemed to betray an unhealthy fascination with things like favorite foods and turn-ons. Arronaugh testified that I had made several intemperate remarks during Hurtado and other court personnel testified to other alleged breaches of etiquette. Some D.A.s testified including McSlappahan. Cymbeline even got on the stand to testify at one point, replacing her wig and jumping back on the bench whenever a ruling was required. But basically, without Soldera, they had nothing and Cymbeline seemed surprised, often shooting glares at her nebbishy law secretary who wouldn't meet her eyes.

After about an hour of that, during which Quackmire fell asleep several times, Cymbeline banged the giant gavel down, adjusted her wig, stood up clearing her throat and began:

"I find counsel's arguments regarding his alleged insanity to be specious and delivered in bad faith. He's as sane as all get out." I was going to protest that Quackmire had argued that on his own but thought better of it. "Moreover there can be no doubt that the accused more than meets the legal definition of a first-class wiseass. That said I see that a Justice from the Appellate Division is in the audience so I cannot as a matter of law rule that his misconduct is so grave as to warrant the term of imprisonment sought by the People. Regrettably, I now rule that the entire matter will be resolved and dropped with an apology from the accused. Counsel is there something you'd like to tell this court? Counsel?"

The second hearing was in the office's seventh-floor conference room and I was late. In front of and facing a long rectangular table was a tiny stool I was urged to sit on. At the center of the table sat Debi. To her left were Troie Liszt and Father Cleary and to her right were Conley and Lee Graham looking like he might faint again. Together, as the neon sign above their heads attested, they fully comprised C.O.C.K. or the Committee to Oust Casi Kwickly. "We're going to begin," Debi announced. She was wearing a robe but not a judge's robe, more like a silk one. She looked real good. I wondered how old she was. She wasn't very wrinkly. "Would you like to make an opening statement Casi?"

"Well I don't know if this is properly part of my opening or not but the list of alleged offenses that I received refers to an incident with Troie as the aggrieved party."

"That's correct, Mr Liszt, what's your point?"

"Well only that it now appears he will be part of the body making a determination as to my guilt or innocence."

"Again, is there a point?"

"Yes, the obvious one that he probably isn't the best choice to serve as an impartial finder of fact where he is also alleging that I caused him personal harm."

"Well I'm sure that would be a very convenient state of affairs for you. Then maybe you could go around assaulting every individual who works in this office until there was no-one left who could sit on the C.O.C.K. Is that what you're saying?"

"No but—"

"Liszt stays. He's an invaluable member of this committee and has been since its inception. Anything else?"

"Guess not," I said. I looked at Conley with squint but he looked away.

"Good, then we'll begin. Each charge will be read to you individually and you will be given an opportunity to respond. Response times will not exceed one minute and each member of C.O.C.K. will have the opportunity to interject questions or comments without time limitation. In all instances, the reading of the charge will constitute full, complete, and irrefutable evidentiary proof of that charge in and of itself, meaning no further corroboration will be required. Any questions?"

"Yes, if they're irrefutable why should I bother to respond? In fact, why even stay here?"

"C.O.C.K. isn't here to advise you how to run your defense Casi. And the time it took you to ask that question is coming off your first minute. Anything else?"

"No." Cleary wouldn't look at me either.

"Good. Firstly, it is alleged that the following two people have been subjected to egregious and unwarranted verbal abuse. Clarke Sealey and Solomon Grinn. Go ahead."

"That's it? That's all the specificity I get?"

"..."

"Well?"

"..."

"Who's Clarke Sealey anyway? I don't even know."

"..."

"Who is that Lee? That the guy on the elevator that time?"

"..."

"Well if it *is* that guy, he was like all happy that a client of mine had gotten fucked up in the arraignment pens so fuck him's what I say. Bring him in here and I'll say so to his dopey face. Or better yet I'll do to him what they did to my client! Wait did I say that out loud? This isn't going well. If I said anything offensive to him I apologize is what I meant to say. Yes I see that, twenty seconds, I know. As for Grinn. Solomon. The situation—"

"Time!"

"I'm sorry."

"Strike that from the record," she said. "That statement was made past the time limit." I looked around but I didn't see anybody transcribing. "Continuing," she continued, "you forged Thomas Swathmore's signature on a minutes order form costing this office two thousand dollars not including tax."

"Untrue in every meaningful respect but I needed the minutes and he wasn't around, sorry."

"Moving on."

"Hey, I thought I get a minute."

"Fine, go on."

"Nothing further."

"It is further alleged that you attempted a vicious assault against fellow committee member Troie Liszt and that said assault was only averted due to Mr Liszt's above-average reflexes. What do you say in response?"

"About his reflexes?"

". . ."

"Well what really happened was—"

"That this assault was completely without provocation and unusually vicious."

"In my defense I should—"

"That significant expense was incurred by this office in repairing a large patch of wall."

"Well I can reimburse, if only the office would see fit to disburse a slight loan—"

"That Mr Liszt has suffered such severe psychological damage as a result of these actions that today is only the second day he has been able to set foot on these premises since the incident."

"Really? I hadn't noticed."

"You have twenty seconds remaining in which to respond."

"Unprovoked I don't know. I had just lost a case and he said something like welcome to the world of the mediocre or something similar as I recall. What would you do?"

"Time!"

"Well I feel I must interject something at this point," said Conley finally. "Basically that there have been several instances where even I myself have felt inclined towards violence against Mr Liszt." Cleary and Graham were nodding in agreement and even Debi seemed a bit chastened. The momentum had clearly swung in my favor, should've known I could count on Conley. Everything was going to be alright.

"Nevertheless that does not conclude the charges!" said Liszt.

"No it doesn't," added Debi. "For it is further alleged that you have paid the bail for a client in clear contravention of office policy." There was a clearly audible gasp from the rest of the committee. "How do you respond?"

"That's absurd. Well, that is, unless you have clear proof I did so in which case I aver that I didn't know it was wrong." They all looked at Debi.

"I hold in my manicured hand a bail slip for $5,000 cash signed by one Lord Windsor of Chesternut securing the release of one Glenda Deeble. I have in my other similarly manicured hand a receipt indicating that the accused took out a credit card cash advance for that amount on that same date."

"Sounds circumstantial no?" offered Conley.

"Until you see this affidavit from the private investigator hired by this committee in which the affiant affirms that he personally observed the accused pay that bail in person and use that alias. Casi?"

"I'm really going to have to insist you employ my hard-earned honorific when you address me, you collectively owe me at least that, and odd that you flatly denied being on this committee Con."

"You see?" she looked at the other members. "Even at this late stage he continues to joke, even as his career hangs in the balance. But what do you say we stick to the evidence rather than your ad hominem attacks Casi? Because that same investigator would testify that in the last seven business days the accused has spent approximately three hours in this building. That he has refused to enter his office during that time but rather has employed Ms Julia Ellis to retrieve his files. That he has repeatedly asked her to burn everything on his desk, which request she has rightly resisted."

"Maybe give him a moment to respond Debi," said Conley.

"That he has likely played a pivotal role in the loss by this office of one its finest attorneys ever in one Melvyn Toomberg."

"Huh?" I said.

"What?" said Conley.

"That Mr Toomberg was last seen seven days ago coming out of the accused's office and muttering about letters. That he subsequently resigned and is in Bora Bora."

"No, Bali," said Cleary.

"I thought Belize," said Graham.

"Are you prepared to level with this committee about your role in the resignation of Mr Toomberg?" said Debi.

"No."

"You had no role?" suggested Conley hopefully.

"No, I refuse to level about it."

"Then we'll proceed to closing statements," said Debi looking side to side. "You have fifteen seconds."

"Well O.K., with respect to these charges, I guess I'll take them one by one. I took some notes along the way. Let's see . . . Liszt . . . Grinn."

"Time!" shouted Debi. "We will now confer and render a decision." They turned to each other and started whispering loudly. In the doorway to the conference room I saw Julia. She met my eyes and shrugged, her palms rotating outward as in *how's it going*? I gestured that I was ignorantly waiting and she half-pout-smiled yummily before looking left and leaving right.

I looked at the whisperers when a phone in their area rang then back at the doorway just in time to see an enormous figure cross it. The figure's passage momentarily occluded every extant photon of light and this eclipse so degraded the air in the room that I had difficulty breathing as I pretended, to myself, that I wasn't sure what I'd seen. Those at the table paused their deliberations to stare at the passing dark and in their sudden silence I think they half-expected an announcement of some sort. When nothing tangible happened next they went back to their perfectly audible whispering. Then Debi rose, tightened the belt to her robe and spoke in a strange stentorian voice:

"Hear ye thricewise! For by the power vested in me by C.O.C.K. and by the newly elected commander-in-chief of this office, Sir Lechuga McSorley, hath the forthcoming been unanimously declared by a vote of four to one with five abstentions. That the herein accused, charged with conduct detrimental to the crown, is hereby separated from his official capacities, said separation to endure throughout the existence of time immemorial."

I said nothing.

"Congratulations Casi," she said but this time in a normal voice. "You just became the first attorney ever fired in the history of this office." The rest of C.O.C.K. nodded in agreement. "I should add for the record that I have just received the minutes of the contempt hearing held earlier today in Judge Cymbeline's courtroom and judging from your response to the court's request for an apology I think it is exceedingly apparent that we made the right decision here today. That said, you do have the right to appeal this committee's decision. Here's a booklet that—"

"Well it's more like a pamphlet really," said Conley.

"Fine, here's a *pamphlet* detailing the procedures to be followed in the appellate process. If you do appeal a committee will be formed—"

"Never mind all that," I said. "I was going to quit anyway."

I got up and started to leave. "Oh well Casi," said Debi. "Look on the bright side."

"What's that?"

"That was lobby security before, seems there's a disturbing giant of some sort down there and he's looking for you."

When I got to the lobby I did some intense skulking whereby I determined that the relevant coast was clear. But not so fast because as I approached the main exit there emerged just past the doors an unnatural series of shadows, their cause so troubling nearby pedestrians that they seemed to think better of any plan that involved proximity to the obscurant. I didn't wait for the shadows to realize I just turned and booked out a side door where I was forced to do an evasive little 180° spin, pointed to the stranger who forced it, said *how'd you like that move*, then disappeared into the subway.

By the time I got to my building I was well-disguised having purchased a Yosemite Sam hat and giant novelty sunglasses at the subway station. At the top of the stairs to the second floor I started seeing shattered pieces of wood every few steps until I came to the door to Ralph's apartment. What I came to really was the remains of that door strewn across the doorway and barely attached to the doorjamb. I stepped on and through those remains and into the apartment. I saw no-one.

"Ralph? You here?" I said. I was looking around in a creepy stillness. I was about to give up and take a load off when an icy aggressive hand seized my shoulder from behind. I spun around and fell back a couple steps.

"Take it easy, it's me," the owner of the hand said.

"Who?" I said.

"Who he says. Angus, who else?"

"Angus?"

"Yeah man."

"You look different."

"It's me dude."

"Scared me, where you been man?"

"I'm baaack."

"What happened to your door?"

"You tell me."

"What do you mean?"

"I mean that about an hour ago I get a knock on my door. Only I'm not feeling very social or anything so I decide to ignore it, you know, pretend I'm not here. Well the knocking gets more and more insistent and shit and now this crazy voice is saying it knows I'm in there and I better open up, it must have heard me moving you know? Now I'm more determined than ever not to open the door if only based on the sound of that voice which was downright scary, and not in a corny horror movie way either, no I mean really scary and disconcerting like you're hearing something you're not supposed to be hearing. Well the

836

thing starts banging harder and harder then suddenly I don't know any other way to put it other than it just all at once eviscerated the door and came right in. And I don't know how to break this to you man but it was looking for you."

"What did he look like?"

"He? Was it a human? If so, the biggest one I've ever seen. As for the face I really couldn't tell you. First of all it's hard to explain but I was afraid to look at it directly. Second of all it was as if it was in shadows the whole time, only shadows it was itself creating if that makes any sense. Anyway it zipped through here, turned the beds over, then just like that it was gone. So what the hell was that Casi?"

"Did you call the police?"

"Crazy? I highly doubt it would like that and I really don't want to upset it."

"What about your door?"

"Forget the door man, what was that?"

"Nothing really, just some guy who wants to literally rip my head off with his bare hands."

"He could probably do it from what I saw!"

"Not a question of probability really, more like certitude."

"Why does it want to, you know, do that ripping thing?"

"Long story."

"How fucking bizarre."

"Actually one of the less bizarre things currently happening to me."

I heard the sound of rain and went to the window to see it pouring.

"What do you mean?"

"Never mind."

"No what's going on?"

I was so tired. I wondered if so many sharp lines of rain might not devolve all that was solid into non-aqueous liquid. I turned back to Angus.

"What's going on you say?"

"Yes, what?"

"Well for starters where the fuck you guys been? In all the time I've been here I can't recall this apartment being empty for so much as a minute now suddenly all three of you gone for weeks? With no warning? And then the apartment's not empty but it's suddenly inhabited by a fat guy named Ralph? You animated Ralph Kramden didn't you you fuck? That's what you were so proud of that night, wasn't it? He said he was a bus driver and even dressed like one. He wanted to go bowling and golfing. What the fuck? Where is he now? What have you done with him? And I just had a teenager represent me at an insane hearing with a giant gavel. And before with the attacking chimps and giant hot dogs! And don't forget the not so minor detail of what is occurring outside this very window as we speak."

"Slow down dude, you're not making any sense."

"Of course not, that's the point!"

"First of all, we didn't just disappear. We told you we were going to Panama City for spring break remember?"

"No."

"Yeah we stayed a lot longer than originally planned but you would too if you saw this place. My God, the women."

"So where's Alyona? And Louie?"

"Still there dude, I'm the only one came back."

"What about Ralph?"

"Ralph. Ralph."

"There was a fat guy living here, I talked to him multiple times. I didn't imagine it!"

"Oh you must mean John."

"Who?"

"John, he's a friend of mine. I told him he could stay here while we were gone. Good guy John. You're right, he's pretty fat. I tried to introduce him to you the night of the blackout."

838

"He said to call him Ralph. But it was even more than that really."

"What do you mean?"

"Never mind."

"Well I should add that John is an actor, not that you would have seen him in anything. The point being that he'll sometimes *do* whatever character he's playing even when he's not on stage. Dig? So he *will* get a little weird at times if you're not expecting it and come to think of it I think he did mention he had just landed a big part at the Bushwick Y or something."

"Whatever happened with that Honeymooners thing you were doing Angus?"

"Nothing."

"Nothing?"

"Well you don't want to know, let's put it that way, especially if you already think things are getting a little weird."

"So everything has an explanation's what you're saying?"

"That's what I'm saying."

"You guys didn't vanish."

"Nope."

"And the chubby guy was an actor."

"Yup, a poor one too by all accounts."

"I guess I feel better."

"Good."

I felt better I guessed. I stared out the window and tapped on the glass making drops of water fly off like jumpers from a plane. "Wait a goddamned minute!" I said. "You almost had me fooled."

"What?"

"Come here."

"What?"

"What do you see?"

"Wow it's really coming down huh?"

"It sure is, that doesn't bother you?"

"Well I don't like rain if that's what you mean."

"It isn't. Look *through* the rain. Up there. See where I'm pointing? What does that say?"

"Citibank?"

"No, the display below it."

"O.K. 6:08 p.m. Well 6:08 but I know it's p.m."

"O.K. but keep looking. Wait. See that?"

"Yeah?"

"What does it say?"

"Six."

"Six what?"

"Six degrees. It's six degrees out, what's your point?"

"What's my point? It's pouring rain out there and the temperature is six fucking degrees! How can that be? Does water not freeze at thirty-two degrees anymore? Is that what you're telling me?"

"Hmm, maybe it's not rain?"

"Oh no? What is it then?"

"It's like a type of snow or sleet."

"It is?"

"Let me see. No you're right, that's pure rain baby. Maybe the temperature's wrong."

"I just came in from out there and if it is it's too high."

"You're right again. I hate rain Casi. When I was a kid whenever it would rain my mom would say it was God crying. Believe that? Then one time when I was thirteen I said something like *fuck him, we're the ones should be crying.* You can imagine how that one went over."

"I'm waiting on that explanation, this is no fat actor."

"Shh, it's starting." Angus made Television louder and sat on the floor. "Did you know Tula is mostly a local story? Thank God I came back when I did huh?"

"What the hell is *this* now?" I said.

"Shh!"

On the screen was a genuine red carpet in front of black limos. A disembodied voice came on to explain that we were live at the legendary Ed Sullivan Theater in Times Square where a select list of invited guests was preparing to view the world premiere of the Tula Abduction Video. And as the voice spoke tuxedoed men opened car doors to let smiling actresses out and the cameraman would capture the precise yummy moment when their outer leg would first pierce the slit on their black dresses. The voice gave the background: about the crime and the Vigilantes and how the footage was originally to be shown at a City Hall press conference but how that plan was foiled by an untimely power outage, how said outage damaged the footage to the point that only *the dedication and tireless expertise* of the F.B.I.'s Video Reclamation Lab was able to restore the clip so that it was fit for viewing but how such great expense was incurred in doing so that an enterprising F.B.I. intern came up with the *inspired and unprecedented* idea of hiring a hot young Bollywood director to cut the footage into a P.G.-13 feature length film to be released in New York only, with children and senior citizens charged double and all proceeds going to the restoring lab. This was the premiere of that film and the proud mayor was set to take the opportunity to make a major announcement as well.

So it was that, under a giant red Campbell's Tomato Soup canopy erected to shield speaker and audience from the rain, Toad announced the formation of T.O.A.D. or the Team to heap assistance On Actors and other Destitutes. He began by identifying what he called the two biggest problems facing New York: homeless people and unemployed actors. Seems the *inhumanly frigid nature* of the past few weeks was causing the homeless to drop like flies or *attrit at record numbers*. The crowd didn't seem to know how to respond to that information but then Toad began to describe the difficulties of *making it* as an actor in the city and his audience voiced audible support.

Toad's solution called for the city to pay unemployed actors to attend funerals for the recently dead homeless and play the part of bereaved friends and relatives. In that manner would *the homeless be afforded the final dignity of an appropriate funeral ceremony complete with the illusion of concern while needy actors will gain valuable experience not to mention a nice paycheck to boot*. Congratulations were exchanged and everyone went inside, where it was warm and dry, to see the highly anticipated movie.

"I suppose that was O.K. huh Angus?"

"A little weird maybe but that's to be expected."

"And the rain? There's just no explanation."

"Oh there's an explanation. For the rain and everything else. I'm just not sure it's one you're going to like."

"What is it then? What's the explanation for these people?"

"People? Surely you can't think this is about anything as jejune as people or human nature can you? Because it isn't. This is exactly why I had to switch from Psychology to Physics. People like you always trying to explain and understand human conduct. The fault, dear Casi, lies not in ourselves but in our stars."

"Huh? How's that?"

"Physics my friend. Only Physics can adequately explain what's occurring. Don't look to the person across from you or even the one in the mirror, look to the cosmos. Don't look closely, look out and afar into the great distance. Because to explain you need a telescope not a microscope as the explanation lies in the very nature of our universe."

"So what is it then?"

"Singularities. You know what they are."

"Singularities?"

"Right. Picture a star turning into a black hole as happens from time to time. It does this through gravitational collapse right? In other words, we know that, put crudely, the term gravity refers to the attraction by matter of other matter. Obviously then in a massive object such as a star its component matter is constantly attracting itself while other forces generally counteract gravity to keep the entity from collapsing in on itself. Now with gravitational collapse the counteracting forces don't do their job well enough and the object begins to shrink, for lack of a better word, and become denser. Of course as the object's density increases so logically does its core's gravitational pull so that the shrinking continues at an accelerating rate. Ultimately the shrinking will end in a point so dense, with an internal gravitational pull so strong, that nothing, not even light, can overcome its pull, thus forming a black hole, black because even light is irretrievably sucked into it if it gets past the hole's event horizon. And at the center of this black hole is a spacetime singularity right? A point of infinite density. A point where concepts such as space and time have no meaning, where the laws of science break down and the future lacks even the slightest predictability. Singularities like these are not mere inventions Casi. They are predicted by a little thing called the General Theory of Relativity. They are, as I've said, the centerpiece of black holes, another actual and verified phenomenon, and they are thought to be in some sense the origin of the universe just before The Big Bang and its likely end after The Big Crunch. Now fortunately until now singularities have only existed in black holes, locations that by definition prevented them from having any effect on our world since remember that no information can escape a black hole."

"Until now?"

"Well you wanted the explanation man and that's it. Our universe is collapsing into a singularity. Slowly, I admit, but it's happening. And not the kind of singularities found in black holes either. No. What we're headed for is what theorists call a naked singularity. One not cloaked by the shadow of a surrounding black hole. One apparent and visible with effects we're all feeling. Predictability, Space, Time, the physical laws, they mean less with every passing second and soon enough they'll mean absolutely nothing. Why now? Why the collapse? Too much matter dude, causing too great a pull. My theory is that certain things that used to have no mass now suddenly do and they're multiplying. Either that or the mysterious invisible force that had previously served to combat gravity and drive universal expansion has now abandoned us or otherwise failed."

"You were doing O.K. until the end man. Are you high right now?"

"Insult away but how else can you explain that rain and I didn't want to mention this but . . ."

"What?"

"That night of the blackout?"

"Yeah."

"I swear I saw Time itself. I saw it and it was hideous man. Do you understand? I saw Time!"

I didn't tell him I had as well.

"So how do you explain those things if I'm wrong?" he continued. "Not to mention Ralph Kramden traipsing around here."

"You said it was an actor!"

"Maybe it was, what do I know? I'm no expert."

"It's not a question of expertise. Was it an actor friend of yours or not?"

"Two seven-year-olds kidnap and kill a baby, people carving each other up like inexpensive deli meat and others lining up to profit from it? The way I see it it's either my explanation or Alyona's."

"Alyona's?"

"Yeah you remember, healthy kept from the sick and we're the sick? Does it really matter which of us is right anyway since we both agree on the ending? You don't even need a theory to agree on the ending right?"

" . . . "

"Anyway Casi, I got to go."

"Go? What about your door?"

"Some dude's on the way to fix it."

"I don't get it, where you going?"

"Back to P.C. man where else? Thought I told you."

"No."

"I just came back to get some things."

"Now though? Stay at least tonight."

"No can do dude. You don't seem to understand. Hundreds of college girls clad scantily and constantly being urged to show even more SKIN TO WIN! And this cold and rain? You get the picture."

"What about school? Spring break's a week not a month."

"Oh, we're dropping out."

"What?"

"Yeah, I can get a job without it, I know a guy."

"What about Physics?"

"You serious? Look, in Psychology I could've been a leading light. In Physics I'll be carrying the spit bucket. No dice. Anyway, I'm going man. You should come too dude, New York's over. Nobody lives here anymore, it's too crowded." He was grabbing a bag and starting down the stairs.

"Hey Angus wait up?"

"Yeah."

"What you said about the singularity and stuff."

"Yeah?"

"Do you really believe in it?"

"Believe in it? Heck I seen it done!"

As soon as I got into my apartment I saw that the roof was leaking, in more than one spot and all over my sad pathetic stuff. In a manner of minutes every pot I owned was catching water but every time I started to relax a new leak sprouted. The water flowed in at a greater and greater rate until I realized I had no way to stop it or even catch it anymore; so that finally I just opened my door hoping that, pursuant to the rules of animation, it would take longer for the water to rise above my head, inch by inch, and drown me. Not that I expected to last that long. Whether or not Angus and Alyona agreed on an ending it was clear they expected theirs in maybe half a century whereas I expected mine in about half an hour. I thought about getting out of there and going back to the hotel but I had no money and my cards were all maxed. I was like a sitting duck, wading in actual water. This ending wasn't going to be a happy one.

The way few in Boxing ever are for example. Marvelous Marvin Hagler, for one, never fought again after the Leonard fight – an altogether intelligent move to be sure but still meaning that his ending consisted of losing a highly disputed decision to a man he hated with the knowledge that he gave away some early rounds and allowed Leonard to steal others with that lame tactic of using late-round, pitty-pat flurries.

Leonard himself fought in the nineties and the results weren't pretty. After the third Duran fight a thirty-four-year-old Leonard was dominated by Terry Norris and dropped multiple times in losing a unanimous decision. He retired after the fight only to return six years later against Hector "Macho" Camacho. Leonard's end would involve being viciously K.O.'d in the fifth round by the obnoxious and notoriously feather-fisted Camacho and there was nothing sweet about that.

Hearns too fought on way past any sense. His name still drew crowds and he won the occasional title until at age forty-one he was knocked out in the second round in front of his native Detroit crowd by the awful Uriah Grant. It can be difficult to understand The Hitman when he talks now but if he's talking into a microphone chances are good he's talking about maybe fighting again.

The way Roberto Duran fought Hector Camacho when he was forty-five and again at fifty, competing well against the same fighter who had starched Leonard. In fact, despite fighting often at ridiculous ages like that, the only fighter to have ever truly iced Duran remains Hearns. Nevertheless, Duran's record after the third Leonard fight was an ugly eighteen wins (only seven by knockout) and eight losses. Ultimately it took a very serious car accident to finally end his immense career.

Wilfred also regrettably fought in the nineties. After retiring in 1986, he must have started to think he was the only person in human history to physically improve with age because after almost four years of sitting around and wondering where the money went he launched a comeback on March 8, 1990, against someone named Ariel Conde. Conde was no great threat, having lost all ten of his fights to that point, but Wilfred had trouble with him anyway. Trouble, that is, until the seventh round when he suddenly smoked Conde with a rare one-punch K.O. It would be the most memorable fight of Conde's twenty-nine fight career: a career that included one draw and twenty-eight losses, twenty of them by knockout.

Feeling good, Wilfred next took on Pat Lawlor two months later in Tucson. Lawlor was 13-1 at the time so he could fight at least a little, while the same could probably no longer be said for Wilfred, who dropped a ten-round decision. (Lawlor continued his non-calendar annus mirabilis in his next fight with a victory over Duran, giving him one of those accomplishments that looks great on paper as long as you don't look too closely; of course, the victory over Duran was more a product of a shoulder injury as was established many years later when Duran won their rematch on his forty-ninth birthday [Lawlor was then stopped in five of his last six fights to finish with 23 wins and 16 losses].) Wilfred's plan for a triumphant and lucrative return to the ring had clearly been derailed but still he wouldn't quit.

Instead, on August 24, 1990, he returned to the ring and added the last victory he would ever earn by winning a ten-round decision against the execrable Sam Wilson. Wilfred heard the announcement of the scores and raised his fists for the last time. The referee came over to raise his right arm and Wilfred smiled that smile once again. People congratulated him and it didn't feel all that different from Puerto Rico in say '74 although sixteen years later it maybe did seem harder to do simple things like express a thought clearly or walk a perfectly straight line.

And when the end came it came in his next fight, held in Canada against someone named Scott Papsadora. On September 18, 1990, Wilfred lost a clear ten-round decision to Papsadora then retired for good with a record of 53-8-1. It was over.

Although there *was* one more nice day. In 1996 Wilfred became just the sixth fighter to be inducted into the International Boxing Hall of Fame in Canastota, New York in his first year of eligibility and although he had already started to have seizures by then he was still strong enough to raise his arms one more time in victory and call his induction *the best and most prestigious honor of my career.*

But then came the doctors. Later that year, Wilfred slipped into a coma while lying on his bed and was taken to a San Juan hospital. Doctors looked at Wilfred and ran tests on the contents of his skull. They used words like *pugilistic dementia* and *post-traumatic encephalitis,* terms that Wilfred, with his junior-high education, would've had trouble understanding even were he conscious. They could have just said too much Boxing really even though others had fought more, certainly been hit more, and remained relatively healthy. He could have easily died then, he spent days in critical condition, but he didn't. Instead he recovered and was released.

Now he needed constant care but this Man, who had let his very blood to earn millions for himself and others, had no money left. Years later, immediately after attending a benefit dinner held in his honor at Tito Puente's restaurant nightclub in the Bronx, near where he was born, Benitez suffered a stroke and ended up in the intensive care unit of nearby Jacobi Hospital. He again survived but this stroke

848

led to some paralysis and greater speech difficulties.

Today Wilfred lives in Saint Just, Puerto Rico; the barrio where his boxing career began in that makeshift backyard ring. The father who in those days put his arm around his seven-year-old son and showed him what to do is now dead. The wife he had when he was one of the strongest men in the world has abandoned him. He has few friends and fewer fans and his name is rarely mentioned anymore outside his own house.

And in that house Wilfred trembles and shakes and can't walk so great. His speech has deteriorated greatly and he sometimes can't say the simplest words. His memory is severely damaged.

He cannot, if alone, find his way home.

He is not, however, alone. Clara Benitez is with him, feeding and cleaning her son, keeping him steady as he stands and whispering in his ear when needed, promising everything will be alright *mijo* like she did the days Wilfred was her baby and she a far stronger woman.

Nature and Nature's laws lay hid in night;
God said, Let Newton be! And all was light.
– Alexander Pope

Chapter 32

The morning the blackout lifted and the lights in Times Square were so bright you couldn't properly see, the first person I saw after I climbed in through the window was my mother looking very tired and sufficiently aged that I quickly tried to mentally calculate her number but realized I lacked even a clue because she guarded that secret zealously. And my face was stinging because it wasn't just warm inside it was *hot* with the fireplace blaring and the baseboard's heat actually visible so that the room seemed almost foggy. I stood in the middle of that steam and looked at them silently until Alana saw me and spoke:

"Casi," she said. "We assumed you were dead."

My mother looked at me and smiled, said I was underdressed. She hugged me and I dropped just about all my weight into her as she laughed. Then she went into the kitchen to look for food because I looked *espantoso*.

I took off my jacket and fell on the sofa. Alana was asking me where I had been and I was rubbing my face and looking up when Mary came into the room and jumped on the sofa.

"Casi, Casi! I have a baby brother!" she said.

"I know baby."

"And he's cute and chubby but can't open his eyes yet." The sound of her voice after so long was strange but sweet. "Do you want to see him?"

"I do Mary."

"Good because he's cooooming," she sang and skipped away.

"The hell?" I said looking at Alana, meaning how did we go from stone silence to that.

"That's not the half of it either," she said and before I could ask what she meant Buela and Buelo were coming down the noisy stairs in the deliberate way they did everything. I stood up and walked over to meet them. I gave them hugs and kisses and didn't want to let go of my grandmother. When they sat down I went to the floor. "Help Alana, I'm being roasted alive in my own juice," I said and took off a shirt.

Buela had a list of things Buelo had to do to help my mother get the house ready for the baby. She said that the baby was *un regalo de Dios* and that it was a miracle that all three – the baby, Marcela, and my mother – were healthy. She gave Buelo more orders and said she *gave light* to all five of her children in her home in Colombia armed with just a midwife. She talked about how as a young girl she watched her mother do the same, how some lived and were entrusted to her in varying degrees and could be referred to as later adults and how others didn't so couldn't. She started crying a little and my mother came in with food that mostly I devoured.

That night Marcela lay on that same sofa, yellow-faced and too tired to move. Beneath her was a red yarn slipcover Buela had sewn by hand. The house was full of those kinds of things. Tons of knick knacks everywhere and all of them covered by or sitting atop hand-sewn, by my mother or Buela, pieces of frilly material. My mother in particular felt she could make *anything* that consisted of cloth-type material. She bought nothing in that area and so great was her confidence that we knew from experience to lie about the cost of any new clothing she asked us about else she gasp and declare she could've made the item for us at a tenth of that then chide us for being wasteful.

Three feet from Marcela, in the same modest bassinet Alana slept in two decades earlier, lay my new nephew. Alana knelt before the oval, absently running her fingers along its border then looking in and gurgling. She looked at Marcela.

"My God," she said. "Three. You're like a baby machine. I doubt seriously I could ever have even one. Did it hurt like crazy?"

"Not like Timmy my God. And less than Mary too. By now I guess I'm so loose down there that they just slip right out."

"That's far more detail than I need," I said. "Or want. Or can bear."

"He's gorgeous Marcela," Alana said. "I don't mean cute either like all babies. I mean he's actually good-looking, like handsome. Who has a handsome infant?"

I went over to see for myself and it was true. The squirt had like this tiny chiseled jaw and everything. I leaned over, put my hand on the back of Marcela's neck and kissed her on the forehead.

"What do you see when you look at him Marcela?" Alana asked. "What do you feel?"

"Love. I feel love."

"Don't give me that. What do you *feel*?"

"That's what I feel, I'm sorry."

"What is it though?"

"It's Love. That thing that takes all these different forms. I feel it strongly when I look at him, the way your body feels cold."

"Not now it doesn't, it's like a sauna in here."

"Sorry, I made the mistake of telling ma that the baby needs a few days to adjust to the loss of the womb's warmth."

"Ah," Alana said. "It all falls into place."

"My fault."

"*Love* you say, hmm."

"What?" I said.

"Nothing, just that love is an inarguably good thing it seems."

"And?"

"Well there didn't have to be Love you know. Love didn't have to exist, right Mar?"

"I don't know if it had to exist or not but I'm not sure it's all you're cracking it up to be," she said.

"Huh?"

"I know this is going to sound weird but this kind of love is almost too intense. It hurts a bit. It feels almost like loss."

"Well you've lost me."

"What's so hard to understand Alana?" I said. "This little sucker came out of her very body. What's Bill for example? Some fat guy she met in a bar?"

Marcela laughed but raised her palm and winced. It hurt to laugh she said and Alana wondered aloud what laughter was anyway.

"I've never been in a bar in my life by the way," Marcela added when the pain had subsided. "And Bill's not fat either. I mean it Casi, don't say anything to him about his weight, he's very sensitive about how fat he's gotten."

"Oh man," said Alana. "I think I know what you mean about the tinge of loss in love and what's worse I think I can explain it." She waited for us to ask her to do so but we said nothing and she continued anyway. "It's not *like* loss, it is loss. What you're feeling, and this is neither the time nor place of course, is the actual loss that is the inevitable end of all love, barely discernible but nagging."

"What? You mean like glimpsing the future?"

"I guess but what does that really mean, *the future*? What do you think Casi?"

"What do I know?" I said and just then we were interrupted by the gleeful screaming of Mary and Timmy in the other room. "And what's up with that Marcela? Now she's talking nonstop? What the hell?"

"That's what I said, what the heck. Well that's what I said after I broke down in tears of relief, hugged her, and thanked God."

"Ask her what Mary's first words were," said Alana.

"Huh?"

"Go ahead, ask her."

"O.K., I'm asking."

"Well I tell ma to bring her to the hospital. She says she told Mary in the car that she was going to meet her new brother. Nothing. Anyway they get there. Mary comes into the room and gives me a hug and kiss. Still nothing. Then she walks over to the little glass bassinet where the baby's sleeping, takes one look at him, smiles and says *this is something nice.*"

"This is something nice?"

"*This is something nice,* exactly like that."

"O.K., and she's been talking since?"

"More than ever, like nothing ever happened."

"Tell him the kicker," said Alana.

"What kicker?"

"Obviously I'm curious but I don't want to mess with a good thing either so I don't really say anything at first. Finally this morning I got up the nerve to ask her, you know, why she hadn't talked in months. Know what she says?"

"What?"

"She goes, *you told me if I didn't have something nice to say not to say anything at all.*"

"Get out."

"Swear."

"..."

"So it was good news all around that day."

"Serious," said Alana.

"Although one thing's for sure, it'll be a long time before I use a saying around that kid again."

"Oh and ma's lumps were nothing either," Alana said to my still slack jaw.

Then that thing happened where everyone in the room is suddenly uncomfortably quiet and doesn't know where to look because the person they're talking about walks in. And beautiful Mary walked confidently with her chin held high, cutting through that silence and into my lap as I began to make out a bizarrely illustrated book in her little hand.

Chapter 33

Everything in lower Manhattan looked different, almost unreal, that day – like Vancouver dressed as New York. Truthfully, I was surprised to see that the old buildings and people still existed in any recognizable form since someone like me believes that when they stop going to a place it immediately changes and everyone else stops going as well. And I had planned on never returning but Soldera was going to be sentenced that day and I had to go back and see what would happen.

The cold had remained and even intensified in a way that defied calendars, the changing of the seasons, or any other logic, until finally it seemed everyone would just quit and petrify in their place. Then suddenly, the day before, the sun had reappeared – without warning and at the seemingly last possible moment – to burn off the sky's gray and warm the air until by the end of the day people could be heard to complain of the heat. And that next day, the first of life's cruelest month, had been more of the same, with some even wearing shorts in a gesture that seemed more symbolic than anything.

From behind two of these individuals, who wore inexplicable smiles along with their shorts, emerged a solitary black figure taking impatient purposeful strides directly toward me as I stood outside of 111 Centre. I watched his every move, frozen in that spot, as the distance between us shrank rapidly and when he stopped three feet away from me I looked near his face but without focusing.

"I guess you're pissed," he said. "I wondered, not an especially long time, what your reaction would be and I suppose I have my answer now."

I didn't say anything and even kind of looked away a bit.

"At any rate, this should smooth things over between us," he said, extending his upturned palm with a gold key in the center.

"Dane!"

"Yeah, who else?"

"I didn't even recognize you until just now."

"What are you insane? It hasn't been that long. I look the same don't I?"

"The hell you been?"

"Take the key Casi."

"What is it?"

"A key."

"To?"

"To a storage locker. You'll find the address right on the key itself. Inside the locker is the money just waiting for you to go rescue it. It'll be safe in there for a while but I wouldn't wait too long. You'll see I spent some of it, a man's got to eat, but it's basically all there."

"Where've you been?"

"Well that's a long story. Let's go get breakfast, I'll tell you all about it."

"No, I can't."

"Why not?"

"I'm going in here about a case."

"Dressed like that?"

"I'm only going because I want to see what happens, not in any official capacity. I don't work there anymore."

"Yeah I heard. So why do you care then?"

"Where'd you go?"

"Look don't think I abandoned you at a difficult time or anything like that. There's twenty million or so reasons for you not to think that. Truth is I had to go a little underground for a bit but now I'm back, in the flesh, before your very eyes. Now forget about what's going on in there and let's go share a last meal. Many of your questions will be answered there."

"No I need to see."

"Need? Casi, man, I guess some things won't change. Forget about that building will you? Go get your money is my sage advice. Bottom line is you'll never be the true subject of anything that happens in that or any similar building and as I repeatedly tried to impart to you in our limited time together nothing else matters the least."

"I guess I won't be."

"No you won't, at least judging from that picture of Assado losing his head."

"You saw that before going underground huh?"

"Ah Ballena, you should say what you think directly. I suppose The Whale's still lurking, true, but that's no longer a concern of mine if it ever was."

"Why would it be our last meal? You going somewhere? Or just still dying?"

"Going somewhere, going back down. Truth is I only came up here because of the cold. I love the cold. But now it's getting hot here as well and if it's going to be hot anyway I might as well be in Florida where I'm more comfortable. Fact is you should come with me. It's much better down there than here, you are aware of that right?" I motioned like I had to go. "Like I said, go get your money Casi. I took enough to live on for a little while then I'll do something else to get more you know? Maybe our future paths will cross who knows? You don't want to come now? Cool. If you change your mind later we can always hook up then. 410? You did the right thing there. It's all how you define *right*. That's the key. Look around you, everyone's adopting our definition Casi. With every passing moment any given individual is being stripped of significance, either being herded together with a great number of others only to be slaughtered en masse or else being severely isolated, left to fend for itself with only its meager gifts for protection. And make no mistake but that this state of affairs is as it should be. Let us continue to hone and hone the methods by which man hangs his fellow man and be done, once and for all, with any hypocrisy." He smiled and grabbed my hand by the wrist. He turned my palm up and slapped the key into it then clasped it closed with his two hands. Just then a woman let out a hurtful scream to my left. I looked over and saw that she was actually laughing, bent over at the waist exaggeratedly as a man hugged her from behind and smiled. When I turned back Dane was gone. I moved my head quickly looking everywhere for him but it was as if he'd never appeared at all. I dropped the key into my pocket and went inside.

As I neared the outside of Cymbeline's courtroom the atmosphere seemed a lot looser than I remembered it. My chin was down as I was hoping to avoid anybody I knew and when I went inside I sat in the last row of a surprisingly full courtroom. Hours passed and nothing happened, Cymbeline didn't take the bench and no cases were done.

At quarter to one I figured I would have to come back in the afternoon. But then some clown I didn't know walked in followed closely by Sam Gold who didn't see me. The Sergeant nodded when he saw them then motioned to the clerk. The clerk in turn called Cymbeline to say the defense attorney had appeared then he called for a D.A. to stand. Said defense attorney looked nervous and Gold kept whispering in his ear.

Then a D.A., looking just as green, arrived followed soon thereafter by a court reporter. And when the judge materialized it wasn't Cymbeline. It was a new judge I hadn't seen before and I didn't catch his name but I heard say he had come over from the Bronx and would be taking over Cymbeline's part indefinitely. And I heard more, that the nervous attorney in the well was a new lateral hire bought in to

858

replace the fired Casi. Don't ask. That before leaving mysteriously Cymbeline had decreed that all of this Casi's cases were to be transferred to her part but that such move had been rendered moot by his subsequent firing, although this new attorney had taken over all those cases just the same.

Only three cases were on the calendar that day and as each was called the new judge would ask the clerk and the parties for a little background. And I had never thought to look at the calendar so I was more than a little surprised when calendar number one was called and Glenda Deeble was brought out from the back, her manacled hands trailing her as she entered. Save for the considerably more swollen stomach, she looked no better or worse, just the way she would apparently always look. The clerk explained that she had two cases. That she had somehow inexplicably made bail on the original methadone sale only to pick up a felony assault on a police officer stemming from another prostitution arrest. Which was the D.A.'s cue to insert that there would be no offer on either case and they were recommending consecutive time for something approaching a ten-year minimum. The attorney wiped some sweat off his meaty brow, the judge made a face that was hard to interpret, and Glenda said something no-one understood as they led her back in.

Number two on the calendar was a codefendant drug case. I watched Terrens Lake and Malkum Jenkins come out together followed by an explanation that even I had a hard time following at first about how Jenkins had a pending V.O.P. and sale in Sizygy and was in a program but picked up another sale in which it was alleged he sold with Lake who himself had two other cases, one of which he had already pled guilty on but had yet to be sentenced. The numbers thrown around then weren't pretty either and my replacement perspired some more. It was agreed that Lake needed a new attorney since the guy who took the plea was nowhere to be found and there was a conflict on his newest case. They were put back in as one.

The last case was The People (I thought every last one the city had) versus timorous Raul Soldera. I stood up out of habit then sat back down quickly. He looked worse, his time flowing more rapidly than ours and the wear apparent. The D.A. did the little synopsis this time. He explained that Soldera needed to be sentenced then and there. That he had warranted and had to be returned involuntarily.

"Why wasn't he sentenced at the time of the plea?" the judge said having lowered his chin to see above his eyeglasses.

"He was sick your honor."

"Was? Have you looked at him?"

"Yes judge but he warranted."

The judge looked up and stared at the D.A. He shuffled some papers and mumbled then looked at the defense table where Soldera sat.

And what took place next I wasn't sure was really happening at first. Because that judge was asking Soldera's new attorney if he had an application with respect to *the interests of justice and this defendant's conviction*, to which the attorney responded with true bewilderment but the D.A. somehow caught on pretty quickly and started protesting that *any such motion has to be in writing*. The judge looked at the D.A. then started scribbling furiously. He told a court officer to give the paper to defense counsel and have him sign it, which even this guy knew enough to do but only after first looking at Gold. And when the paper was returned to the judge he turned immediately to the D.A. and asked him if he wanted to respond to defendant's motion to dismiss in the interests of justice. Then the D.A. rambled a bit off his cuff, not normally a D.A. strength, until the judge looked up and verbally wondered *are you done?* When the D.A. indicated that he guessed he was, the judge gave his ruling:

"I have before me a so-called Clayton motion to dismiss in the interests of justice just submitted by the defense," he said looking at Raul. "I also have before me a defendant who frankly looks like he should welcome death and who is here on a non-violent charge that probably should never have been indicted in the first place. The defendant is released and his case is dismissed."

Soldera looked at his attorney, this man he'd likely met minutes before, with a look that seemed to say *does that mean what I think it means?* Gold went up to the rail and spoke words I couldn't hear. The judge got up to leave.

"Mr Soldera," he said, "go and sin no more. Or at the very least, what do you say we avoid this particular sin?" Then he left through the back and the part closed for lunch. Soldera, Gold, and the new attorney walked by without seeing me and I heard Raul tell the new guy he was the best attorney he'd ever had. I thought about going up to the court officers and asking for the judge's name but decided that, really, it didn't matter.

When I stepped out into the hall I looked to my right in response to a low guttural moan and saw something looking at me from down the hall.

It was Ballena.

It looked at my face.

I jumped back into the courtroom, went straight for the well where I flashed my attorney pass at the clerk, and disappeared into the area behind the courtroom before anyone could voice an objection. This time I knew where I was going and before long I was running down the stairs taking two and three at a time. By the time I opened the door to the street I was covered in sweat. I climbed out of that pit the door opened into and although the area appeared to be safe for the moment I thought I should get the hell out of there as soon as possible. I walked towards Centre Street and saw no-one at all.

Then I hit Centre and looked to the left to see the back of The Whale maybe half a block away. I felt a great fear then. It caught and strangled the breath in my throat and wouldn't let go. I put my back to the building and watched The Whale walk away from me. And anyone who passed it coming toward me would invariably look back in horrified disbelief while others even crossed the street to avoid coming near it so that human traffic appeared to involuntarily part before the immense figure. I twirled the gold key in my pocket a couple of times just watching.

Then I let it go and followed The Whale.

I thought then that Alyona couldn't be right because, while you would certainly expect to find someone like me in a world that had been quarantined from the healthy, there was no way someone like Marcela or Mary would be there with me. Along with a lot of other people I could think of.

Ballena made a left on Canal and I followed less than a block away. The paper that morning had a little feature called This Date in History and I thought of the first time Benitez had one of his fights go the distance. This was against Victor Mangual and it must have been the first time Wilfred began to grasp that he couldn't just do whatever he wanted in the ring. That Life didn't work that way. I wondered if he could even remember that day anymore and I guessed that Mangual probably felt pretty good when he recalled that day so there was that too. I thought how despite what Benitez and others look like today, people still slip in between ropes and into boxing rings. How every week, somewhere in the world, someone gets caught with a vicious left to the liver that steals their breath. How they grimace and drop and are then presented with a choice. How, unlike those who are barely conscious and obey their first instinct to try and rise, these fighters have a real choice to make. And they're O.K. to the head so they know fully what's happening and also often know they're not going to be anything near the next Benitez so ultimately it doesn't really matter if they get up or stay down. But they get up anyway. A lot of them stand up through the pain and get ready to absorb more if only because they think that's what they're supposed to do.

I quickened my pace and the distance between The Whale and I lessened a bit. I realized I never found out where in Florida Dane was from and where he would be returning to and I wondered if maybe he and Angus might not meet one day. Maybe Toomberg was in Boca Raton and they could all get together there.

Then I thought that if Dane was right then the person assigned to hang me had better hope I didn't see him coming. And I was going to do something about that girl with the distended stomach too. I decided then that I would maybe keep practicing law. Yeah I'd lost my way a bit there but there was still time to get a cozy office in that area where I could wait for leggy women in black veiled hats to appear with cases that would involve me in all sorts of madcap adventures. I let the space to The Whale grow. I didn't worry he would suddenly turn and spot me since I knew from experience that any such movement by him would announce itself in advance and with enough warning for me to duck out of sight.

The distance between us grew. The restorative sun that shines on sinner and saint alike warmed my face and I resolved to leave. Everywhere around me was in a still quiet. Then the slow soft strains of an actual violin filled the air. When I turned my head I saw a luminous girl no older than twelve standing behind an open violin case at her feet. She held the end of the bow with just three fingers and her perfect circle of a face seemed to comment on every note. The Missa Solemnis? Maybe. I stared at her as if from a spell and heard what I can only describe as Truth.

But when I looked back it was no ephemeron but rather The Whale, immense and eternal, staring directly at me. It displayed its version of a smile as surrounding people stopped what they were doing, looked grimly at the distorted scabrous face, then followed its eyesight-line to me. They looked at me as if with pity. Ballena stood perfectly still, waiting, I thought, to see which way I would run before pursuing. At first I moved nothing except my head and mouth and that only to tell the violinist to beat it, which she sort of did.

Then I took, on unsteady legs, tentative steps towards Ballena. The snarl smile on The Whale grew as it came forward to meet me. I kept walking and the beast continued to grow before me until even the slightest detail of its face could be discerned. The eyes didn't line up, the chin seemed almost serrated, and the teeth were more like fangs. And the few people in the immediate area had no idea what they were about to see but seemed to shy away from us nonetheless. We were maybe eleven feet apart.

At that instant in Time, from that location in Space, I heard the beginnings of a menacing noise off to the margins of where we stood, like scores of cosmic locomotives loosed and gathering in the distance, a low rumble that swelled with the passing seconds but otherwise remained the same, and the sky managed to darken with the sun lit brighter than ever; I saw the horizons rise as if to merge directly above us while the ground beneath our feet began to sink; jagged swaths of earth along with the structures and people atop were disappearing concentrically as if into a drain and countless humans whistled by making sounds that were either pleas for mercy or yelps of celebration; I saw events and deeds displaced from their proper setting and from notions like past or future and I stared, through regret, at all the ill I'd wrought.

There I stood, rooted, waiting for the disordered wave to arrive.

The wave sped in approach and would either carry stellar material from the farthest reaches of the universe and bury it violently into our very bodies or else take what was already within us, that which was central to our core, and from it form new stars.